P9-DXS-688

3-78   Library of America   58-4000

GERTRUDE STEIN

GERTRUDE STEIN

WRITINGS 1903–1932

Q.E.D.
Three Lives
Portraits and Other Short Works
The Autobiography of Alice B. Toklas

THE LIBRARY OF AMERICA

WEST BRIDGEWATER PUBLIC LIBRARY
80 Howard Street
West Bridgewater, MA 02379

Volume compilation, notes, and chronology copyright © 1998 by
Literary Classics of the United States, Inc., New York, N.Y.
All rights reserved.
No part of this book may be reproduced commercially
by offset-lithographic or equivalent copying devices without
the permission of the publisher.

Texts copyright by the Estate of Gertrude Stein. Selections
from *Composition as Explanation* and *Operas and Plays* and
The Autobiography of Alice B. Toklas reprinted by permission
of Random House, Inc. All other selections reprinted by
permission of the Estate of Gertrude Stein.
Typescripts from The Yale Collection of American Literature,
Beinecke Rare Book and Manuscript Library, Yale University.

The paper used in this publication meets the
minimum requirements of the American National Standard for
Information Sciences—Permanence of Paper for Printed
Library Materials, ANSI Z39.48—1984.

Distributed to the trade
in the United States by Penguin Putnam Inc.
and in Canada by Penguin Books Canada Ltd.

Library of Congress Catalog Number: 97–28915
For cataloging information, see end of Notes.
ISBN 1–883011–40–X

First Printing
The Library of America—99

Manufactured in the United States of America

WEST BRIDGEWATER PUBLIC LIBRARY
80 Howard Street
West Bridgewater, MA 02379

CATHARINE R. STIMPSON
AND
HARRIET CHESSMAN
SELECTED THE CONTENTS AND WROTE THE NOTES
FOR THIS VOLUME

Contents

Q.E.D.

PHE: Good shepherd, tell this youth what 'tis to love.
SIL: It is to be all made of sighs and tears;
   And so am I for Phebe.
PHE: And I for Ganymede.
ORL: And I for Rosalind.
ROS: And I for no woman.
SIL: It is to be all made of faith and service;
   And so am I for Phebe.
PHE: And I for Ganymede.
ORL: And I for Rosalind.
ROS: And I for no woman.
SIL: It is to be all made of fantasy,
   All made of passion, and all made of wishes;
   All adoration, duty, and observance,
   All humbleness, all patience and impatience,
   All purity, all trial, all observance;
   And so am I for Phebe.
PHE: And so am I for Ganymede.
ORL: And so am I for Rosalind.
ROS: And so am I for no woman.
PHE: If this be so why blame you me to love you?
SIL: If this be so why blame you me to love you?
ORL: If this be so why blame you me to love you?
ROS: Who do you speak to, 'Why blame you me to love you'
ORL: To her that is not here, nor doth not hear.
ROS: Pray you, no more of this: tis like the howling of Irish wolves against the moon.

As You Like It 5:2

Adele

The last month of Adele's life in Baltimore had been such a succession of wearing experiences that she rather regretted that she was not to have the steamer all to herself. It was very easy to think of the rest of the passengers as mere wooden objects; they were all sure to be of some abjectly familiar type that one knew so well that there would be no need of recognising their existence, but these two people who would be equally familiar if they were equally little known would as the acquaintance progressed, undoubtedly expose large tracts of unexplored and unknown qualities, filled with new and strange excitements. A little knowledge is not a dangerous thing, on the contrary it gives the most cheerful sense of completeness and content.

"Oh yes" Adele said to a friend the morning of her sailing "I would rather be alone just now but I dare say they will be amusing enough. Mabel Neathe of course I know pretty well; that is we haven't any very vital relations but we have drunk much tea together and sentimentalised over it in a fashion more or less interesting. As for Helen Thomas I don't know her at all although we have met a number of times. Her talk is fairly amusing and she tells very good stories, but she isn't my kind much. Still I don't think it will be utterly hopeless. Heigho its an awful grind; new countries, new people and new experiences all to see, to know and to understand; old countries, old friends and old experiences to keep on seeing knowing and understanding."

They had been several days on the ship and had learned to make themselves very comfortable. Their favorite situation had some disadvantages; it was directly over the screw and they felt the jar every time that it left the water, but then the weather was not very rough and so that did not happen very frequently.

All three of them were college bred American women of the wealthier class but with that all resemblance between them ended. Their appearance, their attitudes and their talk both as to manner and to matter showed the influence of different localities, different forebears and different family ideals. They were distinctly American but each one at the same time bore definitely the stamp of one of the older civilisations, incomplete and frustrated in this American version but still always insistent.

The upright figure was that of Helen Thomas. She was the American version of the English handsome girl. In her ideal completeness she would have been unaggressively determined, a trifle brutal and entirely impersonal; a woman of passions but not of emotions, capable of long sustained action, incapable of regrets. In this American edition it amounted at its best to no more than a brave bluff. In the strength of her youth Helen still thought of herself as the unfrustrated ideal; she had as yet no suspicion of her weakness, she had never admitted to herself her defeats.

As Mabel Neathe lay on the deck with her head in Helen's lap, her attitude of awkward discomfort and the tension of her long angular body sufficiently betrayed her New England origin. It is one of the peculiarities of American womanhood that the body of a coquette often encloses the soul of a prude and the angular form of a spinster is possessed by a nature of the tropics. Mabel Neathe had the angular body of a spinster but the face told a different story. It was pale yellow brown in complexion and thin in the temples and forehead; heavy about the mouth, not with the weight of flesh but with the drag of unidealised passion, continually sated and continually craving. The long formless chin accentuated the lack of moral significance. If the contour had been a little firmer the face would have been baleful. It was a face that in its ideal completeness would have belonged to the decadent days of Italian greatness. It would never now express completely a nature that could hate subtly and poison deftly. In the American woman the aristocracy had become vulgarised and the power weakened. Having gained nothing moral, weakened by lack of adequate development of its strongest instincts, this nature expressed itself in a face no longer dangerous but only unillumined and unmoral, but yet with enough suggestion of the

older aristocratic use to keep it from being merely contempt-
ibly dishonest.

The third member of the group had thrown herself prone
on the deck with the freedom of movement and the simple
instinct for comfort that suggested a land of laziness and sunshine. She nestled close to the bare boards as if accustomed
to make the hard earth soft by loving it. She made just a few
wriggling movements to adapt her large curves to the pro-
jecting boards of the deck, gave a sigh of satisfaction and murmured "How good it is in the sun."

They all breathed in the comfort of it for a little time and
then Adele raising herself on her arm continued the interrupted talk. "Of course I am not logical," she said "logic is
all foolishness. The whole duty of man consists in being reasonable and just. I know Mabel that you don't consider that
an exact portrait of me but nevertheless it is true. I am reasonable because I know the difference between understanding
and not understanding and I am just because I have no opinion about things I don't understand."

"That sounds very well indeed" broke in Helen "but somehow I don't feel that your words really express you. Mabel
tells me that you consider yourself a typical middle-class person, that you admire above all things the middle class ideals
and yet you certainly don't seem one in thoughts or opinions.
When you show such a degree of inconsistency how can you
expect to be believed."

"The contradiction isn't in me," Adele said sitting up to
the occasion and illustrating her argument by vigorous ges-
tures "It is in your perverted ideas. You have a foolish notion
that to be middle-class is to be vulgar, that to cherish the
ideals of respectability and decency is to be commonplace and
that to be the mother of children is to be low. You tell me
that I am not middle class and that I can believe in none of
these things because I am not vulgar, common-place and low,
but it is just there where you make your mistake. You don't
realise the important fact that virtue and vice have it in common that they are vulgar when not passionately given. You
think that they carry within them a different power. Yes they
do because they have different world-values, but as for their

relation to vulgarity, it is as true of vice as of virtue that you can't sell what should be passionately given without forcing yourself into many acts of vulgarity and the chances are that in endeavoring to escape the vulgarity of virtue, you will find yourselves engulfed in the vulgarity of vice. Good gracious! here I am at it again. I never seem to know how to keep still, but you both know already that I have the failing of my tribe. I believe in the sacred rites of conversation even when it is a monologue."

"Oh don't stop yourself" Mabel said quietly "it is entertaining and we know you don't believe it." "Alright" retorted Adele "you think that I have no principles because I take everything as it comes but that is where you are wrong. I say bend again and again but retain your capacity for regaining an upright position, but you will have to learn it in your own way, I am going to play with the sunshine," and then there was a long silence.

They remained there quietly in the warm sunshine looking at the bluest of blue oceans, with the wind moulding itself on their faces in great soft warm chunks. At last Mabel sat up with a groan. "No," she declared, "I cannot any longer make believe to myself that I am comfortable. I haven't really believed it any of the time and the jar of that screw is unbearable. I am going back to my steamer chair." Thereupon ensued between Helen and Mabel the inevitable and interminable offer and rejection of companionship that politeness demands and the elaborate discussion and explanation that always ensues when neither offer nor rejection are sincere. At last Adele broke in with an impatient "I always did thank God I wasn't born a woman" whereupon Mabel hastily bundled her wraps and disappeared down the companion-way.

The two who were left settled down again quietly but somehow the silence now subtly suggested the significance of their being alone together. This consciousness was so little expected by either of them that each was uncertain of the other's recognition of it. Finally Adele lifted her head and rested it on her elbow. After another interval of silence she began to talk very gently without looking at her companion.

"One hears so much of the immensity of the ocean but that isn't at all the feeling that it gives me," she began. "My quarrel with it is that it is the most confined space in the world. A room just big enough to turn around in is immensely bigger. Being on the ocean is like being placed under a nice clean white inverted saucer. All the boundaries are so clear and hard. There is no escape from the knowledge of the limits of your prison. Doesn't it give you too a sensation of intolerable confinement?" She glanced up at her companion who was looking intently at her but evidently had not been hearing her words. After a minute Helen continued the former conversation as if there had been no interruption. "Tell me" she said "what do you really mean by calling yourself middle-class? From the little that I have seen of you I think that you are quite right when you say that you are reasonable and just but surely to understand others and even to understand oneself is the last thing a middle class person cares to do." "I never claimed to be middle class in my intellect and in truth" and Adele smiled brightly "I probably have the experience of all apostles, I am rejected by the class whose cause I preach but that has nothing to do with the case. I simply contend that the middle class ideal which demands that people be affectionate, respectable, honest and content, that they avoid excitements and cultivate serenity is the ideal that appeals to me, it is in short the ideal of affectionate family life, of honorable business methods."

"But that means cutting passion quite out of your scheme of things!"

"Not simple moral passions, they are distinctly of it but really my chief point is a protest against this tendency of so many of you to go in for things simply for the sake of an experience. I believe strongly that one should do things either for the sake of the thing done or because of definite future power which is the legitimate result of all education. Experience for the paltry purpose of having had it is to me both trivial and immoral. As for passion" she added with increasing earnestness "you see I don't understand much about that. It has no reality for me except as two varieties, affectionate comradeship on the one hand and physical passion in greater or less complexity on the other and against the cultivation of that latter I have an almost puritanic horror and that includes an objection to the cultivation of it in any of its many disguised forms. I have a sort of notion that to be capable of anything more worth while one must have the power of idealising another and I don't seem to have any of that."

After a pause Helen explained it. "That is what makes it possible for a face as thoughtful and strongly built as yours to be almost annoyingly unlived and youthful and to be almost foolishly happy and content." There was another silence and then Adele said with conviction, "I could undertake to be an efficient pupil if it were possible to find an efficient teacher;" and then they left it there between them.

In the long idle days that followed an affectionate relation gradually grew between these two. In the chilly evenings as Adele lay at her side on the deck, Helen would protect her from the wind and would allow her hand to rest gently on her face and her fingers to flutter vaguely near her lips. At such times Adele would have dimly a sense of inward resistance, a feeling that if she were not so sluggish she would try to decide whether she should yield or resist but she felt too tired to think, to yield or to resist and so she lay there quite quiet, quite dulled.

These relations formed themselves so gradually and gently that only the nicest observer could have noted any change in the relations of the three. Their intercourse was apparently very much what it had been. There were long conversations in which Adele vehemently and with much picturesque vividness explained her views and theories of manners, people and things, in all of which she was steadily opposed by Helen who differed fundamentally in all her convictions, aspirations and illusions.

Mabel would listen always with immense enjoyment as if it were a play and enacted for her benefit and queerly enough although the disputants were much in earnest in their talk and in their oppositions, it was a play and enacted for her benefit.

One afternoon Adele was lying in her steamer chair yielding herself to a sense of physical weariness and to the disillusionment of recent failures. Looking up she saw Helen looking down at her. Adele's expression changed. "I beg your pardon" she said "I didn't know any one was near. Forgive the indecency of my having allowed the dregs of my soul to appear on the surface." "It is I who ought to apologise for having observed you" Helen answered gravely. Adele gave her a long look of unimpassioned observation. "I certainly never expected to find you one of the most gentle and considerate of human kind," she commented quietly and then Helen made it clearer. "I certainly did not expect that you would find me so," she answered.

This unemphasised interchange still left them as before quite untouched. It was an impartial statement from each one, a simple observation on an event. Time passed and still no charged words, glances or movements passed between them, they gave no recognition of each other's consciousness.

One evening lying there in the darkness yielding to a suggestion rather than to an impulse Adele pressed the fluttering fingers to her lips. The act was to herself quite without emphasis and without meaning.

The next night as she lay down in her berth, she suddenly awakened out of her long emotional apathy. For the first time she recognised the existence of Helen's consciousness and realised how completely ignorant she was both as to its extent and its meaning. She meditated a long time. Finally she began to explain to herself. "No I don't understand it at all," she said. "There are so many possibilities and then there is Mabel," and she dropped into another meditation. Finally it took form. "Of course Helen may be just drifting as I was, or else she may be interested in seeing how far I will go before my principles get in my way or whether they will get in my way at all,—and then again its barely possible that she may really care for me and again she may be playing some entirely different game.—And then there is Mabel.—Apparently she is not to know, but is that real; does it make any difference; does Helen really care or is she only doing it secretly for the sense of mystery. Surely she is right. I am very ignorant. Here after ten days of steady companionship I haven't the vaguest conception of her, I haven't the slightest clue to her or her meanings. Surely I must be very stupid" and she shook her head disconsolately "and to-morrow is our last day together and I am not likely to find out then. I would so much like to know"

she continued "but I can see no way to it, none at all except,"
and she smiled to herself "except by asking her and then I
have no means of knowing whether she is telling me the truth.
Surely all is vanity for I once thought I knew something about
women," and with a long sigh of mystification she composed
herself to sleep.

The next afternoon leaving Mabel comfortable with a book,
Adele, with a mind attuned to experiment wandered back with
Helen to their favorite outlook. It was a sparkling day and
Adele threw herself on the deck joyous with the sunshine and
the blue. She looked up at Helen for a minute and then began
to laugh, her eyes bright with amusement. "Now what?"
asked Helen. "Oh nothing much, I was just thinking of the
general foolishness, Mabel and you and I. Don't you think its
pretty foolish?" There was nothing mocking in her face nothing but simple amusement.

Helen's face gave no response and made no comment but
soon she hit directly with words. "I am afraid" she said "that
after all you haven't a nature much above passionettes. You
are so afraid of losing your moral sense that you are not willing
to take it through anything more dangerous than a mud-
puddle."

Adele took it frankly, her smile changed to meditation. "Yes
there is something in what you say," she returned "but after
all if one has a moral sense there is no necessity in being fool-
hardy with it. I grant you it ought to be good for a swim of
a mile or two, but surely it would be certain death to let it
loose in mid-ocean. Its not a heroic point of view I admit,
but then I never wanted to be a hero, but on the other hand,"
she added "I am not anxious to cultivate cowardice. I wonder—" and then she paused. Helen gave her a little while and
then left her.

Adele continued a long time to look out on the water. "I
wonder" she said to herself again. Finally it came more definitely. "Yes I wonder. There isn't much use in wondering
about Helen. I know no more now than I did last night and
I am not likely to be much wiser. She gives me no means of
taking hold and the key of the lock is surely not in me. It

can't be that she really cares enough to count, no thats impossible," and she relapsed once more into silence.

Her meditations again took form. "As for me is it another little indulgence of my superficial emotions or is there any possibility of my really learning to realise stronger feelings. If its the first I will call a halt promptly and at once. If its the second I won't back out, no not for any amount of moral sense," and she smiled to herself. "Certainly it is very difficult to tell. The probabilities are that this is only another one of the many and so I suppose I had better quit and leave it. Its the last day together and so to be honorable I must quit at once." She then dismissed it all and for some time longer found it very pleasant there playing with the brightness. At last she went forward and joined the others. She sat down by Helen's side and promptly changed her mind. It was really quite different, her moral sense had lost its importance.

Helen was very silent that evening all through the tedious table d'hôte dinner. The burden of the entertainment rested on Adele and she supported it vigorously. After dinner they all went back to their old station. It was a glorious night that last one on the ship. They lay on the deck the stars bright overhead and the wine-colored sea following fast behind the ploughing screw. Helen continued silent, and Adele all through her long discourse on the superior quality of California starlight and the incidents of her childhood with which she was regaling Mabel, all through this talk she still wondered if Helen really cared.

"Was I brutal this afternoon?" she thought it in definite words "and does she really care? If she does it would be only decent of me to give some sign of contrition for if she does care I am most woefully ashamed of my levity, but if she doesn't and is just playing with me then I don't want to apologise." Her mind slowly alternated between these two possibilities. She was beginning to decide in favor of the more generous one, when she felt Helen's hand pressing gently over her eyes. At once the baser interpretation left her mind quite completely. She felt convinced of Helen's rare intensity and generosity of feeling. It was the first recognition of mutual dependence.

*

Steadily the night grew colder clearer and more beautiful. Finally Mabel left them. They drew closer together and in a little while Adele began to question. "You were very generous," she said "tell me how much do you care for me." "Care for you my dear" Helen answered "more than you know and less than you think." She then began again with some abruptness "Adele you seem to me capable of very genuine friendship. You are at once dispassionate in your judgments and loyal in your feelings; tell me will we be friends." Adele took it very thoughtfully. "One usually knows very definitely when there is no chance of an acquaintance becoming a friendship but on the other hand it is impossible to tell in a given case whether there is. I really don't know," she said. Helen answered her with fervor. "I honor you for being honest." "Oh honest," returned Adele lightly. "Honesty is a selfish virtue. Yes I am honest enough." After a long pause she began again meditatively, "I wonder if either of us has the slightest idea what is going on in the other's head." "That means that you think me very wicked" Helen asked. "Oh no" Adele responded "I really don't know enough about you to know whether you are wicked or not. Forgive me I don't mean to be brutal" she added earnestly "but I really don't know."

There was a long silence and Adele looked observingly at the stars. Suddenly she felt herself intensely kissed on the eyes and on the lips. She felt vaguely that she was apathetically unresponsive. There was another silence. Helen looked steadily down at her. "Well!" she brought out at last. "Oh" began Adele slowly "I was just thinking." "Haven't you ever stopped thinking long enough to feel" Helen questioned gravely. Adele shook her head in slow negation. "Why I suppose if one can't think at the same time I will never accomplish the feat of feeling. I always think. I don't see how one can stop it. Thinking is a pretty continuous process" she continued "sometimes its more active than at others but its always pretty much there." "In that case I had better leave you to your thoughts" Helen decided. "Ah! don't go," exclaimed Adele. "I don't want to stir." "Why not" demanded Helen. "Well" Adele put it tentatively "I suppose its simply inertia." "I really must go" repeated Helen gently, there was no abruptness in her voice or movement. Adele sat up, Helen bent down, kissed her warmly and left.

Adele sat for awhile in a dazed fashion. At last she shook her head dubiously and murmured, "I wonder if it was inertia." She sat some time longer among the tossed rugs and finally with another dubious head-shake said with mock sadness, "I asked the unavailing stars and they replied not, I am afraid its too big for me" and then she stopped thinking. She kept quiet some time longer watching the pleasant night. At last she gathered the rugs together and started to go below. Suddenly she stopped and dropped heavily on a bench. "Why" she said in a tone of intense interest, "its like a bit of mathematics. Suddenly it does itself and you begin to see," and then she laughed. "I am afraid Helen wouldn't think much of that if its only seeing. However I never even thought I saw before and I really do think I begin to see. Yes its very strange but surely I do begin to see."

All during the summer Adele did not lose the sense of having seen, but on the other hand her insight did not deepen. She meditated abundantly on this problem and it always ended with a childlike pride in the refrain "I did see a little I certainly did catch a glimpse."

She thought of it as she and her brother lay in the evenings on the hill-side at Tangiers feeling entirely at home with the Moors who in their white garments were rising up and down in the grass like so many ghostly rabbits. As they lay there agreeing and disagreeing in endless discussion with an intensity of interest that long familiarity had in no way diminished, varied by indulgence in elaborate foolishness and reminiscent jokes, she enjoyed to the full the sense of family friendship. She felt that her glimpse had nothing to do with all this. It belonged to another less pleasant and more incomplete emotional world. It didn't illuminate this one and as yet it was not very alluring in itself but as she remarked to herself at the end of one of her unenlightening discussions on this topic, "It is something one ought to know. It seems almost a duty."

*

Sitting in the court of the Alhambra watching the swallows fly in and out of the crevices of the walls, bathing in the soft air filled with the fragrance of myrtle and oleander and letting the hot sun burn her face and the palms of her hands, losing herself thus in sensuous delight she would murmur again and again "No it isn't just this, its something more, something different. I haven't really felt it but I have caught a glimpse."

One day she was sitting on a hill-side looking down at Granada desolate in the noon-day sun. A young Spanish girl carrying a heavy bag was climbing up the dry, brown hill. As she came nearer they smiled at each other and exchanged greetings. The child sat down beside her. She was one of those motherly little women found so often in her class, full of gentle dignity and womanly responsibility.

They sat there side by side with a feeling of complete companionship, looking at each other with perfect comprehension and their intercourse saved from the interchange of commonplaces by their ignorance of each other's language. For some time they sat there, finally they arose and walked on together. They parted as quiet friends part, and as long as they remained in sight of each other they turned again and again and signed a gentle farewell.

After her comrade had disappeared Adele returned to her insistent thought. "A simple experience like this is very perfect, can my new insight give me realler joys" she questioned. "I doubt it very much" she said. "It doesn't deepen such experiences in fact it rather annoyingly gets in my way and disturbs my happy serenity. Heavens what an egotist I am!" she exclaimed and then she devoted herself to the sunshine on the hills.

Later on she was lying on the ground reading again Dante's *Vita Nuova*. She lost herself completely in the tale of Dante and Beatrice. She read it with absorbed interest for it seemed now divinely illuminated. She rejoiced abundantly in her new understanding and exclaimed triumphantly "At last I begin to see what Dante is talking about and so there is something in my glimpse and its alright and worth while" and she felt within herself a great content.

BOOK 2:

Mabel Neathe

I

Mabel Neathe's room fully met the habit of many hours of unaggressive lounging. She had command of an exceptional talent for atmosphere. The room with its very good shape, dark walls but mediocre furnishings and decorations was more than successfully unobtrusive, it had perfect quality. It had always just the amount of light necessary to make mutual observation pleasant and yet to leave the decorations in obscurity or rather to inspire a faith in their being good.

It is true of rooms as of human beings that they are bound to have one good feature and as a Frenchwoman dresses to that feature in such fashion that the observer must see that and notice nothing else, so Mable Neathe had arranged her room so that one enjoyed one's companions and observed consciously only the pleasant fire-place.

But the important element in the success of the room as atmosphere consisted in Mabel's personality. The average guest expressed it in the simple comment that she was a perfect hostess, but the more sympathetic observers put it that it was not that she had the manners of a perfect hostess but the more unobtrusive good manners of a gentleman.

The chosen and they were a few individuals rather than a set found this statement inadequate although it was abundantly difficult for them to explain their feeling. Such an Italian type frustrated by its setting in an unimpassioned and moral community was of necessity misinterpreted although its charm was valued. Mabel's ancestry did not supply any explanation of her character. Her kinship with decadent Italy was purely spiritual.

The capacity for composing herself with her room in unaccented and perfect values was the most complete attribute of that kinship that her modern environment had developed. As for the rest it after all amounted to failure, failure as power, failure as an individual. Her passions in spite of their intensity failed to take effective hold on the objects of her desire. The

15

subtlety and impersonality of her atmosphere which in a position of recognised power would have had compelling attraction, here in a community of equals where there could be no mystery as the seeker had complete liberty in seeking she lacked the vital force necessary to win. Although she was unscrupulous the weapons she used were too brittle, they could always be broken in pieces by a vigorous guard.

Modern situations never endure for a long enough time to allow subtle and elaborate methods to succeed. By the time they are beginning to bring about results the incident is forgotten. Subtlety moreover in order to command efficient power must be realised as dangerous and the modern world is a difficult place in which to be subtly dangerous, the risks are too great. Mabel might now compel by inspiring pity she could never in her world compel by inspiring fear.

Adele had been for some time one of Mabel's selected few. Her enjoyment of ease and her habit of infinite leisure, combined with her vigorous personality and a capacity for endless and picturesque analysis of all things human had established a claim which her instinct for intimacy without familiarity and her ready adjustment to the necessary impersonality which a relation with Mabel demanded, had confirmed.

"Its more or less of a bore getting back for we are all agreed that Baltimore isn't much of a town to live in, but this old habit is certainly very pleasant" she remarked as she stretched herself comfortably on the couch "and after all, it is much more possible to cultivate such joys when a town isn't wildly exciting. No my tea isn't quite right" she continued "Its worth while making a fuss you know when there is a possibility of obtaining perfection, otherwise any old tea is good enough. Anyhow whats the use of anything as long as it isn't Spain? You must really go there some time." They continued to make the most of their recent experiences in this their first meeting.

"Did you stay long in New York after you landed" Mabel finally asked. "Only a few days" Adele replied "I suppose Helen wrote you that I saw her for a little while. We lunched together before I took my train," she added with a consciousness of the embarrassment that that meeting had caused her. "You didn't expect to like her so much, did you?" Mabel suggested. "I remember you used to say that she impressed you as almost coarse and rather decadent and that you didn't even find her interesting. And you know" she added "how much you dislike decadence."

Adele met her with frank bravado. "Of course I said that and as yet I don't retract it. I am far from sure that she is not both coarse and decadent and I don't approve of either of those qualities. I do grant you however that she is interesting, at least as a character, her talk interests me no more than it ever did" and then facing the game more boldly, she continued "But you know I really know very little about her except that she dislikes her parents and goes in for society a good deal. What else is there?"

Mabel drew a very unpleasant picture of that parentage. Her description of the father a successful lawyer and judge, and an excessively brutal and at the same time small-minded man who exercised great ingenuity in making himself unpleasant was not alluring, nor that of the mother who was very religious and spent most of her time mourning that it was not Helen that had been taken instead of the others a girl and boy whom she remembered as sweet gentle children.

One day when Helen was a young girl she heard her mother say to the father "Isn't it sad that Helen should have been the one to be left."

Mabel described their attempts to break Helen's spirit and their anger at their lack of success. "And now" Mabel went on "they object to everything that she does, to her friends and to everything she is interested in. Mrs. T. always sides with her husband. Of course they are proud of her good looks, her cleverness and social success but she won't get married and she doesn't care to please the people her mother wants her to belong to. They don't dare to say anything to her now because she is so much better able to say things that hurt than they are."

"I suppose there is very little doubt that Helen can be uncommonly nasty when she wants to be," laughed Adele, "and if she isn't sensitive to other people's pain, a talent for being successful in bitter repartee might become a habit that would make her a most uncomfortable daughter. I believe I might condole with the elders if they were to confide their sorrows

to me. By the way doesn't Helen address them the way children commonly do their parents, she always speaks of them
as Mr. and Mrs. T." "Oh yes" Mabel explained, "they observe
the usual forms."

"Its a queer game," Adele commented, "coming as I do
from a community where all no matter how much they may
quarrel and disagree have strong family affection and great
respect for the ties of blood, I find it difficult to realise." "Yes
there you come in with your middle class ideals again" retorted Mabel.

She then lauded Helen's courage and daring. "Whenever
there is any difficulty with the horses or anything dangerous
to be done they always call in Helen. Her father is also very
small-minded in money matters. He gives her so little and
whenever anything happens to the carriage if she is out in it,
he makes her pay and she has to get the money as best she
can. Her courage never fails and that is what makes her father
so bitter, that she never gives any sign of yielding and if she
decides to do a thing she is perfectly reckless, nothing stops
her."

"That sounds very awful" mocked Adele "not being myself
of an heroic breed, I don't somehow realise that type much
outside of story-books. That sort of person in real life doesn't
seem very real, but I guess its alright. Helen has courage I
don't doubt that."

Mabel then described Helen's remarkable endurance of
pain. She fell from a hay stack one day and broke her arm.
After she got home, her father was so angry that he wouldn't
for some time have it attended and she faced him boldly to
the end. "She never winces or complains no matter how much
she is hurt," Mabel concluded. "Yes I can believe that" Adele
answered thoughtfully.

Throughout the whole of Mabel's talk of Helen, there was
an implication of ownership that Adele found singularly irritating. She supposed that Mabel had a right to it but in that
thought she found little comfort.

As the winter advanced, Adele took frequent trips to New
York. She always spent some of her time with Helen. For some
undefined reason a convention of secrecy governed their re-

lations. They seemed in this way to emphasise their intention of working the thing out completely between them. To Adele's consciousness the necessity of this secrecy was only apparent when they were together. She felt no obligation to conceal this relation from her friends.

They arranged their meetings in the museums or in the park and sometimes they varied it by lunching together and taking interminable walks in the long straight streets. Adele was always staying with relatives and friends and although there was no reason why Helen should not have come to see her there, something seemed somehow to serve as one. As for Helen's house it seemed tacitly agreed between them that they should not complicate the situation by any relations with Helen's family and so they continued their homeless wanderings.

Adele spent much of their time together in announcing with great interest the results of her endless meditations. She would criticise and examine herself and her ideas with tireless interest. "Helen," she said one day, "I always had an impression that you talked a great deal but apparently you are a most silent being. What is it? Do I talk so hopelessly much that you get discouraged with it as a habit?" "No," answered Helen, "although I admit one might look upon you in the light of a warning, but really I am very silent when I know people well. I only talk when I am with superficial acquaintances." Adele laughed. "I am tempted to say for the sake of picturesque effect, that in that respect I am your complete opposite, but honesty compels me to admit in myself an admirable consistency. I don't know that the quantity is much affected by any conditions in which I find myself, but really Helen why don't you talk more to me?" "Because you know well enough that you are not interested in my ideas, in fact that they bore you. Its always been very evident. You know" Helen continued affectionately, "that you haven't much talent for concealing your feelings and impressions." Adele smiled, "Yes you are certainly right about most of your talk, it does bore me," she admitted. "But that is because its about stuff that you are not really interested in. You don't really care about general ideas and art values and musical development and surgical operations and Heaven knows what all and naturally your talk about those things doesn't interest me. No talking is interesting that one hasn't hammered out one's self. I know I always bore myself unutterably when I talk the thoughts that I hammered out some time ago and that are no longer meaningful to me, for quoting even oneself lacks a flavor of reality, but you, you always make me feel that at no period did you ever have the thoughts that you converse with. Surely one has to hit you awfully hard to shake your realler things to the surface."

These meetings soon became impossible. It was getting cold and unpleasant and it obviously wouldn't do to continue in that fashion and yet neither of them undertook to break the convention of silence which they had so completely adopted concerning the conditions of their relation.

One day after they had been lunching together they both felt strongly that restaurants had ceased to be amusing. They didn't want to stay there any longer but outside there was an unpleasant wet snow-storm, it was dark and gloomy and the streets were slushy. Helen had a sudden inspiration. "Let us go and see Jane Fairfield," she said, "You don't know her of course but that makes no difference. She is queer and will interest you and you are queer and will interest her. Oh! I don't want to listen to your protests, you are queer and interesting even if you don't know it and you like queer and interesting people even if you think you don't and you are not a bit bashful in spite of your convictions to the contrary, so come along." Adele laughed and agreed.

They wandered up to the very top of an interminable New York apartment house. It was one of the variety made up apparently of an endless number of unfinished boxes of all sizes piled up in a great oblong leaving an elevator shaft in the centre. There is a strange effect of bare wood and uncovered nails about these houses and no amount of upholstery really seems to cover their hollow nakedness.

Jane Fairfield was not at home but the elevator boy trustingly let them in to wait. They looked out of the windows at the city all gloomy and wet and white stretching down to the river, and they watched the long tracks of the elevated making such wonderful perspective that it never really seemed to disappear, it just infinitely met.

Finally they sat down on the couch to give their hostess just another quarter of an hour in which to return, and then for the first time in Adele's experience something happened in which she had no definite consciousness of beginnings. She found herself at the end of a passionate embrace.

Some weeks after when Adele came again to New York they agreed to meet at Helen's house. It had been arranged quite as a matter of course as if no objection to such a proceeding had ever been entertained. Adele laughed to herself as she thought of it. "Why we didn't before and why we do now are to me equally mysterious" she said shrugging her shoulders. "Great is Allah, Mohammed is no Shodah (fool)! though I dimly suspect that sometimes he is."

When the time came for keeping her engagement Adele for some time delayed going and remained lying on her friend's couch begging to be detained. She realised that her certain hold on her own frank joyousness and happy serenity was weakened. She almost longed to back out, she did so dread emotional complexities. "Oh for peace and a quiet life!" she groaned as she rang Helen's door-bell.

In Helen's room she found a note explaining that being worried as it was so much past the hour of appointment, she had gone to the Museum as Adele had perhaps misunderstood the arrangement. If she came in she was to wait. "It was very bad of me to fool around so long" Adele said to herself gravely and then sat down very peacefully to read.

"I am awfully sorry" Adele greeted Helen as she came into the room somewhat intensely, "it never occurred to me that you would be bothered, it was just dilatoriness on my part," and then they sat down. After a while Helen came and sat on the arm of Adele's chair. She took her head between tense arms and sent deep into her eyes a long straight look of concentrated question. "Haven't you anything to say to me?" she asked at last. "Why no, nothing in particular," Adele answered slowly. She met Helen's glance for a moment, returned it with simple friendliness and then withdrew from it.

"You are very chivalrous," Helen said with sad self-defiance. "You realise that there ought to be shame somewhere between us and as I have none you generously undertake it all." "No I am not chivalrous" Adele answered, "but I realise my deficiencies. I know that I always take an everlasting time to arrive anywhere really and that the rapidity of my superficial observation keeps it from being realised. It is certainly all my fault. I am so very deceptive. I arouse false expectations. You see," she continued meeting her again with pleasant friendliness, "you haven't yet learned that I am at once impetuous and slow-minded."

Time passed and they renewed their habit of desultory meetings at public places, but these were not the same as before. There was between them now a consciousness of strain, a sense of new adjustments, of uncertain standards and of changing values.

Helen was patient but occasionally moved to trenchant criticism, Adele was irritable and discursive but always ended with a frank almost bald apology for her inadequacy.

In the course of time they again arranged to meet in Helen's room. It was a wet rainy, sleety day and Adele felt chilly and unresponsive. Throwing off her hat and coat, she sat down after a cursory greeting and looked meditatively into the fire. "How completely we exemplify entirely different types" she began at last without looking at her companion. "You are a blooming Anglo Saxon. You know what you want and you go and get it without spending your days and nights changing backwards and forwards from yes to no. If you want to stick a knife into a man you just naturally go and stick straight and hard. You would probably kill him but it would soon be over while I, I would have so many compunctions and considerations that I would cut up all his surface anatomy and make it a long drawn agony but unless he should bleed to death quite by accident, I wouldn't do him any serious injury. No you are the very brave man, passionate but not emotional, capable of great sacrifice but not tender-hearted.

"And then you really want things badly enough to go out and get them and that seems to me very strange. I want things too but only in order to understand them and I never go and get them. I am a hopeless coward, I hate to risk hurting myself or anybody else. All I want to do is to meditate endlessly and think and talk. I know you object because you believe it necessary to feel something to think about and you contend that

I don't give myself time to find it. I recognise the justice of that criticism and I am doing my best these days to let it come."

She relapsed into silence and sat there smiling ironically into the fire. The silence grew longer and her smile turned into a look almost of disgust. Finally she wearily drew breath, shook her head and got up. "Ah! don't go," came from Helen in quick appeal. Adele answered the words. "No I am not going. I just want to look at these books." She wandered about a little. Finally she stopped by Helen's side and stood looking down at her with a gentle irony that wavered on the edge of scorn.

"Do you know" she began in her usual tone of dispassionate inquiry "you are a wonderful example of double personality. The you that I used to know and didn't like, and the occasional you that when I do catch a glimpse of it seems to me so very wonderful, haven't any possible connection with each other. It isn't as if my conception of you had gradually changed because it hasn't. I realise always one whole you consisting of a laugh so hard that it rattles, a voice that suggests a certain brutal coarseness and a point of view that is aggressively unsympathetic, and all that is one whole you and it alternates with another you that possesses a purity and intensity of feeling that leaves me quite awe-struck and a gentleness of voice and manner and an infinitely tender patience that entirely overmasters me. Now the question is which is really you because these two don't seem to have any connections. Perhaps when I really know something about you, the whole will come together but at present it is always either the one or the other and I haven't the least idea which is reallest. You certainly are one too many for me." She shrugged her shoulders, threw out her hands helplessly and sat down again before the fire. She aroused at last and became conscious that Helen was trembling bitterly. All hesitations were swept away by Adele's instant passionate sympathy for a creature obviously in pain and she took her into her arms with pure maternal tenderness. Helen gave way utterly. "I tried to be adequate to your experiments" she said at last "but you had no mercy. You were not content until you had dissected out every nerve in my body and left it quite exposed and it was too much, too much.

You should give your subjects occasional respites even in the ardor of research." She said it without bitterness. "Good God" cried Adele utterly dumbfounded "did you think that I was deliberately making you suffer in order to study results? Heavens and earth what do you take me for! Do you suppose that I for a moment realised that you were in pain. No! no! it is only my cursed habit of being concerned only with my own thoughts, and then you know I never for a moment believed that you really cared about me, that is one of the things that with all my conceit I never can believe. Helen how could you have had any use for me if you thought me capable of such wanton cruelty?" "I didn't know," she answered "I was willing that you should do what you liked if it interested you and I would stand it as well as I could." "Oh! Oh!" groaned Adele yearning over her with remorseful sympathy "surely dear you believe that I had no idea of your pain and that my brutality was due to ignorance and not intention." "Yes! yes! I know" whispered Helen, nestling to her. After a while she went on, "You know dear you mean so very much to me for with all your inveterate egotism you are the only person with whom I have ever come into close contact, whom I could continue to respect." "Faith" said Adele ruefully "I confess I can't see why. After all even at my best I am only tolerably decent. There are plenty of others, your experience has been unfortunate thats all, and then you know you have always shut yourself off by that fatal illusion of yours that you could stand completely alone." And then she chanted with tender mockery, "And the very strong man Kwasind and he was a very strong man" she went on "even if being an unconquerable solitary wasn't entirely a success."

2

All through the winter Helen at intervals spent a few days with Mabel Neathe in Baltimore. Adele was always more or less with them on these occasions. On the surface they preserved the same relations as had existed on the steamer. The only evidence that Mabel gave of a realisation of a difference was in never if she could avoid it leaving them alone together.

It was tacitly understood between them that on these rare

occasions they should give each other no sign. As the time drew near when Adele was once more to leave for Europe this time for an extended absence, the tension of this self-imposed inhibition became unendurable and they as tacitly ceased to respect it.

Some weeks before her intended departure Adele was one afternoon as usual taking tea with Mabel. "You have never met Mr. and Mrs. T. have you?" Mabel asked quite out of the air. They had never definitely avoided talking of Helen but they had not spoken of her unnecessarily. "No" Adele answered, "I haven't wanted to. I don't like perfunctory civilities and I know that I belong to the number of Helen's friends of whom they do not approve." "You would not be burdened by their civility, they never take the trouble to be as amiable as that." "Are your experiences so very unpleasant when you are stopping there? I shouldn't think that you would care to do it often." "Sometimes I feel as if it couldn't be endured but if I didn't, Helen would leave them and I think she would regret that and so I don't want her to do it. I have only to say the word and she would leave them at once and sometimes I think she will do it anyway. If she once makes up her mind she won't reconsider it. Of course I wouldn't say such things to any one but you, you know." "I can quite believe that," said Adele rather grimly, "Isn't there anything else that you would like to tell me just because I am I. If so don't let me get in your way." "I have never told you about our early relations" Mabel continued "You know Helen cared for me long before I knew anything about it. We used to be together a great deal at College and every now and then she would disappear for a long time into the country and it wasn't until long afterwards that I found out the reason of it. You know Helen never gives way. You have no idea how wonderful she is. I have been so worried lately" she went on "lest she should think it necessary to leave home for my sake because it is so uncomfortable for me in the summer when I spend a month with her." "Well then why don't you make a noble sacrifice and stay away. Apparently Helen's heroism is great enough to carry her through the ordeal." Adele felt herself to be quite satisfactorily vulgar. Mabel accepted it literally. "Do you really advise it?" she asked. "Oh yes" said Adele "there is nothing

so good for the soul as self imposed periods of total absti-
nence." "Well, I will think about it" Mabel answered "it is
such a comfort that you understand everything and one can
speak to you openly about it all." "Thats where you are entirely mistaken" Adele said decisively, "I understand nothing.
But after all" she added, "it isn't any of my business anyway.
Adios," and she left.

When she got home she saw a letter of Helen's on the table.
She felt no impulse to read it. She put it well away. "Not that
it is any of my business whether she is bound and if so how,"
she said to herself "That is entirely for her to work out with
her own conscience. For me it is only a question of what exists
between us two. I owe Mabel nothing;" and she resolutely
relegated it all quite to the background of her mind.

Mabel however did not allow the subject to rest. At the
very next opportunity she again asked Adele for advice. "Oh
hang it all" Adele broke out "what do I know about it? I
understand nothing of the nature of the bond between you."
"Don't you really?" Mabel was seriously incredulous. "No I
don't." Adele answered with decision, and the subject
dropped.

Adele communed with herself dismally. "I was strong-
minded enough to put it out of my head once, but this time
apparently it has come to stay. I can't deny that I do badly
want to know and I know well enough that if I continue to
want to know the only decent thing for me to do is to ask
the information of Helen. But I do so hate to do that. Why?
well I suppose because it would hurt so to hear her admit that
she was bound. It would be infinitely pleasanter to have Mabel
explain it but it certainly would be very contemptible of me
to get it from her. Helen is right, its not easy this business of
really caring about people. I seem to be pretty deeply in it"
and she smiled to herself "because now I don't regret the
bother and the pain. I wonder if I am really beginning to
care" and she lost herself in a revery.

Mabel's room was now for Adele always filled with the atmosphere of the unasked question. She could dismiss it when
alone but Mabel was clothed with it as with a garment although nothing concerning it passed between them.

Adele now received a letter from Helen asking why she had not written, whether it was that faith had again failed her. Adele at first found it impossible to answer, finally she wrote a note at once ambiguous and bitter.

At last the tension snapped. "Tell me then" Adele said to Mabel abruptly one evening. Mabel made no attempt to mis-understand but she did attempt to delay. "Oh well if you want to go through the farce of a refusal and an insistence, why help yourself," Adele broke out harshly, "but supposing all that done, I say again tell me." Mabel was dismayed by Adele's hot directness and she vaguely fluttered about as if to escape. "Drop your intricate delicacy" Adele said sternly "you wanted to tell, now tell." Mabel was cowed. She sat down and explained.

The room grew large and portentous and to Mabel's eyes Adele's figure grew almost dreadful in its concentrated repul-sion. There was a long silence that seemed to roar and menace and Mabel grew afraid. "Good-night" said Adele and left her.

Adele had now at last learned to stop thinking. She went home and lay motionless a long time. At last she got up and sat at her desk. "I guess I must really care a good deal about Helen" she said at last, "but oh Lord," she groaned and it was very bitter pain. Finally she roused herself. "Poor Mabel" she said "I could almost find it in my heart to be sorry for her. I must have looked very dreadful."

On the next few occasions nothing was said. Finally Mabel began again. "I really supposed Adele that you knew, or else I wouldn't have said anything about it at all and after I once mentioned it, you know you made me tell." "Oh yes I made you tell." Adele could admit it quite cheerfully; Mabel seemed so trivial. "And then you know," Mabel continued "I never would have mentioned it if I had not been so fond of you." Adele laughed, "Yes its wonderful what an amount of devotion to me there is lying around the universe; but what will Helen think of the results of this devotion of yours." "That is what worries me" Mabel admitted "I must tell her that I have told you and I am afraid she won't like it." "I rather suspect she won't" and Adele laughed again "but there is nothing like seizing an opportunity before your courage has a chance to ooze. Helen will be down next week, you know, and that will give you your chance but I guess now there has been enough said," and she definitely dismissed the matter.

Adele found it impossible to write to Helen, she felt too sore and bitter but even in spite of her intense revulsion of feeling, she realised that she did still believe in that other Helen that she had attempted once to describe to her. In spite of all evidence she was convinced that something real existed there, something that she was bound to reverence.

She spent a painful week struggling between revulsion and respect. Finally two days before Helen's visit, she heard from her. "I am afraid I can bear it no longer" Helen wrote. "As long as I believed there was a chance of your learning to be something more than your petty complacent self, I could willingly endure everything, but now you remind me of an ignorant mob. You trample everything ruthlessly under your feet without considering whether or not you kill something precious and without being changed or influenced by what you so brutally destroy. I am like Diogenes in quest of an honest man; I want so badly to find some one I can respect and I find them all worthy of nothing but contempt. You have done your best. I am sorry."

For some time Adele was wholly possessed by hot anger, but that changed to intense sympathy for Helen's pain. She realised the torment she might be enduring and so sat down at once to answer. "Perhaps though she really no longer cares" she thought to herself and hesitated "Well whether she does or not makes no difference I will at least do my part."

"I can make no defence" she wrote "except only that in spite of all my variations there has grown within me steadily an increasing respect and devotion to you. I am not surprised at your bitterness but your conclusions from it are not justified. It is hardly to be expected that such a changed estimate of values, such a complete departure from established convictions as I have lately undergone could take place without many revulsions. That you have been very patient I fully realise but on the other hand you should recognise that I too have done my best and your word to the contrary notwithstanding that best has not been contemptible. So don't talk any more nonsense about mobs. If your endurance is not equal to this task, why admit it and have done with it, if it is I will try to be adequate."

Adele knew that Helen would receive her letter but there would not be time to answer it as she was to arrive in Baltimore the following evening. They were all three to meet at the opera that night so for a whole day Adele would be uncertain of Helen's feeling toward her. She spent all her strength throughout the day in endeavoring to prepare herself to find that Helen still held her in contempt. It had always been her habit to force herself to realise the worst that was likely to befall her and to submit herself before the event. She was never content with simply thinking that the worst might happen and having said it to still expect the best but she had always accustomed herself to bring her mind again and again to this worst possibility until she had really mastered herself to bear it. She did this because she always doubted her own courage and distrusted her capacity to meet a difficulty if she had not inured herself to it beforehand.

All through this day she struggled for her accustomed definite resignation and the tremendous difficulty of accomplishment made her keenly realise how much she valued Helen's regard.

She did not arrive at the opera until after it had commenced. She knew how little command she had of her expression when deeply moved and she preferred that the first greeting should take place in the dark. She came in quietly to her place. Helen leaned across Mabel and greeted her. There was nothing in her manner to indicate anything and Adele realised by her sensation of sick disappointment that she had really not prepared herself at all. Now that the necessity was more imperative she struggled again for resignation and by the time the act was over she had pretty well gained it. She had at least mastered herself enough to entertain Mabel with elaborate discussion of music and knife fights. She avoided noticing Helen but that was comparatively simple as Mabel sat between them.

Carmen that night was to her at once the longest and the shortest performance that she had ever sat through. It was short because the end brought her nearer to hopeless certainty. It was long because she could only fill it with suspense.

The opera was at last or already over, Adele was uncertain which phrase expressed her feeling most accurately, and then they went for a little while to Mabel's room. Adele was by this time convinced that all her relation with Helen was at an end.

"You look very tired to-night, what's the matter?" Mabel asked her. "Oh!" she explained "there's been a lot of packing and arranging and good-bys to say and farewell lunches and dinners to eat. How I hate baked shad, its a particular delicacy now and I have lunched and dined on it for three days running so I think its quite reasonable for me to be worn out. Good-by no don't come downstairs with me. Hullo Helen has started down already to do the honors. Good-by I will see you again to-morrow." Mabel went back to her room and Helen was already lost in the darkness of the lower hall. Adele slowly descended the stairs impressing herself with the necessity of self-restraint.

"Can you forgive me?" and Helen held her close. "I haven't anything to forgive if you still care," Adele answered. They were silent together a long time. "We will certainly have earned our friendship when it is finally accomplished," Adele said at last.

"Well good-by," Mabel began as the next day Adele was leaving for good. "Oh! before you go I want to tell you that its alright. Helen was angry but its alright now. You will be in New York for a few days before you sail" she continued. "I know you won't be gone for a whole year, you will be certain to come back to us before long. I will think of your advice" she concluded. "You know it carries so much weight coming from you." "Oh of course" answered Adele and thought to herself, "What sort of a fool does Mabel take me for anyway."

Adele was in Helen's room the eve of her departure. They had been together a long time. Adele was sitting on the floor her head resting against Helen's knee. She looked up at Helen and then broke the silence with some effort. "Before I go" she said "I want to tell you myself what I suppose you know already, that Mabel has told me of the relations existing between you." Helen's arms dropped away. "No I didn't know." She was very still. "Mabel didn't tell you then?" Adele asked. "No" replied Helen. There was a sombre silence. "If you were not wholly selfish, you would have exercised self-restraint enough to spare me this," Helen said. Adele hardly heard the words, but the power of the mood that possessed Helen awed her. She broke through it at last and began with slow resolution.

"I do not admit" she said, "that I was wrong in wanting to know. I suppose one might in a spirit of Quixotic gener-osity deny oneself such a right but as a reasonable being, I feel that I had a right to know. I realise perfectly that it was hopelessly wrong to learn it from Mabel instead of from you. I admit I was a coward, I was simply afraid to ask you." Helen laughed harshly "You need not have been," she said "I would have told you nothing." "I think you are wrong, I am quite sure that you would have told me and I wanted to spare myself that pain, perhaps spare you it too, I don't know. I repeat I cannot believe that I was wrong in wanting to know."

They remained there together in an unyielding silence. When an irresistible force meets an immovable body what happens? Nothing. The shadow of a long struggle inevitable as their different natures lay drearily upon them. This incident however decided was only the beginning. All that had gone before was only a preliminary. They had just gotten into position.

The silence was not oppressive but it lasted a long time. "I am very fond of you Adele" Helen said at last with a deep embrace.

It was an hour later when Adele drew a deep breath of resolution, "What foolish people those poets are who say that parting is such sweet sorrow. Although it isn't for ever I can't find a bit of sweetness in it not one tiny little speck. Helen I don't like at all this business of leaving you." "And I" Helen exclaimed "when in you I seem to be taking farewell of par-ents, brothers sisters my own child, everything at once. No dear you are quite right there is nothing pleasant in it."

"Then why do they put it into the books?" Adele asked with dismal petulance. "Oh dear! but at least its some comfort to have found out that they are wrong. Its one fact discovered anyway. Dear we are neither of us sorry that we know enough to find it out, are we?" "No," Helen answered "We are neither of us sorry."

On the steamer Adele received a note of farewell from Mabel in which she again explained that nothing but her great regard for Adele would have made it possible for her to speak as she had done. Adele lost her temper. "I am willing to fight in any way that Mabel likes" she said to herself "underhand or overhand, in the dark, or in the light, in a room or out of doors but at this I protest. She unquestionably did that for a purpose even if the game was not successful. I don't blame her for the game, a weak man must fight with such weapons as he can hold but I don't owe it to her to endure the hypocrisy of a special affection. I can't under the circumstances be very straight but I'll not be unnecessarily crooked. I'll make it clear to her but I'll complicate it in the fashion that she loves."

"My dear Mabel" she wrote, "Either you are duller than I would like to think you or you give me credit for more good-natured stupidity than I possess. If the first supposition is correct then you have nothing to say and I need say nothing; if the second then nothing that you would say would carry weight so it is equally unnecessary for you to say anything. If you don't understand what I am talking about then I am talking about nothing and it makes no difference, if you do then there's enough said." Mabel did not answer for several months and then began again to write friendly letters.

It seemed incredible to Adele this summer that it was only one year ago that she had seemed to herself so simple and all morality so easily reducible to formula. In these long lazy Italian days she did not discuss these matters with herself. She realised that at present morally and mentally she was too complex, and that complexity too much astir. It would take much time and strength to make it all settle again. It might, she thought, be eventually understood, it might even in a great deal of time again become simple but at present it gave little promise.

She poured herself out fully and freely to Helen in their

ardent correspondence. At first she had had some hesitation about this. She knew that Helen and Mabel were to be together the greater part of the summer and she thought it possible that both the quantity and the matter of the correspondence, if it should come to Mabel's notice would give Helen a great deal of bother. She hesitated a long time whether to suggest this to Helen and to let her decide as to the expediency of being more guarded.

There were many reasons for not mentioning the matter. She realised that not alone Helen but that she herself was still uncertain as to the fidelity of her own feeling. She could not as yet trust herself and hesitated to leave herself alone with a possible relapse.

"After all," she said to herself, "it is Helen's affair and not mine. I have undertaken to follow her lead even into very devious and underground ways but I don't know that it is necessary for me to warn her. She knows Mabel as well as I do. Perhaps she really won't be sorry if the thing is brought to a head."

She remembered the reluctance that Helen always showed to taking precautions or to making any explicit statement of conditions. She seemed to satisfy her conscience and keep herself from all sense of wrong-doing by never allowing herself to expect a difficulty. When it actually arrived the active necessity of using whatever deception was necessary to cover it, drowned her conscience in the violence of action. Adele did not as yet realise this quality definitely but she was vaguely aware that Helen would shut her mind to any explicit statement of probabilities, that she would take no precautions and would thus avoid all sense of guilt. In this fashion she could safeguard herself from her own conscience.

Adele recognised all this dimly. She did not formulate it but it aided to keep her from making any statement to Helen.

She herself could not so avoid her conscience, she simply had to admit a change in moral basis. She knew what she was doing, she realised what was likely to happen and the way in which the new developments would have to be met.

She acknowledged to herself that her own defence lay simply in the fact that she thought the game was worth the candle. "After all" she concluded, "there is still the most important reason for saying nothing. The stopping of the correspondence would make me very sad and lonely. In other words I simply don't want to stop it and so I guess I won't."

For several months the correspondence continued with vigor and ardour on both sides. Then there came a three week interval and no word from Helen then a simple friendly letter and then another long silence.

Adele lying on the green earth on a sunny English hill-side communed with herself on these matters day after day. She had no real misgiving but she was deeply unhappy. Her unhappiness was the unhappiness of loneliness not of doubt. She saved herself from intense misery only by realising that the sky was still so blue and the country-side so green and beautiful. The pain of passionate longing was very hard to bear. Again and again she would bury her face in the cool grass to recover the sense of life in the midst of her sick despondency.

"There are many possibilities but to me only one probability," she said to herself. "I am not a trustful person in spite of an optimistic temperament but I am absolutely certain in the face of all the facts that Helen is unchanged. Unquestionably there has been some complication. Mabel has gotten hold of some letters and there has been trouble. I can't blame Mabel much. The point of honor would be a difficult one to decide between the three of us."

As time passed she did not doubt Helen but she began to be much troubled about her responsibility in the matter. She felt uncertain as to the attitude she should take.

"As for Mabel" she said to herself "I admit quite completely that I simply don't care. I owe her nothing. She wanted me when it was pleasant to have me and so we are quits. She entered the fight and must be ready to bear the results. We were never bound to each other, we never trusted each other and so there has been no breach of faith. She would show me no mercy and I need grant her none, particularly as she would wholly misunderstand it. It is very strange how very different one's morality and one's temper are when one wants something really badly. Here am I who have always been hopelessly soft-hearted and good-natured and who have always really preferred letting the other man win find myself quite cold-blooded and relentless. Its a lovely morality that in which we believe even in serious matters when we are not deeply stirred, its so delightfully noble and gentle." She sighed and then laughed. "Well, I hope some day to find a morality that can stand the wear and tear of real desire to take the place of the nice one that I have lost, but morality or no morality the fact remains that I have no compunctions on the score of Mabel.

"About Helen thats a very different matter. I unquestionably do owe her a great deal but just how to pay it is the difficult point to discover. I can't forget that to me she can never be the first consideration as she is to Mabel for I have other claims that I would always recognise as more important. I have neither the inclination or the power to take Mabel's place and I feel therefor that I have no right to step in between them. On the other hand morally and mentally she is in urgent need of a strong comrade and such in spite of all evidence I believe myself to be. Some day if we continue she will in spite of herself be compelled to choose between us and what have I to offer. Nothing but an elevating influence.

"Bah! what is the use of an elevating influence if one hasn't bread and butter. Her possible want of butter if not of bread, considering her dubious relations with her family must be kept in mind. Mabel could and would always supply them and I neither can nor will. Alas for an unbuttered influence say I. What a grovelling human I am anyway. But I do have occasional sparkling glimpses of faith and those when they come I truly believe to be worth much bread and butter. Perhaps Helen also finds them more delectable. Well I will state the case to her and abide by her decision."

She timed her letter to arrive when Helen would be once more at home alone. "I can say to you now" she wrote "what I found impossible in the early summer. I am now convinced and I think you are too that my feeling for you is genuine and loyal and whatever may be our future difficulties we are now at least on a basis of understanding and trust. I know therefor that you will not misunderstand when I beg you to consider carefully whether on the whole you had not better give me up. I can really amount to so little for you and yet will inevitably cause you so much trouble. That I dread your giving me up I do not deny but I dread more being the cause of serious annoyance to you. Please believe that this statement is sincere and is to be taken quite literally."

"Hush little one" Helen answered "Oh you stupid child, don't you realise that you are the only thing in the world that makes anything seem real or worth while to me. I have had a dreadful time this summer. Mabel read a letter of mine to you and it upset her completely. She said that she found it but I can hardly believe that. She asked me if you cared for me and I told her that I didn't know and I really don't dearest. She did not ask me if I cared for you. The thing upset her completely and she was jealous of my every thought and I could not find a moment even to feel alone with you. But don't please don't say any more about giving you up. You are not any trouble to me if you will only not leave me. Its alright now with Mabel, she says that she will never be jealous again." "Oh Lord!" groaned Adele "well if she isn't she would be a hopeless fool. Anyhow I said I would abide by Helen's decision and I certainly will but how so proud a woman can permit such control is more than I can understand."

BOOK 3:

Helen

I

There is no passion more dominant and instinctive in the human spirit than the need of the country to which one belongs. One often speaks of homesickness as if in its intense form it were the peculiar property of Swiss mountaineers, Scandinavians, Frenchmen and those other nations that too have a poetic back-ground, but poetry is no element in the case. It is simply a vital need for the particular air that is native, whether it is the used up atmosphere of London, the clean-cut cold of America or the rarefied air of Swiss mountains. The time comes when nothing in the world is so important as a breath of one's own particular climate. If it were one's last penny it would be used for that return passage.

An American in the winter fogs of London can realise this passionate need, this desperate longing in all its completeness. The dead weight of that fog and smoke laden air, the sky that never suggests for a moment the clean blue distance that has been the accustomed daily comrade, the dreary sun, moon and stars that look like painted imitations on the ceiling of a smoke-filled room, the soggy, damp, miserable streets, and the women with bedraggled, frayed out skirts, their faces swollen and pimply with sordid dirt ground into them until it has become a natural part of their ugly surface all become day after day a more dreary weight of hopeless oppression.

A hopeful spirit resists. It feels that it must be better soon, it cannot last so forever; this afternoon, to-morrow this dead weight must lift, one must soon again realise a breath of clean air, but day after day the whole weight of fog, smoke and low brutal humanity rests a weary load on the head and back and one loses the power of straightening the body to actively bear the burden, it becomes simply a despairing endurance.

Just escaped from this oppression, Adele stood in the saloon of an ocean steamer looking at the white snow line of New York harbor. A little girl one of a family who had also fled from England after a six months trial, stood next to her. They stayed side by side their faces close to the glass. A government ship passed flying the flag. The little girl looked deeply at it and then with slow intensity said quite to herself, "There is the American flag, it looks good." Adele echoed it, there was all America and it looked good; the clean sky and the white snow and the straight plain ungainly buildings all in a cold and brilliant air without spot or stain.

Adele's return had been unexpected and she landed quite alone. "No it wasn't to see you much as I wanted you," she explained to Helen long afterwards, "it was just plain America. I landed quite alone as I had not had time to let any of my friends know of my arrival but I really wasn't in a hurry to go to them much as I had longed for them all. I simply rejoiced in the New York streets, in the long spindling legs of the elevated, in the straight high undecorated houses, in the empty upper air and in the white surface of the snow. It was such a joy to realise that the whole thing was without mystery and without complexity, that it was clean and straight and meagre and hard and white and high. Much as I wanted you I was not eager for after all you meant to me a turgid and complex world, difficult yet necessary to understand and for the moment I wanted to escape all that, I longed only for obvious, superficial, clean simplicity."

Obeying this need Adele after a week of New York went to Boston. She steeped herself in the very essence of clear eyed Americanism. For days she wandered about the Boston streets rejoicing in the passionless intelligence of the faces. She revelled in the American street-car crowd with its ready intercourse, free comments and airy persiflage all without double meanings which created an atmosphere that never suggested for a moment the need to be on guard.

It was a cleanliness that began far inside of these people and was kept persistently washed by a constant current of clean cold water. Perhaps the weight of stains necessary to the deepest understanding might be washed away, it might well be that it was not earthy enough to be completely satisfying, but it was a delicious draught to a throat choked with soot and fog.

For a month Adele bathed herself in this cleanliness and then she returned to New York eager again for a world of greater complexity.

For some time after her return a certain estrangement existed between Helen and herself. Helen had been much hurt at her long voluntary absence and Adele as yet did not sufficiently understand her own motives to be able to explain. It had seemed to her only that she rather dreaded losing herself again with Helen.

This feeling between them gradually disappeared. In their long sessions in Helen's room, Adele now too cultivated the habit of silent intimacy. As time went on her fear of Helen and of herself gradually died away and she yielded herself to the complete joy of simply being together.

One day they agreed between them that they were very near the state of perfect happiness. "Yes I guess its alright" Adele said with a fond laugh "and when its alright it certainly is very good. Am I not a promising pupil?" she asked. "Not nearly so good a pupil as so excellent a teacher as I am deserves" Helen replied. "Oh! Oh!" cried Adele, "I never realised it before but compared with you I am a model of humility. There is nothing like meeting with real arrogance. It makes one recognise a hitherto hidden virtue," and then they once more lost themselves in happiness.

It was a very real oblivion. Adele was aroused from it by a kiss that seemed to scale the very walls of chastity. She flung away on the instant filled with battle and revulsion. Utterly regardless of Helen she lay her face buried in her hands. "I never dreamed that after all that has come I was still such a virgin soul" she said to herself, "and that like Parsifal a kiss could make me frantic with realisation" and then she lost herself in the full tide of her fierce disgust.

She lay long in this new oblivion. At last she turned. Helen lay very still but on her face were bitter tears. Adele with her usual reaction of repentance tried to comfort. "Forgive me!" she said "I don't know what possessed me. No you didn't do anything it was all my fault." "And we were so happy" Helen said. After a long silence she asked "Was it that you felt your old distrust of me again?" "Yes," replied Adele briefly. "I am afraid I can't forgive this," Helen said. "I didn't suppose that you could," Adele replied.

They continued to meet but each one was filled with her own struggle. Adele finally reopened the subject. "You see" she explained "my whole trouble lies in the fact that I don't know on what ground I am objecting, whether it is morality or a meaingless instinct. You know I have always had a conviction that no amount of reasoning will help in deciding what is right and possible for one to do. If you don't begin with some theory of obligation, anything is possible and no rule of right and wrong holds. One must either accept some theory or else believe one's instinct or follow the world's opinion.

"Now I have no theory and much as I would like to, I can't really regard the world's opinion. As for my instincts they have always been opposed to the indulgence of any feeling of passion. I suppose that is due to the Calvinistic influence that dominates American training and has interfered with my natural temperament. Somehow you have made me realise that my attitude in the matter was degrading and material, instead of moral and spiritual but in spite of you my puritan instincts again and again say no and I get into a horrible mess. I am beginning to distrust my instincts and I am about convinced that my objection was not a deeply moral one. I suppose after all it was a good deal cowardice. Anyhow" she concluded, "I guess I haven't any moral objection any more and now if I have lost my instincts it will be alright and we can begin a new deal." "I am afraid I can't help you much" Helen answered "I can only hold by the fact that whatever you do and however much you hurt me I seem to have faith in you, in spite of yourself." Adele groaned. "How hopelessly inadequate I am," she said.

This completeness of revulsion never occurred again, but a new opposition gradually arose between them. Adele realised that Helen demanded of her a response and always before that response was ready. Their pulses were differently timed. She could not go so fast and Helen's exhausted nerves could no longer wait. Adele found herself constantly forced on by Helen's pain. She went farther than she could in honesty because she was unable to refuse anything to one who had given all. It was a false position. All reactions had now to be concealed as it was evident that Helen could no longer support that struggle. Their old openness was no longer possible and Adele ceased to express herself freely.

She realised that her attitude was misunderstood and that

Helen interpreted her slowness as essential deficiency. This was the inevitable result of a situation in which she was forced constantly ahead of herself. She was sore and uneasy and the greater her affection for Helen became the more irritable became her discontent.

One evening they had agreed to meet at a restaurant and dine before going to Helen's room. Adele arriving a half hour late found Helen in a state of great excitement. "Why what's the matter" Adele asked. "Matter" Helen repeated "you kept me waiting for you and a man came in and spoke to me and its the first time that I have ever been so insulted." Adele gazed at her in astonishment "Great guns!" she exclaimed "what do you expect if you go out alone at night. You must be willing to accept the consequences. The men are quite within their rights." "Their rights they have no right to insult me." Adele shook her head in slow wonderment. "Will we ever understand each other's point of view," she said. "A thing that seems to unworldly, unheroic me so simple and inevitable and which I face quietly a score of times seems to utterly unnerve you while on the other hand,—but then we won't go into that, have something to eat and you will feel more cheerful."

"If you had been much later," Helen said as they were walking home, "I would have left and never have had anything farther to do with you until you apologised." "Bah!" exclaimed Adele. "I haven't any objection to apologising, the only thing I object to is being in the wrong. You are quite like a story-book" she continued, "you still believe in the divine right of heroics and of ladies. You think there is some higher power that makes the lower world tremble, when you say, Man how dare you! Thats all very well when the other man wants to be scared but when he doesn't its the strongest man that wins."

They had been together for some time in the room, when Helen broke the silence. "I wonder," she said, "why I am doomed always to care for people who are so hopelessly inadequate." Adele looked at her a few moments and then wandered about the room. She returned to her seat, her face very still and set. "Oh! I didn't mean anything" said Helen, "I was only thinking about it all." Adele made no reply. "I think

you might be patient with me when I am nervous and tired"
Helen continued petulantly "and not be angry at everything
I say." "I could be patient enough if I didn't think that you
really meant what you have said," Adele answered. "I don't
care what you say, the trouble is that you do believe it." "But
you have said it yourself again and again" Helen complained.
"That is perfectly true" returned Adele "but it is right for me
to say it and to believe it too, but not for you. If you believe
it, it puts a different face on the whole matter. It makes the
situation intolerable." They were silent, Helen nervous and
uneasy, and Adele rigid and quiet. "Oh why can't you forget
it?" Helen cried at last. Adele roused herself. "Its alright" she
said "don't bother. You are all tired out come lie down and
go to sleep." She remained with her a little while and then
went into another room to read. She was roused from an
unpleasant revery by Helen's sudden entrance. "I had such a
horrible dream" she said "I thought that you were angry and
had left me never to come back. Don't go away, please stay
with me."

"You haven't forgiven me yet" Helen asked the next morning as Adele was about to leave her. "It isn't a question of
forgiveness, its a question of your feeling," Adele replied
steadily. "You have given no indication as yet that you did not
believe what you said last night." "I don't know what I said,"
Helen evaded "I am worried and pestered and bothered and
you just make everything harder for me and then accuse me
of saying things that I shouldn't. Well perhaps I shouldn't
have said it." "But nevertheless you believe it," Adele returned stubbornly. "Oh I don't know what I believe. I am so
torn and bothered, can't you leave me alone." "You have no
right to constantly use your pain as a weapon," Adele flashed
out angrily. "What do you mean by that?" Helen demanded.
"I mean that you force me on by your pain and then hold me
responsible for the whole business. I am willing to stand for
my own trouble but I will not endure the whole responsibility
of yours." "Well aren't you responsible," asked Helen, "have
I done anything but be passive while you did as you pleased.
I have been willing to endure it all, but I have not taken one
step to hold you." Adele stared at her. "So thats your version

of the situation is it? Oh well then there is no use in saying another word." She started to go and then stood irresolutely by the door. Helen dropped her head on her arms. Adele returned and remained looking down at her stubborn and unhappy. "Oh I shall go mad," Helen moaned. Adele stood motionless. Helen's hand dropped and Adele kneeling beside her took her into her arms with intense fondness, but they both realised that neither of them had yielded.

They were each too fond of the other ever to venture on an ultimatum for they realised that they would not be constant to it. The question of relative values and responsibilities was not again openly discussed between them. Subtly perhaps unconsciously but nevertheless persistently Helen now threw the burden of choice upon Adele. Just how it came about she never quite realised but inevitably now it was always Adele that had to begin and had to ask for the next meeting. Helen's attitude became that of one anxious to give all but unfortunately prevented by time and circumstances. Adele was sure that it was not that Helen had ceased to care but that intentionally or not she was nevertheless taking full advantage of the fact that Adele now cared equally as much.

Adele chafed under this new dispensation but nevertheless realised that it was no more than justice. In fact her submission went deeper. On the night of their quarrel she had realised for the first time Helen's understanding of what their relations had been and she now spent many weary nights in endeavoring to decide whether that interpretation was just and if she really was to that degree responsible. As time went on she became hopelessly confused and unhappy about the whole matter.

One night she was lying on her bed gloomy and disconsolate. Suddenly she burst out, "No I am not a cad. Helen has come very near to persuading me that I am but I really am not. We both went into this with our eyes open, and Helen fully as deliberately as myself. I never intentionally made her suffer however much she may think I did. No if one goes in, one must be willing to stand for the whole game and take the full responsibility of their own share."

*

"You know I don't understand your attitude at all," Adele said to Helen the next day. "I am thinking of your indignation at those men speaking to you that night when we had the quarrel. It seems to me one must be prepared to stand not only the actual results of one's acts but also all the implications of them. People of your heroic kind consider yourselves heroes when you are doing no more than the rest of us who look upon it only as humbly submitting to inevitable necessity." "What do you mean?" asked Helen. "Why simply that when one goes out of bounds one has no claim to righteous indignation if one is caught." "That depends somewhat on the method of going," answered Helen, "one can go out of bounds in such a manner that one's right must be respected." "One's right to do wrong?" Adele asked. "No for when it is done so it isn't wrong. You have not yet learned that things are not separated by such hard and fast lines, but I understand your meaning. You object because I have stopped enduring everything from you. You have no understanding of all that I have forgiven." "I have said it in fun and now I say it in earnest," Adele answered angrily "you are too hopelessly arrogant. Are you the only one that has had to endure and forgive." "Oh yes I suppose that you think that you too have made serious sacrifices but I tell you that I never realised what complete scorn I was capable of feeling as that night when I kissed you and you flung me off in that fashion because you didn't know what it was that you wanted." "You are intolerable" Adele answered fiercely, "I at least realise that I am not always in the right, but you, you are incapable of understanding anything except your own point of view, or realising even distantly the value of a humility which acknowledges an error." "Humility" Helen repeated, "that is a strange claim for you to make for yourself." "May be," Adele answered "all things are relative. I never realised my virtue until it was brought out by contrast." "Oh I could be humble too," Helen retorted "if I could see any one who had made good a superior claim, but that hasn't come yet." "No, and with your native blindness it isn't likely that it ever will, thats quite true." "No it isn't blindness, its because I understand values before I act on them. Oh yes I know you are generous enough after you have gone home and have had time to think it over, but its the generosity of instinctive acts that count and as to that I don't think there is much doubt as to who is the better man." "As you will!" cried Adele bursting violently from her chair with a thundering imprecation and then with the same movement and a feeling of infinite tenderness and sorrow she took Helen into her arms and kissed her. "What a great goose you are," said Helen fondly. "Oh yes I know it" Adele answered drearily, "but its no use I can't remain angry even for one long moment. Repentance comes too swiftly but nevertheless I have a hopelessly persistent mind and after the pressure is removed I return to the old refrain. Dear don't forget, you really are in the wrong."

In spite of this outburst of reconciliation, things did not really improve between them. Helen still pursued her method of granting in inverse ratio to the strength of Adele's desire, and Adele's unhappiness and inward resistance grew steadily with the increase of her affection.

Before long the old problem of Mabel's claims further complicated the situation. "I am going abroad this summer again with Mabel," Helen said one day. Adele made no comment but the question "At whose expense?" was insistently in her mind.

In spite of the conviction that she owed Mabel nothing, she had had an uneasy sense concerning her during the whole winter. She had avoided going to Boston again as she did not wish to see her. She realised a sense of shame at the thought of meeting her. In spite of the clearness of her reasoning, she could not get rid of the feeling that she had stolen the property of another.

On the few occasions when the matter was spoken of between them, Helen while claiming her right to act as she pleased, admitted the validity of Mabel's claim. She declared repeatedly that in the extreme case if she had to give up some one it would be Adele and not Mabel, as Mabel would be unable to endure it, and Adele and herself were strong enough to support such a trial.

Just how Helen reconciled these conflicting convictions, Adele did not understand but as her own reconcilements were far from convincing to herself, she could ask for no explana-

tions of the other's conscience. This statement of a foreign
trip, probably at Mabel's expense made her once more face
the situation. She had a strong sense of the sanctity of money
obligations. She recognised as paramount the necessary return
for value received in all cash considerations. Perhaps Helen
had her own money but of this Adele was exceedingly doubtful. She wanted badly to know but she admitted to herself
that this question she dared not ask.

The recognition of Helen's willingness to accept this of
Mabel brought her some comfort. She lost her own sense of
shame toward Mabel. "After all" she thought, "I haven't
really robbed her of anything. She will win out eventually so
I can meet her with a clearer conscience." She then told Helen
that she intended going to Boston for a week before her return to Europe. Helen said nothing but it was evident that
she did not wish her to go.

In this last month together there was less openness and
confidence between them than at any time in their whole relation. Helen seemed content and indifferent but yet persisted
always in answer to any statement of doubt from Adele that
she was quite unchanged. Adele felt that her own distrust,
stubbornness and affection were all steadily increasing. She
deeply resented Helen's present attitude which was that of
one granting all and more than all to a discontented peti-
tioner. She felt Helen's continued statement of the sacrifices
that she was making and even then the impossibility of satisfying her as both untruthful and insulting, but the conditions
between them had become such that no explanations were
possible.

Helen's attitude was now a triumph of passivity. Adele was
forced to accept it with what grace she might. Her only consolation lay in the satisfaction to her pride in realising Helen's
inadequacy in a real trial of generosity. When together now
they seemed quite to have changed places. Helen was irritating and unsatisfying, Adele patient and forbearing.

"I wonder if we will see each other in Italy" Adele said one
day. "I certainly very much hope so" answered Helen. "It is
only a little over a week and then I go to Boston and then I
will be in New York only a few days before I sail," continued

Adele, "when will I see you." "On Monday evening" suggested Helen. "Good" agreed Adele.

On Monday morning Adele received a note from Helen explaining that the arrival of a friend made it impossible for her to see her alone before the end of the week but she would be glad if she would join them at lunch. Adele was deeply hurt and filled with bitter resentment. She understood Helen's intention whether conscious or not in this delay. The realisation that in order to accomplish her ends Helen would not hesitate to cause her any amount of pain gave her a sense of sick despondency. She wrote a brief note saying that she did not think her presence at this lunch would tend greatly to the gayety of nations but that she would be at home in the evening if Helen cared to come. She got a hurried reply full of urgent protest but still holding to the original plan. "I guess this is the end of the story," Adele said to herself.

"The situation seems utterly hopeless" she wrote, "we are more completely unsympathetic and understand each other less than at any time in our whole acquaintance. It may be my fault but nevertheless I find your attitude intolerable. You need feel no uneasiness about my going to Boston. I will not cause any trouble and as for the past I realise that as a matter of fact I have in no way interfered as you both still have all that is really vital to you."

"I guess that settles it," she said drearily as she dropped the letter into the mail-box. Helen made no sign. The days passed very quickly for Adele. All her actual consciousness found the definite ending of the situation a great relief. As long as one is firmly grasping the nettles there is no sting. The bitter pain begins when the hold begins to relax. At the actual moment of a calamity the undercurrents of pain, repentance and vain regret are buried deep under the ruins of the falling buildings and it is only when the whole mass begins to settle that they begin to well up here and there and at last rush out in an overwhelming flood of bitter pain. Adele in these first days that passed so quickly was peaceful and almost content. It was almost the end of the week when walking down town one day she saw Helen in the distance. It gave her a sudden shock and at first she was dazed but not moved by it, but gradually she became entirely possessed by the passion of her own longing and the pity of Helen's possible pain. Without giving herself time for consideration she wrote to her and told her that having seen her she had realised the intensity of her own affection but that she did not feel that she had been in the wrong either in feeling or expressing resentment but that if Helen cared to come, she would be at home in the morning to see her. "Certainly I will come," Helen answered.

When they met they tried to cover their embarrassment with commonplaces. Suddenly Adele frankly gave it up and went to the window and stared bravely out at the trees. Helen left standing in the room fought it out, finally she yielded and came to the window.

There was no ardor in their reconciliation, they had both wandered too far. Gradually they came together more freely but even then there was no openness of explanation between them. "As long as you have a soreness within that you don't express, nothing can be right between us," Helen said but to this appeal Adele could not make an open answer. There were things in her mind which she knew absolutely that Helen would not endure to hear spoken and so they could meet in mutual fondness but not in mutual honesty.

"Your letter upset me rather badly," Helen said some hours later. "In fact I am rather afraid I fainted." "But you would not have said a word to me, no matter how much you knew I longed for it," Adele asked. "No" answered Helen "how could I?" "We are both proud women," Adele said "but mine doesn't take that form. As long as I thought there was a possibility of your caring, no amount of pain or humiliation would keep me from coming to you. But you do realise don't you," she asked earnestly "that however badly I may behave or whatever I may say or do that my devotion and loyalty to you are absolute." "Yes" answered Helen "I know it. I have learned my lesson too and I do trust you always." They both realised this clearly, Adele had learned to love and Helen to trust but still there was no real peace between them.

"Don't worry about me, I won't get into any trouble in Boston" Adele said cheerily as they parted. "You come back on Sunday" Helen asked. "Yes and will see you Sunday evening and then only a few days and then I will be on the ocean.

Unless we Marconi to each other we will then for some little time be unable to get into difficulties."

From Boston Adele wrote a letter to Helen full of nonsense and affection. She received just before her return a curt and distant answer.

"Well now what's gone wrong" she said impatiently, "will there never be any peace?"

When she arrived at Helen's room Sunday evening, Helen had not yet returned. She sat down and waited impatiently. Helen came in after a while radiant and cordial but very unfamiliar. Adele quietly watched her. Helen moved about and talked constantly. Adele was unresponsive and looked at her quite stolidly. At last Helen became quiet. Adele looked at her some time longer and then laughed. "Aren't you ashamed of yourself" she asked. Helen made an effort to be heroic but failed. "Yes I am" she admitted "but your letter was so cocky and you had caused me so much trouble that I couldn't resist that temptation. There yes I am ashamed but it comes hard for me to say it." Adele laughed joyously "Well its the first and probably the last time in your history that you have ever realised your wrong-doing so lets celebrate" and there was peace between them.

It was not however a peace of long duration for soon it had all come back. Helen was once more inscrutable and Adele resentful and unhappy.

Adele was to sail on the next day and they were spending this last morning together. Adele was bitterly unhappy at the uncertainty of it all and Helen quite peaceful and content. Adele to conceal her feelings wandered up to a book-case and began to read. She stuck to it resolutely until Helen annoyed came up to her. "Pshaw" she said "why do you spend our last morning together in this fashion?" "Because I am considerably unhappy," Adele replied. "Well you had better do as I do, wait to be unhappy until after you are gone," Helen answered. Adele remembered their parting a year ago when Helen's point of view had been different. "I might reply" she began, "but then I guess I won't" she added. "That I won't be unhappy even then, were you going to say," Helen asked. "No I wasn't going to be quite as obvious as that." Adele answered and then wandered disconsolately about the room.

She came back finally and sat on the arm of Helen's chair but held herself drearily aloof. "Why do you draw away from me, when you are unhappy?" Helen finally burst out. "Don't you trust me at all."

A little later Adele was about to leave. They were standing at the door looking intently at each other. "Do you really care for me any more," Adele asked at last. Helen was angry and her arms dropped. "You are impossible" she answered. "I have never before in my life ever given anybody more than one chance, and you, you have had seventy times seven and are no better than at first." She kissed her resignedly. "You have succeeded in killing me" she said drearily, "and now you are doing your best to kill yourself. Good-by I will come to see you this evening for a little while."

In the evening they began to discuss a possible meeting in Italy. "If I meet you there" Adele explained "I must do it deliberately for in the natural course of things I would be in France as my brother does not intend going South this summer. Its a question that you absolutely must decide. There is no reason why I should not come except only as it would please or displease you. As for Mabel she knows that I am fond of you and so it isn't necessary for me to conceal my emotions. It is only a question of you and your desires. You can't leave it to me" she concluded, "for you know, I have no power of resisting temptation, but I am strong enough to do as you say, so you must settle it." "I can certainly conceal my emotions so it would be perfectly safe even if you can't," answered Helen. "I am afraid though I haven't any more power of resisting temptation than you but I will think it over." Just as they parted Helen decided. "I think dear that you had better come" she said. "Alright" answered Adele.

2

There was nothing to distinguish Mabel Neathe and Helen Thomas as they walked down the Via Nazionale from the average American woman tourist. Their shirt-waists trimly pinned down, their veils depending in graceless folds from their hats, the little bags with the steel chain firmly grasped in the left hand, the straightness of their backs and the determination of their observation all marked them an integral part of that national sisterhood which shows a more uncompromising family likeness than a continental group of sisters with all their dresses made exactly alike.

This general American sisterhood has a deeper conformity than the specific European, because in the American it is a conformity from within out. They all look alike not because they want to or because they are forced to do it, but simply because they lack individual imagination.

The European sisterhood conform to a common standard for economy or because it is a tradition to which they must submit but there is always the pathetic attempt to assert individual feeling in the difference of embroidery on a collar, or in a variation in tying of a bow and sometimes in the very daring by a different flower in the hat.

These two Americans then were like all the others. There was the same want of abundant life, the same inwardly compelled restrained movement, which kept them aloof from the life about them and the same intensely serious but unenthusiastic interest in the things to be observed. It was the walking of a dutiful purpose full of the necessity of observing many things among an alien mass of earthy spontaneity whose ideal expression is enthusiasm.

Behind them out of a side street came a young woman, the cut of whose shirt-waist alone betrayed her American origin. Large, abundant, full-busted and joyous, she seemed a part of the rich Roman life. She moved happily along, her white Panama hat well back on her head and an answering smile on her face as she caught the amused glances that fell upon her. Seeing the two in front she broke into a run, clapped them on the shoulder and as they turned with a start, she gave the national greeting "Hullo."

"Why Adele" exclaimed Helen, "where did you come from, you look as brown and white and clean as if you had just sprung out of the sea." With that they all walked on together. Adele kept up a lively talk with Mabel until they came to the Pilgrimage church of the Santa Maria Maggiore. In the shelter of that great friendly hall she exchanged a word with Helen. "How are things going" she asked. "Very badly" Helen replied.

They wandered about all together for awhile and then they agreed to take a drive out into the Campagna. They were all keenly conscious of the fact that this combination of themselves all together was most undesirable but this feeling was covered by an enthusiastic and almost convincing friendly spontaneity, and indeed the spontaneity and the friendliness were not forced or hypocritical for if it had not been that they all wanted something else so much more they would have had great enjoyment in what they had. As it was the friendliness was almost enough to give a substantial basis to many moments of their companionship.

They spent that day together and then the next and by that time the tension of this false position began to tell on all of them.

The burden of constant entertainment and continual peace-keeping began to exhaust Adele's good-nature, and she was beginning to occasionally show signs of impatient boredom. Mabel at first accepted eagerly enough all the entertainment offered her by Adele but gradually there came a change. Helen was constantly depressed and silent and Adele wishing to give her time to recover devoted herself constantly to Mabel's amusement. This seemed to suggest to Mabel for the first time that Adele's devotion was not only accepted but fully returned. This realisation grew steadily in her mind. She now ceased to observe Adele and instead kept constant and insistent watch on Helen. She grew irritable and almost insolent. She had never before in their triple intercourse resented Adele's presence but she began now very definitely to do so.

On the evening of their second day together Helen and Adele had a half hours stroll alone. "Things do seem to be going badly, what's the trouble?" Adele asked. "I don't know exactly why but this summer Mabel is more jealous than ever before. It isn't only you" she hastened to explain, "it is the same with everybody in whom I am ever so slightly interested. As for you nothing can induce her to believe that you came here simply because you had never been here before and wanted to see Rome. She positively refused to read your letter to me which I wanted to show her." Adele laughed. "How you do keep it up!" she said. "What do you expect? Mabel would be a fool if she believed anything but the truth for after all I could have struggled along without Rome for another year." After a while Adele began again. "I don't want you to have me at all on your mind. I am fully able to take care of myself. If you think it will be better if I clear out I will go." "No" said Helen wearily "that would not help matters now." "I owe you so much for all that you have taught me," Adele went on earnestly "and my faith in you is now absolute. As long as you give me that nothing else counts." "You are very generous" murmured Helen. "No its not generosity" Adele insisted "its nothing but justice for really you do mean very much to me. You do believe that." "Yes I believe it," Helen answered.

Adele fulfilled very well the duty that devolved upon her that of keeping the whole thing moving but it was a severe strain to be always enlivening and yet always on guard. One morning she began one of her old time lively disputes with Helen who soon became roused and interested. In the midst Mabel got up and markedly left them. Helen stopped her talk. "This won't do," she said "we must be more careful," and for the rest of the day she exerted herself to cajole, flatter and soothe Mabel back to quiescence.

"Why in the name of all that is wonderful should we both be toadying to Mabel in this fashion," Adele said to herself disgustedly. "What is it anyway that Helen wants. If its the convenience of owning Mabel, Jupiter, she comes high. Helen doesn't love her and if she were actuated by pure kindness and duty and she really wanted to spare her she would tell me to leave. And as for Mabel it is increasing all her native hypocrisy and underhand hatreds and selfishness and surely she is already overly endowed with these qualities. As for me the case is simple enough. I owe Mabel nothing but I want Helen and Helen wants me to do this. It certainly does come high." She was disgusted and exasperated and kept aloof from them for a while. Helen upon this grew restless. She instinctively endeavored to restimulate Adele by accidental momentary contacts, by inflections of voice and shades of manner, by all delicate charged signs such as had for some time been definitely banished between them.

"What a condemned little prostitute it is," Adele said to herself between a laugh and a groan. "I know there is no use in asking for an explanation. Like Kate Croy she would tell me 'I shall sacrifice nothing and nobody' and thats just her situation she wants and will try for everything, and hang it all, I am so fond of her and do somehow so much believe in her that I am willing to help as far as within me lies. Besides I certainly get very much interested in the mere working of the machinery. Bah! it would be hopelessly unpleasant if it didn't have so many compensations."

The next morning she found herself in very low spirits. "I suppose the trouble with me is that I am sad with longing and sick with desire," she said to herself drearily and then went out to meet the others.

Helen on that day seemed even more than ever worn and tired and she even admitted to not feeling very well. Adele in spite of all her efforts continued irritable and depressed. Mabel made no comments but was evidently observant. Adele's mood reacted on Helen whose eyes followed her about wearily and anxiously. "Helen" said Adele hurriedly in the shadow of a church corner. "Don't look at me like that, you utterly unnerve me and I won't be able to keep it up. I am alright, just take care of yourself."

"I wonder whether Helen has lost her old power of control or whether the difference lies in me" she said to herself later. "Perhaps it is that I have learned to read more clearly the small variations in her looks and manner. I am afraid though it isn't that. I think she is really becoming worn out. There would be no use in my going away now for then Mabel would be equally incessant as she was last summer. Now at least I can manage Helen a little time to herself by employing Mabel. Good Heavens she is certainly paying a big price for her whistle."

The situation did not improve. Helen became constantly more and more depressed and Adele found it always more and more difficult to keep it all going. She yearned over Helen with passionate tenderness but dared not express it. She recognised that nothing would be more complete evidence for Mabel than such signs of Helen's dependence, so she was compelled to content herself with brief passionate statements of love, sympathy and trust in those very occasional moments when they were alone. Helen had lost the power of quickly recovering and so even these rare moments could only be sparingly used.

One afternoon they were all three lounging in Helen's and Mabel's room taking the usual afternoon siesta. Adele was lying on the bed looking vacantly out of the window at the blue sky filled with warm sunshine. Mabel was on a couch in a darkened corner and Helen was near her sitting at a table. Adele's eyes after a while came back into the room. Helen was sitting quietly but unconsciously her eyes turned toward Adele as if looking for help and comfort.

Adele saw Mabel's eyes grow large and absorbent. They took in all of Helen's weariness, her look of longing and all the meanings of it all. The drama of the eyes was so complete that for the moment Adele lost herself in the spectacle.

Helen was not conscious that there had been any betrayal and Adele did not enlighten her. She realised that such consciousness would still farther weaken her power of control.

On the next day Mabel decided that they should leave Rome the following day and on that evening Helen and Adele managed a farewell talk.

"I suppose it would be better if we did not meet again" Adele said "but somehow I don't like the thought of that. Well anyhow I must be in Florence and in Sienna as that is the arrangement that I have made with Hortense Block, and I will let you know full particulars, and then we will let it work itself out." "Yes its all very unhappy" answered Helen "but I suppose I would rather see you than not." Adele laughed drearily and then stood looking at her and her mind filled as always with its eternal doubt. "But you do care for me" she broke out abruptly. "You know" she added "somehow I never can believe that since I have learned to care for you." "I don't care for you passionately any more, I am afraid you have killed all that in me as you know, but I never wanted you so much before and I have learned to trust you and depend upon you." Adele was silent, this statement hurt her more keenly than she cared to show. "Alright" she said at last "I must accept what you are able to give and even then I am hopelessly in your debt." After a while she began again almost timidly. "Must you really do for Mabel all that you are doing?" she asked. "Must you submit yourself so? I hate to speak of it to you but it does seem such a hopeless evil for you both." Helen made no reply. "I do love you very much" Adele said at last. "I know it" murmured Helen.

In the week that Adele now spent wandering alone about Rome, in spite of the insistent pain of the recent separation, she was possessed of a great serenity. She felt that now at last she and Helen had met as equals. She was no longer in the position, that she had so long resented, that of an unworthy recipient receiving a great bounty. She had proved herself capable of patience, endurance and forbearance. She had shown herself strong enough to realise power and yet be generous and all this gave her a sense of peace and contentment in the very midst of her keen sorrow and hopeless perplexity.

She abandoned herself now completely to the ugly, barren sun-burned desolation of mid-summer Rome. Her mood of loneliness and bitter sorrow mingled with a sense of recovered dignity and strength found deep contentment in the big desert spaces, in the huge ugly dignified buildings and in the great friendly church halls.

It was several weeks before they met again and in that time the exaltation of her Roman mood had worn itself out and Adele found herself restless and unhappy. She had endeavored to lose her melancholy and perplexity by endless tramping over the Luccan hills but had succeeded only in becoming more lonely sick and feverish.

Before leaving Rome she had written a note stating exactly at what time she was to be in Florence and in Sienna so that if Mabel desired and Helen were willing they might avoid her.

She came to Florence and while waiting for a friend with whom she was to walk to Sienna, she wandered disconsolately about the streets endeavoring to propitiate the gods by forcing herself to expect the worst but finding it difficult to discover what that worst would be whether a meeting or an absence.

One day she was as usual indulging in this dismal self-mockery. She went into a restaurant for lunch and there unexpectedly found Mabel and Helen. Adele gave a curt "Hullo where did you come from?" and then sat down weary and disconsolate. The others gave no sign of surprise. "Why you look badly, whats the matter with you?" Mabel asked. "Oh I am sick and I've got fever and malaise thats all. I suppose I caught a cold in the Luccan hills," Adele answered indifferently, and then she relapsed into a blank silence. They parted after lunch. "When will we see you again?" Mabel asked. "Oh I'll come around this evening after dinner for awhile" answered Adele and left them.

"Its no joke," she said dismally to herself "I am a whole lot sick, and as for Helen she seems less successfully than ever to support the strain, while Mabel is apparently taking command of the situation. Well the game begins again to-night" and she went home to gather strength for it.

That evening there was neither more nor less constraint among them than before but it was evident that in this interval the relative positions had somewhat changed. Helen had less control than ever of the situation. Adele's domination was on the wane and Mabel was becoming the controlling power.

When Adele left Helen accompanied her down-stairs. She realised as Helen kissed her that they had not been as discreet as usual in their choice of position for they stood just under a bright electric light. She said nothing to Helen but as she was going home she reflected that if Mabel had the courage to attack she would this evening from her window have seen this and be able to urge it as a legitimate grievance.

All the next day Adele avoided them but in the evening she again went to their room as had been agreed.

Mabel was now quite completely in possession and Helen as completely in abeyance. Adele disregarded them both and devoted herself to the delivery of a monologue on the disadvantages of foreign residence. As she arose to leave, Helen made no movement. "The fat is on the fire sure enough," she said to herself as she left.

The next day they met in a gallery and lunched together. Mabel was insistently domineering, Helen subservient and Adele disgusted and irritable. "Isn't Helen wonderfully good-natured" Mabel said to Adele as Helen returned from obeying one of her petulant commands. Adele looked at Helen and laughed. "That isn't exactly the word I should use," she said with open scorn.

Later in the day Helen found a moment to say to Adele,

"Mabel saw us the other night and we had an awful scene. She said it was quite accidentally but I don't see how that can be." "What is the use of keeping up that farce, of course I knew all about it," Adele answered without looking at her.

The situation did not change. On the next day Helen showed an elaborate piece of antique jewelry that Mabel had just given her. Adele's eyes rested a moment on Helen and then she turned away filled with utter scorn and disgust. "Oh its simply prostitution" she said to herself bitterly. "How a proud woman and Helen is a proud woman can yield such degrading submission and tell such abject lies for the sake of luxuries beats me. Seems to me I would rather starve or at least work for a living. Still one can't tell if one were hard driven. Its easy talking when you have everything you want and independence thrown in. I don't know if I were hard pressed I too might do it for a competence but it certainly comes high."

From now on Adele began to experience still lower depths of unhappiness. Her previous revulsions and perplexities were gentle compared to those that she now endured. Helen was growing more anxious as she saw Adele's sickness and depression increase but she dared not make any sign for Mabel was carrying things with a high hand.

On the afternoon of Adele's last day in Florence, Mabel and Helen came over to her room and while they were there Mabel left the room for a minute. Adele took Helen's hand and kissed it. "I am afraid I do still care for you" she said mournfully. "I know you do but I cannot understand why," Helen answered. "No more do I" and Adele smiled drearily, "but I simply don't seem to be able to help it. Not that I would even if I could" she hastened to add. "I am sorry I can't do more for you" Helen said, "but I find it impossible." "Oh you have no right to say that to me" Adele exclaimed angrily. "I have made no complaint and I have asked you for nothing and I want nothing of you except what you give me of your need and not because of mine," and she impatiently paced the room. Before anything further could be added Mabel had returned. Helen now looked so pale and faint that Mabel urged her to lie down and rest. Adele roused herself and suggested an errand to Mabel in such fashion that a refusal would have been an open confession of espionage and this Mabel was not willing to admit and so she departed.

Adele soothed Helen and after a bit they both wandered to the window and stood staring blankly into the street. "Yes" said Adele gravely and steadily "in spite of it all I still do believe in you and do still tremendously care for you." "I don't understand how you manage it" Helen answered. "Oh I don't mean that I find it possible to reconcile some of the things that you do even though I remember constantly that it is easy for those who have everything to condemn the errors of the less fortunate." "I don't blame your doubts" said Helen "I find it difficult to reconcile myself to my own actions, but how is it that you don't resent more the pain I am causing you?" "Dearest" Adele broke out vehemently "don't you see that that is why I used to be so angry with you because of your making so much of your endurance. There is no question of forgiveness. Pain doesn't count. Oh it's unpleasant enough and Heaven knows I hate and dread it but it isn't a thing to be remembered. It is only the loss of faith, the loss of joy that count."

In that succeeding week of steady tramping, glorious sunshine, free talk and simple comradeship Adele felt all the cobwebs blow out of her heart and brain. While winding joyously up and down the beautiful Tuscan hills and swinging along the hot dusty roads all foulness and bitterness were burned away. She became once more the embodiment of joyous content. She realised that when Mabel and Helen arrived at Sienna it would all begin again and she resolved to take advantage of this clean interval to set herself in order. She tried to put the whole matter clearly and dispassionately before her mind.

It occurred to her now that it was perhaps some past money obligation which bound Helen to endure everything rather than force honesty into her relations with Mabel. She remembered that when she first began to know Helen that she had heard something about a debt for a considerable sum of money which Helen had contracted. She remembered also that one day in Rome in answer to a statement of hers Helen had admitted that she knew Mabel was constantly growing more hypocritical and selfish but that she herself had never felt it for toward her in every respect Mabel had always been most generous.

Adele longed to ask Helen definitely whether this was the real cause of her submission but now as always she felt that Helen would not tolerate an open discussion of a practical matter.

To Adele this excuse was the only one that seemed valid for Helen's submission. For any reason except love or a debt contracted in the past such conduct was surely indefensible. There was no hope of finding out for Adele realised that she had not the courage to ask the question but in this possible explanation she found much comfort.

In the course of time Mabel and Helen arrived in Sienna and Adele found herself torn from the peaceful contemplation of old accomplishment to encounter the turgid complexity of present difficulties. She soon lost the health and joyousness of her week of peace and sunshine and became again restless and unhappy. The situation was absolutely unchanged. Mabel was still insolent in her power and Helen still humbly obedient. Adele found this spectacle too much for patient endurance and she resolved to attempt once more to speak to Helen about it.

The arranging of reasonably long periods of privacy was now comparatively easy as it was a party of four instead of a party of three.

One evening all four went out for a walk and soon this separation was effected. "You looked pretty well when we came but now you are all worn out again" Helen said as they stood looking over the walls of the fortress at the distant lights. Adele laughed. "What do you expect under the stimulation of your society" she said, "but you know you used to object to my disagreeably youthful contentment. You ought to be satisfied now and you certainly don't look very blooming yourself.—No things haven't improved" Adele went on with visible effort, and then it came with a burst. "Dear don't you realise what a degrading situation you are putting both yourself and Mabel in by persisting in your present course. Can't you manage to get on some sort of an honest footing. Every day you are increasing her vices and creating new ones

of your own." "I don't think thats quite true" Helen said
coldly "I don't think your statement is quite fair." "I think it
is," Adele answered curtly. They walked home together in
silence. They arrived in the room before the others. Helen
came up to Adele for a minute and then broke away. "Oh if
she would only be happy" she moaned. "You are wrong, you
are hideously wrong!" Adele burst out furiously and left her.

For some days Adele avoided her for she could not find it
in her heart to endure this last episode. The cry "if she would
only be happy" rang constantly in her ears. It expressed a
recognition of Mabel's preeminent claim which Adele found
it impossible to tolerate. It made plain to her that after all in
the supreme moment Mabel was Helen's first thought and
on such a basis she found herself unwilling to carry on the
situation.

Finally Helen sought her out and a partial reconciliation
took place between them.

From now on it was comparatively easy for them to be alone
together, for as the constraint between them grew, so Mabel's
civility and generosity returned. Their intercourse in these interviews consisted in impersonal talk with long intervals of
oppressive silences. "Won't you speak to me" Adele exclaimed
crushed under the weight of one of these periods. "But I
cannot think of anything to say," Helen answered gently.

"It is evident enough what happened that evening in Florence" Adele said to herself after a long succession of these
uncomfortable interviews. "Helen not only denied loving me
but she also promised in the future not to show me any affection and now when she does and when she doesn't she is
equally ashamed, so this already hopeless situation is becoming well-nigh intolerable."

Things progressed in this fashion of steadily continuous discomfort. Helen preserved a persistent silence and Adele developed an increasing resentment toward that silence. Mabel
grew always more civil and considerate and trustful. The day
before their final parting Adele and Helen went together for
a long walk. Their intercourse as was usual now consisted in
a succession of oppressive silences.

Just as they were returning to the town Adele stopped
abruptly and faced Helen. "Tell me" she said "do you really

care for me any more?" "Do you suppose I would have stayed on here in Sienna if I didn't," Helen answered angrily. "Won't you ever learn that it is facts that tell." Adele laughed ruefully. "But you forget," she said, "that there are many facts and it isn't easy to know just what they tell." They walked on for awhile and then Adele continued judicially, "No you are wrong in your theory of the whole duty of silence. I admit that I have talked too much but you on the other hand have not talked enough. You hide yourself behind your silences. I know you hate conclusions but that isn't a just attitude. Nothing is too good or holy for clear thinking and definite expression. You hate conclusions because you may be compelled to change them. You stultify yourself to any extent rather than admit that you too have been in the wrong."

"It doesn't really matter" Helen said that night of their final separation, "in what mood we part for sooner or later I know we are bound to feel together again." "I suppose so," answered Adele joylessly. Their last word was characteristic. "Good-by" said Adele "I do love you very much." "And I you" answered Helen "although I don't say so much about it."

For many weeks now there was no communication between them and Adele fought it out with her conscience her pain and her desire.

"I really hardly know what to say to you" she wrote at last. "I don't dare say what I think because I am afraid you might find that an impertinence and on the other hand I feel rather too bitterly toward you to write a simple friendly letter.

"Oh you know well enough what I want. I don't want you ever again to deny that you care for me. The thought of your doing it again takes all the sunshine out of the sky for me. Dear I almost wish sometimes that you did not trust me so completely because then I might have some influence with you for now as you know you have my faith quite absolutely and as that is to you abundantly satisfying I lose all power of coming near you."

Helen answered begging her not to destroy the effect of her patient endurance all the summer and assuring her that such conditions could not again arise.

Adele read the letter impatiently. "Hasn't she yet learned that things do happen and she isn't big enough to stave them off" she exclaimed. "Can't she see things as they are and not as she would make them if she were strong enough as she plainly isn't.

"I am afraid it comes very near being a dead-lock," she groaned dropping her head on her arms.

FINIS.

Oct. 24, 1903.

THREE LIVES

*Stories of the Good Anna,
Melanctha and the Gentle Lena*

*Donc je suis un malheureux et ce
n'est ni ma faute ni celle de la vie.*
JULES LAFORGUE

CONTENTS

The Good Anna

PART I

THE tradesmen of Bridgepoint learned to dread the sound of "Miss Mathilda", for with that name the good Anna always conquered.

The strictest of the one price stores found that they could give things for a little less, when the good Anna had fully said that "Miss Mathilda" could not pay so much and that she could buy it cheaper "by Lindheims."

Lindheims was Anna's favorite store, for there they had bargain days, when flour and sugar were sold for a quarter of a cent less for a pound, and there the heads of the departments were all her friends and always managed to give her the bargain prices, even on other days.

Anna led an arduous and troubled life.

Anna managed the whole little house for Miss Mathilda. It was a funny little house, one of a whole row of all the same kind that made a close pile like a row of dominoes that a child knocks over, for they were built along a street which at this point came down a steep hill. They were funny little houses, two stories high, with red brick fronts and long white steps.

This one little house was always very full with Miss Mathilda, an under servant, stray dogs and cats and Anna's voice that scolded, managed, grumbled all day long.

"Sallie! can't I leave you alone a minute but you must run to the door to see the butcher boy come down the street and there is Miss Mathilda calling for her shoes. Can I do everything while you go around always thinking about nothing at all? If I ain't after you every minute you would be forgetting all the time, and I take all this pains, and when you come to me you was as ragged as a buzzard and as dirty as a dog. Go and find Miss Mathilda her shoes where you put them this morning."

"Peter!",—her voice rose higher,—"Peter!",—Peter was the youngest and the favorite dog,—"Peter, if you don't leave Baby alone,"—Baby was an old, blind terrier that Anna had loved for many years,—"Peter if you don't leave Baby alone, I take a rawhide to you, you bad dog."

The good Anna had high ideals for canine chastity and discipline. The three regular dogs, the three that always lived with Anna, Peter and old Baby, and the fluffy little Rags, who was always jumping up into the air just to show that he was happy, together with the transients, the many stray ones that Anna always kept until she found them homes, were all under strict orders never to be bad one with the other.

A sad disgrace did once happen in the family. A little transient terrier for whom Anna had found a home suddenly produced a crop of pups. The new owners were certain that this Foxy had known no dog since she was in their care. The good Anna held to it stoutly that her Peter and her Rags were guiltless, and she made her statement with so much heat that Foxy's owners were at last convinced that these results were due to their neglect.

"You bad dog," Anna said to Peter that night, "you bad dog."

"Peter was the father of those pups," the good Anna explained to Miss Mathilda, "and they look just like him too, and poor little Foxy, they were so big that she could hardly have them, but Miss Mathilda, I would never let those people know that Peter was so bad."

Periods of evil thinking came very regularly to Peter and to Rags and to the visitors within their gates. At such times Anna would be very busy and scold hard, and then too she always took great care to seclude the bad dogs from each other whenever she had to leave the house. Sometimes just to see how good it was that she had made them, Anna would leave the room a little while and leave them all together, and then she would suddenly come back. Back would slink all the wicked-minded dogs at the sound of her hand upon the knob, and then they would sit desolate in their corners like a lot of disappointed children whose stolen sugar has been taken from them.

Innocent blind old Baby was the only one who preserved the dignity becoming in a dog.

You see that Anna led an arduous and troubled life.

The good Anna was a small, spare, german woman, at this time about forty years of age. Her face was worn, her cheeks were thin, her mouth drawn and firm, and her light blue eyes were very bright. Sometimes they were full of lightning and sometimes full of humor, but they were always sharp and clear.

Her voice was a pleasant one, when she told the histories of bad Peter and of Baby and of little Rags. Her voice was a high and piercing one when she called to the teamsters and to the other wicked men, what she wanted that should come to them, when she saw them beat a horse or kick a dog. She did not belong to any society that could stop them and she told them so most frankly, but her strained voice and her glittering eyes, and her queer piercing german english first made them afraid and then ashamed. They all knew too, that all the policemen on the beat were her friends. These always respected and obeyed Miss Annie, as they called her, and promptly attended to all of her complaints.

For five years Anna managed the little house for Miss Mathilda. In these five years there were four different under servants.

The one that came first was a pretty, cheerful irish girl. Anna took her with a doubting mind. Lizzie was an obedient, happy servant, and Anna began to have a little faith. This was not for long. The pretty, cheerful Lizzie disappeared one day without her notice and with all her baggage and returned no more.

This pretty, cheerful Lizzie was succeeded by a melancholy Molly.

Molly was born in America, of german parents. All her people had been long dead or gone away. Molly had always been alone. She was a tall, dark, sallow, thin-haired creature, and she was always troubled with a cough, and she had a bad temper, and always said ugly dreadful swear words.

Anna found all this very hard to bear, but she kept Molly a long time out of kindness. The kitchen was constantly a battle-ground. Anna scolded and Molly swore strange oaths, and then Miss Mathilda would shut her door hard to show that she could hear it all.

At last Anna had to give it up. "Please Miss Mathilda won't you speak to Molly," Anna said, "I can't do a thing with her.

WEST BRIDGEWATER PUBLIC LIBRARY
80 Howard Street
West Bridgewater, MA 02379

I scold her, and she don't seem to hear and then she swears so that she scares me. She loves you Miss Mathilda, and you scold her please once."

"But Anna," cried poor Miss Mathilda, "I don't want to," and that large, cheerful, but faint hearted woman looked all aghast at such a prospect. "But you must, please Miss Mathilda!" Anna said.

Miss Mathilda never wanted to do any scolding. "But you must please Miss Mathilda," Anna said.

Miss Mathilda every day put off the scolding, hoping always that Anna would learn to manage Molly better. It never did get better and at last Miss Mathilda saw that the scolding simply had to be.

It was agreed between the good Anna and her Miss Mathilda that Anna should be away when Molly would be scolded. The next evening that it was Anna's evening out, Miss Mathilda faced her task and went down into the kitchen.

Molly was sitting in the little kitchen leaning her elbows on the table. She was a tall, thin, sallow girl, aged twenty-three, by nature slatternly and careless but trained by Anna into superficial neatness. Her drab striped cotton dress and gray black checked apron increased the length and sadness of her melancholy figure. "Oh, Lord!" groaned Miss Mathilda to herself as she approached her.

"Molly, I want to speak to you about your behaviour to Anna!", here Molly dropped her head still lower on her arms and began to cry.

"Oh! Oh!" groaned Miss Mathilda.

"It's all Miss Annie's fault, all of it," Molly said at last, in a trembling voice, "I do my best."

"I know Anna is often hard to please," began Miss Mathilda, with a twinge of mischief, and then she sobered herself to her task, "but you must remember, Molly, she means it for your good and she is really very kind to you."

"I don't want her kindness," Molly cried, "I wish you would tell me what to do, Miss Mathilda, and then I would be all right. I hate Miss Annie."

"This will never do Molly," Miss Mathilda said sternly, in her deepest, firmest tones, "Anna is the head of the kitchen and you must either obey her or leave."

WEST BRIDGEWATER PUBLIC LIBRARY
80 Howard Street
West Bridgewater, MA 02379

"I don't want to leave you," whimpered melancholy Molly. "Well Molly then try and do better," answered Miss Mathilda, keeping a good stern front, and backing quickly from the kitchen.

"Oh! Oh!" groaned Miss Mathilda, as she went back up the stairs.

Miss Mathilda's attempt to make peace between the constantly contending women in the kitchen had no real effect. They were very soon as bitter as before.

At last it was decided that Molly was to go away. Molly went away to work in a factory in the town, and she went to live with an old woman in the slums, a very bad old woman Anna said.

Anna was never easy in her mind about the fate of Molly. Sometimes she would see or hear of her. Molly was not well, her cough was worse, and the old woman really was a bad one.

After a year of this unwholesome life, Molly was completely broken down. Anna then again took her in charge. She brought her from her work and from the woman where she lived, and put her in a hospital to stay till she was well. She found a place for her as nursemaid to a little girl out in the country, and Molly was at last established and content.

Molly had had, at first, no regular successor. In a few months it was going to be the summer and Miss Mathilda would be gone away, and old Katy would do very well to come in every day and help Anna with her work.

Old Katy was a heavy, ugly, short and rough old german woman, with a strange distorted german-english all her own. Anna was worn out now with her attempt to make the younger generation do all that it should and rough old Katy never answered back, and never wanted her own way. No scolding or abuse could make its mark on her uncouth and aged peasant hide. She said her "Yes, Miss Annie," when an answer had to come, and that was always all that she could say.

"Old Katy is just a rough old woman, Miss Mathilda," Anna said, "but I think I keep her here with me. She can work and she don't give me trouble like I had with Molly all the time."

Anna always had a humorous sense from this old Katy's twisted peasant english, from the roughness on her tongue of buzzing s's and from the queer ways of her brutish servile humor. Anna could not let old Katy serve at table—old Katy was too coarsely made from natural earth for that—and so Anna had all this to do herself and that she never liked, but even then this simple rough old creature was pleasanter to her than any of the upstart young.

Life went on very smoothly now in these few months before the summer came. Miss Mathilda every summer went away across the ocean to be gone for several months. When she went away this summer old Katy was so sorry, and on the day that Miss Mathilda went, old Katy cried hard for many hours. An earthy, uncouth, servile peasant creature old Katy surely was. She stood there on the white stone steps of the little red brick house, with her bony, square dull head with its thin, tanned, toughened skin and its sparse and kinky grizzled hair, and her strong, squat figure a little overmade on the right side, clothed in her blue striped cotton dress, all clean and always washed but rough and harsh to see—and she stayed there on the steps till Anna brought her in, blubbering, her apron to her face, and making queer guttural broken moans.

When Miss Mathilda early in the fall came to her house again old Katy was not there.

"I never thought old Katy would act so Miss Mathilda," Anna said, "when she was so sorry when you went away, and I gave her full wages all the summer, but they are all alike Miss Mathilda, there isn't one of them that's fit to trust. You know how Katy said she liked you, Miss Mathilda, and went on about it when you went away and then she was so good and worked all right until the middle of the summer, when I got sick, and then she went away and left me all alone and took a place out in the country, where they gave her some more money. She didn't say a word, Miss Mathilda, she just went off and left me there alone when I was sick after that awful hot summer that we had, and after all we done for her when she had no place to go, and all summer I gave her better things to eat than I had for myself. Miss Mathilda, there isn't one of them has any sense of what's the right way for a girl to do, not one of them."

Old Katy was never heard from any more.

No under servant was decided upon now for several months. Many came and many went, and none of them would do. At last Anna heard of Sallie.

Sallie was the oldest girl in a family of eleven and Sallie was just sixteen years old. From Sallie down they came always littler and littler in her family, and all of them were always out at work excepting only the few littlest of them all.

Sallie was a pretty blonde and smiling german girl, and stupid and a little silly. The littler they came in her family the brighter they all were. The brightest of them all was a little girl of ten. She did a good day's work washing dishes for a man and wife in a saloon, and she earned a fair day's wage, and then there was one littler still. She only worked for half the day. She did the house work for a bachelor doctor. She did it all, all of the housework and received each week her eight cents for her wage. Anna was always indignant when she told that story.

"I think he ought to give her ten cents Miss Mathilda any way. Eight cents is so mean when she does all his work and she is such a bright little thing too, not stupid like our Sallie. Sallie would never learn to do a thing if I didn't scold her all the time, but Sallie is a good girl, and I take care and she will do all right."

Sallie was a good, obedient german child. She never answered Anna back, no more did Peter, old Baby and little Rags and so though always Anna's voice was sharply raised in strong rebuke and worn expostulation, they were a happy family all there together in the kitchen.

Anna was a mother now to Sallie, a good incessant german mother who watched and scolded hard to keep the girl from any evil step. Sallie's temptations and transgressions were much like those of naughty Peter and jolly little Rags, and Anna took the same way to keep all three from doing what was bad.

Sallie's chief badness besides forgetting all the time and never washing her hands clean to serve at table, was the butcher boy.

He was an unattractive youth enough, that butcher boy. Suspicion began to close in around Sallie that she spent the evenings when Anna was away, in company with this bad boy.

"Sallie is such a pretty girl, Miss Mathilda," Anna said, "and she is so dumb and silly, and she puts on that red waist, and she crinkles up her hair with irons so I have to laugh, and then I tell her if she only washed her hands clean it would be better than all that fixing all the time, but you can't do a thing with the young girls nowadays Miss Mathilda. Sallie is a good girl but I got to watch her all the time."

Suspicion closed in around Sallie more and more, that she spent Anna's evenings out with this boy sitting in the kitchen. One early morning Anna's voice was sharply raised.

"Sallie this ain't the same banana that I brought home yesterday, for Miss Mathilda, for her breakfast, and you was out early in the street this morning, what was you doing there?"

"Nothing, Miss Annie, I just went out to see, that's all and that's the same banana, 'deed it is Miss Annie."

"Sallie, how can you say so and after all I do for you, and Miss Mathilda is so good to you. I never brought home no bananas yesterday with specks on it like that. I know better, it was that boy was here last night and ate it while I was away, and you was out to get another this morning. I don't want no lying Sallie."

Sallie was stout in her defence but then she gave it up and she said it was the boy who snatched it as he ran away at the sound of Anna's key opening the outside door. "But I will never let him in again, Miss Annie, 'deed I won't," said Sallie.

And now it was all peaceful for some weeks and then Sallie with fatuous simplicity began on certain evenings to resume her bright red waist, her bits of jewels and her crinkly hair.

One pleasant evening in the early spring, Miss Mathilda was standing on the steps beside the open door, feeling cheerful in the pleasant, gentle night. Anna came down the street, returning from her evening out. "Don't shut the door, please, Miss Mathilda," Anna said in a low voice, "I don't want Sallie to know I'm home."

Anna went softly through the house and reached the kitchen door. At the sound of her hand upon the knob there was a wild scramble and a bang, and then Sallie sitting there alone when Anna came into the room, but, alas, the butcher boy forgot his overcoat in his escape.

You see that Anna led an arduous and troubled life.

Anna had her troubles, too, with Miss Mathilda. "And I slave and slave to save the money and you go out and spend it all on foolishness," the good Anna would complain when her mistress, a large and careless woman, would come home with a bit of porcelain, a new etching and sometimes even an oil painting on her arm.

"But Anna," argued Miss Mathilda, "if you didn't save this money, don't you see I could not buy these things," and then Anna would soften and look pleased until she learned the price, and then wringing her hands, "Oh, Miss Mathilda, Miss Mathilda," she would cry, "and you gave all that money out for that, when you need a dress to go out in so bad." "Well, perhaps I will get one for myself next year, Anna," Miss Mathilda would cheerfully concede. "If we live till then Miss Mathilda, I see that you do," Anna would then answer darkly.

Anna had great pride in the knowledge and possessions of her cherished Miss Mathilda, but she did not like her careless way of wearing always her old clothes. "You can't go out to dinner in that dress, Miss Mathilda," she would say, standing firmly before the outside door, "You got to go and put on your new dress you always look so nice in." "But Anna, there isn't time." "Yes there is, I go up and help you fix it, please Miss Mathilda you can't go out to dinner in that dress and next year if we live till then, I make you get a new hat, too. It's a shame Miss Mathilda to go out like that."

The poor mistress sighed and had to yield. It suited her cheerful, lazy temper to be always without care but sometimes it was a burden to endure, for so often she had it all to do again unless she made a rapid dash out of the door before Anna had a chance to see.

Life was very easy always for this large and lazy Miss Mathilda, with the good Anna to watch and care for her and all her clothes and goods. But, alas, this world of ours is after all much what it should be and cheerful Miss Mathilda had her troubles too with Anna.

It was pleasant that everything for one was done, but annoying often that what one wanted most just then, one could not have when one had foolishly demanded and not suggested one's desire. And then Miss Mathilda loved to go out on joyous, country tramps when, stretching free and far with cheerful comrades, over rolling hills and cornfields, glorious in the setting sun, and dogwood white and shining underneath the moon and clear stars over head, and brilliant air and tingling blood, it was hard to have to think of Anna's anger at the late return, though Miss Mathilda had begged that there might be no hot supper cooked that night. And then when all the happy crew of Miss Mathilda and her friends, tired with fullness of good health and burning winds and glowing sunshine in the eyes, stiffened and justly worn and wholly ripe for pleasant food and gentle content, were all come together to the little house—it was hard for all that tired crew who loved the good things Anna made to eat, to come to the closed door and wonder there if it was Anna's evening in or out, and then the others must wait shivering on their tired feet, while Miss Mathilda softened Anna's heart, or if Anna was well out, boldly ordered youthful Sallie to feed all the hungry lot.

Such things were sometimes hard to bear and often grievously did Miss Mathilda feel herself a rebel with the cheerful Lizzies, the melancholy Mollies, the rough old Katies and the stupid Sallies.

Miss Mathilda had other troubles too, with the good Anna. Miss Mathilda had to save her Anna from the many friends, who in the kindly fashion of the poor, used up her savings and then gave her promises in place of payments.

The good Anna had many curious friends that she had found in the twenty years that she had lived in Bridgepoint, and Miss Mathilda would often have to save her from them all.

PART II

THE LIFE OF THE GOOD ANNA

ANNA FEDERNER, this good Anna, was of solid lower middle-class south german stock.

When she was seventeen years old she went to service in a

bourgeois family, in the large city near her native town, but she did not stay there long. One day her mistress offered her maid—that was Anna—to a friend, to see her home. Anna felt herself to be a servant, not a maid, and so she promptly left the place.

Anna had always a firm old world sense of what was the right way for a girl to do.

No argument could bring her to sit an evening in the empty parlour, although the smell of paint when they were fixing up the kitchen made her very sick, and tired as she always was, she never would sit down during the long talks she held with Miss Mathilda. A girl was a girl and should act always like a girl, both as to giving all respect and as to what she had to eat.

A little time after she left this service, Anna and her mother made the voyage to America. They came second-class, but it was for them a long and dreary journey. The mother was already ill with consumption.

They landed in a pleasant town in the far South and there the mother slowly died.

Anna was now alone and she made her way to Bridgepoint where an older half brother was already settled. This brother was a heavy, lumbering, good natured german man, full of the infirmity that comes of excess of body.

He was a baker and married and fairly well to do.

Anna liked her brother well enough but was never in any way dependent on him.

When she arrived in Bridgepoint, she took service with Miss Mary Wadsmith.

Miss Mary Wadsmith was a large, fair, helpless woman, burdened with the care of two young children. They had been left her by her brother and his wife who had died within a few months of each other.

Anna soon had the household altogether in her charge.

Anna found her place with large, abundant women, for such were always lazy, careless or all helpless, and so the burden of their lives could fall on Anna, and give her just content. Anna's superiors must be always these large helpless women, or be men, for none others could give themselves to be made so comfortable and free.

Anna had no strong natural feeling to love children, as she

had to love cats and dogs, and a large mistress. She never became deeply fond of Edgar and Jane Wadsmith. She naturally preferred the boy, for boys love always better to be done for and made comfortable and full of eating, while in the little girl she had to meet the feminine, the subtle opposition, showing so early always in a young girl's nature.

For the summer, the Wadsmiths had a pleasant house out in the country, and the winter months they spent in hotel apartments in the city.

Gradually it came to Anna to take the whole direction of their movements, to make all the decisions as to their journeyings to and fro, and for the arranging of the places where they were to live.

Anna had been with Miss Mary for three years, when little Jane began to raise her strength in opposition. Jane was a neat, pleasant little girl, pretty and sweet with a young girl's charm, and with two blonde braids carefully plaited down her back.

Miss Mary, like her Anna, had no strong natural feeling to love children, but she was fond of these two young ones of her blood, and yielded docilely to the stronger power in the really pleasing little girl. Anna always preferred the rougher handling of the boy, while Miss Mary found the gentle force and the sweet domination of the girl to please her better.

In a spring when all the preparations for the moving had been made, Miss Mary and Jane went together to the country home, and Anna, after finishing up the city matters was to follow them in a few days with Edgar, whose vacation had not yet begun.

Many times during the preparations for this summer, Jane had met Anna with sharp resistance, in opposition to her ways. It was simple for little Jane to give unpleasant orders, not from herself but from Miss Mary, large, docile, helpless Miss Mary Wadsmith who could never think out any orders to give Anna from herself.

Anna's eyes grew slowly sharper, harder, and her lower teeth thrust a little forward and pressing strongly up, framed always more slowly the "Yes, Miss Jane," to the quick, "Oh Anna! Miss Mary says she wants you to do it so!"

On the day of their migration, Miss Mary had been already

put into the carriage. "Oh, Anna!" cried little Jane running back into the house, "Miss Mary says that you are to bring along the blue dressings out of her room and mine." Anna's body stiffened, "We never use them in the summer, Miss Jane," she said thickly. "Yes Anna, but Miss Mary thinks it would be nice, and she told me to tell you not to forget, good-by!" and the little girl skipped lightly down the steps into the carriage and they drove away.

Anna stood still on the steps, her eyes hard and sharp and shining, and her body and her face stiff with resentment. And then she went into the house, giving the door a shattering slam.

Anna was very hard to live with in those next three days. Even Baby, the new puppy, the pride of Anna's heart, a present from her friend the widow, Mrs. Lehntman—even this pretty little black and tan felt the heat of Anna's scorching flame. And Edgar, who had looked forward to these days, to be for him filled full of freedom and of things to eat—he could not rest a moment in Anna's bitter sight.

On the third day, Anna and Edgar went to the Wadsmith country home. The blue dressings out of the two rooms remained behind.

All the way, Edgar sat in front with the colored man and drove. It was an early spring day in the South. The fields and woods were heavy from the soaking rains. The horses dragged the carriage slowly over the long road, sticky with brown clay and rough with masses of stones thrown here and there to be broken and trodden into place by passing teams. Over and through the soaking earth was the feathery new spring growth of little flowers, of young leaves and of ferns. The tree tops were all bright with reds and yellows, with brilliant gleaming whites and gorgeous greens. All the lower air was full of the damp haze rising from heavy soaking water on the earth, mingled with a warm and pleasant smell from the blue smoke of the spring fires in all the open fields. And above all this was the clear, upper air, and the songs of birds and the joy of sunshine and of lengthening days.

The languor and the stir, the warmth and weight and the strong feel of life from the deep centres of the earth that

comes always with the early, soaking spring, when it is not
answered with an active fervent joy, gives always anger, irri-
tation and unrest.

To Anna alone there in the carriage, drawing always nearer
to the struggle with her mistress, the warmth, the slowness,
the jolting over stones, the steaming from the horses, the cries
of men and animals and birds, and the new life all round about
were simply maddening. "Baby! if you don't lie still, I think
I kill you. I can't stand it any more like this."

At this time Anna, about twenty-seven years of age, was not
yet all thin and worn. The sharp bony edges and corners of
her head and face were still rounded out with flesh, but already the temper and the humor showed sharply in her clean
blue eyes, and the thinning was begun about the lower jaw,
that was so often strained with the upward pressure of resolve.

To-day, alone there in the carriage, she was all stiff and yet
all trembling with the sore effort of decision and revolt.

As the carriage turned into the Wadsmith gate, little Jane
ran out to see. She just looked at Anna's face; she did not say
a word about blue dressings.

Anna got down from the carriage with little Baby in her
arms. She took out all the goods that she had brought and
the carriage drove away. Anna left everything on the porch,
and went in to where Miss Mary Wadsmith was sitting by the
fire.

Miss Mary was sitting in a large armchair by the fire. All
the nooks and crannies of the chair were filled full of her soft
and spreading body. She was dressed in a black satin morning
gown, the sleeves, great monster things, were heavy with the
mass of her soft flesh. She sat there always, large, helpless,
gentle. She had a fair, soft, regular, good-looking face, with
pleasant, empty, grey-blue eyes, and heavy sleepy lids.

Behind Miss Mary was the little Jane, nervous and jerky
with excitement as she saw Anna come into the room.

"Miss Mary," Anna began. She had stopped just within the
door, her body and her face stiff with repression, her teeth
closed hard and the white lights flashing sharply in the pale,
clean blue of her eyes. Her bearing was full of the strange
coquetry of anger and of fear, the stiffness, the bridling, the
suggestive movement underneath the rigidity of forced

control, all the queer ways the passions have to show themselves all one.

"Miss Mary," the words came slowly with thick utterance
and with jerks, but always firm and strong. "Miss Mary, I can't
stand it any more like this. When you tell me anything to do,
I do it. I do everything I can and you know I work myself
sick for you. The blue dressings in your room makes too much
work to have for summer. Miss Jane don't know what work
is. If you want to do things like that I go away."

Anna stopped still. Her words had not the strength of
meaning they were meant to have, but the power in the mood
of Anna's soul frightened and awed Miss Mary through and
through.

Like in all large and helpless women, Miss Mary's heart beat
weakly in the soft and helpless mass it had to govern. Little
Jane's excitements had already tried her strength. Now she
grew pale and fainted quite away.

"Miss Mary!" cried Anna running to her mistress and supporting all her helpless weight back in the chair. Little Jane,
distracted, flew about as Anna ordered, bringing smelling salts
and brandy and vinegar and water and chafing poor Miss
Mary's wrists.

Miss Mary slowly opened her mild eyes. Anna sent the
weeping little Jane out of the room. She herself managed to
get Miss Mary quiet on the couch.

There was never a word more said about blue dressings.

Anna had conquered, and a few days later little Jane gave
her a green parrot to make peace.

For six more years little Jane and Anna lived in the same
house. They were careful and respectful to each other to the
end.

Anna liked the parrot very well. She was fond of cats too
and of horses, but best of all animals she loved the dog and
best of all dogs, little Baby, the first gift from her friend, the
widow Mrs. Lehntman.

The widow Mrs. Lehntman was the romance in Anna's life.

Anna met her first at the house of her half brother, the
baker, who had known the late Mr. Lehntman, a small grocer,
very well.

Mrs. Lehntman had been for many years a midwife. Since

her husband's death she had herself and two young children to support.

Mrs. Lehntman was a good looking woman. She had a plump well rounded body, clear olive skin, bright dark eyes and crisp black curling hair. She was pleasant, magnetic, efficient and good. She was very attractive, very generous and very amiable.

She was a few years older than our good Anna, who was soon entirely subdued by her magnetic, sympathetic charm.

Mrs. Lehntman in her work loved best to deliver young girls who were in trouble. She would take these into her own house and care for them in secret, till they could guiltlessly go home or back to work, and then slowly pay her the money for their care. And so through this new friend Anna led a wider and more entertaining life, and often she used up her savings in helping Mrs. Lehntman through those times when she was giving very much more than she got.

It was through Mrs. Lehntman that Anna met Dr. Shonjen who employed her when at last it had to be that she must go away from her Miss Mary Wadsmith.

During the last years with her Miss Mary, Anna's health was very bad, as indeed it always was from that time on until the end of her strong life.

Anna was a medium sized, thin, hard working, worrying woman.

She had always had bad headaches and now they came more often and more wearing.

Her face grew thin, more bony and more worn, her skin stained itself pale yellow, as it does with working sickly women, and the clear blue of her eyes went pale.

Her back troubled her a good deal, too. She was always tired at her work and her temper grew more difficult and fretful.

Miss Mary Wadsmith often tried to make Anna see a little to herself, and get a doctor, and the little Jane, now blossoming into a pretty, sweet young woman, did her best to make Anna do things for her good. Anna was stubborn always to Miss Jane, and fearful of interference in her ways. Miss Mary Wadsmith's mild advice she easily could always turn aside.

Mrs. Lehntman was the only one who had any power over Anna. She induced her to let Dr. Shonjen take her in his care.

No one but a Dr. Shonjen could have brought a good and german Anna first to stop her work and then submit herself to operation, but he knew so well how to deal with german and poor people. Cheery, jovial, hearty, full of jokes that made much fun and yet were full of simple common sense and reasoning courage, he could persuade even a good Anna to do things that were for her own good.

Edgar had now been for some years away from home, first at a school and then at work to prepare himself to be a civil engineer. Miss Mary and Jane promised to take a trip for all the time that Anna was away and so there would be no need for Anna's work, nor for a new girl to take Anna's place.

Anna's mind was thus a little set at rest. She gave herself to Mrs. Lehntman and the doctor to do what they thought best to make her well and strong.

Anna endured the operation very well, and was patient, almost docile, in the slow recovery of her working strength. But when she was once more at work for her Miss Mary Wadsmith, all the good effect of these several months of rest were soon worked and worried well away.

For all the rest of her strong working life Anna was never really well. She had bad headaches all the time and she was always thin and worn.

She worked away her appetite, her health and strength, and always for the sake of those who begged her not to work so hard. To her thinking, in her stubborn, faithful, german soul, this was the right way for a girl to do.

Anna's life with Miss Mary Wadsmith was now drawing to an end.

Miss Jane, now altogether a young lady, had come out into the world. Soon she would become engaged and then be married, and then perhaps Miss Mary Wadsmith would make her home with her.

In such a household Anna was certain that she would never take a place. Miss Jane was always careful and respectful and very good to Anna, but never could Anna be a girl in a household where Miss Jane would be the head. This much was very certain in her mind, and so these last two years with her Miss Mary were not as happy as before.

The change came very soon.

Miss Jane became engaged and in a few months was to marry a man from out of town, from Curden, an hour's railway ride from Bridgepoint.

Poor Miss Mary Wadsmith did not know the strong resolve Anna had made to live apart from her when this new household should be formed. Anna found it very hard to speak to her Miss Mary of this change.

The preparations for the wedding went on day and night.

Anna worked and sewed hard to make it all go well.

Miss Mary was much fluttered, but content and happy with Anna to make everything so easy for them all.

Anna worked so all the time to drown her sorrow and her conscience too, for somehow it was not right to leave Miss Mary so. But what else could she do? She could not live as her Miss Mary's girl, in a house where Miss Jane would be the head.

The wedding day grew always nearer. At last it came and passed.

The young people went on their wedding trip, and Anna and Miss Mary were left behind to pack up all the things.

Even yet poor Anna had not had the strength to tell Miss Mary her resolve, but now it had to be.

Anna every spare minute ran to her friend Mrs. Lehntman for comfort and advice. She begged her friend to be with her when she told the news to Miss Mary.

Perhaps if Mrs. Lehntman had not been in Bridgepoint, Anna would have tried to live in the new house. Mrs. Lehntman did not urge her to this thing nor even give her this advice, but feeling for Mrs. Lehntman as she did made even faithful Anna not quite so strong in her dependence on Miss Mary's need as she would otherwise have been.

Remember, Mrs. Lehntman was the romance in Anna's life.

All the packing was now done and in a few days Miss Mary was to go to the new house, where the young people were ready for her coming.

At last Anna had to speak.

Mrs. Lehntman agreed to go with her and help to make the matter clear to poor Miss Mary.

The two women came together to Miss Mary Wadsmith sitting placid by the fire in the empty living room. Miss Mary had seen Mrs. Lehntman many times before, and so her coming in with Anna raised no suspicion in her mind.

It was very hard for the two women to begin.

It must be very gently done, this telling to Miss Mary of the change. She must not be shocked by suddenness or with excitement.

Anna was all stiff, and inside all a quiver with shame, anxiety and grief. Even courageous Mrs. Lehntman, efficient, impulsive and complacent as she was and not deeply concerned in the event, felt awkward, abashed and almost guilty in that large, mild, helpless presence. And at her side to make her feel the power of it all, was the intense conviction of poor Anna, struggling to be unfeeling, self righteous and suppressed.

"Miss Mary"—with Anna when things had to come they came always sharp and short—"Miss Mary, Mrs. Lehntman has come here with me, so I can tell you about not staying with you there in Curden. Of course I go help you to get settled and then I think I come back and stay right here in Bridgepoint. You know my brother he is here and all his family, and I think it would be not right to go away from them so far, and you know you don't want me now so much Miss Mary when you are all together there in Curden."

Miss Mary Wadsmith was puzzled. She did not understand what Anna meant by what she said.

"Why Anna of course you can come to see your brother whenever you like to, and I will always pay your fare. I thought you understood all about that, and we will be very glad to have your nieces come to stay with you as often as they like. There will always be room enough in a big house like Mr. Goldthwaite's."

It was now for Mrs. Lehntman to begin her work.

"Miss Wadsmith does not understand just what you mean Anna," she began. "Miss Wadsmith, Anna feels how good and kind you are, and she talks about it all the time, and what you do for her in every way you can, and she is very grateful and

never would want to go away from you, only she thinks it
would be better now that Mrs. Goldthwaite has this big new
house and will want to manage it in her own way, she thinks
perhaps it would be better if Mrs. Goldthwaite had all new
servants with her to begin with, and not a girl like Anna who
knew her when she was a little girl. That is what Anna feels
about it now, and she asked me and I said to her that I
thought it would be better for you all and you knew she
liked you so much and that you were so good to her, and
you would understand how she thought it would be better in
the new house if she stayed on here in Bridgepoint, anyway
for a little while until Mrs. Goldthwaite was used to her new
house. Isn't that it Anna that you wanted Miss Wadsmith to
know?"

"Oh Anna," Miss Mary Wadsmith said it slowly and in a
grieved tone of surprise that was very hard for the good Anna
to endure, "Oh Anna, I didn't think that you would ever want
to leave me after all these years."

"Miss Mary!" it came in one tense jerky burst, "Miss Mary
it's only working under Miss Jane now would make me leave
you so. I know how good you are and I work myself sick for
you and for Mr. Edgar and for Miss Jane too, only Miss Jane
she will want everything different from like the way we always
did, and you know Miss Mary I can't have Miss Jane watching
at me all the time, and every minute something new. Miss
Mary, it would be very bad and Miss Jane don't really want
me to come with you to the new house, I know that all the
time. Please Miss Mary don't feel bad about it or think I ever
want to go away from you if I could do things right for you
the way they ought to be."

Poor Miss Mary. Struggling was not a thing for her to do.
Anna would surely yield if she would struggle, but struggling
was too much work and too much worry for peaceful Miss
Mary to endure. If Anna would do so she must. Poor Miss
Mary Wadsmith sighed, looked wistfully at Anna and then
gave it up.

"You must do as you think best Anna," she said at last
letting all of her soft self sink back into the chair. "I am very
sorry and so I am sure will be Miss Jane when she hears what
you have thought it best to do. It was very good of Mrs.

Lehntman to come with you and I am sure she does it for your good. I suppose you want to go out a little now. Come back in an hour Anna and help me go to bed." Miss Mary closed her eyes and rested still and placid by the fire.

The two women went away.

This was the end of Anna's service with Miss Mary Wadsmith, and soon her new life taking care of Dr. Shonjen was begun.

Keeping house for a jovial bachelor doctor gave new elements of understanding to Anna's maiden german mind. Her habits were as firm fixed as before, but it always was with Anna that things that had been done once with her enjoyment and consent could always happen any time again, such as her getting up at any hour of the night to make a supper and cook hot chops and chicken fry for Dr. Shonjen and his bachelor friends.

Anna loved to work for men, for they could eat so much and with such joy. And when they were warm and full, they were content, and let her do whatever she thought best. Not that Anna's conscience ever slept, for neither with interference or without would she strain less to keep on saving every cent and working every hour of the day. But truly she loved it best when she could scold. Now it was not only other girls and the colored man, and dogs, and cats, and horses and her parrot, but her cheery master, jolly Dr. Shonjen, whom she could guide and constantly rebuke to his own good.

The doctor really loved her scoldings as she loved his wickednesses and his merry joking ways.

These days were happy days with Anna.

Her freakish humor now first showed itself, her sense of fun in the queer ways that people had, that made her later find delight in brutish servile Katy, in Sallie's silly ways and in the badness of Peter and of Rags. She loved to make sport with the skeletons the doctor had, to make them move and make strange noises till the negro boy shook in his shoes and his eyes rolled white in his agony of fear.

Then Anna would tell these histories to her doctor. Her worn, thin, lined, determined face would form for itself new and humorous creases, and her pale blue eyes would kindle with humour and with joy as her doctor burst into his hearty laugh. And the good Anna full of the coquetry of pleasing would bridle with her angular, thin, spinster body, straining her stories and herself to please.

These early days with jovial Dr. Shonjen were very happy days with the good Anna.

All of Anna's spare hours in these early days she spent with her friend, the widow Mrs. Lehntman. Mrs. Lehntman lived with her two children in a small house in the same part of the town as Dr. Shonjen. The older of these two children was a girl named Julia and was now about thirteen years of age. This Julia Lehntman was an unattractive girl enough, harsh featured, dull and stubborn as had been her heavy german father. Mrs. Lehntman did not trouble much with her, but gave her always all she wanted that she had, and let the girl do as she liked. This was not from indifference or dislike on the part of Mrs. Lehntman, it was just her usual way.

Her second child was a boy, two years younger than his sister, a bright, pleasant, cheery fellow, who too, did what he liked with his money and his time. All this was so with Mrs. Lehntman because she had so much in her head and in her house that clamoured for her concentration and her time.

This slackness and neglect in the running of the house, and the indifference in this mother for the training of her young was very hard for our good Anna to endure. Of course she did her best to scold, to save for Mrs. Lehntman, and to put things in their place the way they ought to be.

Even in the early days when Anna was first won by the glamour of Mrs. Lehntman's brilliancy and charm, she had been uneasy in Mrs. Lehntman's house with a need of putting things to rights. Now that the two children growing up were of more importance in the house, and now that long acquaintance had brushed the dazzle out of Anna's eyes, she began to struggle to make things go here as she thought was right.

She watched and scolded hard these days to make young Julia do the way she should. Not that Julia Lehntman was pleasant in the good Anna's sight, but it must never be that a young girl growing up should have no one to make her learn to do things right.

The boy was easier to scold, for scoldings never sank in very deep, and indeed he liked them very well for they brought with them new things to eat, and lively teasing, and good jokes.

Julia, the girl, grew very sullen with it all, and very often won her point, for after all Miss Annie was no relative of hers and had no business coming there and making trouble all the time. Appealing to the mother was no use. It was wonderful how Mrs. Lehntman could listen and not hear, could answer and yet not decide, could say and do what she was asked and yet leave things as they were before.

One day it got almost too bad for even Anna's friendship to bear out.

"Well, Julia, is your mamma out?" Anna asked, one Sunday summer afternoon, as she came into the Lehntman house.

Anna looked very well this day. She was always careful in her dress and sparing of new clothes. She made herself always fulfill her own ideal of how a girl should look when she took her Sundays out. Anna knew so well the kind of ugliness appropriate to each rank in life.

It was interesting to see how when she bought things for Miss Wadsmith and later for her cherished Miss Mathilda and always entirely from her own taste and often as cheaply as she bought things for her friends or for herself, that on the one hand she chose the things having the right air for a member of the upper class, and for the others always the things having the awkward ugliness that we call Dutch. She knew the best thing in each kind, and she never in the course of her strong life compromised her sense of what was the right thing for a girl to wear.

On this bright summer Sunday afternoon she came to the Lehntmans', much dressed up in her new, brick red, silk waist trimmed with broad black beaded braid, a dark cloth skirt and a new stiff, shiny, black straw hat, trimmed with colored ribbons and a bird. She had on new gloves, and a feather boa about her neck.

Her spare, thin, awkward body and her worn, pale yellow face though lit up now with the pleasant summer sun made a queer discord with the brightness of her clothes.

She came to the Lehntman house, where she had not been for several days, and opening the door that is always left unlatched in the houses of the lower middle class in the pleasant

cities of the South, she found Julia in the family sitting-room
alone.

"Well, Julia, where is your mamma?" Anna asked. "Ma is
out but come in, Miss Annie, and look at our new brother."
"What you talk so foolish for Julia," said Anna sitting down.
"I ain't talkin' foolish, Miss Annie. Didn't you know mamma
has just adopted a cute, nice little baby boy?" "You talk so
crazy, Julia, you ought to know better than to say such
things." Julia turned sullen. "All right Miss Annie, you don't
need to believe what I say, but the little baby is in the kitchen
and ma will tell you herself when she comes in."

It sounded most fantastic, but Julia had an air of truth and
Mrs. Lehntman was capable of doing stranger things. Anna
was disturbed. "What you mean Julia," she said. "I don't
mean nothin' Miss Annie, you don't believe the baby is in
there, well you can go and see it for yourself."

Anna went into the kitchen. A baby was there all right
enough, and a lusty little boy he seemed. He was very tight
asleep in a basket that stood in the corner by the open door.

"You mean your mamma is just letting him stay here a little
while," Anna said to Julia who had followed her into the
kitchen to see Miss Annie get real mad. "No that ain't it Miss
Annie. The mother was that girl, Lily that came from Bishop's
place out in the country, and she don't want no children, and
ma liked the little boy so much, she said she'd keep him here
and adopt him for her own child."

Anna, for once, was fairly dumb with astonishment and
rage. The front door slammed.

"There's ma now," cried Julia in an uneasy triumph, for she
was not quite certain in her mind which side of the question
she was on, "There's ma now, and you can ask her for yourself
if I ain't told you true."

Mrs. Lehntman came into the kitchen where they were. She
was bland, impersonal and pleasant, as it was her wont to be.
Still to-day, through this her usual manner that gave her
such success in her practice as a midwife, there shone an
uneasy consciousness of guilt, for like all who had to do
with the good Anna, Mrs. Lehntman dreaded her firm character, her vigorous judgments and the bitter fervour of her
tongue.

It had been plain to see in the six years these women were together, how Anna gradually had come to lead. Not really lead, of course, for Mrs. Lehntman never could be led, she was so very devious in her ways; but Anna had come to have direction whenever she could learn what Mrs. Lehntman meant to do before the deed was done. Now it was hard to tell which would win out. Mrs. Lehntman had her unhearing mind and her happy way of giving a pleasant well diffused attention, and then she had it on her side that, after all, this thing was already done.

Anna was, as usual, determined for the right. She was stiff and pale with her anger and her fear, and nervous, and all a tremble as was her usual way when a bitter fight was near.

Mrs. Lehntman was easy and pleasant as she came into the room. Anna was stiff and silent and very white.

"We haven't seen you for a long time, Anna," Mrs. Lehntman cordially began. "I was just gettin' worried thinking you was sick. My! but it's a hot day to-day. Come into the sittin'-room, Anna, and Julia will make us some ice tea."

Anna followed Mrs. Lehntman into the other room in a stiff silence, and when there she did not, as invited, take a chair.

As always with Anna when a thing had to come it came very short and sharp. She found it hard to breathe just now, and every word came with a jerk.

"Mrs. Lehntman, it ain't true what Julia said about your taking that Lily's boy to keep. I told Julia when she told me she was crazy to talk so."

Anna's real excitements stopped her breath, and made her words come sharp and with a jerk. Mrs. Lehntman's feelings spread her breath, and made her words come slow, but more pleasant and more easy even than before.

"Why Anna," she began, "don't you see Lily couldn't keep her boy for she is working at the Bishops' now, and he is such a cute dear little chap, and you know how fond I am of little fellers, and I thought it would be nice for Julia and for Willie to have a little brother. You know Julia always loves to play with babies, and I have to be away so much, and Willie he is running in the streets every minute all the time, and you see a baby would be sort of nice company for Julia, and you know

you are always saying Anna, Julia should not be on the streets
so much and the baby will be so good to keep her in."

Anna was every minute paler with indignation and with
heat.

"Mrs. Lehntman, I don't see what business it is for you to
take another baby for your own, when you can't do what's
right by Julia and Willie you got here already. There's Julia,
nobody tells her a thing when I ain't here, and who is going
to tell her now how to do things for that baby? She ain't got
no sense what's the right way to do with children, and you
out all the time, and you ain't got no time for your own
neither, and now you want to be takin' up with strangers. I
know you was careless, Mrs. Lehntman, but I didn't think
that you could do this so. No, Mrs. Lehntman, it ain't your
duty to take up with no others, when you got two children
of your own, that got to get along just any way they can, and
you know you ain't got any too much money all the time, and
you are all so careless here and spend it all the time, and
Julia and Willie growin' big. It ain't right, Mrs. Lehntman, to
do so."

This was as bad as it could be. Anna had never spoken her
mind so to her friend before. Now it was too harsh for Mrs.
Lehntman to allow herself to really hear. If she really took the
meaning in these words she could never ask Anna to come
into her house again, and she liked Anna very well, and was
used to depend on her savings and her strength. And then
too Mrs. Lehntman could not really take in harsh ideas. She
was too well diffused to catch the feel of any sharp firm edge.

Now she managed to understand all this in a way that made
it easy for her to say, "Why, Anna, I think you feel too bad
about seeing what the children are doing every minute in the
day. Julia and Willie are real good, and they play with all the
nicest children in the square. If you had some, all your own,
Anna, you'd see it don't do no harm to let them do a little
as they like, and Julia likes this baby so, and sweet dear little
boy, it would be so kind of bad to send him to a 'sylum now,
you know it would Anna, when you like children so yourself,
and are so good to my Willie all the time. No indeed Anna,
it's easy enough to say I should send this poor, cute little boy
to a 'sylum when I could keep him here so nice, but you know

Anna, you wouldn't like to do it yourself, now you really know you wouldn't, Anna, though you talk to me so hard. —My, it's hot to-day, what you doin' with that ice tea in there Julia, when Miss Annie is waiting all this time for her drink?"

Julia brought in the ice tea. She was so excited with the talk she had been hearing from the kitchen, that she slopped it on the plate out of the glasses a good deal. But she was safe, for Anna felt this trouble so deep down that she did not even see those awkward, bony hands, adorned to-day with a new ring, those stupid, foolish hands that always did things the wrong way.

"Here Miss Annie," Julia said, "Here, Miss Annie, is your glass of tea, I know you like it good and strong."

"No, Julia, I don't want no ice tea here. Your mamma ain't able to afford now using her money upon ice tea for her friends. It ain't right she should now any more. I go out now to see Mrs. Drehten. She does all she can, and she is sick now working so hard taking care of her own children. I go there now. Good by Mrs. Lehntman, I hope you don't get no bad luck doin' what it ain't right for you to do."

"My, Miss Annie is real mad now," Julia said, as the house shook, as the good Anna shut the outside door with a concentrated shattering slam.

It was some months now that Anna had been intimate with Mrs. Drehten.

Mrs. Drehten had had a tumor and had come to Dr. Shonjen to be treated. During the course of her visits there, she and Anna had learned to like each other very well. There was no fever in this friendship, it was just the interchange of two hard working, worrying women, the one large and motherly, with the pleasant, patient, soft, worn, tolerant face, that comes with a german husband to obey, and seven solid girls and boys to bear and rear, and the other was our good Anna with her spinster body, her firm jaw, her humorous, light, clean eyes and her lined, worn, thin, pale yellow face.

Mrs. Drehten lived a patient, homely, hard-working life. Her husband an honest, decent man enough, was a brewer, and somewhat given to over drinking, and so he was often surly and stingy and unpleasant.

The family of seven children was made up of four stalwart, cheery, filial sons, and three hard working obedient simple daughters.

It was a family life the good Anna very much approved and also she was much liked by them all. With a german woman's feeling for the masterhood in men, she was docile to the surly father and rarely rubbed him the wrong way. To the large, worn, patient, sickly mother she was a sympathetic listener, wise in council and most efficient in her help. The young ones too, liked her very well. The sons teased her all the time and roared with boisterous pleasure when she gave them back sharp hits. The girls were all so good that her scoldings here were only in the shape of good advice, sweetened with new trimmings for their hats, and ribbons, and sometimes on their birthdays, bits of jewels.

It was here that Anna came for comfort after her grievous stroke at her friend the widow, Mrs. Lehntman. Not that Anna would tell Mrs. Drehten of this trouble. She could never lay bare the wound that came to her through this idealised affection. Her affair with Mrs. Lehntman was too sacred and too grievous ever to be told. But here in this large household, in busy movement and variety in strife, she could silence the uneasiness and pain of her own wound.

The Drehtens lived out in the country in one of the wooden, ugly houses that lie in groups outside of our large cities.

The father and the sons all had their work here making beer, and the mother and her girls scoured and sewed and cooked.

On Sundays they were all washed very clean, and smelling of kitchen soap. The sons, in their Sunday clothes, loafed around the house or in the village, and on special days went on picnics with their girls. The daughters in their awkward, colored finery went to church most of the day and then walking with their friends.

They always came together for their supper, where Anna always was most welcome, the jolly Sunday evening supper that german people love. Here Anna and the boys gave it to each other in sharp hits and hearty boisterous laughter, the girls made things for them to eat, and waited on them all, the mother loved all her children all the time, and the father joined in with his occasional unpleasant word that made a bitter feeling but which they had all learned to pass as if it were not said.

It was to the comfort of this house that Anna came that Sunday summer afternoon, after she had left Mrs. Lehntman and her careless ways.

The Drehten house was open all about. No one was there but Mrs. Drehten resting in her rocking chair, out in the pleasant, scented, summer air.

Anna had had a hot walk from the cars.

She went into the kitchen for a cooling drink, and then came out and sat down on the steps near Mrs. Drehten.

Anna's anger had changed. A sadness had come to her. Now with the patient, friendly, gentle mother talk of Mrs. Drehten, this sadness changed to resignation and to rest.

As the evening came on the young ones dropped in one by one. Soon the merry Sunday evening supper was begun.

It had not been all comfort for our Anna, these months of knowing Mrs. Drehten. It had made trouble for her with the family of her half brother, the fat baker.

Her half brother, the fat baker, was a queer kind of a man. He was a huge, unwieldy creature, all puffed out all over, and no longer able to walk much, with his enormous body and the big, swollen, bursted veins in his great legs. He did not try to walk much now. He sat around his place, leaning on his great thick stick, and watching his workmen at their work.

On holidays, and sometimes of a Sunday, he went out in his bakery wagon. He went then to each customer he had and gave them each a large, sweet, raisined loaf of caky bread. At every house with many groans and gasps he would descend his heavy weight out of the wagon, his good featured, black haired, flat, good natured face shining with oily perspiration, with pride in labor and with generous kindness. Up each stoop he hobbled with the help of his big stick, and into the nearest chair in the kitchen or in the parlour, as the fashion of the house demanded, and there he sat and puffed, and then presented to the mistress or the cook the raisined german loaf his boy supplied him.

Anna had never been a customer of his. She had always lived in another part of the town, but he never left her out in these bakery progresses of his, and always with his own hand he gave her her festive loaf.

Anna liked her half brother well enough. She never knew him really well, for he rarely talked at all and least of all to women, but he seemed to her, honest, and good and kind, and he never tried to interfere in Anna's ways. And then Anna liked the loaves of raisined bread, for in the summer she and the second girl could live on them, and not be buying bread with the household money all the time.

But things were not so simple with our Anna, with the other members of her half brother's house.

Her half brother's family was made up of himself, his wife, and their two daughters.

Anna never liked her brother's wife.

The youngest of the two daughters was named after her aunt Anna.

Anna never liked her half brother's wife. This woman had been very good to Anna, never interfering in her ways, always glad to see her and to make her visits pleasant, but she had not found favour in our good Anna's sight.

Anna had too, no real affection for her nieces. She never scolded them or tried to guide them for their good. Anna never criticised or interfered in the running of her half brother's house.

Mrs. Federner was a good looking, prosperous woman, a little harsh and cold within her soul perhaps, but trying always to be pleasant, good and kind. Her daughters were well trained, quiet, obedient, well dressed girls, and yet our good Anna loved them not, nor their mother, nor any of their ways.

It was in this house that Anna had first met her friend, the widow, Mrs. Lehntman.

The Federners had never seemed to feel it wrong in Anna, her devotion to this friend and her care of her and of her children. Mrs. Lehntman and Anna and her feelings were all somehow too big for their attack. But Mrs. Federner had the mind and tongue that blacken things. Not really to blacken black, of course, but just to roughen and to rub on a little smut. She could somehow make even the face of the Almighty seem pimply and a little coarse, and so she always did this with her friends, though not with the intent to interfere.

This was really true with Mrs. Lehntman that Mrs. Federner did not mean to interfere, but Anna's friendship with the Drehtens was a very different matter.

Why should Mrs. Drehten, that poor common working wife of a man who worked for others in a brewery and who always drank too much, and was not like a thrifty, decent german man, why should that Mrs. Drehten and her ugly, awkward daughters be getting presents from her husband's sister all the time, and her husband always so good to Anna, and one of the girls having her name too, and those Drehtens all strangers to her and never going to come to any good? It was not right for Anna to do so.

Mrs. Federner knew better than to say such things straight out to her husband's fiery, stubborn sister, but she lost no chance to let Anna feel and see what they all thought.

It was easy to blacken all the Drehtens, their poverty, the husband's drinking, the four big sons carrying on and always lazy, the awkward, ugly daughters dressing up with Anna's help and trying to look so fine, and the poor, weak, hard-working sickly mother, so easy to degrade with large dosings of contemptuous pity.

Anna could not do much with these attacks for Mrs. Federner always ended with, "And you so good to them Anna all the time. I don't see how they could get along at all if you didn't help them all the time, but you are so good Anna, and got such a feeling heart, just like your brother, that you give anything away you got to anybody that will ask you for it, and that's shameless enough to take it when they ain't no relatives of yours. Poor Mrs. Drehten, she is a good woman. Poor thing it must be awful hard for her to have to take things from strangers all the time, and her husband spending it on drink. I was saying to Mrs. Lehntman, Anna, only yesterday, how I never was so sorry for any one as Mrs. Drehten, and how good it was for you to help them all the time."

All this meant a gold watch and chain to her god daughter for her birthday, the next month, and a new silk umbrella for the elder sister. Poor Anna, and she did not love them very much, these relatives of hers, and they were the only kin she had.

Mrs. Lehntman never joined in, in these attacks. Mrs.

Lehntman was diffuse and careless in her ways, but she never worked such things for her own ends, and she was too sure of Anna to be jealous of her other friends.

All this time Anna was leading her happy life with Dr. Shonjen. She had every day her busy time. She cooked and saved and sewed and scrubbed and scolded. And every night she had her happy time, in seeing her Doctor like the fine things she bought so cheap and cooked so good for him to eat. And then he would listen and laugh so loud, as she told him stories of what had happened on that day.

The Doctor, too, liked it better all the time and several times in these five years he had of his own motion raised her wages.

Anna was content with what she had and grateful for all her doctor did for her.

So Anna's serving and her giving life went on, each with its varied pleasures and its pains.

The adopting of the little boy did not put an end to Anna's friendship for the widow Mrs. Lehntman. Neither the good Anna nor the careless Mrs. Lehntman would give each other up excepting for the gravest cause.

Mrs. Lehntman was the only romance Anna ever knew. A certain magnetic brilliancy in person and in manner made Mrs. Lehntman a woman other women loved. Then, too, she was generous and good and honest, though she was so careless always in her ways. And then she trusted Anna and liked her better than any of her other friends, and Anna always felt this very much.

No, Anna could not give up Mrs. Lehntman, and soon she was busier than before making Julia do things right for little Johnny.

And now new schemes were working strong in Mrs. Lehntman's head, and Anna must listen to her plans and help her make them work.

Mrs. Lehntman always loved best in her work to deliver young girls who were in trouble. She would keep these in her house until they could go to their homes or to their work, and slowly pay her back the money for their care.

Anna had always helped her friend to do this thing, for like all the good women of the decent poor, she felt it hard that girls should not be helped, not girls that were really bad of course, these she condemned and hated in her heart and with her tongue, but honest, decent, good, hard working, foolish girls who were in trouble.

For such as these Anna always liked to give her money and her strength.

Now Mrs. Lehntman thought that it would pay to take a big house for herself to take in girls and to do everything in a big way.

Anna did not like this plan.

Anna was never daring in her ways. Save and you will have the money you have saved, was all that she could know.

Not that the good Anna had it so.

She saved and saved and always saved, and then here and there, to this friend and to that, to one in her trouble and to the other in her joy, in sickness, death, and weddings, or to make young people happy, it always went, the hard earned money she had saved.

Anna could not clearly see how Mrs. Lehntman could make a big house pay. In the small house where she had these girls, it did not pay, and in a big house there was so much more that she would spend.

Such things were hard for the good Anna to very clearly see. One day she came into the Lehntman house. "Anna," Mrs. Lehntman said, "you know that nice big house on the next corner that we saw to rent. I took it for a year just yesterday. I paid a little down you know so I could have it sure all right and now you fix it up just like you want. I let you do just what you like with it."

Anna knew that it was now too late. However, "But Mrs. Lehntman you said you would not take another house, you said so just last week. Oh, Mrs. Lehntman I didn't think that you would do this so!"

Anna knew so well it was too late.

"I know, Anna, but it was such a good house, just right you know and some one else was there to see, and you know you said it suited very well, and if I didn't take it the others said they would, and I wanted to ask you only there wasn't time, and really Anna, I don't need much help, it will go so well I know. I just need a little to begin and to fix up with and that's all Anna that I need, and I know it will go awful well. You wait Anna and you'll see, and I let you fix it up just like you want, and you will make it look so nice, you got such sense in all these things. It will be a good place. You see Anna if I ain't right in what I say."

Of course Anna gave the money for this thing though she could not believe that it was best. No, it was very bad. Mrs. Lehntman could never make it pay and it would cost so much to keep. But what could our poor Anna do? Remember Mrs. Lehntman was the only romance Anna ever knew.

Anna's strength in her control of what was done in Mrs. Lehntman's house, was not now what it had been before that Lily's little Johnny came. That thing had been for Anna a defeat. There had been no fighting to a finish but Mrs. Lehntman had very surely won.

Mrs. Lehntman needed Anna just as much as Anna needed Mrs. Lehntman, but Mrs. Lehntman was more ready to risk Anna's loss, and so the good Anna grew always weaker in her power to control.

In friendship, power always has its downward curve. One's strength to manage rises always higher until there comes a time one does not win, and though one may not really lose, still from the time that victory is not sure, one's power slowly ceases to be strong. It is only in a close tie such as marriage, that influence can mount and grow always stronger with the years and never meet with a decline. It can only happen so when there is no way to escape.

Friendship goes by favour. There is always danger of a break or of a stronger power coming in between. Influence can only be a steady march when one can surely never break away.

Anna wanted Mrs. Lehntman very much and Mrs. Lehntman needed Anna, but there were always other ways to do and if Anna had once given up she might do so again, so why should Mrs. Lehntman have real fear?

No, while the good Anna did not come to open fight she had been stronger. Now Mrs. Lehntman could always hold out longer. She knew too, that Anna had a feeling heart. Anna could never stop doing all she could for any one that really needed help. Poor Anna had no power to say no.

And then, too, Mrs. Lehntman was the only romance Anna

ever knew. Romance is the ideal in one's life and it is very lonely living with it lost.

So the good Anna gave all her savings for this place, although she knew that this was not the right way for her friend to do.

For some time now they were all very busy fixing up the house. It swallowed all Anna's savings fixing up this house, for when Anna once began to make it nice, she could not leave it be until it was as good as for the purpose it should be.

Somehow it was Anna now that really took the interest in the house. Mrs. Lehntman, now the thing was done seemed very lifeless, without interest in the house, uneasy in her mind and restless in her ways, and more diffuse even than before in her attention. She was good and kind to all the people in her house, and let them do whatever they thought best.

Anna did not fail to see that Mrs. Lehntman had something on her mind that was all new. What was it that disturbed Mrs. Lehntman so? She kept on saying it was all in Anna's head. She had no trouble now at all. Everybody was so good and it was all so nice in the new house. But surely there was something here that was all wrong.

Anna heard a good deal of all this from her half brother's wife, the hard speaking Mrs. Federner.

Through the fog of dust and work and furnishing in the new house, and through the disturbed mind of Mrs. Lehntman, and with the dark hints of Mrs. Federner, there loomed up to Anna's sight a man, a new doctor that Mrs. Lehntman knew.

Anna had never met the man but she heard of him very often now. Not from her friend, the widow Mrs. Lehntman. Anna knew that Mrs. Lehntman made of him a mystery that Anna had not the strength just then to vigorously break down.

Mrs. Federner gave always dark suggestions and unpleasant hints. Even good Mrs. Drehten talked of it.

Mrs. Lehntman never spoke of the new doctor more than she could help. This was most mysterious and unpleasant and very hard for our good Anna to endure.

Anna's troubles came all of them at once.

Here in Mrs. Lehntman's house loomed up dismal and forbidding, a mysterious, perhaps an evil man. In Dr. Shonjen's house were beginning signs of interest in the doctor in a woman.

This, too, Mrs. Federner often told to the poor Anna. The doctor surely would be married soon, he liked so much now to go to Mr. Weingartner's house where there was a daughter who loved Doctor, everybody knew.

In these days the living room in her half brother's house was Anna's torture chamber. And worst of all there was so much reason for her half sister's words. The Doctor certainly did look like marriage and Mrs. Lehntman acted very queer.

Poor Anna. Dark were these days and much she had to suffer.

The Doctor's trouble came to a head the first. It was true Doctor was engaged and to be married soon. He told Anna so himself.

What was the good Anna now to do? Dr. Shonjen wanted her of course to stay. Anna was so sad with all these troubles. She knew here in the Doctor's house it would be bad when he was married, but she had not the strength now to be firm and go away. She said at last that she would try and stay.

Doctor got married now very soon. Anna made the house all beautiful and clean and she really hoped that she might stay. But this was not for long.

Mrs. Shonjen was a proud, unpleasant woman. She wanted constant service and attention and never even a thank you to a servant. Soon all Doctor's old people went away. Anna went to Doctor and explained. She told him what all the servants thought of his new wife. Anna bade him a sad farewell and went away.

Anna was now most uncertain what to do. She could go to Curden to her Miss Mary Wadsmith who always wrote how much she needed Anna, but Anna still dreaded Miss Jane's interfering ways. Then too, she could not yet go away from Bridgepoint and from Mrs. Lehntman, unpleasant as it always was now over there.

Through one of Doctor's friends Anna heard of Miss Mathilda. Anna was very doubtful about working for a Miss Mathilda. She did not think it would be good working for a woman any more. She had found it very good with Miss Mary but she did not think that many women would be so.

Most women were interfering in their ways.

Anna heard that Miss Mathilda was a great big woman, not so big perhaps as her Miss Mary, still she was big, and the good Anna liked them better so. She did not like them thin and small and active and always looking in and always prying.

Anna could not make up her mind what was the best thing now for her to do. She could sew and this way make a living, but she did not like such business very well.

Mrs. Lehntman urged the place with Miss Mathilda. She was sure Anna would find it better so. The good Anna did not know.

"Well Anna," Mrs. Lehntman said, "I tell you what we do. I go with you to that woman that tells fortunes, perhaps she tell us something that will show us what is the best way for you now to do."

It was very bad to go to a woman who tells fortunes. Anna was of strong South German Catholic religion and the german priests in the churches always said that it was very bad to do things so. But what else now could the good Anna do? She was so mixed and bothered in her mind, and troubled with this life that was all wrong, though she did try so hard to do the best she knew. "All right, Mrs. Lehntman," Anna said at last, "I think I go there now with you."

This woman who told fortunes was a medium. She had a house in the lower quarter of the town. Mrs. Lehntman and the good Anna went to her.

The medium opened the door for them herself. She was a loose made, dusty, dowdy woman with a persuading, conscious and embracing manner and very greasy hair.

The woman let them come into the house.

The street door opened straight into the parlor, as is the way in the small houses of the south. The parlor had a thick and flowered carpet the floor. The room was full of dirty things all made by hand. Some hung upon the wall, some were on the seats and over backs of chairs and some on tables and on those what-nots that poor people love. And everywhere were little things that break. Many of these little things were broken and the place was stuffy and not clean.

No medium uses her parlor for her work. It is always in her eating room that she has her trances.

The eating room in all these houses is the living room in winter. It has a round table in the centre covered with a decorated woolen cloth, that has soaked in the grease of many dinners, for though it should be always taken off, it is easier to spread the cloth upon it than change it for the blanket deadener that one owns. The upholstered chairs are dark and worn, and dirty. The carpet has grown dingy with the food that's fallen from the table, the dirt that's scraped from off the shoes, and the dust that settles with the ages. The sombre greenish colored paper on the walls has been smoked a dismal dirty grey, and all pervading is the smell of soup made out of onions and fat chunks of meat.

The medium brought Mrs. Lehntman and our Anna into this eating room, after she had found out what it was they wanted. They all three sat around the table and then the medium went into her trance.

The medium first closed her eyes and then they opened very wide and lifeless. She took a number of deep breaths, choked several times and swallowed very hard. She waved her hand back every now and then, and she began to speak in a monotonous slow, even tone.

"I see—I see—don't crowd so on me,—I see—I see—too many forms—don't crowd so on me—I see—I see—you are thinking of something—you don't know whether you want to do it now. I see—I see—don't crowd so on me—I see—I see—you are not sure,—I see—I see—a house with trees around it,—it is dark—it is evening—I see—I see—you go in the house—I see—I see you come out—it will be all right—you go and do it—do what you are not certain about—it will come out all right—it is best and you should do it now."

She stopped, she made deep gulps, her eyes rolled back into her head, she swallowed hard and then she was her former dingy and bland self again.

"Did you get what you wanted that the spirit should tell you?" the woman asked. Mrs. Lehntman answered yes, it was just what her friend had wanted so bad to know. Anna was uneasy in this house with superstition, with fear of her good priest, and with disgust at all the dirt and grease, but she was most content for now she knew what it was best for her to do.

Anna paid the woman for her work and then they came away.

"There Anna didn't I tell you how it would all be? You see the spirit says so too. You must take the place with Miss Mathilda, that is what I told you was the best thing for you to do. We go out and see her where she lives to-night. Ain't you glad, Anna, that I took you to this place, so you know now what you will do?"

Mrs. Lehntman and Anna went that evening to see Miss Mathilda. Miss Mathilda was staying with a friend who lived in a house that did have trees about. Miss Mathilda was not there herself to talk with Anna.

If it had not been that it was evening, and so dark, and that this house had trees all round about, and that Anna found herself going in and coming out just as the woman that day said that she would do, had it not all been just as the medium said, the good Anna would never have taken the place with Miss Mathilda.

Anna did not see Miss Mathilda and she did not like the friend who acted in her place.

This friend was a dark, sweet, gentle little mother woman, very easy to be pleased in her own work and very good to servants, but she felt that acting for her young friend, the careless Miss Mathilda, she must be very careful to examine well and see that all was right and that Anna would surely do the best she knew. She asked Anna all about her ways and her intentions and how much she would spend, and how often she went out and whether she could wash and cook and sew.

The good Anna set her teeth fast to endure and would hardly answer anything at all. Mrs. Lehntman made it all go fairly well.

The good Anna was all worked up with her resentment, and Miss Mathilda's friend did not think that she would do.

However, Miss Mathilda was willing to begin and as for Anna, she knew that the medium said it must be so. Mrs. Lehntman, too, was sure, and said she knew that this was the best thing for Anna now to do. So Anna sent word at last to

Miss Mathilda, that if she wanted her, she would try if it would do.

So Anna began a new life taking care of Miss Mathilda.

Anna fixed up the little red brick house where Miss Mathilda was going to live and made it very pleasant, clean and nice. She brought over her dog, Baby, and her parrot. She hired Lizzie for a second girl to be with her and soon they were all content. All except the parrot, for Miss Mathilda did not like its scream. Baby was all right but not the parrot. But then Anna never really loved the parrot, and so she gave it to the Drehten girls to keep.

Before Anna could really rest content with Miss Mathilda, she had to tell her good german priest what it was that she had done, and how very bad it was that she had been and how she would never do so again.

Anna really did believe with all her might. It was her fortune never to live with people who had any faith, but then that never worried Anna. She prayed for them always as she should, and she was very sure that they were good. The doctor loved to tease her with his doubts and Miss Mathilda liked to do so too, but with the tolerant spirit of her church, Anna never thought that such things were bad for them to do.

Anna found it hard to always know just why it was that things went wrong. Sometimes her glasses broke and then she knew that she had not done her duty by the church, just in the way that she should do.

Sometimes she was so hard at work that she would not go to mass. Something always happened then. Anna's temper grew irritable and her ways uncertain and distraught. Everybody suffered and then her glasses broke. That was always very bad because they cost so much to fix. Still in a way it always ended Anna's troubles, because she knew then that all this was because she had been bad. As long as she could scold it might be just the bad ways of all the thoughtless careless world, but when her glasses broke that made it clear. That meant that it was she herself who had been bad.

No, it was no use for Anna not to do the way she should, for things always then went wrong and finally cost money to make whole, and this was the hardest thing for the good Anna to endure.

Anna almost always did her duty. She made confession and her mission whenever it was right. Of course she did not tell the father when she deceived people for their good, or when she wanted them to give something for a little less.

When Anna told such histories to her doctor and later to her cherished Miss Mathilda, her eyes were always full of humor and enjoyment as she explained that she had said it so, and now she would not have to tell the father for she had not really made a sin.

But going to a fortune teller Anna knew was really bad. That had to be told to the father just as it was and penance had then to be done.

Anna did this and now her new life was well begun, making Miss Mathilda and the rest do just the way they should.

Yes, taking care of Miss Mathilda were the happiest days of all the good Anna's strong hard working life.

With Miss Mathilda Anna did it all. The clothes, the house, the hats, what she should wear and when and what was always best for her to do. There was nothing Miss Mathilda would not let Anna manage, and only be too glad if she would do.

Anna scolded and cooked and sewed and saved so well, that Miss Matilda had so much to spend, that it kept Anna still busier scolding all the time about the things she bought, that made so much work for Anna and the other girl to do. But for all the scolding, Anna was proud almost to bursting of her cherished Miss Mathilda with all her knowledge and her great possessions, and the good Anna was always telling of it all to everybody that she knew.

Yes these were the happiest days of all her life with Anna, even though with her friends there were great sorrows. But these sorrows did not hurt the good Anna now, as they had done in the years that went before.

Miss Mathilda was not a romance in the good Anna's life, but Anna gave her so much strong affection that it almost filled her life as full.

It was well for the good Anna that her life with Miss Mathilda was so happy, for now in these days, Mrs. Lehntman went altogether bad. The doctor she had learned to know, was too certainly an evil as well as a mysterious man, and he had power over the widow and midwife, Mrs. Lehntman.

Anna never saw Mrs. Lehntman at all now any more.

Mrs. Lehntman had borrowed some more money and had given Anna a note then for it all, and after that Anna never saw her any more. Anna now stopped altogether going to the Lehntmans'. Julia, the tall, gawky, good, blonde, stupid daughter, came often to see Anna, but she could tell little of her mother.

It certainly did look very much as if Mrs. Lehntman had now gone altogether bad. This was a great grief to the good Anna, but not so great a grief as it would have been had not Miss Mathilda meant so much to her now.

Mrs. Lehntman went from bad to worse. The doctor, the mysterious and evil man, got into trouble doing things that were not right to do.

Mrs. Lehntman was mixed up in this affair.

It was just as bad as it could be, but they managed, both the doctor and Mrs. Lehntman, finally to come out safe.

Everybody was so sorry about Mrs. Lehntman. She had been really a good woman before she met this doctor, and even now she certainly had not been really bad.

For several years now Anna never even saw her friend.

But Anna always found new people to befriend, people who, in the kindly fashion of the poor, used up her savings and then gave promises in place of payments. Anna never really thought that these people would be good, but when they did not do the way they should, and when they did not pay her back the money she had loaned, and never seemed the better for her care, then Anna would grow bitter with the world.

No, none of them had any sense of what was the right way for them to do. So Anna would repeat in her despair.

The poor are generous with their things. They give always what they have, but with them to give or to receive brings with it no feeling that they owe the giver for the gift.

Even a thrifty german Anna was ready to give all that she had saved, and so not be sure that she would have enough to take care of herself if she fell sick, or for old age, when she could not work. Save and you will have the money you have saved was true only for the day of saving, even for a thrifty german Anna. There was no certain way to have it for old age, for the taking care of what is saved can never be relied on, for it must always be in strangers' hands in a bank or in investments by a friend.

And so when any day one might need life and help from others of the working poor, there was no way a woman who had a little saved could say them no.

So the good Anna gave her all to friends and strangers, to children, dogs and cats, to anything that asked or seemed to need her care.

It was in this way that Anna came to help the barber and his wife who lived around the corner, and who somehow could never make ends meet. They worked hard, were thrifty, had no vices, but the barber was one of them who never can make money. Whoever owed him money did not pay. Whenever he had a chance at a good job he fell sick and could not take it. It was never his own fault that he had trouble, but he never seemed to make things come out right.

His wife was a blonde, thin, pale, german little woman, who bore her children very hard, and worked too soon, and then till she was sick. She too, always had things that went wrong.

They both needed constant help and patience, and the good Anna gave both to them all the time.

Another woman who needed help from the good Anna, was one who was in trouble from being good to others.

This woman's husband's brother, who was very good, worked in a shop where there was a Bohemian, who was getting sick with a consumption. This man got so much worse he could not do his work, but he was not so sick that he could stay in a hospital. So this woman had him living there with her. He was not a nice man, nor was he thankful for all the woman did for him. He was cross to her two children and made a great mess always in her house. The doctor said he must have many things to eat, and the woman and the brother of the husband got them for him.

There was no friendship, no affection, no liking even for the man this woman cared for, no claim of common country or of kin, but in the kindly fashion of the poor this woman gave her all and made her house a nasty place, and for a man who was not even grateful for the gift.

Then, of course, the woman herself got into trouble. Her

husband's brother was now married. Her husband lost his job. She did not have the money for the rent. It was the good Anna's savings that were handy.

So it went on. Sometimes a little girl, sometimes a big one was in trouble and Anna heard of them and helped them to find places.

Stray dogs and cats Anna always kept until she found them homes. She was always careful to learn whether these people would be good to animals.

Out of the whole collection of stray creatures, it was the young Peter and the jolly little Rags, Anna could not find it in her heart to part with. These became part of the household of the good Anna's Miss Mathilda.

Peter was a very useless creature, a foolish, silly, cherished, coward male. It was wild to see him rush up and down in the back yard, barking and bouncing at the wall, when there was some dog out beyond, but when the very littlest one there was got inside of the fence and only looked at Peter, Peter would retire to his Anna and blot himself out between her skirts.

When Peter was left downstairs alone, he howled. "I am all alone," he wailed, and then the good Anna would have to come and fetch him up. Once when Anna stayed a few nights in a house not far away, she had to carry Peter all the way, for Peter was afraid when he found himself on the street outside his house. Peter was a good sized creature and he sat there and he howled, and the good Anna carried him all the way in her own arms. He was a coward was this Peter, but he had kindly, gentle eyes and a pretty collie head, and his fur was very thick and white and nice when he was washed. And then Peter never strayed away, and he looked out of his nice eyes and he liked it when you rubbed him down, and he forgot you when you went away, and he barked whenever there was any noise.

When he was a little pup he had one night been put into the yard and that was all of his origin she knew. The good Anna loved him well and spoiled him as a good german mother always does her son.

Little Rags was very different in his nature. He was a lively creature made out of ends of things, all fluffy and dust color, and he was always bounding up into the air and darting all about over and then under silly Peter and often straight into solemn fat, blind, sleepy Baby, and then in a wild rush after some stray cat.

Rags was a pleasant, jolly little fellow. The good Anna liked him very well, but never with her strength as she loved her good looking coward, foolish young man, Peter.

Baby was the dog of her past life and she held Anna with old ties of past affection. Peter was the spoiled, good looking young man, of her middle age, and Rags was always something of a toy. She liked him but he never struck in very deep. Rags had strayed in somehow one day and then when no home for him was quickly found, he had just stayed right there.

It was a very happy family there all together in the kitchen, the good Anna and Sally and old Baby and young Peter and the jolly little Rags.

The parrot had passed out of Anna's life. She had really never loved the parrot and now she hardly thought to ask for him, even when she visited the Drehtens.

Mrs. Drehten was the friend Anna always went to, for her Sundays. She did not get advice from Mrs. Drehten as she used to from the widow, Mrs. Lehntman, for Mrs. Drehten was a mild, worn, unaggressive nature that never cared to influence or to lead. But they could mourn together for the world these two worn, working german women, for its sadness and its wicked ways of doing. Mrs. Drehten knew so well what one could suffer.

Things did not go well in these days with the Drehtens. The children were all good, but the father with his temper and his spending kept everything from being what it should.

Poor Mrs. Drehten still had trouble with her tumor. She could hardly do any work now any more. Mrs. Drehten was a large, worn, patient german woman, with a soft face, lined, yellow brown in color and the look that comes from a german husband to obey, and many solid girls and boys to bear and rear, and from being always on one's feet and never having any troubles cured.

Mrs. Drehten was always getting worse, and now the doctor thought it would be best to take the tumor out.

It was no longer Dr. Shonjen who treated Mrs. Drehten. They all went now to a good old german doctor they all knew.

"You see, Miss Mathilda," Anna said, "All the old german patients don't go no more now to Doctor. I stayed with him just so long as I could stand it, but now he is moved away up town too far for poor people, and his wife, she holds her head up so and always is spending so much money just for show, and so he can't take right care of us poor people any more. Poor man, he has got always to be thinking about making money now. I am awful sorry about Doctor, Miss Mathilda, but he neglected Mrs. Drehten shameful when she had her trouble, so now I never see him any more. Doctor Herman is a good, plain, german doctor and he would never do things so, and Miss Mathilda, Mrs. Drehten is coming in to-morrow to see you before she goes to the hospital for her operation. She could not go comfortable till she had seen you first to see what you would say."

All Anna's friends reverenced the good Anna's cherished Miss Mathilda. How could they not do so and still remain friends with the good Anna? Miss Mathilda rarely really saw them but they were always sending flowers and words of admiration through her Anna. Every now and then Anna would bring one of them to Miss Mathilda for advice.

It is wonderful how poor people love to take advice from people who are friendly and above them, from people who read in books and who are good.

Miss Mathilda saw Mrs. Drehten and told her she was glad that she was going to the hospital for operation for that surely would be best, and so good Mrs. Drehten's mind was set at rest.

Mrs. Drehten's tumor came out very well. Mrs. Drehten was afterwards never really well, but she could do her work a little better, and be on her feet and yet not get so tired.

And so Anna's life went on, taking care of Miss Mathilda and all her clothes and goods, and being good to every one that asked or seemed to need her help.

Now, slowly, Anna began to make it up with Mrs. Lehntman. They could never be as they had been before. Mrs. Lehntman could never be again the romance in the good

Anna's life, but they could be friends again, and Anna could help all the Lehntmans in their need. This slowly came about.

Mrs. Lehntman had now left the evil and mysterious man who had been the cause of all her trouble. She had given up, too, the new big house that she had taken. Since her trouble her practice had been very quiet. Still she managed to do fairly well. She began to talk of paying the good Anna. This, however, had not gotten very far.

Anna saw Mrs. Lehntman a good deal now. Mrs. Lehntman's crisp, black, curly hair had gotten streaked with gray. Her dark, full, good looking face had lost its firm outline, gone flabby and a little worn. She had grown stouter and her clothes did not look very nice. She was as bland as ever in her ways, and as diffuse as always in her attention, but through it all there was uneasiness and fear and uncertainty lest some danger might be near.

She never said a word of her past life to the good Anna, but it was very plain to see that her experience had not left her easy, nor yet altogether free.

It had been hard for this good woman, for Mrs. Lehntman was really a good woman, it had been a very hard thing for this german woman to do what everybody knew and thought was wrong. Mrs. Lehntman was strong and she had courage, but it had been very hard to bear. Even the good Anna did not speak to her with freedom. There always remained a mystery and a depression in Mrs. Lehntman's affair.

And now the blonde, foolish, awkward daughter, Julia was in trouble. During the years the mother gave her no attention, Julia kept company with a young fellow who was a clerk somewhere in a store down in the city. He was a decent, dull young fellow, who did not make much money and could never save it for he had an old mother he supported. He and Julia had been keeping company for several years and now it was needful that they should be married. But then how could they marry? He did not make enough to start them and to keep on supporting his old mother too. Julia was not used to working much and she said, and she was stubborn, that she would not live with Charley's dirty, cross, old mother. Mrs. Lehntman had no money. She was just beginning to get on her feet. It was of course, the good Anna's savings that were handy.

However it paid Anna to bring about this marriage, paid her in scoldings and in managing the dull, long, awkward Julia, and her good, patient, stupid Charley. Anna loved to buy things cheap, and fix up a new place.

Julia and Charley were soon married and things went pretty well with them. Anna did not approve their slack, expensive ways of doing.

"No Miss Mathilda," she would say, "The young people nowadays have no sense for saving and putting money by so they will have something to use when they need it. There's Julia and her Charley. I went in there the other day, Miss Mathilda, and they had a new table with a marble top and on it they had a grand new plush album. 'Where you get that album?' I asked Julia. 'Oh, Charley he gave it to me for my birthday,' she said, and I asked her if it was paid for and she said not all yet but it would be soon. Now I ask you what business have they Miss Mathilda, when they ain't paid for anything they got already, what business have they to be buying new things for her birthdays. Julia she don't do no work, she just sits around and thinks how she can spend the money, and Charley he never puts one cent by. I never see anything like the people nowadays Miss Mathilda, they don't seem to have any sense of being careful about money. Julia and Charley when they have any children they won't have nothing to bring them up with right. I said that to Julia, Miss Mathilda, when she showed me those silly things that Charley bought her, and she just said in her silly, giggling way, perhaps they won't have any children. I told her she ought to be ashamed of talking so, but I don't know, Miss Mathilda, the young people nowadays have no sense at all of what's the right way for them to do, and perhaps its better if they don't have any children, and then Miss Mathilda you know there is Mrs. Lehntman. You know she regular adopted little Johnny just so she could pay out some more money just as if she didn't have trouble enough taking care of her own children. No Miss Mathilda, I never see how people can do things so. People don't seem to have no sense of right or wrong or anything these days Miss Mathilda, they are just careless and thinking always of themselves and how they can always have a happy time. No, Miss Mathilda I don't see how people can go on and do things so."

The good Anna could not understand the careless and bad ways of all the world and always she grew bitter with it all. No, not one of them had any sense of what was the right way for them to do.

Anna's past life was now drawing to an end. Her old blind dog, Baby, was sick and like to die. Baby had been the first gift from her friend the widow, Mrs. Lehntman in the old days when Anna had been with Miss Mary Wadsmith, and when these two women had first come together.

Through all the years of change, Baby had stayed with the good Anna, growing old and fat and blind and lazy. Baby had been active and a ratter when she was young, but that was so long ago it was forgotten, and for many years now Baby had wanted only her warm basket and her dinner.

Anna in her active life found need of others, of Peter and the funny little Rags, but always Baby was the eldest and held her with the ties of old affection. Anna was harsh when the young ones tried to keep poor Baby out and use her basket. Baby had been blind now for some years as dogs get, when they are no longer active. She got weak and fat and breathless and she could not even stand long any more. Anna had always to see that she got her dinner and that the young active ones did not deprive her.

Baby did not die with a real sickness. She just got older and more blind and coughed and then more quiet, and then slowly one bright summer's day she died.

There is nothing more dreary than old age in animals. Somehow it is all wrong that they should have grey hair and withered skin, and blind old eyes, and decayed and useless teeth. An old man or an old woman almost always has some tie that seems to bind them to the younger, realer life. They have children or the remembrance of old duties, but a dog that's old and so cut off from all its world of struggle, is like a dreary, deathless Struldbrug, the dreary dragger on of death through life.

And so one day old Baby died. It was dreary, more than sad, for the good Anna. She did not want the poor old beast to linger with its weary age, and blind old eyes and dismal shaking cough, but this death left Anna very empty. She had the foolish young man Peter, and the jolly little Rags for comfort, but Baby had been the only one that could remember.

The good Anna wanted a real graveyard for her Baby, but this could not be in a Christian country, and so Anna all alone took her old friend done up in decent wrappings and put her into the ground in some quiet place that Anna knew of.

The good Anna did not weep for poor old Baby. Nay, she had not time even to feel lonely, for with the good Anna it was sorrow upon sorrow. She was now no longer to keep house for Miss Mathilda.

When Anna had first come to Miss Mathilda she had known that it might only be for a few years, for Miss Mathilda was given to much wandering and often changed her home, and found new places where she went to live. The good Anna did not then think much about this, for when she first went to Miss Mathilda she had not thought that she would like it and so she had not worried about staying. Then in those happy years that they had been together, Anna had made herself forget it. This last year when she knew that it was coming she had tried hard to think it would not happen.

"We won't talk about it now Miss Mathilda, perhaps we all be dead by then," she would say when Miss Mathilda tried to talk it over. Or, "If we live till then Miss Mathilda, perhaps you will be staying on right here."

No, the good Anna could not talk as if this thing were real, it was too weary to be once more left with strangers.

Both the good Anna and her cherished Miss Mathilda tried hard to think that this would not really happen. Anna made missions and all kinds of things to keep her Miss Mathilda and Miss Mathilda thought out all the ways to see if the good Anna could not go with her, but neither the missions nor the plans had much success. Miss Mathilda would go, and she was going far away to a new country where Anna could not live, for she would be too lonesome.

There was nothing that these two could do but part. Perhaps we all be dead by then, the good Anna would repeat, but even that did not really happen. If we all live till then Miss

Mathilda, came out truer. They all did live till then, all except poor old blind Baby, and they simply had to part.

Poor Anna and poor Miss Mathilda. They could not look at each other that last day. Anna could not keep herself busy working. She just went in and out and sometimes scolded.

Anna could not make up her mind what she should do now for her future. She said that she would for a while keep this little red brick house that they had lived in. Perhaps she might just take in a few boarders. She did not know, she would write about it later and tell it all to Miss Mathilda.

The dreary day dragged out and then all was ready and Miss Mathilda left to take her train. Anna stood strained and pale and dry eyed on the white stone steps of the little red brick house that they had lived in. The last thing Miss Mathilda heard was the good Anna bidding foolish Peter say good bye and be sure to remember Miss Mathilda.

PART III

THE DEATH OF THE GOOD ANNA

EVERY ONE who had known of Miss Mathilda wanted the good Anna now to take a place with them, for they all knew how well Anna could take care of people and all their clothes and goods. Anna too could always go to Curden to Miss Mary Wadsmith, but none of all these ways seemed very good to Anna.

It was not now any longer that she wanted to stay near Mrs. Lehntman. There was no one now that made anything important, but Anna was certain that she did not want to take a place where she would be under some new people. No one could ever be for Anna as had been her cherished Miss Mathilda. No one could ever again so freely let her do it all. It would be better Anna thought in her strong strained weary body, it would be better just to keep on there in the little red brick house that was all furnished, and make a living taking in some boarders. Miss Mathilda had let her have the things, so it would not cost any money to begin. She could perhaps manage to live on so. She could do all the work and do every-thing as she thought best, and she was too weary with the changes to do more than she just had to, to keep living. So she stayed on in the house where they had lived, and she found some men, she would not take in women, who took her rooms and who were her boarders.

Things soon with Anna began to be less dreary. She was very popular with her few boarders. They loved her scoldings and the good things she made for them to eat. They made good jokes and laughed loud and always did whatever Anna wanted, and soon the good Anna got so that she liked it very well. Not that she did not always long for Miss Mathilda. She hoped and waited and was very certain that sometime, in one year or in another Miss Mathilda would come back, and then of course would want her, and then she could take all good care of her again.

Anna kept all Miss Mathilda's things in the best order. The boarders were well scolded if they ever made a scratch on Miss Mathilda's table.

Some of the boarders were hearty good south german fel-lows and Anna always made them go to mass. One boarder was a lusty german student who was studying in Bridgepoint to be a doctor. He was Anna's special favourite and she scolded him as she used to her old doctor so that he always would be good. Then, too, this cheery fellow always sang when he was washing, and that was what Miss Mathilda always used to do. Anna's heart grew warm again with this young fellow who seemed to bring back to her everything she needed.

And so Anna's life in these days was not all unhappy. She worked and scolded, she had her stray dogs and cats and people, who all asked and seemed to need her care, and she had hearty german fellows who loved her scoldings and ate so much of the good things that she knew so well the way to make.

No, the good Anna's life in these days was not all unhappy. She did not see her old friends much, she was too busy, but once in a great while she took a Sunday afternoon and went to see good Mrs. Drehten.

The only trouble was that Anna hardly made a living. She charged so little for her board and gave her people such good things to eat, that she could only just make both ends meet. The good german priest to whom she always told her troubles tried to make her have the boarders pay a little higher, and Miss Mathilda always in her letters urged her to this thing, but the good Anna somehow could not do it. Her boarders were nice men but she knew they did not have much money, and then she could not raise on those who had been with her and she could not ask the new ones to pay higher, when those who were already there were paying just what they had paid before. So Anna let it go just as she had begun it. She worked and worked all day and thought all night how she could save, and with all the work she just managed to keep living. She could not make enough to lay any money by.

Anna got so little money that she had all the work to do herself. She could not pay even the little Sallie enough to keep her with her.

Not having little Sallie nor having any one else working with her, made it very hard for Anna ever to go out, for she never thought that it was right to leave a house all empty. Once in a great while of a Sunday, Sallie who was now working in a factory would come and stay in the house for the good Anna, who would then go out and spend the afternoon with Mrs. Drehten.

No, Anna did not see her old friends much any more. She went sometimes to see her half brother and his wife and her nieces, and they always came to her on her birthdays to give presents, and her half brother never left her out of his festive raisined bread giving progresses. But these relatives of hers had never meant very much to the good Anna. Anna always did her duty by them all, and she liked her half brother very well and the loaves of raisined bread that he supplied her were most welcome now, and Anna always gave her god daughter and her sister handsome presents, but no one in this family had ever made a way inside to Anna's feelings.

Mrs. Lehntman she saw very rarely. It is hard to build up new on an old friendship when in that friendship there has been bitter disillusion. They did their best, both these women, to be friends, but they were never able to again touch one another nearly. There were too many things between them that they could not speak of, things that had never been explained nor yet forgiven. The good Anna still did her best for foolish Julia and still every now and then saw Mrs. Lehntman, but this family had now lost all its real hold on Anna.

Mrs. Drehten was now the best friend that Anna knew. Here there was never any more than the mingling of their sorrows. They talked over all the time the best way for Mrs. Drehten now to do; poor Mrs. Drehten who with her chief trouble, her bad husband, had really now no way that she could do. She just had to work and to be patient and to love her children and be very quiet. She always had a soothing mother influence on the good Anna who with her irritable, strained, worn-out body would come and sit by Mrs. Drehten and talk all her troubles over.

Of all the friends that the good Anna had had in these twenty years in Bridgepoint, the good father and patient Mrs. Drehten were the only ones that were now near to Anna and with whom she could talk her troubles over.

Anna worked, and thought, and saved, and scolded, and took care of all the boarders, and of Peter and of Rags, and all the others. There was never any end to Anna's effort and she grew always more tired, more pale yellow, and in her face more thin and worn and worried. Sometimes she went farther in not being well, and then she went to see Dr. Herman who had operated on good Mrs. Drehten.

The things that Anna really needed were to rest sometimes and eat more so that she could get stronger, but these were the last things that Anna could bring herself to do. Anna could never take a rest. She must work hard through the summer as well as through the winter, else she could never make both ends meet. The doctor gave her medicines to make her stronger but these did not seem to do much good.

Anna grew always more tired, her headaches came oftener and harder, and she was now almost always feeling very sick. She could not sleep much in the night. The dogs with their noises disturbed her and everything in her body seemed to pain her.

The doctor and the good father tried often to make her give herself more care. Mrs. Drehten told her that she surely would not get well unless for a little while she would stop working. Anna would then promise to take care, to rest in bed a little longer and to eat more so that she would get stronger, but really how could Anna eat when she always did the cooking and was so tired of it all, before it was half ready for the table?

Anna's only friendship now was with good Mrs. Drehten who was too gentle and too patient to make a stubborn faithful german Anna ever do the way she should, in the things that were for her own good.

Anna grew worse all through this second winter. When the summer came the doctor said that she simply could not live on so. He said she must go to his hospital and there he would operate upon her. She would then be well and strong and able to work hard all next winter.

Anna for some time would not listen. She could not do this so, for she had her house all furnished and she simply could not let it go. At last a woman came and said she would take care of Anna's boarders and then Anna said that she was prepared to go.

Anna went to the hospital for her operation. Mrs. Drehten was herself not well but she came into the city, so that some friend would be with the good Anna. Together, then, they went to this place where the doctor had done so well by Mrs. Drehten.

In a few days they had Anna ready. Then they did the operation, and then the good Anna with her strong, strained, worn-out body died.

Mrs. Drehten sent word of her death to Miss Mathilda.

"Dear Miss Mathilda," wrote Mrs. Drehten, "Miss Annie died in the hospital yesterday after a hard operation. She was talking about you and Doctor and Miss Mary Wadsmith all the time. She said she hoped you would take Peter and the little Rags to keep when you came back to America to live. I will keep them for you here Miss Mathilda. Miss Annie died easy, Miss Mathilda, and sent you her love."

FINIS

Melanctha

EACH ONE AS SHE MAY

ROSE JOHNSON made it very hard to bring her baby to its birth.

Melanctha Herbert who was Rose Johnson's friend, did everything that any woman could. She tended Rose, and she was patient, submissive, soothing, and untiring, while the sullen, childish, cowardly, black Rosie grumbled and fussed and howled and made herself to be an abomination and like a simple beast.

The child though it was healthy after it was born, did not live long. Rose Johnson was careless and negligent and selfish, and when Melanctha had to leave for a few days, the baby died. Rose Johnson had liked the baby well enough and perhaps she just forgot it for awhile, anyway the child was dead and Rose and Sam her husband were very sorry but then these things came so often in the negro world in Bridgepoint, that they neither of them thought about it very long.

Rose Johnson and Melanctha Herbert had been friends now for some years. Rose had lately married Sam Johnson a decent honest kindly fellow, a deck hand on a coasting steamer.

Melanctha Herbert had not yet been really married.

Rose Johnson was a real black, tall, well built, sullen, stupid, childlike, good looking negress. She laughed when she was happy and grumbled and was sullen with everything that troubled.

Rose Johnson was a real black negress but she had been brought up quite like their own child by white folks.

Rose laughed when she was happy but she had not the wide, abandoned laughter that makes the warm broad glow of negro sunshine. Rose was never joyous with the earth-born, boundless joy of negroes. Hers was just ordinary, any sort of woman laughter.

Rose Johnson was careless and was lazy, but she had been brought up by white folks and she needed decent comfort.

Her white training had only made for habits, not for nature. Rose had the simple, promiscuous unmorality of the black people.

Rose Johnson and Melanctha Herbert like many of the twos with women were a curious pair to be such friends.

Melanctha Herbert was a graceful, pale yellow, intelligent, attractive negress. She had not been raised like Rose by white folks but then she had been half made with real white blood.

She and Rose Johnson were both of the better sort of negroes, there, in Bridgepoint.

"No, I ain't no common nigger," said Rose Johnson, "for I was raised by white folks, and Melanctha she is so bright and learned so much in school, she ain't no common nigger either, though she ain't got no husband to be married to like I am to Sam Johnson."

Why did the subtle, intelligent, attractive, half white girl Melanctha Herbert love and do for and demean herself in service to this coarse, decent, sullen, ordinary, black childish Rose, and why was this unmoral, promiscuous, shiftless Rose married, and that's not so common either, to a good man of the negroes, while Melanctha with her white blood and attraction and her desire for a right position had not yet been really married.

Sometimes the thought of how all her world was made, filled the complex, desiring Melanctha with despair. She wondered, often, how she could go on living when she was so blue.

Melanctha told Rose one day how a woman whom she knew had killed herself because she was so blue. Melanctha said, sometimes, she thought this was the best thing for her herself to do.

Rose Johnson did not see it the least bit that way.

"I don't see Melanctha why you should talk like you would kill yourself just because you're blue. I'd never kill myself Melanctha just 'cause I was blue. I'd maybe kill somebody else Melanctha 'cause I was blue, but I'd never kill myself. If I ever killed myself Melanctha it'd be by accident, and if I ever killed myself by accident Melanctha, I'd be awful sorry."

Rose Johnson and Melanctha Herbert had first met, one night, at church. Rose Johnson did not care much for religion.

She had not enough emotion to be really roused by a revival. Melanctha Herbert had not come yet to know how to use religion. She was still too complex with desire. However, the two of them in negro fashion went very often to the negro church, along with all their friends, and they slowly came to know each other very well.

Rose Johnson had been raised not as a servant but quite like their own child by white folks. Her mother who had died when Rose was still a baby, had been a trusted servant in the family. Rose was a cute, attractive, good looking little black girl and these people had no children of their own and so they kept Rose in their house.

As Rose grew older she drifted from her white folks back to the colored people, and she gradually no longer lived in the old house. Then it happened that these people went away to some other town to live, and somehow Rose stayed behind in Bridgepoint. Her white folks left a little money to take care of Rose, and this money she got every little while.

Rose now in the easy fashion of the poor lived with one woman in her house, and then for no reason went and lived with some other woman in her house. All this time, too, Rose kept company, and was engaged, first to this colored man and then to that, and always she made sure she was engaged, for Rose had strong the sense of proper conduct.

"No, I ain't no common nigger just to go around with any man, nor you Melanctha shouldn't neither," she said one day when she was telling the complex and less sure Melanctha what was the right way for her to do. "No Melanctha, I ain't no common nigger to do so, for I was raised by white folks. You know very well Melanctha that I'se always been engaged to them."

And so Rose lived on, always comfortable and rather decent and very lazy and very well content.

After she had lived some time this way, Rose thought it would be nice and very good in her position to get regularly really married. She had lately met Sam Johnson somewhere, and she liked him and she knew he was a good man, and then he had a place where he worked every day and got good wages. Sam Johnson liked Rose very well and he was quite ready to be married. One day they had a grand real wedding and were married. Then with Melanctha Herbert's help to do the sewing and the nicer work, they furnished comfortably a little red brick house. Sam then went back to his work as deck hand on a coasting steamer, and Rose stayed home in her house and sat and bragged to all her friends how nice it was to be married really to a husband.

Life went on very smoothly with them all the year. Rose was lazy but not dirty and Sam was careful but not fussy, and then there was Melanctha to come in every day and help to keep things neat.

When Rose's baby was coming to be born, Rose came to stay in the house where Melanctha Herbert lived just then, with a big good natured colored woman who did washing.

Rose went there to stay, so that she might have the doctor from the hospital near by to help her have the baby, and then, too, Melanctha could attend to her while she was sick.

Here the baby was born, and here it died, and then Rose went back to her house again with Sam.

Melanctha Herbert had not made her life all simple like Rose Johnson. Melanctha had not found it easy with herself to make her wants and what she had, agree.

Melanctha Herbert was always losing what she had in wanting all the things she saw. Melanctha was always being left when she was not leaving others.

Melanctha Herbert always loved too hard and much too often. She was always full with mystery and subtle movements and denials and vague distrusts and complicated disillusions. Then Melanctha would be sudden and impulsive and unbounded in some faith, and then she would suffer and be strong in her repression.

Melanctha Herbert was always seeking rest and quiet, and always she could only find new ways to be in trouble.

Melanctha wondered often how it was she did not kill herself when she was so blue. Often she thought this would be really the best way for her to do.

Melanctha Herbert had been raised to be religious, by her mother. Melanctha had not liked her mother very well. This mother, 'Mis' Herbert, as her neighbors called her, had been a sweet appearing and dignified and pleasant, pale yellow, colored woman. 'Mis' Herbert had always been a little wandering and mysterious and uncertain in her ways.

Melanctha was pale yellow and mysterious and a little pleasant like her mother, but the real power in Melanctha's nature came through her robust and unpleasant and very unendurable black father.

Melanctha's father only used to come to where Melanctha and her mother lived, once in a while.

It was many years now that Melanctha had not heard or seen or known of anything her father did.

Melanctha Herbert almost always hated her black father, but she loved very well the power in herself that came through him. And so her feeling was really closer to her black coarse father, than her feeling had ever been toward her pale yellow, sweet-appearing mother. The things she had in her of her mother never made her feel respect.

Melanctha Herbert had not loved herself in childhood. All of her youth was bitter to remember.

Melanctha had not loved her father and her mother and they had found it very troublesome to have her.

Melanctha's mother and her father had been regularly married. Melanctha's father was a big black virile negro. He only came once in a while to where Melanctha and her mother lived, but always that pleasant, sweet-appearing, pale yellow woman, mysterious and uncertain and wandering in her ways, was close in sympathy and thinking to her big black virile husband.

James Herbert was a common, decent enough, colored workman, brutal and rough to his one daughter, but then she was a most disturbing child to manage.

The young Melanctha did not love her father and her mother, and she had a break neck courage, and a tongue that could be very nasty. Then, too, Melanctha went to school and was very quick in all the learning, and she knew very well how to use this knowledge to annoy her parents who knew nothing.

Melanctha Herbert had always had a break neck courage. Melanctha always loved to be with horses; she loved to do wild things, to ride the horses and to break and tame them.

Melanctha, when she was a little girl, had had a good chance to live with horses. Near where Melanctha and her mother lived was the stable of the Bishops, a rich family who always had fine horses.

John, the Bishops' coachman, liked Melanctha very well and he always let her do anything she wanted with the horses. John was a decent, vigorous mulatto with a prosperous house and wife and children. Melanctha Herbert was older than any of his children. She was now a well grown girl of twelve and just beginning as a woman.

James Herbert, Melanctha's father, knew this John, the Bishops' coachman very well.

One day James Herbert came to where his wife and daughter lived, and he was furious.

"Where's that Melanctha girl of yours," he said fiercely, "if she is to the Bishops' stables again, with that man John, I swear I kill her. Why don't you see to that girl better you, you're her mother."

James Herbert was a powerful, loose built, hard handed, black, angry negro. Herbert never was a joyous negro. Even when he drank with other men, and he did that very often, he was never really joyous. In the days when he had been most young and free and open, he had never had the wide abandoned laughter that gives the broad glow to negro sunshine.

His daughter, Melanctha Herbert, later always made a hard forced laughter. She was only strong and sweet and in her nature when she was really deep in trouble, when she was fighting so with all she really had, that she did not use her laughter. This was always true of poor Melanctha who was so certain that she hated trouble. Melanctha Herbert was always seeking peace and quiet, and she could always only find new ways to get excited.

James Herbert was often a very angry negro. He was fierce and serious, and he was very certain that he often had good reason to be angry with Melanctha, who knew so well how to be nasty, and to use her learning with a father who knew nothing.

James Herbert often drank with John, the Bishops' coachman. John in his good nature sometimes tried to soften Herbert's feeling toward Melanctha. Not that Melanctha ever complained to John of her home life or her father. It was never Melanctha's way, even in the midst of her worst trouble to complain to any one of what happened to her, but nevertheless somehow every one who knew Melanctha always knew how much she suffered. It was only while one really loved Melanctha that one understood how to forgive her, that she never once complained nor looked unhappy, and was always handsome and in spirits, and yet one always knew how much she suffered.

The father, James Herbert, never told his troubles either, and he was so fierce and serious that no one ever thought of asking.

'Mis' Herbert as her neighbors called her was never heard even to speak of her husband or her daughter. She was always pleasant, sweet-appearing, mysterious and uncertain, and a little wandering in her ways.

The Herberts were a silent family with their troubles, but somehow every one who knew them always knew everything that happened.

The morning of one day when in the evening Herbert and the coachman John were to meet to drink together, Melanctha had to come to the stable joyous and in the very best of humors. Her good friend John on this morning felt very firmly how good and sweet she was and how very much she suffered.

John was a very decent colored coachman. When he thought about Melanctha it was as if she were the eldest of his children. Really he felt very strongly the power in her of a woman. John's wife always liked Melanctha and she always did all she could to make things pleasant. And Melanctha all her life loved and respected kind and good and considerate people. Melanctha always loved and wanted peace and gentleness and goodness and all her life for herself poor Melanctha could only find new ways to be in trouble.

This evening after John and Herbert had drunk awhile together, the good John began to tell the father what a fine girl he had for a daughter. Perhaps the good John had been drinking a good deal of liquor, perhaps there was a gleam of something softer than the feeling of a friendly elder in the way John then spoke of Melanctha. There had been a good deal of drinking and John certainly that very morning had felt strongly Melanctha's power as a woman. James Herbert was always a fierce, suspicious, serious negro, and drinking never made him feel more open. He looked very black and evil as he sat and listened while John grew more and more admiring as he talked half to himself, half to the father, of the virtues and the sweetness of Melanctha.

Suddenly between them there came a moment filled full with strong black curses, and then sharp razors flashed in the black hands, that held them flung backward in the negro fashion, and then for some minutes there was fierce slashing.

John was a decent, pleasant, good natured, light brown negro, but he knew how to use a razor to do bloody slashing.

When the two men were pulled apart by the other negroes who were in the room drinking, John had not been much wounded but James Herbert had gotten one good strong cut that went from his right shoulder down across the front of his whole body. Razor fighting does not wound very deeply, but it makes a cut that looks most nasty, for it is so very bloody.

Herbert was held by the other negroes until he was cleaned and plastered, and then he was put to bed to sleep off his drink and fighting.

The next day he came to where his wife and daughter lived and he was furious.

"Where's that Melanctha, of yours?" he said to his wife, when he saw her. "If she is to the Bishops' stables now with that yellow John, I swear I kill her. A nice way she is going for a decent daughter. Why don't you see to that girl better you, ain't you her mother!"

Melanctha Herbert had always been old in all her ways and she knew very early how to use her power as a woman, and yet Melanctha with all her inborn intense wisdom was really very ignorant of evil. Melanctha had not yet come to understand what they meant, the things she so often heard around her, and which were just beginning to stir strongly in her.

Now when her father began fiercely to assail her, she did not really know what it was that he was so furious to force from her. In every way that he could think of in his anger, he tried to make her say a thing she did not really know. She held out and never answered anything he asked her, for

Melanctha had a breakneck courage and she just then badly hated her black father.

When the excitement was all over, Melanctha began to know her power, the power she had so often felt stirring within her and which she now knew she could use to make her stronger.

James Herbert did not win this fight with his daughter. After awhile he forgot it as he soon forgot John and the cut of his sharp razor.

Melanctha almost forgot to hate her father, in her strong interest in the power she now knew she had within her.

Melanctha did not care much now, any longer, to see John or his wife or even the fine horses. This life was too quiet and accustomed and no longer stirred her to any interest or excitement.

Melanctha now really was beginning as a woman. She was ready, and she began to search in the streets and in dark corners to discover men and to learn their natures and their various ways of working.

In these next years Melanctha learned many ways that lead to wisdom. She learned the ways, and dimly in the distance she saw wisdom. These years of learning led very straight to trouble for Melanctha, though in these years Melanctha never did or meant anything that was really wrong.

Girls who are brought up with care and watching can always find moments to escape into the world, where they may learn the ways that lead to wisdom. For a girl raised like Melanctha Herbert, such escape was always very simple. Often she was alone, sometimes she was with a fellow seeker, and she strayed and stood, sometimes by railroad yards, sometimes on the docks or around new buildings where many men were working. Then when the darkness covered everything all over, she would begin to learn to know this man or that. She would advance, they would respond, and then she would withdraw a little, dimly, and always she did not know what it was that really held her. Sometimes she would almost go over, and then the strength in her of not really knowing, would stop the average man in his endeavor. It was a strange experience of ignorance and power and desire. Melanctha did not know what it was that she so badly wanted. She was afraid, and yet she did not understand that here she really was a coward.

Boys had never meant much to Melanctha. They had always been too young to content her. Melanctha had a strong respect for any kind of successful power. It was this that always kept Melanctha nearer, in her feeling toward her virile and unendurable black father, than she ever was in her feeling for her pale yellow, sweet-appearing mother. The things she had in her of her mother, never made her feel respect.

In these young days, it was only men that for Melanctha held anything there was of knowledge and power. It was not from men however that Melanctha learned to really understand this power.

From the time that Melanctha was twelve until she was sixteen she wandered, always seeking but never more than very dimly seeing wisdom. All this time Melanctha went on with her school learning; she went to school rather longer than do most of the colored children.

Melanctha's wanderings after wisdom she always had to do in secret and by snatches, for her mother was then still living and 'Mis' Herbert always did some watching, and Melanctha with all her hard courage dreaded that there should be much telling to her father, who came now quite often to where Melanctha lived with her mother.

In these days Melanctha talked and stood and walked with many kinds of men, but she did not learn to know any of them very deeply. They all supposed her to have world knowledge and experience. They, believing that she knew all, told her nothing, and thinking that she was deciding with them, asked for nothing, and so though Melanctha wandered widely, she was really very safe with all the wandering.

It was a very wonderful experience this safety of Melanctha in these days of her attempted learning. Melanctha herself did not feel the wonder, she only knew that for her it all had no real value.

Melanctha all her life was very keen in her sense for real experience. She knew she was not getting what she so badly wanted, but with all her break neck courage Melanctha here was a coward, and so she could not learn to really understand.

Melanctha liked to wander, and to stand by the railroad yard, and watch the men and the engines and the switches and everything that was busy there, working. Railroad yards are a ceaseless fascination. They satisfy every kind of nature. For the lazy man whose blood flows very slowly, it is a steady soothing world of motion which supplies him with the sense of a strong moving power. He need not work and yet he has it very deeply; he has it even better than the man who works in it or owns it. Then for natures that like to feel emotion without the trouble of having any suffering, it is very nice to get the swelling in the throat, and the fullness, and the heart beats, and all the flutter of excitement that comes as one watches the people come and go, and hears the engine pound and give a long drawn whistle. For a child watching through a hole in the fence above the yard, it is a wonder world of mystery and movement. The child loves all the noise, and then it loves the silence of the wind that comes before the full rush of the pounding train, that bursts out from the tunnel where it lost itself and all its noise in darkness, and the child loves all the smoke, that sometimes comes in rings, and always puffs with fire and blue color.

For Melanctha the yard was full of the excitement of many men, and perhaps a free and whirling future.

Melanctha came here very often and watched the men and all the things that were so busy working. The men always had time for, "Hullo sis, do you want to sit on my engine," and, "Hullo, that's a pretty lookin' yaller girl, do you want to come and see him cookin.'"

All the colored porters liked Melanctha. They often told her exciting things that had happened; how in the West they went through big tunnels where there was no air to breathe, and then out and winding around edges of great canyons on thin high spindling trestles, and sometimes cars, and sometimes whole trains fell from the narrow bridges, and always up from the dark places death and all kinds of queer devils looked up and laughed in their faces. And then they would tell how sometimes when the train went pounding down steep slippery mountains, great rocks would racket and roll down around them, and sometimes would smash in the car and kill men; and as the porters told these stories their round, black, shining faces would grow solemn, and their color would go grey beneath the greasy black, and their eyes would roll white in the fear and wonder of the things they could scare themselves by telling.

There was one, big, serious, melancholy, light brown porter who often told Melanctha stories, for he liked the way she had of listening with intelligence and sympathetic feeling, when he told how the white men in the far South tried to kill him because he made one of them who was drunk and called him a damned nigger, and who refused to pay money for his chair to a nigger, get off the train between stations. And then this porter had to give up going to that part of the Southern country, for all the white men swore that if he ever came there again they would surely kill him.

Melanctha liked this serious, melancholy light brown negro very well, and all her life Melanctha wanted and respected gentleness and goodness, and this man always gave her good advice and serious kindness, and Melanctha felt such things very deeply, but she could never let them help her or affect her to change the ways that always made her keep herself in trouble.

Melanctha spent many of the last hours of the daylight with the porters and with other men who worked hard, but when darkness came it was always different. Then Melanctha would find herself with the, for her, gentlemanly classes. A clerk, or a young express agent would begin to know her, and they would stand, or perhaps, walk a little while together.

Melanctha always made herself escape but often it was with an effort. She did not know what it was that she so badly wanted, but with all her courage Melanctha here was a coward, and so she could not learn to understand.

Melanctha and some man would stand in the evening and would talk together. Sometimes Melanctha would be with another girl and then it was much easier to stay or to escape, for then they could make way for themselves together, and by throwing words and laughter to each other, could keep a man from getting too strong in his attention.

But when Melanctha was alone, and she was so, very often, she would sometimes come very near to making a long step on the road that leads to wisdom. Some man would learn a

good deal about her in the talk, never altogether truly, for
Melanctha all her life did not know how to tell a story wholly.
She always, and yet not with intention, managed to leave out
big pieces which make a story very different, for when it came
to what had happened and what she had said and what it was
that she had really done, Melanctha never could remember
right. The man would sometimes come a little nearer, would
detain her, would hold her arm or make his jokes a little
clearer, and then Melanctha would always make herself escape.
The man thinking that she really had world wisdom would
not make his meaning clear, and believing that she was deciding with him he never went so fast that he could stop her
when at last she made herself escape.

And so Melanctha wandered on the edge of wisdom. "Say,
Sis, why don't you when you come here stay a little longer?"
they would all ask her, and they would hold her for an answer,
and she would laugh, and sometimes she did stay longer, but
always just in time she made herself escape.

Melanctha Herbert wanted very much to know and yet she
feared the knowledge. As she grew older she often stayed a
good deal longer, and sometimes it was almost a balanced
struggle, but she always made herself escape.

Next to the railroad yard it was the shipping docks that
Melanctha loved best when she wandered. Often she was
alone, sometimes she was with some better kind of black girl,
and she would stand a long time and watch the men working
at unloading, and see the steamers do their coaling, and she
would listen with full feeling to the yowling of the free swinging negroes, as they ran, with their powerful loose jointed
bodies and their childish savage yelling, pushing, carrying,
pulling great loads from the ships to the warehouses.

The men would call out, "Say, Sis, look out or we'll come
and catch yer," or "Hi, there, you yaller girl, come here and
we'll take you sailin'." And then, too, Melanctha would learn
to know some of the serious foreign sailors who told her all
sorts of wonders, and a cook would sometimes take her and
her friends over a ship and show where he made his messes
and where the men slept, and where the shops were, and how
everything was made by themselves, right there, on ship
board.

Melanctha loved to see these dark and smelly places. She always loved to watch and talk and listen with men who worked hard. But it was never from these rougher people that Melanctha tried to learn the ways that lead to wisdom. In the daylight she always liked to talk with rough men and to listen to their lives and about their work and their various ways of doing, but when the darkness covered everything all over, Melanctha would meet, and stand, and talk with a clerk or a young shipping agent who had seen her watching, and so it was that she would try to learn to understand.

And then Melanctha was fond of watching men work on new buildings. She loved to see them hoisting, digging, sawing and stone cutting. Here, too, in the daylight, she always learned to know the common workmen. "Heh, Sis, look out or that rock will fall on you and smash you all up into little pieces. Do you think you would make a nice jelly?" And then they would all laugh and feel that their jokes were very funny. And "Say, you pretty yaller girl, would it scare you bad to stand up here on top where I be? See if you've got grit and come up here where I can hold you. All you got to do is to sit still on that there rock that they're just hoistin', and then when you get here I'll hold you tight, don't you be scared Sis."

Sometimes Melanctha would do some of these things that had much danger, and always with such men, she showed her power and her break neck courage. Once she slipped and fell from a high place. A workman caught her and so she was not killed, but her left arm was badly broken.

All the men crowded around her. They admired her boldness in doing and in bearing pain when her arm was broken. They all went along with her with great respect to the doctor, and then they took her home in triumph and all of them were bragging about her not squealing.

James Herbert was home where his wife lived, that day. He was furious when he saw the workmen and Melanctha. He drove the men away with curses so that they were all very nearly fighting, and he would not let a doctor come in to attend Melanctha. "Why don't you see to that girl better, you, you're her mother."

James Herbert did not fight things out now any more with

his daughter. He feared her tongue, and her school learning, and the way she had of saying things that were very nasty to a brutal black man who knew nothing. And Melanctha just then hated him very badly in her suffering.

And so this was the way Melanctha lived the four years of her beginning as a woman. And many things happened to Melanctha, but she knew very well that none of them had led her on to the right way, that certain way that was to lead her to world wisdom.

Melanctha Herbert was sixteen when she first met Jane Harden. Jane was a negress, but she was so white that hardly any one could guess it. Jane had had a good deal of education. She had been two years at a colored college. She had had to leave because of her bad conduct. She taught Melanctha many things. She taught her how to go the ways that lead to wisdom.

Jane Harden was at this time twenty-three years old and she had had much experience. She was very much attracted by Melanctha, and Melanctha was very proud that this Jane would let her know her.

Jane Harden was not afraid to understand. Melanctha who had strong the sense for real experience, knew that here was a woman who had learned to understand.

Jane Harden had many bad habits. She drank a great deal, and she wandered widely. She was safe though now, when she wanted to be safe, in this wandering.

Melanctha Herbert soon always wandered with her. Melanctha tried the drinking and some of the other habits, but she did not find that she cared very much to do them. But every day she grew stronger in her desire to really understand.

It was now no longer, even in the daylight, the rougher men that these two learned to know in their wanderings, and for Melanctha the better classes were now a little higher. It was no longer express agents and clerks that she learned to know, but men in business, commercial travelers, and even men above these, and Jane and she would talk and walk and laugh and escape from them all very often. It was still the same, the knowing of them and the always just escaping, only now for Melanctha somehow it was different, for though it was always the same thing that happened it had a different flavor, for now Melanctha was with a woman who had wisdom, and dimly she began to see what it was that she should understand.

It was not from the men that Melanctha learned her wisdom. It was always Jane Harden herself who was making Melanctha begin to understand.

Jane was a roughened woman. She had power and she liked to use it, she had much white blood and that made her see clear, she liked drinking and that made her reckless. Her white blood was strong in her and she had grit and endurance and a vital courage. She was always game, however much she was in trouble. She liked Melanctha Herbert for the things that she had like her, and then Melanctha was young, and she had sweetness, and a way of listening with intelligence and sympathetic interest, to the stories that Jane Harden often told out of her experience.

Jane grew always fonder of Melanctha. Soon they began to wander, more to be together than to see men and learn their various ways of working. Then they began not to wander, and Melanctha would spend long hours with Jane in her room, sitting at her feet and listening to her stories, and feeling her strength and the power of her affection, and slowly she began to see clear before her one certain way that would be sure to lead to wisdom.

Before the end came, the end of the two years in which Melanctha spent all her time when she was not at school or in her home, with Jane Harden, before these two years were finished, Melanctha had come to see very clear, and she had come to be very certain, what it is that gives the world its wisdom.

Jane Harden always had a little money and she had a room in the lower part of the town. Jane had once taught in a colored school. She had had to leave that too on account of her bad conduct. It was her drinking that always made all the trouble for her, for that can never be really covered over.

Jane's drinking was always growing worse upon her. Melanctha had tried to do the drinking but it had no real attraction for her.

In the first year, between Jane Harden and Melanctha

Herbert, Jane had been much the stronger. Jane loved Melanctha and she found her always intelligent and brave and sweet and docile, and Jane meant to, and before the year was over she had taught Melanctha what it is that gives many people in the world their wisdom.

Jane had many ways in which to do this teaching. She told Melanctha many things. She loved Melanctha hard and made Melanctha feel it very deeply. She would be with other people and with men and with Melanctha, and she would make Melanctha understand what everybody wanted, and what one did with power when one had it.

Melanctha sat at Jane's feet for many hours in these days and felt Jane's wisdom. She learned to love Jane and to have this feeling very deeply. She learned a little in these days to know joy, and she was taught too how very keenly she could suffer. It was very different this suffering from that Melanctha sometimes had from her mother and from her very unendurable black father. Then she was fighting and she could be strong and valiant in her suffering, but here with Jane Harden she was longing and she bent and pleaded with her suffering.

It was a very tumultuous, very mingled year, this time for Melanctha, but she certainly did begin to really understand.

In every way she got it from Jane Harden. There was nothing good or bad in doing, feeling, thinking or in talking, that Jane spared her. Sometimes the lesson came almost too strong for Melanctha, but somehow she always managed to endure it and so slowly, but always with increasing strength and feeling, Melanctha began to really understand.

Then slowly, between them, it began to be all different. Slowly now between them, it was Melanctha Herbert, who was stronger. Slowly now they began to drift apart from one another.

Melanctha Herbert never really lost her sense that it was Jane Harden who had taught her, but Jane did many things that Melanctha now no longer needed. And then, too, Melanctha never could remember right when it came to what she had done and what had happened. Melanctha now sometimes quarreled with Jane, and they no longer went about together, and sometimes Melanctha really forgot how much she owed to Jane Harden's teaching.

Melanctha began now to feel that she had always had world wisdom. She really knew of course, that it was Jane who had taught her, but all that began to be covered over by the trouble between them, that was now always getting stronger.

Jane Harden was a roughened woman. Once she had been very strong, but now she was weakened in all her kinds of strength by her drinking. Melanctha had tried the drinking but it had had no real attraction for her.

Jane's strong and roughened nature and her drinking made it always harder for her to forgive Melanctha, that now Melanctha did not really need her any longer. Now it was Melanctha who was stronger and it was Jane who was dependent on her.

Melanctha was now come to be about eighteen years old. She was a graceful, pale yellow, good looking, intelligent, attractive negress, a little mysterious sometimes in her ways, and always good and pleasant, and always ready to do things for people.

Melanctha from now on saw very little of Jane Harden. Jane did not like that very well and sometimes she abused Melanctha, but her drinking soon covered everything all over.

It was not in Melanctha's nature to really lose her sense for Jane Harden. Melanctha all her life was ready to help Jane out in any of her trouble, and later, when Jane really went to pieces, Melanctha always did all that she could to help her.

But Melanctha Herbert was ready now herself to do teaching. Melanctha could do anything now that she wanted. Melanctha knew now what everybody wanted.

Melanctha had learned how she might stay a little longer; she had learned that she must decide when she wanted really to stay longer, and she had learned how when she wanted to, she could escape.

And so Melanctha began once more to wander. It was all now for her very different. It was never rougher men now that she talked to, and she did not care much now to know white men of the, for her, very better classes. It was now something realler that Melanctha wanted, something that would move her very deeply, something that would fill her fully with the wisdom that was planted now within her, and that she wanted badly, should really wholly fill her.

Melanctha these days wandered very widely. She was always alone now when she wandered. Melanctha did not need help now to know, or to stay longer, or when she wanted, to escape.

Melanctha tried a great many men, in these days before she was really suited. It was almost a year that she wandered and then she met with a young mulatto. He was a doctor who had just begun to practice. He would most likely do well in the future, but it was not this that concerned Melanctha. She found him good and strong and gentle and very intellectual, and all her life Melanctha liked and wanted good and considerate people, and then too he did not at first believe in Melanctha. He held off and did not know what it was that Melanctha wanted. Melanctha came to want him very badly. They began to know each other better. Things began to be very strong between them. Melanctha wanted him so badly that now she never wandered. She just gave herself to this experience.

Melanctha Herbert was now, all alone, in Bridgepoint. She lived now with this colored woman and now with that one, and she sewed, and sometimes she taught a little in a colored school as substitute for some teacher. Melanctha had now no home nor any regular employment. Life was just commencing for Melanctha. She had youth and had learned wisdom, and she was graceful and pale yellow and very pleasant, and always ready to do things for people, and she was mysterious in her ways and that only made belief in her more fervent.

During the year before she met Jefferson Campbell, Melanctha had tried many kinds of men but they had none of them interested Melanctha very deeply. She met them, she was much with them, she left them, she would think perhaps this next time it would be more exciting, and always she found that for her it all had no real meaning. She could now do everything she wanted, she knew now everything that everybody wanted, and yet it all had no excitement for her. With these men, she knew she could learn nothing. She wanted some one that could teach her very deeply and now at last she was sure that she had found him, yes she really had it, before she had thought to look if in this man she would find it.

During this year 'Mis' Herbert as her neighbors called her,

Melanctha's pale yellow mother was very sick, and in this year she died.

Melanctha's father during these last years did not come very often to the house where his wife lived and Melanctha. Melanctha was not sure that her father was now any longer here in Bridgepoint. It was Melanctha who was very good now to her mother. It was always Melanctha's way to be good to any one in trouble.

Melanctha took good care of her mother. She did everything that any woman could, she tended and soothed and helped her pale yellow mother, and she worked hard in every way to take care of her, and make her dying easy. But Melanctha did not in these days like her mother any better, and her mother never cared much for this daughter who was always a hard child to manage, and who had a tongue that always could be very nasty.

Melanctha did everything that any woman could, and at last her mother died, and Melanctha had her buried. Melanctha's father was not heard from, and Melanctha in all her life after, never saw or heard or knew of anything that her father did.

It was the young doctor, Jefferson Campbell, who helped Melanctha toward the end, to take care of her sick mother. Jefferson Campbell had often before seen Melanctha Herbert, but he had never liked her very well, and he had never believed that she was any good. He had heard something about how she wandered. He knew a little too of Jane Harden, and he was sure that this Melanctha Herbert, who was her friend and who wandered, would never come to any good.

Dr. Jefferson Campbell was a serious, earnest, good young joyous doctor. He liked to take care of everybody and he loved his own colored people. He always found life very easy did Jeff Campbell, and everybody liked to have him with them. He was so good and sympathetic, and he was so earnest and so joyous. He sang when he was happy, and he laughed, and his was the free abandoned laughter that gives the warm broad glow to negro sunshine.

Jeff Campbell had never yet in his life had real trouble. Jefferson's father was a good, kind, serious, religious man. He was a very steady, very intelligent, and very dignified, light brown, grey haired negro. He was a butler and he had worked for the Campbell family many years, and his father and his mother before him had been in the service of this family as free people.

Jefferson Campbell's father and his mother had of course been regularly married. Jefferson's mother was a sweet, little, pale brown, gentle woman who reverenced and obeyed her good husband, and who worshipped and admired and loved hard her good, earnest, cheery, hard working doctor boy who was her only child.

Jeff Campbell had been raised religious by his people but religion had never interested Jeff very much. Jefferson was very good. He loved his people and he never hurt them, and he always did everything they wanted and that he could to please them, but he really loved best science and experimenting and to learn things, and he early wanted to be a doctor, and he was always very interested in the life of the colored people.

The Campbell family had been very good to him and had helped him on with his ambition. Jefferson studied hard, he went to a colored college, and then he learnt to be a doctor.

It was now two or three years, that he had started in to practice. Everybody liked Jeff Campbell, he was so strong and kindly and cheerful and understanding, and he laughed so with pure joy, and he always liked to help all his own colored people.

Dr. Jeff knew all about Jane Harden. He had taken care of her in some of her bad trouble. He knew about Melanctha too, though until her mother was taken sick he had never met her. Then he was called in to help Melanctha to take care of her sick mother. Dr. Campbell did not like Melanctha's ways and he did not think that she would ever come to any good.

Dr. Campbell had taken care of Jane Harden in some of her bad trouble. Jane sometimes had abused Melanctha to him. What right had that Melanctha Herbert who owed everything to her, Jane Harden, what right had a girl like that to go away to other men and leave her, but Melanctha Herbert never had any sense of how to act to anybody. Melanctha had a good mind, Jane never denied her that, but she never used it to do anything decent with it. But what could you expect when Melanctha had such a brute of a black nigger father, and Melanctha was always abusing her father and yet she was just like him, and really she admired him so much and he never had any sense of what he owed to anybody, and Melanctha was just like him and she was proud of it too, and it made Jane so tired to hear Melanctha talk all the time as if she wasn't. Jane Harden hated people who had good minds and didn't use them, and Melanctha always had that weakness, and wanting to keep in with people, and never really saying that she wanted to be like her father, and it was so silly of Melanctha to abuse her father, when she was so much like him and she really liked it. No, Jane Harden had no use for Melanctha. Oh yes, Melanctha always came around to be good to her. Melanctha was always sure to do that. She never really went away and left one. She didn't use her mind enough to do things straight out like that. Melanctha Herbert had a good mind, Jane never denied that to her, but she never wanted to see or hear about Melanctha Herbert any more, and she wished Melanctha wouldn't come in any more to see her. She didn't hate her, but she didn't want to hear about her father and all that talk Melanctha always made, and that just meant nothing to her. Jane Harden was very tired of all that now. She didn't have any use now any more for Melanctha, and if Dr. Campbell saw her he better tell her Jane didn't want to see her, and she could take her talk to somebody else, who was ready to believe her. And then Jane Harden would drop away and forget Melanctha and all her life before, and then she would begin to drink and so she would cover everything all over.

Jeff Campbell heard all this very often, but it did not interest him very deeply. He felt no desire to know more of this Melanctha. He heard her, once, talking to another girl outside of the house, when he was paying a visit to Jane Harden. He did not see much in the talk that he heard her do. He did not see much in the things Jane Harden said when she abused Melanctha to him. He was more interested in Jane herself than in anything he heard about Melanctha. He knew Jane Harden had a good mind, and she had had power, and she could really have done things, and now this drinking covered everything all over. Jeff Campbell was always very sorry when he had to see it. Jane Harden was a roughened woman, and yet Jeff found a great many strong good things in her, that still made him like her.

Jeff Campbell did everything he could for Jane Harden. He did not care much to hear about Melanctha. He had no feeling, much, about her. He did not find that he took any interest in her. Jane Harden was so much a stronger woman, and Jane really had had a good mind, and she had used it to do things with it, before this drinking business had taken such a hold upon her.

Dr. Campbell was helping Melanctha Herbert to take care of her sick mother. He saw Melanctha now for long times and very often, and they sometimes talked a good deal together, but Melanctha never said anything to him about Jane Harden. She never talked to him about anything that was not just general matters, or about medicine, or to tell him funny stories. She asked him many questions and always listened very well to all he told her, and she always remembered everything she heard him say about doctoring, and she always remembered everything that she had learned from all the others.

Jeff Campbell never found that all this talk interested him very deeply. He did not find that he liked Melanctha when he saw her so much, any better. He never found that he thought much about Melanctha. He never found that he believed much in her having a good mind, like Jane Harden. He found he liked Jane Harden always better, and that he wished very much that she had never begun that bad drinking.

Melanctha Herbert's mother was now always getting sicker. Melanctha really did everything that any woman could. Melanctha's mother never liked her daughter any better. She never said much, did 'Mis' Herbert, but anybody could see that she did not think much of this daughter.

Dr. Campbell now often had to stay a long time to take care of 'Mis' Herbert. One day 'Mis' Herbert was much sicker and Dr. Campbell thought that this night, she would surely die. He came back late to the house, as he had said he would, to sit up and watch 'Mis' Herbert, and to help Melanctha, if she should need anybody to be with her. Melanctha Herbert and Jeff Campbell sat up all that night together. 'Mis' Herbert did not die. The next day she was a little better.

This house where Melanctha had always lived with her

mother was a little red brick, two story house. They had not much furniture to fill it and some of the windows were broken and not mended. Melanctha did not have much money to use now on the house, but with a colored woman, who was their neighbor and good natured and who had always helped them, Melanctha managed to take care of her mother and to keep the house fairly clean and neat.

Melanctha's mother was in bed in a room upstairs, and the steps from below led right up into it. There were just two rooms on this upstairs floor. Melanctha and Dr. Campbell sat down on the steps, that night they watched together, so that they could hear and see Melanctha's mother and yet the light would be shaded, and they could sit and read, if they wanted to, and talk low some, and yet not disturb 'Mis' Herbert.

Dr. Campbell was always very fond of reading. Dr. Campbell had not brought a book with him that night. He had just forgotten it. He had meant to put something in his pocket to read, so that he could amuse himself, while he was sitting there and watching. When he was through with taking care of 'Mis' Herbert, he came and sat down on the steps just above where Melanctha was sitting. He spoke about how he had forgotten to bring his book with him. Melanctha said there were some old papers in the house, perhaps Dr. Campbell could find something in them that would help pass the time for a while for him. All right, Dr. Campbell said, that would be better than just sitting there with nothing. Dr. Campbell began to read through the old papers that Melanctha gave him. When anything amused him in them, he read it out to Melanctha. Melanctha was now pretty silent, with him. Dr. Campbell began to feel a little, about how she responded to him. Dr. Campbell began to see a little that perhaps Melanctha had a good mind. Dr. Campbell was not sure yet that she had a good mind, but he began to think a little that perhaps she might have one.

Jefferson Campbell always liked to talk to everybody about the things he worked at and about his thinking about what he could do for the colored people. Melanctha Herbert never thought about these things the way that he did. Melanctha had never said much to Dr. Campbell about what she thought about them. Melanctha did not feel the same as he did about being good and regular in life, and not having excitements all the time, which was the way that Jefferson Campbell wanted that everybody should be, so that everybody would be wise and yet be happy. Melanctha always had strong the sense for real experience. Melanctha Herbert did not think much of this way of coming to real wisdom.

Dr. Campbell soon got through with his reading, in the old newspapers, and then somehow he began to talk along about the things he was always thinking. Dr. Campbell said he wanted to work so that he could understand what troubled people, and not to just have excitements, and he believed you ought to love your father and your mother and to be regular in all your life, and not to be always wanting new things and excitements, and to always know where you were, and what you wanted, and to always tell everything just as you meant it. That's the only kind of life he knew or believed in, Jeff Campbell repeated. "No I ain't got any use for all the time being in excitements and wanting to have all kinds of experience all the time. I got plenty of experience just living regular and quiet and with my family, and doing my work, and taking care of people, and trying to understand it. I don't believe much in this running around business and I don't want to see the colored people do it. I am a colored man and I ain't sorry, and I want to see the colored people like what is good and what I want them to have, and that's to live regular and work hard and understand things, and that's enough to keep any decent man excited." Jeff Campbell spoke now with some anger. Not to Melanctha, he did not think of her at all when he was talking. It was the life he wanted that he spoke to, and the way he wanted things to be with the colored people.

But Melanctha Herbert had listened to him say all this. She knew he meant it, but it did not mean much to her, and she was sure some day he would find out, that it was not all, of real wisdom. Melanctha knew very well what it was to have real wisdom. "But how about Jane Harden?" said Melanctha to Jeff Campbell, "seems to me Dr. Campbell you find her to have something in her, and you go there very often, and you talk to her much more than you do to the nice girls that stay at home with their people, the kind you say you are really wanting. It don't seem to me Dr. Campbell, that what you say and what you do seem to have much to do with each other. And about your being so good Dr. Campbell," went on Melanctha, "You don't care about going to church much yourself, and yet you always are saying you believe so much in things like that, for people. It seems to me, Dr. Campbell you want to have a good time just like all us others, and then you just keep on saying that it's right to be good and you ought not to have excitements, and yet you really don't want to do it Dr. Campbell, no more than me or Jane Harden. No, Dr. Campbell, it certainly does seem to me you don't know very well yourself, what you mean, when you are talking."

Jefferson had been talking right along, the way he always did when he got started, and now Melanctha's answer only made him talk a little harder. He laughed a little, too, but very low, so as not to disturb 'Mis' Herbert who was sleeping very nicely, and he looked brightly at Melanctha to enjoy her, and then he settled himself down to answer.

"Yes," he began, "it certainly does sound a little like I didn't know very well what I do mean, when you put it like that to me, Miss Melanctha, but that's just because you don't understand enough about what I meant, by what I was just saying to you. I don't say, never, I don't want to know all kinds of people, Miss Melanctha, and I don't say there ain't many kinds of people, and I don't say ever, that I don't find some like Jane Harden very good to know and talk to, but it's the strong things I like in Jane Harden, not all her excitements. I don't admire the bad things she does, Miss Melanctha, but Jane Harden is a strong woman and I always respect that in her. No I know you don't believe what I say, Miss Melanctha, but I mean it, and it's all just because you don't understand it when I say it. And as for religion, that just ain't my way of being good, Miss Melanctha, but it's a good way for many people to be good and regular in their way of living, and if they believe it, it helps them to be good, and if they're honest in it, I like to see them have it. No, what I don't like, Miss Melanctha, is this what I see so much with the colored people, their always wanting new things just to get excited."

Jefferson Campbell here stopped himself in this talking.

Melanctha Herbert did not make any answer. They both sat there very quiet.

Jeff Campbell then began again on the old papers. He sat there on the steps just above where Melanctha was sitting, and he went on with his reading, and his head went moving up and down, and sometimes he was reading, and sometimes he was thinking about all the things he wanted to be doing, and then he would rub the back of his dark hand over his mouth, and in between he would be frowning with his thinking, and sometimes he would be rubbing his head hard to help his thinking. And Melanctha just sat still and watched the lamp burning, and sometimes she turned it down a little, when the wind caught it and it would begin to get to smoking.

And so Jeff Campbell and Melanctha Herbert sat there on the steps, very quiet, a long time, and they didn't seem to think much, that they were together. They sat there so, for about an hour, and then it came to Jefferson very slowly and as a strong feeling that he was sitting there on the steps, alone, with Melanctha. He did not know if Melanctha Herbert was feeling very much about their being there alone together. Jefferson began to wonder about it a little. Slowly he felt that surely they must both have this feeling. It was so important that he knew that she must have it. They both sat there, very quiet, a long time.

At last Jefferson began to talk about how the lamp was smelling. Jefferson began to explain what it is that makes a lamp get to smelling. Melanctha let him talk. She did not answer, and then he stopped in his talking. Soon Melanctha began to sit up straighter and then she started in to question.

"About what you was just saying Dr. Campbell about living regular and all that, I certainly don't understand what you meant by what you was just saying. You ain't a bit like good people Dr. Campbell, like the good people you are always saying are just like you. I know good people Dr. Campbell, and you ain't a bit like men who are good and got religion. You are just as free and easy as any man can be Dr. Campbell, and you always like to be with Jane Harden, and she is a pretty bad one and you don't look down on her and you never tell her she is a bad one. I know you like her just like a friend Dr.

Campbell, and so I certainly don't understand just what it is you mean by all that you was just saying to me. I know you mean honest Dr. Campbell, and I am always trying to believe you, but I can't say as I see just what you mean when you say you want to be good and real pious, because I am very certain Dr. Campbell that you ain't that kind of a man at all, and you ain't never ashamed to be with queer folks Dr. Campbell, and you seem to be thinking what you are doing is just like what you are always saying, and Dr. Campbell, I certainly don't just see what you mean by what you say."

Dr. Campbell almost laughed loud enough to wake 'Mis' Herbert. He did enjoy the way Melanctha said these things to him. He began to feel very strongly about it that perhaps Melanctha really had a good mind. He was very free now in his laughing, but not so as to make Melanctha angry. He was very friendly with her in his laughing, and then he made his face get serious, and he rubbed his head to help him in his thinking.

"I know Miss Melanctha" he began, "It ain't very easy for you to understand what I was meaning by what I was just saying to you, and perhaps some of the good people I like so wouldn't think very much, any more than you do, Miss Melanctha, about the ways I have to be good. But that's no matter Miss Melanctha. What I mean Miss Melanctha by what I was just saying to you is, that I don't, no, never, believe in doing things just to get excited. You see Miss Melanctha I mean the way so many of the colored people do it. Instead of just working hard and caring about their working and living regular with their families and saving up all their money, so they will have some to bring up their children better, instead of living regular and doing like that and getting all their new ways from just decent living, the colored people just keep running around and perhaps drinking and doing everything bad they can ever think of, and not just because they like all those bad things that they are always doing, but only just because they want to get excited. No Miss Melanctha, you see I am a colored man myself and I ain't sorry, and I want to see the colored people being good and careful and always honest and living always just as regular as can be, and I am sure Miss Melanctha, that that way everybody can have a good time, and be happy and keep right and be busy, and not always have to be doing bad things for new ways to get excited. Yes Miss Melanctha, I certainly do like everything to be good, and quiet, and I certainly do think that is the best way for all us colored people. No, Miss Melanctha too, I don't mean this except only just the way I say it. I ain't got any other meaning Miss Melanctha, and it's that what I mean when I am saying about being really good. It ain't Miss Melanctha to be pious and not liking every kind of people, and I don't say ever Miss Melanctha that when other kind of people come regular into your life you shouldn't want to know them always. What I mean Miss Melanctha by what I am always saying is, you shouldn't try to know everybody just to run around and get excited. It's that kind of way of doing that I hate so always Miss Melanctha, and that is so bad for all us colored people. I don't know as you understand now any better what I mean by what I was just saying to you. But you certainly do know now Miss Melanctha, that I always mean it what I say when I am talking."

"Yes I certainly do understand you when you talk so Dr. Campbell. I certainly do understand now what you mean by what you was always saying to me. I certainly do understand Dr. Campbell that you mean you don't believe it's right to love anybody." "Why sure no, yes I do Miss Melanctha, I certainly do believe strong in loving, and in being good to everybody, and trying to understand what they all need, to help them." "Oh I know all about that way of doing Dr. Campbell, but that certainly ain't the kind of love I mean when I am talking. I mean real, strong, hot love Dr. Campbell, that makes you do anything for somebody that loves you." "I don't know much about that kind of love yet Miss Melanctha. You see it's this way with me always Miss Melanctha. I am always so busy with my thinking about my work I am doing and so I don't have time for just fooling, and then too, you see Miss Melanctha, I really certainly don't ever like to get excited, and that kind of loving hard does seem always to mean just getting all the time excited. That certainly is what I always think from what I see of them that have it bad Miss Melanctha, and that certainly would never suit a man like me. You see Miss Melanctha I am a very quiet kind of fellow, and I believe in a quiet life for all the colored people. No Miss Melanctha I certainly never have mixed myself up in that kind of trouble."

"Yes I certainly do see that very clear Dr. Campbell," said Melanctha, "I see that's certainly what it is always made me not know right about you and that's certainly what it is that makes you really mean what you was always saying. You certainly are just too scared Dr. Campbell to really feel things way down in you. All you are always wanting Dr. Campbell, is just to talk about being good, and to play with people just to have a good time, and yet always to certainly keep yourself out of trouble. It don't seem to me Dr. Campbell that I admire that way to do things very much. It certainly ain't really to me being very good. It certainly ain't any more to me Dr. Campbell, but that you certainly are awful scared about really feeling things way down in you, and that's certainly the only way Dr. Campbell I can see that you can mean, by what it is that you are always saying to me."

"I don't know about that Miss Melanctha, I certainly don't think I can't feel things very deep in me, though I do say I certainly do like to have things nice and quiet, but I don't see harm in keeping out of danger Miss Melanctha, when a man knows he certainly don't want to get killed in it, and I don't know anything that's more awful dangerous Miss Melanctha than being strong in love with somebody. I don't mind sickness or real trouble Miss Melanctha, and I don't want to be talking about what I can do in real trouble, but you know something about that Miss Melanctha, but I certainly don't see much in mixing up just to get excited, in that awful kind of danger. No Miss Melanctha I certainly do only know just two kinds of ways of loving. One kind of loving seems to me, is like one has a good quiet feeling in a family when one does his work, and is always living good and being regular, and then the other way of loving is just like having it like any animal that's low in the streets together, and that don't seem to me very good Miss Melanctha, though I don't say ever that it's not all right when anybody likes it, and that's all the kinds of love I know Miss Melanctha, and I certainly don't care very much to get mixed up in that kind of a way just to be in trouble."

Jefferson stopped and Melanctha thought a little.

"That certainly does explain to me Dr. Campbell what I been thinking about you this long time. I certainly did wonder how you could be so live, and knowing everything, and everybody, and talking so big always about everything, and everybody always liking you so much, and you always looking as if you was thinking, and yet you really was never knowing about anybody and certainly not being really very understanding. It certainly is all Dr. Campbell because you is so afraid you will be losing being good so easy, and it certainly do seem to me Dr. Campbell that it certainly don't amount to very much that kind of goodness."

"Perhaps you are right Miss Melanctha," Jefferson answered. "I don't say never, perhaps you ain't right Miss Melanctha. Perhaps I ought to know more about such ways Miss Melanctha. Perhaps it would help me some, taking care of the colored people, Miss Melanctha. I don't say, no, never, but perhaps I could learn a whole lot about women the right way, if I had a real good teacher."

'Mis' Herbert just then stirred a little in her sleep. Melanctha went up the steps to the bed to attend her. Dr. Campbell got up too and went to help her. 'Mis' Herbert woke up and was a little better. Now it was morning and Dr. Campbell gave his directions to Melanctha, and then left her.

Melanctha Herbert all her life long, loved and wanted good, kind and considerate people. Jefferson Campbell was all the things that Melanctha had ever wanted. Jefferson was a strong, well built, good looking, cheery, intelligent and good mulatto. And then at first he had not cared to know Melanctha, and when he did begin to know her he had not liked her very well, and he had not thought that she would ever come to any good. And then Jefferson Campbell was so very gentle. Jefferson never did some things like other men, things that now were beginning to be ugly, for Melanctha. And then too Jefferson Campbell did not seem to know very well what it was that Melanctha really wanted, and all this was making Melanctha feel his power with her always getting stronger.

Dr. Campbell came in every day to see 'Mis' Herbert. 'Mis'

Herbert, after that night they watched together, did get a little better, but 'Mis' Herbert was really very sick, and soon it was pretty sure that she would have to die. Melanctha certainly did everything, all the time, that any woman could. Jefferson never thought much better of Melanctha while she did it. It was not her being good, he wanted to find in her. He knew very well Jane Harden was right, when she said Melanctha was always being good to everybody but that that did not make Melanctha any better for her. Then too, 'Mis' Herbert never liked Melanctha any better, even on the last day of her living, and so Jefferson really never thought much of Melanctha's always being good to her mother.

Jefferson and Melanctha now saw each other, very often. They now always liked to be with each other, and they always now had a good time when they talked to one another. They, mostly in their talking to each other, still just talked about outside things and what they were thinking. Except just in little moments, and not those very often, they never said anything about their feeling. Sometimes Melanctha would tease Jefferson a little just to show she had not forgotten, but mostly she listened to his talking, for Jefferson still always liked to talk along about the things he believed in. Melanctha was liking Jefferson Campbell better every day, and Jefferson was beginning to know that Melanctha certainly had a good mind, and he was beginning to feel a little her real sweetness. Not in her being good to 'Mis' Herbert, that never seemed to Jefferson to mean much in her, but there was a strong kind of sweetness in Melanctha's nature that Jefferson began now to feel when he was with her.

'Mis' Herbert was now always getting sicker. One night again Dr. Campbell felt very certain that before it was morning she would surely die. Dr. Campbell said he would come back to help Melanctha watch her, and to do anything he could to make 'Mis' Herbert's dying more easy for her. Dr. Campbell came back that evening, after he was through with his other patients, and then he made 'Mis' Herbert easy, and then he came and sat down on the steps just above where Melanctha was sitting with the lamp, and looking very tired. Dr. Campbell was pretty tired too, and they both sat there very quiet.

"You look awful tired to-night, Dr. Campbell," Melanctha said at last, with her voice low and very gentle, "Don't you want to go lie down and sleep a little? You're always being much too good to everybody, Dr. Campbell. I like to have you stay here watching to-night with me, but it don't seem right you ought to stay here when you got so much always to do for everybody. You are certainly very kind to come back, Dr. Campbell, but I can certainly get along to-night without you. I can get help next door sure if I need it. You just go 'long home to bed, Dr. Campbell. You certainly do look as if you need it."

Jefferson was silent for some time, and always he was looking very gently at Melanctha.

"I certainly never did think, Miss Melanctha, I would find you to be so sweet and thinking, with me." "Dr. Campbell" said Melanctha, still more gentle, "I certainly never did think that you would ever feel it good to like me. I certainly never did think you would want to see for yourself if I had sweet ways in me."

They both sat there very tired, very gentle, very quiet, a long time. At last Melanctha in a low, even tone began to talk to Jefferson Campbell.

"You are certainly a very good man, Dr. Campbell, I certainly do feel that more every day I see you. Dr. Campbell, I sure do want to be friends with a good man like you, now I know you. You certainly, Dr. Campbell, never do things like other men, that's always ugly for me. Tell me true, Dr. Campbell, how you feel about being always friends with me. I certainly do know, Dr. Campbell, you are a good man, and if you say you will be friends with me, you certainly never will go back on me, the way so many kinds of them do to every girl they ever get to like them. Tell me for true, Dr. Campbell, will you be friends with me."

"Why, Miss Melanctha," said Campbell slowly, "why you see I just can't say that right out that way to you. Why sure you know Miss Melanctha, I will be very glad if it comes by and by that we are always friends together, but you see, Miss Melanctha, I certainly am a very slow-minded quiet kind of fellow though I do say quick things all the time to everybody, and when I certainly do want to mean it what I am saying to you, I can't say things like that right out to everybody till I know really more for certain all about you, and how I like you, and what I really mean to do better for you. You certainly do see what I mean, Miss Melanctha." "I certainly do admire you for talking honest to me, Jeff Campbell," said Melanctha. "Oh, I am always honest, Miss Melanctha. It's easy enough for me always to be honest, Miss Melanctha. All I got to do is always just to say right out what I am thinking. I certainly never have got any real reason for not saying it right out like that to anybody."

They sat together, very silent. "I certainly do wonder, Miss Melanctha," at last began Jeff Campbell, "I certainly do wonder, if we know very right, you and me, what each other is really thinking. I certainly do wonder, Miss Melanctha, if we know at all really what each other means by what we are always saying." "That certainly do mean, by what you say, that you think I am a bad one, Jeff Campbell," flashed out Melanctha. "Why no, Miss Melanctha, why sure I don't mean any thing like that at all, by what I am saying to you. You know well as I do, Miss Melanctha, I think better of you every day I see you, and I like to talk with you all the time now, Miss Melanctha, and I certainly do think we both like it very well when we are together, and it seems to me always more, you are very good and sweet always to everybody. It only is, I am really so slow-minded in my ways, Miss Melanctha, for all I talk so quick to everybody, and I don't like to say to you what I don't know for very sure, and I certainly don't know for sure I know just all what you mean by what you are always saying to me. And you see, Miss Melanctha, that's what makes me say what I was just saying to you when you asked me."

"I certainly do thank you again for being honest to me, Dr. Campbell," said Melanctha. "I guess I leave you now, Dr. Campbell. I think I go in the other room and rest a little. I leave you here, so perhaps if I ain't here you will maybe sleep and rest yourself a little. Good night now, Dr. Campbell, I call you if I need you later to help me, Dr. Campbell, I hope you rest well, Dr. Campbell."

Jeff Campbell, when Melanctha left him, sat there and he was very quiet and just wondered. He did not know very well just what Melanctha meant by what she was always saying to him. He did not know very well how much he really knew about Melanctha Herbert. He wondered if he should go on being so much all the time with her. He began to think about what he should do now with her. Jefferson Campbell was a man who liked everybody and many people liked very much to be with him. Women liked him, he was so strong, and good, and understanding, and innocent, and firm, and gentle. Sometimes they seemed to want very much he should be with them. When they got so, they always had made Campbell very tired. Sometimes he would play a little with them, but he never had had any strong feeling for them. Now with Melanctha Herbert everything seemed different. Jefferson was not sure that he knew here just what he wanted. He was not sure he knew just what it was that Melanctha wanted. He knew if it was only play, with Melanctha, that he did not want to do it. But he remembered always how she had told him he never knew how to feel things very deeply. He remembered how she told him he was afraid to let himself ever know real feeling, and then too, most of all to him, she had told him he was not very understanding. That always troubled Jefferson very keenly, he wanted very badly to be really understanding. If Jefferson only knew better just what Melanctha meant by what she said. Jefferson always had thought he knew something about women. Now he found that really he knew nothing. He did not know the least bit about Melanctha. He did not know what it was right that he should do about it. He wondered if it was just a little play that they were doing. If it was a play he did not want to go on playing, but if it was really that he was not very understanding, and that with Melanctha Herbert he could learn to really understand, then he was very certain he did not want to be a coward. It was very hard for him to know what he wanted. He thought and thought, and always he did not seem to know any better what he wanted. At last he gave up this thinking. He felt sure it was only play with Melanctha. "No, I certainly won't go on fooling with her any more this way," he said at last out loud to himself, when he was through with this thinking. "I certainly will stop fooling, and begin to go on with my thinking about my work and what's the matter with people like 'Mis' Herbert," and Jefferson took out his book from his pocket, and drew near to the lamp, and began with some hard scientific reading.

Jefferson sat there for about an hour reading, and he had really forgotten all about his trouble with Melanctha's meaning. Then 'Mis' Herbert had some trouble with her breathing. She woke up and was gasping. Dr. Campbell went to her and gave her something that would help her. Melanctha came out from the other room and did things as he told her. They together made 'Mis' Herbert more comfortable and easy, and soon she was again in her deep sleep.

Dr. Campbell went back to the steps where he had been sitting. Melanctha came and stood a little while beside him, and then she sat down and watched him reading. By and by they began with their talking. Jeff Campbell began to feel that perhaps it was all different. Perhaps it was not just play, with Melanctha. Anyway he liked it very well that she was with him. He began to tell her about the book he was just reading.

Melanctha was very intelligent always in her questions. Jefferson knew now very well that she had a good mind. They were having a very good time, talking there together. And then they began again to get quiet.

"It certainly was very good in you to come back and talk to me Miss Melanctha," Jefferson said at last to her, for now he was almost certain, it was no game she was playing. Melanctha really was a good woman, and she had a good mind, and she had a real, strong sweetness, and she could surely really teach him. "Oh I always like to talk to you Dr. Campbell" said Melanctha, "And then you was only just honest to me, and I always like it when a man is really honest to me." Then they were again very silent, sitting there together, with the lamp between them, that was always smoking. Melanctha began to lean a little more toward Dr. Campbell, where he was sitting, and then she took his hand between her two and pressed it hard, but she said nothing to him. She let it go then and leaned a little nearer to him. Jefferson moved a little but did not do anything in answer. At last, "Well," said Melanctha sharply to him. "I was just thinking" began Dr. Campbell slowly, "I was just wondering," he was beginning to get ready to go on with his talking. "Don't you ever stop with your thinking long enough ever to have any feeling

Jeff Campbell," said Melanctha a little sadly. "I don't know," said Jeff Campbell slowly, "I don't know Miss Melanctha much about that. No, I don't stop thinking much Miss Melanctha and if I can't ever feel without stopping thinking, I certainly am very much afraid Miss Melanctha that I never will do much with that kind of feeling. Sure you ain't worried Miss Melanctha, about my really not feeling very much all the time. I certainly do think I feel some, Miss Melanctha, even though I always do it without ever knowing how to stop with my thinking." "I am certainly afraid I don't think much of your kind of feeling Dr. Campbell." "Why I think you certainly are wrong Miss Melanctha I certainly do think I feel as much for you Miss Melanctha, as you ever feel about me, sure I do. I don't think you know me right when you talk like that to me. Tell me just straight out how much do you care about me, Miss Melanctha." "Care about you Jeff Campbell," said Melanctha slowly. "I certainly do care for you Jeff Campbell less than you are always thinking and much more than you are ever knowing."

Jeff Campbell paused on this, and he was silent with the power of Melanctha's meaning. They sat there together very silent, a long time. "Well Jeff Campbell," said Melanctha. "Oh," said Dr. Campbell and he moved himself a little, and then they were very silent a long time. "Haven't you got nothing to say to me Jeff Campbell?" said Melanctha. "Why yes, what was it we were just saying about to one another. You see Miss Melanctha I am a very quiet, slow minded kind of fellow, and I am never sure I know just exactly what you mean by all that you are always saying to me. But I do like you very much Miss Melanctha and I am very sure you got very good things in you all the time. You sure do believe what I am saying to you Miss Melanctha." "Yes I believe it when you say it to me, Jeff Campbell," said Melanctha, and then she was silent and there was much sadness in it. "I guess I go in and lie down again Dr. Campbell," said Melanctha. "Don't go leave me Miss Melanctha," said Jeff Campbell quickly. "Why not, what you want of me Jeff Campbell?" said Melanctha. "Why," said Jeff Campbell slowly, "I just want to go on talking with you. I certainly do like talking about all kinds of things with you. You certainly know that all right,

Miss Melanctha." "I guess I go lie down again and leave you here with your thinking," said Melanctha gently. "I certainly am very tired to night Dr. Campbell. Good night I hope you rest well Dr. Campbell." Melanctha stooped over him, where he was sitting, to say this good night, and then, very quick and sudden, she kissed him and then, very quick again, she went away and left him.

Dr. Campbell sat there very quiet, with only a little thinking and sometimes a beginning feeling, and he was alone until it began to be morning, and then he went, and Melanctha helped him, and he made 'Mis' Herbert more easy in her dying. 'Mis' Herbert lingered on till about ten o'clock the next morning, and then slowly and without much pain she died away. Jeff Campbell staid till the last moment, with Melanctha, to make her mother's dying easy for her. When it was over he sent in the colored woman from next door to help Melanctha fix things, and then he went away to take care of his other patients. He came back very soon to Melanctha. He helped her to have a funeral for her mother. Melanctha then went to live with the good natured woman, who had been her neighbor. Melanctha still saw Jeff Campbell very often. Things began to be very strong between them.

Melanctha now never wandered, unless she was with Jeff Campbell. Sometimes she and he wandered a good deal together. Jeff Campbell had not got over his way of talking to her all the time about all the things he was always thinking. Melanctha never talked much, now, when they were together. Sometimes Jeff Campbell teased her about her not talking to him. "I certainly did think Melanctha you was a great talker from the way Jane Harden and everybody said things to me, and from the way I heard you talk so much when I first met you. Tell me true Melanctha, why don't you talk more now to me, perhaps it is I talk so much I don't give you any chance to say things to me, or perhaps it is you hear me talk so much you don't think so much now of a whole lot of talking. Tell me honest Melanctha, why don't you talk more to me." "You know very well Jeff Campbell," said Melanctha "You certainly do know very well Jeff, you don't think really much, of my talking. You think a whole lot more about everything than I do Jeff, and you don't care much what I got to say about it.

You know that's true what I am saying Jeff, if you want to be real honest, the way you always are when I like you so much." Jeff laughed and looked fondly at her. "I don't say ever I know, you ain't right, when you say things like that to me, Melanctha. You see you always like to be talking just what you think everybody wants to be hearing from you, and when you are like that, Melanctha, honest, I certainly don't care very much to hear you, but sometimes you say something that is what you are really thinking, and then I like a whole lot to hear you talking." Melanctha smiled, with her strong sweetness, on him, and she felt her power very deeply. "I certainly never do talk very much when I like anybody really, Jeff. You see, Jeff, it ain't much use to talk about what a woman is really feeling in her. You see all that, Jeff, better, by and by, when you get to really feeling. You won't be so ready then always with your talking. You see, Jeff, if it don't come true what I am saying." "I don't ever say you ain't always right, Melanctha," said Jeff Campbell. "Perhaps what I call my thinking ain't really so very understanding. I don't say, no never now any more, you ain't right, Melanctha, when you really say things to me. Perhaps I see it all to be very different when I come to really see what you mean by what you are always saying to me." "You is very sweet and good to me always, Jeff Campbell," said Melanctha. "'Deed I certainly am not good to you, Melanctha. Don't I bother you all the time with my talking, but I really do like you a whole lot, Melanctha." "And I like you, Jeff Campbell, and you certainly are mother, and father, and brother, and sister, and child and everything, always to me. I can't say much about how good you been to me, Jeff Campbell, I never knew any man who was good and didn't do things ugly, before I met you to take care of me, Jeff Campbell. Good-by, Jeff, come see me to-morrow, when you get through with your working." "Sure Melanctha, you know that already," said Jeff Campbell, and then he went away and left her.

These months had been an uncertain time for Jeff Camp-bell. He never knew how much he really knew about Melanctha. He saw her now for long times and very often. He was beginning always more and more to like her. But he did not seem to himself to know very much about her. He was beginning to feel he could almost trust the goodness in her. But then, always, really, he was not very sure about her. Melanctha always had ways that made him feel uncertain with her, and yet he was so near, in his feeling for her. He now never thought about all this in real words any more. He was always letting it fight itself out in him. He was now never taking any part in this fighting that was always going on inside him.

Jeff always loved now to be with Melanctha and yet he always hated to go to her. Somehow he was always afraid when he was to go to her, and yet he had made himself very certain that here he would not be a coward. He never felt any of this being afraid, when he was with her. Then they always were very true, and near to one another. But always when he was going to her, Jeff would like anything that could happen that would keep him a little longer from her.

It was a very uncertain time, all these months, for Jeff Campbell. He did not know very well what it was that he really wanted. He was very certain that he did not know very well what it was that Melanctha wanted. Jeff Campbell had always all his life loved to be with people, and he had loved all his life always to be thinking, but he was still only a great boy, was Jeff Campbell, and he had never before had any of this funny kind of feeling. Now, this evening, when he was free to go and see Melanctha, he talked to anybody he could find who would detain him, and so it was very late when at last he came to the house where Melanctha was waiting to receive him.

Jeff came in to where Melanctha was waiting for him, and he took off his hat and heavy coat, and then drew up a chair and sat down by the fire. It was very cold that night, and Jeff sat there, and rubbed his hands and tried to warm them. He had only said "How do you do" to Melanctha, he had not yet begun to talk to her. Melanctha sat there, by the fire, very quiet. The heat gave a pretty pink glow to her pale yellow and attractive face. Melanctha sat in a low chair, her hands, with their long, fluttering fingers, always ready to show her strong feeling, were lying quiet in her lap. Melanctha was very tired with her waiting for Jeff Campbell. She sat there very quiet and just watching. Jeff was a robust, dark, healthy, cheery negro. His hands were firm and kindly and unimpassioned. He touched women always with his big hands, like a brother. He always had a warm broad glow, like southern sunshine. He never had anything mysterious in him. He was open, he was pleasant, he was cheery, and always he wanted, as Melanctha once had wanted, always now he too wanted really to understand.

Jeff sat there this evening in his chair and was silent a long time, warming himself with the pleasant fire. He did not look at Melanctha who was watching. He sat there and just looked into the fire. At first his dark, open face was smiling, and he was rubbing the back of his black-brown hand over his mouth to help him in his smiling. Then he was thinking, and he frowned and rubbed his head hard, to help him in his thinking. Then he smiled again, but now his smiling was not very pleasant. His smile was now wavering on the edge of scorning. His smile changed more and more, and then he had a look as if he were deeply down, all disgusted. Now his face was darker, and he was bitter in his smiling, and he began, without looking from the fire, to talk to Melanctha, who was now very tense with her watching.

"Melanctha Herbert", began Jeff Campbell, "I certainly after all this time I know you, I certainly do know little, real about you. You see, Melanctha, it's like this way with me"; Jeff was frowning, with his thinking and looking very hard into the fire, "You see it's just this way, with me now, Melanctha. Sometimes you seem like one kind of a girl to me, and sometimes you are like a girl that is all different to me, and the two kinds of girls is certainly very different to each other, and I can't see any way they seem to have much to do, to be together in you. They certainly don't seem to be made much like as if they could have anything really to do with each other. Sometimes you are a girl to me I certainly never would be trusting, and you got a laugh then so hard, it just rattles, and you got ways so bad, I can't believe you mean them hardly, and yet all that I just been saying is certainly you one way I often see you, and it's what your mother and Jane Harden always found you, and it's what makes me hate so, to come near you. And then certainly sometimes, Melanctha, you certainly is all a different creature, and sometimes then there comes out in you what is certainly a thing, like a real beauty. I certainly, Melanctha, never can tell just how it is that it comes so lovely. Seems to me when it comes it's got a real sweetness, that is more wonderful than a pure flower, and a gentleness, that is more tender than the sunshine, and a kindness, that makes one feel like summer, and then a way to know, that makes everything all over, and all that, and it does certainly seem to be real for the little while it's lasting, for the little while that I can surely see it, and it gives me to feel like I certainly had got real religion. And then when I got rich with such a feeling, comes all that other girl, and then that seems more likely that that is really you what's honest, and then I certainly do get awful afraid to come to you, and I certainly never do feel I could be very trusting with you. And then I certainly don't know anything at all about you, and I certainly don't know which is a real Melanctha Herbert, and I certainly don't feel no longer, I ever want to talk to you. Tell me honest, Melanctha, which is the way that is you really, when you are alone, and real, and all honest. Tell me, Melanctha, for I certainly do want to know it."

Melanctha did not make him any answer, and Jeff, without looking at her, after a little while, went on with his talking. "And then, Melanctha, sometimes you certainly do seem sort of cruel, and not to care about people being hurt or in trouble, something so hard about you it makes me sometimes real nervous, sometimes somehow like you always, like your being, with 'Mis' Herbert. You sure did do everything that any woman could, Melanctha, I certainly never did see anybody do things any better, and yet, I don't know how to say just what I mean, Melanctha, but there was something awful hard about your feeling, so different from the way I'm always used to see good people feeling, and so it was the way Jane Harden and 'Mis' Herbert talked when they felt strong to talk about you, and yet, Melanctha, somehow I feel so really near to you, and you certainly have got an awful wonderful, strong kind of sweetness. I certainly would like to know for sure, Melanctha, whether I got really anything to be afraid for. I certainly did think once, Melanctha, I knew something about all kinds of women. I certainly know now really, how I don't know anything sure at all about you, Melanctha, though I been with you so long, and so many times for whole hours with you, and I like so awful much to be with you, and I can always say anything I am thinking to you. I certainly do awful wish, Melanctha, I really was more understanding. I certainly do that same, Melanctha."

Jeff stopped now and looked harder than before into the fire. His face changed from his thinking back into that look that was so like as if he was all through and through him, disgusted with what he had been thinking. He sat there a long time, very quiet, and then slowly, somehow, it came strongly to him that Melanctha Herbert, there beside him, was trembling and feeling it all to be very bitter. "Why, Melanctha," cried Jeff Campbell, and he got up and put his arm around her like a brother. "I stood it just so long as I could bear it, Jeff," sobbed Melanctha, and then she gave herself away, to her misery, "I was awful ready, Jeff, to let you say anything you liked that gave you any pleasure. You could say all about me what you wanted, Jeff, and I would try to stand it, so as you would be sure to be liking it, Jeff, but you was too cruel to me. When you do that kind of seeing how much you can make a woman suffer, you ought to give her a little rest, once sometimes, Jeff. They can't any of us stand it so for always, Jeff. I certainly did stand it just as long as I could, so you would like it, but I,—oh Jeff, you went on too long to-night Jeff. I couldn't stand it not a minute longer the way you was doing of it, Jeff. When you want to be seeing how the way a woman is really made of, Jeff, you shouldn't never be so cruel, never to be thinking how much she can stand, the strong way you always do it, Jeff." "Why, Melanctha," cried Jeff Campbell, in his horror, and then he was very tender to her, and like a good, strong, gentle brother in his soothing of her, "Why Melanctha dear, I certainly don't now see what it is you mean by what you was just saying to me. Why Melanctha, you poor little girl, you certainly never did believe I ever knew I was giving you real suffering. Why, Melanctha, how could you ever like me if you thought I ever could be so like a red Indian?" "I didn't just know, Jeff," and Melanctha nestled to him, "I certainly never did know just what it was you wanted to be doing with me, but I certainly wanted you should do anything you liked, you wanted, to make me more understanding for you. I tried awful hard to stand it, Jeff, so as you could do anything you wanted with me." "Good Lord and Jesus Christ, Melanctha!" cried Jeff Campbell. "I certainly never can know anything about you real, Melanctha, you poor little girl," and Jeff drew her closer to him, "But I certainly do admire and trust you a whole lot now, Melanctha. I certainly do, for I certainly never did think I was hurting you at all, Melanctha, by the things I always been saying to you. Melanctha, you poor little, sweet, trembling baby now, be good, Melanctha. I certainly can't ever tell you how awful sorry I am to hurt you so, Melanctha. I do anything I can to show you how I never did mean to hurt you, Melanctha." "I know, I know," murmured Melanctha, clinging to him. "I know you are a good man, Jeff. I always know that, no matter how much you can hurt me." "I sure don't see how you can think so, Melanctha, if you certainly did think I was trying so hard just to hurt you." "Hush, you are only a great big boy, Jeff Campbell, and you don't know nothing yet about real hurting," said Melanctha, smiling up through her crying, at him. "You see, Jeff, I never knew anybody I could know real well and yet keep on always respecting, till I came to know you real well, Jeff." "I sure don't understand that very well, Melanctha. I ain't a bit better than just lots of others of the colored people. You certainly have been unlucky with the kind you met before me, that's all, Melanctha. I certainly ain't very good, Melanctha." "Hush, Jeff, you don't know nothing at all about what you are," said Melanctha. "Perhaps you are right, Melanctha. I don't say ever any more, you ain't right, when you say things to me, Melanctha," and Jefferson sighed, and then he smiled, and then they were quiet a long time together, and then after some more kindness, it was late, and then Jeff left her.

Jeff Campbell, all these months, had never told his good mother anything about Melanctha Herbert. Somehow he always kept his seeing her so much now, to himself. Melanctha too had never had any of her other friends meet him. They always acted together, these two, as if their being so much together was a secret, but really there was no one who would have made it any harder for them. Jeff Campbell did not really know how it had happened that they were so secret. He did

not know if it was what Melanctha wanted. Jeff had never
spoken to her at all about it. It just seemed as if it were well
understood between them that nobody should know that they
were so much together. It was as if it were agreed between
them, that they should be alone by themselves always, and so
they would work out together what they meant by what they
were always saying to each other.

Jefferson often spoke to Melanctha about his good mother.
He never said anything about whether Melanctha would want
to meet her. Jefferson never quite understood why all this had
happened so, in secret. He never really knew what it was that
Melanctha really wanted. In all these ways he just, by his nature, did, what he sort of felt Melanctha wanted. And so they
continued to be alone and much together, and now it had
come to be the spring time, and now they had all out-doors
to wander.

They had many days now when they were very happy. Jeff
every day found that he really liked Melanctha better. Now
surely he was beginning to have real, deep feeling in him. And
still he loved to talk himself out to Melanctha, and he loved
to tell her how good it all was to him, and how he always
loved to be with her, and to tell her always all about it. One
day, now Jeff arranged, that Sunday they would go out and
have a happy, long day in the bright fields, and they would be
all day just alone together. The day before, Jeff was called in
to see Jane Harden.

Jane Harden was very sick almost all day and Jeff Campbell
did everything he could to make her better. After a while Jane
became more easy and then she began to talk to Jeff about
Melanctha. Jane did not know how much Jeff was now seeing
of Melanctha. Jane these days never saw Melanctha. Jane began to talk of the time when she first knew Melanctha. Jane
began to tell how in these days Melanctha had very little understanding. She was young then and she had a good mind.
Jane Harden never would say Melanctha never had a good
mind, but in those days Melanctha certainly had not been very
understanding. Jane began to explain to Jeff Campbell how
in every way, she Jane, had taught Melanctha. Jane then began
to explain how eager Melanctha always had been for all that
kind of learning. Jane Harden began to tell how they had

wandered. Jane began to tell how Melanctha once had loved her, Jane Harden. Jane began to tell Jeff of all the bad ways Melanctha had used with her. Jane began to tell all she knew of the way Melanctha had gone on, after she had left her. Jane began to tell all about the different men, white ones and blacks, Melanctha never was particular about things like that, Jane Harden said in passing, not that Melanctha was a bad one, and she had a good mind, Jane Harden never would say that she hadn't, but Melanctha always liked to use all the understanding ways that Jane had taught her, and so she wanted to know everything, always, that they knew how to teach her.

Jane was beginning to make Jeff Campbell see much clearer. Jane Harden did not know what it was that she was really doing with all this talking. Jane did not know what Jeff was feeling. Jane was always honest when she was talking, and now it just happened she had started talking about her old times with Melanctha Herbert. Jeff understood very well that it was all true what Jane was saying. Jeff Campbell was beginning now to see very clearly. He was beginning to feel very sick inside him. He knew now many things Melanctha had not yet taught him. He felt very sick and his heart was very heavy, and Melanctha certainly did seem very ugly to him. Jeff was at last beginning to know what it was to have deep feeling. He took care a little longer of Jane Harden, and then he went to his other patients, and then he went home to his room, and he sat down and at last he had stopped thinking. He was very sick and his heart was very heavy in him. He was very tired and all the world was very dreary to him, and he knew very well now at last, he was really feeling. He knew it now from the way it hurt him. He knew very well that now at last he was beginning to really have understanding. The next day he had arranged to spend, long and happy, all alone in the spring fields with Melanctha, wandering. He wrote her a note and said he could not go, he had a sick patient and would have to stay home with him. For three days after, he made no sign to Melanctha. He was very sick all these days, and his heart was very heavy in him, and he knew very well that now at last he had learned what it was to have deep feeling.

At last one day he got a letter from Melanctha. "I certainly don't rightly understand what you are doing now to me Jeff

Campbell," wrote Melanctha Herbert. "I certainly don't rightly understand Jeff Campbell why you ain't all these days been near me, but I certainly do suppose it's just another one of the queer kind of ways you have to be good, and repenting of yourself all of a sudden. I certainly don't say to you Jeff Campbell I admire very much the way you take to be good Jeff Campbell. I am sorry Dr. Campbell, but I certainly am afraid I can't stand it no more from you the way you have been just acting. I certainly can't stand it any more the way you act when you have been as if you thought I was always good enough for anybody to have with them, and then you act as if I was a bad one and you always just despise me. I certainly am afraid Dr. Campbell I can't stand it any more like that. I certainly can't stand it any more the way you are always changing. I certainly am afraid Dr. Campbell you ain't man enough to deserve to have anybody care so much to be always with you. I certainly am awful afraid Dr. Campbell I don't ever any more want to really see you. Good-by Dr. Campbell I wish you always to be real happy."

Jeff Campbell sat in his room, very quiet, a long time, after he got through reading this letter. He sat very still and first he was very angry. As if he, too, did not know very badly what it was to suffer keenly. As if he had not been very strong to stay with Melanctha when he never knew what it was that she really wanted. He knew he was very right to be angry, he knew he really had not been a coward. He knew Melanctha had done many things it was very hard for him to forgive her. He knew very well he had done his best to be kind, and to trust her, and to be loyal to her, and now;—and then Jeff suddenly remembered how one night Melanctha had been so strong to suffer, and he felt come back to him the sweetness in her, and then Jeff knew that really, he always forgave her, and that really, it all was that he was so sorry he had hurt her, and he wanted to go straight away and be a comfort to her. Jeff knew very well, that what Jane Harden had told him about Melanctha and her bad ways, had been a true story, and yet he wanted very badly to be with Melanctha. Perhaps she could teach him to really understand it better. Perhaps she could teach him how it could be all true, and yet how he could be right to believe in her and to trust her.

Jeff sat down and began his answer to her. "Dear Melanctha," Jeff wrote to her. "I certainly don't think you got
it all just right in the letter, I just been reading, that you
just wrote me. I certainly don't think you are just fair or very
understanding to all I have to suffer to keep straight on to
really always to believe in you and trust you. I certainly don't
think you always are fair to remember right how hard it is for
a man, who thinks like I was always thinking, not to think
you do things very bad very often. I certainly don't think,
Melanctha, I ain't right when I was so angry when I got your
letter to me. I know very well, Melanctha, that with you, I
never have been a coward. I find it very hard, and I never said
it any different, it is hard to me to be understanding, and to
know really what it is you wanted, and what it is you are
meaning by what you are always saying to me. I don't say
ever, it ain't very hard for you to be standing that I ain't very
quick to be following whichever way that you are always leading. You know very well, Melanctha, it hurts me very bad and
way inside me when I have to hurt you, but I always got to
be real honest with you. There ain't no other way for me to
be, with you, and I know very well it hurts me too, a whole
lot, when I can't follow so quick as you would have me. I
don't like to be a coward to you, Melanctha, and I don't like
to say what I ain't meaning to you. And if you don't want me
to do things honest, Melanctha, why I can't ever talk to you,
and you are right when you say, you never again want to see
me, but if you got any real sense of what I always been feeling
with you, and if you got any right sense, Melanctha, of how
hard I been trying to think and to feel right for you, I will be
very glad to come and see you, and to begin again with you.
I don't say anything now, Melanctha, about how bad I been
this week, since I saw you, Melanctha. It don't ever do any
good to talk such things over. All I know is I do my best,
Melanctha, to you, and I don't say, no, never, I can do any
different than just to be honest and come as fast as I think
it's right for me to be going in the ways you teach me to be
really understanding. So don't talk any more foolishness,
Melanctha, about my always changing. I don't change, never,
and I got to do what I think is right and honest to me, and
I never told you any different, and you always knew it very

well that I always would do just so. If you like me to come
and see you to-morrow, and go out with you, I will be very
glad to, Melanctha. Let me know right away, what it is you
want me to be doing for you, Melanctha.

Very truly yours,

JEFFERSON CAMPBELL

"Please come to me, Jeff." Melanctha wrote back for her
answer. Jeff went very slowly to Melanctha, glad as he was,
still to be going to her. Melanctha came, very quick, to meet
him, when she saw him from where she had been watching
for him. They went into the house together. They were very
glad to be together. They were very good to one another.

"I certainly did think, Melanctha, this time almost really,
you never did want me to come to you at all any more to see
you," said Jeff Campbell to her, when they had begun again
with their talking to each other. "You certainly did make me
think, perhaps really this time, Melanctha, it was all over, my
being with you ever, and I was very mad, and very sorry, too,
Melanctha."

"Well you certainly was very bad to me, Jeff Campbell,"
said Melanctha, fondly.

"I certainly never do say any more you ain't always right,
Melanctha," Jeff answered and he was very ready now with
cheerful laughing, "I certainly never do say that any more,
Melanctha, if I know it, but still, really, Melanctha, honest, I
think perhaps I wasn't real bad to you any more than you just
needed from me."

Jeff held Melanctha in his arms and kissed her. He sighed
then and was very silent with her. "Well, Melanctha," he said
at last, with some more laughing, "well, Melanctha, any way
you can't say ever it ain't, if we are ever friends good and
really, you can't say, no, never, but that we certainly have
worked right hard to get both of us together for it, so we
shall sure deserve it then, if we can ever really get it." "We
certainly have worked real hard, Jeff, I can't say that ain't all
right the way you say it," said Melanctha. "I certainly never
can deny it, Jeff, when I feel so worn with all the trouble you
been making for me, you bad boy, Jeff," and then Melanctha
smiled and then she sighed, and then she was very silent with
him.

At last Jeff was to go away. They stood there on the steps for a long time trying to say good-by to each other. At last Jeff made himself really say it. At last he made himself, that he went down the steps and went away.

On the next Sunday they arranged, they were to have the long happy day of wandering that they had lost last time by Jane Harden's talking. Not that Melanctha Herbert had heard yet of Jane Harden's talking.

Jeff saw Melanctha every day now. Jeff was a little uncertain all this time inside him, for he had never yet told to Melanctha what it was that had so nearly made him really want to leave her. Jeff knew that for him, it was not right he should not tell her. He knew they could only have real peace between them when he had been honest, and had really told her. On this long Sunday Jeff was certain that he would really tell her.

They were very happy all that day in their wandering. They had taken things along to eat together. They sat in the bright fields and they were happy, they wandered in the woods and they were happy. Jeff always loved in this way to wander. Jeff always loved to watch everything as it was growing, and he loved all the colors in the trees and on the ground, and the little, new, bright colored bugs he found in the moist ground and in the grass he loved to lie on and in which he was always so busy searching. Jeff loved everything that moved and that was still, and that had color, and beauty, and real being.

Jeff loved very much this day while they were wandering. He almost forgot that he had any trouble with him still inside him. Jeff loved to be there with Melanctha Herbert. She was always so sympathetic to him for the way she listened to everything he found and told her, the way she felt his joy in all this being, the way she never said she wanted anything different from the way they had it. It was certainly a busy and a happy day, this their first long day of really wandering.

Later they were tired, and Melanctha sat down on the ground, and Jeff threw himself his full length beside her. Jeff lay there, very quiet, and then he pressed her hand and kissed it and murmured to her, "You certainly are very good to me, Melanctha." Melanctha felt it very deep and did not answer. Jeff lay there a long time, looking up above him. He was counting all the little leaves he saw above him. He was following all the little clouds with his eyes as they sailed past him. He watched all the birds that flew high beyond him, and all the time Jeff knew he must tell to Melanctha what it was he knew now, that which Jane Harden, just a week ago, had told him. He knew very well that for him it was certain that he had to say it. It was hard, but for Jeff Campbell the only way to lose it was to say it, the only way to know Melanctha really, was to tell her all the struggle he had made to know her, to tell her so she could help him to understand his trouble better, to help him so that never again he could have any way to doubt her.

Jeff lay there a long time, very quiet, always looking up above him, and yet feeling very close now to Melanctha. At last he turned a little toward her, took her hands closer in his to make him feel it stronger, and then very slowly, for the words came very hard for him, slowly he began his talk to her.

"Melanctha," began Jeff, very slowly, "Melanctha, it ain't right I shouldn't tell you why I went away last week and almost never got the chance again to see you. Jane Harden was sick, and I went in to take care of her. She began to tell everything she ever knew about you. She didn't know how well now I know you. I didn't tell her not to go on talking. I listened while she told me everything about you. I certainly found it very hard with what she told me. I know she was talking truth in everything she said about you. I knew you had been free in your ways, Melanctha, I knew you liked to get excitement the way I always hate to see the colored people take it. I didn't know, till I heard Jane Harden say it, you had done things so bad, Melanctha. When Jane Harden told me, I got very sick, Melanctha. I couldn't bear hardly, to think, perhaps I was just another like them to you, Melanctha. I was wrong not to trust you perhaps, Melanctha, but it did make things very ugly to me. I try to be honest to you, Melanctha, the way you say you really want it from me."

Melanctha drew her hands from Jeff Campbell. She sat there, and there was deep scorn in her anger.

"If you wasn't all through just selfish and nothing else, Jeff Campbell, you would take care you wouldn't have to tell me things like this, Jeff Campbell."

Jeff was silent a little, and he waited before he gave his

answer. It was not the power of Melanctha's words that held him, for, for them, he had his answer, it was the power of the mood that filled Melanctha, and for that he had no answer. At last he broke through this awe, with his slow fighting resolution, and he began to give his answer.

"I don't say ever, Melanctha," he began, "it wouldn't have been more right for me to stop Jane Harden in her talking and to come to you to have you tell me what you were when I never knew you. I don't say it, no never to you, that that would not have been the right way for me to do, Melanctha. But I certainly am without any kind of doubting, I certainly do know for sure, I had a good right to know about what you were and your ways and your trying to use your understanding, every kind of way you could to get your learning. I certainly did have a right to know things like that about you, Melanctha. I don't say it ever, Melanctha, and I say it very often, I don't say ever I shouldn't have stopped Jane Harden in her talking and come to you and asked you yourself to tell me all about it, but I guess I wanted to keep myself from how much it would hurt me more, to have you yourself say it to me. Perhaps it was I wanted to keep you from having it hurt you so much more, having you to have to tell it to me. I don't know, I don't say it was to help you from being hurt most, or to help me. Perhaps I was a coward to let Jane Harden tell me 'stead of coming straight to you, to have you tell me, but I certainly am sure, Melanctha, I certainly had a right to know such things about you. I don't say it ever, ever, Melanctha, I hadn't the just right to know those things about you." Melanctha laughed her harsh laugh. "You needn't have been under no kind of worry, Jeff Campbell, about whether you should have asked me. You could have asked, it wouldn't have hurt nothing. I certainly never would have told you nothing." "I am not so sure of that, Melanctha," said Jeff Campbell. "I certainly do think you would have told me. I certainly do think I could make you feel it right to tell me. I certainly do think all I did wrong was to let Jane Harden tell me. I certainly do know I never did wrong, to learn what she told me. I certainly know very well, Melanctha, if I had come here to you, you would have told it all to me, Melanctha."

He was silent, and this struggle lay there, strong, between

them. It was a struggle, sure to be going on always between them. It was a struggle that was as sure always to be going on between them, as their minds and hearts always were to have different ways of working.

At last Melanctha took his hand, leaned over him and kissed him. "I sure am very fond of you, Jeff Campbell," Melanctha whispered to him.

Now for a little time there was not any kind of trouble between Jeff Campbell and Melanctha Herbert. They were always together now for long times, and very often. They got much joy now, both of them, from being all the time together.

It was summer now, and they had warm sunshine to wander. It was summer now, and Jeff Campbell had more time to wander, for colored people never get sick so much in summer. It was summer now, and there was a lovely silence everywhere, and all the noises, too, that they heard around them were lovely ones, and added to the joy, in these warm days, they loved so much to be together.

They talked some to each other in these days, did Jeff Campbell and Melanctha Herbert, but always in these days their talking more and more was like it always is with real lovers. Jeff did not talk so much now about what he before always had been thinking. Sometimes Jeff would be, as if he was just waking from himself to be with Melanctha, and then he would find he had been really all the long time with her, and he had really never needed to be doing any thinking.

It was sometimes pure joy Jeff would be talking to Melanctha, in these warm days he loved so much to wander with her. Sometimes Jeff would lose all himself in a strong feeling. Very often now, and always with more joy in his feeling, he would find himself, he did not know how or what it was he had been thinking. And Melanctha always loved very well to make him feel it. She always now laughed a little at him, and went back a little in him to his before, always thinking, and she teased him with his always now being so good with her in his feeling, and then she would so well and freely, and with her pure, strong ways of reaching, she would give him all the love she knew now very well, how much he always wanted to be sure he really had it.

And Jeff took it straight now, and he loved it, and he felt, strong, the joy of all this being, and it swelled out full inside him, and he poured it all out back to her in freedom, in tender kindness, and in joy, and in gentle brother fondling. And Melanctha loved him for it always, her Jeff Campbell now, who never did things ugly, for her, like all the men she always knew before always had been doing to her. And they loved it always, more and more, together, with this new feeling they had now, in these long summer days so warm; they, always together now, just these two so dear, more and more to each other always, and the summer evenings when they wandered, and the noises in the full streets, and the music of the organs, and the dancing, and the warm smell of the people, and of dogs and of the horses, and all the joy of the strong, sweet pungent, dirty, moist, warm negro southern summer.

Every day now, Jeff seemed to be coming nearer, to be really loving. Every day now, Melanctha poured it all out to him, with more freedom. Every day now, they seemed to be having more and more, both together, of this strong, right feeling. More and more every day now they seemed to know more really, what it was each other one was always feeling. More and more now every day Jeff found in himself, he felt more trusting. More and more every day now, he did not think anything in words about what he was always doing. Every day now more and more Melanctha would let out to Jeff her real, strong feeling.

One day there had been much joy between them, more than they ever yet had had with their new feeling. All the day they had lost themselves in warm wandering. Now they were lying there and resting, with a green, bright, light-flecked world around them.

What was it that now really happened to them? What was it that Melanctha did, that made everything get all ugly for them? What was it that Melanctha felt then, that made Jeff remember all the feeling he had had in him when Jane Harden told him how Melanctha had learned to be so very understanding? Jeff did not know how it was that it had happened to him. It was all green, and warm, and very lovely to him, and now Melanctha somehow had made it all so ugly for him. What was it Melanctha was now doing with him? What was it he used to be thinking was the right way for him and all the colored people to be always trying to make it right, the way they should be always living? Why was Melanctha Herbert now all so ugly for him?

Melanctha Herbert somehow had made him feel deeply just then, what very more it was that she wanted from him. Jeff Campbell now felt in him what everybody always had needed to make them really understanding, to him. Jeff felt a strong disgust inside him; not for Melanctha herself, to him, not for himself really, in him, not for what it was that everybody wanted, in them; he only had disgust because he never could know really in him, what it was he wanted, to be really right in understanding, for him, he only had disgust because he never could know really what it was really right to him to be always doing, in the things he had before believed in, the things he before had believed in for himself and for all the colored people, the living regular, and the never wanting to be always having new things, just to keep on, always being in excitements. All the old thinking now came up very strong inside him. He sort of turned away then, and threw Melanctha from him.

Jeff never, even now, knew what it was that moved him. He never, even now, was ever sure, he really knew what Melanctha was, when she was real herself, and honest. He thought he knew, and then there came to him some moment, just like this one, when she really woke him up to be strong in him. Then he really knew he could know nothing. He knew then, he never could know what it was she really wanted with him. He knew then he never could know really what it was he felt inside him. It was all so mixed up inside him. All he knew was he wanted very badly Melanctha should be there beside him, and he wanted very badly, too, always to throw her from him. What was it really that Melanctha wanted with him? What was it really, he, Jeff Campbell, wanted she should give him? "I certainly did think now," Jeff Campbell groaned inside him, "I certainly did think now I really was knowing all right, what I wanted. I certainly did really think now I was knowing how to be trusting with Melanctha. I certainly did think it was like that now with me sure, after all I've been through all this time with her. And now I certainly do know I don't know anything that's very real about her. Oh the good

Lord help and keep me!'' and Jeff groaned hard inside him, and he buried his face deep in the green grass underneath him, and Melanctha Herbert was very silent there beside him.

Then Jeff turned to look and see her. She was lying very still there by him, and the bitter water on her face was biting. Jeff was so very sorry then, all over and inside him, the way he always was when Melanctha had been deep hurt by him. "I didn't mean to be so bad again to you, Melanctha, dear one," and he was very tender to her. "I certainly didn't never mean to go to be so bad to you, Melanctha, darling. I certainly don't know, Melanctha, darling, what it is makes me act so to you sometimes, when I certainly ain't meaning anything like I want to hurt you. I certainly don't mean to be so bad, Melanctha, only it comes so quick on me before I know what I am acting to you. I certainly am all sorry, hard, to be so bad to you, Melanctha, darling." "I suppose, Jeff," said Melanctha, very low and bitter, "I suppose you are always thinking, Jeff, somebody had ought to be ashamed with us two together, and you certainly do think you don't see any way to it, Jeff, for me to be feeling that way ever, so you certainly don't see any way to it, only to do it just so often for me. That certainly is the way always with you, Jeff Campbell, if I understand you right the way you are always acting to me. That certainly is right the way I am saying it to you now, Jeff Campbell. You certainly didn't anyway trust me now no more, did you, when you just acted so bad to me. I certainly am right the way I say it Jeff now to you. I certainly am right when I ask you for it now, to tell me what I ask you, about not trusting me more then again, Jeff, just like you never really knew me. You certainly never did trust me just then, Jeff, you hear me?" "Yes, Melanctha," Jeff answered slowly. Melanctha paused. "I guess I certainly never can forgive you this time, Jeff Campbell," she said firmly. Jeff paused too, and thought a little. "I certainly am afraid you never can no more now again, Melanctha," he said sadly.

They lay there very quiet now a long time, each one thinking very hard on their own trouble. At last Jeff began again to tell Melanctha what it was he was always thinking with her. "I certainly do know, Melanctha, you certainly now don't want any more to be hearing me just talking, but you see,

Melanctha, really, it's just like this way always with me. You
see, Melanctha, its like this way now all the time with me. You
remember, Melanctha, what I was once telling to you, when
I didn't know you very long together, about how I certainly
never did know more than just two kinds of ways of loving,
one way the way it is good to be in families and the other
kind of way, like animals are all the time just with each other,
and how I didn't ever like that last kind of way much for any
of the colored people. You see Melanctha, it's like this way
with me. I got a new feeling now, you been teaching to me,
just like I told you once, just like a new religion to me, and
I see perhaps what really loving is like, like really having everything together, new things, little pieces all different, like I
always before been thinking was bad to be having, all go together like, to make one good big feeling. You see, Melanctha,
it's certainly like that you make me been seeing, like I never
know before any way there was of all kinds of loving to come
together to make one way really truly lovely. I see that now,
sometimes, the way you certainly been teaching me, Melanctha, really, and then I love you those times, Melanctha,
like a real religion, and then it comes over me all sudden, I
don't know anything real about you Melanctha, dear one, and
then it comes over me sudden, perhaps I certainly am wrong
now, thinking all this way so lovely, and not thinking now any
more the old way I always before was always thinking, about
what was the right way for me, to live regular and all the
colored people, and then I think, perhaps, Melanctha you are
really just a bad one, and I think, perhaps I certainly am doing
it so because I just am too anxious to be just having all the
time excitements, like I don't ever like really to be doing when
I know it, and then I always get so bad to you, Melanctha,
and I can't help it with myself then, never, for I want to be
always right really in the ways, I have to do them. I certainly
do very badly want to be right, Melanctha, the only way I
know is right Melanctha really, and I don't know any way,
Melanctha, to find out really, whether my old way, the way I
always used to be thinking, or the new way, you make so like
a real religion to me sometimes, Melanctha, which way certainly is the real right way for me to be always thinking, and
then I certainly am awful good and sorry, Melanctha, I always

give you so much trouble, hurting you with the bad ways I am acting. Can't you help me to any way, to make it all straight for me, Melanctha, so I know right and real what it is I should be acting. You see, Melanctha, I don't want always to be a coward with you, if I only could know certain what was the right way for me to be acting. I certainly am real sure, Melanctha, that would be the way I would be acting, if I only knew it sure for certain now, Melanctha. Can't you help me any way to find out real and true, Melanctha, dear one. I certainly do badly want to know always, the way I should be acting."

"No, Jeff, dear, I certainly can't help you much in that kind of trouble you are always having. All I can do now, Jeff, is to just keep certainly with my believing you are good always, Jeff, and though you certainly do hurt me bad, I always got strong faith in you, Jeff, more in you certainly, than you seem to be having in your acting to me, always so bad, Jeff."

"You certainly are very good to me, Melanctha, dear one," Jeff said, after a long, tender silence. "You certainly are very good to me, Melanctha, darling, and me so bad to you always, in my acting. Do you love me good, and right, Melanctha, always?" "Always and always, you be sure of that now you have me. Oh you Jeff, you always be so stupid." "I certainly never can say now you ain't right, when you say that to me so, Melanctha," Jeff answered. "Oh, Jeff dear, I love you always, you know that now, all right, for certain. If you don't know it right now, Jeff, really, I prove it to you now, for good and always." And they lay there a long time in their loving, and then Jeff began again with his happy free enjoying.

"I sure am a good boy to be learning all the time the right way you are teaching me, Melanctha, darling," began Jeff Campbell, laughing, "You can't say no, never, I ain't a good scholar for you to be teaching now, Melanctha, and I am always so ready to come to you every day, and never playing hooky ever from you. You can't say ever, Melanctha, now can you, I ain't a real good boy to be always studying to be learning to be real bright, just like my teacher. You can't say ever to me, I ain't a good boy to you now, Melanctha." "Not near so good, Jeff Campbell, as such a good, patient kind of teacher, like me, who never teaches any ways it ain't good her scholars should be knowing, ought to be really having, Jeff, you hear me? I certainly don't think I am right for you, to be forgiving always, when you are so bad, and I so patient, with all this hard teaching always." "But you do forgive me always, sure, Melanctha, always?" "Always and always, you be sure Jeff, and I certainly am afraid I never can stop with my forgiving, you always are going to be so bad to me, and I always going to have to be so good with my forgiving." "Oh! Oh!" cried Jeff Campbell, laughing, "I ain't going to be so bad for always, sure I ain't, Melanctha, my own darling. And sure you do forgive me really, and sure you love me true and really, sure, Melanctha?" "Sure, sure, Jeff, boy, sure now and always, sure now you believe me, sure you do, Jeff, always." "I sure hope I does, with all my heart, Melanctha, darling." "I sure do that same, Jeff, dear boy, now you really know what it is to be loving, and I prove it to you now so, Jeff, you never can be forgetting. You see now, Jeff, good and certain, what I always before been saying to you, Jeff, now." "Yes, Melanctha, darling," murmured Jeff, and he was very happy in it, and so the two of them now in the warm air of the sultry, southern, negro sunshine, lay there for a long time just resting.

And now for a real long time there was no open trouble any more between Jeff Campbell and Melanctha Herbert. Then it came that Jeff knew he could not say out any more, what it was he wanted, he could not say out any more, what it was, he wanted to know about, what Melanctha wanted.

Melanctha sometimes now, when she was tired with being all the time so much excited, when Jeff would talk a long time to her about what was right for them both to be always doing, would be, as if she gave way in her head, and lost herself in a bad feeling. Sometimes when they had been strong in their loving, and Jeff would have rise inside him some strange feeling, and Melanctha felt it in him as it would soon be coming, she would lose herself then in this bad feeling that made her head act as if she never knew what it was they were doing. And slowly now, Jeff soon always came to be feeling that his Melanctha would be hurt very much in her head in the ways he never liked to think of, if she would ever now again have to listen to his trouble, when he was telling about what it was he still was wanting to make things for himself really understanding.

Now Jeff began to have always a strong feeling that Melanctha could no longer stand it, with all her bad suffering, to let him fight out with himself what was right for him to be doing. Now he felt he must not, when she was there with him, keep on, with this kind of fighting that was always going on inside him. Jeff Campbell never knew yet, what he thought was the right way, for himself and for all the colored people to be living. Jeff was coming always each time closer to be really understanding, but now Melanctha was so bad in her suffering with him, that he knew she could not any longer have him with her while he was always showing that he never really yet was sure what it was, the right way, for them to be really loving.

Jeff saw now he had to go so fast, so that Melanctha never would have to wait any to get from him always all that she ever wanted. He never could be honest now, he never could be now, any more, trying to be really understanding, for always every moment now he felt it to be a strong thing in him, how very much it was Melanctha Herbert always suffered.

Jeff did not know very well these days, what it was, was really happening to him. All he knew every now and then, when they were getting strong to get excited, the way they used to when he gave his feeling out so that he could be always honest, that Melanctha somehow never seemed to hear him, she just looked at him and looked as if her head hurt with him, and then Jeff had to keep himself from being honest, and he had to go so fast, and to do everything Melanctha ever wanted from him.

Jeff did not like it very well these days, in his true feeling. He knew now very well Melanctha was not strong enough inside her to stand any more of his slow way of doing. And yet now he knew he was not honest in his feeling. Now he always had to show more to Melanctha than he was ever feeling. Now she made him go so fast, and he knew it was not real with his feeling, and yet he could not make her suffer so any more because he always was so slow with his feeling.

It was very hard for Jeff Campbell to make all this way of doing, right, inside him. If Jeff Campbell could not be straight out, and real honest, he never could be very strong inside him. Now Melanctha, with her making him feel, always, how good she was and how very much she suffered in him, made him always go so fast then, he could not be strong then, to feel things out straight then inside him. Always now when he was with her, he was being more, than he could already yet, be feeling for her. Always now, with her, he had something inside him always holding in him, always now, with her, he was far ahead of his own feeling.

Jeff Campbell never knew very well these days what it was that was going on inside him. All he knew was, he was uneasy now always to be with Melanctha. All he knew was, that he was always uneasy when he was with Melanctha, not the way he used to be from just not being very understanding, but now, because he never could be honest with her, because he was now always feeling her strong suffering, in her, because he knew now he was having a straight, good feeling with her, but she went so fast, and he was so slow to her; Jeff knew his right feeling never got a chance to show itself as strong, to her.

All this was always getting harder for Jeff Campbell. He was very proud to hold himself to be strong, was Jeff Campbell. He was very tender not to hurt Melanctha, when he knew she would be sure to feel it badly in her head a long time after, he hated that he could not now be honest with her, he wanted to stay away to work it out all alone, without her, he was afraid she would feel it to suffer, if he kept away now from her. He was uneasy always, with her, he was uneasy when he thought about her, he knew now he had a good, straight, strong feeling of right loving for her, and yet now he never could use it to be good and honest with her.

Jeff Campbell did not know, these days, anything he could do to make it better for her. He did not know anything he could do, to set himself really right in his acting and his thinking toward her. She pulled him so fast with her, and he did not dare to hurt her, and he could not come right, so fast, the way she always needed he should be doing it now, for her.

These days were not very joyful ones now any more, to Jeff Campbell, with Melanctha. He did not think it out to himself now, in words, about her. He did not know enough, what was his real trouble, with her.

Sometimes now and again with them, and with all this trouble for a little while well forgotten by him, Jeff, and Melanctha with him, would be very happy in a strong, sweet loving. Sometimes then, Jeff would find himself to be soaring very high in his true loving. Sometimes Jeff would find then, in his loving, his soul swelling out full inside him. Always Jeff felt now in himself, deep feeling.

Always now Jeff had to go so much faster than was real with his feeling. Yet always Jeff knew now he had a right, strong feeling. Always now when Jeff was wondering, it was Melanctha he was doubting, in the loving. Now he would often ask her, was she real now to him, in her loving. He would ask her often, feeling something queer about it all inside him, though yet he was never really strong in his doubting, and always Melanctha would answer to him, "Yes Jeff, sure, you know it, always," and always Jeff felt a doubt now, in her loving.

Always now Jeff felt in himself, deep loving. Always now he did not know really, if Melanctha was true in her loving.

All these days Jeff was uncertain in him, and he was uneasy about which way he should act so as not to be wrong and put them both into bad trouble. Always now he was, as if he must feel deep into Melanctha to see if it was real loving he would find she now had in her, and always he would stop himself, with her, for always he was afraid now that he might badly hurt her.

Always now he liked it better when he was detained when he had to go and see her. Always now he never liked to go to be with her, although he never wanted really, not to be always with her. Always now he never felt really at ease with her, even when they were good friends together. Always now he felt, with her, he could not be really honest to her. And Jeff never could be happy with her when he could not feel strong to tell all his feeling to her. Always now every day he found it harder to make the time pass, with her, and not let his feeling come so that he would quarrel with her.

And so one evening, late, he was to go to her. He waited a little long, before he went to her. He was afraid, in himself, to-night, he would surely hurt her. He never wanted to go when he might quarrel with her.

Melanctha sat there looking very angry, when he came in to her. Jeff took off his hat and coat and then sat down by the fire with her.

"If you come in much later to me just now, Jeff Campbell, I certainly never would have seen you no more never to speak to you, 'thout your apologising real humble to me." "Apologising Melanctha," and Jeff laughed and was scornful to her, "Apologising, Melanctha, I ain't proud that kind of way, Melanctha, I don't mind apologising to you, Melanctha, all I mind, Melanctha is to be doing of things wrong, to you." "That's easy, to say things that way, Jeff to me. But you never was very proud Jeff, to be courageous to me." "I don't know about that Melanctha. I got courage to say some things hard, when I mean them, to you." "Oh, yes, Jeff, I know all about that, Jeff, to me. But I mean real courage, to run around and not care nothing about what happens, and always to be game in any kind of trouble. That's what I mean by real courage, to me, Jeff, if you want to know it." "Oh, yes, Melanctha, I know all that kind of courage. I see plenty of it all the time with some kinds of colored men and with some girls like you Melanctha, and Jane Harden. I know all about how you are always making a fuss to be proud because you don't holler so much when you run in to where you ain't got any business to be, and so you get hurt, the way you ought to. And then, you kind of people are very brave then, sure, with all your kinds of suffering, but the way I see it, going round with all my patients, that kind of courage makes all kind of trouble, for them who ain't so noble with their courage, and then they got it, always to be bearing it, when the end comes, to be hurt the hardest. It's like running around and being game to spend all your money always, and then a man's wife and children are the ones do all the starving and they don't ever get a name for being brave, and they don't ever want to be doing all that suffering, and they got to stand it and say nothing. That's the way I see it a good deal now with all that kind of braveness in some of the colored people. They always make a lot of noise to show they are so brave not to holler, when they got so much suffering they always bring all on themselves, just by doing things they got no business to be doing. I don't say, never, Melanctha, they ain't got good courage not to holler, but I never did see much in looking for that kind of trouble just to show you ain't going to holler. No its all right being brave every day, just living regular and not having new ways all the time just to get excitements, the way I hate to see it in all the colored people. No I don't see much, Melanctha, in being brave just to get it good, where you've got no business. I ain't ashamed Melanctha, right here to tell you, I ain't ashamed ever to say I ain't got no longing to be brave, just to go around and look for trouble." "Yes that's just like you always, Jeff, you never understand things right, the way you are always feeling in you. You ain't got no way to understand right, how it depends what way somebody goes to look for new things, the way it makes it right for them to get excited." "No Melanctha, I certainly never do say I understand much anybody's got a right to think they won't have real bad trouble, if they go and look hard where they are certain sure to find it. No Melanctha, it certainly does sound very pretty all this talking about danger and being game and never hollering, and all that way of talking, but when two men are just fighting, the strong man mostly gets on top with doing good hard pounding, and the man that's getting all that pounding, he mostly never likes it so far as I have been able yet to see it, and I don't see much difference what kind of noble way they are made of when they ain't got any kind of business to get together there to be fighting. That certainly is the only way I ever see it happen right, Melanctha, whenever I happen to be anywhere I can be looking." "That's because you never can see anything that ain't just so simple, Jeff, with everybody, the way you always think it. It do make all the difference the kind of way anybody is made to do things game Jeff Campbell." "Maybe Melanctha, I certainly never say no you ain't right, Melanctha. I just been telling it to you all straight, Melanctha, the way I always see it. Perhaps if you run around where you ain't got any business, and you stand up very straight and say, I am so brave, nothing can ever ever hurt me, maybe nothing will ever hurt you then Melanctha. I never have seen it do so. I never can say truly any differently to you Melanctha, but I always am ready to be learning from you, Melanctha. And perhaps when somebody cuts into you real hard, with a brick he is throwing, perhaps you never will do any hollering then, Melanctha. I certainly don't ever say no, Melanctha to you, I only say that ain't the way yet I ever see it happen when I had a chance to be there looking."

They sat there together, quiet by the fire, and they did not seem to feel very loving.

"I certainly do wonder," Melanctha said dreamily, at last breaking into their long unloving silence. "I certainly do wonder why always it happens to me I care for anybody who ain't no ways good enough for me ever to be thinking to respect him."

Jeff looked at Melanctha. Jeff got up then and walked a little up and down the room, and then he came back, and his face was set and dark and he was very quiet to her.

"Oh dear, Jeff, sure, why you look so solemn now to me. Sure Jeff I never am meaning anything real by what I just been saying. What was I just been saying Jeff to you. I only certainly was just thinking how everything always was just happening to me."

Jeff Campbell sat very still and dark, and made no answer.

"Seems to me, Jeff you might be good to me a little to-night when my head hurts so, and I am so tired with all the hard work I have been doing, thinking, and I always got so many things to be a trouble to me, living like I do with no-body ever who can help me. Seems to me you might be good to me Jeff to-night, and not get angry, every little thing I am ever saying to you."

"I certainly would not get angry ever with you, Melanctha, just because you say things to me. But now I certainly been thinking you really mean what you have been just then saying to me." "But you say all the time to me Jeff, you ain't no ways good enough in your loving to me, you certainly say to me all the time you ain't no ways good or understanding to me." "That certainly is what I say to you always, just the way I feel it to you Melanctha always, and I got it right in me to say it, and I have got a right in me to be very strong and feel it, and to be always sure to believe it, but it ain't right for you Melanctha to feel it. When you feel it so Melanctha, it does certainly make everything all wrong with our loving. It makes it so I certainly never can bear to have it."

They sat there then a long time by the fire, very silent, and not loving, and never looking to each other for it. Melanctha was moving and twitching herself and very nervous with it. Jeff was heavy and sullen and dark and very serious in it.

"Oh why can't you forget I said it to you Jeff now, and I certainly am so tired, and my head and all now with it."

Jeff stirred, "All right Melanctha, don't you go make your-self sick now in your head, feeling so bad with it," and Jeff made himself do it, and he was a patient doctor again now with Melanctha when he felt her really having her head hurt with it. "It's all right now Melanctha darling, sure it is now I tell you. You just lie down now a little, dear one, and I sit here by the fire and just read awhile and just watch with you so I will be here ready, if you need me to give you something to help you resting." And then Jeff was a good doctor to her, and very sweet and tender with her, and Melanctha loved him to be there to help her, and then Melanctha fell asleep a little, and Jeff waited there beside her until he saw she was really sleeping, and then he went back and sat down by the fire.

And Jeff tried to begin again with his thinking, and he could not make it come clear to himself, with all his thinking, and he felt everything all thick and heavy and bad, now inside him, everything that he could not understand right, with all the hard work he made, with his thinking. And then he moved himself a little, and took a book to forget his thinking, and then as always, he loved it when he was reading, and then very soon he was deep in his reading, and so he forgot now for a little while that he never could seem to be very under-standing.

And so Jeff forgot himself for awhile in his reading, and Melanctha was sleeping. And then Melanctha woke up and she was screaming. "Oh, Jeff, I thought you gone away for always from me. Oh, Jeff, never now go away no more from me. Oh, Jeff, sure, sure, always be just so good to me."

There was a weight in Jeff Campbell from now on, always with him, that he could never lift out from him, to feel easy. He always was trying not to have it in him and he always was trying not to let Melanctha feel it, with him, but it was always there inside him. Now Jeff Campbell always was serious, and dark, and heavy, and sullen, and he would often sit a long time with Melanctha without moving.

"You certainly never have forgiven to me, what I said to you that night, Jeff, now have you?" Melanctha asked him after a long silence, late one evening with him. "It ain't ever with me a question like forgiving, Melanctha, I got in me. It's just only what you are feeling for me, makes any difference to me. I ain't ever seen anything since in you, makes me think you didn't mean it right, what you said about not thinking now any more I was good, to make it right for you to be really caring so very much to love me."

"I certainly never did see no man like you, Jeff. You always wanting to have it all clear out in words always, what everybody is always feeling. I certainly don't see a reason, why I should always be explaining to you what I mean by what I am just saying. And you ain't got no feeling ever for me, to ask me what I meant, by what I was saying when I was so tired, that night. I never know anything right I was saying." "But you don't ever tell me now, Melanctha, so I really hear you say it, you don't mean it the same way, the way you said it to me." "Oh Jeff, you so stupid always to me and always just bothering with your always asking to me. And I don't never any way remember ever anything I been saying to you, and I am always my head, so it hurts me it half kills me, and my heart jumps so, sometimes I think I die so when it hurts me, and I am so blue always, I think sometimes I take something to just kill me, and I got so much to bother thinking always and doing, and I got so much to worry, and all that, and then you come and ask me what I mean by what I was just saying to you. I certainly don't know, Jeff, when you ask me. Seems to me, Jeff, sometimes you might have some kind of a right feeling to be careful to me." "You ain't got no right Melanctha Herbert," flashed out Jeff through his dark, frowning anger, "you certainly ain't got no right always to be using your being hurt and being sick, and having pain, like a weapon, so as to make me do things it ain't never right for me to be doing for you. You certainly ain't got no right to be always holding your pain out to show me." "What do you mean by them words, Jeff Campbell." "I certainly do mean them just like I am saying them, Melanctha. You act always, like I been responsible all myself for all our loving one another. And if its anything anyway that ever hurts you, you act like as if it was me made you just begin it all with me. I ain't no coward, you hear me, Melanctha? I never put my trouble back on anybody, thinking that they made me. I certainly am right ready always, Melanctha, you certainly had ought to know me, to stand all my own trouble for me, but I tell you straight now, the way I think it Melanctha, I ain't going to be as if I was the reason why you wanted to be loving, and to be suffering so now with me." "But ain't you certainly ought to be feeling it so, to be right, Jeff Campbell. Did I ever do anything but just let you do everything you wanted to me. Did I ever try to make you be loving to me. Did I ever do nothing except just sit there ready to endure your loving with me. But I certainly never, Jeff Campbell, did make any kind of way as if I wanted really to be having you for me."

Jeff stared at Melanctha. "So that's the way you say it when you are thinking right about it all, Melanctha. Well I certainly ain't got a word to say ever to you any more, Melanctha, if that's the way its straight out to you now, Melanctha." And Jeff almost laughed out to her, and he turned to take his hat and coat, and go away now forever from her.

Melanctha dropped her head on her arms, and she trembled all over and inside her. Jeff stopped a little and looked very sadly at her. Jeff could not so quickly make it right for himself, to leave her.

"Oh, I certainly shall go crazy now, I certainly know that," Melanctha moaned as she sat there, all fallen and miserable and weak together.

Jeff came and took her in his arms, and held her. Jeff was very good then to her, but they neither of them felt inside all right, as they once did, to be together.

From now on, Jeff had real torment in him.

Was it true what Melanctha had said that night to him? Was it true that he was the one had made all this trouble for them?

Was it true, he was the only one, who always had had wrong ways in him? Waking or sleeping Jeff now always had this torment going on inside him.

Jeff did not know now any more, what to feel within him. He did not know how to begin thinking out this trouble that must always now be bad inside him. He just felt a confused struggle and resentment always in him, a knowing, no, Melanctha was not right in what she had said that night to him, and then a feeling, perhaps he always had been wrong in the way he never could be understanding. And then would come strong to him, a sense of the deep sweetness in Melanctha's loving and a hating the cold slow way he always had to feel things in him.

Always Jeff knew, sure, Melanctha was wrong in what she had said that night to him, but always Melanctha had had deep feeling with him, always he was poor and slow in the only way he knew how to have any feeling. Jeff knew Melanctha was wrong, and yet he always had a deep doubt in him. What could he know, who had such slow feeling in him? What could he ever know, who always had to find his way with just thinking. What could he know, who had to be taught such a long time to learn about what was really loving? Jeff now always had this torment in him.

Melanctha was now always making him feel her way, strong whenever she was with him. Did she go on to do it just to show him, did she do it so now because she was no longer loving, did she do it so because that was her way to make him be really loving. Jeff never did know how it was that it all happened so to him.

Melanctha acted now the way she had said it always had been with them. Now it was always Jeff who had to do the asking. Now it was always Jeff who had to ask when would be the next time he should come to see her. Now always she was good and patient to him, and now always she was kind and loving with him, and always Jeff felt it was, that she was good to give him anything he ever asked or wanted, but never now any more for her own sake to make her happy in him. Now she did these things, as if it was just to please her Jeff Campbell who needed she should now have kindness for him. Always now he was the beggar, with them. Always now

Melanctha gave it, not of her need, but from her bounty to him. Always now Jeff found it getting harder for him.

Sometimes Jeff wanted to tear things away from before him, always now he wanted to fight things and be angry with them, and always now Melanctha was so patient to him.

Now, deep inside him, there was always a doubt with Jeff, of Melanctha's loving. It was not a doubt yet to make him really doubting, for with that, Jeff never could be really loving, but always now he knew that something, and that not in him, something was wrong with their loving. Jeff Campbell could not know any right way to think out what was inside Melanctha with her loving, he could not use any way now to reach inside her to find if she was true in her loving, but now something had gone wrong between them, and now he never felt sure in him, the way once she had made him, that now at last he really had got to be understanding.

Melanctha was too many for him. He was helpless to find out the way she really felt now for him. Often Jeff would ask her, did she really love him. Always she said, "Yes Jeff, sure, you know that," and now instead of a full sweet strong love with it, Jeff only felt a patient, kind endurance in it.

Jeff did not know. If he was right in such a feeling, he certainly never any more did want to have Melanctha Herbert with him. Jeff Campbell hated badly to think Melanctha ever would give him love, just for his sake, and not because she needed it herself, to be with him. Such a way of loving would be very hard for Jeff to be enduring.

"Jeff what makes you act so funny to me. Jeff you certainly now are jealous to me. Sure Jeff, now I don't see ever why you be so foolish to look so to me." "Don't you ever think I can be jealous of anybody ever Melanctha, you hear me. It's just, you certainly don't ever understand me. It's just this way with me always now Melanctha. You love me, and I don't care anything what you do or what you ever been to anybody. You don't love me, then I don't care any more about what you ever do or what you ever be to anybody. But I never want you to be being good Melanctha to me, when it ain't your loving makes you need it. I certainly don't ever want to be having any of your kind of kindness to me. If you don't love me, I can stand it. All I never want to have is your being good to me from kindness. If you don't love me, then you and I certainly do quit right here Melanctha, all strong feeling, to be always living to each other. It certainly never is anybody I ever am thinking about when I am thinking with you Melanctha darling. That's the true way I am telling you Melanctha, always. It's only your loving me ever gives me anything to bother me Melanctha, so all you got to do, if you don't really love me, is just certainly to say so to me. I won't bother you more then than I can help to keep from it Melanctha. You certainly need never to be in any worry, never, about me Melanctha. You just tell me straight out Melanctha, real, the way you feel it. I certainly can stand it all right, I tell you true Melanctha. And I never will care to know why or nothing Melanctha. Loving is just living Melanctha to me, and if you don't really feel it now Melanctha to me, there ain't ever nothing between us then Melanctha, is there? That's straight and honest just the way I always feel it to you now Melanctha. Oh Melanctha, darling, do you love me? Oh Melanctha, please, please, tell me honest, tell me, do you really love me?"

"Oh you so stupid Jeff boy, of course I always love you. Always and always Jeff and I always just so good to you. Oh you so stupid Jeff and don't know when you got it good with me. Oh dear, Jeff I certainly am so tired Jeff to-night, don't you go be a bother to me. Yes I love you Jeff, how often you want me to tell you. Oh you so stupid Jeff, but yes I love you. Now I won't say it no more now tonight Jeff, you hear me. You just be good Jeff now to me or else I certainly get awful angry with you. Yes I love you, sure, Jeff, though you don't any way deserve it from me. Yes, yes I love you. Yes Jeff I say it till I certainly am very sleepy. Yes I love you now Jeff, and you certainly must stop asking me to tell you. Oh you great silly boy Jeff Campbell, sure I love you, oh you silly stupid, my own boy Jeff Campbell. Yes I love you and I certainly never won't say it one more time to-night Jeff, now you hear me."

Yes Jeff Campbell heard her, and he tried hard to believe her. He did not really doubt her but somehow it was wrong now, the way Melanctha said it. Jeff always now felt baffled with Melanctha. Something, he knew, was not right now in her. Something in her always now was making stronger the torment that was tearing every minute at the joy he once always had had with her.

Always now Jeff wondered did Melanctha love him. Always now he was wondering, was Melanctha right when she said, it was he had made all their beginning. Was Melanctha right when she said, it was he had the real responsibility for all the trouble they had and still were having now between them. If she was right, what a brute he always had been in his acting. If she was right, how good she had been to endure the pain he had made so bad so often for her. But no, surely she had made herself to bear it, for her own sake, not for his to make him happy. Surely he was not so twisted in all his long thinking. Surely he could remember right what it was had happened every day in their long loving. Surely he was not so poor a coward as Melanctha always seemed to be thinking. Surely, surely, and then the torment would get worse every minute in him.

One night Jeff Campbell was lying in his bed with his thinking, and night after night now he could not do any sleeping for his thinking. To-night suddenly he sat up in his bed, and it all came clear to him, and he pounded his pillow with his fist, and he almost shouted out alone there to him, "I ain't a brute the way Melanctha has been saying. Its all wrong the way I been worried thinking. We did begin fair, each not for the other but for ourselves, what we were wanting. Melanctha Herbert did it just like I did it, because she liked it bad enough to want to stand it. It's all wrong in me to think it any way except the way we really did it. I certainly don't know now whether she is now real and true in her loving. I ain't got any way ever to find out if she is real and true now always to me. All I know is I didn't ever make her to begin to be with me. Melanctha has got to stand for her own trouble, just like I got to stand for my own trouble. Each man has got to do it for himself when he is in real trouble. Melanctha, she certainly don't remember right when she says I made her begin and then I made her trouble. No by God, I ain't no coward nor a brute either ever to her. I been the way I felt it honest, and that certainly is all about it now between us, and everybody always has just got to stand for their own trouble.

I certainly am right this time the way I see it." And Jeff lay down now, at last in comfort, and he slept, and he was free from his long doubting torment.

"You know Melanctha," Jeff Campbell began, the next time he was alone to talk a long time to Melanctha. "You know Melanctha, sometimes I think a whole lot about what you like to say so much about being game and never doing any hollering. Seems to me Melanctha, I certainly don't understand right what you mean by not hollering. Seems to me it certainly ain't only what comes right away when one is hit, that counts to be brave to be bearing, but all that comes later from your getting sick from the shock of being hurt once in a fight, and all that, and all the being taken care of for years after, and the suffering of your family, and all that, you certainly must stand and not holler, to be certainly really brave the way I understand it." "What you mean Jeff by your talking." "I mean, seems to me really not to holler, is to be strong not to show you ever have been hurt. Seems to me, to get your head hurt from your trouble and to show it, ain't certainly no braver than to say, oh, oh, how bad you hurt me, please don't hurt me mister. It just certainly seems to me, like many people think themselves so game just to stand what we all of us always just got to be standing, and everybody stands it, and we don't certainly none of us like it, and yet we don't ever most of us think we are so much being game, just because we got to stand it."

"I know what you mean now by what you are saying to me now Jeff Campbell. You make a fuss now to me, because I certainly just have stopped standing everything you like to be always doing so cruel to me. But that's just the way always with you Jeff Campbell, if you want to know it. You ain't got no kind of right feeling for all I always been forgiving to you." "I said it once for fun, Melanctha, but now I certainly do mean it, you think you got a right to go where you got no business, and you say, I am so brave nothing can hurt me, and then something, like always, it happens to hurt you, and you show your hurt always so everybody can see it, and you say, I am so brave nothing did hurt me except he certainly didn't have any right to, and see how bad I suffer, but you never hear me make a holler, though certainly anybody got any feeling, to see me suffer, would certainly never touch me except to take good care of me. Sometimes I certainly don't rightly see Melanctha, how much more game that is than just the ordinary kind of holler." "No, Jeff Campbell, and made the way you is you certainly ain't likely ever to be much more understanding." "No, Melanctha, nor you neither. You think always, you are the only one who ever can do any way to really suffer." "Well, and ain't I certainly always been the only person knows how to bear it. No, Jeff Campbell, I certainly be glad to love anybody really worthy, but I made so, I never seem to be able in this world to find him." "No, and your kind of way of thinking, you certainly Melanctha never going to any way be able ever to be finding of him. Can't you understand Melanctha, ever, how no man certainly ever really can hold your love for long times together. You certainly Melanctha, you ain't got down deep loyal feeling, true inside you, and when you ain't just that moment quick with feeling, then you certainly ain't ever got anything more there to keep you. You see Melanctha, it certainly is this way with you, it is, that you ain't ever got any way to remember right what you been doing, or anybody else that has been feeling with you. You certainly Melanctha, never can remember right, when it comes what you have done and what you think happens to you." "It certainly is all easy for you Jeff Campbell to be talking. You remember right, because you don't remember nothing till you get home with your thinking everything all over, but I certainly don't think much ever of that kind of way of remembering right, Jeff Campbell. I certainly do call it remembering right Jeff Campbell, to remember right just when it happens to you, so you have a right kind of feeling not to act the way you always been doing to me, and then you go home Jeff Campbell, and you begin with your thinking, and then it certainly is very easy for you to be good and forgiving with it. No, that ain't to me, the way of remembering Jeff Campbell, not as I can see it not to make people always suffer, waiting for you certainly to get to do it. Seems to me like Jeff Campbell, I never could feel so like a man was low and to be scorning of him, like that day in the summer, when you threw me off just because you got one of those fits of your remembering. No, Jeff Campbell, its real feeling every moment when its needed, that certainly does seem to me like real remembering. And that way, certainly, you don't never know nothing like what should be right Jeff Campbell. No Jeff, it's me that always certainly has had to bear it with you. It's always me that certainly has had to suffer, while you go home to remember. No you certainly ain't got no sense yet Jeff, what you need to make you really feeling. No, it certainly is me Jeff Campbell, that always has got to be remembering for us both, always. That's what's the true way with us Jeff Campbell, if you want to know what it is I am always thinking." "You is certainly real modest Melanctha, when you do this kind of talking, you sure is Melanctha," said Jeff Campbell laughing. "I think sometimes Melanctha I am certainly awful conceited, when I think sometimes I am all out doors, and I think I certainly am so bright, and better than most everybody I ever got anything now to do with, but when I hear you talk this way Melanctha, I certainly do think I am a real modest kind of fellow." "Modest!" said Melanctha, angry, "Modest, that certainly is a queer thing for you Jeff to be calling yourself even when you are laughing." "Well it certainly does depend a whole lot what you are thinking with," said Jeff Campbell. "I never did use to think I was so much on being real modest Melanctha, but now I know really I am, when I hear you talking. I see all the time there are many people living just as good as I am, though they are a little different to me. Now with you Melanctha if I understand you right what you are talking, you don't think that way of no other one that you are ever knowing." "I certainly could be real modest too, Jeff Campbell," said Melanctha, "If I could meet somebody once I could keep right on respecting when I got so I was really knowing with them. But I certainly never met anybody like that yet, Jeff Campbell, if you want to know it." "No, Melanctha, and with the way you got of thinking, it certainly don't look like as if you ever will Melanctha, with your never remembering anything only what you just then are feeling in you, and you not understanding what any one else is ever feeling, if they don't holler just the way you are doing. No Melanctha, I certainly don't see any ways you are likely ever to meet one, so good as you are always thinking you be."

"No, Jeff Campbell, it certainly ain't that way with me at all the way you say it. It's because I am always knowing what it is I am wanting, when I get it. I certainly don't never have to wait till I have it, and then throw away what I got in me, and then come back and say, that's a mistake I just been making, it ain't that never at all like I understood it, I want to have, bad, what I didn't think it was I wanted. It's that way of knowing right what I am wanting, makes me feel nobody can come right with me, when I am feeling things, Jeff Campbell. I certainly do say Jeff Campbell, I certainly don't think much of the way you always do it, always never knowing what it is you are ever really wanting and everybody always got to suffer. No Jeff, I don't certainly think there is much doubting which is better and the stronger with us two, Jeff Campbell."

"As you will, Melanctha Herbert," cried Jeff Campbell, and he rose up, and he thundered out a black oath, and he was fierce to leave her now forever, and then with the same movement, he took her in his arms and held her.

"What a silly goose boy you are, Jeff Campbell," Melanctha whispered to him fondly.

"Oh yes," said Jeff, very dreary. "I never could keep really mad with anybody, not when I was a little boy and playing. I used most to cry sometimes, I couldn't get real mad and keep on a long time with it, the way everybody always did it. It's certainly no use to me Melanctha, I certainly can't ever keep mad with you Melanctha, my dear one. But don't you ever be thinking it's because I think you right in what you been just saying to me. I don't Melanctha really think it that way, honest, though I certainly can't get mad the way I ought to. No Melanctha, little girl, really truly, you ain't right the way you think it. I certainly do know that Melanctha, honest. You certainly don't do me right Melanctha, the way you say you are thinking. Good-bye Melanctha, though you certainly is my own little girl for always." And then they were very good a little to each other, and then Jeff went away for that evening, from her.

Melanctha had begun now once more to wander. Melanctha did not yet always wander, but a little now she needed to begin to look for others. Now Melanctha Herbert began again to be with some of the better kind of black girls, and with them she sometimes wandered. Melanctha had not yet come again to need to be alone, when she wandered.

Jeff Campbell did not know that Melanctha had begun again to wander. All Jeff knew, was that now he could not be so often with her.

Jeff never knew how it had come to happen to him, but now he never thought to go to see Melanctha Herbert, until he had before, asked her if she could be going to have time then to have him with her. Then Melanctha would think a little, and then she would say to him, "Let me see Jeff, to-morrow, you was just saying to me. I certainly am awful busy you know Jeff just now. It certainly does seem to me this week Jeff, I can't anyways fix it. Sure I want to see you soon Jeff. I certainly Jeff got to do a little more now, I been giving so much time, when I had no business, just to be with you when you asked me. Now I guess Jeff, I certainly can't see you no more this week Jeff, the way I got to do things." "All right Melanctha," Jeff would answer and he would be very angry. "I want to come only just certainly as you want me now Melanctha." "Now Jeff you know I certainly can't be neglecting always to be with everybody just to see you. You come see me next week Tuesday Jeff, you hear me. I don't think Jeff I certainly be so busy, Tuesday." Jeff Campbell would then go away and leave her, and he would be hurt and very angry, for it was hard for a man with a great pride in himself, like Jeff Campbell, to feel himself no better than a beggar. And yet he always came as she said he should, on the day she had fixed for him, and always Jeff Campbell was not sure yet that he really understood what it was Melanctha wanted. Always Melanctha said to him, yes she loved him, sure he knew that. Always Melanctha said to him, she certainly did love him just the same as always, only sure he knew now she certainly did seem to be right busy with all she certainly now had to be doing.

Jeff never knew what Melanctha had to do now, that made her always be so busy, but Jeff Campbell never cared to ask Melanctha such a question. Besides Jeff knew Melanctha Herbert would never, in such a matter, give him any kind of a real answer. Jeff did not know whether it was that Melanctha did not know how to give a simple answer. And then how could he, Jeff, know what was important to her. Jeff Campbell always felt strongly in him, he had no right to interfere with Melanctha in any practical kind of a matter. There they had always, never asked each other any kind of question. There they had felt always in each other, not any right to take care of one another. And Jeff Campbell now felt less than he had ever, any right to claim to know what Melanctha thought it right that she should do in any of her ways of living. All Jeff felt a right in himself to question, was her loving.

Jeff learned every day now, more and more, how much it was that he could really suffer. Sometimes it hurt so in him, when he was alone, it would force some slow tears from him. But every day, now that Jeff Campbell, knew more how it could hurt him, he lost his feeling of deep awe that he once always had had for Melanctha's feeling. Suffering was not so much after all, thought Jeff Campbell, if even he could feel it so it hurt him. It hurt him bad, just the way he knew he once had hurt Melanctha, and yet he too could have it and not make any kind of a loud holler with it.

In tender hearted natures, those that mostly never feel strong passion, suffering often comes to make them harder. When these do not know in themselves what it is to suffer, suffering is then very awful to them and they badly want to help everyone who ever has to suffer, and they have a deep reverence for anybody who knows really how to always suffer. But when it comes to them to really suffer, they soon begin to lose their fear and tenderness and wonder. Why it isn't so very much to suffer, when even I can bear to do it. It isn't very pleasant to be having all the time, to stand it, but they are not so much wiser after all, all the others just because they know too how to bear it.

Passionate natures who have always made themselves, to suffer, that is all the kind of people who have emotions that come to them as sharp as a sensation, they always get more tender-hearted when they suffer, and it always does them good to suffer. Tender-hearted, unpassionate, and comfortable natures always get much harder when they suffer, for so they lose the fear and reverence and wonder they once had for everybody who ever has to suffer, for now they know themselves what it is to suffer and it is not so awful any longer to them when they know too, just as well as all the others, how to have it.

And so it came in these days to Jeff Campbell. Jeff knew now always, way inside him, what it is to really suffer, and now every day with it, he knew how to understand Melanctha better. Jeff Campbell still loved Melanctha Herbert and he still had a real trust in her and he still had a little hope that some day they would once more get together, but slowly, every day, this hope in him would keep growing always weaker. They still were a good deal of time together, but now they never any more were really trusting with each other. In the days when they used to be together, Jeff had felt he did not know much what was inside Melanctha, but he knew very well, how very deep always was his trust in her; now he knew Melanctha Herbert better, but now he never felt a deep trust in her. Now Jeff never could be really honest with her. He never doubted yet, that she was steady only to him, but somehow he could not believe much really in Melanctha's loving.

Melanctha Herbert was a little angry now when Jeff asked her, "I never give nobody before Jeff, ever more than one chance with me, and I certainly been giving you most a hundred Jeff, you hear me." "And why shouldn't you Melanctha, give me a million, if you really love me!" Jeff flashed out very angry. "I certainly don't know as you deserve that anyways from me, Jeff Campbell." "It ain't deserving, I am ever talking about to you Melanctha. Its loving, and if you are really loving to me you won't certainly never any ways call them chances." "Deed Jeff, you certainly are getting awful wise Jeff now, ain't you, to me." "No I ain't Melanctha, and I ain't jealous either to you. I just am doubting from the way you are always acting to me." "Oh yes Jeff, that's what they all say, the same way, when they certainly got jealousy all through them. You ain't got no cause to be jealous with me Jeff, and I am awful tired of all this talking now, you hear me."

Jeff Campbell never asked Melanctha any more if she loved him. Now things were always getting worse between them. Now Jeff was always very silent with Melanctha. Now Jeff never wanted to be honest to her, and now Jeff never had much to say to her.

Now when they were together, it was Melanctha always did most of the talking. Now she often had other girls there with her. Melanctha was always kind to Jeff Campbell but she never seemed to need to be alone now with him. She always treated Jeff, like her best friend, and she always spoke so to him and yet she never seemed now to very often want to see him.

Every day it was getting harder for Jeff Campbell. It was as if now, when he had learned to really love Melanctha, she did not need any more to have him. Jeff began to know this very well inside him.

Jeff Campbell did not know yet that Melanctha had begun again to wander. Jeff was not very quick to suspect Melanctha. All Jeff knew was, that he did not trust her to be now really loving to him.

Jeff was no longer now in any doubt inside him. He knew very well now he really loved Melanctha. He knew now very well she was not any more a real religion to him. Jeff Campbell knew very well too now inside him, he did not really want Melanctha, now if he could no longer trust her, though he loved her hard and really knew now what it was to suffer.

Every day Melanctha Herbert was less and less near to him. She always was very pleasant in her talk and to be with him, but somehow now it never was any comfort to him.

Melanctha Herbert now always had a lot of friends around her. Jeff Campbell never wanted to be with them. Now Melanctha began to find it, she said it often to him, always harder to arrange to be alone now with him. Sometimes she would be late for him. Then Jeff always would try to be patient in his waiting, for Jeff Campbell knew very well how to remember, and he knew it was only right that he should now endure this from her.

Then Melanctha began to manage often not to see him, and once she went away when she had promised to be there to meet him.

Then Jeff Campbell was really filled up with his anger. Now he knew he could never really want her. Now he knew he never any more could really trust her.

Jeff Campbell never knew why Melanctha had not come to meet him. Jeff had heard a little talking now, about how

Melanctha Herbert had commenced once more to wander. Jeff Campbell still sometimes saw Jane Harden, who always needed a doctor to be often there to help her. Jane Harden always knew very well what happened to Melanctha. Jeff Campbell never would talk to Jane Harden anything about Melanctha. Jeff was always loyal to Melanctha. Jeff never let Jane Harden say much to him about Melanctha, though he never let her know that now he loved her. But somehow Jeff did know now about Melanctha, and he knew about some men that Melanctha met with Rose Johnson very often.

Jeff Campbell would not let himself really doubt Melanctha, but Jeff began to know now very well, he did not want her. Melanctha Herbert did not love him ever, Jeff knew it now, the way he once had thought that she could feel it. Once she had been greater for him than he had thought he could ever know how to feel it. Now Jeff had come to where he could understand Melanctha Herbert. Jeff was not bitter to her because she could not really love him, he was bitter only that he had let himself have a real illusion in him. He was a little bitter too, that he had lost now, what he had always felt real in the world, that had made it for him always full of beauty, and now he had not got this new religion really, and he had lost what he before had to know what was good and had real beauty.

Jeff Campbell was so angry now in him, because he had begged Melanctha always to be honest to him. Jeff could stand it in her not to love him, he could not stand it in her not to be honest to him.

Jeff Campbell went home from where Melanctha had not met him, and he was sore and full of anger in him.

Jeff Campbell could not be sure what to do, to make it right inside him. Surely he must be strong now and cast this loving from him, and yet, was he sure he now had real wisdom in him. Was he sure that Melanctha Herbert never had had a real deep loving for him. Was he sure Melanctha Herbert never had deserved a reverence from him. Always now Jeff had this torment in him, but always now he felt more that Melanctha never had real greatness for him.

Jeff waited to see if Melanctha would send any word to him. Melanctha Herbert never sent a line to him.

At last Jeff wrote his letter to Melanctha. "Dear Melanctha, I certainly do know you ain't been any way sick this last week when you never met me right the way you promised, and never sent me any word to say why you acted a way you certainly never could think was the right way you should do it to me. Jane Harden said she saw you that day and you went out walking with some people you like now to be with. Don't be misunderstanding me now any more Melanctha. I love you now because that's my slow way to learn what you been teaching, but I know now you certainly never had what seems to me real kind of feeling. I don't love you Melanctha any more now like a real religion, because now I know you are just made like all us others. I know now no man can ever really hold you because no man can ever be real to trust in you, because you mean right Melanctha, but you never can remember, and so you certainly never have got any way to be honest. So please you understand me right now Melanctha, it never is I don't know how to love you. I do know now how to love you, Melanctha, really. You sure do know that, Melanctha, in me. You certainly always can trust me. And so now Melanctha, I can say to you certainly real honest with you, I am better than you are in my right kind of feeling. And so Melanctha, I don't never any more want to be a trouble to you. You certainly make me see things Melanctha, I never any other way could be knowing. You been very good and patient to me, when I was certainly below you in my right feeling. I certainly never have been near so good and patient to you ever any way Melanctha, I certainly know that Melanctha. But Melanctha, with me, it certainly is, always to be good together, two people certainly must be thinking each one as good as the other, to be really loving right Melanctha. And it certainly must never be any kind of feeling, of one only taking, and one only just giving, Melanctha, to me. I know you certainly don't really ever understand me now Melanctha, but that's no matter. I certainly do know what I am feeling now with you real Melanctha. And so good-bye now for good Melanctha. I say I can never ever really trust you real Melanctha, that's only just certainly from your way of not being ever equal in your feeling to anybody real, Melanctha, and your way never to know right how to remember. Many ways I really trust you deep Melanctha, and I certainly do feel deep all the good sweetness you certainly got real in you Melanctha. Its only just in your loving me Melanctha. You never can be equal to me and that way I certainly never can bear any more to have it. And so now Melanctha, I always be your friend, if you need me, and now we never see each other any more to talk to."

And then Jeff Campbell thought and thought, and he could never make any way for him now, to see it different, and so at last he sent this letter to Melanctha.

And now surely it was all over in Jeff Campbell. Surely now he never any more could know Melanctha. And yet, perhaps Melanctha really loved him. And then she would know how much it hurt him never any more, any way, to see her, and perhaps she would write a line to tell him. But that was a foolish way for Jeff ever to be thinking. Of course Melanctha never would write a word to him. It was all over now for always, everything between them, and Jeff felt it a real relief to him.

For many days now Jeff Campbell only felt it as a relief in him. Jeff was all locked up and quiet now inside him. It was all settling down heavy in him, and these days when it was sinking so deep in him, it was only the rest and quiet of not fighting that he could really feel inside him. Jeff Campbell could not think now, or feel anything else in him. He had no beauty nor any goodness to see around him. It was a dull, pleasant kind of quiet he now had inside him. Jeff almost began to love this dull quiet in him, for it was more nearly being free for him than anything he had known in him since Melanctha Herbert first had moved him. He did not find it a real rest yet for him, he had not really conquered what had been working so long in him, he had not learned to see beauty and real goodness yet in what had happened to him, but it was rest even if he was sodden now all through him. Jeff Campbell liked it very well, not to have fighting always going on inside him.

And so Jeff went on every day, and he was quiet, and he began again to watch himself in his working; and he did not see any beauty now around him, and it was dull and heavy always now inside him, and yet he was content to have gone so far in keeping steady to what he knew was the right way for him to come back to, to be regular, and see beauty in every kind of quiet way of living, the way he had always wanted it for himself and for all the colored people. He knew he had lost the sense he once had of joy all through him, but he could work, and perhaps he would bring some real belief back into him about the beauty that he could not now any more see around him.

And so Jeff Campbell went on with his working, and he staid home every evening, and he began again with his reading, and he did not do much talking, and he did not seem to himself to have any kind of feeling.

And one day Jeff thought perhaps he really was forgetting, one day he thought he could soon come back and be happy in his old way of regular and quiet living.

Jeff Campbell had never talked to any one of what had been going on inside him. Jeff Campbell liked to talk and he was honest, but it never came out from him, anything he was ever really feeling, it only came out from him, what it was that he was always thinking. Jeff Campbell always was very proud to hide what he was really feeling. Always he blushed hot to think things he had been feeling. Only to Melanctha Herbert, had it ever come to him, to tell what it was that he was feeling.

And so Jeff Campbell went on with this dull and sodden, heavy, quiet always in him, and he never seemed to be able to have any feeling. Only sometimes he shivered hot with shame when he remembered some things he once had been feeling. And then one day it all woke up, and was sharp in him.

Dr. Campbell was just then staying long times with a sick man who might soon be dying. One day the sick man was resting. Dr. Campbell went to the window to look out a little, while he was waiting. It was very early now in the southern springtime. The trees were just beginning to get the little zig-zag crinkles in them, which the young buds always give them. The air was soft and moist and pleasant to them. The earth was wet and rich and smelling for them. The birds were making sharp fresh noises all around them. The wind was very gentle and yet urgent to them. And the buds and the long earthworms, and the negroes, and all the kinds of children, were coming out every minute farther into the new spring, watery, southern sunshine.

Jeff Campbell too began to feel a little his old joy inside him. The sodden quiet began to break up in him. He leaned far out of the window to mix it all up with him. His heart went sharp and then it almost stopped inside him. Was it Melanctha Herbert he had just seen passing by him? Was it Melanctha, or was it just some other girl, who made him feel so bad inside him? Well, it was no matter, Melanctha was there in the world around him, he did certainly always know that in him. Melanctha Herbert was always in the same town with him, and he could never any more feel her near him. What a fool he was to throw her from him. Did he know she did not really love him. Suppose Melanctha was now suffering through him. Suppose she really would be glad to see him. And did anything else he did, really mean anything now to him? What a fool he was to cast her from him. And yet did Melanctha Herbert want him, was she honest to him, had Melanctha ever loved him, and did Melanctha now suffer by him? Oh! Oh! Oh! and the bitter water once more rose up in him.

All that long day, with the warm moist young spring stirring in him, Jeff Campbell worked, and thought, and beat his breast, and wandered, and spoke aloud, and was silent, and was certain, and then in doubt and then keen to surely feel, and then all sodden in him; and he walked, and he sometimes ran fast to lose himself in his rushing, and he bit his nails to pain and bleeding, and he tore his hair so that he could be sure he was really feeling, and he never could know what it was right, he now should be doing. And then late that night he wrote it all out to Melanctha Herbert, and he made himself quickly send it without giving himself any time to change it.

"It has come to me strong to-day Melanctha, perhaps I am wrong the way I now am thinking. Perhaps you do want me badly to be with you. Perhaps I have hurt you once again the way I used to. I certainly Melanctha, if I ever think that really, I certainly do want bad not to be wrong now ever any more to you. If you do feel the way to-day it came to me strong may-be you are feeling, then say so Melanctha to me, and I come again to see you. If not, don't say anything any more ever to me. I don't want ever to be bad to you Melanctha, really. I never want ever to be a bother to you. I never can stand it to think I am wrong; really, thinking you don't want me to come to you. Tell me Melanctha, tell me honest to me, shall I come now any more to see you." "Yes" came the answer from Melanctha, "I be home Jeff to-night to see you."

Jeff Campbell went that evening late to see Melanctha Herbert. As Jeff came nearer to her, he doubted that he wanted really to be with her, he felt that he did not know what it was he now wanted from her. Jeff Campbell knew very well now, way inside him, that they could never talk their trouble out between them. What was it Jeff wanted now to tell Melanctha Herbert? What was it that Jeff Campbell now could tell her? Surely he never now could learn to trust her. Surely Jeff knew very well all that Melanctha always had inside her. And yet it was awful, never any more to see her.

Jeff Campbell went in to Melanctha, and he kissed her, and he held her, and then he went away from her and he stood still and looked at her. "Well Jeff!" "Yes Melanctha!" "Jeff what was it made you act so to me?" "You know very well Melanctha, it's always I am thinking you don't love me, and you are acting to me good out of kindness, and then Melanctha you certainly never did say anything to me why you never came to meet me, as you certainly did promise to me you would that day I never saw you!" "Jeff don't you really know for certain, I always love you?" "No Melanctha, deed I don't know it in me. Deed and certain sure Melanctha, if I only know that in me, I certainly never would give you any bother." "Jeff, I certainly do love you more seems to me always, you certainly had ought to feel that in you." "Sure Melanctha?" "Sure Jeff boy, you know that." "But then Melanctha why did you act so to me?" "Oh Jeff you certainly been such a bother to me. I just had to go away that day Jeff, and I certainly didn't mean not to tell you, and then that letter you wrote came to me and something happened to me. I don't know right what it was Jeff, I just kind of fainted, and what could I do Jeff, you said you certainly never any more wanted to come and see me!" "And no matter Melanctha, even if you knew, it was just killing me to act so to you, you never would have said nothing to me?" "No of course, how could I Jeff when you wrote that way to me. I know how you was feeling Jeff to me, but I certainly couldn't say nothing to you." "Well Melanctha, I certainly know I am right proud too in me, but I certainly never could act so to you Melanctha, if I ever knew any way at all you ever really loved me. No Melanctha darling, you and me certainly don't feel much the same way ever. Any way Melanctha, I certainly do love you true Melanctha." "And I love you too Jeff, even though you don't never certainly seem to believe me." "No I certainly don't any way believe you Melanctha, even when you say it to me. I don't know Melanctha how, but sure I certainly do trust you, only I don't believe now ever in your really being loving to me. I certainly do know you trust me always Melanctha, only somehow it ain't ever all right to me. I certainly don't know any way otherwise Melanctha, how I can say it to you." "Well I certainly can't help you no ways any more Jeff Campbell, though you certainly say it right when you say I trust you Jeff now always. You certainly is the best man Jeff Campbell, I ever can know, to me. I never been anyways thinking it can be ever different to me." "Well you trust me then Melanctha, and I certainly love you Melanctha, and seems like to me Melanctha, you and me had ought to be a little better than we certainly ever are doing now to be together. You certainly do think that way, too, Melanctha to me. But may be you do really love me. Tell me, please, real honest now Melanctha darling, tell me so I really always know it in me, do you really truly love me?" "Oh you stupid, stupid boy, Jeff Campbell. Love you, what do you think makes me always to forgive you. If I certainly didn't always love you Jeff, I certainly never would let you be always being all the time such a bother to me the way you certainly Jeff always are to me. Now don't you dass ever any more say words like that ever to me. You hear me now Jeff, or I do something real bad sometime, so I really hurt you. Now Jeff you just be good to me. You know Jeff how bad I need it, now you should always be good to me!"

Jeff Campbell could not make an answer to Melanctha. What was it he should now say to her? What words could help him to make their feeling any better? Jeff Campbell knew that he had learned to love deeply, that, he always knew very well now in him, Melanctha had learned to be strong to be always trusting, that he knew too now inside him, but Melanctha did not really love him, that he felt always too strong for him. That fact always was there in him, and it always thrust itself firm, between them. And so this talk did not make things really better for them.

Jeff Campbell was never any more a torment to Melanctha, he was only silent to her. Jeff often saw Melanctha and he was very friendly with her and he never any more was a bother to her. Jeff never any more now had much chance to be loving with her. Melanctha never was alone now when he saw her.

Melanctha Herbert had just been getting thick in her trouble with Jeff Campbell, when she went to that church where she first met Rose, who later was married regularly to Sam Johnson. Rose was a good-looking, better kind of black girl, and had been brought up quite like their own child by white folks. Rose was living now with colored people. Rose was staying just then with a colored woman, who had known 'Mis' Herbert and her black husband and this girl Melanctha.

Rose soon got to like Melanctha Herbert and Melanctha now always wanted to be with Rose, whenever she could do it. Melanctha Herbert always was doing everything for Rose that she could think of that Rose ever wanted. Rose always liked to be with nice people who would do things for her. Rose had strong common sense and she was lazy. Rose liked Melanctha Herbert, she had such kind of fine ways in her. Then, too, Rose had it in her to be sorry for the subtle, sweet-natured, docile, intelligent Melanctha Herbert who always was so blue sometimes, and always had had so much trouble. Then, too, Rose could scold Melanctha, for Melanctha Herbert never could know how to keep herself from trouble, and Rose was always strong to keep straight, with her simple selfish wisdom.

But why did the subtle, intelligent, attractive, half white girl Melanctha Herbert, with her sweetness and her power and her wisdom, demean herself to do for and to flatter and to be scolded, by this lazy, stupid, ordinary, selfish black girl. This was a queer thing in Melanctha Herbert.

And so now in these new spring days, it was with Rose that Melanctha began again to wander. Rose always knew very well in herself what was the right way to do when you wandered. Rose knew very well, she was not just any common kind of black girl, for she had been raised by white folks, and Rose always saw to it that she was engaged to him when she had any one man with whom she ever always wandered. Rose always had strong in her the sense for proper conduct. Rose always was telling the complex and less sure Melanctha, what was the right way she should do when she wandered.

Rose never knew much about Jeff Campbell with Melanctha Herbert. Rose had not known about Melanctha Herbert when she had been almost all her time with Dr. Campbell.

Jeff Campbell did not like Rose when he saw her with Melanctha. Jeff would never, when he could help it, meet her. Rose did not think much about Dr. Campbell. Melanctha never talked much about him to her. He was not important now to be with her.

Rose did not like Melanctha's old friend Jane Harden when she saw her. Jane despised Rose for an ordinary, stupid, sullen black girl. Jane could not see what Melanctha could find in that black girl, to endure her. It made Jane sick to see her. But then Melanctha had a good mind, but she certainly never did care much to really use it. Jane Harden now really never cared any more to see Melanctha, though Melanctha still always tried to be good to her. And Rose, she hated that stuck up, mean speaking, nasty, drunk thing, Jane Harden. Rose did not see how Melanctha could bear to ever see her, but Melanctha always was so good to everybody, she never would know how to act to people the way they deserved that she should do it.

Rose did not know much about Melanctha, and Jeff Campbell and Jane Harden. All Rose knew about Melanctha was her old life with her mother and her father. Rose was always glad to be good to poor Melanctha, who had had such an awful time with her mother and her father, and now she was alone and had nobody who could help her. "He was a awful black man to you Melanctha, I like to get my hands on him so he certainly could feel it. I just would Melanctha, now you hear me."

Perhaps it was this simple faith and simple anger and simple moral way of doing in Rose, that Melanctha now found such a comfort to her. Rose was selfish and was stupid and was lazy, but she was decent and knew always what was the right way she should do, and what she wanted, and she certainly did admire how bright was her friend Melanctha Herbert, and she certainly did feel how very much it was she always suffered and she scolded her to keep her from more trouble, and she never was angry when she found some of the different ways Melanctha Herbert sometimes had to do it.

And so always Rose and Melanctha were more and more together, and Jeff Campbell could now hardly ever any more be alone with Melanctha.

Once Jeff had to go away to another town to see a sick man. "When I come back Monday Melanctha, I come Monday evening to see you. You be home alone once Melanctha to see me." "Sure Jeff, I be glad to see you!"

When Jeff Campbell came to his house on Monday there was a note there from Melanctha. Could Jeff come day after to-morrow, Wednesday? Melanctha was so sorry she had to go out that evening. She was awful sorry and she hoped Jeff would not be angry.

Jeff was angry and he swore a little, and then he laughed, and then he sighed. "Poor Melanctha, she don't know any way to be real honest, but no matter, I sure do love her and I be good if only she will let me."

Jeff Campbell went Wednesday night to see Melanctha. Jeff Campbell took her in his arms and kissed her. "I certainly am awful sorry not to see you Jeff Monday, the way I promised, but I just couldn't Jeff, no way I could fix it." Jeff looked at her and then he laughed a little at her. "You want me to believe that really now Melanctha. All right I believe it if you want me to Melanctha. I certainly be good to you to-night the way you like it. I believe you certainly did want to see me Melanctha, and there was no way you could fix it." "Oh Jeff dear," said Melanctha, "I sure was wrong to act so to you. It's awful hard for me ever to say it to you, I have been wrong in my acting to you, but I certainly was bad this time Jeff to you. It do certainly come hard to me to say it Jeff, but I certainly was wrong to go away from you the way I did it. Only you always certainly been so bad Jeff, and such a bother to me, and making everything always so hard for me, and I certainly got some way to do it to make it come back sometimes to you. You bad boy Jeff, now you hear me, and this certainly is the first time Jeff I ever yet said it to anybody, I ever been wrong, Jeff, you hear me!" "All right Melanctha, I sure do forgive you, cause it's certainly the first time I ever heard you say you ever did anything wrong the way you shouldn't," and Jeff Campbell laughed and kissed her, and Melanctha laughed and loved him, and they really were happy now for a little time together.

And now they were very happy in each other and then they were silent and then they became a little sadder and then they were very quiet once more with each other.

"Yes I certainly do love you Jeff!" Melanctha said and she was very dreamy. "Sure, Melanctha." "Yes Jeff sure, but not the way you are now ever thinking. I love you more and more seems to me Jeff always, and I certainly do trust you more and more always to me when I know you. I do love you Jeff, sure yes, but not the kind of way of loving you are ever thinking it now Jeff with me. I ain't got certainly no hot passion any more now in me. You certainly have killed all that kind of feeling now Jeff in me. You certainly do know that Jeff, now the way I am always, when I am loving with you. You certainly do know that Jeff, and that's the way you certainly do like it now in me. You certainly don't mind now Jeff, to hear me say this to you."

Jeff Campbell was hurt so that it almost killed him. Yes he certainly did know now what it was to have real hot love in him, and yet Melanctha certainly was right, he did not deserve she should ever give it to him. "All right Melanctha I ain't ever kicking. I always will give you certainly always everything you want that I got in me. I take anything you want now to give me. I don't say never Melanctha it don't hurt me, but I certainly don't say ever Melanctha it ought ever to be any different to me." And the bitter tears rose up in Jeff Campbell, and they came and choked his voice to be silent, and he held himself hard to keep from breaking.

"Good-night Melanctha," and Jeff was very humble to her. "Good-night Jeff, I certainly never did mean any way to hurt you. I do love you, sure Jeff every day more and more, all the time I know you." "I know Melanctha, I know, it's never nothing to me. You can't help it, anybody ever the way they are feeling. It's all right now Melanctha, you believe me, good-night now Melanctha, I got now to leave you, good-by Melanctha, sure don't look so worried to me, sure Melanctha I come again soon to see you." And then Jeff stumbled down the steps, and he went away fast to leave her.

And now the pain came hard and harder in Jeff Campbell, and he groaned, and it hurt him so, he could not bear it. And the tears came, and his heart beat, and he was hot and worn and bitter in him.

Now Jeff knew very well what it was to love Melanctha. Now Jeff Campbell knew he was really understanding. Now Jeff knew what it was to be good to Melanctha. Now Jeff was good to her always.

Slowly Jeff felt it a comfort in him to have it hurt so, and to be good to Melanctha always. Now there was no way Melanctha ever had had to bear things from him, worse than he now had it in him. Now Jeff was strong inside him. Now with all the pain there was peace in him. Now he knew he was understanding, now he knew he had a hot love in him, and he was good always to Melanctha Herbert who was the one had made him have it. Now he knew he could be good, and not cry out for help to her to teach him how to bear it. Every day Jeff felt himself more a strong man, the way he once had thought was his real self, the way he knew it. Now Jeff Campbell had real wisdom in him, and it did not make him bitter when it hurt him, for Jeff knew now all through him that he was really strong to bear it.

And so now Jeff Campbell could see Melanctha often, and he was patient, and always very friendly to her, and every day Jeff Campbell understood Melanctha Herbert better. And always Jeff saw Melanctha could not love him the way he needed she should do it. Melanctha Herbert had no way she ever really could remember.

And now Jeff knew there was a man Melanctha met very often, and perhaps she wanted to try to have this man to be good, for her. Jeff Campbell never saw the man Melanctha

Herbert perhaps now wanted. Jeff Campbell only knew very well that there was one. Then there was Rose that Melanctha now always had with her when she wandered.

Jeff Campbell was very quiet to Melanctha. He said to her, now he thought he did not want to come any more especially to see her. When they met, he always would be glad to see her, but now he never would go anywhere any more to meet her. Sure he knew she always would have a deep love in him for her. Sure she knew that. "Yes Jeff, I always trust you Jeff, I certainly do know that all right." Jeff Campbell said, all right he never could say anything to reproach her. She knew always that he really had learned all through him how to love her. "Yes, Jeff, I certainly do know that." She knew now she could always trust him. Jeff always would be loyal to her though now she never was any more to him like a religion, but he never could forget the real sweetness in her. That Jeff must remember always, though now he never can trust her to be really loving to any man for always, she never did have any way she ever could remember. If she ever needed anybody to be good to her, Jeff Campbell always would do anything he could to help her. He never can forget the things she taught him so he could be really understanding, but he never any more wants to see her. He be like a brother to her always, when she needs it, and he always will be a good friend to her. Jeff Campbell certainly was sorry never any more to see her, but it was good that they now knew each other really. "Good-by Jeff you always been very good always to me." "Good-by Melanctha you know you always can trust yourself to me." "Yes, I know, I know Jeff, really." "I certainly got to go now Melanctha, from you. I go this time, Melanctha really," and Jeff Campbell went away and this time he never looked back to her. This time Jeff Campbell just broke away and left her.

Jeff Campbell loved to think now he was strong again to be quiet, and to live regular, and to do everything the way he wanted it to be right for himself and all the colored people. Jeff went away for a little while to another town to work there, and he worked hard, and he was very sad inside him, and sometimes the tears would rise up in him, and then he would work hard, and then he would begin once more to see some beauty in the world around him. Jeff had behaved right and he had learned to have a real love in him. That was very good to have inside him.

Jeff Campbell never could forget the sweetness in Melanctha Herbert, and he was always very friendly to her, but they never any more came close to one another. More and more Jeff Campbell and Melanctha fell away from all knowing of each other, but Jeff never could forget Melanctha. Jeff never could forget the real sweetness she had in her, but Jeff never any more had the sense of a real religion for her. Jeff always had strong in him the meaning of all the new kind of beauty Melanctha Herbert once had shown him, and always more and more it helped him with his working for himself and for all the colored people.

Melanctha Herbert, now that she was all through with Jeff Campbell, was free to be with Rose and the new men she met now.

Rose was always now with Melanctha Herbert. Rose never found any way to get excited. Rose always was telling Melanctha Herbert the right way she should do, so that she would not always be in trouble. But Melanctha Herbert could not help it, always she would find new ways to get excited.

Melanctha was all ready now to find new ways to be in trouble. And yet Melanctha Herbert never wanted not to do right. Always Melanctha Herbert wanted peace and quiet, and always she could only find new ways to get excited.

"Melanctha," Rose would say to her, "Melanctha, I certainly have got to tell you, you ain't right to act so with that kind of feller. You better just had stick to black men now, Melanctha, you hear me what I tell you, just the way you always see me do it. They're real bad men, now I tell you Melanctha true, and you better had hear to me. I been raised by real nice kind of white folks, Melanctha, and I certainly knows awful well, soon as ever I can see 'em acting, what is a white man will act decent to you and the kind it ain't never no good to a colored girl to ever go with. Now you know real Melanctha how I always mean right good to you, and you ain't got no way like me Melanctha, what was raised by white folks, to know right what is the way you should be acting with men. I don't never want to see you have bad trouble come hard to you now Melanctha, and so you just hear to me now Melanctha, what I tell you, for I knows it. I don't say never certainly to you Melanctha, you never had ought to have nothing to do ever with no white men, though it ain't never to me Melanctha, the best kind of a way a colored girl can have to be acting, no I never do say to you Melanctha, you hadn't never ought to be with white men, though it ain't never the way I feel it ever real right for a decent colored girl to be always doing, but not never Melanctha, now you hear me, no not never no kind of white men like you been with always now Melanctha when I see you. You just hear to me Melanctha, you certainly had ought to hear to me Melanctha, I say it just like I knows it awful well, Melanctha, and I knows you don't know no better, Melanctha, how to act so, the ways I seen it with them kind of white fellers, them as never can know what to do right by a decent girl they have ever got to be with them. Now you hear to me Melanctha, what I tell you."

And so it was Melanctha Herbert found new ways to be in trouble. But it was not very bad this trouble, for these white men Rose never wanted she should be with, never meant very much to Melanctha. It was only that she liked it to be with them, and they knew all about fine horses, and it was just good to Melanctha, now a little, to feel real reckless with them. But mostly it was Rose and other better kind of colored girls and colored men with whom Melanctha Herbert now always wandered.

It was summer now and the colored people came out into the sunshine, full blown with the flowers. And they shone in the streets and in the fields with their warm joy, and they glistened in their black heat, and they flung themselves free in their wide abandonment of shouting laughter.

It was very pleasant in some ways, the life Melanctha Herbert now led with Rose and all the others. It was not always that Rose had to scold her.

There was not anybody of all these colored people, excepting only Rose, who ever meant much to Melanctha Herbert. But they all liked Melanctha, and the men all liked to see her do things, she was so game always to do anything anybody ever could do, and then she was good and sweet to do anything anybody ever wanted from her.

These were pleasant days then, in the hot southern negro sunshine, with many simple jokes and always wide abandonment of laughter. "Just look at that Melanctha there a running. Don't she just go like a bird when she is flying. Hey Melanctha there, I come and catch you, hey Melanctha, I put salt on your tail to catch you," and then the man would try to catch her, and he would fall full on the earth and roll in an agony of wide-mouthed shouting laughter. And this was the kind of way Rose always liked to have Melanctha do it, to be engaged to him, and to have a good warm nigger time with colored men, not to go about with that kind of white man, never could know how to act right, to any decent kind of girl they could ever get to be with them.

Rose, always more and more, liked Melanctha Herbert better. Rose often had to scold Melanctha Herbert, but that only made her like Melanctha better. And then Melanctha always listened to her, and always acted every way she could to please her. And then Rose was so sorry for Melanctha, when she was so blue sometimes, and wanted somebody should come and kill her.

And Melanctha Herbert clung to Rose in the hope that Rose could save her. Melanctha felt the power of Rose's selfish, decent kind of nature. It was so solid, simple, certain to her. Melanctha clung to Rose, she loved to have her scold her, she always wanted to be with her. She always felt a solid safety in her. Rose always was, in her way, very good to let Melanctha be loving to her. Melanctha never had any way she could really be a trouble to her. Melanctha never had any way that she could ever get real power, to come close inside to her. Melanctha was always very humble to her. Melanctha was always ready to do anything Rose wanted from her. Melanctha needed badly to have Rose always willing to let Melanctha cling to her. Rose was a simple, sullen, selfish, black girl, but she had a solid power in her. Rose had strong the sense of decent conduct, she had strong the sense for decent comfort. Rose always knew very well what it was she wanted, and she knew very well what was the right way to do to get everything she wanted, and she never had any kind of trouble to perplex her. And so the subtle intelligent attractive half white girl Melanctha Herbert loved and did for, and demeaned herself in service to this coarse, decent, sullen, ordinary, black, childish Rose and now this unmoral promiscuous shiftless Rose was to be married to a good man of the negroes, while Melanctha Herbert with her white blood and attraction and her desire for a right position was perhaps never to be really regularly married. Sometimes the thought of how all her world was made filled the complex, desiring Melanctha with despair. She wondered often how she could go on living when she was so blue. Sometimes Melanctha thought she would just kill herself, for sometimes she thought this would be really the best thing for her to do.

Rose was now to be married to a decent good man of the negroes. His name was Sam Johnson, and he worked as a deck-hand on a coasting steamer, and he was very steady, and he got good wages.

Rose first met Sam Johnson at church, the same place where she had met Melanctha Herbert. Rose liked Sam when she saw him, she knew he was a good man and worked hard and got good wages, and Rose thought it would be very nice and very good now in her position to get really, regularly married.

Sam Johnson liked Rose very well and he always was ready to do anything she wanted. Sam was a tall, square shouldered, decent, a serious, straightforward, simple, kindly, colored workman. They got on very well together, Sam and Rose, when they were married. Rose was lazy, but not dirty, and Sam was careful but not fussy. Sam was a kindly, simple, earnest, steady workman, and Rose had good common decent sense in her, of how to live regular, and not to have excitements, and to be saving so you could be always sure to have money, so as to have everything you wanted.

It was not very long that Rose knew Sam Johnson, before they were regularly married. Sometimes Sam went into the country with all the other young church people, and then he would be a great deal with Rose and with her Melanctha Herbert. Sam did not care much about Melanctha Herbert. He liked Rose's ways of doing, always better. Melanctha's mystery had no charm for Sam ever. Sam wanted a nice little house to come to when he was tired from his working, and a little baby all his own he could be good to. Sam Johnson was ready to marry as soon as ever Rose wanted he should do it. And so Sam Johnson and Rose one day had a grand real wedding and were married. Then they furnished completely, a little red brick house and then Sam went back to his work as deck hand on a coasting steamer.

Rose had often talked to Sam about how good Melanctha was and how much she always suffered. Sam Johnson never really cared about Melanctha Herbert, but he always did almost everything Rose ever wanted, and he was a gentle, kindly creature, and so he was very good to Rose's friend Melanctha. Melanctha Herbert knew very well Sam did not like her, and so she was very quiet, and always let Rose do the talking for her. She only was very good to always help Rose, and to do anything she ever wanted from her, and to be very good and listen and be quiet whenever Sam had anything to say to her. Melanctha liked Sam Johnson, and all her life Melanctha loved and wanted good and kind and considerate people, and always Melanctha loved and wanted people to be gentle to her, and always she wanted to be regular, and to have peace and quiet in her, and always Melanctha could only find new ways to be in trouble. And Melanctha needed badly to have Rose, to believe her, and to let her cling to her. Rose was the only steady thing Melanctha had to cling to and so Melanctha demeaned herself to be like a servant, to wait on, and always to be scolded, by this ordinary, sullen, black, stupid, childish woman.

Rose was always telling Sam he must be good to poor Melanctha. "You know Sam," Rose said very often to him, "You certainly had ought to be very good to poor Melanctha, she always do have so much trouble with her. You know Sam how I told you she had such a bad time always with that father, and he was awful mean to her always that awful black man, and he never took no kind of care ever to her, and he never helped her when her mother died so hard, that poor Melanctha. Melanctha's ma you know Sam, always was just real religious. One day Melanctha was real little, and she heard her ma say to her pa, it was awful sad to her, Melanctha had not been the one the Lord had took from them stead of the little brother who was dead in the house there from fever. That hurt Melanctha awful when she heard her ma say it. She never could feel it right, and I don't no ways blame Melanctha, Sam, for not feeling better to her ma always after, though Melanctha, just like always she is, always was real good to her ma after, when she was so sick, and died so hard, and nobody never to help Melanctha do it, and she just all alone to do everything without no help come to her no way, and that ugly awful black man she have for a father never all the time come near her. But that's always the way Melanctha is just doing Sam, the way I been telling to you. She always is being just so good to everybody and nobody ever there to thank her for it. I never did see nobody ever Sam, have such bad luck, seems to me always with them, like that poor Melanctha always has it, and she always so good with it, and never no murmur in her, and never no complaining from her, and just never saying nothing with it. You be real good to her Sam, now you hear me, now you and me is married right together. He certainly was an awful black man to her Sam, that father she had, acting always just like a brute to her and she so game and never to tell anybody how it hurt her. And she so sweet and good always to do anything anybody ever can be wanting. I don't see Sam how some men can be to act so awful. I told you Sam, how once Melanctha broke her arm bad and she was so sick and it hurt her awful and he never would let no doctor come near to her and he do some things so awful to her, she don't never want to tell nobody how bad he hurt her. That's just the way Sam with Melanctha always, you never can know how bad it is, it hurts her. You hear me Sam, you always be real good to her now you and me is married right to each other."

And so Rose and Sam Johnson were regularly married, and Rose sat at home and bragged to all her friends how nice it was to be married really to a husband.

Rose did not have Melanctha to live with her, now Rose was married. Melanctha was with Rose almost as much as ever but it was a little different now their being together.

Rose Johnson never asked Melanctha to live with her in the house, now Rose was married. Rose liked to have Melanctha come all the time to help her, Rose liked Melanctha to be almost always with her, but Rose was shrewd in her simple selfish nature, she did not ever think to ask Melanctha to live with her.

Rose was hard headed, she was decent, and she always knew what it was she needed. Rose needed Melanctha to be with her, she liked to have her help her, the quick, good Melanctha to do for the slow, lazy, selfish, black girl, but Rose could have Melanctha to do for her and she did not need her to live with her.

Sam never asked Rose why she did not have her. Sam always took what Rose wanted should be done for Melanctha, as the right way he should act toward her.

It could never come to Melanctha to ask Rose to let her. It never could come to Melanctha to think that Rose would ask her. It would never ever come to Melanctha to want it, if Rose should ask her, but Melanctha would have done it for the safety she always felt when she was near her. Melanctha Herbert wanted badly to be safe now, but this living with her, that, Rose would never give her. Rose had strong the sense for decent comfort, Rose had strong the sense for proper conduct, Rose had strong the sense to get straight always what she wanted, and she always knew what was the best thing she needed, and always Rose got what she wanted.

And so Rose had Melanctha Herbert always there to help her, and she sat and was lazy and she bragged and she complained a little and she told Melanctha how she ought to do, to get good what she wanted like she Rose always did it, and always Melanctha was doing everything Rose ever needed. "Don't you bother so, doing that Melanctha, I do it or Sam when he comes home to help me. Sure you don't mind lifting it Melanctha? You is very good Melanctha to do it, and when you go out Melanctha, you stop and get some rice to bring me to-morrow when you come in. Sure you won't forget Melanctha. I never see anybody like you Melanctha to always do things so nice for me." And then Melanctha would do some more for Rose, and then very late Melanctha would go home to the colored woman where she lived now.

And so though Melanctha still was so much with Rose Johnson, she had times when she could not stay there. Melanctha now could not really cling there. Rose had Sam,

and Melanctha more and more lost the hold she had had
there.

Melanctha Herbert began to feel she must begin again to
look and see if she could find what it was she had always
wanted. Now Rose Johnson could no longer help her.

And so Melanctha Herbert began once more to wander and
with men Rose never thought it was right she should be with.

One day Melanctha had been very busy with the different
kinds of ways she wandered. It was a pleasant late afternoon
at the end of a long summer. Melanctha was walking along,
and she was free and excited. Melanctha had just parted from
a white man and she had a bunch of flowers he had left with
her. A young buck, a mulatto, passed by and snatched them
from her. "It certainly is real sweet in you sister, to be giving
me them pretty flowers," he said to her.

"I don't see no way it can make them sweeter to have with
you," said Melanctha. "What one man gives, another man had
certainly just as much good right to be taking." "Keep your
old flowers then, I certainly don't never want to have them."
Melanctha Herbert laughed at him and took them. "No, I
didn't nohow think you really did want to have them. Thank
you kindly mister, for them. I certainly always do admire to
see a man always so kind of real polite to people." The man
laughed, "You ain't nobody's fool I can say for you, but you
certainly are a damned pretty kind of girl, now I look at you.
Want men to be polite to you? All right, I can love you, that's
real polite now, want to see me try it." "I certainly ain't got
no time this evening just only left to thank you. I certainly
got to be real busy now, but I certainly always will admire to
see you." The man tried to catch and stop her, Melanctha
Herbert laughed and dodged so that he could not touch her.
Melanctha went quickly down a side street near her and so
the man for that time lost her.

For some days Melanctha did not see any more of her mulatto. One day Melanctha was with a white man and they saw
him. The white man stopped to speak to him. Afterwards
Melanctha left the white man and she then soon met him.
Melanctha stopped to talk to him. Melanctha Herbert soon
began to like him.

Jem Richards, the new man Melanctha had begun to know

now, was a dashing kind of fellow, who had to do with fine horses and with racing. Sometimes Jem Richards would be betting and would be good and lucky, and be making lots of money. Sometimes Jem would be betting badly, and then he would not be having any money.

Jem Richards was a straight man. Jem Richards always knew that by and by he would win again and pay it, and so Jem mostly did win again, and then he always paid it.

Jem Richards was a man other men always trusted. Men gave him money when he lost all his, for they all knew Jem Richards would win again, and when he did win they knew, and they were right, that he would pay it.

Melanctha Herbert all her life had always loved to be with horses. Melanctha liked it that Jem knew all about fine horses. He was a reckless man was Jem Richards. He knew how to win out, and always all her life, Melanctha Herbert loved successful power.

Melanctha Herbert always liked Jem Richards better. Things soon began to be very strong between them.

Jem was more game even than Melanctha. Jem always had known what it was to have real wisdom. Jem had always all his life been understanding.

Jem Richards made Melanctha Herbert come fast with him. He never gave her any time with waiting. Soon Melanctha always had Jem with her. Melanctha did not want anything better. Now in Jem Richards, Melanctha found everything she had ever needed to content her.

Melanctha was now less and less with Rose Johnson. Rose did not think much of the way Melanctha now was going. Jem Richards was all right, only Melanctha never had no sense of the right kind of way she should be doing. Rose often was telling Sam now, she did not like the fast way Melanctha was going. Rose told it to Sam, and to all the girls and men, when she saw them. But Rose was nothing just then to Melanctha. Melanctha Herbert now only needed Jem Richards to be with her.

And things were always getting stronger between Jem Richards and Melanctha Herbert. Jem Richards began to talk now as if he wanted to get married to her. Jem was deep in his love now for her. And as for Melanctha, Jem was all the world now to her. And so Jem gave her a ring, like white folks, to show he was engaged to her, and would by and by be married to her. And Melanctha was filled full with joy to have Jem so good to her.

Melanctha always loved to go with Jem to the races. Jem had been lucky lately with his betting, and he had a swell turn-out to drive in, and Melanctha looked very handsome there beside him.

Melanctha was very proud to have Jem Richards want her. Melanctha loved it the way Jem knew how to do it. Melanctha loved Jem and loved that he should want her. She loved it too, that he wanted to be married to her. Jem Richards was a straight decent man, whom other men always looked up to and trusted. Melanctha needed badly a man to content her.

Melanctha's joy made her foolish. Melanctha told everybody about how Jem Richards, that swell man who owned all those fine horses and was so game, nothing ever scared him, was engaged to be married to her, and that was the ring he gave her.

Melanctha let out her joy very often to Rose Johnson. Melanctha had begun again now to go there.

Melanctha's love for Jem made her foolish. Melanctha had to have some one always now to talk to and so she went often to Rose Johnson.

Melanctha put all herself into Jem Richards. She was mad and foolish in the joy she had there.

Rose never liked the way Melanctha did it. "No Sam I don't say never Melanctha ain't engaged to Jem Richards the way she always says it, and Jem he is all right for that kind of a man he is, though he do think himself so smart and like he owns the earth and everything he can get with it, and he sure gave Melanctha a ring like he really meant he should be married right soon with it, only Sam, I don't ever like it the way Melanctha is going. When she is engaged to him Sam, she ain't not right to take on so excited. That ain't no decent kind of a way a girl ever should be acting. There ain't no kind of a man going stand that, not like I knows men Sam, and I sure does know them. I knows them white and I knows them colored, for I was raised by white folks, and they don't none of them like a girl to act so. That's all right to be so when you is just only loving, but it ain't no ways right to be acting so when you is engaged to him, and when he says, all right he get really regularly married to you. You see Sam I am right like I am always and I knows it. Jem Richards, he ain't going to the last to get real married, not if I knows it right, the way Melanctha now is acting to him. Rings or anything ain't nothing to them, and they don't never do no good for them, when a girl acts foolish like Melanctha always now is acting. I certainly will be right sorry Sam, if Melanctha has real bad trouble come now to her, but I certainly don't no ways like it Sam the kind of way Melanctha is acting to him. I don't never say nothing to her Sam. I just listens to what she is saying always, and I thinks it out like I am telling to you Sam but I don't never say nothing no more now to Melanctha. Melanctha didn't say nothing to me about that Jem Richards till she was all like finished with him, and I never did like it Sam, much, the way she was acting, not coming here never when she first ran with those men and met him. And I didn't never say nothing to her, Sam, about it, and it ain't nothing ever to me, only I don't never no more want to say nothing to her, so I just listens to what she got to tell like she wants it. No Sam, I don't never want to say nothing to her. Melanctha just got to go her own way, not as I want to see her have bad trouble ever come hard to her, only it ain't in me never Sam, after Melanctha did so, ever to say nothing more to her how she should be acting. You just see Sam like I tell you, what way Jem Richards will act to her, you see Sam I just am right like I always am when I knows it."

Melanctha Herbert never thought she could ever again be in trouble. Melanctha's joy had made her foolish.

And now Jem Richards had some bad trouble with his betting. Melanctha sometimes felt now when she was with him that there was something wrong inside him. Melanctha knew he had had trouble with his betting but Melanctha never felt that that could make any difference to them.

Melanctha once had told Jem, sure he knew she always would love to be with him, if he was in jail or only just a beggar. Now Melanctha said to him, "Sure you know Jem that it don't never make any kind of difference you're having any kind of trouble, you just try me Jem and be game, don't look so worried to me. Jem sure I know you love me like I love you always, and its all I ever could be wanting Jem to me, just your wanting me always to be with you. I get married Jem to you soon ever as you can want me, if you once say it Jem to me. It ain't nothing to me ever, anything like having any money Jem, why you look so worried to me."

Melanctha Herbert's love had surely made her mad and foolish. She thrust it always deep into Jem Richards and now that he had trouble with his betting, Jem had no way that he ever wanted to be made to feel it. Jem Richards never could want to marry any girl while he had trouble. That was no way a man like him should do it. Melanctha's love had made her mad and foolish, she should be silent now and let him do it. Jem Richards was not a kind of man to want a woman to be strong to him, when he was in trouble with his betting. That was not the kind of a time when a man like him needed to have it.

Melanctha needed so badly to have it, this love which she had always wanted, she did not know what she should do to save it. Melanctha saw now, Jem Richards always had something wrong inside him. Melanctha soon dared not ask him. Jem was busy now, he had to sell things and see men to raise money. Jem could not meet Melanctha now so often.

It was lucky for Melanctha Herbert that Rose Johnson was coming now to have her baby. It had always been understood between them, Rose should come and stay then in the house where Melanctha lived with an old colored woman, so that Rose could have the Doctor from the hospital near by to help her, and Melanctha there to take care of her the way Melanctha always used to do it.

Melanctha was very good now to Rose Johnson. Melanctha did everything that any woman could, she tended Rose, and she was patient, submissive, soothing and untiring, while the sullen, childish, cowardly, black Rosie grumbled, and fussed, and howled, and made herself to be an abomination and like a simple beast.

All this time Melanctha was always being every now and then with Jem Richards. Melanctha was beginning to be stronger with Jem Richards. Melanctha was never so strong and sweet and in her nature as when she was deep in trouble, when she was fighting so with all she had, she could not do any foolish thing with her nature.

Always now Melanctha Herbert came back again to be nearer to Rose Johnson. Always now Melanctha would tell all about her troubles to Rose Johnson. Rose had begun now a little again to advise her.

Melanctha always told Rose now about the talks she had with Jem Richards, talks where they neither of them liked very well what the other one was saying. Melanctha did not know what it was Jem Richards wanted. All Melanctha knew was, he did not like it when she wanted to be good friends and get really married, and then when Melanctha would say, "all right, I never wear your ring no more Jem, we ain't not any more to meet ever like we ever going to get really regular married," then Jem did not like it either. What was it Jem Richards really wanted?

Melanctha stopped wearing Jem's ring on her finger. Poor Melanctha, she wore it on a string she tied around her neck so that she could always feel it, but Melanctha was strong now with Jem Richards, and he never saw it. And sometimes Jem seemed to be awful sorry for it, and sometimes he seemed kind of glad of it. Melanctha never could make out really what it was Jem Richards wanted.

There was no other woman yet to Jem, that Melanctha knew, and so she always trusted that Jem would come back to her, deep in his love, the way once he had had it and had made all the world like she once had never believed anybody could really make it. But Jem Richards was more game than Melanctha Herbert. He knew how to fight to win out, better. Melanctha really had already lost it, in not keeping quiet and waiting for Jem to do it.

Jem Richards was not yet having better luck in his betting. He never before had had such a long time without some good coming to him in his betting. Sometimes Jem talked as if he wanted to go off on a trip somewhere and try some other place for luck with his betting. Jem Richards never talked as if he wanted to take Melanctha with him.

And so Melanctha sometimes was really trusting, and sometimes she was all sick inside her with her doubting. What was it Jem really wanted to do with her? He did not have any other woman, in that Melanctha could be really trusting, and when she said no to him, no she never would come near him, now he did not want to have her, then Jem would change and swear, yes sure he did want her, now and always right here near him, but he never now any more said he wanted to be married soon to her. But then Jem Richards never would marry a girl, he said that very often, when he was in this kind of trouble, and now he did not see any way he could get out of his trouble. But Melanctha ought to wear his ring, sure she knew he never had loved any kind of woman like he loved her. Melanctha would wear the ring a little while, and then they would have some more trouble, and then she would say to him, no she certainly never would any more wear anything he gave her, and then she would wear it on the string so nobody could see it but she could always feel it on her.

Poor Melanctha, surely her love had made her mad and foolish.

And now Melanctha needed always more and more to be with Rose Johnson, and Rose had commenced again to advise her, but Rose could not help her. There was no way now that anybody could advise her. The time when Melanctha could have changed it with Jem Richards was now all past for her. Rose knew it, and Melanctha too, she knew it, and it almost killed her to let herself believe it.

The only comfort Melanctha ever had now was waiting on Rose till she was so tired she could hardly stand it. Always Melanctha did everything Rose ever wanted. Sam Johnson began now to be very gentle and a little tender to Melanctha. She was so good to Rose and Sam was so glad to have her there to help Rose and to do things and to be a comfort to her.

Rose had a hard time to bring her baby to its birth and Melanctha did everything that any woman could.

The baby though it was healthy after it was born did not live long. Rose Johnson was careless and negligent and selfish and when Melanctha had to leave for a few days the baby died. Rose Johnson had liked her baby well enough and perhaps she just forgot it for a while, anyway the child was dead and Rose and Sam were very sorry, but then these things came so often in the negro world in Bridgepoint that they neither of them thought about it very long. When Rose had become strong again she went back to her house with Sam. And Sam Johnson was always now very gentle and kind and good to Melanctha who had been so good to Rose in her bad trouble.

Melanctha Herbert's troubles with Jem Richards were never getting any better. Jem always now had less and less time to be with her. When Jem was with Melanctha now he was good enough to her. Jem Richards was worried with his betting. Never since Jem had first begun to make a living had he ever had so much trouble for such a long time together with his betting. Jem Richards was good enough now to Melanctha but he had not much strength to give her. Melanctha could never any more now make him quarrel with her. Melanctha never now could complain of his treatment of her, for surely, he said it always by his actions to her, surely she must know how a man was when he had trouble on his mind with trying to make things go a little better.

Sometimes Jem and Melanctha had long talks when they neither of them liked very well what the other one was saying, but mostly now Melanctha could not make Jem Richards quarrel with her, and more and more, Melanctha could not find any way to make it right to blame him for the trouble she now always had inside her. Jem was good to her, and she knew, for he told her, that he had trouble all the time now with his betting. Melanctha knew very well that for her it was all wrong inside Jem Richards, but Melanctha had now no way that she could really reach him.

Things between Melanctha and Jem Richards were now never getting any better. Melanctha now more and more needed to be with Rose Johnson. Rose still liked to have Melanctha come to her house and do things for her, and Rose liked to grumble to her and to scold her and to tell Melanctha what was the way Melanctha always should be doing so she could make things come out better and not always be so much in trouble. Sam Johnson in these days was always very good and gentle to Melanctha. Sam was now beginning to be very sorry for her.

Jem Richards never made things any better for Melanctha. Often Jem would talk so as to make Melanctha almost certain that he never any more wanted to have her. Then Melanctha would get very blue, and she would say to Rose, sure she would kill herself, for that certainly now was the best way she could do.

Rose Johnson never saw it the least bit that way. "I don't see Melanctha why you should talk like you would kill yourself just because you're blue. I'd never kill myself Melanctha cause I was blue. I'd maybe kill somebody else but I'd never kill myself. If I ever killed myself, Melanctha it'd be by accident and if I ever killed myself by accident, Melanctha, I'd be awful sorry. And that certainly is the way you should feel it Melanctha, now you hear me, not just talking foolish like you always do. It certainly is only your way just always being foolish makes you all that trouble to come to you always now, Melanctha, and I certainly right well knows that. You certainly never can learn no way Melanctha ever with all I certainly been telling to you, ever since I know you good, that it ain't never no way like you do always is the right way you be acting ever and talking, the way I certainly always have seen you do so Melanctha always. I certainly am right Melanctha about them ways you have to do it, and I knows it; but you certainly never can noways learn to act right Melanctha, I certainly do know that, I certainly do my best Melanctha to help you with it only you certainly never do act right Melanctha, not to nobody ever, I can see it. You never act right by me Melanctha no more than by everybody. I never say nothing to you Melanctha when you do so, for I certainly never do like it when I just got to say it to you, but you just certainly done with that Jem Richards you always say wanted real bad to be married to you, just like I always said to Sam you certainly was going to do it. And I certainly am real kind of sorry like for you Melanctha, but you certainly had ought to have come to see me to talk to you, when you first was engaged to him so I could show you, and now you got all this trouble come to you Melanctha like I certainly know you always catch it. It certainly ain't never Melanctha I ain't real sorry to see trouble come so hard to you, but I certainly can see Melanctha it all is always just the way you always be having it in you not never to do right. And now you always talk like you just kill yourself because you are so blue, that certainly never is Melanctha, no kind of a way for any decent kind of a girl to do."

Rose had begun to be strong now to scold Melanctha and she was impatient very often with her, but Rose could now never any more be a help to her. Melanctha Herbert never could know now what it was right she should do. Melanctha always wanted to have Jem Richards with her and now he never seemed to want her, and what could Melanctha do. Surely she was right now when she said she would just kill herself, for that was the only way now she could do.

Sam Johnson always, more and more, was good and gentle to Melanctha. Poor Melanctha, she was so good and sweet to do anything anybody ever wanted, and Melanctha always liked it if she could have peace and quiet, and always she could only find new ways to be in trouble. Sam often said this now to Rose about Melanctha.

"I certainly don't never want Sam to say bad things about Melanctha, for she certainly always do have most awful kind of trouble come hard to her, but I never can say I like it real right Sam the way Melanctha always has to do it. Its now just the same with her like it is always she has got to do it, now the way she is with that Jem Richards. He certainly now don't never want to have her but Melanctha she ain't got no right kind of spirit. No Sam I don't never like the way any more Melanctha is acting to him, and then Sam, she ain't never real right honest, the way she always should do it. She certainly just don't kind of never Sam tell right what way she is doing with it. I don't never like to say nothing Sam no more to her about the way she always has to be acting. She always say, yes all right Rose, I do the way you say it, and then Sam she don't never noways do it. She certainly is right sweet and good, Sam, is Melanctha, nobody ever can hear me say she ain't always ready to do things for everybody any way she ever can see to do it, only Sam some ways she never does act real right ever, and some ways, Sam, she ain't ever real honest with it. And Sam sometimes I hear awful kind of things she been doing, some girls know about her how she does it, and sometimes they tell me what kind of ways she has to do it, and Sam it certainly do seem to me like more and more I certainly am awful afraid Melanctha never will come to any good. And then Sam, sometimes, you hear it, she always talk like she kill herself all the time she is so blue, and Sam that certainly never is no kind of way any decent girl ever had ought to do. You see Sam, how I am right like I always is when I knows it. You just be careful, Sam, now you hear me, you be careful Sam sure, I tell you, Melanctha more and more I see her I certainly do feel Melanctha no way is really honest. You be careful, Sam now, like I tell you, for I knows it, now you hear to me, Sam, what I tell you, for I certainly always is right, Sam, when I knows it."

At first Sam tried a little to defend Melanctha, and Sam always was good and gentle to her, and Sam liked the ways Melanctha had to be quiet to him, and to always listen as if she was learning, when she was there and heard him talking, and then Sam liked the sweet way she always did everything so nicely for him; but Sam never liked to fight with anybody ever, and surely Rose knew best about Melanctha and anyway Sam never did really care much about Melanctha. Her mystery never had had any interest for him. Sam liked it that she was sweet to him and that she always did everything Rose ever wanted that she should be doing, but Melanctha never could be important to him. All Sam ever wanted was to have a little house and to live regular and to work hard and to come home to his dinner, when he was tired with his working and by and by he wanted to have some children all his own to be good to, and so Sam was real sorry for Melanctha, she was so good and so sweet always to them, and Jem Richards was a bad man to behave so to her, but that was always the way a girl got it when she liked that kind of a fast fellow. Anyhow Melanctha was Rose's friend, and Sam never cared to have anything to do with the kind of trouble always came to women, when they wanted to have men, who never could know how to behave good and steady to their women.

And so Sam never said much to Rose about Melanctha. Sam was always very gentle to her, but now he began less and less to see her. Soon Melanctha never came any more to the house to see Rose and Sam never asked Rose anything about her.

Melanctha Herbert was beginning now to come less and less to the house to be with Rose Johnson. This was because Rose seemed always less and less now to want her, and Rose would not let Melanctha now do things for her. Melanctha was always humble to her and Melanctha always wanted in every way she could to do things for her. Rose said no, she guessed she do that herself like she likes to have it better. Melanctha is real good to stay so long to help her, but Rose guessed perhaps Melanctha better go home now, Rose don't need nobody to help her now, she is feeling real strong, not like just after she had all that trouble with the baby, and then Sam, when he comes home for his dinner he likes it when Rose is all alone there just to give him his dinner. Sam always is so tired now, like he always is in the summer, so many people always on the steamer, and they make so much work so Sam is real tired now, and he likes just to eat his dinner and never have people in the house to be a trouble to him.

Each day Rose treated Melanctha more and more as if she never wanted Melanctha any more to come there to the house to see her. Melanctha dared not ask Rose why she acted in this way to her. Melanctha badly needed to have Rose always there to save her. Melanctha wanted badly to cling to her and Rose had always been so solid for her. Melanctha did not dare to ask Rose if she now no longer wanted her to come and see her.

Melanctha now never any more had Sam to be gentle to her. Rose always sent Melanctha away from her before it was time for Sam to come home to her. One day Melanctha had stayed a little longer, for Rose that day had been good to let Melanctha begin to do things for her. Melanctha then left her and Melanctha met Sam Johnson who stopped a minute to speak kindly to her.

The next day Rose Johnson would not let Melanctha come in to her. Rose stood on the steps, and there she told Melanctha what she thought now of her.

"I guess Melanctha it certainly ain't no ways right for you to come here no more just to see me. I certainly don't Melanctha no ways like to be a trouble to you. I certainly think Melanctha I get along better now when I don't have nobody like you are, always here to help me, and Sam he do so good now with his working, he pay a little girl something to come every day to help me. I certainly do think Melanctha I don't never want you no more to come here just to see me." "Why Rose, what I ever done to you, I certainly don't think you is right Rose to be so bad now to me." "I certainly

don't no ways Melanctha Herbert think you got any right ever
to be complaining the way I been acting to you. I certainly
never do think Melanctha Herbert, you hear to me, nobody
ever been more patient to you than I always been to like you,
only Melanctha, I hear more things now so awful bad about
you, everybody always is telling to me what kind of a way you
always have been doing so much, and me always so good to
you, and you never no ways, knowing how to be honest to
me. No Melanctha it ain't ever in me, not to want you to have
good luck come to you, and I like it real well Melanctha when
you some time learn how to act the way it is decent and right
for a girl to be doing, but I don't no ways ever like it the kind
of things everybody tell me now about you. No Melanctha, I
can't never any more trust you. I certainly am real sorry to
have never any more to see you, but there ain't no other way,
I ever can be acting to you. That's all I ever got any more to
say to you now Melanctha." "But Rose, deed; I certainly
don't know, no more than the dead, nothing I ever done to
make you act so to me. Anybody say anything bad about me
Rose, to you, they just a pack of liars to you, they certainly is
Rose, I tell you true. I certainly never done nothing I ever
been ashamed to tell you. Why you act so bad to me Rose.
Sam he certainly don't think ever like you do, and Rose I
always do everything I can, you ever want me to do for you."
"It ain't never no use standing there talking, Melanctha
Herbert. I just can tell it to you, and Sam, he don't know
nothing about women ever the way they can be acting. I certainly am very sorry Melanctha, to have to act so now to you,
but I certainly can't do no other way with you, when you do
things always so bad, and everybody is talking so about you.
It ain't no use to you to stand there and say it different to
me Melanctha. I certainly am always right Melanctha Herbert,
the way I certainly always have been when I knows it, to you.
No Melanctha, it just is, you never can have no kind of a way
to act right, the way a decent girl has to do, and I done my
best always to be telling it to you Melanctha Herbert, but it
don't never do no good to tell nobody how to act right; they
certainly never can learn when they ain't got no sense right
to know it, and you never have no sense right Melanctha to
be honest, and I ain't never wishing no harm to you ever

Melanctha Herbert, only I don't never want any more to see you come here. I just say to you now, like I always been saying to you, you don't know never the right way, any kind of decent girl has to be acting, and so Melanctha Herbert, me and Sam, we don't never any more want you to be setting your foot in my house here Melanctha Herbert, I just tell you. And so you just go along now, Melanctha Herbert, you hear me, and I don't never wish no harm to come to you."

Rose Johnson went into her house and closed the door behind her. Melanctha stood like one dazed, she did not know how to bear this blow that almost killed her. Slowly then Melanctha went away without even turning to look behind her.

Melanctha Herbert was all sore and bruised inside her. Melanctha had needed Rose always to believe her, Melanctha needed Rose always to let her cling to her, Melanctha wanted badly to have somebody who could make her always feel a little safe inside her, and now Rose had sent her from her. Melanctha wanted Rose more than she had ever wanted all the others. Rose always was so simple, solid, decent, for her. And now Rose had cast her from her. Melanctha was lost, and all the world went whirling in a mad weary dance around her.

Melanctha Herbert never had any strength alone ever to feel safe inside her. And now Rose Johnson had cast her from her, and Melanctha could never any more be near her. Melanctha Herbert knew now, way inside her, that she was lost, and nothing any more could ever help her.

Melanctha went that night to meet Jem Richards who had promised to be at the old place to meet her. Jem Richards was absent in his manner to her. By and by he began to talk to her, about the trip he was going to take soon, to see if he could get some luck back in his betting. Melanctha trembled, was Jem too now going to leave her. Jem Richards talked some more then to her, about the bad luck he always had now, and how he needed to go away to see if he could make it come out any better.

Then Jem stopped, and then he looked straight at Melanctha.

"Tell me Melanctha right and true, you don't care really nothing more about me now Melanctha," he said to her.

"Why you ask me that, Jem Richards," said Melanctha.

"Why I ask you that Melanctha, God Almighty, because I just don't give a damn now for you any more Melanctha. That the reason I was asking."

Melanctha never could have for this an answer. Jem Richards waited and then he went away and left her.

Melanctha Herbert never again saw Jem Richards. Melanctha never again saw Rose Johnson, and it was hard to Melanctha never any more to see her. Rose Johnson had worked in to be the deepest of all Melanctha's emotions.

"No, I don't never see Melanctha Herbert no more now," Rose would say to anybody who asked her about Melanctha. "No, Melanctha she never comes here no more now, after we had all that trouble with her acting so bad with them kind of men she liked so much to be with. She don't never come to no good Melanctha Herbert don't, and me and Sam don't want no more to see her. She didn't do right ever the way I told her. Melanctha just wouldn't, and I always said it to her, if she don't be more kind of careful, the way she always had to be acting, I never did want no more she should come here in my house no more to see me. I ain't no ways ever against any girl having any kind of a way, to have a good time like she wants it, but not that kind of a way Melanctha always had to do it. I expect some day Melanctha kill herself, when she act so bad like she do always, and then she get so awful blue. Melanctha always says that's the only way she ever can think it a easy way for her to do. No, I always am real sorry for Melanctha, she never was no just common kind of nigger, but she don't never know not with all the time I always was telling it to her, no she never no way could learn, what was the right way she should do. I certainly don't never want no kind of harm to come bad to Melanctha, but I certainly do think she will most kill herself some time, the way she always say it would be easy way for her to do. I never see nobody ever could be so awful blue."

But Melanctha Herbert never really killed herself because she was so blue, though often she thought this would be really the best way for her to do. Melanctha never killed herself, she only got a bad fever and went into the hospital where they took good care of her and cured her.

When Melanctha was well again, she took a place and began to work and to live regular. Then Melanctha got very sick again, she began to cough and sweat and be so weak she could not stand to do her work.

Melanctha went back to the hospital, and there the Doctor told her she had the consumption, and before long she would surely die. They sent her where she would be taken care of, a home for poor consumptives, and there Melanctha stayed until she died.

The Gentle Lena

LENA WAS patient, gentle, sweet and german. She had been a servant for four years and had liked it very well.

Lena had been brought from Germany to Bridgepoint by a cousin and had been in the same place there for four years.

This place Lena had found very good. There was a pleasant, unexacting mistress and her children, and they all liked Lena very well.

There was a cook there who scolded Lena a great deal but Lena's german patience held no suffering and the good incessant woman really only scolded so for Lena's good.

Lena's german voice when she knocked and called the family in the morning was as awakening, as soothing, and as appealing, as a delicate soft breeze in midday, summer. She stood in the hallway every morning a long time in her unexpectant and unsuffering german patience calling to the young ones to get up. She would call and wait a long time and then call again, always even, gentle, patient, while the young ones fell back often into that precious, tense, last bit of sleeping that gives a strength of joyous vigor in the young, over them that have come to the readiness of middle age, in their awakening.

Lena had good hard work all morning, and on the pleasant, sunny afternoons she was sent out into the park to sit and watch the little two year old girl baby of the family.

The other girls, all them that make the pleasant, lazy crowd, that watch the children in the sunny afternoons out in the park, all liked the simple, gentle, german Lena very well. They all, too, liked very well to tease her, for it was so easy to make her mixed and troubled, and all helpless, for she could never learn to know just what the other quicker girls meant by the queer things they said.

The two or three of these girls, the ones that Lena always sat with, always worked together to confuse her. Still it was pleasant, all this life for Lena.

The little girl fell down sometimes and cried, and then Lena had to soothe her. When the little girl would drop her hat,

Lena had to pick it up and hold it. When the little girl was bad and threw away her playthings, Lena told her she could not have them and took them from her to hold until the little girl should need them.

It was all a peaceful life for Lena, almost as peaceful as a pleasant leisure. The other girls, of course, did tease her, but then that only made a gentle stir within her.

Lena was a brown and pleasant creature, brown as blonde races often have them brown, brown, not with the yellow or the red or the chocolate brown of sun burned countries, but brown with the clear color laid flat on the light toned skin beneath, the plain, spare brown that makes it right to have been made with hazel eyes, and not too abundant straight, brown hair, hair that only later deepens itself into brown from the straw yellow of a german childhood.

Lena had the flat chest, straight back and forward falling shoulders of the patient and enduring working woman, though her body was now still in its milder girlhood and work had not yet made these lines too clear.

The rarer feeling that there was with Lena, showed in all the even quiet of her body movements, but in all it was the strongest in the patient, old-world ignorance, and earth made pureness of her brown, flat, soft featured face. Lena had eyebrows that were a wondrous thickness. They were black, and spread, and very cool, with their dark color and their beauty, and beneath them were her hazel eyes, simple and human, with the earth patience of the working, gentle, german woman.

Yes it was all a peaceful life for Lena. The other girls, of course, did tease her, but then that only made a gentle stir within her.

"What you got on your finger Lena," Mary, one of the girls she always sat with, one day asked her. Mary was good natured, quick, intelligent and Irish.

Lena had just picked up the fancy paper made accordion that the little girl had dropped beside her, and was making it squeak sadly as she pulled it with her brown, strong, awkward finger.

"Why, what is it, Mary, paint?" said Lena, putting her finger to her mouth to taste the dirt spot.

"That's awful poison Lena, don't you know?" said Mary, "that green paint that you just tasted."

Lena had sucked a good deal of the green paint from her finger. She stopped and looked hard at the finger. She did not know just how much Mary meant by what she said.

"Ain't it poison, Nellie, that green paint, that Lena sucked just now," said Mary. "Sure it is Lena, its real poison, I ain't foolin' this time anyhow."

Lena was a little troubled. She looked hard at her finger where the paint was, and she wondered if she had really sucked it.

It was still a little wet on the edges and she rubbed it off a long time on the inside of her dress, and in between she wondered and looked at the finger and thought, was it really poison that she had just tasted.

"Ain't it too bad, Nellie, Lena should have sucked that," Mary said.

Nellie smiled and did not answer. Nellie was dark and thin, and looked Italian. She had a big mass of black hair that she wore high up on her head, and that made her face look very fine.

Nellie always smiled and did not say much, and then she would look at Lena to perplex her.

And so they all three sat with their little charges in the pleasant sunshine a long time. And Lena would often look at her finger and wonder if it was really poison that she had just tasted and then she would rub her finger on her dress a little harder.

Mary laughed at her and teased her and Nellie smiled a little and looked queerly at her.

Then it came time, for it was growing cooler, for them to drag together the little ones, who had begun to wander, and to take each one back to its own mother. And Lena never knew for certain whether it was really poison, that green stuff that she had tasted.

During these four years of service, Lena always spent her Sundays out at the house of her aunt, who had brought her four years before to Bridgepoint.

This aunt, who had brought Lena, four years before, to

Bridgepoint, was a hard, ambitious, well meaning, german woman. Her husband was a grocer in the town, and they were very well to do. Mrs. Haydon, Lena's aunt, had two daughters who were just beginning as young ladies, and she had a little boy who was not honest and who was very hard to manage.

Mrs. Haydon was a short, stout, hard built, german woman. She always hit the ground very firmly and compactly as she walked. Mrs. Haydon was all a compact and well hardened mass, even to her face, reddish and darkened from its early blonde, with its hearty, shiny, cheeks, and doubled chin well covered over with the up-roll from her short, square neck.

The two daughters, who were fourteen and fifteen, looked like unkneaded, unformed mounds of flesh beside her.

The elder girl, Mathilda, was blonde, and slow, and simple, and quite fat. The younger, Bertha, who was almost as tall as her sister, was dark, and quicker, and she was heavy, too, but not really fat.

These two girls the mother had brought up very firmly. They were well taught for their position. They were always both well dressed, in the same kinds of hats and dresses, as is becoming in two german sisters. The mother liked to have them dressed in red. Their best clothes were red dresses, made of good heavy cloth, and strongly trimmed with braid of a glistening black. They had stiff, red felt hats, trimmed with black velvet ribbon, and a bird. The mother dressed matronly, in a bonnet and in black, always sat between her two big daughters, firm, directing, and repressed.

The only weak spot in this good german woman's conduct was the way she spoiled her boy, who was not honest and who was very hard to manage.

The father of this family was a decent, quiet, heavy, and uninterfering german man. He tried to cure the boy of his bad ways, and make him honest, but the mother could not make herself let the father manage, and so the boy was brought up very badly.

Mrs. Haydon's girls were now only just beginning as young ladies, and so to get her niece, Lena, married, was just then the most important thing that Mrs. Haydon had to do.

Mrs. Haydon had four years before gone to Germany to

see her parents, and had taken the girls with her. This visit had been for Mrs. Haydon most successful, though her children had not liked it very well.

Mrs. Haydon was a good and generous woman, and she patronized her parents grandly, and all the cousins who came from all about to see her. Mrs. Haydon's people were of the middling class of farmers. They were not peasants, and they lived in a town of some pretension, but it all seemed very poor and smelly to Mrs. Haydon's american born daughters.

Mrs. Haydon liked it all. It was familiar, and then here she was so wealthy and important. She listened and decided, and advised all of her relations how to do things better. She arranged their present and their future for them, and showed them how in the past they had been wrong in all their methods.

Mrs. Haydon's only trouble was with her two daughters, whom she could not make behave well to her parents. The two girls were very nasty to all their numerous relations. Their mother could hardly make them kiss their grandparents, and every day the girls would get a scolding. But then Mrs. Haydon was so very busy that she did not have time to really manage her stubborn daughters.

These hard working, earth-rough german cousins were to these american born children, ugly and dirty, and as far below them as were italian or negro workmen, and they could not see how their mother could ever bear to touch them, and then all the women dressed so funny, and were worked all rough and different.

The two girls stuck up their noses at them all, and always talked in English to each other about how they hated all these people and how they wished their mother would not do so. The girls could talk some German, but they never chose to use it.

It was her eldest brother's family that most interested Mrs. Haydon. Here there were eight children, and out of the eight, five of them were girls.

Mrs. Haydon thought it would be a fine thing to take one of these girls back with her to Bridgepoint and get her well started. Everybody liked that she should do so, and they were all willing that it should be Lena.

Lena was the second girl in her large family. She was at this time just seventeen years old. Lena was not an important daughter in the family. She was always sort of dreamy and not there. She worked hard and went very regularly at it, but even good work never seemed to bring her near.

Lena's age just suited Mrs. Haydon's purpose. Lena could first go out to service, and learn how to do things, and then, when she was a little older, Mrs. Haydon could get her a good husband. And then Lena was so still and docile, she would never want to do things her own way. And then, too, Mrs. Haydon, with all her hardness had wisdom, and she could feel the rarer strain there was in Lena.

Lena was willing to go with Mrs. Haydon. Lena did not like her german life very well. It was not the hard work but the roughness that disturbed her. The people were not gentle, and the men when they were glad were very boisterous, and would lay hold of her and roughly tease her. They were good people enough around her, but it was all harsh and dreary for her.

Lena did not really know that she did not like it. She did not know that she was always dreamy and not there. She did not think whether it would be different for her away off there in Bridgepoint. Mrs. Haydon took her and got her different kinds of dresses, and then took her with them to the steamer. Lena did not really know what it was that had happened to her.

Mrs. Haydon, and her daughters, and Lena traveled second class on the steamer. Mrs. Haydon's daughters hated that their mother should take Lena. They hated to have a cousin, who was to them, little better than a nigger, and then everybody on the steamer there would see her. Mrs. Haydon's daughters said things like this to their mother, but she never stopped to hear them, and the girls did not dare to make their meaning very clear. And so they could only go on hating Lena hard, together. They could not stop her from going back with them to Bridgepoint.

Lena was very sick on the voyage. She thought, surely before it was over that she would die. She was so sick she could not even wish that she had not started. She could not eat, she could not moan, she was just blank and scared, and sure that every minute she would die. She could not hold herself in, nor help herself in her trouble. She just staid where she had been put, pale, and scared, and weak, and sick, and sure that she was going to die.

Mathilda and Bertha Haydon had no trouble from having Lena for a cousin on the voyage, until the last day that they were on the ship, and by that time they had made their friends and could explain.

Mrs. Haydon went down every day to Lena, gave her things to make her better, held her head when it was needful, and generally was good and did her duty by her.

Poor Lena had no power to be strong in such trouble. She did not know how to yield to her sickness nor endure. She lost all her little sense of being in her suffering. She was so scared, and then at her best, Lena, who was patient, sweet and quiet, had not self-control, nor any active courage.

Poor Lena was so scared and weak, and every minute she was sure that she would die.

After Lena was on land again a little while, she forgot all her bad suffering. Mrs. Haydon got her the good place, with the pleasant unexacting mistress, and her children, and Lena began to learn some English and soon was very happy and content.

All her Sundays out Lena spent at Mrs. Haydon's house. Lena would have liked much better to spend her Sundays with the girls she always sat with, and who often asked her, and who teased her and made a gentle stir within her, but it never came to Lena's unexpectant and unsuffering german nature to do something different from what was expected of her, just because she would like it that way better. Mrs. Haydon had said that Lena was to come to her house every other Sunday, and so Lena always went there.

Mrs. Haydon was the only one of her family who took any interest in Lena. Mr. Haydon did not think much of her. She was his wife's cousin and he was good to her, but she was for him stupid, and a little simple, and very dull, and sure some day to need help and to be in trouble. All young poor relations, who were brought from Germany to Bridgepoint were sure, before long, to need help and to be in trouble.

The little Haydon boy was always very nasty to her. He was

a hard child for any one to manage, and his mother spoiled him very badly. Mrs. Haydon's daughters as they grew older did not learn to like Lena any better. Lena never knew that she did not like them either. She did not know that she was only happy with the other quicker girls, she always sat with in the park, and who laughed at her and always teased her.

Mathilda Haydon, the simple, fat, blonde, older daughter felt very badly that she had to say that this was her cousin Lena, this Lena who was little better for her than a nigger. Mathilda was an overgrown, slow, flabby, blonde, stupid, fat girl, just beginning as a woman; thick in her speech and dull and simple in her mind, and very jealous of all her family and of other girls, and proud that she could have good dresses and new hats and learn music, and hating very badly to have a cousin who was a common servant. And then Mathilda remembered very strongly that dirty nasty place that Lena came from and that Mathilda had so turned up her nose at, and where she had been made so angry because her mother scolded her and liked all those rough cow-smelly people.

Then, too, Mathilda would get very mad when her mother had Lena at their parties, and when she talked about how good Lena was, to certain german mothers in whose sons, perhaps, Mrs. Haydon might find Lena a good husband. All this would make the dull, blonde, fat Mathilda very angry. Sometimes she would get so angry that she would, in her thick, slow way, and with jealous anger blazing in her light blue eyes, tell her mother that she did not see how she could like that nasty Lena; and then her mother would scold Mathilda, and tell her that she knew her cousin Lena was poor and Mathilda must be good to poor people.

Mathilda Haydon did not like relations to be poor. She told all her girl friends what she thought of Lena, and so the girls would never talk to Lena at Mrs. Haydon's parties. But Lena in her unsuffering and unexpectant patience never really knew that she was slighted. When Mathilda was with her girls in the street or in the park and would see Lena, she always turned up her nose and barely nodded to her, and then she would tell her friends how funny her mother was to take care of people like that Lena, and how, back in Germany, all Lena's people lived just like pigs.

The younger daughter, the dark, large, but not fat, Bertha Haydon, who was very quick in her mind, and in her ways, and who was the favorite with her father, did not like Lena, either. She did not like her because for her Lena was a fool and so stupid, and she would let those Irish and Italian girls laugh at her and tease her, and everybody always made fun of Lena, and Lena never got mad, or even had sense enough to know that they were all making an awful fool of her.

Bertha Haydon hated people to be fools. Her father, too, thought Lena was a fool, and so neither the father nor the daughter ever paid any attention to Lena, although she came to their house every other Sunday.

Lena did not know how all the Haydons felt. She came to her aunt's house all her Sunday afternoons that she had out, because Mrs. Haydon had told her she must do so. In the same way Lena always saved all of her wages. She never thought of any way to spend it. The german cook, the good woman who always scolded Lena, helped her to put it in the bank each month, as soon as she got it. Sometimes before it got into the bank to be taken care of, somebody would ask Lena for it. The little Haydon boy sometimes asked and would get it, and sometimes some of the girls, the ones Lena always sat with, needed some more money; but the german cook, who always scolded Lena, saw to it that this did not happen very often. When it did happen she would scold Lena very sharply, and for the next few months she would not let Lena touch her wages, but put it in the bank for her on the same day that Lena got it.

So Lena always saved her wages, for she never thought to spend them, and she always went to her aunt's house for her Sundays because she did not know that she could do anything different.

Mrs. Haydon felt more and more every year that she had done right to bring Lena back with her, for it was all coming out just as she had expected. Lena was good and never wanted her own way, she was learning English, and saving all her wages, and soon Mrs. Haydon would get her a good husband.

All these four years Mrs. Haydon was busy looking around

among all the german people that she knew for the right man to be Lena's husband, and now at last she was quite decided.

The man Mrs. Haydon wanted for Lena was a young german-american tailor, who worked with his father. He was good and all the family were very saving, and Mrs. Haydon was sure that this would be just right for Lena, and then too, this young tailor always did whatever his father and his mother wanted.

This old german tailor and his wife, the father and the mother of Herman Kreder, who was to marry Lena Mainz, were very thrifty, careful people. Herman was the only child they had left with them, and he always did everything they wanted. Herman was now twenty-eight years old, but he had never stopped being scolded and directed by his father and his mother. And now they wanted to see him married.

Herman Kreder did not care much to get married. He was a gentle soul and a little fearful. He had a sullen temper, too. He was obedient to his father and his mother. He always did his work well. He often went out on Saturday nights and on Sundays, with other men. He liked it with them but he never became really joyous. He liked to be with men and he hated to have women with them. He was obedient to his mother, but he did not care much to get married.

Mrs. Haydon and the elder Kreders had often talked the marriage over. They all three liked it very well. Lena would do anything that Mrs. Haydon wanted, and Herman was always obedient in everything to his father and his mother. Both Lena and Herman were saving and good workers and neither of them ever wanted their own way.

The elder Kreders, everybody knew, had saved up all their money, and they were hard, good german people, and Mrs. Haydon was sure that with these people Lena would never be in any trouble. Mr. Haydon would not say anything about it. He knew old Kreder had a lot of money and owned some good houses, and he did not care what his wife did with that simple, stupid Lena, so long as she would be sure never to need help or to be in trouble.

Lena did not care much to get married. She liked her life very well where she was working. She did not think much about Herman Kreder. She thought he was a good man and she always found him very quiet. Neither of them ever spoke much to the other. Lena did not care much just then about getting married.

Mrs. Haydon spoke to Lena about it very often. Lena never answered anything at all. Mrs. Haydon thought, perhaps Lena did not like Herman Kreder. Mrs. Haydon could not believe that any girl not even Lena, really had no feeling about getting married.

Mrs. Haydon spoke to Lena very often about Herman. Mrs. Haydon sometimes got very angry with Lena. She was afraid that Lena, for once, was going to be stubborn, now when it was all fixed right for her to be married.

"Why you stand there so stupid, why don't you answer, Lena," said Mrs. Haydon one Sunday, at the end of a long talking that she was giving Lena about Herman Kreder, and about Lena's getting married to him.

"Yes ma'am," said Lena, and then Mrs. Haydon was furious with this stupid Lena. "Why don't you answer with some sense, Lena, when I ask you if you don't like Herman Kreder. You stand there so stupid and don't answer just like you ain't heard a word what I been saying to you. I never see anybody like you, Lena. If you going to burst out at all, why don't you burst out sudden instead of standing there so silly and don't answer. And here I am so good to you, and find you a good husband so you can have a place to live in all your own. Answer me, Lena, don't you like Herman Kreder? He is a fine young fellow, almost too good for you, Lena, when you stand there so stupid and don't make no answer. There ain't many poor girls that get the chance you got now to get married."

"Why, I do anything you say, Aunt Mathilda. Yes, I like him. He don't say much to me, but I guess he is a good man, and I do anything you say for me to do."

"Well then Lena, why you stand there so silly all the time and not answer when I asked you."

"I didn't hear you say you wanted I should say anything to you. I didn't know you wanted me to say nothing. I do whatever you tell me it's right for me to do. I marry Herman Kreder, if you want me."

And so for Lena Mainz the match was made.

Old Mrs. Kreder did not discuss the matter with her Herman. She never thought that she needed to talk such things over with him. She just told him about getting married to Lena Mainz who was a good worker and very saving and never wanted her own way, and Herman made his usual little grunt in answer to her.

Mrs. Kreder and Mrs. Haydon fixed the day and made all the arrangements for the wedding and invited everybody who ought to be there to see them married.

In three months Lena Mainz and Herman Kreder were to be married.

Mrs. Haydon attended to Lena's getting all the things that she needed. Lena had to help a good deal with the sewing. Lena did not sew very well. Mrs. Haydon scolded because Lena did not do it better, but then she was very good to Lena, and she hired a girl to come and help her. Lena still stayed on with her pleasant mistress, but she spent all her evenings and her Sundays with her aunt and all the sewing.

Mrs. Haydon got Lena some nice dresses. Lena liked that very well. Lena liked having new hats even better, and Mrs. Haydon had some made for her by a real milliner who made them very pretty.

Lena was nervous these days, but she did not think much about getting married. She did not know really what it was, that, which was always coming nearer.

Lena liked the place where she was with the pleasant mistress and the good cook, who always scolded, and she liked the girls she always sat with. She did not ask if she would like being married any better. She always did whatever her aunt said and expected, but she was always nervous when she saw the Kreders with their Herman. She was excited and she liked her new hats, and everybody teased her and every day her marrying was coming nearer, and yet she did not really know what it was, this that was about to happen to her.

Herman Kreder knew more what it meant to be married and he did not like it very well. He did not like to see girls and he did not want to have to have one always near him. Herman always did everything that his father and his mother wanted and now they wanted that he should be married.

Herman had a sullen temper; he was gentle and he never

said much. He liked to go out with other men, but he never wanted that there should be any women with them. The men all teased him about getting married. Herman did not mind the teasing but he did not like very well the getting married and having a girl always with him.

Three days before the wedding day, Herman went away to the country to be gone over Sunday. He and Lena were to be married Tuesday afternoon. When the day came Herman had not been seen or heard from.

The old Kreder couple had not worried much about it. Herman always did everything they wanted and he would surely come back in time to get married. But when Monday night came, and there was no Herman, they went to Mrs. Haydon to tell her what had happened.

Mrs. Haydon got very much excited. It was hard enough to work so as to get everything all ready, and then to have that silly Herman go off that way, so no one could tell what was going to happen. Here was Lena and everything all ready, and now they would have to make the wedding later so that they would know that Herman would be sure to be there.

Mrs. Haydon was very much excited, and then she could not say much to the old Kreder couple. She did not want to make them angry, for she wanted very badly now that Lena should be married to their Herman.

At last it was decided that the wedding should be put off a week longer. Old Mr. Kreder would go to New York to find Herman, for it was very likely that Herman had gone there to his married sister.

Mrs. Haydon sent word around, about waiting until a week from that Tuesday, to everybody that had been invited, and then Tuesday morning she sent for Lena to come down to see her.

Mrs. Haydon was very angry with poor Lena when she saw her. She scolded her hard because she was so foolish, and now Herman had gone off and nobody could tell where he had gone to, and all because Lena always was so dumb and silly. And Mrs. Haydon was just like a mother to her, and Lena always stood there so stupid and did not answer what anybody asked her, and Herman was so silly too, and now his father had to go and find him. Mrs. Haydon did not think that any old people should be good to their children. Their children always were so thankless, and never paid any attention, and older people were always doing things for their good. Did Lena think it gave Mrs. Haydon any pleasure, to work so hard to make Lena happy, and get her a good husband, and then Lena was so thankless and never did anything that anybody wanted. It was a lesson to poor Mrs. Haydon not to do things any more for anybody. Let everybody take care of themselves and never come to her with any troubles; she knew better now than to meddle to make other people happy. It just made trouble for her and her husband did not like it. He always said she was too good, and nobody ever thanked her for it, and there Lena was always standing stupid and not answering anything anybody wanted. Lena could always talk enough to those silly girls she liked so much, and always sat with, but who never did anything for her except to take away her money, and here was her aunt who tried so hard and was so good to her and treated her just like one of her own children and Lena stood there, and never made any answer and never tried to please her aunt, or to do anything that her aunt wanted. "No, it ain't no use your standin' there and cryin', now, Lena. Its too late now to care about that Herman. You should have cared some before, and then you wouldn't have to stand and cry now, and be a disappointment to me, and then I get scolded by my husband for taking care of everybody, and nobody ever thankful. I am glad you got the sense to feel sorry now, Lena, anyway, and I try to do what I can to help you out in your trouble, only you don't deserve to have anybody take any trouble for you. But perhaps you know better next time. You go home now and take care you don't spoil your clothes and that new hat, you had no business to be wearin' that this morning, but you ain't got no sense at all, Lena. I never in my life see anybody be so stupid."

Mrs. Haydon stopped and poor Lena stood there in her hat, all trimmed with pretty flowers, and the tears coming out of her eyes, and Lena did not know what it was that she had done, only she was not going to be married and it was a disgrace for a girl to be left by a man on the very day she was to be married.

Lena went home all alone, and cried in the street car.

Poor Lena cried very hard all alone in the street car. She almost spoiled her new hat with her hitting it against the window in her crying. Then she remembered that she must not do so.

The conductor was a kind man and he was very sorry when he saw her crying. "Don't feel so bad, you get another feller, you are such a nice girl," he said to make her cheerful. "But Aunt Mathilda said now, I never get married," poor Lena sobbed out for her answer. "Why you really got trouble like that," said the conductor, "I just said that now to josh you. I didn't ever think you really was left by a feller. He must be a stupid feller. But don't you worry, he wasn't much good if he could go away and leave you, lookin' to be such a nice girl. You just tell all your trouble to me, and I help you." The car was empty and the conductor sat down beside her to put his arm around her, and to be a comfort to her. Lena suddenly remembered where she was, and if she did things like that her aunt would scold her. She moved away from the man into the corner. He laughed, "Don't be scared," he said, "I wasn't going to hurt you. But you just keep up your spirit. You are a real nice girl, and you'll be sure to get a real good husband. Don't you let nobody fool you. You're all right and I don't want to scare you."

The conductor went back to his platform to help a passenger get on the car. All the time Lena stayed in the street car, he would come in every little while and reassure her, about her not to feel so bad about a man who hadn't no more sense than to go away and leave her. She'd be sure yet to get a good man, she needn't be so worried, he frequently assured her.

He chatted with the other passenger who had just come in, a very well dressed old man, and then with another who came in later, a good sort of a working man, and then another who came in, a nice lady, and he told them all about Lena's having trouble, and it was too bad there were men who treated a poor girl so badly. And everybody in the car was sorry for poor Lena and the workman tried to cheer her, and the old man looked sharply at her, and said she looked like a good girl, but she ought to be more careful and not to be so careless, and things like that would not happen to her, and the nice lady went and sat beside her and Lena liked it, though she shrank away from being near her.

So Lena was feeling a little better when she got off the car, and the conductor helped her, and he called out to her, "You be sure you keep up a good heart now. He wasn't no good that feller and you were lucky for to lose him. You'll get a real man yet, one that will be better for you. Don't you be worried, you're a real nice girl as I ever see in such trouble," and the conductor shook his head and went back into his car to talk it over with the other passengers he had there.

The german cook, who always scolded Lena, was very angry when she heard the story. She never did think Mrs. Haydon would do so much for Lena, though she was always talking so grand about what she could do for everybody. The good german cook always had been a little distrustful of her. People who always thought they were so much never did really do things right for anybody. Not that Mrs. Haydon wasn't a good woman. Mrs. Haydon was a real, good, german woman, and she did really mean to do well by her niece Lena. The cook knew that very well, and she had always said so, and she always had liked and respected Mrs. Haydon, who always acted very proper to her, and Lena was so backward, when there was a man to talk to, Mrs. Haydon did have hard work when she tried to marry Lena. Mrs. Haydon was a good woman, only she did talk sometimes too grand. Perhaps this trouble would make her see it wasn't always so easy to do, to make everybody do everything just like she wanted. The cook was very sorry now for Mrs. Haydon. All this must be such a disappointment, and such a worry to her, and she really had always been very good to Lena. But Lena had better go and put on her other clothes and stop with all that crying. That wouldn't do nothing now to help her, and if Lena would be a good girl, and just be real patient, her aunt would make it all come out right yet for her. "I just tell Mrs. Aldrich, Lena, you stay here yet a little longer. You know she is always so good to you, Lena, and I know she let you, and I tell her all about that stupid Herman Kreder. I got no patience, Lena, with anybody who can be so stupid. You just stop now with your crying, Lena, and take off them good clothes and put them away so you don't spoil them when you need them, and you can help me with the dishes and everything will come off better for you. You see if I ain't right by what I tell you. You just stop crying now Lena quick, or else I scold you."

Lena still choked a little and was very miserable inside her but she did everything just as the cook told her.

The girls Lena always sat with were very sorry to see her look so sad with her trouble. Mary the Irish girl sometimes got very angry with her. Mary was always very hot when she talked of Lena's aunt Mathilda, who thought she was so grand, and had such stupid, stuck up daughters. Mary wouldn't be a fat fool like that ugly tempered Mathilda Haydon, not for anything anybody could ever give her. How Lena could keep on going there so much when they all always acted as if she was just dirt to them, Mary never could see. But Lena never had any sense of how she should make people stand round for her, and that was always all the trouble with her. And poor Lena, she was so stupid to be sorry for losing that gawky fool who didn't ever know what he wanted and just said "ja" to his mamma and his papa, like a baby, and was scared to look at a girl straight, and then sneaked away the last day like as if somebody was going to do something to him. Disgrace, Lena talking about disgrace! It was a disgrace for a girl to be seen with the likes of him, let alone to be married to him. But that poor Lena, she never did know how to show herself off for what she was really. Disgrace to have him go away and leave her. Mary would just like to get a chance to show him. If Lena wasn't worth fifteen like Herman Kreder, Mary would just eat her own head all up. It was a good riddance Lena had of that Herman Kreder and his stingy, dirty parents, and if Lena didn't stop crying about it,—Mary would just naturally despise her.

Poor Lena, she knew very well how Mary meant it all, this she was always saying to her. But Lena was very miserable inside her. She felt the disgrace it was for a decent german girl that a man should go away and leave her. Lena knew very well that her aunt was right when she said the way Herman had acted to her was a disgrace to everyone that knew her. Mary and Nellie and the other girls she always sat with were always very good to Lena but that did not make her trouble any better. It was a disgrace the way Lena had been left, to any decent family, and that could never be made any different to her.

And so the slow days wore on, and Lena never saw her Aunt Mathilda. At last on Sunday she got word by a boy to go and see her aunt Mathilda. Lena's heart beat quick for she was very nervous now with all this that had happened to her. She went just as quickly as she could to see her Aunt Mathilda.

Mrs. Haydon quick, as soon as she saw Lena, began to scold her for keeping her aunt waiting so long for her, and for not coming in all the week to see her, to see if her aunt should need her, and so her aunt had to send a boy to tell her. But it was easy, even for Lena, to see that her aunt was not really angry with her. It wasn't Lena's fault, went on Mrs. Haydon, that everything was going to happen all right for her. Mrs. Haydon was very tired taking all this trouble for her, and when Lena couldn't even take trouble to come and see her aunt, to see if she needed anything to tell her. But Mrs. Haydon really never minded things like that when she could do things for anybody. She was tired now, all the trouble she had been taking to make things right for Lena, but perhaps now Lena heard it she would learn a little to be thankful to her. "You get all ready to be married Tuesday, Lena, you hear me," said Mrs. Haydon to her. "You come here Tuesday morning and I have everything all ready for you. You wear your new dress I got you, and your hat with all them flowers on it, and you be very careful coming you don't get your things all dirty, you so careless all the time, Lena, and not thinking, and you act sometimes you never got no head at all on you. You go home now, and you tell your Mrs. Aldrich that you leave her Tuesday. Don't you go forgetting now, Lena, anything I ever told you what you should do to be careful. You be a good girl, now Lena. You get married Tuesday to Herman Kreder." And that was all Lena ever knew of what had happened all this week to Herman Kreder. Lena forgot there was anything to know about it. She was really to be married Tuesday, and her Aunt Mathilda said she was a good girl, and now there was no disgrace left upon her.

Lena now fell back into the way she always had of being always dreamy and not there, the way she always had been, except for the few days she was so excited, because she had been left by a man the very day she was to have been married. Lena was a little nervous all these last days, but she did not think much about what it meant for her to be married.

Herman Kreder was not so content about it. He was quiet and was sullen and he knew he could not help it. He knew now he just had to let himself get married. It was not that Herman did not like Lena Mainz. She was as good as any other girl could be for him. She was a little better perhaps than other girls he saw, she was so very quiet, but Herman did not like to always have to have a girl around him. Herman had always done everything that his mother and his father wanted. His father had found him in New York, where Herman had gone to be with his married sister.

Herman's father when he had found him coaxed Herman a long time and went on whole days with his complaining to him, always troubled but gentle and quite patient with him, and always he was worrying to Herman about what was the right way his boy Herman should always do, always whatever it was his mother ever wanted from him, and always Herman never made him any answer.

Old Mr. Kreder kept on saying to him, he did not see how Herman could think now, it could be any different. When you make a bargain you just got to stick right to it, that was the only way old Mr. Kreder could ever see it, and saying you would get married to a girl and she got everything all ready, that was a bargain just like one you make in business and Herman he had made it, and now Herman he would just have to do it, old Mr. Kreder didn't see there was any other way a good boy like his Herman had, to do it. And then too that Lena Mainz was such a nice girl and Herman hadn't ought to really give his father so much trouble and make him pay out all that money, to come all the way to New York just to find him, and they both lose all that time from their working, when all Herman had to do was just to stand up, for an hour, and then he would be all right married, and it would be all over for him, and then everything at home would never be any different to him.

And his father went on; there was his poor mother saying always how her Herman always did everything before she ever wanted, and now just because he got notions in him, and wanted to show people how he could be stubborn, he was making all this trouble for her, and making them pay all that money just to run around and find him. "You got no idea Herman, how bad mama is feeling about the way you been acting Herman," said old Mr. Kreder to him. "She says she never can understand how you can be so thankless Herman. It hurts her very much you been so stubborn, and she find you such a nice girl for you, like Lena Mainz who is always just so quiet and always saves up all her wages, and she never wanting her own way at all like some girls are always all the time to have it, and your mama trying so hard, just so you could be comfortable Herman to be married, and then you act so stubborn Herman. You like all young people Herman, you think only about yourself, and what you are just wanting, and your mama she is thinking only what is good for you to have, for you in the future. Do you think your mama wants to have a girl around to be a bother, for herself, Herman. Its just for you Herman she is always thinking, and she talks always about how happy she will be, when she sees her Herman married to a nice girl, and then when she fixed it all up so good for you, so it never would be any bother to you, just the way she wanted you should like it, and you say yes all right, I do it, and then you go away like this and act stubborn, and make all this trouble everybody to take for you, and we spend money, and I got to travel all round to find you. You come home now with me Herman and get married, and I tell your mama she better not say anything to you about how much it cost me to come all the way to look for you—Hey Herman," said his father coaxing, "Hey, you come home now and get married. All you got to do Herman is just to stand up for an hour Herman, and then you don't never to have any more bother to it—Hey Herman!—you come home with me to-morrow and get married. Hey Herman."

Herman's married sister liked her brother Herman, and she had always tried to help him, when there was anything she knew he wanted. She liked it that he was so good and always did everything that their father and their mother wanted, but still she wished it could be that he could have more his own way, if there was anything he ever wanted.

But now she thought Herman with his girl was very funny. She wanted that Herman should be married. She thought it would do him lots of good to get married. She laughed at Herman when she heard the story. Until his father came to find him, she did not know why it was Herman had come just then to New York to see her. When she heard the story she laughed a good deal at her brother Herman and teased him a good deal about his running away, because he didn't want to have a girl to be all the time around him.

Herman's married sister liked her brother Herman, and she did not want him not to like to be with women. He was good, her brother Herman, and it would surely do him good to get married. It would make him stand up for himself stronger. Herman's sister always laughed at him and always she would try to reassure him. "Such a nice man as my brother Herman acting like as if he was afraid of women. Why the girls all like a man like you Herman, if you didn't always run away when you saw them. It do you good really Herman to get married, and then you got somebody you can boss around when you want to. It do you good Herman to get married, you see if you don't like it, when you really done it. You go along home now with papa, Herman and get married to that Lena. You don't know how nice you like it Herman when you try once how you can do it. You just don't be afraid of nothing, Herman. You good enough for any girl to marry, Herman. Any girl be glad to have a man like you to be always with them Herman. You just go along home with papa and try it what I say, Herman. Oh you so funny Herman, when you sit there, and then run away and leave your girl behind you. I know she is crying like anything Herman for to lose you. Don't be bad to her Herman. You go along home with papa now and get married Herman. I'd be awful ashamed Herman, to really have a brother didn't have spirit enough to get married, when a girl is just dying for to have him. You always like me to be with you Herman. I don't see why you say you don't want a girl to be all the time around you. You always been good to me Herman, and I know you always be good to that Lena, and you soon feel just like as if she had always been there with you. Don't act like as if you wasn't a nice strong man, Herman. Really I laugh at you Herman, but you know

I like awful well to see you real happy. You go home and get married to that Lena, Herman. She is a real pretty girl and real nice and good and quiet and she make my brother Herman very happy. You just stop your fussing now with Herman, papa. He go with you to-morrow papa, and you see he like it so much to be married, he make everybody laugh just to see him be so happy. Really truly, that's the way it will be with you Herman. You just listen to me what I tell you Herman." And so his sister laughed at him and reassured him, and his father kept on telling what the mother always said about her Herman, and he coaxed him and Herman never said anything in answer, and his sister packed his things up and was very cheerful with him, and she kissed him, and then she laughed and then she kissed him, and his father went and bought the tickets for the train, and at last late on Sunday he brought Herman back to Bridgepoint with him.

It was always very hard to keep Mrs. Kreder from saying what she thought, to her Herman, but her daughter had written her a letter, so as to warn her not to say anything about what he had been doing, to him, and her husband came in with Herman and said, "Here we are come home mama, Herman and me, and we are very tired it was so crowded coming," and then he whispered to her. "You be good to Herman, mama, he didn't mean to make us so much trouble," and so old Mrs. Kreder, held in what she felt was so strong in her to say to her Herman. She just said very stiffly to him, "I'm glad to see you come home to-day, Herman." Then she went to arrange it all with Mrs. Haydon.

Herman was now again just like he always had been, sullen and very good, and very quiet, and always ready to do whatever his mother and his father wanted. Tuesday morning came, Herman got his new clothes on and went with his father and his mother to stand up for an hour and get married. Lena was there in her new dress, and her hat with all the pretty flowers, and she was very nervous for now she knew she was really very soon to be married. Mrs. Haydon had everything all ready. Everybody was there just as they should be and very soon Herman Kreder and Lena Mainz were married.

When everything was really over, they went back to the Kreder house together. They were all now to live together,

Lena and Herman and the old father and the old mother, in
the house where Mr. Kreder had worked so many years as a
tailor, with his son Herman always there to help him.

Irish Mary had often said to Lena she never did see how
Lena could ever want to have anything to do with Herman
Kreder and his dirty stingy parents. The old Kreders were to
an Irish nature, a stingy, dirty couple. They had not the
free-hearted, thoughtless, fighting, mud bespattered, ragged,
peat-smoked cabin dirt that irish Mary knew and could forgive
and love. Theirs was the german dirt of saving, of being
dowdy and loose and foul in your clothes so as to save them
and yourself in washing, having your hair greasy to save it in
the soap and drying, having your clothes dirty, not in freedom, but because so it was cheaper, keeping the house close
and smelly because so it cost less to get it heated, living so
poorly not only so as to save money but so they should never
even know themselves that they had it, working all the time
not only because from their nature they just had to and because it made them money but also that they never could be
put in any way to make them spend their money.

This was the place Lena now had for her home and to her
it was very different than it could be for an irish Mary. She
too was german and was thrifty, though she was always so
dreamy and not there. Lena was always careful with things
and she always saved her money, for that was the only way she
knew how to do it. She never had taken care of her own
money and she never had thought how to use it.

Lena Mainz had been, before she was Mrs. Herman Kreder,
always clean and decent in her clothes and in her person, but
it was not because she ever thought about it or really needed
so to have it, it was the way her people did in the german
country where she came from, and her Aunt Mathilda and the
good german cook who always scolded, had kept her on and
made her, with their scoldings, always more careful to keep
clean and to wash real often. But there was no deep need in
all this for Lena and so, though Lena did not like the old
Kreders, though she really did not know that, she did not
think about their being stingy dirty people.

Herman Kreder was cleaner than the old people, just because it was his nature to keep cleaner, but he was used to his

mother and his father, and he never thought that they should keep things cleaner. And Herman too always saved all his money, except for that little beer he drank when he went out with other men of an evening the way he always liked to do it, and he never thought of any other way to spend it. His father had always kept all the money for them and he always was doing business with it. And then too Herman really had no money, for he always had worked for his father, and his father had never thought to pay him.

And so they began all four to live in the Kreder house together, and Lena began soon with it to look careless and a little dirty, and to be more lifeless with it, and nobody ever noticed much what Lena wanted, and she never really knew herself what she needed.

The only real trouble that came to Lena with their living all four there together, was the way old Mrs. Kreder scolded. Lena had always been used to being scolded, but this scolding of old Mrs. Kreder was very different from the way she ever before had had to endure it.

Herman, now he was married to her, really liked Lena very well. He did not care very much about her but she never was a bother to him being there around him, only when his mother worried and was nasty to them because Lena was so careless, and did not know how to save things right for them with their eating, and all the other ways with money, that the old woman had to save it.

Herman Kreder had always done everything his mother and his father wanted but he did not really love his parents very deeply. With Herman it was always only that he hated to have any struggle. It was all always all right with him when he could just go along and do the same thing over every day with his working, and not to hear things, and not to have people make him listen to their anger. And now his marriage, and he just knew it would, was making trouble for him. It made him hear more what his mother was always saying, with her scolding. He had to really hear it now because Lena was there, and she was so scared and dull always when she heard it. Herman knew very well with his mother, it was all right if one ate very little and worked hard all day and did not hear her when she scolded, the way Herman always had done before they were so foolish about his getting married and having a girl there to be all the time around him, and now he had to help her so the girl could learn too, not to hear it when his mother scolded, and not to look so scared, and not to eat much, and always to be sure to save it.

Herman really did not know very well what he could do to help Lena to understand it. He could never answer his mother back to help Lena, that never would make things any better for her, and he never could feel in himself any way to comfort Lena, to make her strong not to hear his mother, in all the awful ways she always scolded. It just worried Herman to have it like that all the time around him. Herman did not know much about how a man could make a struggle with a mother, to do much to keep her quiet, and indeed Herman never knew much how to make a struggle against anyone who really wanted to have anything very badly. Herman all his life never wanted anything so badly, that he would really make a struggle against any one to get it. Herman all his life only wanted to live regular and quiet, and not talk much and to do the same way every day like every other with his working. And now his mother had made him get married to this Lena and now with his mother making all that scolding, he had all this trouble and this worry always on him.

Mrs. Haydon did not see Lena now very often. She had not lost her interest in her niece Lena, but Lena could not come much to her house to see her, it would not be right, now Lena was a married woman. And then too Mrs. Haydon had her hands full just then with her two daughters, for she was getting them ready to find them good husbands, and then too her own husband now worried her very often about her always spoiling that boy of hers, so he would be sure to turn out no good and be a disgrace to a german family, and all because his mother always spoiled him. All these things were very worrying now to Mrs. Haydon, but still she wanted to be good to Lena, though she could not see her very often. She only saw her when Mrs. Haydon went to call on Mrs. Kreder or when Mrs. Kreder came to see Mrs. Haydon, and that never could be very often. Then too these days Mrs. Haydon could not scold Lena, Mrs. Kreder was always there with her, and it would not be right to scold Lena when Mrs. Kreder was there, who had now the real right to do it. And so her aunt always said nice things now to Lena, and though Mrs. Haydon sometimes was a little worried when she saw Lena looking sad and not careful, she did not have time just then to really worry much about it.

Lena now never any more saw the girls she always used to sit with. She had no way now to see them and it was not in Lena's nature to search out ways to see them, nor did she now ever think much of the days when she had been used to see them. They never any of them had come to the Kreder house to see her. Not even Irish Mary had ever thought to come to see her. Lena had been soon forgotten by them. They had soon passed away from Lena and now Lena never thought any more that she had ever known them.

The only one of her old friends who tried to know what Lena liked and what she needed, and who always made Lena come to see her, was the good german cook who had always scolded. She now scolded Lena hard for letting herself go so, and going out when she was looking so untidy. "I know you going to have a baby Lena, but that's no way for you to be looking. I am ashamed most to see you come and sit here in my kitchen, looking so sloppy and like you never used to Lena. I never see anybody like you Lena. Herman is very good to you, you always say so, and he don't treat you bad ever though you don't deserve to have anybody good to you, you so careless all the time, Lena, letting yourself go like you never had anybody tell you what was the right way you should know how to be looking. No, Lena, I don't see no reason you should let yourself go so and look so untidy Lena, so I am ashamed to see you sit there looking so ugly, Lena. No Lena that ain't no way ever I see a woman make things come out better, letting herself go so every way and crying all the time like as if you had real trouble. I never wanted to see you marry Herman Kreder, Lena, I knew what you got to stand with that old woman always, and that old man, he is so stingy too and he don't say things out but he ain't any better in his heart than his wife with her bad ways, I know that Lena, I know they don't hardly give you enough to eat, Lena, I am real sorry for you Lena, you know that Lena, but that ain't any way to be going round so untidy Lena, even if you have got all that trouble. You never see me do like that Lena, though sometimes I got a headache so I can't see to stand to be working hardly, and nothing comes right with all my cooking, but I always see Lena, I look decent. That's the only way a german girl can make things come out right Lena. You hear me what I am saying to you Lena. Now you eat something nice Lena, I got it all ready for you, and you wash up and be careful Lena and the baby will come all right to you, and then I make your Aunt Mathilda see that you live in a house soon all alone with Herman and your baby, and then everything go better for you. You hear me what I say to you Lena. Now don't let me ever see you come looking like this any more Lena, and you just stop with that always crying. You ain't got no reason to be sitting there now with all that crying, I never see anybody have trouble it did them any good to do the way you are doing, Lena. You hear me Lena. You go home now and you be good the way I tell you Lena, and I see what I can do. I make your Aunt Mathilda make old Mrs. Kreder let you be till you get your baby all right. Now don't you be scared and so silly Lena. I don't like to see you act so Lena when really you got a nice man and so many things really any girl should be grateful to be having. Now you go home Lena to-day and you do the way I say, to you, and I see what I can do to help you."

"Yes Mrs. Aldrich" said the good german woman to her mistress later, "Yes Mrs. Aldrich that's the way it is with them girls when they want so to get married. They don't know when they got it good Mrs. Aldrich. They never know what it is they're really wanting when they got it, Mrs. Aldrich. There's that poor Lena, she just been here crying and looking so careless so I scold her, but that was no good that marrying for that poor Lena, Mrs. Aldrich. She do look so pale and sad now Mrs. Aldrich, it just break my heart to see her. She was a good girl was Lena, Mrs. Aldrich, and I never had no trouble with her like I got with so many young girls nowadays, Mrs. Aldrich, and I never see any girl any better to work right than our Lena, and now she got to stand it all the time with that old woman Mrs. Kreder. My! Mrs. Aldrich, she is a bad old woman to her. I never see Mrs. Aldrich how old people can be so bad to young girls and not have no kind of patience with them. If Lena could only live with her Herman, he ain't so bad the way men are, Mrs. Aldrich, but he is just the way always his mother wants him, he ain't got no spirit in him, and so I don't really see no help for that poor Lena. I know her aunt, Mrs. Haydon, meant it all right for her Mrs. Aldrich, but poor Lena, it would be better for her if her Herman had stayed there in New York that time he went away to leave her. I don't like it the way Lena is looking now, Mrs. Aldrich. She looks like as if she don't have no life left in her hardly, Mrs. Aldrich, she just drags around and looks so dirty and after all the pains I always took to teach her and to keep her nice in her ways and looking. It don't do no good to them, for them girls to get married Mrs. Aldrich, they are much better when they only know it, to stay in a good place when they got it, and keep on regular with their working. I don't like it the way Lena looks now Mrs. Aldrich. I wish I knew some way to help that poor Lena, Mrs. Aldrich, but she is a bad old woman, that old Mrs. Kreder, Herman's mother. I speak to Mrs. Haydon real soon, Mrs. Aldrich, I see what we can do now to help that poor Lena."

These were really bad days for poor Lena. Herman always was real good to her and now he even sometimes tried to stop his mother from scolding Lena. "She ain't well now mama, you let her be now you hear me. You tell me what it is you want she should be doing, I tell her. I see she does it right just the way you want it mama. You let be, I say now mama, with that always scolding Lena. You let be, I say now, you wait till she is feeling better." Herman was getting really strong to struggle, for he could see that Lena with that baby working hard inside her, really could not stand it any longer with his mother and the awful ways she always scolded.

It was a new feeling Herman now had inside him that made him feel he was strong to make a struggle. It was new for Herman Kreder really to be wanting something, but Herman wanted strongly now to be a father, and he wanted badly that his baby should be a boy and healthy. Herman never had cared really very much about his father and his mother, though always, all his life, he had done everything just as they wanted, and he had never really cared much about his wife, Lena, though he always had been very good to her, and had always tried to keep his mother off her, with the awful way she always scolded, but to be really a father of a little baby, that feeling took hold of Herman very deeply. He was almost ready, so as to save his baby from all trouble, to really make a strong struggle with his mother and with his father, too, if he would not help him to control his mother.

Sometimes Herman even went to Mrs. Haydon to talk all this trouble over. They decided then together, it was better to wait there all four together for the baby, and Herman could make Mrs. Kreder stop a little with her scolding, and then when Lena was a little stronger, Herman should have his own house for her, next door to his father, so he could always be there to help him in his working, but so they could eat and sleep in a house where the old woman could not control them and they could not hear her awful scolding.

And so things went on, the same way, a little longer. Poor Lena was not feeling any joy to have a baby. She was scared the way she had been when she was so sick on the water. She was scared now every time when anything would hurt her. She was scared and still and lifeless, and sure that every minute she would die. Lena had no power to be strong in this kind of trouble, she could only sit still and be scared, and dull, and lifeless, and sure that every minute she would die.

Before very long, Lena had her baby. He was a good, healthy little boy, the baby. Herman cared very much to have the baby. When Lena was a little stronger he took a house next door to the old couple, so he and his own family could eat and sleep and do the way they wanted. This did not seem to make much change now for Lena. She was just the same as when she was waiting with her baby. She just dragged around and was careless with her clothes and all lifeless, and she acted always and lived on just as if she had no feeling. She always did everything regular with the work, the way she always had had to do it, but she never got back any spirit in her. Herman was always good and kind, and always helped her with her working. He did everything he knew to help her. He always did all the active new things in the house and for the baby. Lena did what she had to do the way she always had been taught it. She always just kept going now with her working, and she was always careless, and dirty, and a little dazed, and lifeless. Lena never got any better in herself of this way of being that she had had ever since she had been married.

Mrs. Haydon never saw any more of her niece, Lena. Mrs. Haydon had now so much trouble with her own house, and her daughters getting married, and her boy, who was growing up, and who always was getting so much worse to manage. She knew she had done right by Lena. Herman Kreder was a good man, she would be glad to get one so good, sometimes, for her own daughters, and now they had a home to live in together, separate from the old people, who had made their trouble for them. Mrs. Haydon felt she had done very well by her niece, Lena, and she never thought now she needed any more to go and see her. Lena would do very well now without her aunt to trouble herself any more about her.

The good german cook who had always scolded, still tried to do her duty like a mother to poor Lena. It was very hard now to do right by Lena. Lena never seemed to hear now what anyone was saying to her. Herman was always doing everything he could to help her. Herman always, when he was home, took good care of the baby. Herman loved to take care of his baby. Lena never thought to take him out or to do anything she didn't have to.

The good cook sometimes made Lena come to see her. Lena would come with her baby and sit there in the kitchen, and watch the good woman cooking, and listen to her sometimes a little, the way she used to, while the good german woman scolded her for going around looking so careless when now she had no trouble, and sitting there so dull, and always being just so thankless. Sometimes Lena would wake up a little and get back into her face her old, gentle, patient, and unsuffering sweetness, but mostly Lena did not seem to hear much when the good german woman scolded. Lena always liked it when Mrs. Aldrich her good mistress spoke to her kindly, and then Lena would seem to go back and feel herself to be like she was when she had been in service. But mostly Lena just lived along and was careless in her clothes, and dull, and lifeless.

By and by Lena had two more little babies. Lena was not so much scared now when she had the babies. She did not seem to notice very much when they hurt her, and she never seemed to feel very much now about anything that happened to her.

They were very nice babies, all these three that Lena had, and Herman took good care of them always. Herman never really cared much about his wife, Lena. The only things Herman ever really cared for were his babies. Herman always was very good to his children. He always had a gentle, tender way when he held them. He learned to be very handy with them. He spent all the time he was not working, with them. By and by he began to work all day in his own home so that he could have his children always in the same room with him.

Lena always was more and more lifeless and Herman now mostly never thought about her. He more and more took all the care of their three children. He saw to their eating right and their washing, and he dressed them every morning, and he taught them the right way to do things, and he put them to their sleeping, and he was now always every minute with them. Then there was to come to them, a fourth baby. Lena went to the hospital near by to have the baby. Lena seemed to be going to have much trouble with it. When the baby was come out at last, it was like its mother lifeless. While it was coming, Lena had grown very pale and sicker. When it was all over Lena had died, too, and nobody knew just how it had happened to her.

The good german cook who had always scolded Lena, and had always to the last day tried to help her, was the only one who ever missed her. She remembered how nice Lena had looked all the time she was in service with her, and how her voice had been so gentle and sweet-sounding, and how she always was a good girl, and how she never had to have any trouble with her, the way she always had with all the other girls who had been taken into the house to help her. The good cook sometimes spoke so of Lena when she had time to have a talk with Mrs. Aldrich, and this was all the remembering there now ever was of Lena.

Herman Kreder now always lived very happy, very gentle, very quiet, very well content alone with his three children. He never had a woman any more to be all the time around him. He always did all his own work in his house, when he was through every day with the work he was always doing for his father. Herman always was alone, and he always worked alone, until his little ones were big enough to help him. Herman Kreder was very well content now and he always lived very regular and peaceful, and with every day just like the next one, always alone now with his three good, gentle children.

FINIS

PORTRAITS AND
OTHER SHORT WORKS

Ada

Barnes Colhard did not say he would not do it but he did not do it. He did it and then he did not do it, he did not ever think about it. He just thought some time he might do something.

His father Mr. Abram Colhard spoke about it to every one and very many of them spoke to Barnes Colhard about it and he always listened to them.

Then Barnes fell in love with a very nice girl and she would not marry him. He cried then, his father Mr. Abram Colhard comforted him and they took a trip and Barnes promised he would do what his father wanted him to be doing. He did not do the thing, he thought he would do another thing, he did not do the other thing, his father Mr. Colhard did not want him to do the other thing. He really did not do anything then. When he was a good deal older he married a very rich girl. He had thought perhaps he would not propose to her but his sister wrote to him that it would be a good thing. He married the rich girl and she thought he was the most wonderful man and one who knew everything. Barnes never spent more than the income of the fortune he and his wife had then, that is to say they did not spend more than the income and this was a surprise to very many who knew about him and about his marrying the girl who had such a large fortune. He had a happy life while he was living and after he was dead his wife and children remembered him.

He had a sister who also was successful enough in being one being living. His sister was one who came to be happier than most people come to be in living. She came to be a completely happy one. She was twice as old as her brother. She had been a very good daughter to her mother. She and her mother had always told very pretty stories to each other. Many old men loved to hear her tell these stories to her mother. Every one who ever knew her mother liked her mother. Many were sorry later that not every one liked the daughter. Many did like the daughter but not every one as every one had liked the mother. The daughter was charming inside in her, it did not show outside in her to every one, it certainly did to some. She did sometimes think her mother would be pleased with a story that did not please her mother, when her mother later was sicker the daughter knew that there were some stories she could tell her that would not please her mother. Her mother died and really mostly altogether the mother and the daughter had told each other stories very happily together.

The daughter then kept house for her father and took care of her brother. There were many relations who lived with them. The daughter did not like them to live with them and she did not like them to die with them. The daughter, Ada they had called her after her grandmother who had delightful ways of smelling flowers and eating dates and sugar, did not like it at all then as she did not like so much dying and she did not like any of the living she was doing then. Every now and then some old gentlemen told delightful stories to her. Mostly then there were not nice stories told by any one then in her living. She told her father Mr. Abram Colhard that she did not like it at all being one being living then. He never said anything. She was afraid then, she was one needing charming stories and happy telling of them and not having that thing she was always trembling. Then every one who could live with them were dead and there were then the father and the son a young man then and the daughter coming to be that one then. Her grandfather had left some money to them each one of them. Ada said she was going to use it to go away from them. The father said nothing then, then he said something and she said nothing then, then they both said nothing and then it was that she went away from them. The father was quite tender then, she was his daughter then. He wrote her tender letters then, she wrote him tender letters then, she never went back to live with him. He wanted her to come and she wrote him tender letters then. He liked the tender letters she wrote to him. He wanted her to live with him. She answered him by writing tender letters to him and telling very nice stories indeed in them. He wrote nothing and then he wrote again and there was some waiting and then he wrote tender letters again and again.

She came to be happier than anybody else who was living then. It is easy to believe this thing. She was telling some one, who was loving every story that was charming. Some one who was living was almost always listening. Some one who was loving was almost always listening. That one who was loving was almost always listening. That one who was loving was telling about being one then listening. That one being loving was then telling stories having a beginning and a middle and an ending. That one was then one always completely listening. Ada was then one and all her living then one completely telling stories that were charming, completely listening to stories having a beginning and a middle and an ending. Trembling was all living, living was all loving, some one was then the other one. Certainly this one was loving this Ada then. And certainly Ada all her living then was happier in living than any one else who ever could, who was, who is, who ever will be living.

Matisse

One was quite certain that for a long part of his being one being living he had been trying to be certain that he was wrong in doing what he was doing and then when he could not come to be certain that he had been wrong in doing what he had been doing, when he had completely convinced himself that he would not come to be certain that he had been wrong in doing what he had been doing he was really certain then that he was a great one and he certainly was a great one. Certainly every one could be certain of this thing that this one is a great one.

Some said of him, when anybody believed in him they did not then believe in any other one. Certainly some said this of him.

He certainly very clearly expressed something. Some said that he did not clearly express anything. Some were certain that he expressed something very clearly and some of such of them said that he would have been a greater one if he had not been one so clearly expressing what he was expressing. Some said he was not clearly expressing what he was expressing and some of such of them said that the greatness of struggling which was not clear expression made of him one being a completely great one.

Some said of him that he was greatly expressing something struggling. Some said of him that he was not greatly expressing something struggling.

He certainly was clearly expressing something, certainly sometime any one might come to know that of him. Very many did come to know it of him that he was clearly expressing what he was expressing. He was a great one. Any one might come to know that of him. Very many did come to know that of him. Some who came to know that of him, that he was a great one, that he was clearly expressing something, came then to be certain that he was not greatly expressing something being struggling. Certainly he was expressing something being struggling. Any one could be certain that he was expressing something being struggling. Some were certain that he was greatly expressing this thing. Some were certain that he was not greatly expressing this thing. Every one could come to be certain that he was a great man. Any one could come to be certain that he was clearly expressing something.

Some certainly were wanting to be needing to be doing what he was doing, that is clearly expressing something. Certainly they were willing to be wanting to be a great one. They were, that is some of them, were not wanting to be needing expressing anything being struggling. And certainly he was one not greatly expressing something being struggling, he was a great one, he was clearly expressing something. Some were wanting to be doing what he was doing that is clearly expressing something. Very many were doing what he was doing, not greatly expressing something being struggling. Very many who were wanting to be doing what he was doing were not wanting to be expressing anything being struggling.

There were very many wanting to be doing what he was doing that is to be one clearly expressing something. He was certainly a great man, any one could be really certain of this thing, every one could be certain of this thing. There were very many who were wanting to be ones doing what he was doing that is to be ones clearly expressing something and then very many of them were not wanting to be being ones doing that thing, that is clearly expressing something, they wanted to be ones expressing something being struggling, something being going to be some other thing, something being going to be something some one sometime would be clearly expressing and that would be something that would be a thing then that would then be greatly expressing some other thing then that thing, certainly very many were then not wanting to be doing what this one was doing clearly expressing something and some of them had been ones wanting to be doing that thing wanting to be ones clearly expressing something. Some were wanting to be ones doing what this one was doing wanted to be ones clearly expressing something. Some of such of them were ones certainly clearly expressing something, that was in them a thing not really interesting then any other one. Some of such of them went on being all their living ones wanting to be clearly expressing something and some of them were clearly expressing something.

This one was one very many were knowing some and very many were glad to meet him, very many sometimes listened to him, some listened to him very often, there were some who listened to him, and he talked then and he told them then that certainly he had been one suffering and he was then being one trying to be certain that he was wrong in doing what he was doing and he had come then to be certain that he never would be certain that he was doing what it was wrong for him to be doing then and he was suffering then and he was certain that he would be one doing what he was doing and he was certain that he should be one doing what he was doing and he was certain that he would always be one suffering and this then made him certain this, that he would always be one being suffering, this made him certain that he was expressing something being struggling and certainly very many were quite certain that he was greatly expressing something being struggling. This one was one knowing some who were listening to him and he was telling very often about being one suffering and this was not a dreary thing to any one hearing that then, it was not a saddening thing to any one hearing it again and again, to some it was quite an interesting thing hearing it again and again, to some it was an exciting thing hearing it again and again, some knowing this one and being certain that this one was a great man and was one clearly expressing something were ones hearing this one telling about being one being living were hearing this one telling this thing again and again. Some who were ones knowing this one and were ones certain that this one was one who was clearly telling something, was a great man, were not listening very often to this one telling again and again about being one being living. Certainly some who were certain that this one was a great man and one clearly expressing something and greatly expressing something being struggling were listening to this one telling about being living telling about this again and again and again. Certainly very many knowing this one and being certain that this one was a great man and that this one was clearly telling something were not listening to this one telling about being living, were not listening to this one telling this again and again.

This one was certainly a great man, this one was certainly

clearly expressing something. Some were certain that this one was clearly expressing something being struggling, some were certain that this one was not greatly expressing something being struggling.

Very many were not listening again and again to this one telling about being one being living. Some were listening again and again to this one telling about this one being one being in living.

Some were certainly wanting to be doing what this one was doing that is were wanting to be ones clearly expressing something. Some of such of them did not go on in being ones wanting to be doing what this one was doing that is in being ones clearly expressing something. Some went on being ones wanting to be doing what this one was doing that is, being ones clearly expressing something. Certainly this one was one who was a great man. Any one could be certain of this thing. Every one would come to be certain of this thing. This one was one certainly clearly expressing something. Any one could come to be certain of this thing. Every one would come to be certain of this thing. This one was one, some were quite certain, one greatly expressing something being struggling. This one was one, some were quite certain, one not greatly expressing something being struggling.

Picasso

One whom some were certainly following was one who was completely charming. One whom some were certainly following was one who was charming. One whom some were following was one who was completely charming. One whom some were following was one who was certainly completely charming.

Some were certainly following and were certain that the one they were then following was one working and was one bringing out of himself then something. Some were certainly following and were certain that the one they were then following was one bringing out of himself then something that was coming to be a heavy thing, a solid thing and a complete thing.

One whom some were certainly following was one working and certainly was one bringing something out of himself then and was one who had been all his living had been one having something coming out of him.

Something had been coming out of him, certainly it had been coming out of him, certainly it was something, certainly it had been coming out of him and it had meaning, a charming meaning, a solid meaning, a struggling meaning, a clear meaning.

One whom some were certainly following and some were certainly following him, one whom some were certainly following was one certainly working.

One whom some were certainly following was one having something coming out of him something having meaning and this one was certainly working then.

This one was working and something was coming then, something was coming out of this one then. This one was one and always there was something coming out of this one and always there had been something coming out of this one. This one had never been one not having something coming out of this one. This one was one having something coming out of this one. This one had been one whom some were following. This one was one whom some were following. This one was

282

being one whom some were following. This one was one who was working.

This one was one who was working. This one was one being one having something being coming out of him. This one was one going on having something come out of him. This one was one going on working. This one was one whom some were following. This one was one who was working.

This one always had something being coming out of this one. This one was working. This one always had been working. This one was always having something that was coming out of this one that was a solid thing, a charming thing, a lovely thing, a perplexing thing, a disconcerting thing, a simple thing, a clear thing, a complicated thing, an interesting thing, a disturbing thing, a repellant thing, a very pretty thing. This one was one certainly being one having something coming out of him. This one was one whom some were following. This one was one who was working.

This one was one who was working and certainly this one was needing to be working so as to be one being working. This one was one having something coming out of him. This one would be one all his living having something coming out of him. This one was working and then this one was working and this one was needing to be working, not to be one having something coming out of him something having meaning, but was needing to be working so as to be one working.

This one was certainly working and working was something this one was certain this one would be doing and this one was doing that thing, this one was working. This one was not one completely working. This one was not ever completely working. This one certainly was not completely working.

This one was one having always something being coming out of him, something having completely a real meaning. This one was one whom some were following. This one was one who was working. This one was one who was working and he was one needing this thing needing to be working so as to be one having some way of being one having some way of working. This one was one who was working. This one was one having something come out of him something having meaning. This one was one always having something come out of him and this thing the thing coming out of him always had real meaning. This one was one who was working. This one was one who was almost always working. This one was not one completely working. This one was one not ever completely working. This one was not one working to have anything come out of him. This one did have something having meaning that did come out of him. He always did have something come out of him. He was working, he was not ever completely working. He did have some following. They were always following him. Some were certainly following him. He was one who was working. He was one having something coming out of him something having meaning. He was not ever completely working.

Orta or One Dancing

Even if one was one she might be like some other one. She was like one and then was like another one and then was like another one and then was like another one and then was one who was one having been one and being one who was one then, one being like some.

Even if she was one and she was one, even if she was one she was changing. She was one and was then like some one. She was one and she had then come to be like some other one. She was then one and she had come then to be like some other one. She was then one and she had come then to be like some other one. She was then one and she had come then to be like a kind of a one.

Even if she was one being one, and she was one being one, she was one being one and even if she was one being one she was one who was then being a kind of a one.

Even if she was one being one and she was being one being one, even if she was one being one she was one having come to be one of another kind of a one.

Even if she was then being one and she was then one being one, even if she was then being the one she was one being, she was one who had come to be one being of another kind of a one.

Even if she was one being one and she was one being one, even if she was one being the one she was one being she was then another kind of a one, she was then being another kind of a one.

Even if she was one being one, even if she was one being one and being that one in being one, even if she was being the one she was being in being that one, even if she was being that one she was being a kind of a one she was come to be of a kind of a one, she was coming to be quite of a kind of a one.

Even if she was one being the one she was being, even if she was being that one the one she was being, the one she had been being, even if she was being that one, that one she was being, even if in being that one the one she was being she was being that one, being the one she was being, even if

she was being the one she was being, even if she was being
that one, even if she was being that one she was one coming
to be of a kind of a one, coming to be and being of a kind
of a one, quite coming to be of a kind of a one, of another
kind of a one, of that kind of a one.

She was one being one. She was one having been that one.
She was one going on being that one. She was one being one.
She was one being of one kind of a one. She was one being
that kind of a one. She was one being another kind of a one.
She was one being another kind of a one. She was one being
another kind of a one. She was one being another kind of a
one.

She was one being one. She was one going on being that
one. She was one being that one.

She was one being one. She was one always being that one.
She was one always having being that one. She was one always
going on being that one. She was one being one.

She was one being one and that thing, being that one was
a thing that had come to be something. She was one being
one and that thing, being that one was a thing that did then
go on being existing. She was one being that one. She was
being one.

She was one believing that thing, believing being the one
she was being. She was one always believing that thing, always
believing being the one she was being.

She was one who had been believing being the one she was
being. She had been one believing being the one she was
being. She is believing being the one she is believing. She has
been believing this thing. She always has been, she always is
believing being the one she is being.

She is one doing that thing, doing believing being the one
she is being. She is one being the one she is being. She is one
being one. She is one being that one.

She is one being the one she is being. She is one doing
something. She is one being the one she is being. She is one
being that one.

In doing something that one is being the one doing that
thing. In doing something, the one doing the thing is the one
being one doing that thing. This one is one doing something.
This one is being the one doing the thing. That one is doing

the thing. That one has been doing the thing. That one is dancing.

Meaning that thing, meaning being the one doing that thing is something the one doing that thing is doing. Meaning doing dancing is the thing this one is doing. This one is doing dancing. This one is the one meaning to be doing that thing meaning to be doing dancing.

This one is one having been doing dancing. This one is one doing dancing. This one is one. This one is one doing that thing. This one is one doing dancing. This one is one having been meaning to be doing dancing. This one is one meaning to be doing dancing.

This one being one meaning to be doing dancing, this one being one dancing, this one is one, this one is being that one. This one is one. This one is one being one. This one is being one and has been one being one having a kind of a way of being one believing anything, this one is being one and has been one being one having a kind of way of meaning anything. This one is one being one having a way of being one thinking of anything. This one is one having a kind of way of meaning everything.

This one is one being that one. This one is one and is that one and is one having had and having a way of being one believing something and meaning something and dancing. This is one being one having a way of dancing. This is one being that one.

This is one being one and having been one who is one being one showing being that one in being one changing and being that one, that kind of a one, the one that is the kind of a one that is meaning and believing the way this one is meaning and believing. This one is not changing. This one is changing, that is to say this one is looking like different ones of them who are ones who are believing and feeling and meaning the way this one is meaning and feeling and believing. This one is one who has been, who is meaning and feeling and believing. This one is one who is meaning. This one is one who has been meaning. This one is one who has a way of meaning. This one is one who has been one who is one meaning in the kind of way that some looking like this one are meaning. This one has a way of believing, this one has a way of feeling. This one has a way of feeling, this one has a way of believing and that is a way of feeling, and that is a way of believing that some have who sometimes look very much like this one looks some of the time. This one is one being one. This one is one dancing. This one has a way of believing and feeling and meaning. This one has a way of feeling, believing and meaning in dancing.

Being one having meaning, being one believing, being one dancing, being that one is what this one is one doing. This one is one who has meaning, this one is one who is dancing and is one having meaning in that thing in dancing. This one is one meaning to be having meaning in dancing. This one is one believing in having meaning. This one is one thinking in believing in having meaning.

This one is the one being dancing. This one is the one thinking in believing in dancing having meaning. This one is one believing in thinking. This one is one thinking in dancing having meaning. This one is one believing in dancing having meaning. This one is one dancing. This one is one being that one. This one is one being in being one being dancing. This one is one being in being one who is dancing. This one is one being one. This one is one being in being one.

This one is one changing. This one is one who has been, who always has been one being living in being that one. This one was one quite living in being that one. This one is one finishing living in being that one. This one is that one. This one has been that one. This one is one having been in the beginning been that one. This one has been going on being that one. This one is quite finishing being living in being that one.

This one is one who has been one being dancing. This one has been one beginning in being one being dancing. This one has been going on being living in being one being dancing. This one has been ending in being one going to be dancing. This one is finishing living in being one dancing.

This one is one not changing. This one is one coming to be one completely believing in thinking. This one is one beginning in being one coming to be believing. This one is going on in being one believing in meaning. This one is one going on thinking in believing in meaning. This one is going on believing in thinking in having meaning. This one is going on in believing, this one is one going on in believing in thinking, this one is one going on in believing in having meaning. This one is one going on. This one is one finishing in thinking in believing having meaning in dancing. This one is finishing in being one thinking in believing in meaning. This one is finishing in believing in thinking. This one is finishing in believing in having meaning. This one is finishing in believing. This one is finishing in thinking in believing. This one is finishing in believing.

This one is one who is that one, who is one dancing, who is one being one doing that thing, who is one being one believing in meaning. This one is one being one believing in thinking having meaning. This one is one being one believing that meaning is existing. This one is one meaning to be thinking in believing. This one is one believing in meaning.

She was not needing to be one believing in meaning being existing. She was not one needing this thing, needing being such a one. Needing being such a one, needing that meaning is existing is something, needing that meaning is existing is something that some one being one is having. Very many being one are having that thing, are having that needing of meaning being existing. Very many are being one having it that being that one they are the one the one that is needing that meaning is existing. This one is one being one having it that being that one she is one the one needing that meaning is existing.

She was one beginning being living and there were then others who were ones doing that thing, being living. Her mother was being living and was living then with four children. The mother was one having been married to some one and she was one then not needing that thing enough not needing that thing so that the one to whom she had been married could then marry another one.

She was living then with four children and all of them all the four children were being living then, were quite commencing then being ones being living. There were four children. The oldest one was a son, the second one was not a son, the third one was this one, the fourth one was a boy and all four of them were living then and the mother was living then and all five of them were living together then.

The mother came to be one believing that meaning was something that could be exciting to any one. She had come to be one knowing that meaning was completely interesting to her youngest one and to the one who was a little older than her youngest one. She had come to be forgetting that her oldest son had not any meaning, was not remembering that he was the oldest one, was not forgetting that he was being one having been in the family living. She had come to be remembering that her daughter, the one who had not been a son was one who could be supporting that meaning is existing, could be quite supporting some. She went on then being living and she was finishing in being one fading in meaning, fading and meaning and greeting meaning and fading and being then anything being faded and having meaning. She was then one not completely fading, she was then knowing that every one could be greeting meaning being existing. She was then still not yet being come to be a dead one.

She was fading then and asking any one to be one greeting meaning being existing. She was asking any one to do this thing. She was fading enough then. She was a dead one sometime.

She was not living with any children then when she was greeting meaning being existing. She was then not living with any child she had been having. All four were being living then. All four of them were being living and any one of them might be one being dancing. Any one of the four of them might then be one being dancing. The oldest one of them was not then being one dancing. He was not doing that thing, he was not dancing. The second one was one not then dancing, she was then completely knowing everything about all dancing. She was then being one living in dancing being existing. She was then living in this thing.

The third one was one dancing. She was quite doing that thing quite dancing. She was one dancing.

The fourth was one who in a way was one dancing. He was in a way being one doing that thing. He was one in a way completely meaning that thing completely meaning being one being dancing. He was in a way then dancing. He was one being one asking and answering in dancing being asking. He was one asking in dancing being existing. He was one answering in dancing being existing. He was one in a way dancing that is he was one coming to be one asking and answering. He was one asking. Dancing was existing. He was one answering. Dancing was existing. He was one asking and answering. He was one meaning that thing meaning that dancing had come to be existing. He was one not dancing. He certainly was not dancing. Any one could be one dancing. He was not then dancing. He was then meaning the thing meaning that something is existing and that something is one thing. In a way he was doing nothing that was not something that was meaning something had been existing, that dancing had been existing. He could be one dancing. Dancing was existing.

She, Orta Davray, was one being of a kind of a one. That is to say she was one looking like some. She was changing. In the beginning she was one and then she was one having the same look as some other one and that one is of a kind of a one. Then she was changing and she was looking as another one was looking and that one was of a kind of a one. Then she was changing and she was looking as another one was looking and that one was of a kind of one. Then she was changing and she was looking like another one who was of a kind of a one. All four of them were quite different kinds of ones all four whom she was resembling. All four were in a way of a kind of a one. All four could be ones being ones needing believing that meaning is existing. All four could be ones expecting something from such thing. All four of them could be ones expecting something in meaning being existing. They were quite different ones these four of them.

She was one beginning being living and then she was one being that one being dancing. She was beginning then being one being existing. She was then being one and every one in her family living was needing then needing being completing that thing, completing her being one being dancing. She was then beginning being living. She was then one being like some and she was then one being existing, being one who was a young one and family living was being existing and she was then one completing that thing completing family living in being one being dancing and being the one each one was then completing as being one being dancing. She was being then quite like some. She was then feeling anything in any one being one completing her being one being dancing. She was then being one feeling anything in being one completing the family living in being one being dancing. She was then being one feeling anything in being one needing being that one, the one she was then.

She was then an older one, she was then like some. She was then dancing. She was then creating family living being existing. She was then completely creating that thing. She was then one of them one of all of them who were all ones who had been ones completing her being one being dancing.

She was then one being dancing. She was then being one exceeding in being that one. She was then being one who was being dominated by being one dominating anything. She was dancing then. She was exceeding everything. She was one dancing.

She was one who would be contradicting any one if she had not been one exceeding in affirming everything. She was one not contradicting every one. She was one contradicting. She could contradict any one. She was dancing. She was not contradicting she was dancing. She was exceedingly dancing. She was not contradicting every one. She was one dancing.

She was one meaning something in being one not contradicting every one. She was one meaning something in being one contradicting any one. She was one being one meaning in being one not contradicting any one. She was one having meaning in being one who was contradicting any one. She was one having meaning in being one who was not contradicting every one. She was one having meaning in dancing. She was one having meaning in exceeding in being the one being one dancing. She was having meaning in being that one the one contradicting every one. She was having meaning in being that one the one not contradicting every one. She was having meaning in being the one contradicting any one. She was having meaning in being the one not contradicting any one. Contradicting every one was existing. She was affirming dancing. She was exceeding in not contradicting every one. She was exceeding in not contradicting any one.

Dancing was what she was doing then. She was doing dancing. She was doing dancing and she was that one she was the one dancing. She was doing dancing and she was then one having meaning in being that one. She was then one being that one, she was then one being dancing, she was then one having meaning, she was then one dancing in being that one, she was then one being one dancing in being that one the one having meaning. She was dancing then. She was being that one. She was meaning that thing quite meaning being that one. She was dancing.

She was being that one. She was dancing. She was one needing meaning being existing. She was not then showing needing meaning being existing. Not anything then was showing anything in her being one then needing that meaning is existing.

She was thinking then. She was not then meaning everything in thinking. She was thinking then. She was dancing. She was thinking then and dancing had been existing. She was dancing then, she was thinking then, she was meaning everything, she was completely then being dancing, she was exceeding then exceeding in being that one the one then dancing.

She was dancing then. She certainly was thinking then. She had been thinking some. She was meaning everything then. She was completely then meaning everything then and thinking then thinking that meaning is existing and she was dancing then, quite dancing then. She was dancing then, she was meaning that thing, meaning dancing, she was dancing then, she was meaning thinking then, she was thinking then, she was meaning everything, she was dancing.

She went on then dancing. She was dancing again and again. She went on then being one being dancing. She went on then being that one. She went on then being one being dancing. She went on then being that one being that one being dancing. She went on dancing.

She was then one looking like some one. She was then one looking like some. She was then one looking like some one

who was one needing to be thinking in meaning being existing. She was then one looking like some one and that one
was one living in believing in thinking in meaning being existing. She was then one looking like some one and that one
was one moving in every direction in believing meaning is
existing. She was then one looking like one and that one was
straining in being one thinking in believing that meaning is
existing. She was looking like this one and she was dancing
then, she was quite dancing then.

She was dancing then she was being strained then quite
strained then by meaning being existing. She was strained
then quite strained then in believing in thinking in meaning
being existing. She was quite strained then. She was dancing
then. She was quite moving in every direction in meaning
being existing.

She was dancing, she was answering, she was carelessly
domineering, she was domineering, she was dancing, she was
answering.

She was dancing, she was that one then, the one dancing
and answering, the one domineering and answering, the one
having meaning in believing in thinking in meaning having
the condition of being in a direction. She was one dancing,
she was one answering. She was that one the one dancing.
She was that one the one dancing, the one answering. She
was that one the one answering and dancing. She was that
one the one dancing and answering. She was worn some then,
she was not quite at all worn then, she was dancing then, she
was answering then, she was moving in every direction in being one being worn some then. She was believing in thinking
having meaning in meaning being existing.

She was thinking, she was believing, she was dancing, she
was meaning. She was thinking, she was believing in thinking,
she was thinking in believing, she was believing in dancing,
she was thinking in believing in dancing. She was thinking in
believing in dancing having meaning. She was believing in
thinking in dancing having meaning. She was dancing in having meaning, she was having meaning in dancing, she was
dancing, she was believing, she was thinking, she was answering, she was domineering, she was going on answering, she
was worn with believing, she was careless in domineering, she

was energetic in answering, she was believing in going in any direction, she went on in changing, she was simple in not going on questioning, she was moving changing, she was changing in connecting, she was seeing feeling in connecting dancing, she was feeling in careless domineering, she was needing dancing in believing.

She would be dancing in being that one the one having been dancing. She was that one the one having been dancing. She was dancing. She was dancing in being that one the one dancing. She was dancing.

She was dancing in being that one believing that thinking in having meaning in meaning being existing. She was dancing in this thing. She was dancing. She was dancing in moving in every direction being something having meaning. She was dancing in this thing. She was dancing. She was dancing, she was using then being one believing in meaning being existing. She was dancing in being one having feeling of anything being cheering. She was dancing in feeling that something had been coming. She was dancing in feeling that something having been coming is having meaning. She was dancing in feeling that feeling has a meaning. She was dancing in feeling that any one coming to be one being asked something would be one answering that meaning is existing. She was one dancing in feeling certain that some doing something are ones being certain that meaning is existing. She was one dancing in being one being that one being the one dancing then.

Being that one being the one dancing then was then being something, was then being some one. She was that one, she was the one dancing, she was then one being that one that is being something, she was the one being that one that is being some one.

Being that one being that one dancing was then being one quite completing that thing quite completing being that one, that one dancing. Being that one, the one dancing, being that one was being some one, was being something. Being that one dancing was then being that one. She was that one, she was completely being that one being the one dancing. She was quite being that one, quite completely being that one, the one dancing, the one meaning everything, the one moving in that direction, the one thinking in believing in meaning being existing, the one moving in every direction, the one feeling in thinking in meaning having existence, the dancing, the one being that one.

Remembering being dancing is something. Completely remembering being dancing is something. Completely remembering being dancing is what she was doing in being that one the one dancing. She completely remembered something of being one being dancing.

She completely remembered dancing. She was that one, she was one dancing, she was dancing, she was that one the one dancing.

She went on being that one, the one dancing. She went on being that one. She went on being that one, the one dancing.

She was that one, the one dancing. She went on being that one, the one having been dancing, the one dancing, the one being that one the one having been dancing and being dancing, the one being the one that one was.

She went on being one. She was one. She was then resembling some one, one who was not dancing, she was then resembling some all of whom were ones believing in thinking, believing in meaning being existing, believing in worrying, believing in not worrying, believing in not needing remembering that some meaning has been existing, believing in moving in any direction, feeling in thinking in meaning being existing, feeling in believing in thinking being existing, feeling in moving in every direction, believing in being one thinking, believing in being one moving in a direction, feeling in being any one, feeling in being that one the one the one is being, believing in feeling in being that one the one each one has been and is being.

She was one dancing and she was one not dancing. She was one not dancing. She was one dancing. She was one believing in meaning being existing. She was dancing.

She had been dancing. She was dancing. She could be dancing. Being dancing was something every one was needing and she was being one dancing. Being dancing was what every one expressing meaning being existing was assisting to be existing, she was dancing, any one expressing meaning being existing was one needing to be one understanding anything of assisting to dancing being existing.

She had been dancing. She was dancing. She could be dancing. She could remember that she could be dancing. She did
remember something of that thing. She did remember anything of that thing. She did remember everything of being
one who could be dancing.

She was dancing. She had been dancing. She could be dancing. She could remember everything of dancing. She could
remember everything of having been dancing. She could remember everything of being one who could be dancing.

She was dancing. She was remembering this thing. She was
dancing. She was asking any one who had been one expressing
that meaning is existing to be one assisting dancing to be
existing. She was dancing. Any one was then assisting that
dancing be existing. Some were then assisting so that dancing
could be existing. She could be dancing. She was remembering then everything of being one who could be dancing. She
was dancing then. She was remembering then, remembering
everything of being dancing. She had been dancing then. She
was remembering everything of dancing then. She was dancing then.

In being that one, one dancing, she was one who was one
being that one the one seeing thinking in meaning being existing. In being that one the one dancing then she was such
a one, one believing in thinking being in meaning being
existing.

In being one then being dancing she was being then one
who might be one worrying to be exerting thinking being in
meaning being existing. In being one then being dancing she
would be one worrying to winning thinking being existing in
meaning being existing if she had not been one winning some
to be ones expressing meaning being existing who were ones
having been ones feeling in believing in meaning being existing. She might have been one worrying in continuing thinking in feeling in believing in meaning being existing if she had
not been one remembering something of having been one
being dancing. She might have been one being worrying in
feeling in believing that meaning is existing if she had not
been one believing that sometime any one could be learning
what she might have been one teaching. She might have been
one worrying in thinking in feeling in meaning being existing

if she had not been one who could be one teaching anything
of meaning being existing. She might have been worrying if
she had not been one remembering anything of what she had
been one doing in being living in dancing being existing, in
meaning being existing. She might have been one worrying if
she had not been one forgetting something of thinking in
believing in meaning being existing. She might have been one
worrying if she had not been one not completing coming to
be worrying. She might have been one worrying if she had
not been one who had been dancing. She might have come
to be one worrying if she had not been one being one dancing. She was dancing. She had been dancing. She could be
dancing.

In being dancing she was dancing, she was remembering
having been dancing, she was believing in thinking in meaning
being existing, she was being one being one going to be moving in any direction, she was being one being one who had
not been dancing, she was being one being one leading and
following every moving in any direction, she was being one
being one dancing.

In being one dancing she was being one dancing. In dancing she was doing that thing she was doing dancing. In doing
dancing she was dancing.

In being one dancing she was being that one being one
dancing. In being dancing she was dancing. In dancing she
was quite being that one the one being dancing. In being
dancing she was dancing. She was dancing.

In having been dancing she had been one dancing. In having been dancing she had been being that one the one being
dancing. In having been dancing she had been dancing.

She had been dancing. She had been one dancing. She was
dancing then. She had been doing dancing. When she had
been doing dancing she had been dancing. She had been
dancing when she had been dancing. She had been dancing.

She was always being one who was one who was dancing.
She was dancing then. She was always dancing some. She was
always dancing in being one being dancing. She always would
be one dancing some. She always would be one dancing some
when she was one being one being dancing. She always would
be that one, one having been one being dancing. She always

would be one who was one dancing. She always would be one dancing when she was one being one being dancing. She always would be one being dancing. She always would be one being that one.

She always would be one remembering everything about dancing. She always would be that one. She always would be remembering anything about dancing. She always would be such a one. She always would be thinking in believing in meaning being existing. She always would be that one. She always would be moving in a direction and almost then would be one moving in a direction in being one dancing, in having been one dancing.

In being one remembering everything of dancing she was one coming to be one who was one who was of a kind of them a kind of them remembering everything of something and expressing then that every one is believing in thinking in meaning being existing. In being one remembering that dancing is existing, in being one remembering anything of dancing being existing in meaning being existing she was being one being that one one expressing that thinking in meaning is being existing in dancing being existing. She was then that one. She was then one dancing. She was then one moving in any direction. She was then being that one, the one dancing.

In being that one the one dancing she was being one who was not then one coming to be changing. In being that one the one dancing she was being then one who had not been changing. In being one who had not been changing, in being the one who was not one changing she was being dancing. She was one dancing.

She was one dancing and if she had not been one changing she would always have been one being a young one. She was not always being one being a quite young one.

In being one changing she was one who would be one showing something of being one who was an older one, one doing a little dancing.

She was one not changing. She was one dancing. She was one showing everything of this thing, of being one dancing.

In being one going on being that one the one dancing she was one who would have been one going on dancing if she

had not come to be one showing some that every one could
be needing to be understanding the meaning of believing that
dancing is existing in thinking in meaning being existing. She
would have been one going on being one dancing if she were
not being that one the one dancing. She would have been one
going on being dancing if she had not been that one the one
who had been dancing.

Being one dancing and being one remembering everything
of that thing is something. Being one dancing and being one
going on being one dancing is something. Being one dancing
and being one believing in feeling in thinking in meaning being existing is something. Being one dancing is something. In
being one dancing this one the one dancing is one doing that
thing doing dancing. In being one dancing this one is being
that one the one dancing.

This one in being dancing is one being dancing. In being
one being dancing this one is one who in being dancing is
one expressing that thing expressing being one dancing. In
dancing this one is one expressing that dancing is existing. In
being one dancing this one is expressing that dancing is existing. In dancing this one is expressing anything. In dancing
this one is one feeling the expressing everything. In dancing
this one is dancing. In dancing this one is being one dancing.
In dancing this one is being that one the one dancing.

In being one dancing this one is one being one remembering anything in dancing. In being one dancing this one is one
remembering something in dancing. In being one dancing this
one was dancing and dancing being that thing being dancing
this one was doing that thing was doing dancing. In being one
dancing this one was one being dancing. In being dancing this
one was dancing. In dancing this one was dancing.

In dancing she was dancing. She was dancing and dancing
and in being that one the one dancing and dancing she was
dancing and dancing. In dancing, dancing being existing, she
was dancing, and in being one dancing dancing was being
existing.

She was one and being one she was one in a way being one,
she was one dancing. She was one she was one dancing. She
was one dancing, she was being one, she was in a way one,
she was one, she was one dancing.

In being one, in being in a way one, she was one dancing. In being one dancing, she was in a way one. She was in a way one. She was one dancing, she was one remembering anything of dancing, she was in a way one. She was one dancing. In being one who was one dancing she was in a way one. She was in a way one, that is, she was one and being one who was one dancing and being one dancing she was one being that one the one dancing, and being that one the one dancing she was one. She was one, that is, she was one being one dancing. She was one and she was being dancing, that is in a way she was one. In being dancing, she was one, that is, she was in a way one.

She was in a way one, that is she was dancing, that is she was in a way one, that is she was dancing, and she was one dancing and being that one the one dancing, being that one she was in a way one. She was one, she was in a way one, she was dancing.

She was believing in thinking in meaning being existing, she was in a way one. She was thinking in feeling in believing in meaning being existing. She was in a way one. She was one, she was moving in some directions, she was moving, she was thinking in feeling in meaning being existing. She was that one. She was dancing. She was in a way one. She was that one, she was one. She was in a way one.

In being in a way one she was one being one being the one she was. She was in a way one, she was one dancing. She was that one, she was in a way one. She was in a way one, she was one dancing and dancing was being existing and she was one dancing. She certainly was one dancing. Dancing being existing is something. She was in a way one. She was one dancing. She was that one, she was one dancing. She was dancing. Dancing is being existing. She was in a way one.

In being one she was one completing that thing. In being one she was not completing that thing again and again. She was not completing again and again being that one. In being that one she was not completing that, she was not completing being that one. She was not completing being that one, the one she was.

In not completing being that one, the one she was, she was one doing anything. In not completing being that one, the one she was, she was one moving in some direction. She was one not completing being one, being that one, she was not completing that thing. In not completing that thing, she was being that one, she was being the one she was. She was one being one who being one not being completing being the one she was, was one who was completing something again and again, who was completing being one she was, who was not completing being that one, being one, being the one she was.

She was one resembling some. She was one resembling some and being one resembling some she was one not resembling one kind of a one. She was resembling some and they were one kind of a one, they were a kind of a one not completing being one, not completing being that one, not completing being the kind of a one completing being that one. She was resembling some and each one of them were not resembling the other ones in being ones being the one they were being.

In being one she was being one who being one resembling some was one being one not completing being that one, the one being one. In being one not completing being one she was resembling some.

In being one she was one and in being that one she was one some one was knowing was that one. In some knowing she was that one she was one who would be completing being one and she was completing being one and she was one and she was one who was resembling some and these were ones who were ones who were a kind of one which is a kind which is completing being one who are not completing being one, they being ones being one and not being ones being completed then and being ones then not any one has been completing.

She was one. She was one and knowing one, that one was being one she was knowing and it might be that they were going on knowing one another if they went on knowing one another and going on knowing one another she might be one not going on knowing that one and not going on knowing that one she would come to be knowing some whom she would be knowing and who would not come to be ones being the same ones and they would be ones expressing something for some being ones listening and looking. She would be one telling something and she would be one being one. She was one. She was dancing. She was one. She had been one. She was one. She was being that one. She would be that one.

In being one dancing she was being one and being one who was resembling some and these were of a kind of a one being ones thinking in feeling in meaning being existing she was one who had been, who was dancing and dancing could be, had been existing.

In being one in being that one she was one. She was one and being that one she was that one. She was that one and being that one and being one feeling in believing completing being existing, and being one thinking in feeling in meaning being existing and being one being of a kind of a one and being of that kind of them and they being of a kind of them and complete connection being existing in her being one dancing between dancing being existing and her being one not being one completing being one, she was one dancing and being that one she was that one and being that one she was that one the one dancing and being the one dancing being that one she was the one going on being that one the one dancing. She was dancing. She had been dancing. She would be dancing.

Flirting at the Bon Marche

Some know very well that their way of living is a sad one. Some know that their way of living is a dreary thing. Some know very well that their way of being living is a tedious one. Some know very well that they are living in a very dull way of living. Some do not know that a way of living is a tedious one. Some do not know that a way of living is a sad one. Some do not know that a way of living is a dreary way of living. Some do not know that one way of living is a dull one.

Some live a dull way of living very quickly and they are not then certain that they are living a dull way of living. Some live in a sad way of living and are quicker and quicker and they are certain that they are not living in a sad way of living. Some are certain that they would be living in a dreary way of living if they were not so quickly living. Some are trying to be quick in being living and some of them are very quick then and these are living a very tedious way of living.

Some are slow enough and make a sad way of living lose the sadness of that way of living. Some are slow to make a dull way of living fill up to not being such a dull one. Some make themselves a slow one and these then are having a tedious way of living full up with occupation. Some are making themselves slow ones and they are then not such dreary ones in living in a dreary way of living.

Some are coming to know very well that they are living in a very dreary way of living. Some are coming to know very well that they are living in a very sad way of living. Some are coming to know very well that they are living in a very tedious way of living. Some are coming to know very well that they are living in a very dull way of living.

These go shopping. They go shopping and it always was a thing they were rightly doing. Now everything is changing. Certainly everything is changing. They go shopping, they are being in a different way of living. Everything is changing.

Why is everything changing. Everything is changing because the place where they shop is a place where every one is needing to be finding that there are ways of living that are not dreary ones, ways of living that are not sad ones, ways of living that are not dull ones, ways of living that are not tedious ones. Certainly in a way these are existing.

Certainly in a way some are finding a way of living which is not a dull one, which is not a tedious one, which is not a sad one, which is not a dreary one. These are then living in a way of living that is very nearly a completely dreary one, a completely sad one, a completely tedious one, a completely dull one. These are then shopping. Shopping is a thing that is to them, that has been to them a thing that is quite interesting, they are then living in a way of living that is a dreary one, that is a dull one, that is a tedious one, that is in a way a sad one. These are then shopping, certainly shopping is in a way interesting, certainly it is not changing the living they are having, the way of living in which they are living. They are shopping and that is not so interesting and then they are changing in their way of living. They are shopping and slowly they are changing, there is a way of living that is coming then to be in them and it is not completely exciting but it is quite exciting, it is pretty nearly completely exciting. They are living the way they are living, that is a way of living that is a tedious way, that is a sad way, that is a dull way, that is a dreary way and they are living in this way and they are shopping and shopping is not to them very exciting and then it is to them completely exciting and the place where they are shopping is completely existing to those living there in the way they are living, those who are living being ones selling where very many are buying, very many men and very many women, very many women, very many men, very many women.

Some are knowing very well that the living they are living is dull enough, is dreary enough, is tedious enough, is sad enough, yes is sad enough. Some of such of them are changing, very many of such of them are changing, some of such of them are completely changing, very many of such of them are not ever very completely changing. Some of such of them are pretty nearly changing.

Some do not know very well that their way of living is a dull one, is a tedious enough one, is a dreary enough one. Some of such of them are changing, are shopping, some of such of them are shopping and shopping is something, they are shopping and shopping is something but changing is not in being one buying, changing is in being one having some one be one selling something and not selling that thing, changing is then existing, sometimes in some quite some changing, in some quite completely changing, in some some changing, in some not very much changing.

Miss Furr and Miss Skeene

Helen Furr had quite a pleasant home. Mrs. Furr was quite a pleasant woman. Mr. Furr was quite a pleasant man. Helen Furr had quite a pleasant voice a voice quite worth cultivating. She did not mind working. She worked to cultivate her voice. She did not find it gay living in the same place where she had always been living. She went to a place where some were cultivating something, voices and other things needing cultivating. She met Georgine Skeene there who was cultivating her voice which some thought was quite a pleasant one. Helen Furr and Georgine Skeene lived together then. Georgine Skeene liked travelling. Helen Furr did not care about travelling, she liked to stay in one place and be gay there. They were together then and travelled to another place and stayed there and were gay there.

They stayed there and were gay there, not very gay there, just gay there. They were both gay there, they were regularly working there both of them cultivating their voices there, they were both gay there. Georgine Skeene was gay there and she was regular, regular in being gay, regular in not being gay, regular in being a gay one who was one not being gay longer than was needed to be one being quite a gay one. They were both gay then there and both working there then.

They were in a way both gay there where there were many cultivating something. They were both regular in being gay there. Helen Furr was gay there, she was gayer and gayer there and really she was just gay there, she was gayer and gayer there, that is to say she found ways of being gay there that she was using in being gay there. She was gay there, not gayer and gayer, just gay there, that is to say she was not gayer by using the things she found there that were gay things, she was gay there, always she was gay there.

They were quite regularly gay there, Helen Furr and Georgine Skeene, they were regularly gay there where they were gay. They were very regularly gay.

To be regularly gay was to do every day the gay thing that they did every day. To be regularly gay was to end every day at the same time after they had been regularly gay. They were regularly gay. They were gay every day. They ended every day in the same way, at the same time, and they had been every day regularly gay.

The voice Helen Furr was cultivating was quite a pleasant one. The voice Georgine Skeene was cultivating was, some said, a better one. The voice Helen Furr was cultivating she cultivated and it was quite completely a pleasant enough one then, a cultivated enough one then. The voice Georgine Skeene was cultivating she did not cultivate too much. She cultivated it quite some. She cultivated and she would sometime go on cultivating it and it was not then an unpleasant one, it would not be then an unpleasant one, it would be a quite richly enough cultivated one, it would be quite richly enough to be a pleasant enough one.

They were gay where there were many cultivating something. The two were gay there, were regularly gay there. Georgine Skeene would have liked to do more travelling. They did some travelling, not very much travelling, Georgine Skeene would have liked to do more travelling, Helen Furr did not care about doing travelling, she liked to stay in a place and be gay there.

They stayed in a place and were gay there, both of them stayed there, they stayed together there, they were gay there, they were regularly gay there.

They went quite often, not very often, but they did go back to where Helen Furr had a pleasant enough home and then Georgine Skeene went to a place where her brother had quite some distinction. They both went, every few years, went visiting to where Helen Furr had quite a pleasant home. Certainly Helen Furr would not find it gay to stay, she did not find it gay, she said she would not stay, she said she did not find it gay, she said she would not stay where she did not find it gay, she said she found it gay where she did stay and she did stay there where very many were cultivating something. She did stay there. She always did find it gay there.

She went to see them where she had always been living and where she did not find it gay. She had a pleasant home there, Mrs. Furr was a pleasant enough woman, Mr. Furr was a pleasant enough man, Helen told them and they were not worrying, that she did not find it gay living where she had always been living.

Georgine Skeene and Helen Furr were living where they were both cultivating their voices and they were gay there. They visited where Helen Furr had come from and then they went to where they were living where they were then regularly living.

There were some dark and heavy men there then. There were some who were not so heavy and some who were not so dark. Helen Furr and Georgine Skeene sat regularly with them. They sat regularly with the ones who were dark and heavy. They sat regularly with the ones who were not so dark. They sat regularly with the ones that were not so heavy. They sat with them regularly, sat with some of them. They went with them regularly went with them. They were regular then, they were gay then, they were where they wanted to be then where it was gay to be then, they were regularly gay then. There were men there then who were dark and heavy and they sat with them with Helen Furr and Georgine Skeene and they went with them with Miss Furr and Miss Skeene, and they went with the heavy and dark men Miss Furr and Miss Skeene went with them, and they sat with them, Miss Furr and Miss Skeene sat with them, and there were other men, some were not heavy men and they sat with Miss Furr and Miss Skeene and Miss Furr and Miss Skeene sat with them, and there were other men who were not dark men and they sat with Miss Furr and Miss Skeene and Miss Furr and Miss Skeene sat with them. Miss Furr and Miss Skeene went with them and they went with Miss Furr and Miss Skeene, some who were not heavy men, some who were not dark men. Miss Furr and Miss Skeene sat regularly, they sat with some men. Miss Furr and Miss Skeene went and there were some men with them. There were men and Miss Furr and Miss Skeene went with them, went somewhere with them, went with some of them.

Helen Furr and Georgine Skeene were regularly living where very many were living and cultivating in themselves something. Helen Furr and Georgine Skeene were living very regularly then, being very regular then in being gay then. They did then learn many ways to be gay and they were then being gay being quite regular in being gay, being gay and they were learning little things, little things in ways of being gay, they were very regular then, they were learning very many little things in ways of being gay, they were being gay and using these little things they were learning to have to be gay with regularly gay with then and they were gay the same amount they had been gay. They were quite gay, they were quite regular, they were learning little things, gay little things, they were gay inside them the same amount they had been gay, they were gay the same length of time they had been gay every day.

They were regular in being gay, they learned little things that are things in being gay, they learned many little things that are things in being gay, they were gay every day, they were regular, they were gay, they were gay the same length of time every day, they were gay, they were quite regularly gay.

Georgine Skeene went away to stay two months with her brother. Helen Furr did not go then to stay with her father and her mother. Helen Furr stayed there where they had been regularly living the two of them and she would then certainly not be lonesome, she would go on being gay. She did go on being gay. She was not any more gay but she was gay longer every day than they had been being gay when they were to-gether being gay. She was gay then quite exactly the same way. She learned a few more little ways of being in being gay. She was quite gay and in the same way, the same way she had been gay and she was gay a little longer in the day, more of each day she was gay. She was gay longer every day than when the two of them had been being gay. She was gay quite in the way they had been gay, quite in the same way.

She was not lonesome then, she was not at all feeling any need of having Georgine Skeene. She was not astonished at this thing. She would have been a little astonished by this thing but she knew she was not astonished at anything and so she was not astonished at this thing not astonished at not feeling any need of having Georgine Skeene.

Helen Furr had quite a completely pleasant voice and it was

quite well enough cultivated and she could use it and she did use it but then there was not any way of working at cultivating a completely pleasant voice when it has become a quite completely well enough cultivated one, and there was not much use in using it when one was not wanting it to be helping to make one a gay one. Helen Furr was not needing using her voice to be a gay one. She was gay then and sometimes she used her voice and she was not using it very often. It was quite completely enough cultivated and it was quite completely a pleasant one and she did not use it very often. She was then, she was quite exactly as gay as she had been, she was gay a little longer in the day than she had been.

She was gay exactly the same way. She was never tired of being gay that way. She had learned very many little ways to use in being gay. Very many were telling about using other ways in being gay. She was gay enough, she was always gay exactly the same way, she was always learning little things to use in being gay, she was telling about using other ways in being gay, she was telling about learning other ways in being gay, she was learning other ways in being gay, she would be using other ways in being gay, she would always be gay in the same way, when Georgine Skeene was there not so long each day as when Georgine Skeene was away.

She came to using many ways in being gay, she came to use every way in being gay. She went on living where many were cultivating something and she was gay, she had used every way to be gay.

They did not live together then Helen Furr and Georgine Skeene. Helen Furr lived there the longer where they had been living regularly together. Then neither of them were living there any longer. Helen Furr was living somewhere else then and telling some about being gay and she was gay then and she was living quite regularly then. She was regularly gay then. She was quite regular in being gay then. She remembered all the little ways of being gay. She used all the little ways of being gay. She was quite regularly gay. She told many then the way of being gay, she taught very many then little ways they could use in being gay. She was living very well, she was gay then, she went on living then, she was regular in being gay, she always was living very well and was gay very well and was telling about little ways one could be learning to use in being gay, and later was telling them quite often, telling them again and again.

Tender Buttons

OBJECTS

A carafe, that is a blind glass.

A kind in glass and a cousin, a spectacle and nothing strange a single hurt color and an arrangement in a system to pointing. All this and not ordinary, not unordered in not resembling. The difference is spreading.

Glazed Glitter.

Nickel, what is nickel, it is originally rid of a cover.

The change in that is that red weakens an hour. The change has come. There is no search. But there is, there is that hope and that interpretation and sometime, surely any is unwelcome, sometime there is breath and there will be a sinecure and charming very charming is that clean and cleansing. Certainly glittering is handsome and convincing.

There is no gratitude in mercy and in medicine. There can be breakages in Japanese. That is no programme. That is no color chosen. It was chosen yesterday, that showed spitting and perhaps washing and polishing. It certainly showed no obligation and perhaps if borrowing is not natural there is some use in giving.

A substance in a cushion.

The change of color is likely and a difference a very little difference is prepared. Sugar is not a vegetable.

Callous is something that hardening leaves behind what will be soft if there is a genuine interest in there being present as many girls as men. Does this change. It shows that dirt is clean when there is a volume.

A cushion has that cover. Supposing you do not like to change, supposing it is very clear that there is no change in appearance, supposing that there is regularity and a costume is that any the worse than an oyster and an exchange. Come to season that is there any extreme use in feather and cotton.

Is there not much more joy in a table and more chairs and very likely roundness and a place to put them.

A circle of fine card board and a chance to see a tassel.

What is the use of a violent kind of delightfulness if there is no pleasure in not getting tired of it. The question does not come before there is a quotation. In any kind of place there is a top to covering and it is a pleasure at any rate there is some venturing in refusing to believe nonsense. It shows what use there is in a whole piece if one uses it and it is extreme and very likely the little things could be dearer but in any case there is a bargain and if there is the best thing to do is to take it away and wear it and then be reckless be reckless and re-solved on returning gratitude.

Light blue and the same red with purple makes a change. It shows that there is no mistake. Any pink shows that and very likely it is reasonable. Very likely there should not be a finer fancy present. Some increase means a calamity and this is the best preparation for three and more being together. A little calm is so ordinary and in any case there is sweetness and some of that.

A seal and matches and a swan and ivy and a suit.

A closet, a closet does not connect under the bed. The band if it is white and black, the band has a green string. A sight a whole sight and a little groan grinding makes a trimming such a sweet singing trimming and a red thing not a round thing but a white thing, a red thing and a white thing.

The disgrace is not in carelessness nor even in sewing it comes out out of the way.

What is the sash like. The sash is not like anything mustard it is not like a same thing that has stripes, it is not even more hurt than that, it has a little top.

A box.

Out of kindness comes redness and out of rudeness comes rapid same question, out of an eye comes research, out of selection comes painful cattle. So then the order is that a white way of being round is something suggesting a pin and is it disappointing, it is not, it is so rudimentary to be analysed and see a fine substance strangely, it is so earnest to have a green point not to red but to point again.

A piece of coffee.

More of double.

A place in no new table.

A single image is not splendor. Dirty is yellow. A sign of more in not mentioned. A piece of coffee is not a detainer. The resemblance to yellow is dirtier and distincter. The clean mixture is whiter and not coal color, never more coal color than altogether.

The sight of a reason, the same sight slighter, the sight of a simpler negative answer, the same sore sounder, the intention to wishing, the same splendor, the same furniture.

The time to show a message is when too late and later there is no hanging in a blight.

A not torn rose-wood color. If it is not dangerous then a pleasure and more than any other if it is cheap is not cheaper. The amusing side is that the sooner there are no fewer the more certain is the necessity dwindled. Supposing that the case contained rose-wood and a color. Supposing that there was no reason for a distress and more likely for a number, supposing that there was no astonishment, is it not necessary to mingle astonishment.

The settling of stationing cleaning is one way not to shatter scatter and scattering. The one way to use custom is to use soap and silk for cleaning. The one way to see cotton is to have a design concentrating the illusion and the illustration. The perfect way is to accustom the thing to have a lining and the shape of a ribbon and to be solid, quite solid in standing and to use heaviness in morning. It is light enough in that. It has that shape nicely. Very nicely may not be exaggerating. Very strongly may be sincerely fainting. May be strangely flattering. May not be strange in everything. May not be strange to.

Dirt and not copper.

Dirt and not copper makes a color darker. It makes the shape so heavy and makes no melody harder. It makes mercy and relaxation and even a strength to spread a table fuller. There are more places not empty. They see cover.

Nothing elegant.

A charm a single charm is doubtful. If the red is rose and there is a gate surrounding it, if inside is let in and there places change then certainly something is upright. It is earnest.

Mildred's umbrella.

A cause and no curve, a cause and loud enough, a cause and extra a loud clash and an extra wagon, a sign of extra, a sac a small sac and an established color and cunning, a slender grey and no ribbon, this means a loss a great loss a restitution.

A method of a cloak.

A single climb to a line, a straight exchange to a cane, a desperate adventure and courage and a clock, all this which is a system, which has feeling, which has resignation and success, all makes an attractive black silver.

A red stamp.

If lilies are lily white if they exhaust noise and distance and even dust, if they dusty will dirt a surface that has no extreme grace, if they do this and it is not necessary it is not at all necessary if they do this they need a catalogue.

A box.

A large box is handily made of what is necessary to replace any substance. Suppose an example is necessary, the plainer it is made the more reason there is for some outward recognition that there is a result.

A box is made sometimes and them to see to see to it neatly and to have the holes stopped up makes it necessary to use paper.

A custom which is necessary when a box is used and taken is that a large part of the time there are three which have different connections. The one is on the table. The two are on the table. The three are on the table. The one, one is the same length as is shown by the cover being longer. The other is different there is more cover that shows it. The other is different and that makes the corners have the same shade the eight are in singular arrangement to make four necessary.

Lax, to have corners, to be lighter than some weight, to indicate a wedding journey, to last brown and not curious, to be wealthy, cigarettes are established by length and by doubling.

Left open, to be left pounded, to be left closed, to be circulating in summer and winter, and sick color that is grey that is not dusty and red shows, to be sure cigarettes do measure an empty length sooner than a choice in color.

Winged, to be winged means that white is yellow and pieces pieces that are brown are dust color if dust is washed off, then it is choice that is to say it is fitting cigarettes sooner than paper.

An increase why is an increase idle, why is silver cloister, why is the spark brighter, if it is brighter is there any result, hardly more than ever.

A plate.

An occasion for a plate, an occasional resource is in buying and how soon does washing enable a selection of the same thing neater. If the party is small a clever song is in order.

Plates and a dinner set of colored china. Pack together a string and enough with it to protect the center, cause a considerable haste and gather more as it is cooling, collect more trembling and not any even trembling, cause a whole thing to be a church.

A sad size a size that is not sad is blue as every bit of blue is precocious. A kind of green a game in green and nothing flat nothing quite flat and more round, nothing a particular color strangely, nothing breaking the losing of no little piece.

A splendid address a really splendid address is not shown by giving a flower freely, it is not shown by a mark or by wetting.

Cut cut in white, cut in white so lately. Cut more than any other and show it. Show it in the stem and in starting and in evening coming complication.

A lamp is not the only sign of glass. The lamp and the cake are not the only sign of stone. The lamp and the cake and the cover are not the only necessity altogether.

A plan a hearty plan, a compressed disease and no coffee,

not even a card or a change to incline each way, a plan that has that excess and that break is the one that shows filling.

A seltzer bottle.

Any neglect of many particles to a cracking, any neglect of this makes around it what is lead in color and certainly discolor in silver. The use of this is manifold. Supposing a certain time selected is assured, suppose it is even necessary, suppose no other extract is permitted and no more handling is needed, suppose the rest of the message is mixed with a very long slender needle and even if it could be any black border, supposing all this altogether made a dress and suppose it was actual, suppose the mean way to state it was occasional, if you suppose this in August and even more melodiously, if you suppose this even in the necessary incident of there certainly being no middle in summer and winter, suppose this and an elegant settlement a very elegant settlement is more than of consequence, it is not final and sufficient and substituted. This which was so kindly a present was constant.

A long dress.

What is the current that makes machinery, that makes it crackle, what is the current that presents a long line and a necessary waist. What is this current.

What is the wind, what is it.

Where is the serene length, it is there and a dark place is not a dark place, only a white and red are black, only a yellow and green are blue, a pink is scarlet, a bow is every color. A line distinguishes it. A line just distinguishes it.

A red hat.

A dark grey, a very dark grey, a quite dark grey is monstrous ordinarily, it is so monstrous because there is no red in it. If red is in everything it is not necessary. Is that not an argument for any use of it and even so is there any place that is better, is there any place that has so much stretched out.

A blue coat.

A blue coat is guided guided away, guided and guided away,

that is the particular color that is used for that length and not any width not even more than a shadow.

A piano.

If the speed is open, if the color is careless, if the event is overtaken, if the selection of a strong scent is not awkward, if the button holder is held by all the waving color and there is no color, not any color. If there is no dirt in a pin and there can be none scarcely, if there is not then the place is the same as up standing.

This is no dark custom and it even is not acted in any such a way that a restraint is not spread. That is spread, it shuts and it lifts and awkwardly not awkwardly the center is in standing.

A chair.

A widow in a wise veil and more garments shows that shadows are even. It addresses no more, it shadows the stage and learning. A regular arrangement, the severest and the most preserved is that which has the arrangement not more than always authorised.

A suitable establishment, well housed, practical, patient and staring, a suitable bedding, very suitable and not more particularly than complaining, anything suitable is so necessary.

A fact is that when the direction is just like that, no more, longer, sudden and at the same time not any sofa, the main action is that without a blaming there is no custody.

Practice measurement, practice the sign that means that really means a necessary betrayal, in showing that there is wearing.

Hope, what is a spectacle, a spectacle is the resemblance between the circular side place and nothing else, nothing else.

To choose it is ended, it is actual and more than that it has it certainly has the same treat, and a seat all that is practiced and more easily much more easily ordinarily.

Pick a barn, a whole barn, and bend more slender accents than have ever been necessary, shine in the darkness necessarily.

Actually not aching, actually not aching, a stubborn bloom is so artificial and even more than that, it is a spectacle, it is a binding accident, it is animosity and accentuation.

If the chance to dirty diminishing is necessary, if it is why is there no complexion, why is there no rubbing, why is there no special protection.

A frightful release.

A bag which was left and not only taken but turned away was not found. The place was shown to be very like the last time. A piece was not exchanged, not a bit of it, a piece was left over. The rest was mismanaged.

A purse.

A purse was not green, it was not straw color, it was hardly seen and it has a use a long use and the chain, the chain was never missing, it was not misplaced, it showed that it was open, that is all that it showed.

A mounted umbrella.

What was the use of not leaving it there where it would hang what was the use if there was no chance of ever seeing it come there and show that it was handsome and right in the way it showed it. The lesson is to learn that it does show it, that it shows it and that nothing, that there is nothing, that there is no more to do about it and just so much more is there plenty of reason for making an exchange.

A cloth.

Enough cloth is plenty and more, more is almost enough for that and besides if there is no more spreading is there plenty of room for it. Any occasion shows the best way.

More.

An elegant use of foliage and grace and a little piece of white cloth and oil.

Wondering so winningly in several kinds of oceans is the reason that makes red so regular and enthusiastic. The reason that there is more snips are the same shining very colored rid of no round color.

A new cup and saucer.

Enthusiastically hurting a clouded yellow bud and saucer, enthusiastically so is the bite in the ribbon.

Objects.

Within, within the cut and slender joint alone, with sudden equals and no more than three, two in the center make two one side.

If the elbow is long and it is filled so then the best example is all together.

The kind of show is made by squeezing.

Eye glasses.

A color in shaving, a saloon is well placed in the center of an alley.

A cutlet.

A blind agitation is manly and uttermost.

Careless water.

No cup is broken in more places and mended, that is to say a plate is broken and mending does do that it shows that culture is japanese. It shows the whole element of angels and orders. It does more to choosing and it does more to that ministering counting. It does, it does change in more water.

Supposing a single piece is a hair supposing more of them are orderly, does that show that strength, does that show that joint, does that show that balloon famously. Does it.

A paper.

A courteous occasion makes a paper show no such occasion and this makes readiness and eyesight and likeness and a stool.

A drawing.

The meaning of this is entirely and best to say the mark, best to say it best to show sudden places, best to make bitter, best to make the length tall and nothing broader, anything between the half.

Water raining.

Water astonishing and difficult altogether makes a meadow and a stroke.

Cold climate.

A season in yellow sold extra strings makes lying places.

Malachite.

The sudden spoon is the same in no size. The sudden spoon is the wound in the decision.

An umbrella.

Coloring high means that the strange reason is in front not more in front behind. Not more in front in peace of the dot.

A petticoat.

A light white, a disgrace, an ink spot, a rosy charm.

A waist.

A star glide, a single frantic sullenness, a single financial grass greediness.

Object that is in wood. Hold the pine, hold the dark, hold in the rush, make the bottom.

A piece of crystal. A change, in a change that is remarkable there is no reason to say that there was a time.

A woolen object gilded. A country climb is the best disgrace, a couple of practices any of them in order is so left.

A time to eat.

A pleasant simple habitual and tyrannical and authorised and educated and resumed and articulate separation. This is not tardy.

A little bit of a tumbler.

A shining indication of yellow consists in there having been more of the same color than could have been expected when all four were bought. This was the hope which made the six and seven have no use for any more places and this necessarily spread into nothing. Spread into nothing.

A fire.

What was the use of a whole time to send and not send if there was to be the kind of thing that made that come in. A letter was nicely sent.

A handkerchief.

A winning of all the blessings, a sample not a sample because there is no worry.

Red roses.

A cool red rose and a pink cut pink, a collapse and a sold hole, a little less hot.

In between.

In between a place and candy is a narrow foot path that shows more mounting than anything, so much really that a calling meaning a bolster measured a whole thing with that. A virgin a whole virgin is judged made and so between curves and outlines and real seasons and more out glasses and a perfectly unprecedented arrangement between old ladies and mild colds there is no satin wood shining.

Colored Hats.

Colored hats are necessary to show that curls are worn by an addition of blank spaces, this makes the difference between single lines and broad stomachs, the least thing is lightening, the least thing means a little flower and a big delay a big delay that makes more nurses than little women really little women. So clean is a light that nearly all of it shows pearls and little ways. A large hat is tall and me and all custard whole.

A feather.

A feather is trimmed, it is trimmed by the light and the bug and the post, it is trimmed by little leaning and by all sorts of mounted reserves and loud volumes. It is surely cohesive.

A brown.

A brown which is not liquid not more so is relaxed and yet there is a change, a news is pressing.

A little called Pauline.

A little called anything shows shudders.

Come and say what prints all day. A whole few watermelon. There is no pope.

No cut in pennies and little dressing and choose wide soles and little spats really little spices.

A little lace makes boils. This is not true.

Gracious of gracious and a stamp a blue green white bow a blue green lean, lean on the top.

If it is absurd then it is leadish and nearly set in where there is a tight head.

A peaceful life to arise her, noon and moon and moon. A letter a cold sleeve a blanket a shaving house and nearly the best and regular window.

Nearer in fairy sea, nearer and farther, show white has lime in sight, show a stitch of ten. Count, count more so that thicker and thicker is leaning.

I hope she has her cow. Bidding a wedding, widening received treading, little leading, mention nothing.

Cough out cough out in the leather and really feather it is not for.

Please could, please could, jam it not plus more sit in when.

A sound.

Elephant beaten with candy and little pops and chews all bolts and reckless reckless rats, this is this.

A table.

A table means does it not my dear it means a whole steadiness. Is it likely that a change.

A table means more than a glass even a looking glass is tall. A table means necessary places and a revision a revision of a little thing it means it does mean that there has been a stand, a stand where it did shake.

Shoes.

To be a wall with a damper a stream of pounding way and nearly enough choice makes a steady midnight. It is pus.

A shallow hole rose on red, a shallow hole in and in this makes ale less. It shows shine.

A dog.

A little monkey goes like a donkey that means to say that means to say that more sighs last goes. Leave with it. A little monkey goes like a donkey.

A white hunter.

A white hunter is nearly crazy.

A leave.

In the middle of a tiny spot and nearly bare there is a nice thing to say that wrist is leading. Wrist is leading.

Suppose an eyes.

Suppose it is within a gate which open is open at the hour of closing summer that is to say it is so.

All the seats are needing blackening. A white dress is in sign. A soldier a real soldier has a worn lace a worn lace of different sizes that is to say if he can read, if he can read he is a size to show shutting up twenty-four.

Go red go red, laugh white.

Suppose a collapse in rubbed purr, in rubbed purr get.

Little sales ladies little sales ladies little saddles of mutton.

Little sales of leather and such beautiful beautiful, beautiful beautiful.

A shawl.

A shawl is a hat and hurt and a red ballon and an under coat and a sizer a sizer of talks.

A shawl is a wedding, a piece of wax a little build. A shawl.

Pick a ticket, pick it in strange steps and with hollows. There is hollow hollow belt, a belt is a shawl.

A plate that has a little bobble, all of them, any so.

Please a round it is ticket.

It was a mistake to state that a laugh and a lip and a laid climb and a depot and a cultivator and little choosing is a point it.

Book.

Book was there, it was there. Book was there. Stop it, stop it, it was a cleaner, a wet cleaner and it was not where it was wet, it was not high, it was directly placed back, not back again, back, it was returned, it was needless, it put a bank, a bank when, a bank care.

Suppose a man a realistic expression of resolute reliability suggests pleasing itself white all white and no head does that mean soap. It does not so. It means kind wavers and little chance to beside beside rest. A plain.

Suppose ear rings, that is one way to breed, breed that. Oh chance to say, oh nice old pole. Next best and nearest a pillar. Chest not valuable, be papered.

Cover up cover up the two with a little piece of string and hope rose and green, green.

Please a plate, put a match to the seam and really then really then, really then it is a remark that joins many many lead games. It is a sister and sister and a flower and a flower and a dog and a colored sky a sky colored grey and nearly that nearly that let.

Peeled pencil, choke.

Rub her coke.

It was black, black took.

Black ink best wheel bale brown.

Excellent not a hull house, not a pea soup, no bill no care, no precise no past pearl pearl goat.

This is this dress, aider.

Aider, why aider why whow, whow stop touch, aider whow, aider stop the muncher, muncher munchers.

A jack in kill her, a jack in, makes a meadowed king, makes a to let.

FOOD

STUDIES IN DESCRIPTION.

Roastbeef   Mutton   Breakfast   Sugar   Cranberries   milk   eggs   apple   tails   lunch   cups   rhubarb   single   fish

cake   custard   potatoes   asparagus   butter   end of summer   sausages   celery   veal   vegetable   cooking   chicken
pastry   cream   cucumber   dinner   dining   eating   salad
sauce   salmon   orange   cocoa and clear soup and oranges
and oat-meal   salad dressing and an artichoke   A center in
a table.

Roastbeef.

In the inside there is sleeping, in the outside there is reddening, in the morning there is meaning, in the evening there
is feeling. In the evening there is feeling. In feeling anything
is resting, in feeling anything is mounting, in feeling there is
resignation, in feeling there is recognition, in feeling there is
recurrence and entirely mistaken there is pinching. All the
standards have steamers and all the curtains have bed linen
and all the yellow has discrimination and all the circle has
circling. This makes sand.

Very well. Certainly the length is thinner and the rest, the
round rest has a longer summer. To shine, why not shine, to
shine, to station, to enlarge, to hurry the measure all this
means nothing if there is singing, if there is singing then there
is the resumption.

The change the dirt, not to change dirt means that there is
no beefsteak and not to have that is no obstruction, it is so
easy to exchange meaning, it is so easy to see the difference.
The difference is that a pliant resource is not entangled with
thickness and it does not mean that thickness shows such cutting, it does mean that a meadow is useful and a cow absurd.
It does not mean that there are tears, it does not mean that
exudation is cumbersome, it means no more than a memory,
a choice and a reestablishment, it means more than any escape
from a surrounding extra. All the time that there is use there
is use and any time there is a surface there is a surface, and
every time there is an exception there is an exception and
every time there is a division there is a dividing. Any time
there is a surface there is a surface and every time there is a
suggestion there is a suggestion and every time there is silence
there is silence and every time that is languid there is that
there then and not oftener, not always, not particular, tender
and changing and external and central and surrounded and

singular and simple and the same and the surface and the circle and the shine and the succor and the white and the same and the better and the red and the same and the center and the yellow and the tender and the better, and altogether.

Considering the circumstances there is no occasion for a reduction, considering that there is no pealing there is no occasion for an obligation, considering that there is no outrage there is no necessity for any reparation, considering that there is no particle sodden there is no occasion for deliberation. Considering everything and which way the turn is tending, considering everything why is there no restraint, considering everything what makes the place settle and the plate distinguish some specialties. The whole thing is not understood and this is not strange considering that there is no education, this is not strange because having that certainly does show the difference in cutting, it shows that when there is turning there is no distress.

In kind, in a control, in a period, in the alteration of pigeons, in kind cuts and thick and thin spaces, in kind ham and different colors, the length of leaning a strong thing outside not to make a sound but to suggest a crust, the principal taste is when there is a whole chance to be reasonable, this does not mean that there is overtaking, this means nothing precious, this means clearly that the chance to exercise is a social success. So then the sound is not obtrusive. Suppose it is obtrusive suppose it is. What is certainly the desertion is not a reduced description, a description is not a birthday.

Lovely snipe and tender turn, excellent vapor and slender butter, all the splinter and the trunk, all the poisonous darkning drunk, all the joy in weak success, all the joyful tenderness, all the section and the tea, all the stouter symmetry.

Around the size that is small, inside the stern that is the middle, besides the remains that are praying, inside the between that is turning, all the region is measuring and melting is exaggerating.

Rectangular ribbon does not mean that there is no eruption it means that if there is no place to hold there is no place to spread. Kindness is not earnest, it is not assiduous it is not revered.

Room to comb chickens and feathers and ripe purple, room

to curve single plates and large sets and second silver, room to send everything away, room to save heat and distemper, room to search a light that is simpler, all room has no shadow.

There is no use there is no use at all in smell, in taste, in teeth, in toast, in anything, there is no use at all and the respect is mutual.

Why should that which is uneven, that which is resumed, that which is tolerable why should all this resemble a smell, a thing is there, it whistles, it is not narrower, why is there no obligation to stay away and yet courage, courage is everywhere and the best remains to stay.

If there could be that which is contained in that which is felt there would be a chair where there are chairs and there would be no more denial about a clatter. A clatter is not a smell. All this is good.

The Saturday evening which is Sunday is every week day. That choice is there when there is a difference. A regulation is not active. Thirstiness is not equal division.

Anyway, to be older and ageder is not a surfeit nor a suction, it is not dated and careful, it is not dirty. Any little thing is clean, rubbing is black. Why should ancient lambs be goats and young colts and never beef, why should they, they should because there is so much difference in age.

A sound, a whole sound is not separation, a whole sound is in an order.

Suppose there is a pigeon, suppose there is.

Looseness, why is there a shadow in a kitchen, there is a shadow in a kitchen because every little thing is bigger.

The time when there are four choices and there are four choices in a difference, the time when there are four choices there is a kind and there is a kind. There is a kind. There is a kind. Supposing there is a bone, there is a bone. Supposing there are bones. There are bones. When there are bones there is no supposing there are bones. There are bones and there is that consuming. The kindly way to feel separating is to have a space between. This shows a likeness.

Hope in gates, hope in spoons, hope in doors, hope in tables, no hope in daintiness and determination. Hope in dates.

Tin is not a can and a stove is hardly. Tin is not necessary and neither is a stretcher. Tin is never narrow and thick.

Color is in coal. Coal is outlasting roasting and a spoonful, a whole spoon that is full is not spilling. Coal any coal is copper.

Claiming nothing, not claiming anything, not a claim in everything, collecting claiming, all this makes a harmony, it even makes a succession.

Sincerely gracious one morning, sincerely graciously trembling, sincere in gracious eloping, all this makes a furnace and a blanket. All this shows quantity.

Like an eye, not so much more, not any searching, no compliments.

Please be the beef, please beef, pleasure is not wailing. Please beef, please be carved clear, please be a case of consideration.

Search a neglect. A sale, any greatness is a stall and there is no memory, there is no clear collection.

A satin sight, what is a trick, no trick is mountainous and the color, all the rush is in the blood.

Bargaining for a little, bargain for a touch, a liberty, an estrangement, a characteristic turkey.

Please spice, please no name, place a whole weight, sink into a standard rising, raise a circle, choose a right around make the resonance accounted and gather green any collar.

To bury a slender chicken, to raise an old feather, to surround a garland and to bake a pole splinter, to suggest a repose and to settle simply, to surrender one another, to succeed saving simpler, to satisfy a singularity and not to be blinder, to sugar nothing darker and to read redder, to have the color better, to sort out dinner, to remain together, to surprise no sinner, to curve nothing sweeter, to continue thinner, to increase in resting recreation to design string not dimmer.

Cloudiness what is cloudiness, is it a lining, is it a roll, is it melting.

The sooner there is jerking, the sooner freshness is tender, the sooner the round it is not round the sooner it is withdrawn in cutting, the sooner the measure means service, the sooner there is chinking, the sooner there is sadder than salad, the sooner there is none do her, the sooner there is no choice, the sooner there is a gloom freer, the same sooner and more sooner, this is no error in hurry and in pressure and in opposition to consideration.

A recital, what is a recital, it is an organ and use does not strengthen valor, it soothes medicine.

A transfer, a large transfer, a little transfer, some transfer, clouds and tracks do transfer, a transfer is not neglected.

Pride, when is there perfect pretence, there is no more than yesterday and ordinary.

A sentence of a vagueness that is violence is authority and a mission and stumbling and also certainly also a prison. Calmness, calm is beside the plate and in way in. There is no turn in terror. There is no volume in sound.

There is coagulation in cold and there is none in prudence. Something is preserved and the evening is long and the colder spring has sudden shadows in a sun. All the stain is tender and lilacs really lilacs are disturbed. Why is the perfect reestablishment practiced and prized, why is it composed. The result the pure result is juice and size and baking and exhibition and nonchalance and sacrifice and volume and a section in division and the surrounding recognition and horticulture and no murmur. This is a result. There is no superposition and circumstance, there is hardness and a reason and the rest and remainder. There is no delight and no mathematics.

Mutton.

A letter which can wither, a learning which can suffer and an outrage which is simultaneous is principal.

Student, students are merciful and recognised they chew something.

Hate rests that is solid and sparse and all in a shape and largely very largely. Interleaved and successive and a sample of smell all this makes a certainty a shade.

Light curls very light curls have no more curliness than soup. This is not a subject.

Change a single stream of denting and change it hurriedly, what does it express, it expresses nausea. Like a very strange likeness and pink, like that and not more like that than the same resemblance and not more like that than no middle space in cutting.

An eye glass, what is an eye glass, it is water. A splendid

specimen, what is it when it is little and tender so that there are parts. A center can place and four are no more and two and two are not middle.

Melting and not minding, safety and powder, a particular recollection and a sincere solitude all this makes shunning so thorough and so unrepeated and surely if there is anything left it is a bone. It is not solitary.

Any space is not quiet it is so likely to be shiny. Darkness very dark darkness is sectional. There is a way to see in onion and surely very surely rhubarb and a tomatoe, surely very surely there is that seeding. A little thing in is a little thing.

Mud and water were not present and not any more of either. Silk and stockings were not present and not any more of either. A receptacle and a symbol and no monster were present and no more. This made a piece show and was it a kindness, it can be asked was it a kindness to have it warmer, was it a kindness and does gliding mean more. Does it.

Does it dirty a ceiling. It does not. Is it dainty, it is if prices are sweet. Is it lamentable, it is not if there is no undertaker. Is it curious, it is not when there is youth. All this makes a line, it even makes no more. All this makes cherries. The reason that there is a suggestion in vanity is due to this that there is a burst of mixed music.

A temptation any temptation is an exclamation if there are misdeeds and little bones. It is not astonishing that bones mingle as they vary not at all and in any case why is a bone outstanding, it is so because the circumstance that does not make a cake and character is so easily churned and cherished.

Mouse and mountain and a quiver, a quaint statue and pain in an exterior and silence more silence louder shows salmon a mischief intender. A cake, a real salve made of mutton and liquor, a specially retained rinsing and an established cork and blazing, this which resignation influences and restrains, restrains more altogether. A sign is the specimen spoken.

A meal in mutton, mutton, why is lamb cheaper, it is cheaper because so little is more. Lecture, lecture and repeat instruction.

Breakfast.

A change, a final change includes potatoes. This is no authority for the abuse of cheese. What language can instruct any fellow.

A shining breakfast, a breakfast shining, no dispute, no practice, nothing, nothing at all.

A sudden slice changes the whole plate, it does so suddenly.

An imitation, more imitation, imitation succeed imitations.

Anything that is decent, anything that is present, a calm and a cook and more singularly still a shelter, all these show the need of clamor. What is the custom, the custom is in the center.

What is a loving tongue and pepper and more fish than there is when tears many tears are necessary. The tongue and the salmon, there is not salmon when brown is a color, there is salmon when there is no meaning to an early morning being pleasanter. There is no salmon, there are no tea cups, there are the same kind of mushes as are used as stomachers by the eating hopes that makes eggs delicious. Drink is likely to stir a certain respect for an egg cup and more water melon than was ever eaten yesterday. Beer is neglected and cocoanut is famous. Coffee all coffee and a sample of soup all soup these are the choice of a baker. A white cup means a wedding. A wet cup means a vacation. A strong cup means an especial regulation. A single cup means a capital arrangement between the drawer and the place that is open.

Price a price is not in language, it is not in custom, it is not in praise.

A colored loss, why is there no leisure. If the persecution is so outrageous that nothing is solemn is there any occasion for persuasion.

A grey turn to a top and bottom, a silent pocketful of much heating, all the pliable succession of surrendering makes an ingenious joy.

A breeze in a jar and even then silence, a special anticipation in a rack, a gurgle a whole gurgle and more cheese than almost anything, is this an astonishment, does this incline more than the original division between a tray and a talking arrangement and even then a calling into another room gently with some chicken in any way.

A bent way that is a way to declare that the best is all together, a bent way shows no result, it shows a slight restraint, it shows a necessity for retraction.

Suspect a single buttered flower, suspect it certainly, suspect it and then glide, does that not alter a counting.

A hurt mended stick, a hurt mended cup, a hurt mended article of exceptional relaxation and annoyance, a hurt mended, hurt and mended is so necessary that no mistake is intended.

What is more likely than a roast, nothing really and yet it is never disappointed singularly.

A steady cake, any steady cake is perfect and not plain, any steady cake has a mounting reason and more than that it has singular crusts. A season of more is a season that is instead. A season of many is not more a season than most.

Take no remedy lightly, take no urging intently, take no separation leniently, beware of no lake and no larder.

Burden the cracked wet soaking sack heavily, burden it so that it is an institution in fright and in climate and in the best plan that there can be.

An ordinary color, a color is that strange mixture which makes, which does make which does not make a ripe juice, which does not make a mat.

A work which is a winding a real winding of the cloaking of a relaxing rescue. This which is so cool is not dusting, it is not dirtying in smelling, it could use white water, it could use more extraordinarily and in no solitude altogether. This which is so not winsome and not widened and really not so dipped as dainty and really dainty, very dainty, ordinarily, dainty, a dainty, not in that dainty and dainty. If the time is determined, if it is determined and there is reunion there is reunion with that then outline, then there is in that a piercing shutter, all of a piercing shouter, all of a quite weather, all of a withered exterior, all of that in most violent likely.

An excuse is not dreariness, a single plate is not butter, a single weight is not excitement, a solitary crumbling is not only martial.

A mixed protection, very mixed with the same actual intentional unstrangeness and riding, a single action caused necessarily is not more a sign than a minister.

Seat a knife near a cage and very near a decision and more

nearly a timely working cat and scissors. Do this temporarily and make no more mistake in standing. Spread it all and arrange the white place, does this show in the house, does it not show in the green that is not necessary for that color, does it not even show in the explanation and singularly not at all stationary.

Sugar.

A violent luck and a whole sample and even then quiet.

Water is squeezing, water is almost squeezing on lard. Water, water is a mountain and it is selected and it is so practical that there is no use in money. A mind under is exact and so it is necessary to have a mouth and eye glasses.

A question of sudden rises and more time than awfulness is so easy and shady. There is precisely that noise.

A peck a small piece not privately overseen, not at all not a slice, not at all crestfallen and open, not at all mounting and chaining and evenly surpassing, all the bidding comes to tea.

A separation is not tightly in worsted and sauce, it is so kept well and sectionally.

Put it in the stew, put it to shame. A little slight shadow and a solid fine furnace.

The teasing is tender and trying and thoughtful.

The line which sets sprinkling to be a remedy is beside the best cold.

A puzzle, a monster puzzle, a heavy choking, a neglected Tuesday.

Wet crossing and a likeness, any likeness, a likeness has blisters, it has that and teeth, it has the staggering blindly and a little green, any little green is ordinary.

One, two and one, two, nine, second and five and that.

A blaze, a search in between, a cow, only any wet place, only this tune.

Cut a gas jet uglier and then pierce pierce in between the next and negligence. Choose the rate to pay and pet pet very much. A collection of all around, a signal poison, a lack of languor and more hurts at ease.

A white bird, a colored mine, a mixed orange, a dog.

Cuddling comes in continuing a change.

A piece of separate outstanding rushing is so blind with open delicacy.

A canoe is orderly. A period is solemn. A cow is accepted.

A nice old chain is widening, it is absent, it is laid by.

Cranberries.

Could there not be a sudden date, could there not be in the present settlement of old age pensions, could there not be by a witness, could there be.

Count the chain, cut the grass, silence the noon and murder flies. See the basting undip the chart, see the way the kinds are best seen from the rest, from that and untidy.

Cut the whole space into twenty four spaces and then and then is there a yellow color, there is but it is smelled, it is then put where it is and nothing stolen.

A remarkable degree of red means that, a remarkable exchange is made.

Climbing altogether in when there is a solid chance of soiling no more than a dirty thing, coloring all of it in steadying is jelly.

Just as it is suffering, just as it is succeeded, just as it is moist so is there no countering.

Milk.

A white egg and a colored pan and a cabbage showing settlement, a constant increase.

A cold in a nose, a single cold nose makes an excuse. Two are more necessary.

All the goods are stolen, all the blisters are in the cup.

Cooking, cooking is the recognition between sudden and nearly sudden very little and all large holes.

A real pint, one that is open and closed and in the middle is so bad.

Tender colds, seen eye holders, all work, the best of change, the meaning, the dark red, all this and bitten, really bitten.

Guessing again and golfing again and the best men, the very best men.

Milk.

Climb up in sight climb in the whole utter needles and a guess a whole guess is hanging. Hanging hanging.

Eggs.

Kind height, kind in the right stomach with a little sudden mill.

Cunning shawl, cunning shawl to be steady.

In white in white handkerchiefs with little dots in a white belt all shadows are singular they are singular and procured and relieved.

No that is not the cows shame and a precocious sound, it is a bite.

Cut up alone the paved way which is harm. Harm is old boat and a likely dash.

Apple.

Apple plum, carpet steak, seed clam, colored wine, calm seen, cold cream, best shake, potatoe, potatoe and no no gold work with pet, a green seen is called bake and change sweet is bready, a little piece a little piece please.

A little piece please. Cane again to the presupposed and ready eucalyptus tree, count out sherry and ripe plates and little corners of a kind of ham. This is use.

Tails.

Cold pails, cold with joy no joy.

A tiny seat that means meadows and a lapse of cuddles with cheese and nearly bats, all this went messed. The post placed a loud loose sprain. A rest is no better. It is better yet. All the time.

Lunch.

Luck in loose plaster makes holy gauge and nearly that, nearly more states, more states come in town light kite, blight not white.

A little lunch is a break in skate a little lunch so slimy, a west end of a board line is that which shows a little beneath so that necessity is a silk under wear. That is best wet. It is so natural and why is there flake, there is flake to explain exhaust.

A real cold hen is nervous is nervous with a towel with a spool with real beads. It is mostly an extra sole nearly all that shaved, shaved with an old mountain, more than that bees more than that dinner and a bunch of likes that is to say the hearts of onions aim less.

Cold coffee with a corn a corn yellow and green mass is a gem.

Cups.

A single example of excellence is in the meat. A bent stick is surging and might all might is mental. A grand clothes is searching out a candle not that wheatly not that by more than an owl and a path. A ham is proud of cocoanut.

A cup is neglected by being all in size. It is a handle and meadows and sugar any sugar.

A cup is neglected by being full of size. It shows no shade, in come little wood cuts and blessing and nearly not that not with a wild bought in, not at all so polite, not nearly so behind.

Cups crane in. They need a pet oyster, they need it so hoary and nearly choice. The best slam is utter. Nearly be freeze.

Why is a cup a stir and a behave. Why is it so seen.

A cup is readily shaded, it has in between no sense that is to say music, memory, musical memory.

Pea nuts blame, a half sand is holey and nearly.

Rhubarb.

Rhubarb is susan not susan not seat in bunch toys not wild and laughable not in little places not in neglect and vegetable not in fold coal age not please.

Single fish.

Single fish single fish single fish egg plant single fish sight.

A sweet win and not less noisy than saddle and more ploughing and nearly well painted by little things so.

Please shade it a play. It is necessary and beside the large sort is puff.

Every way oakly, please prune it near. It is so found.

It is not the same.

Cake.

Cake cast in went to be and needles wine needles are such.

This is to-day. A can experiment is that which makes a town, makes a town dirty, it is little please. We came back. Two bore,

bore what, a mussed ash, ash when there is tin. This meant cake. It was a sign.

Another time there was extra a hat pin sought long and this dark made a display. The result was yellow. A caution, not a caution to be.

It is no use to cause a foolish number. A blanket stretch a cloud, a shame, all that bakery can tease, all that is beginning and yesterday yesterday we had it met. It means some change. No some day.

A little leaf upon a scene an ocean any where there, a bland and likely in the stream a recollection green land. Why white.

Custard.

Custard is this. It has aches, aches when. Not to be. Not to be narrowly. This makes a whole little hill.

It is better than a little thing that has mellow real mellow. It is better than lakes whole lakes, it is better than seeding.

Potatoes.

Real potatoes cut in between.

Potatoes.

In the preparation of cheese, in the preparation of crackers, in the preparation of butter, in it.

Roast potatoes.

Roast potatoes for.

Asparagus.

Asparagus in a lean in a lean to hot. This makes it art and it is wet wet weather wet weather wet.

Butter.

Boom in boom in, butter. Leave a grain and show it, show it. I spy.

It is a need it is a need that a flower a state flower. It is a need that a state rubber. It is a need that a state rubber is sweet and sight and a swelled stretch. It is a need. It is a need that state rubber.

Wood a supply. Clean little keep and a strange, estrange on it.

Make a little white, no and not with pit, pit on in within.

End of summer.

Little eyelets that have hammer and a check with stripes between, a lounge, in wit, in a rested development.

Sausages.

Sausages in between a glass.

There is read butter. A loaf of it is managed. Wake a question. Eat an instant, answer.

A reason for bed is this, that a decline, any decline is poison, poison is a toe a toe extractor, this means a solemn change. Hanging.

No evil is wide, any extra in leaf is so strange and singular a red breast.

Celery.

Celery tastes tastes where in curled lashes and little bits and mostly in remains.

A green acre is so selfish and so pure and so enlivened.

Veal.

Very well very well, washing is old, washing is washing.

Cold soup, cold soup clear and particular and a principal a principal question to put into.

Vegetable.

What is cut. What is cut by it. What is cut by it in.

It was a cross a crescent a cross and an unequal scream, it was upslanting, it was radiant and reasonable with little ins and red.

News. News capable of glees, cut in shoes, belike under pump of wide chalk, all this combing.

Way lay vegetable.

Leaves in grass and mow potatoes, have a skin, hurry you up flutter.

Suppose it is ex a cake suppose it is new mercy and leave

charlotte and nervous bed rows. Suppose it is meal. Suppose it is sam.

Cooking.

Alas, alas the pull alas the bell alas the coach in china, alas the little put in leaf alas the wedding butter meat, alas the receptacle, alas the back shape of mussle, mussle and soda.

Chicken.

Pheasant and chicken, chicken is a peculiar third.

Chicken.

Alas a dirty word, alas a dirty third alas a dirty third, alas a dirty bird.

Chicken.

Alas a doubt in case of more go to say what it is cress. What is it. Mean. Why. Potato. Loaves.

Chicken.

Stick stick call then, stick stick sticking, sticking with a chicken. Sticking in a extra succession, sticking in.

Chain-boats.

Chain-boats are merry, are merry blew, blew west, carpet.

Pastry.

Cutting shade, cool spades and little last beds, make violet, violet when.

Cream.

In a plank, in a play sole, in a heated red left tree there is shut in specs with salt be where. This makes an eddy. Necessary.

Cream.

Cream cut. Any where crumb. Left hop chambers.

Cucumber.

Not a razor less, not a razor, ridiculous pudding, red and

relet put in, rest in a slender go in selecting, rest in, rest in in white widening.

Dinner.

Not a little fit, not a little fit sun in sat in shed more mentally.

Let us why, let us why weight, let us why winter chess, let us why way.

Only a moon to soup her, only that in the sell never be the cocups nice be, shatter it they lay.

Egg ear nuts, look a bout. Shoulder. Let it strange, sold in bell next herds.

It was a time when in the acres in late there was a wheel that shot a burst of land and needless are niggers and a sample sample set of old eaten butterflies with spoons, all of it to be are fled and measures make it, make it, yes all the one in that we see where shall not it set with a left and more so, yes there add when the longer not it shall the best in the way when all be with when shall not for there with see and chest how for another excellent and excellent and easy easy excellent and easy express e c, all to be nice all to be no so. All to be no so no so. All to be not a white old chat churner. Not to be any example of an edible apple in.

Dining.

Dining is west.

Eating.

Eat ting, eating a grand old man said roof and never never re soluble burst, not a near ring not a bewildered neck, not really any such bay.

Is it so a noise to be is it a least remain to rest, is it a so old say to be, is it a leading are been. Is it so, is it so, is it so, is it so is it so is it so.

Eel us eel us with no no pea no pea cool, no pea cool cooler, no pea cooler with a land a land cost in, with a land cost in stretches.

Eating he heat eating he heat it eating, he heat it heat eating. He heat eating.

A little piece of pay of pay owls owls such as pie, bolsters.

Will leap beat, willie well all. The rest rest oxen occasion occasion to be so purred, so purred how.

It was a ham it was a square come well it was a square remain, a square remain not it a bundle, not it a bundle so is a grip, a grip to shed bay leave bay leave draught, bay leave draw cider in low, cider in low and george. George is a mass.

Eating.

It was a shame it was a shame to stare to stare and double and relieve relieve be cut up show as by the elevation of it and out out more in the steady where the come and on and the all the shed and that.

It was a garden and belows belows straight. It was a pea, a pea pour it in its not a succession, not it a simple, not it a so election, election with.

Salad.

It is a winning cake.

Sauce.

What is bay labored what is all be section, what is no much. Sauce sam in.

Salmon.

It was a peculiar bin a bin fond in beside.

Orange.

Why is a feel oyster an egg stir. Why is it orange center.

A show at tick and loosen loosen it so to speak sat.

It was an extra leaker with a see spoon, it was an extra licker with a see spoon.

Orange.

A type oh oh new new not no not knealer knealer of old show beefsteak, neither neither.

Oranges.

Build is all right.

Orange in.

Go lack go lack use to her.

Cocoa and clear soup and oranges and oat-meal.

Whist bottom whist close, whist clothes, woodling.

Cocoa and clear soup and oranges and oat-meal.

Pain soup, suppose it is question, suppose it is butter, real is, real is only, only excreate, only excreate a no since.

A no, a no since, a no since when, a no since when since, a no since when since a no since when since, a no since, a no since when since, a no since, a no, a no since a no since, a no since, a no since.

Salad dressing and an artichoke.

Please pale hot, please cover rose, please acre in the red stranger, please butter all the beef-steak with regular feel faces.

Salad dressing and an artichoke.

It was please it was please carriage cup in an ice-cream, in an ice-cream it was too bended bended with scissors and all this time. A whole is inside a part, a part does go away, a hole is red leaf. No choice was where there was and a second and a second.

A center in a table.

It was a way a day, this made some sum. Suppose a cod liver a cod liver is an oil, suppose a cod liver oil is tunny, suppose a cod liver oil tunny is pressed suppose a cod liver oil tunny pressed is china and secret with a bestow a bestow reed, a reed to be a reed to be, in a reed to be.

Next to me next to a folder, next to a folder some waiter, next to a foldersome waiter and re letter and read her. Read her with her for less.

ROOMS

Act so that there is no use in a center. A wide action is not a width. A preparation is given to the ones preparing. They do not eat who mention silver and sweet. There was an occupation.

A whole center and a border make hanging a way of dressing. This which is not why there is a voice is the remains of an offering. There was no rental.

So the tune which is there has a little piece to play and the exercise is all there is of a fast. The tender and true that makes no width to hew is the time that there is question to adopt.

To begin the placing there is no wagon. There is no change lighter. It was done. And then the spreading, that was not accomplishing that needed standing and yet the time was not so difficult as they were not all in place. They had no change. They were not respected. They were that, they did it so much in the matter and this showed that that settlement was not condensed. It was spread there. Any change was in the ends of the center. A heap was heavy. There was no change.

Burnt and behind and lifting a temporary stone and lifting more than a drawer.

The instance of there being more is an instance of more. The shadow is not shining in the way there is a black line. The truth has come. There is a disturbance. Trusting to a baker's boy meant that there would be very much exchanging and anyway what is the use of a covering to a door. There is a use, they are double.

If the center has the place then there is distribution. That is natural. There is a contradiction and naturally returning there comes to be both sides and the center. That can be seen from the description.

The author of all that is in there behind the door and that is entering in the morning. Explaining darkening and expecting relating is all of a piece. The stove is bigger. It was a shape that made no audience bigger if the opening is assumed why should there not be kneeling. Any force which is bestowed on a floor shows rubbing. This is so nice and sweet and yet there comes the change, there comes the time to press more air. This does not mean the same as disappearance.

A little lingering lion and a chinese chair, all the handsome cheese which is stone, all of it and a choice, a choice of a blotter. If it is difficult to do it one way there is no place of similar trouble. None. The whole arrangement is established. The end of which is that there is a suggestion, a suggestion that there can be a different whiteness to a wall. This was thought.

A page to a corner means that the shame is no greater when the table is longer. A glass is of any height, it is higher, it is simpler and if it were placed there would not be any doubt.

Something that is an erection is that which stands and feeds and silences a tin which is swelling. This makes no diversion that is to say what can please exaltation, that which is cooking.

A shine is that which when covered changes permission. An enclosure blends with the same that is to say there is blending. A blend is that which holds no mice and this is not because of a floor it is because of nothing, it is not in a vision.

A fact is that when the place was replaced all was left that was stored and all was retained that would not satisfy more than another. The question is this, is it possible to suggest more to replace anything than there is to replace that thing. This question and this perfect denial does make the time change all the time.

The sister was not a mister. Was this a surprise. It was. The conclusion came when there was no arrangement. All the time that there was a question there was a decision. Replacing a casual acquaintance with an ordinary daughter does not make a son.

It happened in a way that the time was perfect and there was a growth of a whole dividing time so that where formerly there was no mistake there was no mistake now. For instance before when there was a separation there was waiting, now when there is separation there is the division between intending and departing. This made no more mixture than there would be if there had been no change.

A little sign of an entrance is the one that made it alike. If it were smaller it was not alike and it was so much smaller that a table was bigger. A table was much bigger, very much bigger. Changing that made nothing bigger, it did not make anything bigger littler, it did not hinder wood from not being used as leather. And this was so charming. Harmony is so essential. Is there pleasure when there is a passage, there is when every room is open. Every room is open when there are not four, there were there and surely there were four, there were two together. There is no resemblance.

A single speed, the reception of table linen, all the wonder of six little spoons, there is no exercise.

The time came when there was a birthday. Every day was no excitement and a birthday was added, it was added on Monday, this made the memory clear, this which was a speech showed the chair in the middle where there was copper.

Alike and a snail, this means Chinamen, it does there is no doubt that to be right is more than perfect there is no doubt and glass is confusing it confuses the substance which was of a colour. Then came the time for discrimination, it came then and it was never mentioned it was so triumphant, it showed the whole bead that had a hole and should have a hole it showed the resemblance between silver.

Startling a starving husband is not disagreeable. The reason that nothing is hidden is that there is no suggestion of silence. No song is sad. A lesson is of consequence.

Blind and weak and organised and worried and betrothed and resumed and also asked to a fast and always asked to consider and never startled and not at all bloated, this which is no rarer than frequently is not so astonishing when hair brushing is added. There is quiet, there certainly is.

No eye glasses are rotten, no window is useless and yet if air will not come in there is a speech ready, there always is and there is no dimness, not a bit of it.

All along the tendency to deplore the absence of more has not been authorised. It comes to mean that with burning there is that pleasant state of stupefication. Then there is a way of earning a living. Who is a man.

A silence is not indicated by any motion, less is indicated by a motion, more is not indicated it is enthralled. So sullen and so low, so much resignation, so much refusal and so much place for a lower and an upper, so much and yet more silence why is not sleeping a feat why is it not and when is there some discharge when. There never is.

If comparing a piece that is a size that is recognised as not a size but a piece, comparing a piece with what is not recognised but what is used as it is held by holding, comparing these two comes to be repeated. Suppose they are put together, suppose that there is an interruption, supposing that beginning again they are not changed as to position, suppose all this and suppose that any five two of whom are not separating suppose that the five are not consumed. Is there an exchange, is there a resemblance to the sky which is admitted to be there and the stars which can be seen. Is there. That was a question. There was no certainty. Fitting a failing meant that any two were indifferent and yet they were all connecting that, they were all connecting that consideration. This did not determine rejoining a letter. This did not make letters smaller. It did.

The stamp that is not only torn but also fitting is not any symbol. It suggests nothing. A sack that has no opening suggests more and the loss is not commensurate. The season gliding and the torn hangings receiving mending all this shows an example, it shows the force of sacrifice and likeness and disaster and a reason.

The time when there is not the question is only seen when there is a shower. Any little thing is water.

There was a whole collection made. A damp cloth, an oyster, a single mirror, a manikin, a student, a silent star, a single spark, a little movement and the bed is made. This shows the disorder, it does, it shows more likeness than anything else, it shows the single mind that directs an apple. All the coats have a different shape, that does not mean that they differ in colour, it means a union between use and exercise and a horse.

A plain hill, one is not that which is not white and red and green, a plain hill makes no sunshine, it shows that without a disturber. So the shape is there and the colour and the outline and the miserable center, it is not very likely that there is a center, a hill is a hill and no hill is contained in a pink tender descender.

A can containing a curtain is a solid sentimental usage. The trouble in both eyes does not come from the same symmetrical carpet, it comes from there being no more disturbance than in little paper. This does show the teeth, it shows colour.

A measure is that which put up so that it shows the length has a steel construction. Tidiness is not delicacy, it does not destroy the whole piece, certainly not it has been measured and nothing has been cut off and even if that has been lost there is a name, no name is signed and left over, not any space is fitted so that moving about is plentiful. Why is there so much resignation in a package, why is there rain, all the same the chance has come, there is no bell to ring.

A package and a filter and even a funnel, all this together makes a scene and supposing the question arises is hair curly, is it dark and dusty, supposing that question arises, is brushing necessary, is it, the whole special suddenness commences then, there is no delusion.

A cape is a cover, a cape is not a cover in summer, a cape is a cover and the regulation is that there is no such weather. A cape is not always a cover, a cape is not a cover when there is another, there is always something in that thing in establishing a disposition to put wetting where it will not do more harm. There is always that disposition and in a way there is some use in not mentioning changing and in establishing the temperature, there is some use in it as establishing all that lives dimmer freer and there is no dinner in the middle of anything. There is no such thing.

Why is a pale white not paler than blue, why is a connection made by a stove, why is the example which is mentioned not shown to be the same, why is there no adjustment between the place and the separate attention. Why is there a choice in gamboling. Why is there no necessary dull stable, why is there a single piece of any colour, why is there that sensible silence. Why is there the resistance in a mixture, why is there no poster, why is there that in the window, why is there no suggester, why is there no window, why is there no oyster closer. Why is there a circular diminisher, why is there a bather, why is there no scraper, why is there a dinner, why is there a bell ringer, why is there a duster, why is there a section of a similar resemblance, why is there that scissor.

South, south which is a wind is not rain, does silence choke speech or does it not.

Lying in a conundrum, lying so makes the springs restless, lying so is a reduction, not lying so is arrangeable.

Releasing the oldest auction that is the pleasing some still renewing.

Giving it away, not giving it away, is there any difference. Giving it away. Not giving it away.

Almost very likely there is no seduction, almost very likely

there is no stream, certainly very likely the height is pene-
trated, certainly certainly the target is cleaned. Come to sit,
come to refuse, come to surround, come slowly and age is
not lessening. The time which showed that was when there
was no eclipse. All the time that resenting was removal all that
time there was breath. No breath is shadowed, no breath is
painstaking and yet certainly what could be the use of paper,
paper shows no disorder, it shows no desertion.

Why is there a difference between one window and another,
why is there a difference, because the curtain is shorter. There
is no distaste in beefsteak or in plums or in gallons of milk
water, there is no defiance in original piling up over a roof,
there is no daylight in the evening, there is none there empty.

A tribune, a tribune does not mean paper, it means nothing
more than cake, it means more sugar, it shows the state of
lengthening any nose. The last spice is that which shows the
whole evening spent in that sleep, it shows so that walking is
an alleviation, and yet this astonishes everybody the distance
is so sprightly. In all the time there are three days, those are
not passed uselessly. Any little thing is a change that is if nothing is wasted in that cellar. All the rest of the chairs are established.

A success, a success is alright when there are there rooms
and no vacancies, a success is alright when there is a package,
success is alright anyway and any curtain is wholesale. A curtain diminishes and an ample space shows varnish.

One taste one tack, one taste one bottle, one taste one fish,
one taste one barometer. This shows no distinguishing sign
when there is a store.

Any smile is stern and any coat is a sample. Is there any use
in changing more doors than there are committees. This question is so often asked that squares show that they are blotters.
It is so very agreeable to hear a voice and to see all the signs
of that expression.

Cadences, real cadences, real cadences and a quiet colour.
Careful and curved, cake and sober, all accounts and mixture,
a guess at anything is righteous, should there be a call there
would be a voice.

A line in life, a single line and a stairway, a rigid cook, no
cook and no equator, all the same there is higher than that

another evasion. Did that mean shame, it meant memory. Looking into a place that was hanging and was visible looking into this place and seeing a chair did that mean relief, it did, it certainly did not cause constipation and yet there is a melody that has white for a tune when there is straw colour. This shows no face.

Star-light, what is star-light, star-light is a little light that is not always mentioned with the sun, it is mentioned with the moon and the sun, it is mixed up with the rest of the time.

Why is the name changed. The name is changed because in the little space there is a tree, in some space there are no trees, in every space there is a hint of more, all this causes the decision.

Why is there education, there is education because the two tables which are folding are not tied together with a ribbon, string is used and string being used there is a necessity for another one and another one not being used to hearing shows no ordinary use of any evening and yet there is no disgrace in looking, none at all. This came to separate when there was simple selection of an entire preoccupation.

A curtain, a curtain which is fastened discloses mourning, this does not mean sparrows or elocution or even a whole preparation, it means that there are ears and very often more much more altogether.

Climate, climate is not southern, a little glass, a bright winter, a strange supper an elastic tumbler, all this shows that the back is furnished and red which is red is a dark colour. An example of this is fifteen years and a separation of regret.

China is not down when there are plates, lights are not ponderous and incalculable.

Currents, currents are not in the air and on the floor and in the door and behind it first. Currents do not show it plainer. This which is mastered has so thin a space to build it all that there is plenty of room and yet is it quarreling, it is not and the insistence is marked. A change is in a current and there is no habitable exercise.

A religion, almost a religion, any religion, a quintal in religion, a relying and a surface and a service in indecision and a creature and a question and a syllable in answer and more counting and no quarrel and a single scientific statement and no darkness and no question and an earned administration and a single set of sisters and an outline and no blisters and the section seeing yellow and the center having spelling and no solitude and no quaintness and yet solid quite so solid and the single surface centered and the question in the placard and the singularity, is there a singularity, and the singularity, why is there a question and the singularity why is the surface outrageous, why is it beautiful why is it not when there is no doubt, why is anything vacant, why is not disturbing a center no virtue, why is it when it is and why is it when it is and is and there is no doubt, there is no doubt that the singularity shows.

A climate, a single climate, all the time there is a single climate, any time there is a doubt, any time there is music that is to question more and more and there is no politeness, there is hardly any ordeal and certainly there is no tablecloth.

This is a sound and obligingness more obligingness leads to a harmony in hesitation.

A lake a single lake which is a pond and a little water any water which is an ant and no burning, not any burning, all this is sudden.

A cannister that is the remains of furniture and a looking glass and a bed room and a larger size, all the stand is shouted and what is ancient is practical. Should the resemblance be so that any little cover is copied, should it be so that yards are measured, should it be so and there be a sin, should it be so then certainly a room is big enough when it is so empty and the corners are gathered together.

The change is mercenary that settles whitening the colouring and serving dishes where there is metal and making yellow any yellow every colour in a shade which is expressed in a tray. This is a monster and awkward quite awkward and the little design which is flowered which is not strange and yet has visible writing, this is not shown all the time but at once, after that it rests where it is and where it is in place. No change is not needed. That does show design.

Excellent, more excellence is borrowing and slanting very slanting is light and secret and a recitation and emigration. Certainly shoals are shallow and nonsense more nonsense is sullen. Very little cake is water, very little cake has that escape.

Sugar any sugar, anger every anger, lover sermon lover, center no distractor, all order is in a measure.

Left over to be a lamp light, left over in victory, left over in saving, all this and negligence and bent wood and more even much more is not so exact as a pen and a turtle and even, certainly, and even a piece of the same experience as more.

To consider a lecture, to consider it well is so anxious and so much a charity and really supposing there is grain and if a stubble every stubble is urgent, will there not be a chance of legality. The sound is sickened and the price is purchased and golden what is golden, a clergyman, a single tax, a currency and an inner chamber.

Checking an emigration, checking it by smiling and certainly by the same satisfactory stretch of hands that have more use for it than nothing, and mildly not mildly a correction, not mildly even a circumstance and a sweetness and a serenity. Powder, that has no colour, if it did have would it be white.

A whole soldier any whole soldier has no more detail than any case of measles.

A bridge a very small bridge in a location and thunder, any thunder, this is the capture of reversible sizing and more indeed more can be cautious. This which makes monotony careless makes it likely that there is an exchange in principle and more than that, change in organisation.

This cloud does change with the movements of the moon and the narrow the quite narrow suggestion of the building. It does and then when it is settled and no sounds differ then comes the moment when cheerfulness is so assured that there is an occasion.

A plain lap, any plain lap shows that sign, it shows that there is not so much extension as there would be if there were more choice in everything. And why complain of more, why complain of very much more. Why complain at all when it is all arranged that as there is no more opportunity and no more appeal and not even any more clinching that certainly now some time has come.

A window has another spelling, it has "f" all together, it lacks no more then and this is rain, this may even be something else, at any rate there is no dedication in splendour. There is a turn of the stranger.

Catholic to be turned is to venture on youth and a section of debate, it even means that no class where each one over fifty is regular is so stationary that there are invitations.

A curving example makes righteous finger-nails. This is the only object in secretion and speech.

To begin the same four are no more than were taller. The rest had a big chair and a surveyance a cold accumulation of nausea, and even more than that, they had a disappointment.

Nothing aiming is a flower, if flowers are abundant then they are lilac, if they are not they are white in the center.

Dance a clean dream and an extravagant turn up, secure the steady rights and translate more than translate the authority, show the choice and make no more mistakes than yesterday.

This means clearness, it means a regular notion of exercise, it means more than that, it means liking counting, it means more than that, it does not mean exchanging a line.

Why is there more craving than there is in a mountain. This does not seem strange to one, it does not seem strange to an echo and more surely is in there not being a habit. Why is there so much useless suffering. Why is there.

Any wet weather means an open window, what is attaching eating, anything that is violent and cooking and shows weather is the same in the end and why is there more use in something than in all that.

The cases are made and books, back books are used to secure tears and church. They are even used to exchange black slippers. They can not be mended with wax. They show no need of any such occasion.

A willow and no window, a wide place stranger, a wideness makes an active center.

The sight of no pussy cat is so different that a tobacco zone is white and cream.

A lilac, all a lilac and no mention of butter, not even bread and butter, no butter and no occasion, not even a silent resemblance, not more care than just enough haughty.

A safe weight is that which when it pleases is hanging. A

safer weight is one more naughty in a spectacle. The best game is that which is shiny and scratching. Please a pease and a cracker and a wretched use of summer.

Surprise, the only surprise has no occasion. It is an ingredient and the section the whole section is one season.

A pecking which is petting and no worse than in the same morning is not the only way to be continuous often.

A light in the moon the only light is on Sunday. What was the sensible decision. The sensible decision was that notwithstanding many declarations and more music, not even notwithstanding the choice and a torch and a collection, notwithstanding the celebrating hat and a vacation and even more noise than cutting, notwithstanding Europe and Asia and being overbearing, not even withstanding an elephant and a strict occasion, not even withstanding more cultivation and some seasoning, not even with not drowning and with the ocean being encircling, not even with more likeness and any cloud, not even with terrific sacrifice of pedestrianism and a special resolution, not even more likely to be pleasing. The care with which the rain is wrong and the green is wrong and the white is wrong, the care with which there is a chair and plenty of breathing. The care with which there is incredible justice and likeness, all this makes a magnificent asparagus, and also a fountain.

Portrait of Mable Dodge at the Villa Curonia

The days are wonderful and the nights are wonderful and the life is pleasant.

Bargaining is something and there is not that success. The intention is what if application has that accident results are reappearing. They did not darken. That was not an adulteration.

So much breathing has not the same place when there is that much beginning. So much breathing has not the same place when the ending is lessening. So much breathing has the same place and there must not be so much suggestion. There can be there the habit that there is if there is no need of resting. The absence is not alternative.

Any time is the half of all the noise and there is not that disappointment. There is no distraction. An argument is clear.

Packing is not the same when the place which has all that is not emptied. There came there the hall and this was not the establishment. It had not all the meaning.

Blankets are warmer in the summer and the winter is not lonely. This does not assure the forgetting of the intention when there has been and there is every way to send some. There does not happen to be a dislike for water. This is not heartening.

As the expedition is without the participation of the question there will be nicely all that energy. They can arrange that the little color is not bestowed. They can leave it in regaining that intention. It is mostly repaid. There can be an irrigation. They can have the whole paper and they send it in some package. It is not inundated.

A bottle that has all the time to stand open is not so clearly shown when there is green color there. This is not the only way to change it. A little raw potato and then all that softer does happen to show that there has been enough. It changes the expression.

It is not darker and the present time is the best time to agree. This which has been feeling is what has the appetite and the patience and the time to stay. This is not collaborating.

All the attention is when there is not enough to do. This does not determine a question. The only reason that there is not that pressure is that there is a suggestion. There are many going. A delight is not bent. There had been that little wagon. There is that precision when there has not been an imagination. There has not been that kind abandonment. Nobody is alone. If the spread that is not a piece removed from the bed is likely to be whiter then certainly the sprinkling is not drying. There can be the message where the print is pasted and this does not mean that there is that esteem. There can be the likelihood of all the days not coming later and this will not deepen the collected dim version.

It is a gnarled division that which is not any obstruction and the forgotten swelling is certainly attracting, it is attracting the whiter division, it is not sinking to be growing, it is not darkening to be disappearing, it is not aged to be annoying. There can not be sighing. This is this bliss.

Not to be wrapped and then to forget undertaking, the credit and then the resting of that interval, the pressing of the sounding when there is no trinket is not altering, there can be pleasing classing clothing.

A sap that is that adaptation is the drinking that is not increasing. There can be that lack of quivering. That does not originate every invitation. There is not wedding introduction. There is not all that filling. There is the climate that is not existing. There is that plainer. There is the likeliness lying in liking likely likeliness. There is that dispensation. There is the paling that is not reddening, there is the reddening that is not reddening, there is that protection, there is that destruction, there is not the present lessening there is the argument of increasing. There is that that is not that which is that resting. There is not that occupation. There is that particular half of directing that there is that particular whole direction that is not all the measure of any combination. Gliding is not heavily moving. Looking is not vanishing. Laughing is not evaporating. There can be the climax. There can be the same dress. There can be an old dress. There can be the way there is that way there is that which is not that charging what is a regular way of paying. There has been William. All the time is likely. There is the condition. There has been admitting. There is not the print. There is that smiling. There is the season. There is that where there is not that which is where there is what there is which is beguiling. There is a paste.

Abandon a garden and the house is bigger. This is not smiling. This is comfortable. There is the comforting of predilection. An open object is establishing the loss that there was when the vase was not inside the place. It was not wandering.

A plank that was dry was not disturbing the smell of burning and altogether there was the best kind of sitting there could never be all the edging that the largest chair was having. It was not pushed. It moved then. There was not that lifting. There was that which was not any contradiction and there was not the bland fight that did not have that regulation. The contents were not darkening. There was not that hesitation. It was occupied. That was not occupying any exception. Any one had come. There was that distribution.

There was not that velvet spread when there was a pleasant head. The colour was paler. The moving regulating is not a distinction. The place is there.

Likely there is not that departure when the whole place that has that texture is so much in the way. It is not there to stay. It does not change that way. A pressure is not later. There is the same. There is not the shame. There is that pleasure.

In burying that game there is not a change of name. There is not perplexing and co-ordination. The toy that is not round has to be found and looking is not straining such relation. There can be that company. It is not wider when the length is not longer and that does make that way of staying away. Every one is exchanging returning. There is not a prediction. The whole day is that way. Any one is resting to say that the time which is not reverberating is acting in partaking.

A walk that is not stepped where the floor is covered is not in the place where the room is entered. The whole one is the same. There is not any stone. There is the wide door that is narrow on the floor. There is all that place.

There is that desire and there is no pleasure and the place is filling the only space that is placed where all the piling is not adjoining. There is not that distraction.

Praying has intention and relieving that situation is not solemn. There comes that way.

The time that is the smell of the plain season is not showing the water is running. There is not all that breath. There is the use of the stone and there is the place of the stuff and there is the practice of expending questioning. There is not that differentiation. There is that which is in time. There is the room that is the largest place when there is all that is where there is space. There is not that perturbation. The legs that show are not the certain ones that have been used. All legs are used. There is no action meant.

The particular space is not beguiling. There is that participation. It is not passing any way. It has that to show. It is why there is no exhalation.

There is all there is when there has all there has where there is what there is. That is what is done when there is done what is done and the union is won and the division is the explicit visit. There is not all of any visit.

One
Carl Van Vechten

One.

In the ample checked fur in the back and in the house, in the by next cloth and inner, in the chest, in mean wind.

One.

In the best most silk and water much, in the best most silk.

One.

In the best might last and wind that. In the best might last and wind in the best might last.

Ages, ages, all what sat.

One.

In the gold presently, in the gold presently unsuddenly and decapsized and dewalking.

In the gold coming in.

ONE.

One.

None in stable, none at ghosts, none in the latter spot.

ONE.

One.

An oil in a can, an oil and a vial with a thousand stems. An oil in a cup and a steel sofa.

One.

An oil in a cup and a woolen coin, a woolen card and a best satin.

A water house and a hut to speak, a water house and entirely water, water and water.

TWO.

Two.

A touching white shining sash and a touching white green undercoat and a touching white colored orange and a touching piece of elastic. A touching piece of elastic suddenly.

A touching white inlined ruddy hurry, a touching research in all may day. A touching research is an over show.

A touching expartition is in an example of work, a touching beat is in the best way.

A touching box is in a coach seat so that a touching box is on a coach seat so a touching box is on a coach seat, a touching box is on a coat seat, a touching box is on a coach seat.

A touching box is on the touching so helping held.

Two.

Any left in the touch is a scene, a scene. Any left in is left somehow.

FOUR.

Four.

Four between, four between and hacking. Four between and hacking.

Five.

Four between and a saddle, a kind of dim judge and a great big so colored dog.

Susie Asado

Sweet sweet sweet sweet sweet tea.
      Susie Asado.
Sweet sweet sweet sweet sweet tea.
      Susie Asado.
Susie Asado which is a told tray sure.
A lean on the shoe this means slips slips hers.
When the ancient light grey is clean it is yellow, it is a silver seller.
This is a please this is a please there are the saids to jelly. These are the wets these say the sets to leave a crown to Incy.
Incy is short for incubus.
A pot. A pot is a beginning of a rare bit of trees. Trees tremble, the old vats are in bobbles, bobbles which shade and shove and render clean, render clean must.
      Drink pups.
Drink pups drink pups lease a sash hold, see it shine and a bobolink has pins. It shows a nail.
What is a nail. A nail is unison.
Sweet sweet sweet sweet sweet tea.

Yet Dish

I

Put a sun in Sunday, Sunday.
Eleven please ten hoop. Hoop.
Cousin coarse in coarse in soap.
Cousin coarse in soap sew up. soap.
Cousin coarse in sew up soap.

II

A lea ender stow sole lightly.
Not a bet beggar.
Nearer a true set jump hum,
A lamp lander so seen poor lip.

III

Never so round.
A is a guess and a piece.
A is a sweet cent sender.
A is a kiss slow cheese.
A is for age jet.

IV

New deck stairs.
Little in den little in dear den.

V

Polar pole.
Dust winder.
Core see.
A bale a bale o a bale.

VI

Extravagant new or noise peal extravagant.

VII

S a glass.
Roll ups.

VIII

Powder in wails, powder in sails, powder is all next to it is
does wait sack rate all goals like chain in clear.

IX

Negligible old star.
Pour even.
It was a sad per cent.
Does on sun day.
Watch or water.
So soon a moon or a old heavy press.

X

Pearl cat or cat or pill or pour check.
New sit or little.
New sat or little not a wad yet.
Heavy toe heavy sit on head.

XI

Ex, ex, ex.
Bull it bull it bull it bull it.
Ex Ex Ex.

XII

Cousin plates pour a y shawl hood hair.
No see eat.

XIII

They are getting, bad left log lope, should a court say
stream, not a dare long beat a soon port.

XIV

Colored will he.
Calamity.
Colored will he
Is it a soon. Is it a soon. Is it a soon. soon. Is it
a soon. soon.

XV

Nobody's ice.
Nobody's ice to be knuckles.
Nobody's nut soon.
Nobody's seven picks.
Picks soap stacks.
Six in set on seven in seven told, to top.

XVI

A spread chin shone.
A set spread chin shone.

XVII

No people so sat.
Not an eider.
Not either. Not either either.

XVIII

Neglect, neglect use such.
Use such a man.
Neglect use such a man.
Such some here.

XIX

Note tie a stem bone single pair so itching.

XX

Little lane in lay in a circular crest.

XXI

Peace while peace while toast.
Paper eight paper eight or, paper eight ore white.

XXII

Coop pour.
Never a single ham.
Charlie. Charlie.

XXIII

Neglect or.
A be wade.
Earnest care lease.
Least ball sup.

XXIV

Meal dread.
Meal dread so or.
Meal dread so or bounce.
Meal dread so or bounce two sales. Meal dread so or
   bounce two sails. Not a rice. No nor a pray seat,
   not a little muscle, not a nor noble, not a cool
   right more than a song in every period of nails
   and pieces pieces places of places.

XXV

Neat know.
Play in horizontal pet soap.

XXVI

Nice pose.
Supper bell.
Pull a rope pressed.
Color glass.

XXVII

Nice oil pail.
No gold go at.
Nice oil pail.
Near a paper lag sought.
What is an astonishing won door. A please spoon.

XXVIII

Nice knee nick ear.
Not a well pair in day.
Nice knee neck core.
What is a skin pour in day.

XXIX

Climb climb max.
Hundred in wait.
Paper cat or deliver.

XXX

Little drawers of center.
Neighbor of dot light.
Shorter place to make a boom set.
Marches to be bright.

XXXI

Suppose a do sat.
Suppose a negligence.
Suppose a cold character.

XXXII

Suppose a negligence.
Suppose a sell.
Suppose a neck tie.

XXXIII

Suppose a cloth cape.
Suppose letter suppose let a paper.
Suppose soon.

XXXIV

A prim a prim prize.
A sea pin.
A prim a prim prize
A sea pin.

XXXV

Witness a way go.
Witness a way go. Witness a way go. Wetness.
Wetness.

XXXVI

Lessons lettuce.
Let us peer let us polite let us pour, let us polite. Let us
    polite.

XXXVII

Neither is blessings bean.

XXXVIII

Dew Dew Drops.
Leaves kindly Lasts.
Dew Dew Drops.

XXXIX

A R. nuisance.
Not a regular plate.
Are, not a regular plate.

XL

Lock out sandy.
Lock out sandy boot trees.
Lock out sandy boot trees knit glass.
Lock out sandy boot trees knit glass.

XLI

A R not new since.
New since.
Are new since bows less.

XLII

A jell cake.
A jelly cake.
A jelly cake.

XLIII

Peace say ray comb pomp
Peace say ray comb pump
Peace say ray comb pomp
Peace say ray comb pomp.

XLIV

Lean over not a coat low.
Lean over not a coat low by stand.
Lean over net. Lean over net a coat low hour stemmed
Lean over a coat low a great send. Lean over coat low
    extra extend.

XLV

Copying Copying it in.

XLVI

Never second scent never second scent in stand. Never
second scent in stand box or show. Or show me sales.
Or show me sales oak. Oak pet. Oak pet stall.

XLVII

Not a mixed stick or not a mixed stick or glass. Not a mend
stone bender, not a mend stone bender or stain.

XLVIII

Polish polish is it a hand, polish is it a hand or all, or all
poles sick, or all poles sick.

XLIX

Rush in rush in slice.

L

Little gem in little gem in an. Extra.

LI

In the between egg in, in the between egg or on.

LII

Leaves of gas, leaves of get a towel louder.

LIII

Not stretch.

LIV

Tea Fulls.
Pit it pit it little saddle pear say.

LV

Let me see wheat air blossom.
Let me see tea.

LVI

Nestle in glass, nestle in walk, nestle in fur a lining.

LVII

Pale eaten best seek.
Pale eaten best seek, neither has met is a glance.

LVIII

Suppose it is a s. Suppose it is a seal. Suppose it is a
recognised opera.

LIX

Not a sell inch, not a boil not a never seeking cellar.

LX

Little gem in in little gem in an. Extra.

LXI

Catch as catch as coal up.

LXII

Necklaces, neck laces, necklaces, neck laces.

LXIII

Little in in in in.

LXIV

Next or Sunday, next or sunday check.

LXV

Wide in swim, wide in swim pansy.

LXVI

Next to hear next to hear old boat seak, old boat seak next to hear.

LXVII

Ape pail ape pail to glow.

LXVIII

It was in on an each tuck. It was in on an each tuck.

LXIX

Wire lean string, wire lean string excellent miss on one pepper cute. Open so mister soil in to close not a see wind not seat glass.

Americans

Eating and paper.

A laugh in a loop is not dinner. There is so much to pray.

A slight price is a potatoe. A slimness is in length and even in strength.

A capable extravagance that is that which shows no provision is that which when necessity is mild shows a certain distribution of anger. This is no sign of sin.

Five, five are more wonderful than a million. Five million, five million, five million, five are more wonderful than two together. Two together, two together.

A song, if a sad song is in unison and is sung, a sad song is singing. A sign of singing.

A gap what is a gap when there is not any meaning in a slice with a hole in it. What is the exchange between the whole and no more witnesses.

Press juice from a button, press it carelessly, press it with care, press it in a storm. A storm is so waiting and awful and moreover so much the worse for being where there is a storm that the use the whole use of more realization comes out of a narrow bridge and water faucets. This is no plain evidence of disaster. The point of it is that there is a strange straw being in any strange ice-cream.

A legal pencil a really legal pencil is incredible, it fastens the whole strong iron wire calender.

An inherent investigation, does that mean murder or does it only mean a railroad track with plenty of cinders.

Words that cumber nothing and call exceptionally tall people from very far away are those that have the same center as those used by them frequently.

Bale, bale is a thing that surrounding largely means hay, no hay has any more food than it needs to weigh that way henceforward and not more that most likely.

A soap, a whole soap, any piece of a whole soap, more whole soap and not mistily, all this is no outrage and no blessing. A precious thing is an oily thing. In that there is no sugar and silence.

A reason is that a curly house an ordinary curly house is exactly that, it is exactly more than that, it is so exactly no more than more than that.

Waiter, when is a waiter passive and expressed, a waiter is so when there is no more selection and really no more buckets altogether. This is what remains. It does. It is kindly exacted, it is pleased, it is anxious, it is even worthy when a material is like it. It is.

What is a hinge. A hinge is a location. What is a hinge necessarily.

When the butter cup is limited and there are radishes, when radishes are clean and a whole school, a real school is outrageous and more incensed, really more incensed and inclined, when the single satisfaction is so perfect and the pearl is so demure when all this is changed then there is no rattle there is hardly any rattle.

A and B and also nothing of the same direction is the best personal division there is between any laughing. The climate, the whole thing is surrounded, it is not pressed, it is not a vessel, it is not all there is of joining, it is a real anxious needful and it is so seldom circular, so more so than any article in the wire. The cluster is just the same ordinarily.

Supposing a movement is segregated and there is a piece of staging, suppose there is and the present is melted does that mean that any salt is bitter, would it change an investigation suddenly, when it would would it mean a long wide and not particular eddy. Would it and if it did would there be a change. A kind of exercise is hardest and the best excellence is sweet.

Finding a best hat with a hearty hat pin in mid-summer is a reason for being blindly. A smell is not in earth.

A wonder to chew and to eat and to mind and to set into the very tiny glass that is tall. This is that when there is a tenement. All weights are scales.

No put in a closet, no skirt in a closet, no lily, no lily not a lime lily. A solving and learned, awake and highing and a throat and a throat and a short set color, a short set color and a collar and a color. A last degree in the kink in a glove the rest.

A letter to press, a letter to press is not rowdy, it is not sliding, it is not a measure of the increasing swindling of elastic and breaking.

The thread, the thread, the thread is the language of yesterday, it is the resolution of today, it is no pain.

What is pain, pain is so changing the climate and the best ever that it is a time, it is really only a time, it is so winding. It is even.

A warm banana is warm naturally and this makes an ingredient in a mixture which has banana in it.

Cooling in the chasing void, cooling more than milder.

Hold that ho, that is hold the hold.

Pow word, a pow word is organic and sectional and an old man's company.

Win, win, a little bit chickeny, wet, wet, a long last hollow chucking jam, gather, a last butter in a cheese, a lasting surrounding action.

White green, a white green. A looking like that is a most connected piece of example of what it is where there is no choking, no choking in any sign.

Pin in and pin in and point clear and point where.

Breakfast, breakfast is the arrangement that beggars corn, that shows the habit of fishes, that powders aches and stumblings, and any useful thing. The way to say it is to say it.

No counting, no counting in not cousins, no counting for that example and that number of thirty and thirteen and thirty six and thirty.

A blind hobble which makes distress. A place not to put in a foot, a place so called and in close color, a place best and more shape and really a thought.

Cousin why is there no cousin, because it is an article to be preparatory.

Was it green told, was it a pill, was it chased awake, will it sale per, peas are fish, chicken, cold ups, nail poppers, nail pack in hers extra. Look past per. Look past per. Look past per. Look past fer. Look past fer. Look past fer.

No end in yours, knock puzzler palers, no beast in papers, no bird.

Icer cream, ice her steam, ice her icer ice sea excellent, excel gone in front excel sent.

Leaves of wet perfect sharpen setters, leaves of wet purr feet shape for seal weight for shirters.

Leaves of wet for ear pole ache sold hers, ears for sake heat purse change to meeters, change to be a sunk leave to see wet hers, but to why in that peace so not. Knot lot.

Please bell room please bell room fasten a character fasten a care in apter buttons fasten a care in such, in such. Fasten a care in, in in a in.

A lovely life in the center makes a mine in found a lovely pond in the water makes it just a space. A lovely seat in a day lump makes a set to collapse, a lovely light in a grass field makes it see just the early day in when there is a sight of please please please.

Due tie due to die due show the never less more way less. Do, weigh the more do way less.

Let us call a boat, let us call a boat.

Leave little grace to be. Leave little grace to bea, live little grace to bee.

Leave little grace. Leave little.

Leave little grace to be.

Near red reserve leave lavender acre bat.

Shout us, shout horse curve less.

Least bee, least bay alter, alter the sat pan and left all, rest in, resafe in article so fur.

A cannon ball a cigar and a dress in suits, a cannon ball a cigar and a dress suit case, a cannon ball a cigar and a dress suit case, a head a hand a little above, a shake in my and mines.

Let us leaves, moor itch. Bars touch.

Nap old in town inch chair, nap on in term on chain, do deal sack file in for, do bale send on and for, reset the pan old in for same and chew get that all baste for, nice nor call churches, meet by and boot send for in, last when with and by that which for with all do sign call, meet with like shall what shirs not by bought lest, not by bought lest in own see certain, in own so same excellent, excellent hairy, hairy, excellent not excellent not knot excellent, excellent knot.

B r, brute says. A hole, a hole is a true, a true, a true.

Little paper and dolls, little paper and row why, little paper and a thin opera extra.

No use to age mother, no whole wide able recent mouth

parcel, no relief farther, no relief in loosens no relief abler, no relief, no relief pie pepper nights, no relief poor no relief or, no relief, or no relief.

America a merica, a merica the go leading s the go leading s cans, cans be forgot and nigh nigh is a niecer a niecer to bit, a niecer to bit.

It was a peach, it was a long suit, it was heavy harsh singes.

Leave crack his leave crack his eats, all guest all guest a stove. Like bit.

Nuts, when and if the bloom is on next and really really really, it is a team, it is a left and all it cut, it is a so like that between and a shun a shun with a believer, a believer in the extra, extra not, extra a rechange for it more. No sir.

No it sir.

It was a tame in, it was a tame in and a a little vent made a whole simmer simmer a wish.

What is it not to say reach house. Coal mill. Coal mill well. It to lease house. Coal mill tell. Coal in meal tell.

A pill shape with a round center.

Color Cook color him with ready bbs and neat show pole glass and nearly be seen every day more see what all a pearly little not shut, no rail see her.

No peter no rot.

Poles poles are seeds and near the change the change pets are swimming swimming and a plate all a plate is reed pour for the grammar grammar of lake.

Lake in a sad old chimney last and needs needs needs needs needs needs needs, in the mutton and the meat there is a change to pork walk, with a walk mean clean and butter and does it show the feather bench does it mean the actual and not or does it light the cylinder. It is in choice and chosen, it is in choice and knee and knee and knee and just the same two bay.

To irregulate to irregulate gums.

America key america key.

It is too nestle by the pin grove shirr, all agree to the counting ate ate pall. Paul is better.

Vest in restraint in repute.

Shown land in constate.

I am sorry I am awfully sorry, I am so sorry, I am so sorry.

No fry shall it see c bough it.

Nibbling bit, nibbling bit, may the land in awe for.

It is not a particular lamp lights which absolutely so far pull sizes and near by in the change with it not in the behoof.

It was a singe, it was a scene in the in, it was a singe in.

Never sink, never sink sinker, never sink sinker sunk, sink sink sinker sink.

A cattle sheep.

By the white white white white, by the white white white white white white, by the white white white white by the white by the white white white white.

Needless in pins.

In the fence in the for instance, in the fence or how, hold chirp, hold chirp her, hold your paper, hope hop in hit it.

Extra successive.

Little beats of long saturday tileing.

No neck leg ticking.

Peel more such wake next stir day.

Peel heaps pork seldom.

Coiled or red bench.

A soled in a light is not waver. There is for much ash so.

In the second, in the second second second.

Pour were whose has. Pole sack sirs.

A neat not necklace neglect.

A neat not neglect. A neat.

A neat not neglect.

Put a sun in sunday. Sunday.

In the Grass
(On Spain)

Occident all Spain the taste.

Milled cautious and plaster and with the heat her trimmed white. Seat silver, seat it next. Poor it in gold hot hoods.

Be cool inside with a monkey tied, with a monkey tied. Be cool inside the mule. Be cool inside with a surrounded tied, a cast, before, behind again, indeed, many.

What in the cut with any money and so, and so the climate is at stake, all the circular receipts are pears and linen is the stall to peep, likely and more the season's chair and little grasses with a pole all the occasion is the wreath and many houses are baked. Many have the same in came and all the light is many wet all the burst in in the man and best to hide is only sweet. All is that and a little haste, a little pleading with a clouded pup all is chance to be the curl that sets and all the winding causes. All of it cucumber.

Cup of lather and moan moan stone grown corn and lead white and any way culture is power, Culture is power. Culture.

Clambering from a little sea, clambering within bathing, clambering with a necessary rest for eye glasses, clambering beside.

A little green is only seen when they mean to be holder, holder why, coal pepper is a tissue.

Come up shot come up cousin, come up cold salmon pearly, come up, come in, nicely, nicely seen, singing, singing with music, sudden leaves loaves and turtles, taught turtles taught turtles teach hot and cold and little drinks.

Colored huts, cold to din acres of as real birds as stole when. Stole when, it is a lie. It is coming to the seal, it is coming how is it. Language of the hold of the sea sucking dart belt and no gowns in, no gowns in pelting. This is the cane that is short and gold more.

Cold not coin in the ground be sour and special and settled and soiled and a little reason. Come then to sort the kinks in how surrounded is a limb.

Cute numbers, cute to be so bold and so sallow and so in

the cream and furled, furled with chalk and lights and high bees and little legs heady and little least little cups, least little cups bellow, bellow electric shadows, real old teachers with a private cake of bean and numbers those numbers. Do they pack.

Spanish cut that means a squeeze and in place of water oil and water more. Mine in the pin and see cuttle cuttle fish call that it is that it is sardine, that it is in pelts and all the same there is paper in poles paper and scratches and nearly places.

Guess a green. The cloud is too hold, collected necessary pastes in that shine of old boil and much part much part in thread and land with a pile. The closeness of a lesson to shirt and the reason for a pale cullass is what is the revolution and retaliation and serpentine illustration and little eagle. A long little beagle, a long little scissor of a kind that has choice all this makes a collation.

All winter is dutiful. All the short stays are digestion. All lines are cylindrical that means that there is leading.

Any roast is not leading. Enough pale ways are scratched.

Spend a height all up and only pup, spend it with the soon. And this when. More call. Cane seat in bottom choice makes a melon within. A melon within then.

A little return bitten with a cake set white with ink and size and little parlors healthy with a coat. A keen glance wet with accustomed perspiration. No need to dry, no need to current a sand paper with white seams and long shoals. No more mail in splendor and shape to set sights and little steaders in so hat shoot, shut toes, shut toes with a rid of not that, no that, not that.

A peach a peach pear which means a pear early and looking and near near there, exactly pass the light hall where there is no cover no cover to what.

Suppose it is past the mouth which is peculiar and nervous and left and argued and whiled whiled with a tree.

Less a chain than a loss and pieces of pearly paper that means blue not all and the best choice is moreover.

Naturally lovey naturally a period which is regulated by a perfect beam of carpet and more boats does mean something. It is enough.

A handsome beam a handsome beam is quite like the

standing of a little peak shut up and needles all not needles. Rest and zest and powder to shout and color and ball and sweet word black.

Believe, I believe you restruck my cold wet and the dun hit it back choose it set.

Come to why, sit in oil save the sos, all the gone sing in a pin save sit it kit, kit all.

Suppose a little chance to hold a door would leave the door closed would that mean that the sun was in, would it mean messages and a kite, would it mean a sold bone and little pies. The necessary shakes makes a whittle. This is not none.

A little pan, that is to please it, a little which is a point to show that co-incident to a lively boat there is nearly places. That is nobody touching. All the plays garden. Little screen. Not collected and spacious not at all so old. And more places have the behold it. The best example is mustard. A little thing. A little no old shut.

Lot in that which is a place surrounded by a fence. A fence is small it is a wall, a wall is tall it is a tunnel, a tunnel is not necessary to a city. A city is celebrated.

Leave piles steady, show it the moon.

Not cut loud and teasing I bleed you, not quite shadow and niece it lises. This is mike when the land is shooken and left peel short is most to sake and not sublime is moist to ramming and leave it whet is most in chance. Nest bite is way back in the clam of dear gold weights with necessary williams williams wild williams with lamb laden twitches and new-casts and love boosts and most nextily.

Reason with toil and a mark upside down and left boils not knealed with close cracks and moses. A real plume with a no less boiled collander and share.

This is the sport.

Leave it to shut up the right nasal extra ollofactorising sea lights and nearly base more shall sees to the place of the best.

We wide lade the tall tack which squeeze load the no sire and leave more in church maid than rest so to streak.

Mow chases in a spoon and tub, big clam, mow places in a boil a piece. No gas bests.

Look it to peas, loaf it in both spats mean a glass mean in passes in passes a poke and a chair and little cries and a bottle.

A veil and a place seater and a peanut which makes throws so grand.

Never pet never pet a gallon because there is a trunk. A trunk has a bosom. Lead less. Lead prosper pour, poor gold wax and much much tower.

Please place what, place a colored glass. This shows two three eight three nine. This is not sunday. A trouble home.

If a wake means bounded numbers eighty and lately. This is three, show shine five, leave it pare. All that. Seven rough state.

No nuisance is in a married widow with a collection of dear ones in one room nicely. Why is black cooler, black is cooler because spread in makes a little piece of pillow and a coal black lace. This is so best shown.

Suppose it is a parcel of oats and no fat, suppose it is a drill, suppose even that it is a winning centre, this means five and five and five.

Let let let a chief go.

The reason why a laugh is laughed after is that a shed and a shawl and little onions and keys and keys are after all a dog and a curtain and a little less.

Please please please please please.

The more the wet is water the more lilies are tubes and red are rice rows. A little scene and a tall fanner and a flower a hair flower and a shoes and a shoes boots and rubbish all this makes raising please tease and a little likeness noises.

A gain again pounds. Agate in pets, love biscuits, a time.

Again in leaves of potatoes and cuts, cuts with, with in, in him, a length.

A little belly a little belly cold, speed out stuff, stuff alike, alike shirts and goats and get ups and laid car cases.

All a bill, a bill boaster. Suppose it happened when, when a little shadow was a tail and a can a can was gathering. Gathering then.

Suppose a clandestine roof had tires and could neglect a blue spot suppose it was the end and three places were necessary a like view would be charming charming, charming weather.

Cries is, coming, a leg, all a leg, two utter, more children, no narrow, read a little.

If a horse and a bat and a gathering bleed stir and a chin and a cloth and early ear marks and then such such raiding and little lives and a multiplied purple, all the spool all of it cloth and gets gets out and a piece of reasonable white jacket and a hair a long pail and all bone some binding and a little season silk.

Grand mutter grand mutter shell, real core, real oak plate.

Lara Lara Psyche, Lara Lara three brothers and a mother, sister sister and a new year a new year not christmas, christmas is off off of it. Really.

Three brothers and mother. Leave it fit to a string and there is a ball a ball a hat, a hat a special astracan, a kind of loaf, a real old seventeen checkers. Come to be in, see the table and the look and the little day tomorrow, it is Thursday Friday, Friday, Friday in a day to Sunday, Sunday Sunday, Monday Monday Monday Wednesday and seventy failing out sights.

A son what is a son, a son is in the sitting room and in a central carry ball. A son is not a sister diamond, it is so noted.

Whispers, whispers. Whispers not whiskers, whiskers, whiskers and really hair. Hair. Hair is when two are in and show gum.

Kiss a turn, close.

Suppose close is clothes, clothes is close.

Be less be seen, stain in burr and make pressure. This is bit.

Excel a line, a line is in end purple blue, yes guess show packets and it it it.

Spain is a tame name with a track a track so particular to shame, a track a little release in sold out casts a little next to saleable old cream. Able to pass.

A land steam, a cold cake, a received egg check, an oleander.

Lessen pay a corridor, meal passes.

Necklace, strings.

Necklace, strings, shoulder.

Newly set tea, tea be hold.

Tea behold.

If the soiling carries the head, if the baking measures the pint, if the rudening leans on a strand then shutters.

No need to say a little deaf way is a goat, a goat has a pin in him. Leave glasses, glasses are so cactuses.

Able able ever grass her, get up fern case, get up seize.

Noble and no noble and no next burr, net in and bee net in and bee next to shown miner. Next to beat bean, next to beat bean next to be blender, next to between, next to between in intend intender. In tender.

A laugh in cat, coal hot in. A remembrance of a direct realteration with no bust no buster, no bust here.

Suppose it a glaze a glaze of curtain a fetch in pots a news camper, supper the next old meat oak and kneel kneel with excellent excellent least sands and neck stop. That is.

What you call them what you call them say butter butter and let us leaves and a special a realteration lace a realteration lace.

Next all, next all, inks.

It was a strange name that which when a record of a lucine and naughty bent made it by that that nearly any excellent shade of night glasses made a pleasing and regular hair.

A wet syllable is we are, a wet syllable is we are we in.

A Spanish water and a coop shape mine and legs and reed ridiculous red, and little lively hue, little lively hue and copper, little lively hue and copper up.

Guillaume Apollinaire

Give known or pin ware.
Fancy teeth, gas strips.
Elbow elect, sour stout pore, pore caesar, pour state at.
Leave eye lessons I. Leave I. Lessons. I. Leave I lessons, I.

Preciosilla

Cousin to Clare washing.

In the win all the band beagles which have cousin lime sign and arrange a weeding match to presume a certain point to exstate to exstate a certain pass lint to exstate a lean sap prime lo and shut shut is life.

Bait, bait tore, tore her clothes, toward it, toward a bit, to ward a sit, sit down in, in vacant surely lots, a single mingle, bait and wet, wet a single establishment that has a l i l y lily grow. Come to the pen come in the stem, come in the grass grown water.

Lily wet lily wet while. This is so pink so pink in stammer, a long bean which shows bows is collected by a single curly shady, shady get, get set wet bet.

It is a snuff a snuff to be told and have can wither, can is it and sleep sleeps knot, it is a lily scarf the pink and blue yellow, not blue not odor sun, nobles are bleeding bleeding two seats two seats on end. Why is grief. Grief is strange black. Sugar is melting. We will not swim.

Preciosilla.

Please be please be get, please get wet, wet naturally, naturally in weather. Could it be fire more firier. Could it be so in ate struck. Could it be gold up, gold up stringing, in it while while which is hanging, hanging in dingling, dingling in pinning, not so. Not so dots large dressed dots, big sizes, less laced, less laced diamonds, diamonds white, diamonds bright, diamonds in the in the light, diamonds light diamonds door diamonds hanging to be four, two four, all before, this bean, lessly, all most, a best, willow, vest, a green guest, guest, go go go go go go, go. Go go. Not guessed. Go go.

Toasted susie is my ice-cream.

Sacred Emily

Compose compose beds.
Wives of great men rest tranquil.
Come go stay philip philip.
Egg be takers.
Parts of place nuts.
Suppose twenty for cent.
It is rose in hen.
Come one day.
A firm terrible a firm terrible hindering, a firm hindering have a ray nor pin nor.
Egg in places.
Egg in few insists.
In set a place.
I am not missing.
Who is a permit.
I love honor and obey I do love honor and obey I do.
Melancholy do lip sing.
How old is he.
Murmur pet murmur pet murmur.
Push sea push sea push sea push sea push sea push sea push sea push sea.
Sweet and good and kind to all.
Wearing head.
Cousin tip nicely.
Cousin tip.
Nicely.
Wearing head.
Leave us sit.
I do believe it will finish, I do believe it will finish.
Pat ten patent, Pat ten patent.
Eleven and eighteen.
Foolish is foolish is.
Birds measure birds measure stores birds measure stores measure birds measure.
Exceptional firm bites.

How do you do I forgive you everything and there is nothing to forgive.

Never the less.

Leave it to me.

Weeds without papers.

Weeds without papers are necessary.

Left again left again.

Exceptional considerations.

Never the less tenderness.

Resting cow curtain.

Resting bull pin.

Resting cow curtain.

Resting bull pin.

Next to a frame.

The only hat hair.

Leave us mass leave us. Leave us pass. Leave us. Leave us pass leave us.

Humming is.

No climate.

What is a size.

Ease all I can do.

Colored frame.

Couple of canning.

Ease all I can do.

Humming does as

Humming does as humming is.

What is a size.

No climate.

Ease all I can do.

Shall give it, please to give it.

Like to give it, please to give it.

What a surprise.

Not sooner whether.

Cordially yours.

Pause.

Cordially yours.

Not sooner together.

Cordially yours.

In strewing, in strewing.

That is the way we are one and indivisible.

Pay nuts renounce.
Now without turning around.
I will give them to you tonight.
Cunning is and does cunning is and does the most beautiful notes.
I would like a thousand most most.
Center pricking petunia.
Electrics are tight electrics are white electrics are a button.
Singular pressing.
Recent thimble.
Noisy pearls noisy pearl coat.
Arrange.
Arrange wide opposite.
Opposite it.
Lily ice-cream.
Nevertheless.
A hand is Willie.
Henry Henry Henry.
A hand is Henry.
Henry Henry Henry.
A hand is Willie.
Henry Henry Henry.
All the time.
A wading chest.
Do you mind.
Lizzie do you mind.
Ethel.
Ethel.
Ethel.
Next to barber.
Next to barber bury.
Next to barber bury china.
Next to barber bury china glass.
Next to barber china and glass.
Next to barber and china.
Next to barber and hurry.
Next to hurry.
Next to hurry and glass and china.
Next to hurry and glass and hurry.
Next to hurry and hurry.

Next to hurry and hurry.
Plain cases for see.
Tickle tickle tickle you for education.
A very reasonable berry.
Suppose a selection were reverse.
Cousin to sadden.
A coral neck and a little song so very extra so very Susie.
Cow come out cow come out and out and smell a little.
Draw prettily.
Next to a bloom.
Neat stretch.
Place plenty.
Cauliflower.
Cauliflower.
Curtain cousin.
Apron.
Neither best set.
Do I make faces like that at you.
Pinkie.
Not writing not writing another.
Another one.
Think.
Jack Rose Jack Rose.
Yard.
Practically all of them.
Does believe it.
Measure a measure a measure or.
Which is pretty which is pretty which is pretty.
To be top.
Neglect Waldberg.
Sudden say separate.
So great so great Emily.
Sew grate sew grate Emily.
Not a spell nicely.
Ring.
Weigh pieces of pound.
Aged steps.
Stops.
Not a plan bow.
Why is lacings.

Little slam up.
Cold seam peaches.
Begging to state begging to state begging to state alright.
Begging to state begging to state begging to state alright.
Wheels stows wheels stows.
Wickedness.
Cotton could mere less.
Nevertheless.
Anne.
Analysis.
From the standpoint of all white a week is none too much.
Pink coral white coral, coral coral.
Happy happy happy.
All the, chose.
Is a necessity.
Necessity.
Happy happy happy all the.
Happy happy happy all the.
Necessity.
Remain seated.
Come on come on come on on.
All the close.
Remain seated.
Happy.
All the.
Necessity.
Remain seated.
All the, close.
Websters and mines, websters and mines.
Websters and mines.
Trimming.
Gold space gold space of toes.
Twos, twos.
Pinned to the letter.
In accompany.
In a company in.
Received.
Must.
Natural lace.
Spend up.

Spend up length.
Spend up length.
Length thoroughly.
Neatness.
Neatness Neatness.
Excellent cording.
Excellent cording short close.
Close to.
When.
Pin black.
Cough or up.
Shouting.
Shouting.
Neater pin.
Pinned to the letter.
Was it a space was it a space was it a space to see.
Neither things.
Persons.
Transition.
Say say say.
North of the calender.
Window.
Peoples rest.
Preserve pulls.
Cunning piler.
Next to a chance.
Apples.
Apples.
Apples went.
It was a chance to preach Saturday.
Please come to Susan.
Purpose purpose black.
Extra plain silver.
Furious slippers.
Have a reason.
Have a reason candy.
Points of places.
Neat Nezars.
Which is a cream, can cream.
Ink of paper slightly mine breathes a shoulder able shine.

Necessity.
Near glass.
Put a stove put a stove hoarser.
If I was surely if I was surely.
See girl says.
All the same bright.
Brightness.
When a churn say suddenly when a churn say suddenly.
Poor pour percent.
Little branches.
Pale.
Pale.
Pale.
Pale.
Pale.
Pale.
Pale.
Near sights.
Please sorts.
Example.
Example.
Put something down.
Put something down some day.
Put something down some day in.
Put something down some day in my.
In my hand.
In my hand right.
In my hand writing.
Put something down some day in my hand writing.
Needles less.
Never the less.
Never the less.
Pepperness.
Never the less extra stress.
Never the less.
Tenderness.
Old sight.
Pearls.
Real line.
Shoulders.

Upper states.
Mere colors.
Recent resign.
Search needles.
All a plain all a plain show.
White papers.
Slippers.
Slippers underneath.
Little tell.
I chance.
I chance to.
I chance to to.
I chance to.
What is a winter wedding a winter wedding.
Furnish seats.
Furnish seats nicely.
Please repeat.
Please repeat for.
Please repeat.
This is a name to Anna.
Cushions and pears.
Reason purses.
Reason purses to relay to relay carpets.
Marble is thorough fare.
Nuts are spittoons.
That is a word.
That is a word careless.
Paper peaches.
Paper peaches are tears.
Rest in grapes.
Thoroughly needed.
Thoroughly needed signs.
All but.
Relieving relieving.
Argonauts.
That is plenty.
Cunning saxon symbol.
Symbol of beauty.
Thimble of everything.
Cunning clover thimble.

Cunning of everything.
Cunning of thimble.
Cunning cunning.
Place in pets.
Night town.
Night town a glass.
Color mahogany.
Color mahogany center.
Rose is a rose is a rose is a rose.
Loveliness extreme.
Extra gaiters.
Loveliness extreme.
Sweetest ice-cream.
Page ages page ages page ages.
Wiped Wiped wire wire.
Sweeter than peaches and pears and cream.
Wiped wire wiped wire.
Extra extreme.
Put measure treasure.
Measure treasure.
Tables track.
Nursed.
Dough.
That will do.
Cup or cup or.
Excessively illegitimate.
Pussy pussy pussy what what.
Current secret sneezers.
Ever.
Mercy for a dog.
Medal make medal.
Able able able.
A go to green and a letter spoke a go to green or praise or
Worships worships worships.
Door.
Do or.
Table linen.
Wet spoil.
Wet spoil gaiters and knees and little spools little spools or
ready silk lining.

Suppose misses misses.
Curls to butter.
Curls.
Curls.
Settle stretches.
See at till.
Louise.
Sunny.
Sail or.
Sail or rustle.
Mourn in morning.
The way to say.
Patter.
Deal own a.
Robber.
A high b and a perfect sight.
Little things singer.
Jane.
Aiming.
Not in description.
Day way.
A blow is delighted.

Turkey and Bones and Eating and We Liked It

A Play

He was very restless. He does not like to stand while he picks flowers. He does not smell flowers. He has a reasonable liking for herbs. He likes their smell. He is not able to see storms. He can see anything running. He has been able to be praised.

SCENE I.

Polybe and seats.

Straw seats which are so well made that they resemble stools. They are all of straw and thick. They are made with two handles.

Genevieve and cotton.

I do not like cotton drawers. I prefer wool or linen. I admit that linen is damp. Wool is warm. I believe I prefer wool.

Minorca and dogs.

I like a dog which is easily understood as I have never had the habit of going out except on Sunday. Now I go out every day.

Anthony and coal.

I believe that coal is better than wood. If coal is good it burns longer. In any case it is very difficult to get here.

Felix and a letter.

I do not wish to reply to a telegram, not because I find it difficult to explain in it that I wished to see you. I did wish to see you.

Mr. Clement.

It gives me great pleasure to meet you. I am feeling well today and I see that you are enjoying the mild weather. It will continue so. I hope you will be pleased. I will present myself

to you in saying that I am certain that you are deriving pleasure from your winter. I am certainly eager.

William.

He is too difficult. I mean he is too difficult. I don't believe
you understand me yet. He is too difficult.

SCENE II.

She would not insist. We were to have a saddle of mutton.
We were served first with a not distasteful supply of vegetables.
There was ham in it and pork. These had boiling and they
were a sauce. Let me tell you about the german.

A little girl.

I can tell blue when I see it.

A German.

Look.

Italians.

We expect to go home.
When
When the cigarettes come. I know these were stale. If I go
to the war I will be readily excused because I am lame. You
have every reason to be lame. You are a waiter but the out of
door life may do you good.

Genevieve.

I could not leave the house as I was expecting the repara-
tion of a mattress.
You did not find it necessary to leave the house,
Not in the morning.

William and Mary.

William is William and he does not use any precaution. He
is not very adroit.
She.   Will you drink wine.
I do.
I know that but will you take any now.
I don't mind the taste of it.
This is really not wine. It is a concoction of brown sugar
and water and fermented juice. I call it wine it is a drink. I
did not know it was not wine.

The count.

Why does the count wish for this house. He wishes for it because it has all conveniences. It really hasn't but it is better situated than the one he has now.

Raymond and Jenny.

I do like a Spanish name a Spanish name always begins with a V.

We went together.

We went together and we did not go to the Opera. The opera that was being given was Boris Goudonoff.

SCENE III.

A whole collection of stamps. A family meeting.
Where did you get it.
I got it when I saw the envelope.
Where did you see it.
Don't hold it.
Don't spoil it.
Let me see it.
Thanks.
Thanks so much.
I thank you.
I thank you for your kindness.
Please make a collection of flowers.

Collecting flowers is not a misery. You have to carry something a handkerchief will do and more than that is perfectly selfish.

We are not perfectly selfish.
William.   Do be persevering.
Mrs. Clement.   I am. I do not leave my house.
Genevieve.   Don't you leave your house.
Mr. and Mrs. Clement.   We do.
Maud.   The hills would be better than water. We like water.
Mrs. Clement.   Everybody likes water.
Maud.   And fish.
Genevieve.   I do not care for the fish here.
William.   Radishes.
Maud.   Radishes are strong.
Mrs. Clement.   I am glad to have seen you.

SCENE IV.

An interlude.

If you were a Breton and read a book and understood Span-ish would you be richer than a frenchman who talked in a field. If a man talked in a field and told about papers and contraband and laughed would you see a resemblance in him to a Swiss. I would. This is what happened. He says it is very necessary to be young to be young and unmarried and then you can not do as you please. You can not go where you please. He believed that it was alright. I am certain that he understood talking. He also laughed. I am not convinced that ploughing is safe. Ploughing is done with a plough and under a tree. Dogs bark, little dogs bark the horse and sometimes a mule and sometimes a donkey. The people say leave it to me. I will not.

SCENE V.

Farmer.

Listen to me.

I will not.

Then do not listen to me.

I heard you when you said it. I like to see goats feed.

And so do I like to see them lay the tracks.

They are laying them for the electrical railroad.

Sarah. I don't like him. I don't like his ways. I don't like it and I will not say it. I will do as you do and you do it so nicely. I will do as you do and then we were right. We were right to ask him to come in. He will not come in. I will not go out. We will not stay there. We will say yes certainly, we are not very busy. Yes please see that you have the things you want. You have not been given them. Don't fail to come again when you need them.

A Farmer.

A fisherman.

We don't like to look at a wall.

A Fisherman and a farmer.

They both believe in fish. Fish is a fertilizer. It cannot be found in the bay. You do not have to go out far. You have to have a great many boats.

An English mother.
You make me quite afraid of dogs.

SCENE VI.

A water faucet.

We were very likely to meet one another. None of us have running water. The count Rangle had.

We were all fond of winter. We said we liked summer. The trouble with the summer is that it is too hot. You see I am convinced.
Harold.

Harold is your name. I thought it was Martin.
It is Martin or Mark.
Thank you.
You speak English.
Yes certainly.
And french.
Very nicely.
And Hindustani.
My mother does.
I supposed she did.
We had never thought about it.

SCENE VII.

ACT II.

We are deserted. We are left alone. They are going to Paris. We stay here.
Minorca.   And there is such a nice view.
A dinner.
Tomorrow.
Every day.
Yes every day.

In the morning.

We will ride. We will come home. Yes we will. Don't bother. Yes you need to we understand. We will meet you at half past one old time. You need never be drunk. It is an older word.
Do be clear.

Golly Moses it is damp out here.

Any little piece of paper makes a wind.
Yes yes.

Anthony and Cleopatra.

Do you like him. I must go and see the workingmen.
Do you like them they are giving our son a knife.
Whom does he resemble. The son resembles his mother.
Don't say it.
Why not.
Because the father does not prefer to hear it. He prefers to
hear that the son resembles him.
The son resembles him but he looks like his mother.
They wish him to have every advantage.

Change of scene.

In walking home we did not go that way. I had my reason
for not going that way. I did not care about losing a button.
As a matter of fact I didn't lose it.

Winnie and William.

How are they today.
They are going away.
We are going away.
I am sorry.
We are not sorry.
No I cannot say whether we are not sorry.
We are not sorry.

Another climate.

The ponds are frozen. We did not read that today.
Mike wrote it.
We were very careful to look at the water.
It was not cold here.
There are a great many times when there is rain.
Oh yes.
All right.
He.
He came in.
What is the name of it.
I cannot say it.
Do not say it.
I do not care to look at any one.
I do.

Then please yourself.
I do not understand electricity.
I do.
I do not understand hail.
I can explain it.
I do not care for history.
I can read it.
I do not care about individual wishes.
I understand it.
Plenty of people do love another.
She.

Loud voices are attractive. When two people talk together they have to talk louder.

I wish you would not talk about summer. Say anything you please but don't say that you are not to stay here altogether. I do not want it known.

Alright. We will stay here altogether.

That is not my wish. We will stay here for the winter. The summer climate is not possible.

I quite agree with you.
Do you.
Yes I do.
No I can't say that.
What.
You know it is the words of a song.
I know what you mean.
Of course you do.
This is the end of this month.
Next month will be shorter.
Why.
Because it is December.
I understand that.
Of course you do.
They have gone away.

William.   I am drinking.
Maria.   I am so sorry to go.
Henrietta.   I cannot understand departure because if you are french you attend mass.
Sarah.   I quite agree with you I think it unforgiveable.
Mrs. Clement.   And they are.

Mr. Penfield.   We are very often forgetful.

Many of us think of things.

How many times have you been defeated.

Sleeping.

Turning.

Turning and sleeping.

What did you say. I said I am closing the door. Very well.

Henrietta.   John and I are bewildered.

So are William and Monica.

Henrietta.   The difference between us is that we know what we want.

Oh do you.

Henrietta knows.

Henrietta.   Why are you shutting the door.

Because it is the habit. It really isn't necessary.

Then why do you do it.

Henrietta.   Every one knows William and Monica.

Yes and every one knows how they started.

How did they start.

By quarreling with their landlord.

Indeed yes.

It was not a comfortable house in summer.

They knew this.

No they didn't.

You are quite right they didn't.

SCENE IX.

Go on.

Go on and on.

The day I was settled down to making a fire I found that it came very easily. All I had to do was to be here when the wood came. We had not ordered any water.

Tonight.

Mrs. Chambers.   When did you leave him.

I didn't leave you.

I know you didn't then and I am vainly wishing for a postman.

What did you wish of him.

I wish to tell him that I don't want my packages open.

How do you know where they are open.
I know that they are not opened here I mean in this house.
I understand what you mean.

SCENE X.

A mother.   Do not listen to a mass.
Another mother.   I have left my children at home.
A son.   I have no engagement on Wednesday.
A niece.   I go out frequently.
  Do you.
  Oh yes.
  Do you go out with your aunt.
  We go out together.
Mrs. Hitchcock.   I do not understand wishes.
  A large time is not a sentence we use.
  That I understood.
  Two Englishmen have searched for a Polish flag. They
found it not the flag of the nation the flag of war and com-
merce.
  Thank you so much.

SCENE XI.

  The life of the turkey.
  Who is cruel.
  Not the little boy he lifts it in his arms.
  No the other one. He is a guardian. They are all placing
their confidence in them.
  The life of the turkies here exist after Christmas. We were
surprised to see that. So many of them were eaten that we
supposed there were no more.
  The life of the turkey.
  In church.
  Here in church.
  Nonsense I will not say I prefer suckling pig.
  I don't know but that I do.
  I like grouse.
  To eat.
  And also.
  Chicken liver.
  Arthur Llynn.   Come and rest.

Helen Lewis.   We are waiting for the letter carrier.
Is he coming today.
I don't know.

SCENE XII.

Come in Come in
Mary and Susan.   Shall we come again.
Andrew.   Yes that's the name.
What I want you to know is the origin of it all.
The one is a soldier, the other an admiral the third a gypsy.
We were not pleased.
Captain Rose.   You must pronounce after me. A fire in the
kitchen not against the outer wall.
Yes we know that.
I have been convinced.
Don't you like it's appearance.
Very much.
I am not satisfied.
With what with it's appearance.
I expected it to be white.
Oh that can be arranged afterward.
Yes I see.
You are going.
May we stay a little while.

SCENE XIII.

It was rarely neglected. Come in Herbert.
I recognise the name Herbert.
Come in.
We are going out.
Do you like walking.
Very much.
Do you like the sound of the waves.
Yes certainly.
Do you like them near or at distance.
The effect is different far and near.
Yes so it is.
Which do you prefer.
I have no choice.

This evening we will have to be cold.
But not at all.
Yes indeed and I mean to speak to my landlord about it.
Good-night.

SCENE XIV.

Clarence for a change.

If you have as vacation one day a month and you take it every six months you have six days vacation. In those six days you can visit your family in the country or you can work in your garden or you can make changes in the position of the wall you can do all this and then there will be six days in six months. If you are not able to be about this will be counted off of the days.

The french language.

Who is it.

What was I saying.

You were saying that you were able to be at home.

Yes I am able to be at home.

Then this is what troubles you.

No it does not trouble me. It makes me realize that I do not wish to leave.

Of course you do not wish to leave.

Yes that was understood.

Did you say that you listened.

Were you speaking what did you wish.

I wish not to be disturbed.

Oh yes we will leave in the spring.

I am not satisfied with what is right.

SCENE XV.

Come again.
Mr. Picard.   He was dedicated to him.
Was he.
Do you feel happy.
All the time.
Do not be
Neglected.
I was.
And I saw

That
There are mountains.
And the water.
We are really not interested in the country if there is no water.
You mean salt water.
Yes.
Do not dispute about it.
It is unlucky to wish any one happy new year before the new year.

SCENE XVI.

Do you want me to go on.
Yes I want you to go on.
Where shall we walk tomorrow.
Tonight you mean.
Not not this evening.
Yes I understand.
Where shall we walk tomorrow.
To Fernville.
No not to Fernville.
To Arbuthnot.
No not to Arbuthnot.
In the park.
No not the park.
Well then let's walk along by the water.
No let's not go that way.
Then let us walk to Wintersdale.
Yes let's walk to Wintersdale.
Very well then.
Where are you going this afternoon.
We are going down town.
Oh yes you have a good deal to do.
Yes we have a good deal to do.
Will you go in the morning.
As you like.

SCENE XVII.

Come happily.
Yes we come very happily.

There is very good reason for suspecting Mr. Bournville.
Is there.
Yes very good reason.
What is the reason.
The real reason is that he has been incorrect.
How has he been incorrect.
He has been altogether incorrect as to the necessity of having water.
Do you mean to say that he said it would be difficult to have water.
He said so.
But it hasn't been.
No indeed.
That may be because the season is different.
That may be the reason. In any case he is pardonable.
In any case he is pardonable.
You agree with me.
Yes I agree with you.
Do you always agree with me.
You know I always agree with you.
Then that is satisfactory.
To me.
And to me too.

FINIS.

Lifting Belly

I have been heavy and had much selecting. I saw a star which was low. It was so low it twinkled. Breath was in it. Little pieces are stupid.

I want to tell about fire. Fire is that which we have when we have olive. Olive is a wood. We like linen. Linen is ordered. We are going to order linen.

All belly belly well.

Bed of coals made out of wood.

I think this one may be an expression. We can understand heating and burning composition. Heating with wood.

Sometimes we readily decide upon wind we decide that there will be stars and perhaps thunder and perhaps rain and perhaps no moon. Sometimes we decide that there will be a storm and rain. Sometimes we look at the boats. When we read about a boat we know that it has been sunk. Not by the waves but by the sails. Any one knows that rowing is dangerous. Be alright. Be careful. Be angry. Say what you think. Believe in there being the same kind of a dog. Jerk. Jerk him away. Answer that you do not care to think so.

We quarreled with him. We quarreled with him then. Do not forget that I showed you the road. Do not forget that I showed you the road. We will forget it because he does not oblige himself to thank me. Ask him to thank me.

The next time that he came we offered him something to read. There is a great difference of opinion as to whether cooking in oil is or is not healthful.

I don't pardon him. I find him objectionable.

What is it when it's upset. It isn't in the room. Moonlight and darkness. Sleep and not sleep. We sleep every night.

What was it.

I said lifting belly.

You didn't say it.

I said it I mean lifting belly.

Don't misunderstand me.

Do you.

Do you lift everybody in that way.

No.
You are to say No.
Lifting belly.
How are you.
Lifting belly how are you lifting belly.
We like a fire and we don't mind if it smokes.
Do you.
How do you do. The Englishmen are coming. Not here.
No an Englishwoman. An Englishman and an Englishwoman.
What did you say lifting belly. I did not understand you
correctly. It is not well said. For lifting belly. For lifting belly
not to lifting belly.
Did you say, oh lifting belly.
What is my another name.
Representative.
Of what.
Of the evils of eating.
What are they then.
They are sweet and figs.
Do not send them.
Yes we will it will be very easy.

Part II.

Lifting belly. Are you. Lifting.
Oh dear I said I was tender, fierce and tender.
Do it. What a splendid example of carelessness.
It gives me a great deal of pleasure to say yes.
Why do I always smile.
I don't know.
It pleases me.
You are easily pleased.
I am very pleased.
Thank you I am scarcely sunny.
I wish the sun would come out.
Yes.
Do you lift it.
High.
Yes sir I helped to do it.
Did you.
Yes.

Do you lift it.
We cut strangely.
What.
That's it.
Address it say to it that we will never repent.
A great many people come together.
Come together.
I don't think this has anything to do with it.
What I believe in is what I mean.
Lifting belly and roses.
We get a great many roses.
I always smile.
Yes.
And I am happy.
With what.
With what I said.
This evening.
Not pretty.
Beautiful.
Yes beautiful.
Why don't you prettily bow.
Because it shows thought.
It does.
Lifting belly is so strong.
A great many things are weaknesses. You are pleased to say so. I say because I am so well pleased. With what. With what I said.
There are a great many weaknesses.
Lifting belly.
What was it I said.
I can add that.
It's not an excuse.
I do not like bites.
How lift it.
Not so high.
What a question.
I do not understand about ducks.
Do not you.
I don't mean to close.
No of course not.

Dear me. Lifting belly.
Dear me. Lifting belly.
Oh yes.
Alright.
Sing.
Do you hear.
Yes I hear.
Lifting belly is amiss.
This is not the way.
I see.
Lifting belly is alright.
Is it a name.
Yes it's a name.
We were right.
So you weren't pleased.
I see that we are pleased.
It is a great way.
To go.
No not to go.
But to lift.
Not light.
Paint.
No not paint.
All the time we are very happy.
All loud voices are seen. By whom. By the best.
Lifting belly is so erroneous.
I don't like to be teased and worried.
Lifting belly is so accurate.
Yes indeed.
She was educated.
And pleased.
Yes indeed.
Lifting belly is so strong.
I said that to mean that I was very glad.
Why are you very glad.
Because that pleased me.
Baby love.
A great many people are in the war.
I will go there and back again.
What did you say about Lifting belly.

I said lifting belly is so strong.

Yes indeed it is and agreeable and grateful.

We have gratitude.

No one can say we haven't.

Lifting belly is so cold. Not in summer. No nor in winter either.

All of it is a joke.

Lifting belly is no joke. Not after all.

I am so discouraged about it. About lifting belly. I question.

I am so discouraged about lifting belly.

The other day there was a good deal of sunlight.

There often is.

There often is here.

We are very well satisfied at present.

So enthusiastic.

Lifting belly has charm.

Charming.

Alright.

Lifting belly is not very interesting.

To you.

To me.

Say did you see that the wind was from the east.

It usually is from the South.

We like rain.

Sneeze. This is the way to say it.

You meant a pressure.

Indeed yes.

All the time there is a chance to see me. I don't wish it to be said so.

The skirt.

And water.

You mean ocean water.

Not exactly an ocean a sea.

A success.

Was it a success.

Lifting belly is all there.

Lifting belly high.

It is not necessary to repeat the word.

How do you do I forgive you everything and there is nothing to forgive.

Lifting belly is so high.
Do you like lilies.
Do you like lilies.
Use the word lifting belly is so high.
In place of that.
A special case to-day.
Of peaches.
Lifting belly is delightful.
Lifting belly is so high.
To-day.
Yes to-day.
Do you think that said yesterday.
Yes to-day.
Don't be silly.
In that we see that we can please me.
I don't see how you can write on the wall about roses.
Lifting belly a terminus.
What is there to please me.
Alright.
A pocket.
Lifting belly is good.
Rest.
Arrest.
Do you please me.
I do more than that.
When are you most proud of me.
Dare I ask you to be satisfied.
Dear me.
Lifting belly is anxious.
Not about Verdun.
Oh dear no.
The wind whistles that means it whistles just like any one.
I thought it was a whistle.
Lifting belly together.
Do you like that there.
There are not mistakes made.
Not here at any rate.
Not here at any rate.
There are no mistakes made. Not here at any rate.
When do I see the lightning. Every night.

Lifting belly again.

It is a credit to me.

There was an instant of lifting belly.

Lifting belly is an occasion. An occasion to please me. Oh yes. Mention it.

Lifting belly is courteous.

Lifting belly is hilarious gay and favorable.

Oh yes it is.

Indeed it is not a disappointment.

Not to me.

Lifting belly is such an incident. In one's life.

Lifting belly is such an incident in one's life.

I don't mean to be reasonable.

Shall I say thin.

This makes me smile.

Lifting belly is so kind.

A great many clouds for the sun. You mean the sun on high.

Leave me.

See me.

Lifting belly is no joke.

I appreciate that.

Do not show kindness.

Why not.

Because it ruffles me.

Do not say that it is unexpected.

Lifting belly is so scarce.

Not to-day.

Lifting belly is so kind.

To me there are many exceptional cases.

What did you say. I said I had not been disturbed. Neither had we. Lifting belly is so necessary.

Lifting belly is so kind.

I can't say it too often.

Pleasing me.

Lifting belly.

Extraordinary.

Lifting belly is such exercise.

You mean altogether.

Lifting belly is so kind to me.

Lifting belly is so kind to many.

Don't say that please.
If you please.
Lifting belly is right.
And we were right.
Now I say again. I say now again.
What is a whistle.
Miracle you don't know about the miracle.
You mean a meteor.
No I don't I mean everything away.
Away where.
Away here.
Oh yes.
Lifting belly is so strong.
You said that before.
Lifting belly is so strong and willing.
Lifting belly is so strong and yet waiting.
Lifting belly is so soothing. Yes indeed.
It gives me greater pleasure.
Does it.
It gives me great pleasure.
What do you mean by St. John.
A great many churches are visited.
Lifting belly try again.
I will not say what I think about lifting belly. Oh yes you will.
Well then please have it understood that I can't be responsible for doubts. Nobody doubts.
Nobody doubts.
I have no use for lifting belly.
Do you say that to me.
No I don't.
Anybody who is wisely urged to go to Inca goes to the hill.
What hill. The hill above lifting belly.
Is it all hill.
Not very well.
Not very well hill.
Lifting belly is so strong.
And clear.
Why do you say feeding.
Lifting belly is such a windmill.

Do you stare.

Lifting belly to me.

What did he say.

He didn't say that he was waiting.

I have been adequately entertained.

Some when they sigh by accident say poor country she is betrayed.

I didn't say that to-day. No indeed you didn't.

Mixing belly is so kind.

Lifting belly is so a measure of it all.

Lifting belly is a picnic.

On a fine day.

We like the weather it is very beautiful.

Lifting belly is so able.

Lifting belly is so able to be praised.

The act.

The action.

A great many people are excitable.

Mixing belly is so strange.

Lifting belly is so satisfying.

Do not speak to me.

Of it.

Lifting belly is so sweet.

That is the way to separate yourself from the water.

Lifting belly is so kind.

Loud voices discuss pigeons.

Do loud voices discuss pigeons.

Remember me to the hill. What hill. The hill in back of Genova.

Lifting belly is so kind. So very kind.

Lifting belly is so kind.

I never mean to insist to-day.

Lifting belly is so consecutive.

With all of us.

Lifting belly is so clear.

Very clear.

And there is lots of water.

Lifting belly is so impatient.

So impatient to-day.

Lifting belly is all there.

Do I doubt it.
Lifting belly.
What are my plans.
There are some she don't mention.
There are some she doesn't mention. Some others she doesn't mention.
Lifting belly is so careful. Full of care for me. Lifting belly is mean. I see. You mean lifting belly is all right.
Lifting belly is so simple.
Listen to me to-day.
Lifting belly is so warm.
Leave it to me.
Leave what to me.
Lifting belly is such an experiment.
We were thoroughly brilliant.
If I were a postman I would deliver letters. We call them letter carriers.
Lifting belly is so strong. And so judicious.
Lifting belly is an exercise.
Exercise is very good for me.
Lifting belly necessarily pleases the latter.
Lifting belly is necessary.
Do believe me.
Lifting belly quietly.
It is very exciting.
Stand.
Why do you stand.
Did you say you thought it would make any difference.
Lifting belly is not so kind.
Little places to sting.
We used to play star spangled banner.
Lifting belly is so near.
Lifting belly is so dear.
Lifting belly all around.
Lifting belly makes a sound.
Keep still.
Lifting belly is gratifying.
I can't express the hauntingness of Dugny.
I can't express either the obligation I have to say say it.
Lifting belly is so kind.

Dear me lifting belly is so kind.
Am I in it.
That doesn't affect it.
How do you mean.
Lifting belly and a resemblance.
There is no resemblance.
A plain case of misdeed.
Lifting belly is peaceable.
The Cataluna has come home.
Lifting belly is a success.
So is tenderness.
Lifting belly is kind and good and beautiful.
Lifting belly is my joy.
Do you believe in singling. Singing do you mean.
Lifting belly is a special pleasure.
Who can be convinced of this measure.
Lifting belly is perfect.
I know what you mean.
Lifting belly was very fatiguing.
Did you make a note of it of the two donkeys and the three
dogs. The smaller one is the mother of the other two.
Lifting belly.
Exactly.
Lifting belly all the time.
Do be careful of me.
Remarkably so.
Remarkably a recreation.
Lifting belly is so satisfying.
Lifting belly to me.
Large quantities of it.
Say that you see that you are praised.
Lifting belly.
See that.
You have entertained me.
Hurry up.
Hurry up with it.
Lifting belly does that astonish you.
Excuse me.
Why do you wish to hear me.
I wish to hear you because it pleases me.

Yesterday and to-day.

Yesterday and to-day we managed it altogether.

Lifting belly is so long.

It is an expression of opinion.

Conquistador. James I.

It is exceptional.

Lifting belly is current rolling. Lifting belly is so strong.

Lifting belly is so strong.

That is what I say.

I say it to please me.

Please yourself with thunder.

Lifting belly is famous.

So are many celebrations.

Lifting belly is so.

We mean lifting belly.

We mean it and do we care.

We keep all the letters.

Lifting belly is so seen.

You mean here.

Not with spy glasses.

Lifting belly is an expression.

Explain it explain it to me.

Lifting belly is cautious.

Of course these words are said.

To be strong.

Lifting belly.

Yes orchids.

Lifting belly is so adaptable.

That will amuse my baby.

Lifting belly is a way of sitting.

I don't mean to laugh.

Lifting belly is such a reason.

Lifting belly is such a reason.

Why do I say bench.

Because it is laughable.

Lifting belly is so droll.

We have met to-day with every kind of consideration.

Not very good. Of course it is very good.

Lifting belly is so kind.

Why do you say that.

Bouncing belly.

Did you say bouncing belly.

We asked here for a sister.

Lifting belly is not noisy.

We go to Barcelona to-morrow.

Lifting belly is an acquisition.

I forgot to put in a special cake. Love to be.

Very well.

Lifting belly is the understanding.

Sleepy.

Why do you wake up.

Lifting belly keep it.

We will send it off.

She should.

Nothing pleases me except dinner.

I have done as I wished and I do not feel any responsibility to you.

Are you there.

Lifting belly.

What do I say.

Pussy how pretty you are.

That goes very quickly unless you have been there too long.

I told him I would send him Mildred's book. He seemed very pleased at the prospect.

Lifting belly is so strong.

Lifting belly together.

Lifting belly oh yes.

Lifting belly.

Oh yes.

Remember what I say.

I have no occasion to deliberate.

He has no heart but that you can supply.

The fan goes alright.

Lifting belly what is earnest. Expecting an arena to be monumental.

Lifting belly is recognised to be the only spectacle present. Do you mean that.

Lifting belly is a language. It says island. Island a strata. Lifting belly is a repetition.

Lifting belly means me.

I do love roses and carnations.

A mistake. There can be no mistakes

I do not say a mother.

Lifting belly.

Lifting belly.

Cry.

Lifting belly.

Lifting belly. Splendid.

Jack Johnson Henry.

Henry is his name sir.

Jack Johnson Henry is an especially eloquent curtain.

We see a splendid force in mirrors.

Angry we are not angry.

Pleasing.

Lifting belly raining.

I am good looking.

A magazine of lifting belly. Excitement sisters.

Did we see the bird jelly I call it. I call it something religious. You mean beautiful. I do not know that I like large rocks. Sarsen land we call it. Oh yes. Lifting belly is a persuasion. You are satisfied. With it. With it and with you. I am satisfied with your behavior. I call it astonishing. Lifting belly is so exact and audible and Spanish curses. You know I prefer a bird. What bird. Why a yellow bird. I saw it first. That was an accident. You mean by accident. I mean exactly what I said. Lifting belly is a great luxury. Can you imitate a cow.

Lifting belly is so kind.

And so cold.

Lifting belly is a rare instance. I am fond of it. I am attached to the accentuation.

Lifting belly is a third.

Did you say third. No I said Avila.

Listen to him sing.

She is so sweet and thrilling.

Listen to me as yet I have no color. Red white and blue all out but you.

This is the best thing I have ever said. Lifting belly and it, it is not startling. Lifting belly until to-morrow. Lifting belly to-morrow.

I would not be surprised surprised if I added that yet.

Lifting belly to me.

I am fondest of all of lifting belly.

Lifting belly careful don't say anything about lifting belly.

I did not change my mind.

Neither did you carefully.

Lifting belly and again lifting belly.

I have changed my mind about the country.

Lifting belly and action and voices and care to be taken.

Does it make any difference if you pay for paper or not.

Listen to me. Using old automobile tires as sandals is singularly interesting. It is done in Avila.

What did I tell. Lifting belly is so kind.

What kind of a noise does it make. Like the man at night. The man that calls out. We hear him.

Lifting belly is so strong. I love cherish idolise adore and worship you. You are so sweet so tender and so perfect.

Did you believe in sandals. When they are made of old automobile tire. I wish I knew the history of it.

Lifting belly is notorious.

A great many people wish to salute. The general does. So does the leader of the battalion. In spanish. I understand that.

I understand everything.

Lifting belly is to jelly.

Holy most is in the sky.

We see it in three.

Yes we see it every night near the hills. This is so natural. Birds do it. We do not know their name.

Lifting belly or all I can never be pleased with this. Listen to me. Lifting belly is so kind.

Lifting belly is so dear.

Lifting belly is here.

Did we not hear and we were walking leave it to me and say come quickly now. He is not sleepy. At last I know why he laughs. Do you.

I will not imitate colors. From the stand point of white yellow is colored. Do you mean bushes. No I mean acacias. Lilacs do fade. What did you say for lifting belly. Extra. Extra thunder. I can so easily be fastidious.

LIFTING BELLY IS SO KIND
PART TWO

Kiss my lips. She did.
Kiss my lips again she did.
Kiss my lips over and over and over again she did.
I have feathers.
Gentle fishes.
Do you think about apricots. We find them very beautiful.
It is not alone their color it is their seeds that charm us. We
find it a change.
Lifting belly is so strange.
I came to speak about it.
Selected raisins well then grapes grapes are good.
Change your name.
Question and garden.
It's raining. Don't speak about it.
My baby is a dumpling I want to tell her something.
Wax candles. We have bought a great many wax candles.
Some are decorated. They have not been lighted.
I do not mention roses.
Exactly.
Actually.
Question and butter.
I find the butter very good.
Lifting belly is so kind.
Lifting belly fattily.
Doesn't that astonish you.
You did want me.
Say it again.
Strawberry.
Lifting beside belly.
Lifting kindly belly.
Sing to me I say.
Some are wives not heroes.
Lifting belly merely.
Sing to me I say.
Lifting belly. A reflection.
Lifting belly adjoins more prizes.

Fit to be.

I have fit on a hat.

Have you.

What did you say to excuse me. Difficult paper and scattered.

Lifting belly is so kind.

What shall you say about that. Lifting belly is so kind.

What is a veteran.

A veteran is one who has fought.

Who is the best.

The king and the queen and the mistress.

Nobody has a mistress.

Lifting belly is so kind.

To-day we decided to forgive Nellie.

Anybody can describe dresses.

How do you do what is the news.

Lifting belly is so kind.

Lifting belly exactly.

The king and the prince of Montenegro.

Lifting belly is so kind.

Lifting belly to please me.

Excited.

Excited are you.

I can whistle, the train can whistle we can hear the whistle, the boat whistle. The train is not running to-day. Mary whistle whistle for the whim.

Didn't you say you'd write it better.

Mrs. Vettie. It is necessary to have a Ford.

Yes sir.

Dear Mrs. Vettie. Smile to me.

I am.

Dear Mrs. Vettie never better.

Yes indeed so.

Lifting belly is most kind.

What did I say, that I was a great poet like the English only sweeter.

When I think of this afternoon and the garden I see what you mean.

You are not thinking of the pleasure.

Lifting belly again.

What did I mention when I drew a pansy that pansy and petunia both begin with p.

Lifting belly splendidly.

We have wishes.

Let us say we know it.

Did I say anything about it. I know the title. We know the title.

Lifting belly is so kind.

We have made no mistake.

The Montenegrin family.

A condition to a wide admiration.

Lifting belly before all.

You don't mean disobedience.

Lifting belly all around.

Eat the little girl I say.

Listen to me. Did you expect it to go back. Why do you do to stop.

What do you do to stop.

What do you do to go on.

I do the same.

Yes wishes. Oh yes wishes.

What do you do to turn a corner.

What do you do to sing.

We don't mention singing.

What do you do to be reformed.

You know.

Yes wishes.

What do you do to measure.

I do it in such a way.

I hope to see them come.

Lifting belly go around.

I was sorry to be blistered.

We were such company.

Did she say jelly.

Jelly my jelly.

Lifting belly is so round.

Big Caesars.

Two Caesars.

Little seize her.

Too.

Did I do my duty.
Did I wet my knife.
No I don't mean whet.
Exactly four teeth.
Little belly is so kind.
What did you say about accepting.
Yes.
Lifting belly another lifting belly.
I question the weather.
It is not necessary.
Lifting belly oh lifting belly in time.
Yes indeed.
Be to me.
Did you say this was this.
Mr. Louis.
Do not mention Mr. Louis.
Little axes.
Yes indeed little axes and rubbers.
This is a description of an automobile.
I understand all about them.
Lifting belly is so kind.
So is whistling.
A great many whistles are shrill.
Lifting belly connects.
Lifting belly again.
Sympathetic blessing.
Not curls.
Plenty of wishes.
All of them fulfilled.
Lifting belly you don't say so.
Climb trees.
Lifting belly has sparks.
Sparks of anger and money.
Lifting belly naturally celebrates.
We naturally celebrate.
Connect me in places.
Lifting belly.
No no don't say that.
Lifting belly oh yes.
Tax this.

Running behind a mountain.
I fly to thee.
Lifting belly.
Shall I chat.
I mean pugilists.
Oh yes trainer.
Oh yes yes.
Say it again to study.
It has been perfectly fed.
Oh yes I do.
Belly alright.
Lifting belly very well.
Lifting belly this.
So sweet.
To me.
Say anything a pudding made of Caesars.
Lobster. Baby is so good to baby.
I correct blushes. You mean wishes.
I collect pearls. Yes and colors.
All colors are dogs. Oh yes Beddlington.
Now I collect songs.
Lifting belly is so nice.
I wrote about it to him.
I wrote about it to her.
Not likely not very likely that they will seize rubber. Not very likely that they will seize rubber.
Lifting belly yesterday.
And to-day.
And to-morrow.
A train to-morrow.
Lifting belly is so exacting.
Lifting belly asks any more.
Lifting belly captures.
Seating.
Have a swim.
Lifting belly excuses.
Can you swim.
Lifting belly for me.
When this you see remember me.
Oh yes.

Yes.
Researches and a cab.
A cab right.
Lifting belly phlegmatically.
Bathing bathing in bliss.
I am very well satisfied with meat.
Kindness to my wife.
Lifting belly to a throne.
Search it for me.
Yes wishes.
I say it again I am perfection in behavior and circumstance.
Oh yes alright.
Levelheaded fattuski.
I do not wish to be Polish.
Quite right in singing.
Lifting belly is so recherché.
Lifting belly.
Up.
Correct me.
I believe he makes together of pieces.
Lifting belly.
Not that.
Think of me.
Oh yes.
Lifting belly for me.
Right there.
Not that yesterday.
Fetch missions.
Lifting belly or Dora.
Lifting belly.
Yes Misses.
Lifting belly separately all day.
I say lifting belly.
An example.
A good example.
Cut me a slice.
You see what I wish.
I wish a seat and Caesar.
Caesar is plural.
I can think.

And so can I.
And argue.
Oh yes you see.
What I see.
You see me.
Yes stretches.
Stretches and stretches of happiness.
Should you have put it away.
Yes you should have put it away.
Do not think so much.
I do not.
Have you a new title.
Lifting belly articulately.
It is not a problem.
Kissing and singing.
We have the habit when we wash.
In singing we say how do you do how do you like the war.
Little dumps of it.
Did you hear that man. What did he say close it.
Lifting belly lifting pleasure.
What can we say about wings.
Wings and refinement.
Come to me.
Sleepy.
Sleepily we think.
Wings after lunch.
I don't think.
No don't I regret a silver sugar.
And I platinum knitting needles.
And I sherry glasses.
I do not care for sherry I used to use it for castor-oil.
You mean licorice.
He is so fond of coffee.
Let me tell you about kissing. We saw a piece of mistletoe.
We exchanged a pillow. We murmured training and we were
asleep.
This is what happened Saturday.
Another day we said sour grass it grows in fields. So do
daisies and green flowers.
I have never noticed green flowers.

Lifting belly is my joy.

What did I tell Caesars.

That I recognised them.

It is the custom to answer swimming.

Catch a call.

Does the moonlight make any difference to you.

Lifting belly yes Miss.

I can lean upon a pencil.

Lifting belly yes address me.

I address you.

Lifting belly magnetically.

Did you make a mistake.

Wave to me.

Lifting belly permanently.

What did the Caesars.

What did they all say.

They said that they were not deceived.

Lifting belly such a good example. And is so readily watchful.

What do you think of watches.

Collect lobsters.

And sweetbreads.

And a melon.

And salad.

Do not have a term.

You mean what do you call it.

Yes sir.

Sing to me.

Lifting belly is neglected.

The Caesar.

Oh yes the Caesar.

Oh yes the Caesar.

Lifting belly pencils to me.

And pens.

Lifting belly and the intention.

I particularly like what I know.

Lifting belly sublimely.

We made a fire this evening.

Cooking is cheap.

I do not care for Ethel.

That's a very good one. I say that's a very good one.
Yes and we think.
A rhyme, I understand nectarine. I also understand egg.
A special case you are.
Lifting belly and Caesar.
Did I explain it.
Have I explained it to you.
Have I explained it to you in season. Have I perplexed you.
You have not perplexed me nor mixed me. You have addressed
me as Caesar. This is the answer that I expected. When I said
do not mention any words I meant no indifference. I meant
do your duty and do not forget that I establish myself.
You establish yourself.
When this you see believe me.
Lifting belly etcetera.
Lifting belly and a hand. A hand is black and not by toil. I
do not like fat resemblances. There are none such.
Lifting belly and kind.
This is the pencil for me.
Lifting belly squeezes.
Remember what I said about a rhyme.
Don't call it again.
Say white spots.
Do not mention disappointment in cups.
Oh you are so sweet.
Lifting belly believe me.
Believe it is for pleasure that I do it.
Not foreign pleasure.
Oh no.
My pleasure in Susie.
Lifting belly so kind.
So kindly.
Lifting belly gratuitously.
Lifting belly increase.
Do this to me.
Lifting belly famously.
When did I say I thought it.
When you heard it.
Oh yes.
Bright eyes I make you ties.

No mockings.

This is to say I knit woolen stockings for you. And I understand it and I am very grateful.

Making a spectacle.

Drinking prepared water.

Laughing together.

Asking lifting belly to be particular.

Lifting belly is so kind.

She was like that.

Star spangled banner, story of Savannah.

She left because she was going to have the child with her.

Lifting belly don't think of it.

Believe me in truth and marriage.

Believe that I use the best paper that I can get.

Do you believe me.

Lifting belly is not an invitation.

Call me semblances.

I call you a cab sir.

That's the way she tells it.

Lifting belly is so accurate.

I congratulate you in being respectable and respectably married.

Call me Helen.

Not at all.

You may call me Helen.

That's what we said.

Lifting belly with firmness and pride.

Lifting belly with industry beside.

Heated heated with cold.

Some people are heated with linen.

Lifting belly comes extra.

This is a picture of lifting belly having a cow.

Oh yes you can say it of me.

When this you see remember me.

Lifting belly says pardon.

Pardon for what.

For having made a mistake.

Can you imagine what I say.

I say impossible.

Lifting belly is recognised.

Lifting belly presumably.
Do we run together.
I say do we run together.
I do not like stubbornness.
Come and sing.
Lifting belly.
I sing lifting belly.
I say lifting belly and then I say lifting belly and Caesars. I say lifting belly gently and Caesars gently. I say lifting belly again and Caesars again. I say lifting belly and I say Caesars and I say lifting belly Caesars and cow come out. I say lifting belly and Caesars and cow come out.
Can you read my print.
Lifting belly say can you see the Caesars. I can see what I kiss.
Of course you can.
Lifting belly high.
That is what I adore always more and more.
Come out cow.
Little connections.
Yes oh yes cow come out.
Lifting belly unerringly.
A wonderful book.
Baby my baby I backhand for thee.
She is a sweet baby and well baby and me.
This is the way I see it.
Lifting belly can you say it.
Lifting belly persuade me.
Lifting belly persuade me.
You'll find it very easy to sing to me.
What can you say.
Lifting belly set.
I can not pass a door.
You mean odor.
I smell sweetly.
So do you.
Lifting belly plainly.
Can you sing.
Can you sing for me.
Lifting belly settled.

Can you excuse money.
Lifting belly has a dress.
Lifting belly in a mess.
Lifting belly in order.
Complain I don't complain.
She is my sweetheart.
Why doesn't she resemble an other.
This I cannot say here.
Full of love and echoes. Lifting belly is full of love.
Can you.
Can you can you.
Can you buy a Ford.
Did you expect that.
Lifting belly hungrily.
Not lonesomely.
But enthusiastically.
Lifting belly altogether.
Were you wise.
Were you wise to do so.
Can you say winking.
Can you say Francis Ferdinand has gone to the West.
Can you neglect me.
Can you establish the clock.
Yes I can when I am good.
Lifting belly precariously.
Lifting belly is noted.
Are you noted with me.
Come to sing and sit.
This is not the time for discussion.
A splendid table little table.
A splendid little table.
Can you be fortunate.
Yes sir.
What is a man.
What is a woman.
What is a bird.
Lifting belly must please me.
Yes can you think so.
Lifting belly cherished and flattered.
Lifting belly naturally.

Can you extract.
Can you be through so quickly.
No I cannot get through so quickly.
Are you afraid of negro sculpture.
I have my feelings.
Lifting belly is so exact.
Lifting belly is favored by me.
Lifting belly cautiously.
I lift it in place of the music.
You mean it is the same.
I mean everything.
Can you not whistle.
Call me for that.
And sing.
I sing too.
Lifting belly counts.
My idea is.
Yes I know what your idea is.
Lifting belly knows all about the wind.
Yes indeed Miss.
Yes indeed.
Can you suspect me.
We are glad that we do not deceive.
Lifting belly or regular.
Lifted belly behind.
Candidly.
Can you say that there is a mistake.
In the wash.
No in respect to the woman.
Can you say we meant to send her away.
Lifting belly is so orderly.
She makes no mistake.
She does not indeed.
Lifting belly heroically.
Can you think of that.
Can you guess what I mean.
Yes I can.
Lovely sweet.
Calville cow.
And that is it.

Lifting belly resignedly.
Now you laugh.
Lifting belly for me.
When this you see remember me.
Can you be sweet.
You are.
We are so likely.
We are so likely to be sweet.
Lifting belly handy.
Can you mention lifting belly. I can.
Yes indeed I know what I say.
Do you.
Lifting belly is so much.
Lifting belly grandly.
You can be sweet.
We see it.
We are tall.
We are wellbred.
We can say we do like what we have.
Lifting belly is mine.
I am more than ever inclined to how do you do. That's the
way to wish it.
Lifting belly is so good.
That is natural.
Lifting belly exactly.
Calville cow is all to me.
Don't excite me.
Lifting belly exactly.
That's respectable.
Lifting belly is all to me.
Pretty Caesars yes they do.
Can you spell mixing.
I hear you.
How do you do.
Can you tell me about imposing.
When are you careful to speak.
Lifting belly categorically.
Think of it.
Lifting belly in the mind.
The Honorable Graham Murray.

My honorable Graham Murray.
What can you say.
I can say that I find it most useful and very warm, yet light.
Lifting belly astonishingly.
Can you mention her brother.
Yes.
Her father.
Yes.
A married couple.
Yes.
Lifting belly names it.
Look at that.
Yes that's what I said.
I put down something on lifting belly.
Humph.
Lifting belly bells.
Can you think of singing. In the little while in which I say stop it you are not spoiled.
Can you be spoiled. I do not think so.
I think not.
I think everything of you.
Lifting belly is rich.
Chickens are rich.
I cannot disguise nice.
Don't you need to.
I think not.
Lifting belly exactly.
Why can lifting belly please me.
Lifting belly can please me because it is an occupation I enjoy.
Rose is a rose is a rose is a rose.
In print on top.
What can you do.
I can answer my question.
Very well answer this.
Who is Mr. Mc Bride.
In the way of laughing.
Lifting belly is an intention.
You are sure you know the meaning of any word.
Leave me to see.

Pink.

My pink.

Hear me to-day.

It is after noon.

I mean that literally.

It is after noon.

Little lifting belly is a quotation.

Frankly what do you say to me.

I say that I need protection.

You shall have it.

After that what do you wish.

I want you to mean a great deal to me.

Exactly.

And then.

And then blandishment.

We can see that very clearly.

Lifting belly is perfect.

Do you stretch farther.

Come eat it.

What did I say.

To whom.

Calville or a cow.

We were in a fashion deceived in Calville but not in a cow.

I understand when they say they mean something by it.

Lifting belly grandly.

Lifting belly sufficiently.

Come and be awake.

Certainly this morning.

Lifting belly very much.

I do not feel that I will be deceived.

Lifting belly fairly.

You mean follow.

I mean I follow.

Need you wish me to say lifting belly is recognised. No it is not necessary lifting belly is not peculiar. It is recognised. Can you recognise it. In a flash.

Thank you for me.

Can you excuse any one for loving its dearest. I said from. That is eaten.

Can you excuse any one from loving its dearest.
No I cannot.
A special fabric.
Can you begin a new thing.
Can I begin.
We have a dress.
You have a dress.
A dress by him.
Feel me.
I feel you.
Then it is fair to me.
Let me sing.
Certainly.
And you too Miss Polly.
What can you say.
I can say that there is no need of regretting a ball.
Mount Fatty.
That is a tremendous way.
Leave me to sing about it to-day.
And then there was a cake. Please give it to me. She did.
When can there be glasses. We are so pleased with it.
Go on to-morrow.
He cannot understand women. I can.
Believe me in this way.
I can understand the woman.
Lifting belly carelessly. I do not lift baby carelessly.
Lifting belly because there is no mistake. I planned to flour-
ish. Of course you did.
Lifting belly is exacting. You mean exact. I mean exacting.
Lifting belly is exacting.
Can you say see me.
Lifting belly is exciting.
Can you explain a mistake.
There is no mistake.
You have mentioned the flour.
Lifting belly is full of charm.
They are very nice candles.
Lifting belly is resourceful.
What can lifting belly say.

Oh yes I was not mistaken. Were not you indeed.

Lifting belly lifting belly lifting belly oh then lifting belly.

Can you make an expression. Thanks for the cigarette. How pretty.

How fast. What. How fast the cow comes out.

Lifting belly a permanent caress.

Lifting belly bored.

You don't say so.

Lifting belly now.

Cow.

Lifting belly exactly.

I have often been pleased with this thing.

Lifting belly is necessarily venturesome.

You mean by that that you are collected. I hope I am.

What is an evening dress. What is a cape. What is a suit. What is a fur collar.

Lifting belly needs to speak.

Land Rising next time.

Lifting belly has no choice.

Lifting belly seems to me to be remarkably kind.

Can you hear me witness that I was wolfish. I can. And that I do not interfere with you. No I cannot countenance you here. Countenance what do you mean by that. I mean that it is a pleasure to prepare you. Thank you my dear.

Lifting belly is so kind.

Can you recollect this for me.

Lifting belly naturally.

Can you believe the truth.

Fredericka or Frederica.

Can you give me permission.

The Loves.

I never forget the Caesars.

Or the dears.

Lifting belly casually.

Where the head gets thin.

Lifting belly never mind.

You do please me.

Lifting belly restless.

Not at all.

Lifting belly there.

Expand my chest endlessly.
You did not do so.
Lifting belly is loved.
You know I am always ready to please you.
Lifting belly in a breath.
Lifting belly.
You do speak kindly.
We speak very kindly.
Lifting belly is so bold.

LIFTING BELLY

PART THREE

Lifting belly in here.
Able to state whimsies.
Can you recollect mistakes.
I hope not.
Bless you.
Lifting belly the best and only seat.
Lifting belly the reminder of present duties.
Lifting belly the charm.
Lifting belly is easy to me.
Lifting belly naturally.
Of course you lift belly naturally.
I lift belly naturally together.
Lifting belly answers.
Can you think for me.
I can.
Lifting belly endears me.
Lifting belly cleanly. With a wood fire. With a good fire.
Say how do you do to the lady. Which lady. The jew lady.
How do you do. She is my wife.
Can you accuse lifting belly of extras.
Salmon is salmon. Smoked and the most nourishing.
Pink salmon is my favorite color.

To be sure.
We are so necessary.
Can you wish for me.
I never mention it.
You need not resemble me.
But you do.
Of course you do.
That is very well said.
And meant.
And explained.
I explain too much.
And then I say.
She knows everything
And she does.
Lifting belly beneficently.
I can go on with lifting belly forever. And you do.
I said it first. Lifting belly to engage. And then wishes. I wish to be whimsied. I do that.
A worldly system.
A humorous example.
Lindo see me.
Whimsy see me.
See me.
Lifting belly exaggerates. Lifting belly is reproachful.
Oh can you see.
Yes sir.
Lifting belly mentions the bee.
Can you imagine the noise.
Can you whisper to me.
Lifting belly pronouncedly.
Can you imagine me thinking lifting belly.
Safety first.
Thats the trimming.
I hear her snore
On through the door.
I can say that it is my delight.
Lifting belly fairly well.
Lifting belly visibly.
Yes I say visibly.
Lifting belly behind me.

The room is so pretty and clean.
Do you know the rest.
Yes I know the rest.
She knows the rest and will do it.
Lifting belly in eclipse.
There is no such moon for me.
Eclipse indeed can lifting belly be methodical.
In lifting belly yes.
In lifting belly yes.
Can you think of me.
I can and do.
Lifting belly encourages plenty.
Do not speak of San Francisco he is a saint.
Lifting belly shines.
Lifting belly nattily.
Lifting belly to fly.
Not to-day.
Motor.
Lifting belly for wind.
We do not like wind.
We do not mind snow.
Lifting belly partially.
Can you spell for me.
Spell bottle.
Lifting belly remarks.
Can we have the hill.
Of course we can have the hill.
Lifting belly patiently.
Can you see me rise.
Lifting belly says she can.
Lifting belly soundly.
Here is a bun for my bunny.
Every little bun is of honey.
On the little bun is my oney.
My little bun is so funny.
Sweet little bun for my money.
Dear little bun I'm her sunny.
Sweet little bun dear little bun good little bun for my
bunny.
Lifting belly merry Christmas.

Lifting belly has wishes.
And then we please her.
What is the name of that pin.
Not a hat pin.
We use elastic.
As garters.
We are never blamed.
Thank you and see me.
How can I swim.
By not being surprised.
Lifting belly is so kind.
Lifting belly is harmonious.
Can you smile to me.
Lifting belly is prepared.
Can you imagine what I say.
Lifting belly can.
To be remarkable.
To be remarkably so.
Lifting belly and emergencies.
Lifting belly in reading.
Can you say effectiveness.
Lifting belly in reserve.
Lifting belly marches.
There is no song.
Lifting belly marry.
Lifting belly can see the condition.
How do you spell Lindo.
Not to displease.
The dears.
When can I.
When can I.
To-morrow if you like.
Thank you so much.
See you.
We were pleased to receive notes.
In there.
To there.
Can you see spelling.
Anybody can see lines.
Lifting belly is arrogant.

Not with oranges.
Lifting belly inclines me.
To see clearly.
Lifting belly is for me.
I can say truthfully never better.
Believe me lifting belly is not nervous.
Lifting belly is a miracle.
I am with her.
Lifting belly to me.
Very nicely done.
Poetry is very nicely done.
Can you say pleasure.
I can easily say please me.
You do.
Lifting belly is precious.
Then you can sing.
We do not encourage a nightingale.
Do you really mean that.
We literally do.
Then it is an intention.
Not the smell.
Lifting baby is a chance.
Certainly sir.
I please myself.
Can we convince Morlet.
We can.
Then see the way.
We can have a pleasant ford.
And we do.
We will.
See my baby cheerily.
I am celebrated by the lady.
Indeed you are.
I can rhyme
In English.
In loving.
In preparing.
Do not be rough.
I can sustain conversation.
Do you like a title.

Do you like my title.
Do you like my title for you.
Can you agree
We do.
In that way have candles.
And dirt.
Not dirt.
There are two Caesars and there are four Caesars.
Caesars do their duty.
I never make a mistake.
We will be very happy and boastful and we will celebrate Sunday.
How do you like your Aunt Pauline.
She is worthy of a queen.
Will she go as we do dream.
She will do satisfactorily.
And so will we.
Thank you so much.
Smiling to me.
Then we can see him.
Yes we can.
Can we always go.
I think so.
You will be secure.
We are secure.
Then we see.
We see the way.
This is very good for me.
In this way we play.
Then we are pleasing.
We are pleasing to him
We have gone together.
We are in our Ford.
Please me please me.
We go then.
We go when.
In a minute.
Next week.
Yes indeed oh yes indeed.
I can tell you she is charming in a coat.

Yes and we are full of her praises.
Yes indeed.
This is the way to worry. Not it.
Can you smile.
Yes indeed oh yes indeed.
And so can I.
Can we think.
Wrist leading.
Wrist leading.
A kind of exercise.
A brilliant station.
Do you remember its name.
Yes Morlet.
Can you say wishes.
I can.
Winning baby.
Theoretically and practically.
Can we explain a season.
We can when we are right.
Two is too many.
To be right.
One is right and so we mount and have what we want.
We will remember.
Can you mix birthdays.
Certainly I can.
Then do so.
I do so.
Do I remember to write.
Can he paint.
Not after he has driven a car.
I can write.
There you are.
Lifting belly with me.
You inquire.
What do you do then.
Pushing.
Thank you so much.
And lend a hand.
What is lifting belly now.
My baby.

Always sincerely.
Lifting belly says it there.
Thank you for the cream.
Lifting belly tenderly.
A remarkable piece of intuition.
I have forgotten all about it.
Have you forgotten all about it.
Little nature which is mine.
Fairy ham
Is a clam.
Of chowder
Kiss him Louder.
Can you be especially proud of me.
Lifting belly a queen.
In that way I can think.
Thank you so much.
I have,
Lifting belly for me.
I can not forget the name.
Lifting belly for me.
Lifting belly again.
Can you be proud of me.
I am.
Then we say it.
In miracles.
Can we say it and then sing. You mean drive.
I mean to drive.
We are full of pride.
Lifting belly is proud.
Lifting belly my queen.
Lifting belly happy.
Lifting belly see.
Lifting belly.
Lifting belly address.
Little washers.
Lifting belly how do you do.
Lifting belly is famous for recipes.
You mean Genevieve.
I mean I never ask for potatoes.
But you liked them then.

And now.
Now we know about water.
Lifting belly is a miracle.
And the Caesars.
The Caesars are docile.
Not more docile than is right.
No beautifully right.
And in relation to a cow.
And in relation to a cow.
Do believe me when I incline.
You mean obey.
I mean obey.
Obey me.
Husband obey your wife.
Lifting belly is so dear.
To me.
Lifting belly is smooth,
Tell lifting belly about matches.
Matches can be struck with the thumb.
Not by us.
No indeed.
What is it I say about letters.
Twenty six.
And counted.
And counted deliberately.
This is not as difficult as it seems.
Lifting belly is so strange
And quick.
Lifting belly in a minute.
Lifting belly in a minute now.
In a minute.
Not to-day.
No not to-day.
Can you swim.
Lifting belly can perform aquatics.
Lifting belly is astonishing.
Lifting belly for me.
Come together.
Lifting belly near.
I credit you with repetition.

Believe me I will not say it.
And retirement.
I celebrate something.
Do you.
Lifting belly extraordinarily in haste.
I am so sorry I said it.
Lifting belly is a credit. Do you care about poetry.
Lifting belly in spots.
Do you like ink.
Better than butter.
Better than anything.
Any letter is an alphabet.
When this you see you will kiss me.
Lifting belly is so generous.
Shoes.
Servant.
And Florence.
Then we can sing.
We do among.
I like among.
Lifting belly keeps.
Thank you in lifting belly.
Can you wonder that they don't make preserves.
We ask the question and they answer you give us help.
Lifting belly is so successful.
Is she indeed.
I wish you would not be disobliging.
In that way I am.
But in giving.
In giving you always win.
You mean in effect.
In mean in essence.
Thank you so much we are so much obliged.
This may be a case
Have no fear.
Then we can be indeed.
You are and you must.
Thank you so much.
In kindness you excel.
You have obliged me too.

I have done what is necessary.
Then can I say thank you may I say thank you very much.
Thank you again.
Because lifting belly is about baby.
Three eggs in lifting belly.
Eclair.
Think of it.
Think of that
We think of that.
We produce music.
And in sleeping.
Noises.
Can that be she.
Lifting belly is so kind
Darling wifie is so good.
Little husband would.
Be as good.
If he could.
This was said.
Now we know how to differ.
From that.
Certainly.
Now we say.
Little hubbie is good.
Every Day.
She did want a photograph.
Lifting belly changed her mind.
Do I look fat.
Do I look fat and thin.
Blue eyes and windows.
You mean Vera.
Lifting belly can guess.
Quickly.
Lifting belly is so pleased.
Lifting belly seeks pleasure.
And she finds it altogether.
Lifting belly is my love.
Can you say meritorious.
Yes camellia.
Why do you complain.

Postal cards.
And then.
The Louvre.
After that.
After that Francine.
You don't mean by that name.
What is Spain.
Listen lightly.
But you do.
Don't tell me what you call me.
But he is pleased.
But he is pleased.
That is the way it sounds.
In the morning.
By that bright light.
Will you exchange purses.
You know I like to please you.
Lifting belly is so kind.
Then sign.
I sign the bulletin.
Do the boys remember that nicely.
To-morrow we go there.
And the photographs
The photographs will come.
When
You will see.
Will it please me.
Not suddenly
But soon
Very soon.
But you will hear first.
That will take some time.
Not very long.
What do you mean by long.
A few days.
How few days.
One or two days.
Thank you for saying so.
Thank you so much.
Lifting belly waits splendidly.

For essence.
For essence too.
Can you assure me.
I can and do.
Very well it will come
And I will be happy.
You are happy.
And I will be.
You always will be.
Lifting belly sings nicely.
Not nervously.
No not nervously.
Nicely and forcefully.
Lifting belly is so sweet.
Can you say you say.
In this thought.
I do think lifting belly.
Little love lifting.
Little love light.
Little love heavy.
Lifting belly tight.
Thank you.
Can you turn over.
Rapidly.
Lifting belly so meaningly.
Yes indeed the dog.
He watches.
The little boys.
They whistle on their legs,
Little boys have meadows,
Then they are well.
Very well.
Please be the man.
I am the man.
Lifting belly praises.
And she gives
Health.
And fragrance.
And words.
Lifting belly is in bed.

And the bed has been made comfortable.
Lifting belly knows this.
Spain and torn
Whistling.
Can she whistle to me.
Lifting belly in a flash.
You know the word.
Strawberries grown in Perpignan are not particularly good.
These are inferior kinds.
Kind are a kind.
Lifting belly is sugar.
Lifting belly to me.
In this way I can see.
What
Lifting belly dictate.
Daisy dear.
Lifting belly
Lifting belly carelessly.
I didn't.
I see why you are careful
Can you stick a stick. In what In the carpet.
Can you be careful of the corner.
Mrs. the Mrs. indeed yes.
Lifting belly is charming.
Often to-morrow
I'll try again.
This time I will sin
Not by a prophecy.
That is the truth.
Very well.
When will they change.
They have changed.
Then they are coming
Yes.
Soon.
On the way.
I like the smell of gloves.
Lifting belly has money.
Do you mean cuckoo.
A funny noise.

In the meantime there was lots of singing.
And then and then.
We have a new game
Can you fill it.
Alone.
And is it good
And useful
And has it a name
Lifting belly can change to filling petunia.
But not the same.
It is not the same.
It is the same.
Lifting belly.
So high.
And aiming.
Exactly.
And making
A cow
Come out.
Indeed I was not mistaken.
Come do not have a cow.
He has.
Well then.
Dear Daisy.
She is a dish.
A dish of good.
Perfect.
Pleasure,
In the way of dishes.
Willy.
And Milly.
In words.
So loud.
Lifting belly the dear.
Protection.
Protection
Protection
Speculation
Protection
Protection.

Can the furniture shine.
Ask me.
What is my answer.
Beautifully.
Is there a way of being careful
Of what.
Of the South.
By going to it.
We will go.
For them.
For them again.
And is there any likelihood of butter.
We do not need butter.
Lifting belly enormously and with song.
Can you sing about a cow.
Yes.
And about signs.
Yes.
And also about Aunt Pauline.
Yes.
Can you sing at your work.
Yes.
In the meantime listen to Miss Cheetham.
In the midst of writing.
In the midst of writing there is merriment.

Marry Nettie

Alright make it a series and call it Marry Nettie.

Principle calling.
They don't marry.
Land or storm.
This is a chance.
A negress.
Nurse.
Three years.
For three years.
By the time.
He had heard.
He didn't eat.
Well.
What does it cost to sew much.

A cane dropped out of the window. It was sometime before it was searched for. In the meantime the negress had gotten it. It had no value. It was one that did bend. We asked every one. No one would be intended or contented. We gave no peace. At last the day before we left I passed the door. I saw a bamboo cane but I thought the joints were closer together. I said this. Miss Thaddeus looked in. It was my cane. We told the woman who was serving. She said she would get it. She waited and was reasonable. She asked if they found it below as it was the cane of Miss Thaddeus. It was and plain. So there. We leave.

There is no such thing as being good to your wife.

She asked for tissue paper. She wanted to use it as a respirator. I don't understand how so many people can stand the mosquitoes.

It seems unnecessary to have it last two years. We would be so pleased.

We are good.

We are energetic.

459

We will get the little bowls we saw to-day.

The little bowls we saw to-day are quite pretty.

They will do nicely.

We will also get a fan. We will have an electric one. Everything is so reasonable.

It was very interesting to find a sugar bowl with the United States seal on one side and the emblem of liberty on the other.

If you care to talk to the servant do not talk to her while she is serving at table. This does not make me angry nor annoy me. I like salad. I am losing my individuality.

It is a noise.

Plan

All languages.

By means of swimming.

They see English spoken.

They are dark to-day very easily by the sun.

We will go out in the morning. We will go and bring home fish. We will also bring note-books and also three cups. We will see Palma. Shoes are necessary. Shoes with cord at the bottom are white. How can I plan everything.

Sometimes I don't mind putting on iodine and sometimes I do.

This is not the way to be pleasant. I am very careful.

To describe tube-roses.

This is the day.

Pressing.

John.

Eating garlic. Do be careful. Do be careful in eating garlic particularly on an island. There is a fish a devil fish an ink fish which is good to eat. It is prepared with pepper and sauce and we eat it nicely. It is very edible.

How did we please her. A bottle of wine not that doesn't do it.

Oil.

Oil.

To make her shine.

We entwine.

So that.

How do you do.

We don't think highly of Jenny.

SPANISH NEWSPAPER.

A spanish newspaper says that the king went to a place and addressed the artillery officer who was there and told him, artillery is very important in war.

THE COUNT.

Somebody does sleep next door.

The count went to bathe, the little boy had amber beads around him. He went.

I made a mistake.

That's it.

He wanted the towel dried.

They refused.

Towels do not dry down here.

They do up at my place, said the Count.

SHE WAS.
NOT ASTONISHING.

She came upstairs having been sick. It was the effect of the crab.

Was I lost in the market or was she lost in the market.

We were not. We thought that thirty nine was a case of say it. Please try. I could find her. A large piece. Beets. Figs. Egg plants. Fish. We walked up and down. They sold pencils. The soldier what is a soldier. A soldier is readily given a paper. He does not like that pencil. He does not try another. We were so happy. She ought to be a very happy woman. Now we are able to recognise a photograph. We are able to get what we want.

A NEW SUGAR BOWL WITH A CROSS ON TOP.

We said we had it. We will take it to Paris. Please let us take everything.

The sugar bowl with a cross on top now has sugar in it. Not soft sugar but the sugar used in coffee. It is put on the table for that.

It is very pretty. We have not seen many things. We want to be careful. We don't really have to bother about it.

ANOTHER CHANCE.

That's it. Beds. How glad I am. What was I worried about. Was it the weather, was it the sun, was it fatigue was it being tired. It was none of these. It was that wood was used and we did not know.

We blamed each other.

WE BLAMED EACH OTHER.

She said I was nervous. I said I knew she wasn't nervous. The dear of course I wasn't nervous. I said I wasn't nervous. We were sure that steam was coming out of the water. It makes that noise. Our neighbors have a small telescope. They can see the water with it. They can not see the names of ships. They can tell that their little boy is lonesome which he is. He stands there and calls out once in a while to the others. I am so annoyed.

Do we believe the germans.

We do not.

SPANISH PENS.

Spanish pens are falling. They fall there. That makes it rich. That makes Spain richer than ever. Spanish pens are in places. They are in the places which we see. We read about everything. This is by no means an ordeal. A charity is true.

WHY ARE WE PLEASED.

We are pleased because we have an electrical fan.

May the gods of Moses and of Mars help the allies. They do they will.

WE WILL WALK AFTER SUPPER.

We will not have tea. We will rest all day with the electric fan. We will have supper. We can perspire. After supper. This is so humorous.

WE HAD AN EXCITING DAY.

We took a fan out of a man's hand. We complained to the mother of Richard. Not knowing her we went there. They all said it. It was useful. We went to the ball room where there was billiard playing and reading. Then we accepted it. He said it was changed from five to seven and a half.

NOT VERY LIKELY.

We were frightened. We are so brave and we never allow it. We do not allow anything at last. That's the way to say we like ours best.

PAPERS.

Buy me some cheese even if we must throw it away. Buy me some beets. Do not ask them to save any of these things. There will be plenty of them. One reason why we are careful is that carrots are indifferent. They are so and we forgot to say Tuesday. How do you do. Will you give me some of the fruit. It is thoughtless of me to be displeased.

HOT WEATHER.

I don't care for it. Why not. Because it makes me careless. Careless of what. Of the example of church. What is church. Church is not a question. So there is strength and truth and rocking.

PLEASE BE QUICK.

Why do they unload at night. Or is it that one hears it then. Perhaps it has just come. I am not suspicious.

WHY DO YOU LIKE IT.

Because it is all about you. Whom do you marry. Nettie.

WHOM DO YOU SAY YOU SEE.

You see plenty of french people. You see some foolish people. You hear one boasting. What is he saying. He says it takes a hundred men to make a steam boat landing. I am going to say you missed it. Do be still. We are awkward. Not in swimming. We are very strong. We have small touches and we do see our pride. We have earned plates. We are looking for a bell.

YOU LIKE THIS BEST.

Lock me in neatly.
Unlock me sweetly.
I love my baby with a rush rushingly.

SOMETIMES THEY CAN FINISH A BUGLE CALL.

Sometimes they can finish a bugle call when they know it.
They have a very good ear. They are not quick to learn. They
do not have application.

MARRY NETTIE.

Marry who. Marry Nettie. Which Nettie. My Nettie. Marry
whom. Marry Nettie. Marry my Nettie.

I was distinguished by knowing about the flower pot. It
was one that had tube-roses. I put the others down below.
That one will be fixed.

I was also credited with having partiality for the sun. I am
not particular. I do not like to have it said that it is so necessary to hear the next letter. We all wish to go now. Do be
certain that we are cool.

Oh shut up.

Accents in Alsace

A Reasonable Tragedy

ACT I. THE SCHEMILS.

Brother brother go away and stay.
Sister mother believe me I say.
They will never get me as I run away.

He runs away and stays away and strange to say he passes
the lines and goes all the way and they do not find him but
hear that he is there in the foreign legion in distant Algier.

And what happens to the family.

The family manages to get along and then some one of his
comrades in writing a letter which is gotten hold of by the
Boche find he is a soldier whom they cannot touch, so what
do they do they decide to embrew his mother and sister and
father too. And how did they escape by paying somebody
money.

That is what you did with the Boche. You always paid some
money to some one it might be a colonel or it might be a
sergeant but anyway you did it and it was necessary so then
what happened.

THE SCHEMMELS.

Sing so la douse so la dim.
Un deux trois
Can you tell me wha
Is it indeed.
What you call a Petide.
And then what do I say to thee
Let me kiss thee willingly.
Not a mountain not a goat not a door.
Not a whisper not a curl not a gore
In me meeney miney mo.
You are my love and I tell you so.
    In the daylight
    And the night

465

Baby winks and holds me tight.
In the morning and the day and the evening and alway.
I hold my baby as I say.
Completely.
And what is an accent of my wife.
And accent and the present life.
Oh sweet oh my oh sweet oh my
I love you love you and I try
I try not to be nasty and hasty and good
I am my little baby's daily food.

ALSATIA.

In the exercise of greatness there is charm.
Believe me I mean to do you harm.
And except you have a stomach to alarm.
I mean to scatter so you are to arm.
Let me go.
And the Alsatians say.
What has another prince a birthday.

Now we come back to the Schemmils.
Schimmel Schimmel Gott in Himmel
Gott in Himmel There comes Shimmel.
Schimmel is an Alsatian name.

ACT II.

It is a little thing to expect nobody to sell what you give
them.
It is a little thing to be a minister.
It is a little thing to manufacture articles.
All this is modest.

THE BROTHER.

Brother brother here is mother.
We are all very well.

SCENE.

Listen to thee sweet cheerie
Is the pleasure of me.

In the way of being hungry and tired
That is what a depot makes you
A depot is not for trains
Its for us.

What are baby carriages
Household goods
And not the dears.
But dears.

ANOTHER ACT.

Clouds do not fatten with teaching.
They do not fatten at all.
We wonder if it is influence
By the way I guess.
She said. I like it better than Eggland.
What do you mean.
We never asked how many children over eleven.
You cannot imagine what I think about the country.
Any civilians killed.

ACT II.

See the swimmer. He don't swim.
See the swimmer.
My wife is angry when she sees a swimmer.

OPENING II.

We like Hirsing.

III.

We like the mayor of Guebwiller.

IV.

We like the road between Cernay and the railroad.
We go everywhere by automobile.

ACT II.

This is a particular old winter.
Everybody goes back.

Back.
I can clean.
I can clean.
I cannot clean without a change in birds.
I am so pleased that they cheat.

ACT 54.

In silver stars and red crosses.
In paper money and water.
We know a french wine.
Alsatian wine is dearer.
They are not particularly old.
Old men are old.
There are plenty to hear of Schemmel having appendicitis.

SCENE II.

Can you mix with another
Can you be a Christian and a Swiss.
Mr. Zumsteg.   Do I hear a saint.
Louisa.   They call me Lisela.
Mrs. Zumsteg.   Are you going to hear me.
Young Mr. Zumsteg.   I was looking at the snow.
All of them.   Like flowers. They like flowers.

SCENE III.

It is an occasion.
When you see a Hussar.
          A Zouave.
          A soldier
          An antiquary.
Perhaps it is another.
We were surprised with the history of Marguerite's father
and step-father and the American Civil War.
Joseph.   Three three six, six, fifty, six fifty, fifty, seven.
Reading french.
Reading french.
Reading french singing.
Any one can look at pictures.
They explain pictures.

The little children have old birds.
They wish they were women.
Any one can hate a Prussian.
Alphonse what is your name.
Henri what is your name.
Madeleine what is your name.
Louise what is your name.
Rene what is your name.
Berthe what is your name
Charles what is your name
Marguerite what is your name
Jeanne what is your name.

ACT 425.

We see a river and we are glad to say that that is in a way
in the way today.

We see all the windows and we see a souvenir and we see
the best flower. The flower of the truth.

AN INTERLUDE.

Thirty days in April gave a chance to sing at a wedding.
Three days in February gave reality to life.
Fifty days every year do not make substraction.
The Alsations sing anyway.
Forty days in September.
Forty days in September we know what it is to spring.

ACT IN AMERICA.

Alsatians living in America.

FEBRUARY XIV.

On this day the troops who had been at Mulhouse came
again.

They came in the spring.
The spring is late in Alsace.
Water was good and hot anyway.
What are you doing.
Making music and burning the surface of marble.

When the surface of marble is burned it is not much discolored.

No but there is a discussion.

And then the Swiss.

What is amiss.

The Swiss are the origin of Mulhouse.

ALSACE OR ALSATIANS.

We have been deeply interested in the words of the song.

The Alsatians do not sing as well as their storks.

Their storks are their statuettes.

The rule is that angels and food and eggs are all sold by the dozen.

We were astonished.

And potatoes

Potatoes are eaten dry.

This reminds me of another thing I said. A woman likes to use money.

And if not.

She feels it really is her birthday.

Is it her birthday.

God bless her it is her birthday.

Please carry me to Dannemarie.

And what does Herbstadt say.

The names of cities are the names of all.

And pronouncing villages is more of a test than umbrella.

This was the first thing we heard in Alsatia.

Canary, roses, violets and curtains and bags and churches and rubber tires and an examination.

All the leaves are green and babyish.

How many children make a family.

THE WATCH ON THE RHINE.

Sweeter than water or cream or ice. Sweeter than bells of roses. Sweeter than winter or summer or spring. Sweeter than pretty posies. Sweeter than anything is my queen and loving is her nature.

Loving and good and delighted and best is her little King

and Sire whose devotion is entire who has but one desire to express the love which is hers to inspire.

In the photograph the Rhine hardly showed

In what way do chimes remind you of singing. In what way do birds sing. In what way are forests black or white.

We saw them blue.

With for get me nots.

In the midst of our happiness we were very pleased.

A Movie

Eyes are a surprise
Printzess a dream
　　Buzz is spelled with z
　　　Fuss is spelled with s
　　　So is business.
The UNITED STATES is comical.
Now I want to tell you about the Monroe doctrine. We think very nicely we think very well of the Monroe doctrine.

American painter painting in French country near railroad track. Mobilisation locomotive passes with notification for villages.

Where are American tourists to buy my pictures sacre nom d'un pipe says the american painter.

American painter sits in café and contemplates empty pocket book as taxi cabs file through Paris carrying French soldiers to battle of the Marne. I guess I'll be a taxi driver here in gay Paree says the american painter.

Painter sits in studio trying to learn names of streets with help of Brettonne peasant femme de menage. He becomes taxi driver. Ordinary street scenes in war time Paris.

Being lazy about getting up in the mornings he spends some of his dark nights in teaching Brettonne femme de menage peasant girl how to drive the taxi so she can replace him when he wants to sleep.

America comes into the war american painter wants to be american soldier. Personnel officer interviews him. What have you been doing, taxiing. You know Paris, Secret Service for you go on taxiing.

He goes on taxiing and he teaches Brettonne f. m. english so she can take his place if need be.

One night he reads his paper under the light. Police man tells him to move up, don't want to wants to read.

Man comes up wants to go to the station.

Painter has to take him. Gets back, reading again.

Another man comes wants to go to the station. Painter takes him.

Comes back to read again. Two american officers come up. Want to go to the station.

Painter says Tired of the station take you to Berlin if you like. No station.

Officers say Give you a lot if you take us outside town on way to the south, first big town.

He says alright got to stop at home first to get his coat.

Stops at home calls out to Brettonne f. m. Get busy telegraph to all your relations, you have them all over, ask have you any american officers staying forever. Be back to-morrow.

Back to-morrow. Called up by chief secret service. Goes to see him. Money has been disappearing out of quartermaster's department in chunks. You've got a free hand. Find out something.

Goes home. Finds f. m. brettonne surrounded with telegrams and letters from relatives. Americans everywhere but everywhere. She groans. Funny americans everywhere but everywhere they all said. Many funny americans everywhere. Two americans not so funny here my fifth cousin says, she is helping in the hospital at Avignon. Such a sweet american soldier. So young so tall so tender. Not very badly hurt but will stay a long long time. He has been visited by american officers who live in a villa. Two such nice ladies live there too and they spend and they spend, they buy all the good sweet food in Avignon. "Is that something William Sir," says the brettonne f. m.

Its snowing but no matter we will get there in the taxi. Take us two days and two nights you inside and me out. Hurry. They start, the funny little taxi goes over the mountains with and without assistance, all tired out he is inside, she driving when they turn down the hill into Avignon. Just then two americans on motor cycles come on and Brettonne f.m. losing her head grand smash. American painter wakes up burned, he sees the two and says by God and makes believe he is dead. The two are very helpful. A team comes along and takes american painter and all to hospital. Two americans ride off on motor cycles direction of Nimes and Pont du Gard.

Arrival at hospital, interview with the wounded american who described two american officers who had been like brothers to him, didn't think any officer could be so chummy with a soldier. Took me out treated me, cigarettes, everything fine.

Where have they gone on to, to Nimes.

Yes Pont du Gard.

American painter in bed in charge of french nursing nun but manages to escape and leave for Pont du Gard in mended taxi. There under the shadow of that imperishable monument of the might and industry of ancient Rome exciting duel. French gendarme american painter, taxi, f. m. brettonne, two american crooks with motor cycles on which they try to escape over the top of the Pont du Gard, great stunt, they are finally captured. They have been the receivers of the stolen money.

After many other adventures so famous has become the american painter, Brettonne femme de menage and taxi that in the march under the arch at the final triumph of the allies the taxi at the special request of General Pershing brings up the rear of the procession after the tanks, the Brettonne driving and the american painter inside waving the american flag Old Glory and the tricolor.

CURTAIN

Idem the Same

A Valentine to Sherwood Anderson

I knew too that through them I knew too that he was through, I knew too that he threw them. I knew too that they were through, I knew too I knew too, I knew I knew them. I knew to them.

If they tear a hunter through, if they tear through a hunter, if they tear through a hunt and a hunter, if they tear through the different sizes of the six, the different sizes of the six which are these, a woman with a white package under one arm and a black package under the other arm and dressed in brown with a white blouse, the second Saint Joseph the third a hunter in a blue coat and black garters and a plaid cap, a fourth a knife grinder who is full faced and a very little woman with black hair and a yellow hat and an excellently smiling appropriate soldier. All these as you please.

In the meantime examples of the same lily. In this way please have you rung.

WHAT DO I SEE.

A very little snail.
A medium sized turkey.
A small band of sheep.
A fair orange tree.
All nice wives are like that.
Listen to them from here.
Oh.
You did not have an answer.
Here.
Yes.

A VERY VALENTINE.

Very fine is my valentine.
Very fine and very mine.
Very fine is my valentine very mine and very fine.

Very fine is my valentine and mine, very fine very mine and mine is my valentine.

WHY DO YOU FEEL DIFFERENTLY.

Why do you feel differently about a very little snail and a big one.

Why do you feel differently about a medium sized turkey and a very large one.

Why do you feel differently about a small band of sheep and several sheep that are riding.

Why do you feel differently about a fair orange tree and one that has blossoms as well.

Oh very well.

All nice wives are like that.

To Be.
No Please.
To Be
They can please
Not to be
Do they please.
Not to be
Do they not please
Yes please.
Do they please
No please.
Do they not please
No please.
Do they please.
Please.
If you please.
And if you please.
And if they please
And they please.
To be pleased
Not to be pleased.
Not to be displeased.
To be pleased and to please.

KNEELING.

One two three four five six seven eight nine and ten.

The tenth is a little one kneeling and giving away a rooster with this feeling.

I have mentioned one, four five seven eight and nine.

Two is also giving away an animal.

Three is changed as to disposition.

Six is in question if we mean mother and daughter, black and black caught her, and she offers to be three she offers it to me.

That is very right and should come out below and just so.

BUNDLES FOR THEM.
A History Of Giving Bundles.

We were able to notice that each one in a way carried a bundle, they were not a trouble to them nor were they all bundles as some of them were chickens some of them pheasants some of them sheep and some of them bundles, they were not a trouble to them and then indeed we learned that it was the principal recreation and they were so arranged that they were not given away, and to-day they were given away.

I will not look at them again.

They will not look for them again.

They have not seen them here again.

They are in there and we hear them again.

In which way are stars brighter than they are. When we have come to this decision. We mention many thousands of buds. And when I close my eyes I see them.

If you hear her snore

It is not before you love her

You love her so that to be her beau is very lovely

She is sweetly there and her curly hair is very lovely

She is sweetly here and I am very near and that is very lovely.

She is my tender sweet and her little feet are stretched out well which is a treat and very lovely

Her little tender nose is between her little eyes which close and are very lovely.

She is very lovely and mine which is very lovely.

ON HER WAY.

If you can see why she feels that she kneels if you can see why he knows that he shows what he bestows, if you can see why they share what they share, need we question that there is no doubt that by this time if they had intended to come they would have sent some notice of such intention. She and they and indeed the decision itself is not early dissatisfaction.

IN THIS WAY.

Keys please, it is useless to alarm any one it is useless to alarm some one it is useless to be alarming and to get fertility in gardens in salads in heliotrope and in dishes. Dishes and wishes are mentioned and dishes and wishes are not capable of darkness. We like sheep. And so does he.

LET US DESCRIBE.

Let us describe how they went. It was a very windy night and the road although in excellent condition and extremely well graded has many turnings and although the curves are not sharp the rise is considerable. It was a very windy night and some of the larger vehicles found it more prudent not to venture. In consequence some of those who had planned to go were unable to do so. Many others did go and there was a sacrifice, of what shall we, a sheep, a hen, a cock, a village, a ruin, and all that and then that having been blessed let us bless it.

An Instant Answer
or
A Hundred Prominent Men

What is the difference between wandering behind one another or behind each other. One wandered behind the other. They wandered behind each other, they wandered behind one another.

Kings counts and chinamen.

A revival.

I will select a hundred prominent men and look at their photographs hand-writing and career, and then I will earnestly consider the question of synthesis.

Here are the hundred.

The first one is used to something. He is useful and available and has an unclouded intelligence and has the needed contact between Rousseau and pleasure. It is a pleasure to read.

The second one and in this case integrity has not been worshipped, in this case there has been no alternative.

The third one alternates between mountains and mountaineering. He has an anxious time and he wholly fails to appreciate the reason of rainfall. Rainfall sometimes lacks. It sometimes is completely absent and at other times is lacking in the essential quality of distribution. This has spread disaster.

The fourth one illustrates plentifully illustrates the attachments all of us have to what we have. We have that and we are worried. How kind of you to say so.

The fifth one of the fifth it has not been said that there have been three told of the gulf stream and the consul. Frank, where have you been. I have not been to London to see the queen.

The sixth one the sixth one thoroughly a pioneer. He is anchored we do not speak of anchor nor of diving he is readily thoughtful. He has energy and daughters. How often do we dream of daughters. How often. Just how often.

The seventh is mentioned every day.

The eighth. Can you pay the eighth to-day. Can you delay.

Can you say that you went away. Can you colour it to satisfy
the eye. Can you. Can you feel this as an elaborate precaution.
Can you.

The ninth one is vague. Is he vague there where they care
to insist. Is he vague there or is he inclined to tease. Is he
inclined to tease. We know what we show. A little quarter to
eight. I hope you will conduct him to his seat. He does not
need politeness. No and he tells you so. No.

The tenth one the tenth one feels traces of terror. This does
not sound wealthy nor wise nor does he plan otherwise. He
planned very well. There is always this to tell of him. He can
be a king or a queen or a countess or a Katherine Susan. We
know that name. It has always been the same. At the same
time every one shows changes. We arrange this at once.

The eleventh. Who won you. That is very sweet. Who were
you. Expected pages and word of mouth, and by word of
mouth. Expect pages and by word of mouth. Who won one.
Who won won. Mrs. Mrs. kisses, Mrs. kisses most. Mrs. misses
kisses, misses kisses most. Who won you.

And the twelfth. The twelfth was the man who restrained
Abel and Genoa. Why do the men like names. They like names
because they like calling. A calling is something to follow. We
no longer represent absence. I call you. Hullo are you there.
I have not been as intelligent yet as I was yesterday.

Thirteen, the thirteenth has not neglected the zenith. You
know how to invent a word. And so do you. You know how
to oblige him with lilacs. And so do you, you know you do.
And you know how to rectify an expression. Do you build
anew. Oh yes you do.

The fourteenth prominent man is prominent every day of
the year. Do you feel this to be at all queer. He is prominent
and eminent and he is personally severe. He is not amiable.
How can an amiable baby pronounce words. How can they
be predominant. We know why we have reason we reason
because of this.

The fifteenth is wholly exhilarated. Place air and water
where they are.

The sixteenth yes indeed. Have we decreed. Yes indeed.
Have we. Do we need that.

The seventeenth. The seventeenth century is older than the

sixteenth. How much older. A century older. Or older than a century older. The seventeenth is a century older is older than a century older than the sixteenth.

The eighteenth one wishes to annex the Philippines.

The nineteenth one mingles with men. We say he mixes with men. We say he mixes up nothing. He does not mix things up nor does he do the opposed thing. When he does ring and he does ring, what, that is what he says, what. What does he say. He says what did I say. He says. Did I ring. I say, he says, I say did you say anything. How cleverly brothers mingle. We haven't forgotten.

The twentieth. No one forgets anything and he does not forget anything. He does not forget anything when he is here. Does he forget to come again. He does not elaborate exercises. There are witnesses there.

The twenty-first nursed what was to him beaming. I can declare that they are not aware of seeming to share policing. They have increased the number of police in New York.

The twenty-second, how many more days are there in September than there were. This question has been aroused by the question asked by the prominent man who is the subject of the declaration that words may be spoken.

The twenty-third is not indicated by invasion. We all believe that we do invade islands countries homes and fountains. We do believe that the hierarchy of repetition rests with the repeaters. Now we severally antedate the memory. Do you relish powder.

Of the twenty-fourth it has been said that out of sight out of mind is not so blind. Please do not wave me away. Waves and waves they say carry wood away. Carry, does that remind you of anything.

The twenty-fifth is moderately a queen. What did you say. Anger is expressive and so are they.

The twenty-sixth has many ordinary happinesses. He is ordinarily in the enjoyment of his challenge. Do not challenge him to-day. What did you say. Do not challenge him to-day.

The twenty-seventh does measure very well indeed the heights of hills. How high are they when they are negligible. How high are they any way and where do dogs run when they run faster and faster. And why do dog lovers love dogs. Do you know everything about deer. He had a father and they made a window and windows have never been scarce.

The twenty-eighth is perceptibly loving. He has invented perfumes and portraits and he has also reconciled stamina with countenance. I do say that yesterday he was very welcome. And to-day. To-day he is very welcome. We do not say that it is wonderful to be loaned at all.

The twenty-ninth neglects the history of a mute. Mute and unavailing. The twenty-ninth does not add considerably to his expense. He is not needed there. Where is he needed. He is needed here and there. Drive me there.

The thirtieth manages to be lavish. He washes land and water, washes them to be green, wishes them to be clean, his daughter merits her mother and her sister her brother. He himself witnesses this himself and he carries himself by special train. A train of cars. Will there soon be no trains of cars. Did you hear me ask that. Will there pretty soon be no bridling.

The thirty-first remembers that a pump can pump other things than water and because of this he says miles are astray. They have proof of this. Can you solidly measure for pleasure.

The thirty-second is an irresistible pedestrian. He has much choice, he chooses himself and then his brother and then he rides back. He can seem in a dream and he can uncover the lover. I have been so tender to-day.

The thirty-third is incapable of amnesty. Forgive me for that you dear man. Where were you born. I was born in a city and I love the whole land.

The thirty-fourth is second to none in value. Why do you value that more. Why do you value you value that any more.

The thirty-fifth why can there be naturally this one who has found it invigorating to exchange beds for beds and butter for butter. Exchange butter for butter. Do exchange more beds for more beds.

The thirty-sixth has heard of excitement. How can you be excited without a reason. How can you be an adaptable tenth. He is in the tent. There is a tent there.

The thirty-seventh for the thirty-seventh a great many tell the truth, they tell the truth generously. Somebody is generous there where the rest of them care. Do they care for me. Do they. How awfully popular I am.

The thirty-eighth has held enough and he holds the rest there where there are no more edible mushrooms. Do you know how, to tell an edible mushroom. Have you heard all of the number of ways.

The thirty-ninth is contented and alarmed. Why do you share and share alike and where do you share what you share. What do you care.

The fortieth is rapidly rained on. Rain is what is useful in Europe and not necessary where you have irrigation. Do you understand me. And why do you repeat what you say. I like to repeat what I say.

The forty-first one did he duck. Did he say I wish they would go away, did he describe himself, did he feel that he was married, did he entertain on next to nothing and did he furnish houses and did he candidly satisfy enquiries. Did he learn to quiet himself. Did he resemble ready money and did he inquire where they went. How can all shawls be worn all the time. Some say it is very fine to-day.

The forty-second what did you say, the forty-second came every day and yet how can he come every day when they are away. He comes anyway and he replaces what he uses and he uses it there and he promises to share what he has and he is very prominently there. We stay home every day when he comes here. I don't quite understand, I am a little confused. Does he come every day.

The forty-third one is the one that has inevitably established himself in the location which is the one that was intended as the site of the building. Did they build there. No certainly not as he has already arranged it for himself. I understand. He came first. Yes he came first and he stayed which was quite the natural thing for him to do.

The forty-fourth one married again. No one meant to come to the wedding absolutely no one and he said I am marrying and they said who is it to be and he said I know what you believe and they said how can you believe that you are to be married again. What is the marriage ceremony that you refer to. I refer to the marriage ceremony. Is that so.

The forty-fifth, all the immediate present and those immediately present, all those present will please answer that they are present now. And what do they all say. All those who

are present say so. We were very nearly pioneers in this movement. And why are you so frequently referred to, because
when they refer to me they mean me.

The forty-sixth prominent man is the one who connected
them to their country. My country all the same they have their
place there. And why do you tell their names. I tell their
names because in this way I know that one and one and one
and one and one and one and one and one and one and one
and one and one and one and one and one and one and one
and one and one and one and one and one and one and one
and one and one and one and one and one and one and one
and one and one and one and one and one and one and one
and one and one and one and one and one and one and one
and one and one and one and one and one and one and one
and one and one and one and one and one and one and one
and one and one and one and one and one and one and one
and one and one and one and one and one and one and one
and one and one and one and one and one and one and one
and one and one and one and one and one and one and one
and one and one and one and one and one and one and one
and one and one and one and one and one and one and one
and one and one and one and one and one make a
hundred. It is very difficult to count in a foreign language.

The forty-seventh does do what he expected to do. He expected to have what he had include what he was to have and
it did and then when he went again he went again and again.
After that all the same he said all the same I am very well
satisfied.

The forty-eighth placed them there. Where did he place
them. Exactly what do you mean by placing them, he was
asked and he answered, I placed them and they were equally
distant from the different places that were near them. Is this
the way you choose a capital they said. Yes indeed he said,
that is as you may say the result of the influence of Spanish.
Oh yes they replied not entirely understanding but really he
was right. He was undoubtedly in the right.

The forty-ninth, what habits had this one formed, you may
say that he can be mentioned as being the one who was bestowed again and again on elephants and mosses. It is queer
that fountains have mosses and forests elephants. And why is
it astonishing that we have heard him when he was men-

tioning that he went there, we do not know. Show me he said and they opened their eyes. Why do you stare, and why did they. We do not care. Yes do please me. We please ourselves.

The fiftieth, why did you expect me. We expected you because you had announced yourself and you are usually punctual. How did you learn to be punctual, because we have had the habit of waiting for the rain. Does that make one punctual. It does. This is what has been bought. Buying is a vindication of roads. Buy and stay, stay and but. By and by. Yes sir.

The fifty-first one has to say what do you command. What is sweating, that is what I like says Mike, the fifty-first one has an understanding of resisting. He had it said of him that he could countenance alarmingly the destruction of a condition. Why are conditions connected with what I have not said. I said the account, was there an account of it on account of it.

The fifty-second has as an established fact the fact that the account given is the one that makes him furnish everything. Did he furnish it all and was it wise to apprise him that there were many who had religiously speaking an interest in interpretation. This sounds like nonsense. What do you mean by spiritual, what do you. Mike said what do you mean by spiritual what do you. They wished to say that they did not wish anything tried again and again. Be rested. You be rested.

The fifty-third have you heard that fifty and fifty are evenly divided. Have you heard about the way they say it. All of them come again and say it. We say it and they say it. May we say it. I have not forgotten that the fifty-third prominent man is the one that has the most anxious air.

The fifty-fourth one is the one that has been left to study industrialism. No one asks is there merit in that. No one says that there is something noble in that. No one says how do you study a subject. No one idolises Frank. Don't they indeed.

The fifty-fifth is very pretty in any language. How do you do is one way of looking at it. He minds it the most and the shape of it very much. He is very easily offended and he believes in a reference. I refer to you and to you and to you. I always refer to you. I refer to you and I refer you to him and I refer her to them and they refer them to me. Can you see why. Do you understand why they have no need to go and come, to sit down to get up and to walk around.

The fifty-sixth measures what he has done by what he will do. He measures it all and means to react. Action and reaction are equal and possible and we relieve the strain. In this way we arrange for hope and pleasure. This is what we say unites us all to-day.

The fifty-seventh is admirably speaking radiant when he has no annoyances. And why does he continue to know that a lieutenant colonel is in command. Why does he know it. Dear me why does he know it.

The fifty-eighth one is alright. How do the hours come to be longer. Longer than what, longer than English french, Italian, North and South American Japanese and Chinese.

The fifty-ninth marries when he marries, and he is married to me. Do not fail to see him and hear him and rehearse with him and molest him. He has an organic wit.

The sixtieth is actually rested. He has come to be reasonably industrious. He had and he has come to be reasonably industrious. In this way he is successful.

The lieutenant colonel was found dead with a bullet in the back of his head and his handkerchief in his hand.

The sixty-first one has had a very astonishing career. He said that he would never mention another and he never did, he also foresaw the re-establishment of every crisis and he went ahead he went in and out and he foresaw that youth is not young and that the older ones will not seem older and then he imagined expresses. In this way he established his success. I have not mentioned his name.

The sixty-second was just the same. He entered and he came and he came away and no one cared to share expenses. No one cared to share expenses. What did you say. No one cared to share expenses. He was privileged to increase paler nights and he always measured investigation. How can you investigate privileges. By not curtailing expenses. Thank you for all your thoughts. Give your best thoughts. Thank you for all your thoughts.

The sixty-third, we all have heard of regiments called the sixty-third. Reform regiments in time and they have magnificent beginnings. Do not reform them in time and they progress fairly. Do not reform them at all and they will not necessarily decrease. I say the sixty-third one is the one who came to be celebrated because of this. Because of this he came to be the one that one of the ones that are mentioned in this list.

The sixty-fourth we are a nation of sixty-fourth. Do you remember how a great many of them sat together. Do you and do you remember what they said. My impression was that they had not spoken. My impression was that they had not spoken then. Never again. It is hard to love your father-in-law. Hard almost impossible.

The sixty-fifth, there is a standard for the sixty-fifth. This is his standard. He comes to it and he is very well indeed. Is he. Yes he is very well indeed.

The sixty-sixth, how are you when you are steady. He steadily repeats himself. Do you mean he allows you to feel that he does so. He does indeed.

The sixty-seventh has this advantage. It is an advantage that is easily enjoyed.

The sixty-eighth all small culmination meets with this as their reward. We reward when and where we reward and we reward with rewards. And this is the use of a guardian, where it is guarded it is as well guarded as ever.

The sixty-ninth how authoritative he is and he was. He was able to arrange for everything again and again and he said with hesitation why do I like to make sweets. Sweets to the sweet said some one.

The seventieth come again and listen were the origin and the beginning of his success. Come again and do not go away. Come again and stay and in this way he succeeded. He was successful. Have you meant to go away he would say. Oh no indeed he meant to stay they would say. And he meant to stay. He was successful in his hey day and he continued to be successful and he is succeeding to-day. When you say how can you feel as you feel we say, that is the way to succeed. That is just the way to succeed. He says I have succeeded.

The seventieth do I remember whether I do or I don't. I think I usually do that is to say I always have. Does that mean you always will. I think so. I gather from what I saw at the door that you wanted me to come in before.

The seventy-first believe me at first. At first we believed that that was because they were so many that had been equal to this one. And then we accompanied them. They were not regularly identified. Nor was he, why did he and because, why did he, because he did double the pansies. You understand that this is symbolical. No one has really more than doubled the pansies.

The seventy-second for in this way there is a second the seventy-second managed to see me. And where were they all. They were all in there. And why did no one declare themselves faultless. This was very nearly a dish, a nest of dishes. Do you remember that play, A Nest of Dishes. This and the painting of a garden scene made an astonishing measure for measure. Answer blindly to this assurance and be assured that all the pleasure is yours.

The seventy-third has nearly spoken. He said I see rapidly I compose carefully, I follow securely and I arrange dexterously, I predict this for me.

The seventy-fourth how often have both had children. I said that he should not change he should continue with girls. I said she should not change she should continue with girls. She changed and he did not. He continued with girls.

The seventy-fifth very many actually count. They count one two three four five six seven.

The seventy-sixth one is the one that has not often met nor often been met nor very often met them yet. They are there they do declare that they are there. And why publish data.

The seventy-seventh really places it. He places there with a great deal of care. And when he was twelve he sang in public. There are a great many reasons for it. This is one of them. The reason I have given is their reason. Do be satisfied with their reason. Do not be worried do not be worried at all nor do not be at all worried. Be satisfied. Be very well satisfied.

The seventy-eighth do you remember about him do you really explain when you explain that he loved lacing and unlacing and releasing and separate silence. Do you really credit this with that. Do you do so fairly.

The seventy-ninth was originally delicious, delicious as delicious as the excellent repast which was offered. Do you remember how she wrote offer, offered. Do you and do you prefer exchange that is barter to pleasure in reason. I believe in pleasure and the reason the reason for it.

The eightieth how do you manage to mention a number separately. It is a specialty a specialty of wine. That is very fine in you and it all proves to me that I have faith and a future.

The eighty-first at first the eighty-first was the one who had made the fruit house who had the fruit house made there where it was very singular that he could understand that there was land. You see it is like this land is made to be near by so that one can see it. Land is made to be understood to be there. So there was naturally no distribution of land and land. Do you understand, Lizzie do you understand. These were naturally there here there and everywhere. We have principally met whether we need to or not. I do complain of sitting there. Not here. No not here.

The eighty-second, was it we say was it by means of a hammer or by means of a rock, was it by hammer or by rock that we felt that the future was one with the present. Do you know by what means rockets signal pleasure pain and noise and union, do you know by what means a rock is freed when it is not held too tightly held in the hand. Many hold what they hold and he held what was best to settle in Seattle. Why do you care for climate. Why do you. I know.

The eighty-third, tell me about him. I will. He was never neglected nor was he especially willing to sing, a great many ceased to secure singing. You mean they found Saturday intolerable. That is just it that is just what I wish to say, you put it in that way and certainly very certainly a great many kinds of birthdays are taken for granted. Granted.

The eighty-fourth that too might be taken to be the same as if it were one number the more and yet if you think delicately and you do think so you will see why I say no it is not the same. Now supposing he were famous would he understand it as you say he does understand fame. Would he. Oh you question me so narrowly and I might say I didn't mean to and then what would you say. I would say I just want to be praised. There that is permanent.

The eighty-fifth is the one did I mention that this too might be the number of a regiment. You see they say that there are more there you mean as to one thousand and four thousand, there are more there.

He has given as the reason that he knows the difference

between Christmas New Year Easter and Thanksgiving. He has given this as a reason.

The eighty-sixth is the one to measure by animals. A dog another dog and a woman two lions and a man a central surface a lion a dog and a man and two men and more introduction. I introduce you to him and to him. Do you introduce him too often. I do not think so. No I do not think so.

The eighty-seventh study the eighty-seventh one carefully and tell me what it is that you notice. I notice that in different positions one sees a different distinction. You mean you always distinguish him. Oh so readily. And when you smile does he smile at all, he smiles very readily when you smile at all. And does he furnish you with agreeable merriment. Very agreeably so. Tell him so it will please him. I do. I will.

The eighty-eighth furnish the eighty-eighth with the means of furnishing. We furnish everything. He furnishes everything. In this way we cannot mean what has been made clear. We cannot mean that he plans this.

The eighty-ninth remember that when you remember the eighty-ninth it was not so happily bowed to as it might have been if all pages were printed as they came. We like printing it all the same. Now just what do you mean by that. I mean that very rapidly he refreshes himself.

The eighty-ninth, forty made the eighty-ninth clearly the half of that number. There are a number of them aren't they and each one every one more than one, one and one, they all stay over there. If for instance there had been one continuation where then would they place the succession. Where would they. You don't ask where did they. You don't really ask me anything.

The ninetieth is the ninetieth one to-day. To-day come to care to stay. How do you. Dear me how can you use it as if it was a cane. How can you. Please how can you. I can do all this and all the time have you discovered anything. She did, keys and a kitchen. Not a mistake. It was not a mistake.

The ninety-first who knows about this one, it is not easy to plan for it, eat for it or trouble for it. It is not easy to manage to say to-day and yesterday and very likely every other day. It is not easy. I say it isn't easy.

The ninety-second and does he attend to all of it. Do you attend to all of it. I am not easily convinced that they attend to all of it. Do they attend to all of it. All that I know about it is that whether they do or whether they do not we have a system of triple mirrors. In this way we see where they come. Where do they come from. I see abundance geographically.

The ninety-third, every one has heard of the ninety-third. Naturally, and now what do you mean by rushing. What do you mean by rushing in here and saying am I in it. What do you mean by doing that. Even if you were in it you would not be heard from so definitely. Be reasonable, leave it all to me. When this you see remember that you are to wait for me. I can say this very quickly.

The ninety-fourth marries he marries them, now how can you know whether in saying this I mean what you mean does this bother you at all does it annoy you, can you be obstinate in asserting that we have the same meaning that you mean and that I mean that he marries them. Think about this carefully and when you are thoroughly prepared to be generous give me your answer. I answer for him.

The ninety-fifth, remember the ninety-fifth. Ninety-nine is ninety-nine, and the ninety-fifth has a very good evening. Good evening. It is not our custom to say good-evening.

The ninety-sixth and more and more. You were given to reconciling floods with fire. This is a noisy day. May I look again.

The ninety-seventh hears me has heard me when I have said do not care to hear Cornelius Vanderbilt. The ninety-seventh is excellent in his way, he is very excellent in that way and does prepare his share. Do you prepare your share. And do you estimate your share correctly. Have you ever mistaken anything and put it away there with your share. No neither of you have, neither of you have ever done so.

The ninety-eighth, the ninety-eighth and the ninety-ninth, the ninety-eighth is the one we see when we look. We look and we look. How do we look. We look very pretty. Do we look well. We look very well.

The ninety-ninth who is the ninety-ninth, as for me I prefer to call tissue paper silk paper. Do you prefer to do so by the year. Tissue paper is a thin paper, and silk paper is a thin paper.

One might say that tissue paper is a paper made of thin tissue. It is sometimes called silk paper. It is made of the same material but is not quite so thin.

The Hundredth. When you believe me you believe me very often don't you. I believe that Andrew D. White and many worked all day and I believe that Andrew D. White and many others worked all night I believe that many others worked all day and that many others worked all night. I believe that many others are so had I not better say are often an addition. Then can you say that you do like to see. Yes I do like to see you here. And then why do you follow me. You follow me. I follow you follow you follow me. You do follow me.

One hundred and won. When this is done will you make me another one.

Erik Satie

Erick Satie benignly.
Come to Sylvia do.
Sylvia Sybil and Sarah
A bird is for more cookcoo.
And then what spreads thinner, and a letter. It is early for all.

Cezanne

The Irish lady can say, that to-day is every day. Caesar can say that every day is to-day and they say that every day is as they say.

In this way we have a place to stay and he was not met because he was settled to stay. When I said settled I meant settled to stay. When I said settled to stay I meant settled to stay Saturday. In this way a mouth is a mouth. In this way if in as a mouth if in as a mouth where, if in as a mouth where and there. Believe they have water too. Believe they have that water too and blue when you see blue, is all blue precious too, is all that that is precious too is all that and they meant to absolve you. In this way Cezanne nearly did nearly in this way Cezanne nearly did nearly did and nearly did. And was I surprised. Was I very surprised. Was I surprised. I was surprised and in that patient, are you patient when you find bees. Bees in a garden make a specialty of honey and so does honey. Honey and prayer. Honey and there. There where the grass can grow nearly four times yearly.

A Book Concluding With
As a Wife Has a Cow
A Love Story

KEY TO CLOSET.

There is a key.
There is a key to a closet that opens the drawer. And she keeps both so that neither money nor candy will go suddenly, Fancy, baby, new year. She keeps both so that neither money nor candy will go suddenly, Fancy baby New Year, fancy baby mine, fancy.

HAPPEN TO HAVE.

She does happen to have an aunt and in visiting and in taking a flower she shows that she is well supplied with sweet food at home otherwise she would have taken candies to her aunt as it would have been her sister. Her sister did.

RIGHT AWAY.

Active at a glance and said, said it again. Active at a glance and then to change gold right away. Active at a glance and not to change gold right away.

FISH.

Can fish be wives and wives and wives and have as many as that. Can fish be wives and have as many as that.
Ten o'clock or earlier.

PINK.

Pink looks as pink, pink looks as pink, as pink as pink supposes, suppose.

QUICKLY.

She will finish first and come, the second time she will finish first and come. The second time.

DECISION.

He decided when he had a house he would not buy them. By and by. By then.

CHOOSE.

He let it be expected and he let it be expected and she let it be expected and he came and brought them and she did not. Usually she sent them and usually he brought them. They were well-chosen.

HAD A HORSE.

If in place of a nose she had a horse and in place of a flower she had wax and in place of a melon she had a stone and in place of perfume buckles how many days would it be.

JULIA.

She asked for white and it was refused, she asked for pink and it was refused she asked for white and pink and it was agreed, it was agreed it would be pink and it was agreed to.

A COUSIN.

If a mistake as to the other if in mistake as to the brother, if by mistake and it was either if and all of it came and come. To come means partly that.

LOOK LIKE.

Look like look like it and he had twenty and more than twenty of them too. The great question is is it easier to have more than were wanted and in that case what do they do with it.

TO-DAY.

Yesterday not at all. To-day one to each one of four, ten to one two to one fifty to one and none to one. And might be satisfied. So also is the one who not being forgotten had five.

LONGER.

She stayed away longer.

BESIDE.

It can be known that he changed from Friday to Sunday. It can also be known that he changed from year to year. It can also be known that he was worried. It can also be known that his fellow voyager would not only be attentive but would if necessary forget to come. Everybody would be grateful.

IN QUESTION.

How large a mouth has a good singer. He knows. How much better is one colour than another. He knows. How far away is a city from a city. He knows. How often is it delayed. He knows.

MUCH LATER.

Elephants and birds of beauty and a gold-fish. Gold fish or a superstition. They always bring bad luck. He had them and he was not told. Gold fish and he was not old. Gold fish and he was not to scold. Gold fish all told. The result was that the other people never had them and he knows nothing of it.

NEGLECTED AND NEGLECTFUL.

She needed it all very well and pressed her, she needed it all very well and as read, to read it better a letter and better, to read it and let her it all very well.

AND SOUP.

It has always been a test of who made it best, and it has always been a test and who made it best. Who made it best it has always been a test. It has always been a test it has always been a test. Who made it best. Who made it best it has always been a test.

PETER.

Peter said Peter said eyes are always and eyes are always. Peter said Peter said, eyes are always and Peter said eyes are always. Peter said eyes are always.

Peter said eyes are always.

EMILY.

Emily is admitted admittedly, Emily is admittedly Emily is admittedly.

Emily said Emily said, Emily is admittedly Emily. Emily said Emily is admittedly is Emily said Emily is admittedly Emily said Emily is Emily is admittedly.

JULIA AGNES AND EMILY.

Emily is and Julia. Julia is and Agnes. Agnes will entertain Julia. Emily is and Agnes is and will entertain Julia and Agnes will entertain Julia Agnes will entertain Julia.

THERE.

There is an excuse for expecting success there is an excuse. There is an excuse for expecting success and there is an excuse for expecting success. And at once.

IN ENGLISH.

Even in the midst and may be even in the midst and even in the midst and may be. Watched them.

THEY HAD.

They had no children. They had no children but three sister-in-laws a brother which brother and no nephews and no nieces and no other language.

IN ADDITION.

They think that they will they think that they will change their opinion concerning. And it is nearly what they said.

Could and could she be addition.

THESE.

Three mentioned the three mentioned are too much glass too many hyacinths too many horses. Horses are used at once. Why are horses used at once.

A LITTLE BEGINNING.

She says it is a small beginning, she says that partly this and partly that, she says it is partly this and partly that, she says that it is what she is accustomed to.

INTRODUCTION.

When they introduced not at all when they introduced not at all.

A SLATE.

A long time in which to decide that although it is a slate a slate used to mean a slate pencil.

PLACES.

If he came and was at once inclined inclined to have heard that how many places are there in it. How many places are there in it.

IN ENGLISH.

Longer legs than English. In English longer legs than English.

IN HALF.

Half the size of that. This does not refer to a half or a whole or a piece. Half the size of that refers only to the size.

NOT SURPRISING.

It is not at all surprising. Not at all surprising. If he gets it done at all. It is not at all surprising.

HANDS AND GRATEFUL.

Hands and grateful. This does enjoying this. Hands and grateful. Go upstairs go upstairs go upstairs go. Hands and grateful.

SUSPICIONS.

He was suspicious of it and he had every reason to be suspicious of it.

AN AID TO MEMORY.

In aid of memory. Mentioned by itself alone. Butter or flattery. Mentioned by itself. In aid of memory mentioned by itself alone.

ALL.

He was the last and best of all not at all. He was the last of all he was the best of all he was the last and best of all not at all.

FANCY.

Fancy looking at it now and if it resembled he made half of it.

A TRAIT.

He met him. It was very difficult to remember who was here alone.

This decided us to consider it a trait.

READY.

When I was as ready to like it as ever I was ready to account for the difference between and the flowers.

Are you ready yet, not yet.

KNIVES.

Who painted knives first. Who painted knives first. Who said who painted knives first. Who said who painted knives first. And see the difference.

INSISTED.

I insisted upon it in summer as well as in winter. I insisted upon it I insisted upon it in summer I insisted upon it in summer as well as in winter. To remember in winter that it is winter and in summer that it is summer. I insisted upon it in summer as well as in winter not sentimentally with raspberries.

TO REMIND.

She reminded me that I was as ready as not and I said I

will not say that I preferred service to opposition. I will not say what or what is not a pleasure.

SEVEN.

If she follows let her go, one two three four five six seven. She is let go if she follows. If she follows she is let go. If she follows let her go, she is let go if she follows.

A HAT.

It is as pleasant as that to have a hat, to have a hat and it is as pleasant as that. It is as pleasant as that to have a hat. It is as pleasant as that. To have a hat. To have a hat it is as pleasant as that to have a hat. To have had a hat it is as pleasant as that to have a hat.

HOW TO REMEMBER.

A pretty dress and a pretty hat and how to come, leave out two and how to come. A pretty dress and a pretty hat leave out two. How to come and leave out two. A pretty hat and a pretty dress a pretty dress and a pretty hat and leave out two. Leave out two and how to come.

A WISH.

And always not when absently enough and heard and said. He had a wish.

FIFTY.

Fifty fifty and fifty-one, she said she thought so and she was told that that was about what it was. Not in place considered as places. Julia was used only as cake, Julia cake was used only as Julia. In some countries cake is called candy. The next is as much as that. When do they is not the same as why do they.

As a Wife Has a Cow
A Love Story

Nearly all of it to be as a wife has a cow, a love story. All of it to be as a wife has a cow, all of it to be as a wife has a cow, a love story.

As to be all of it as to be a wife as a wife has a cow, a love story, all of it as to be all of it as a wife all of it as to be as a wife has a cow a love story, all of it as a wife has a cow as a wife has a cow a love story.

Has made, as it has made as it has made, has made has to be as a wife has a cow, a love story. Has made as to be as a wife has a cow a love story. As a wife has a cow, as a wife has a cow a love story. Has to be as a wife has a cow a love story. Has made as to be as a wife has a cow a love story.

When he can, and for that when he can, for that. When he can and for that when he can. For that. When he can. For that when he can. For that. And when he can and for that. Or that, and when he can. For that and when he can.

And to in six and another. And to and in and six and another. And to and in and six and another. And to in six and and to and in and six and another. And to and in and six and another. And to and six and in and another and and to and six and another and and to and in and six and and to and six and in and another.

In came in there, came in there come out of there. In came in come out of there. Come out there in came in there. Come out of there and in and come out of there. Came in there. Come out of there.

Feeling or for it, as feeling or for it, came in or come in, or come out of there or feeling as feeling or feeling as for it.

As a wife has a cow.

Came in and come out.

As a wife has a cow a love story.

As a love story, as a wife has a cow, a love story.

Not and now, now and not, not and now, by and by not and now, as not, as soon as not not and now, now as soon now, now as soon, and now as soon as soon as now. Just as soon just now just now just as soon just as soon as now. Just as soon as now.

And in that, as and in that, in that and and in that, so that, so that and in that, and in that and so that and as for that and as for that and that. In that. In that and and for that as for that and in that. Just as soon and in that. In that as that and just as soon. Just as soon as that.

Even now, now and even now and now and even now. Not as even now, therefor, even now and therefor, therefor and even now and even now and therefor even now. So not to and moreover and even now and therefor and moreover and even now and so and even now and therefor even now.

Do they as they do so. And do they do so.

We feel we feel. We feel or if we feel if we feel or if we feel. We feel or if we feel. As it is made made a day made a day or two made a day, as it is made a day or two, as it is made a day. Made a day. Made a day. Not away a day. By day. As it is made a day.

On the fifteenth of October as they say, said any way, what is it as they expect, as they expect it or as they expected it, as they expect it and as they expected it, expect it or for it, expected it and it is expected of it. As they say said anyway. What is it as they expect for it, what is it and it is as they expect of it. What is it. What is it the fifteenth of October as they say as they expect or as they expected as they expect for it. What is it as they say the fifteenth of October as they say and as expected of it, the fifteenth of October as they say, what is it as expected of it. What is it and the fifteenth of October as they say and expected of it.

And prepare and prepare so prepare to prepare and prepare to prepare and prepare so as to prepare, so to prepare and prepare to prepare to prepare for and to prepare for it to prepare, to prepare for it, in preparation, as preparation in preparation by preparation. They will be too busy afterwards to prepare. As preparation prepare, to prepare, as to preparation and to prepare. Out there.

Have it as having having it as happening, happening to have it as having, having to have it as happening. Happening and have it as happening and having it happen as happening and having to have it happen as happening, and my wife has a cow as now, my wife having a cow as now, my wife having a cow as now and having a cow as now and having a cow and having a cow now, my wife has a cow and now. My wife has a cow.

Van or Twenty Years After

A Second Portrait of Carl Van Vechten

Twenty years after, as much as twenty years after in as much as twenty years after, after twenty years and so on. It is it is it is it is.

If it and as if it, if it or as if it, if it is as if it, and it is as if it and as if it. Or as if it. More as if it. As more. As more as if it. And if it. And for and as if it.

If it was to be a prize a surprise if it was to be a surprise to realise, if it was to be if it were to be, was it to be. What was it to be. It was to be what it was. And it was. So it was. As it was. As it is. Is it as it as. It is and as it is and as it is. And so and so as it was.

Keep it in sight alright.

Not to the future but to the fuschia.

Tied and untied and that is all there is about it. And as tied and as beside, and as beside and tied. Tied and untied and beside and as beside and as untied and as tied and as untied and as beside. As beside as by and as beside. As by as by the day. By their day and and as it may, may be they will may be they may. Has it been reestablished as not to weigh. Weigh how. How to weigh. Or weigh. Weight, state, await, state, late state rate state, state await weight state, in state rate at any rate state weight state as stated. In this way as stated. Only as if when the six sat at the table they all looked for those places together. And each one in that direction so as to speak look down and see the same as weight. As weight for weight as state to state as wait to wait as not so. Beside.

For arm absolutely for arm.

They reinstate the act of birth.

Bewildering is a nice word but it is not suitable at present.

They meant to be left as they meant to be left, as they meant to be left left and their center, as they meant to be left and their center. So that in their and do, so that in their and to do. So suddenly and at his request. Get up and give it to him and so suddenly and as his request. Request to request in request, as request, for a request by request, requested, as requested as they requested, or so have it to be nearly there. Why are the three waiting, there are more than three. One two three four five six seven.

As seven.

Seating, regard it as the rapidly increased February.

Seating regard it as the very regard it as their very nearly regard as their very nearly or as the very regard it as the very settled, seating regard it as the very as their very regard it as their very nearly regard it as the very nice, seating regard as their very nearly regard it as the very nice, known and seated seating regard it, seating and regard it, regard it as the very nearly center left and in the center, regard it as the very left and in the center. And so I say so. So and so. That. For. For that. And for that. So and so and for that. And for that and so and so. And so I say so.

Now to fairly see it have, now to fairly see it have and now to fairly see it have. Have and to have. Now to fairly see it have and to have. Naturally.

As naturally, naturally as, as naturally as. As naturally.

Now to fairly see it have as naturally.

If I Told Him

A Completed Portrait of Picasso

If I told him would he like it. Would he like it if I told him.
Would he like it would Napoleon would Napoleon would
would he like it.

If Napoleon if I told him if I told him if Napoleon. Would
he like it if I told him if I told him if Napoleon. Would he
like it if Napoleon if Napoleon if I told him. If I told him if
Napoleon if Napoleon if I told him. If I told him would he
like it would he like it if I told him.

Now.

Not now.

And now.

Now.

Exactly as as kings.

Feeling full for it.

Exactitude as kings.

So to beseech you as full as for it.

Exactly or as kings.

Shutters shut and open so do queens. Shutters shut and
shutters and so shutters shut and shutters and so and so shut-
ters and so shutters shut and so shutters shut and shutters and
so. And so shutters shut and so and also. And also and so and
so and also.

Exact resemblance to exact resemblance the exact resemblance as exact as a resemblance, exactly as resembling, exactly
resembling, exactly in resemblance exactly a resemblance, exactly and resemblance. For this is so. Because.

Now actively repeat at all, now actively repeat at all, now
actively repeat at all.

Have hold and hear, actively repeat at all.

I judge judge.

As a resemblance to him.

Who comes first. Napoleon the first.

Who comes too coming coming too, who goes there, as they
go they share, who shares all, all is as all as as yet or as yet.

Now to date now to date. Now and now and date and the date.

Who came first Napoleon at first. Who came first Napoleon the first. Who came first, Napoleon first.

Presently.

Exactly do they do.

First exactly.

Exactly do they do too.

First exactly.

And first exactly.

Exactly do they do.

And first exactly and exactly.

And do they do.

At first exactly and first exactly and do they do.

The first exactly.

And do they do.

The first exactly.

At first exactly.

First as exactly.

As first as exactly.

Presently

As presently.

As as presently.

He he he he and he and he and and he and he and he and and as and as he and as he and he. He is and as he is, and as he is and he is, he is and as he and he and as he is and he and he and and he and he.

Can curls rob can curls quote, quotable.

As presently.

As exactitude.

As trains.

Has trains.

Has trains.

As trains.

As trains.

Presently.

Proportions.

Presently.

As proportions as presently.

Father and farther.

Was the king or room.
Farther and whether.
Was there was there was there what was there was there
what was there was there there was there.
Whether and in there.
As even say so.
One.
I land.
Two.
I land.
Three.
The land.
Three
The land.
Three.
The land.
Two
I land.
Two
I land.
One
I land.
Two
I land.
As a so.
They cannot.
A note.
They cannot
A float.
They cannot.
They dote.
They cannot.
They as denote.
Miracles play.
Play fairly.
Play fairly well.
A well.
As well.
As or as presently.
Let me recite what history teaches. History teaches.

Geography

As geography return to geography, return geography. Geography. Comes next. Geography. Comes. Comes geography.

As geography returns to geography comes next geography. Comes. Comes geography.

Geography as nice. Comes next geography. Geography as nice comes next geography comes geography.

Geographically, geographical. Geographically to place, geographically in case in case of it.

Looking up under fairly see fairly looking up under as to movement. The movement described. Sucked in met in, met in set in, sent in sent out sucked in sucked out.

An interval.

If it needs if it needs if it needs to do not move, do not move, do not touch, do not touch, do not if it needs to if it needs. That is what she is looking for. Less. Less threads fairly nearly and geography and water. Descriptive emotion. As it can be.

He was terribly deceived about the Jews about Napoleon and about everything else.

If you do not know the meaning of such things do not use them. That is all. Such phrases.

More geography, more than, more geography. Which bird what bird more geography. Than geography.

Geography pleases me that is to say not easily. Beside it is decided. Geographically quickly. Not geographically but geography.

Geographically not inland not an island and the sea. It is what it is good for to sit by it to eat and to go away. Every time then to come again and so there is an interruption.

Plentifully simply. Napoleon is dimply.

If the water comes into the water if the water as it comes into the water makes as much more as it should can snow melt. If the water as it should does snow melt and could it as it has melted could it melt and does it and does it melt and should it, should it melt and would it melt and does it melt and will it melt and can it and does it melt. As water. I often think about seasonable.

Waterfully when the water waterfully when the water come to soften when the water comes and to soften when the water and to soften, waterfully and to soften, when the water and to soften, not wetter. When the water and to soften I know noises. As to noises. When the water and to soften as to water as to soften I know I know noises. I have secretly wished altogether. One two three altogether.

Geographically and inundated, geography and inundated, not inundated.

He says that the rain, he says that for rain he says that for snow he says, he says that the rain he says that the snow he says that the rain that the snow he says that is rain he says that is snow he says it is rain he says it is rain he says that it is snow he says it is snow.

He says it is snow.

Paper very well. Paper and water and very well. Paper and water and very well and paper and water and very well and paper and very well and water. Paper and water very well.

Naturally and water colour the colour of water and naturally. Very naturally the colour and very naturally. It is the best yet.

When this you see remember for me remember it for me if you can.

Once again as we can, once again and as we can, once again and as we can and once again and once again and as we can and can.

New to you. New to us. New. I knew. This is a very interesting thing to ask. To ask if it is new if it is new to you. It is a very interesting thing to ask.

It is a very interesting thing to know. That is a very interesting thing to know. Do you know whether it is new whether it is as new whether it is new to you. It is a very interesting thing to know that it is as new as it is to you.

I stands for Iowa and Italy. M stands for Mexico and Monte Carlo. G stands for geographic and geographically. B stands for best and most. It is very nearly decided.

Immeasurably. Immeasurably and frequently. Frequently and invariably. Invariably and contentedly. Contentedly and indefatigably. Indefatigably and circumstances. Circumstances and circumstantially. Initiative and reference. In reference to it. It needs to be added to, in addition. Additionally as in reduction. In geography and in geography.

As it might be said to be as it might be said to be.

As at this was was was as it was was as it was.

Not to be outdone in kindness.

Can you tell can you really tell it from there, can you really tell it can you tell it can you tell from here. From here to there and from there to there. Put it there. Is he still there.

If to say it if to see it if to say it. If to say it. The point of it, the point is this, that point at that point and twenty at that point and not twenty if you see and if you say it. If you say it and if you see it. As at that point and twenty. Twenty twenty a new figure. And a new finger. As a direction as in a direction. And so in whistling incorrectly. Very near and very near and very nearly and very nearly and very near it was a very near thing, very near to it. Amuse yourself. Vastly.

So much and as much. Much and as much, much and so much. Much and very much, very much and as much. Thank you for it.

Pardon me plainly pardon me. In this and hear. Here. Here at once. Not exactly angry. How exactly angry. Fed as to wheat. Seated by me. Sat and that. If to please. Instead.

Cochin china as Cochin China Tuesday. What is my delight.

No not that and no not that. And designs and the post, postmark. As dark. We know how to feel British. Saving stamps. Excuse me.

To make no allusion to anybody. Spread as glass is, glass is spread and so are colours, colours and pretty ways.

Able and Mabel. Mabel and able.

As outing. As an outing can it please me.

Leave and leave and leave relieve and relieve and relieve, candy as everywhere, but it is if it is, have happened. I touched it.

As through.

Shipping not shipping, shipping not shipping, shipping as shipping, shipping in shipping in shipping it. In shipping it as easily. Famous as a sire.

Notably notably reading.

Fasten as lengthily. As one day.

Smell sweetly. Industriously and indeed. It is apt to be.

Is it very apt to be explained.

I know how to wait. This is a joke. It is a pun.

Feasibly. A market as market to market.

In standing in plenty of ways, attending to it in plenty of ways, as opera glasses in plenty of ways as raining and in plenty of ways, hard as a pear run in the way, ran in this way. Ran away. I know the exact size and shape and surface and use and distance. To place it with them.

Any many many any any many many any any many many any any many many any. Any one.

Geography includes inhabitants and vessels.

Plenty of planning.

Geographically not at all.

The Difference Between the Inhabitants of France and the Inhabitants of the United States of America

There is a difference between France and the United States of America in the character of their inhabitants. There is this difference between France and the United States of America in the character of its inhabitants. The inhabitants of the United States of America have this quality in their character in reference to drama that the things they do and the things that they do do are such things that when they are young are different than when they are older. For instance when they are young and violent, then when they are young and then when they are violent and when they are not young and when they are not young are they not young and not as violent. Drama consists and in this they are so they are so certainly restricted, restricted to that themselves and not any more so. Thank you is not mentioned. In France especially so and for this reason especially when they are young and as an example not at all exacting not at all as exacting and when they are young and not any more so not feverishly so not as exacting exactly and as an instance and in collusion and not in very nearly as many cases secondary. The need of thanking for this is taught by description. Five examples of each will be given.

Five examples of each will be given so that the difference will be as well understood as ever. As ever and so much and so forth for nearly and very nearly all the same in a minute and as connected for it is as it shall should or may be yes. May be it may be as yes as yes so there and so there would have been some noise to-day.

In the beginning did she know her that is to say as she was away from home and as she was away from home did she know her. This makes fountains remain with her too with her too. No one need decide whether it is or is not used by the ones sending or whether in order that the ones sending are able to send whether it is necessary to send them beforehand a written address arranged in the fashion that is habitual and expected by the employees who will have to handle it in the ordinary course of the arrangement. And a letter follows when an envelope and a stamp have both been given and at the request of the giver thanked for. After that we change to America and those who are very much older and have had really have had an entirely different experience not only with all of it but with very much else. In both cases handkerchiefs and Easter and in the one case as a gift and in the other case as reception and careful conditions. Conditions carefully conditions as carefully as carefully as conditions and as ever.

This is the story of an American. An american formerly known as meant as much as that formerly known everywhere where he had been as having been seen often can not replace it all alone and not any more. The reason given is that when can there be a change, changes and occupation. Occupied too. This makes the meaning of what he meant when he had four or five four or five what.

This is the story of a friendship, two sons two and two sons, a man as two and two sons, and a man and as two and two sons. They had neither of them any reason to come again soon. This made it so prettily as an order. Order it. No one sees more than if for distribution. No, no women. No.

Begin again fairly well. An American woman means that she is to say have it, have it, four four and why should four and four why should four and four and why should four and four, fear, four and four, fear.

The frenchwoman comes away, comes away, fifteen fifteen has never meant that, sixteen has never meant that seventeen has never meant that, if as presents, if as presents easter and if as presents. Hopes to stay.

How many examples make addition subtraction division and long division. To continue as advised.

Another case of a frenchman. A frenchman has had an arrangement that makes it possible that he should read and what should he read. He should read and write. What should he read and write. He should read and write and recite. What should he read and write and recite.

Another case is the case of that American the American of whom it is said can he say so. This American of whom it is said can he say so says practically that he practically says that he unites windows and windows when windows and windows are in their place and he wishes to stop that is to remain where he is.

The example of the American lady who has a fan is the one selected for admiration in the same way the example of the french lady who has a fan is the one selected as the one to be chosen to be an example of an admirable frenchwoman.

The next example that is to be noted is that of the french family who nearly came too late for the festival. Every one asked was the celebration as pleasant as it could be and they were all there.

The American family needed no more, no one needed any more nothing more was needed really nothing more was needed at all. All of them and so forth and very kindly. Will they kindly say so also.

The next example is easily disposed of in this way there is no difference.

The next example may not be used to be used, the next example may be used to show that an aunt and two nieces say that they may make up their minds to stay the nieces may make up their minds to stay and the aunt may make up her mind to let them stay and they may or they may not be asked to stay. Anyway the decision has cost them nothing and so forth. This is principally from them and by them and in a way for them and perhaps beside them. This is in a way before them.

The other example American example the other example the American example is this both nieces and their aunt have been separated for some time and quite naturally they do not ask it of each other and if so it is refused. There is always some reason given.

More examples make all of it necessary.

The difference between the examples is this, one example shows this and the same example never shows anything else. Another example shows something else and in this way something is proved. Approved by all.

A Finish.

More difference the more difference it makes the less trouble there is in making any reference to it.

The trouble with it is that they may be mistaken. The marriage and it is a marriage the marriage may mean more. Having met and having met the man and having met the man there he might say that he had never heard of it and he might say that when he heard of it he said that he had not heard of it before. This makes it all the more this makes all the more and as this makes it all the more as much so. Formerly formally, formally and formerly does it mean that indeed as they said she had not thought so.

On the other side as another side this is the other side. If the man should assume that he was to be married would his brother write to him as his father would have written to him. And would the wife say that her husband had written to his brother as the father would have written to the brother and would he. The occasion did not arise as the brother remained unmarried married again.

Another case is this, the father and the mother had a son. The son was young and when he was old enough he married and as his father and his mother said it might easily be that the marriage would be satisfactory.

The American case is this. The father and the mother had not denied it to any one. No one need wonder. And no wonder was and it was no wonder that they all felt that children had that privilege and did not need to remember how often everything was heard. They heard it said.

To say we will wait, to say we wait, waiting for recognition. Take this case. Not excited about that. Take that case. No excitement in that. In that case there is no excitement in that case. That makes what one can out of everything.

The American has nearly five has nearly five has more nearly five. The American has nearly more nearly all five.

The French and almost and almost, almost the french and almost. Two and three and their family for this as this with this to this, to decide all decide and decide. Expect recognition.

The American five times laterally, laterally for five times and not to except and to disturb and not to be all so far and as far as that.

Forty-four and forty, make forty-five which is the same as has expected recognition.

The American has expected recognition.

The difference between there is a difference between, what is the difference and their difference, to add to them to be added to them, to divide from them to be divided from them, to be sent away by them and if sent away by them would they be willing are they willing have they spoken of it and have they acted in a way to make it at all likely that they would be prepared to have it happen. This is partly a beginning.

For any other reason there is more of this for a reason, there is more of this for this reason and for the rest of the time as well.

Thought of it, they thought of it, as they thought it as they thought of it as well.

They thought of it as well and very nearly always for this and on this account. No change was made.

Change it for one change it as perhaps may be necessary. They changed it and they changed it.

Change it in a family early way. This is an example. Three months is an example. This is an example. At the end of three months is an example. This is an example as the three months are more than ended it is an example.

The Americans have heard they have heard the Americans and they have heard, the American has heard as the American has heard this.

A new example of indeed and said so. No one and that.

Has many as many, as many, in case of as many, they went on to say as many has many, as many as they went on to say and so soon as soon and as soon, the one thing necessary is and was that there was a mistake in having it as an impression that one was not going to be told so at all.

After that there is no reason why after that there is no reason why.

Can it be seen that these two last that these last two differ from one another.

Another difference if and another difference.

After that in the middle of it, after that in the middle of it after that in the middle of it they have to as much as if they told you what they would do just as if they had preferred to, preferred to. Changed to preferred to. Just as if they had to changed to preferred to.

The American can say changed to preferred to the American

can say or say the American can say to say, to say can say changed to can say to say changed to to say can say to changed to to preferred to to say to preferred to to changed to to say to say to can say.

Very occupied with that and very occupied with that and here and very occupied with that.

And there and not and there and not and not there.

Here and there and not and very occupied as occupied as that.

And there and there and not as here and there and not and not here and not there, there and not here. There and there and as not here and there.

Here and occupied, occupied and here occupied as that.

There and not there and not and as there and as not there and not, as not there.

And here. For instance as occupied as that. Here and for instance, here in this instance here occupied as that.

There occupied as that there. This is a new this is a nuisance, this is news too, this is new too, this is not new too. As occupied as that in this instance.

Here, come here, no one says come here here.

There, come here, they say come here there.

To guess which is which.

Which is which.

Guess.

Two guess.

Which is which.

Guess which is which.

To guess which is which.

Which is which.

The first one here.

The one here.

Guess which is which.

I guess which is which.

The first there.

Which is which.

Here and there.

Which is which.

To guess which is which.

To guess which is which here which is which there. Which is which.

To guess which is which.

If to guess which is which, if to guess which is which, to guess.

Which is which.

Composition as Explanation

An Address Given in Cambridge and Oxford, June 1926

There is singularly nothing that makes a difference a difference in beginning and in the middle and in ending except that each generation has something different at which they are all looking. By this I mean so simply that anybody knows it that composition is the difference which makes each and all of them then different from other generations and this is what makes everything different otherwise they are all alike and everybody knows it because everybody says it.

It is very likely that nearly every one has been very nearly certain that something that is interesting is interesting them. Can they and do they. It is very interesting that nothing inside in them, that is when you consider the very long history of how every one ever acted or has felt, it is very interesting that nothing inside in them in all of them makes it connectedly different. By this I mean this. The only thing that is different from one time to another is what is seen and what is seen depends upon how everybody is doing everything. This makes the thing we are looking at very different and this makes what those who describe it make of it, it makes a composition, it confuses, it shows, it is, it looks, it likes it as it is, and this makes what is seen as it is seen. Nothing changes from generation to generation except the thing seen and that makes a composition. Lord Grey remarked that when the generals before the war talked about the war they talked about it as a nineteenth century war although to be fought with twentieth century weapons. That is because war is a thing that decides how it is to be when it is to be done. It is prepared and to that degree it is like all academies it is not a thing made by being made it is a thing prepared. Writing and painting and all that, is like that, for those who occupy themselves with it and don't make it as it is made. Now the few who make it as it is made, and it is to be remarked that the most decided of them usually are prepared just as the world around them is preparing, do it in this way and so I if you do not mind I will tell you how it happens. Naturally one does not know how it happened until it is well over beginning happening.

To come back to the part that the only thing that is different is what is seen when it seems to be being seen, in other words, composition and time-sense.

No one is ahead of his time, it is only that the particular variety of creating his time is the one that his contemporaries who also are creating their own time refuse to accept. And they refuse to accept it for a very simple reason and that is that they do not have to accept it for any reason. They themselves that is everybody in their entering the modern composition and they do enter it, if they do not enter it they are not so to speak in it they are out of it and so they do enter it. But in as you may say the non-competitive efforts where if you are not in it nothing is lost except nothing at all except what is not had, there are naturally all the refusals, and the things refused are only important if unexpectedly somebody happens to need them. In the case of the arts it is very definite. Those who are creating the modern composition authentically are naturally only of importance when they are dead because by that time the modern composition having become past is classified and the description of it is classical. That is the reason why the creator of the new composition in the arts is an outlaw until he is a classic, there is hardly a moment in between and it is really too bad very much too bad naturally for the creator but also very much too bad for the enjoyer, they all really would enjoy the created so much better just after it has been made than when it is already a classic, but it is perfectly simple that there is no reason why the contemporaries should see, because it would not make any difference as they lead their lives in the new composition anyway and as every one is naturally indolent why naturally they don't see. For this reason as in quoting Lord Grey it is quite certain that nations not actively threatened are at least several generations behind themselves militarily so authentically they are more than several generations behind themselves and it is very much too bad, it is so very much more exciting and satisfactory for everybody if one can have contemporaries, if all ones contemporaries could be ones contemporaries.

There is almost not an interval.

For a very long time everybody refuses and then almost without a pause almost everybody accepts. In the history of the refused in the arts and literature the rapidity of the change is always startling. Now the only difficulty with the *volte-face* concerning the arts is this. When the acceptance comes, by that acceptance the thing created becomes a classic. It is a natural phenomena a rather extraordinary natural phenomena that a thing accepted becomes a classic. And what is the characteristic quality of a classic. The characteristic quality of a classic is that it is beautiful. Now of course it is perfectly true that a more or less first rate work of art is beautiful but the trouble is that when that first rate work of art becomes a classic because it is accepted the only thing that is important from then on to the majority of the acceptors the enormous majority, the most intelligent majority of the acceptors is that it is so wonderfully beautiful. Of course it is wonderfully beautiful, only when it is still a thing irritating annoying stimulating then all quality of beauty is denied to it.

Of course it is beautiful but first all beauty in it is denied and then all the beauty of it is accepted. If every one were not so indolent they would realise that beauty is beauty even when it is irritating and stimulating not only when it is accepted and classic. Of course it is extremely difficult nothing more so than to remember back to its not being beautiful once it has become beautiful. This makes it so much more difficult to realise its beauty when the work is being refused and prevents every one from realising that they were convinced that beauty was denied, once the work is accepted. Automatically with the acceptance of the time-sense comes the recognition of the beauty and once the beauty is accepted the beauty never fails any one.

Beginning again and again is a natural thing even when there is a series.

Beginning again and again and again explaining composition and time is a natural thing.

It is understood by this time that everything is the same except composition and time, composition and the time of the composition and the time in the composition.

Everything is the same except composition and as the com-

position is different and always going to be different everything is not the same. Everything is not the same as the time
when of the composition and the time in the composition is
different. The composition is different, that is certain.

Composition is the thing seen by every one living in the
living they are doing, they are that composing of the composition that at the time they are living is the composition of
the time in which they are living. It is that that makes living
a thing they are doing. Nothing else is different, of that almost
any one can be certain. The time when and the time of and
the time in that composition is the natural phenomena of that
composition and of that perhaps every one can be certain.

No one thinks these things when they are making when
they are creating what is the composition, naturally no one
thinks, that is no one formulates until what is to be formulated
has been made.

Composition is not there, it is going to be there and we
are here. This is some time ago for us naturally.

The only thing that is different from one time to another
is what is seen and what is seen depends upon how everybody
is doing everything. This makes the thing we are looking at
very different and this makes what those who describe it make
of it, it makes a composition, it confuses, it shows, it is, it
looks, it likes it as it is, and this makes what is seen as it is
seen. Nothing changes from generation to generation except
the thing seen and that makes a composition.

Now the few who make writing as it is made and it is to be
remarked that the most decided of them are those that are
prepared by preparing, are prepared just as the world around
them is prepared and is preparing to do it in this way and so
if you do not mind I will again tell you how it happens. Naturally one does not know how it happened until it is well over
beginning happening.

Each period of living differs from any other period of living
not in the way life is but in the way life is conducted and that
authentically speaking is composition. After life has been
conducted in a certain way everybody knows it but nobody
knows it little by little, nobody knows it as long as nobody
knows it. Any one creating the composition in the arts does
not know it either, they are conducting life and that makes

their composition what it is, it makes their work compose as it does.

Their influence and their influences are the same as that of all of their contemporaries only it must always be remembered that the analogy is not obvious until as I say the composition of a time has become so pronounced that it is past and the artistic composition of it is a classic.

And now to begin as if to begin. Composition is not there, it is going to be there and we are here. This is some time ago for us naturally. There is something to be added afterwards.

Just how much my work is known to you I do not know. I feel that perhaps it would be just as well to tell the whole of it.

In beginning writing I wrote a book called THREE LIVES this was written in 1905. I wrote a negro story called Melanctha. In that there was a constant recurring and beginning there was a marked direction in the direction of being in the present although naturally I had been accustomed to past present and future, and why, because the composition forming around me was a prolonged present. A composition of a prolonged present is a natural composition in the world as it has been these thirty years it was more and more a prolonged present. I created then a prolonged present naturally I knew nothing of a continuous present but it came naturally to me to make one, it was simple it was clear to me and nobody knew why it was done like that, I did not myself although naturally to me it was natural.

After that I did a book called THE MAKING OF AMERICANS it is a long book about 1000 pages.

Here again it was all so natural to me and more and more complicatedly a continuous present. A continuous present is a continuous present. I made almost a thousand pages of a continuous present.

Continuous present is one thing and beginning again and again is another thing. These are both things. And then there is using everything.

This brings us again to composition this the using everything. The using everything brings us to composition and to this composition. A continuous present and using everything and beginning again. In these two books there was elaboration of the complexities of using everything and of a continuous present and of beginning again and again and again.

In the first book there was a groping for a continuous present and for using everything by beginning again and again.

There was a groping for using everything and there was a groping for a continuous present and there was an inevitable beginning of beginning again and again and again.

Having naturally done this I naturally was a little troubled with it when I read it. I became then like the others who read it. One does, you know, excepting that when I reread it myself I lost myself in it again. Then I said to myself this time it will be different and I began. I did not begin again I just began.

In this beginning naturally since I at once went on and on very soon there were pages and pages and pages more and more elaborated creating a more and more continuous present including more and more using of everything and continuing more and more beginning and beginning and beginning.

It went on and to a thousand pages of it.

In the meantime to naturally begin I commenced making portraits of anybody and anything. In making these portraits I naturally made a continuous present an including everything and a beginning again and again within a very small thing. That started me into composing anything into one thing. So then naturally it was natural that one thing an enormously long thing was not everything an enormously short thing was also not everything nor was it all of it a continuously present thing nor was it always and always beginning again. Naturally I would then begin again. I would begin again I would naturally begin. I did naturally begin. This brings me to a great deal that has been begun.

And after that what changes what changes after that, after that what changes and what changes after that and after that and what changes and after that and what changes after that.

The problem from this time on became more definite.

It was all so nearly alike it must be different and it is different, it is natural that if everything is used and there is a continuous present and a beginning again and again if it is all so alike it must be simply different and everything simply different was the natural way of creating it then.

In this natural way of creating it then that it was simply

different everything being alike it was simply different, this kept on leading one to lists. Lists naturally for awhile and by lists I mean a series. More and more in going back over what was done at this time I find that I naturally kept simply different as an intention. Whether there was or whether there was not a continuous present did not then any longer trouble me there was or there was, and using everything no longer troubled me if everything is alike using everything could no longer trouble me and beginning again and again could no longer trouble me because if lists were inevitable if series were inevitable and the whole of it was inevitable beginning again and again could not trouble me so then with nothing to trouble me I very completely began naturally since everything is alike making it as simply different naturally as simply different as possible. I began doing natural phenomena what I call natural phenomena and natural phenomena naturally everything being alike natural phenomena are making things be naturally simply different. This found its culmination later, in the beginning it began in a center confused with lists with series with geography with returning portraits and with particularly often four and three and often with five and four. It is easy to see that in the beginning such a conception as everything being naturally different would be very inarticulate and very slowly it began to emerge and take the form of anything, and then naturally if anything that is simply different is simply different what follows will follow.

So far then the progress of my conceptions was the natural progress entirely in accordance with my epoch as I am sure is to be quite easily realised if you think over the scene that was before us all from year to year.

As I said in the beginning, there is the long history of how every one ever acted or has felt and that nothing inside in them in all of them makes it connectedly different. By this I mean all this.

The only thing that is different from one time to another is what is seen and what is seen depends upon how everybody is doing everything.

It is understood by this time that everything is the same except composition and time, composition and the time of the composition and the time in the composition.

Everything is the same except composition and as the composition is different and always going to be different everything is not the same. So then I as a contemporary creating the composition in the beginning was groping toward a continuous present, a using everything a beginning again and again and then everything being alike then everything very simply everything was naturally simply different and so I as a contemporary was creating everything being alike was creating everything naturally being naturally simply different, everything being alike. This then was the period that brings me to the period of the beginning of 1914. Everything being alike everything naturally would be simply different and war came and everything being alike and everything being simply different brings everything being simply different brings it to romanticism.

Romanticism is then when everything being alike everything is naturally simply different, and romanticism.

Then for four years this was more and more different even though this was, was everything alike. Everything alike naturally everything was simply different and this is and was romanticism and this is and was war. Everything being alike everything naturally everything is different simply different naturally simply different.

And so there was the natural phenomena that was war, which had been, before war came, several generations behind the contemporary composition because it became war and so completely needed to be contemporary became completely contemporary and so created the completed recognition of the contemporary composition. Every one but one may say every one became consciously became aware of the existence of the authenticity of the modern composition. This then the contemporary recognition, because of the academic thing known as war having been forced to become contemporary made every one not only contemporary in act not only contemporary in thought but contemporary in self consciousness made every one contemporary with the modern composition. And so the art creation of the contemporary composition which would have been outlawed normally outlawed several generations more behind even than war, war having been brought so to speak up to date art so to speak was allowed not completely to be up to date, but nearly up to date, in other words we who created the expression of the modern composition were to be recognized before we were dead some of us even quite a long time before we were dead. And so war may be said to have advanced a general recognition of the expression of the contemporary composition by almost thirty years.

And now after that there is no more of that in other words there is peace and something comes then and it follows coming then.

And so now one finds oneself interesting oneself in an equilibration, that of course means words as well as things and distribution as well as between themselves between the words and themselves and the things and themselves, a distribution as distribution. This makes what follows what follows and now there is every reason why there should be an arrangement made. Distribution is interesting and equilibration is interesting when a continuous present and a beginning again and again and using everything and everything alike and everything naturally simply different has been done.

After all this, there is that, there has been that that there is a composition and that nothing changes except composition the composition and the time of and the time in the composition.

The time of the composition is a natural thing and the time in the composition is a natural thing it is a natural thing and it is a contemporary thing.

The time of the composition is the time of the composition. It has been at times a present thing it has been at times a past thing it has been at times a future thing it has been at times an endeavour at parts or all of these things. In my beginning it was a continuous present a beginning again and again and again and again, it was a series it was a list it was a similarity and everything different it was a distribution and an equilibration. That is all of the time some of the time of the composition.

Now there is still something else the time sense in the composition. This is what is always a fear a doubt and a judgement and a conviction. The quality in the creation of expression the quality in a composition that makes it go dead just after it has been made is very troublesome.

The time in the composition is a thing that is very troublesome. If the time in the composition is very troublesome it is because there must even if there is no time at all in the composition there must be time in the composition which is in its quality of distribution and equilibration. In the beginning there was the time in the composition that naturally was in the composition but time in the composition comes now and this is what is now troubling every one the time in the composition is now a part of distribution and equilibration. In the beginning there was confusion there was a continuous present and later there was romanticism which was not a confusion but an extrication and now there is either succeeding or failing there must be distribution and equilibration there must be time that is distributed and equilibrated. This is the thing that is at present the most troubling and if there is the time that is at present the most troublesome the time sense that is at present the most troubling is the thing that is the thing that makes the present the most troubling. There is at present there is distribution, by this I mean expression and time, and in this way at present composition is time that is the reason that at present the time sense is troubling that is the reason why at present the time sense in the composition is the composition that is making what there is in composition.

And afterwards.

Now that is all.

An Acquaintance with Description

Mouths and Wood.

Queens and from a thousand to a hundred.

Description having succeeded deciding, studying description so that there is describing until it has been adjoined and is in a description. Studies in description until in attracting which is a building has been described as an in case of planting. And so studying in description not only but also is not finishing but understood as describing.

To describe it as at all through. Once more. To describe it as not as dew because it is in the trees. To describe it as it is new not because it has come to be for them if it lasts. At last to come to place it where it was not by that time in that way. And what is what is the name. Holly has very little red berries and so have very large fir trees but not at the same time even though in the same place. Not even in houses and gardens not even in woods and why, why because geraniums have one colour and to find it high, high and high up and a little like it was. Once more and more when it was once more and once more when more when it was. When one goes three go and when three go two go. She said she did not believe in there having there having been there having been there having been there before. Refusing to turn away.

A description refusing to turn away a description.

Two older and one very much younger do not make two older and one very much younger. Come again is easily said if they have if they have come back.

A description simply a description.

A sea gull looking at the grain as seen. And then remarkably farming and manufacturing they like wedding and still with horses and it does not matter if you ask they might there might be a choice. This makes that be what a little in the front and not at all what we see. Never having forgotten to be pleased.

What is the difference between not what is the difference between. What is the difference between not what is the difference between. An acquaintance with description or what is the difference between not what is the difference between not an acquaintance in description. An acquaintance in description. First a sea-gull looking into the grain in order to look into the grain it must be flying as if it were looking at the grain. A sea-gull looking at the grain. Second a sea-gull looking into the grain. Any moment at once. Why is the grain that comes again paler so that it is not so high and after awhile there can be very many of a kind to know that kind. Next to find it coming up and down and not when it is directly through around. This comes to be a choice and we are the only choosers. This makes that be what a little in the front and not at all what we see. To have seen very many every time suspended. This can be in black and as grey and surprising. It is not early to be discouraged by their seating. Seating four to a colour.

Acquaintance with description if he holds it to him and it falls toward him.

Every little bit different and to ask did he might it be older might it be did it did it have it as suggested it might be older.

Very often not at all. An acquaintance with description and they might be if it were at all needed not by them fortunately. Fortunately is always understood. There is a difference between forests and the cultivation of cattle. In regard to either there is a choice in one a choice of trees in the other a choice.

An acquaintance with description if and acquaintance with description. Making an acquaintance with description does not begin new begin now. In acquaintance with description. Simply describe that they are married as they were married. They married. She the one and she the one and they and none and they and one and she and one and they they were nearly certain that their daughter had a friend who did not resemble either their daughter's father or their daughter's mother and this was not altogether why they had what they had they had it as if they might of if they had asked it of all of all. Meant to be not left to it as if it was not beside that it could be and best. Best and best can be delighted delighted delighted.

It is very inconvenient when there is that by this because because of this being that by then. An acquaintance with description has not been begun. An acquaintance with description to begin three.

Not it is not it is not it is not it is at all as it is. No one should remember anything if it did not make any difference it did not make any difference if it did not make any difference. No one should remember anything and it should not make any difference. No one should remember anything and it should not make any difference. Who makes this carefully. Who makes this carefully that it should not make any difference that not any one should remember anything. When two horses meet both being driven and they have not turned aside they turn aside. They both turn aside.

When it is not remarkable that it takes longer it does not make it more than they could do. It is not more remarkable that it takes longer than that it is more remarkable than that is what they have to do. It is not more remarkable that it takes longer than that it is they have it to do. It is not more remarkable. After this makes them prepare this. Very well she is very well. I will you will they will he will.

Not finally so much and change it.

They might like it as it is in the sun.

Naming everything every day, this is the way. Naming everything every day. Naming everything every day.

It is a great pleasure to watch it coming.

They might like it, as it is in the sun.

It is a pleasure to watch it coming but it might that she could be unaccustomed to lie down without sleeping it might be that she could be unaccustomed to lie down without sleeping.

What is the difference between three and two in furniture. Three is the third of three and two is the second of two. This makes it as true as a description. And not satisfied. And what is the difference between being on the road and waiting very likely being very likely waiting, a road is connecting and as it is connecting it is intended to be keeping going and waiting everybody can understand puzzling. He said it nicely. This makes it as if they had not been intended and after all who is after all after all it is after all afterwards, as they have left there may be a difference between summer and winter. Everybody makes a part of it part of it and a part of it. If he comes to do it, if he comes to do it and if he comes to do it. He comes to do it. Anybody can be mistaken many times mistaken for it. Turkeys should never be brought any where they belong there where they are turkeys there and this reminds one at once. Acquainted with description is the same as acquainted with turkeys. Acquainted with description is the same as being acquainted with turkeys. Why when the sun is here and there is it here. Acquainted with the sun to be acquainted to be unacquainted and to be unacquainted and to be unacquainted and to be in the sun and to be acquainted to be acquainted with the sun. It can be there.

Look down and see a blue curtain and a white hall. A horse asleep lying surrounded by cows.

There is a great difference not only then but now.

After all after this afterwards it was not only that there had been more than there was differently but it was more often than not recognised there can be instances of difference between recognisable and between recognisable when they had been formidable and in the use of that notwithstanding. Having come along. And not being described as very likely to make it not belong to this at that time and very easily when they were delighted and might it be not only suggested and not only suggested as that could be while they came and after that by nearly very often having when it was that it should be decided. They might not only be very often not more nearly as if they could and should has returned. Not on that account.

Never to be left to add it too. Never to be left to add it to that.

Describing that that trees are as available as they were that trees were as available as they were. And to say that it is not to be more than understood very likely it is very likely to be. To be not only pleased but pleasing and to be not only pleased but to be not only pleased. An acquaintance with description.

What is the difference between a hedge and a tree. A hedge and a tree what is the difference between a hedge and a tree.

Next to that what is there to be more than if it was to be prepared.

In part.

Letting it be not what it is like.

The difference between a small pair and that colour and outside. If blue is pale and green is different how many trees are there in it.

Simply a description and sensibly a description and around and a description.

After all who might be who might be influenced by dahlias and roses, pinks and greens white and another colour. Who might be careful not to think just as well of what they had when they were there. And never having this by now. A plain description so that anyone would know that pears do grow very well on very good on the very best of pear trees. They made it be theirs yet. After a while they knew the difference after a while they knew that difference after a while they knew this difference after a while they knew the difference after a while they knew the difference after a while they knew the difference. Pleasing them with the description of a pear tree. Pleasing them with the description of a pear tree pleasing them with the description of a pear tree. Pleasing them with the description of a pear tree. And pleasing them by having it not made so much as much differently. They might have been and if by this at once.

Not after all.

An acquaintance with description the difference between by that time and why they went. We have left them now.

An acquaintance with description.

Mary Lake is a pretty name. Two five seven nine eleven. And I was to tell you what, about a window, what was it. She thought it was two four six nine eleven but it was not it was two five seven nine eleven. Mary Lake is a pretty name she said it was she said she thought it was she said she said it was. Mary Lake is a pretty name all the same she said she said it was. To change to poplar and trees. Mary Lake is a pretty name to change to poplars to change she said it was to change to she said she thought it was to change to she said she she said it was. Mary Lake is a pretty name to change to poplars and to change she said she said it was.

Now then they then they have to have what after all is a difference to be left alone. Nobody needs to be around and gathering the milk. If they have it here and nearly as if they also differently arranged chickens and to calve how do they need to be so sure sure and be certain that they have theirs there and the same. It is astonishing not to please.

Beginning with the poplars as seed. They grow fruit trees just as well. Beginning with the poplars as seed. Is there any difference between Nelson and a Brazilian admiral is there any difference between Nelson and a Brazilian admiral's son and where they chose it. Not as well as he did he is not only the eldest of five but the eldest of eight. In this way he absolutely has not only not but not gone. When they come to say they come and have spoken of an acquaintance with description in describing that there is no intention to distinguish between looking and looking. An acquaintance with description gives a very pleasant pregramme of fruit and some varieties of carnations. He quotes me. She does not like not only when but how. Not of him but of the time when there is no more relief from irresistible.

How can and how can he climb higher than a house if he can be at that time having had it be as much as that and certain. Never to mention more than never to mention more than that it was like a hat a cardinal can not have a stone hat not have a stone hat a hat and candlesticks of blue green when they are glass and small and a box made at all.

That pleases them and him.

Yes can be mentioned altogether.

Each one can be interested in at a time and added.

There is a difference between whether and leather there is more happening when no one needs to next to a need it for pansies. A watch kept in and there or all the time. Not a mother nor a step-mother but always after all when she did and after all when she did come to be called and they might if they came have it in three different kinds chickens ducks and geese.

Have it in three different kinds before that a sister and a brother and now when at first, at first makes it that they asked him and he said just farther it is a very fearful thing to cross the river Rhone when they might even when they might. They did the second time. The first time they did the second time. Might makes snuff might makes enough enough and snuff. It is very pleasant that a box a little box is just alike.

An acquaintance with description and and an acquaintance with description reconciled.

She is very happy and a farm. She is very happy and a farm. She is very happy and a farm. She is very happy and a farm. She is very happy and a farm.

In and sight if the once and before that could be a hearing heard at most. Might it be needed like it. He can be said if when it might that like it by now. Could he have had a had and have and had a hat. Very every time they were killed for their father. Their father might be their mother. Their mother might be that it might be in their and unison. Unison is not disturbed for their and for their and for their it can be that although they they might if she was here and he was there spoken to by that not alone by slow or snow not alone by snow or slow slowly and snow comes now not by having that it was different from a hollyhock by a chance. He did indeed indeed and might after all his aunt and if she were to be by by and by by and by with the one, they could very often need to select theirs in place. Let it be that his brother was killed altogether his father not his father his mother not his mother the children of his brother and he he was deafened by that and not altogether. He need he need he need he need to not to need to be what if it were differently Perrette and Perrine, that makes it said. Safe is when after all they could eat.

Thank you for a description and would have hesitated to ask.

Did you see him fall. Not at all.

If two and two and she likes it and dew was it that it could be not wishing to be left. Not to be respected as it was not to be respected as it was not why it was and she left them and he said I do too and she said do not bother exactly and around they met met if not likely to be nearly where as if looking. This makes it take a place.

Nicely and seated makes it left again left and right makes it regular and because it was not when they wished. They often know that. There is no difference between she not being comfortable and she comfortable. Never again to be signed and resigned and acquaintance with description. If it were not to use we would choose. If we were not Jews we would choose if it were not to use we would choose. They can be as small as that and there reliability there as counted. Never to like it smaller and a lavender colour. It might make it added one in green. Not fortunately an alignment. Repeat relate and change three and four to two. This makes it more difficult than fluttering. Not to be argued about. Noon is for nooning.

Do you leave it to be mine and nicely. Out of eight there was are how many are there when there are very many.

Seven and two and nearly awake because snuff is useful in little boxes where there are put metal clippers and no snuff. Anybody can be reasonably satisfied with that exactly.

She liked my description of aunt Fanny, she liked my description of hazel nuts she liked my description of the resemblance between pheasants and peacocks she liked my description of how that would be what was wanted. She liked to have them hear it if it was good not only for theirs but for ours and she would not mind it if they could be what they had at that time and easily no one is ever allowed allowed and aroused around and not the difference between the distance between Brazil and France and the difference between whether they made it be what they liked. It might be changed. They might be not at all easily often all arranged so that they would prefer where it actually is and now as pleases it pleases her to please when it can be fortunately not at all as it might be if they were certain that shells and shells did and did make flowers did and did and easily having examined who they had and when they came they thanked. Now can it be two and Tuesday, leaving it alone.

Leaving it alone. From this time on to borrow to borrow is to reply and to reply is to be useful attentively and might as well as might and might as well as might, might it being the same come to be having it for this and that precisely. An interval between when they had this as well when they had this as well. She said and says that when a higher and not a high hill has it as their left and right how can it be told favourably. It can and will. An acquaintance with description or it can and will.

Will it be that they like when they see why it has not as if when it came leaving that in that round and settled so that if it is doubled they might be wrong. Not left to it only by what is after all why they like and had it here. This may be otherwise known. If they are sold as they are sold we might as well but not only really not at all reliably placing if it is as it as it is at all very well very well to do so. Yesterday to say.

Describing where they went. Describing when it was like it. They did put a clock face on the telegraph pole.

Eagerly enough they looked to see the difference between a horse and two oxen and they looked eagerly enough to see the difference between poplars at a distance and walnut trees.

Every little while they made it at that time. Not meaning to have lost it when when it had gone away. They saved it in order that it might be had when it was accepted as a large quantity. Not in order to be kind. They like it fancifully. Might they be placed where they could see. If they were left where they were sent and could be by it when it is fastened and to explain explained that it was that as that had had been theirs too and nearly not while it needed it for it to be arranged by the putting it side by side for them, at least as they had not been very liked and liking that as much as if it had been leaving it near them and coming to have the key put not as now underneath but nearly under all the top so that if when it is not only that he would be releasing sheep releasing sheep they might not only be two who have themselves seated there. Not while it did. Two who have themselves seated there not while it did not come to be four in renown and not be settled to become the next who near and needed did anybody know the difference between their fairly seated and leaving it as seen. Very nearly wrongly so and to be sure and next next can be why they went why they went to stay not as if it was when it is might it be changed changed every day to theirs having if they went and to cross. Back is not why they have called it. She knows what they mean. An acquaintance with description is not earlier and later than they say. They say that they have been as it is why they could. To like it better. I will always describe it where it is at its widest and it will be very well done.

Would it do it any good to be so where they went. To be sure to be so when they leave it to them. And they might have theirs half of the time which is why once and one they make it be that they did not take it then and take it take it apart. Not in this case and would leave it for them to see. Sit is as well as if on top they might have been to change not if it is where where can be separated from while and when it is the same they exchange pleasing it as if very likely when it had not as if she said been heard.

Like and it was if a guinea hen was wild they needed it as well when they had been liked as much if they had need be thought to come as well and it did not. Next to need not be well as well as said need to be seeing it where it is where there is leaving it as very likely well and they might be two having having leaving leaving let it not let it not is nearly around and it did not like that because it was salty because it was salty, not after a very long after a little while after it was there a little while after it was there a little while and might it be theirs for themselves it might. What was it as it said not so what is it as it said and this is why they could be nearly finally theirs in their being nearly when they had it. It need not be so very much. Here I can see it. If it was above and below they could be seen letting it be theirs to think of well why should they when they will be as they were in there and by this with it for the rest they do not need it leaving what it is because if they announced announced readily by the time that it is nearer than that which is very well. Letting it be not leaving it in this way and recommending what they need for it. Letting it be let it alone let it alone and like it. They would never like to let it leave. Continue. They make a mistake it was not that and coming back to it. There is a great difference and when they like it there is a great difference and when they like it. There is a great difference and when they like it. Not taking it away. This is one way to believe their pieces. Very like the water.

There is a difference between the middle and both sides.

They will not be themselves aloud they heard in that with it to leave not when and left, excuse me. If not they wish it.

How can it be left as it will when they know that each one is in some place as if it came to come and leave it likely that it is exactly there. Very often we looked for them. So many ways of forgetting that this is there there where if left to leave it.

Is it likely if it went that it went around it. Is it likely if it did not go and it was in it so that if it was not there it was placed would it be divided. They liked it to be said. Very likely not. It was very encouraging to hear them do it. Not at first it did not at first it did not at first seem to be very likely to be what they would do, to be what they would do it is reasonable that it is more intelligent to see it but not if all at all having not lost it altogether by this time theirs might be easily just as well as if it were. They can be divided between themselves and the others and if they are not only because both sides and pleases but actually when they are identical and left alone it really is too much in a crisis.

There is no difference between what between and at a distance as there is no difference between what between what and at a distance no difference between between and at a distance there is no difference between what between between and at a distance. Next. There is no difference between between and and between at a distance there is no difference between at a distance between and what between there is no difference between what between and at a distance. Next. There is no difference between where and where it is just before never before never between never before never at a distance before, leaving before at a distance between there is no difference between having decided upon thirty, thirty what and having decided upon using both using both how, using both habitually. That makes it difficult that it is not seen from there.

Example and precept, sitting if in sitting they are there they must as if in crossing two at a time and not bound not bound to be used to as in lead lead to it from their having this in use not to be reaching leaving it as well they might be theirs to connect having to indeed now and and turned around if it were to be prepared as if when this is when it is to be and back need and they need leaving it with a change changed to be could it be remembered and left that it might commandingly so not if as it was said come and across they might if they were third and altogether once more felt and after it was not in place but and beside and a little change and this is if if it was when it was to study study could be could be should it have it round and as could be when there is little to be left when separated not all through when it is shorter than it could and and could not be used as so and it was not to be not when it was that length at length and never yet after all when

when is doubtfully repeated in this letting it be as much as if could it be heard coming not in shawl and not in all and after very much after longer not very much shorter and held not very much as held to be coming how often has there been a white one where they could not think to see. It. It is not needing blue having artificially leaves and connecting as stems it is never theirs by right by right winding it later might make not so nearly nearly white and white and white which is just as naturally as every letter. This makes them say delighted. This makes them say delighted. To be liking liked like it like if like like to like like and often often where where is it. It is there just there where I am looking. Very clearly expressed.

Not to leave it be alone and looks like in the way and when it is not left to be themselves have it to say they made it come as if it would be leaving it as fast nicely. One this is to be that it is not here leave it for them by this with whom it is to nicely handle it with what is meant when it is not to be changed what I notice. It is not very nearly that it is not at all it when it is that in the leaving it leave it in not around they might have had it sent it not to come to be theirs when they leave and it was very likely that it had been in that first when it needs to mention how could there in there not so much as that when to be leading it not when it is in front and kept to be sure to be sure. Would it be almost what it is leaving leaving never needs it left because not white it is certainly better than here better than here there.

She would be there if it was very well said that it would be it is would be unsatisfactory it is would be it is would be unsatisfactory and find it from the things as it is done done has been has been it would as it would be is it as it would be unsatisfactory. Find it as it would be unsatisfactory. She said and as it would it it is as it would be as it is in that from this and as it is in this to be and is to be and is to be and is to be unsatisfactory. She said it would be as it is to be unsatisfactory. It is very easily certain that it could happen happen and to be would be would be and to be would be unsatisfactory. Even every thing like in and like and that. In every even like and thing and like and even in and every even in and like and that. There is no difference at all between paper and basket, this has nothing to do with fruit and soap, this has nothing to do

with places and head this has nothing to do with their arrangements. Not to be with it in theirs in hand and now. Now
it is open open and liked liked and to-morrow to-morrow
when then, the Saone.

Would it be nearly as certain that they would like to have
theirs be as much as if when they did by this time if they did
make it. Not to mention what it was when they were altogether part of it because because allowing because allowing it
to be for this reason leaving it aloud and much of it and never
to be what it was when it was opened and very nearly very
little ones and as much more as when it was to be sure to be
sure erected erected to make islands having it not only that it
was sold once and they made it be because of that over and
under over and under makes it be nearly that if spoken to
spoken of spoken of birds birds and very nearly grass in their
and to be sure leaving it as an announcement and readily readily makes it be in tufts and when there are two and when there
are two and once more it was necessary to buy a piece of
ground in order to plant upon it one hundred poplars and to
precisely understand plant upon it one hundred poplars and
to precisely understand moreover not to be exactly and precisely dated when it is not only to be purchased but also to
be purchased planted and very certainly absolutely designed
as one hundred poplars when in any event not only having
been attached to that but very often very favourably needed
needed and needing using using is never adaptable using had
advanced as by and by developed because indeed they might
and they might not, because once at once and as this was to
be new it was also very nearly needed now. One more observation. It does not need need and necessarily and necessarily
and very well understood. And now leave it to be what was
as much interrupted like why is it to be looked looked for it
now when it is not altogether where it was where is it. An
acquaintance with description and not very good. They
planted theirs and have it as it might so that if they and many
wider many wider and as if it could not be as a mistake to be
in certain certain certain certain that then there there is as not
as a mound not as a not as a not as a failing failing that if all
at once at once at least and remaining not in right in right in
right as if with that and sound sound in a leaf a leaf to be who

can be nearly where it was when it was not which needed while it did, telling it as sound as soundly as not by that time to be and when to copy copy which copy which is which is what they could if it could not be in change in change for this at once at once is never nearly why they did not let it be at best at best is what is not when it was change and changed to rest, rest at most thank you. Not an acquaintance with not only with and only with description and only with with it. Is it an and an account of it.

Always wait along never wait so long always wait along always wait along never wait so long never wait as long always wait along always wait along never wait so long never wait so long always wait along always wait as long always wait along never wait so long always wait along. Not to believe it because not to believe it because not to believe that it is here. Come over here now. Left and right white and red and never to be along at all not at all when it is to be nearly left as it was by the time when it shall be so well so well allowed allowed and allowed and leaving it all to that when it is might have been not a little never and a little at all by the time that it is where there is leave it too long have it. Having left it there until there was what seemed to be a little at once like the rest like the rest fairly well finally to be in and in might it have that in change leaving not it not it at last at last differs from the leaving having having never can there not by this about in the way from never there in is they used find it can there is looking at in in comes to let and very well it was not why they did consider it not at all one way.

To find it there yes put it there yes to put it there if to put it there by which not it not it now to see it as it and very adapted to partly leave it there to partly not to partly not put it there it might if a little bit when it is in a corner for the morning so that not to allow allowable around when it is separately not separate to the shore, can a river have a shore or can a little little more before can it be interrupted and not once or twice when too might two be only left to throw it away away from that which was outlined, it was and if wish to wish to a paving it with that. Now to have it in their way when they have it as they will be that they do not mind it.

Why and why often and why often when it is not by the

time that there is much much as much as said as said as will
because of this and thinning of it out and in this is this that
the left is sent by this around and ground and not to leave it
in this might it be the change of that to theirs theirs have this
leave it very nearly place and might it if it not in this pleased
if this when is it in their leave as not all of it can be in this in
theirs and interchange in also not to change and china can be
sought in this in places in this and places places from this two
and uneasy which is why that it must be shown as that in the
next never asked to as coming in delight and relight when this
is that in theirs left it to be not for this in change near neighbour coming in the last and finding it as can it be that it is
right and left so that it is for this and with theirs obligation
nearly by this in the instance that it is arranged for that in the
most and believe in half and kindly kindly give it to them and
away and can it be in theirs and for remaining can and can
not left to be in so much as it is in theirs and added not by
this which is relieved by none and none to add it more than
is not for this openly so seen can in and likely leaving it so
nearly with it in this case can find bequeath and needed in
regularly to that in those and called and layer of that this
below which send sent to the are there why is it as addressed
left it as when as or that come to the last which is for that
not finally incased but surely where as there is that in an allowed now this and here there most come to be supplied with
the whole and share and this and leaves and why and could
and some and nestles and no much and come come in and
that beside the noise and leave and trust and how to. Following it altogether. She it might be come. Not how is it.

I understand that you do not do much in winter with your
land.

Leaving it out when this is seen in the nearest afternoon to
there having had left there that is not to do that which is
might and might it be and for this as their even left it to be
at namely why this is for them considerably liking and like
then when it could be after letting and distributed. Now again
named whenever it is to that beside by and by can if in the
central and why it is not alone nor should it come to theirs
be advised leave when shall it reduce to this coming can leave
where in the not to be altogether where it is placed to be

divided between fish and moths. There to be divided there to be divided divided between find and find out find it in nearly to be sure and more easily if named. When one is what is what is it then it is easier when it is when it is in their name. Leaving out having had it now. They might be while they can if it is can it and they no doubt can leave it leave it at that. There is every day every day every day to be sure to be sure that they can go and have to have very well I thank you. Leave out and account leave it out and account account not to be always to be said that it was there that it was there that it was in there not in there but like in there as it not in there when it was begun begun to be left and left not in that allowance but in that in spite of it being that it was what they could in arrange like it and some to some to some some who have not best at all why not as much as after a while not theirs very well. Remembering everything as seen to like it only is it that it should should come to be what is it when it is no longer theirs at all. To know why we why can it be leave it to be three. There can always be a difference.

If she works then he works but if she reads then he pleads.

If she does knit and he does count how many are there in it. Five in each but unverified and beside beside unverified too and a market too and well left beside the pressure pressure of an earring.

Never deriding anything and then it was not only at a distance but in the distance that it can be many makes it come to be so now. That is not to what it does not have it so to speak that is and said consider it to be theirs aloud.

When it was left. Water was running as large as two firsts eighteen. What is when it is of that to be not green and wheat but green and why and green and it can have it to be that it is a third the next of that which when the come for it too leave why which where they announce amuse leave it for in that way come should it have the never changing most now and then in as not have seen the having thought of three as two to be sure from that where they they might could it be curtain and hat not as much as net not only if it were to be wrapped in and for the which it was by this to come to that it is now known. Excuse me.

To change from what was what to that.

Everything that must be as a bed or hedge must when it is to be had where it was must be what is left to be theirs as they wish come to be left when it is found and farther could be decided that it was not nearly an arrangement that they had if this was theirs as if it were to be not at least and negligent and so to say so to find it naturally where it was to be if there it was does it really have as much when it is not as much and coming to be not at all nearer nearer than it is to it. Thank you for having been so kind.

There he said he had said that it was where there it was and after all nobody should touch it.

Not more than seldom not more than winning not any having this as that and for it in leaving that is what is when it is at the end of the house which is when it is not an end and it does not look differently because they have seen it otherwise it would look differently because I had seen it otherwise it would look otherwise it would be it would be it would be otherwise it otherwise if it is not not what is it every little one larger larger and so much smaller when there is no difference between a white carnation and a white lily both are white when they are here when they are here when they are when they are here in this case not as well not as well long as well charcoal as well water as well leaving as well lambs as well why and when with as well leave as well but as but as well why as well a while as well with what as well the piece as well as if as well three more to four as well and as well as well as as well as well as well when if in as and well and see in to be some to cause could in there be from the one that can be in there by the coming to this to be that it is by that in there with it for in in could leave no more this by for it come to be not while it is shall be come to this if it can leave it in this coming talking be as well as the kind at first should left that it was all could can it as rest the rest of it to be that it is not there theirs as it is should the stand fall at once what is it.

That is one way of that to be new nicely see and seen come come to be alike. We are very grateful that it is so large.

Would anybody be allowed would anybody be allowed to come to ask to have it sent in winter.

This is not theirs to be to be to be to be very much very much left as if as if very well knew and known that it should not be again and again and in again and in again and again and again and in again. Peaches should always be eaten over more over as if strawberries as if papers as if printed papers as printed and papers as if printed and papers as if printed and papers and wool as if printed and papers and peaches as if printed and papers and wool as if printed and papers peaches should always be eaten as if as if papers as if printed and papers as if strawberries as if as if peaches and papers as if as if as if as if papers as if peaches and papers as if printed papers and wool and strawberries and peaches as if papers as if printed papers as if.

Always the same.

Not as to delight.

An acquaintance with description.

If it is to have the leaving as an obligation to be there and come to to the rest that if there is if there is the next to have it leave to to be in that way from three one leaving it around as it might indeed have it that they not as if it were in opposite around let it might and might be considered as two three three there many there how many there how many three two one leaving it as much behind behind to mind letting letting all in theirs for that most when makes what is why it was as much as much for the having having to be interrupted shall it shall it have the name when there is that in two made which is much the more than theirs for that now leaving it in this to be to be sure let it coming coming to have it given given in place of theirs to have it can it be and fairly well at most in that which which when where and light and come to last last and might and might it be in this and change get it is it not what in their might it come to have it in this place it could it be that it is when it when it is in theirs to place and to say need it and it was not only why it came to left and calling this is in the way of any other one which is not only why they left they did not have it to fit in when it was that the two were two were to make four places and a little below to say so if it must be just their in that complete why is it only when it is not only is it is in that increase. There can be no difference between a circus a mason and a mechanic between a horse and cooking a blacksmith and his brother and his places al-together and an electrician. In every other way I am disappointed. Yes when it is not only this and having been not prepared to be so much and wonder they had it and they changed it and they made it be very nearly might it be what is it when it is not after all very little of a having not seen it when it came.

It is not well placed if before they had it there and now they put it there and will they place it there and could it be what it was when it might. It is very nearly intended to be a basket made over.

They might do.

If it after all was not what was it when it came and it might do. When could it leave it in this way and say it for this was to be and like it all thank you to say. They went to see it.

Again Albert again write to Albert again basket again changed to have it again have it basket again again as again as a change again basket again basket again it is again as a change again as a basket again at again larger again as many again as a basket again have it a basket again larger again is it again it is it again a basket again as larger again a basket again get it again is it again a basket again it is.

It is is it. A basket.

Basket it is is it.

Very nearly fairly pleased.

Which is why it is that it is looking is it in it as it it is as it is is it as it is there. There it is.

There is always some difference between nine o'clock and eight o'clock.

An acquaintance with description.

There is an arrangement as berries. There is also an arrangement as loopholes. There is also an arrangement as distance. There is also an arrangement as by the way. There is also an arrangement as at first. There is also an arrangement as to be. There is also an arrangement as disappointed. There is also an arrangement as why and let. There is also an arrangement of poplars that give a great deal of pleasure. There is also an arrangement that it can be twice chosen. There is also an arrangement which is advantageous.

Never be left to be that it can have to be if it could leave it all let it be mine while it came shall it have that to see come again like it while it is much to be relied upon as yet and while and awhile and while and it is not that but what if it is by the breaking of it in the place of that nearly by changing that to make it have it be nearly coming as if there is not more than it could be theirs so much not by that time there is between needing needing not by that and if it is in let it let it in light and might it be very well said that if a cloud is light one could read by it. What can be after all the difference between candles and electricity, they go out one after the other they come one one after the other they go on together. Let it be known. It is.

Not to think of anything which is not what is at least when poplars come to have to be a very little bridge to see at any way if not before when it is well to have a rain bow let alone a wire place and met it. Not easily there chance. After all and met it not easily there chance. An instance of it as a distance from the come to come and have it had and with it with and leave it let leave it as it must be while then for this as it is not for this for this come to be in their choice come to be this is in an angle if it comes come let it with some not perch come left that not as a very good half to help let it let is is let to be there singular relieve it with it for the not there when why cinnamon and come to have it that it is as a district describe while white not so much as if at first a lake as come to come to pride where fair that it is not so have it from the end to end alright.

Six is more than four how many to a door, who can be so late to see if they wait to be to see if it can to have to meet if it does which is as were and left to right and with it as if when it fell so that he was where it could be and in that as could it by the trace of left and right come to the having as and stands that is as bale that is as hay that is as then that is as if letting be it so much care this to then if for and in case fasten and in most fasten and very likely why it was when it was if they had not had it come to be remembering that to run up hill that to run up hill that to run up hill for the heard it come to be. An actual reasonable time. No one must be very lively about it. It is not at all necessary that it is after this so much as much as much way much for much to much in much left much then much there much those this that the under left might join come leaf and left as if it were not not not not not white.

Anybody could be one. One one one one.

This time not uneasily.

An acquaintance with description above all an acquaintance with description above an acquaintance with description above all an acquaintance with description above an acquaintance with description and above and above an acquaintance with description and an acquaintance with description. Please and an acquaintance with description please an acquaintance with description please an acquaintance with description.

They must be as well as ever to be had to be it when they can if it must as well as if and that is what it can be now that it is if in plainly as much as if what is not come to be had if when it is not that if it is not to have to own and then there scare and scarce and this that in that might which can for most where with in much come to be that this with it left to make to me to mention to the same let if that which in candied let it mean that if then where there this is not that now which is when it is left come to this there come have to be not reconsidered. It meant that it was not kept up.

If it and this is wild from this to the neatness of there being larger left and with it could it might if it not if it as lead it lead it there and incorrectly which is at this time. Once more if refused. Make make it left it with with with not with there may may may not be there though though though if left and the same not only had but will have once more having let it fall altogether.

If in way that should left come by it it not must can near to naturally why do it because it is a pleasure.

What you want to do.

What you want to do.

What you want to do.

Left it what you want to do.

Left it what you want to do.

The regular if all much not could lean well settled plus return more than be lighter for that here.

Very well not in might to ran made with it coat for is need banding when is it sense and send not is it come can for this sure that it change makes it always have the had it could must lean leaning as mine there are in are plain plan must it be trees with be find not lying for this time in and a middle while it is very likely there it is what when not come to this walnut tree if you know that a walnut can grow. Say so.

The next which and which to say is how many trees are there in it and what are their ages and their sizes. Who has been counting at a distance. An acquaintance with description is to be used again and again.

And acquaintance with description is to be used again and again. And acquaintance with description is to be used again and again. Always begin an acquaintance with description to be used again and again.

A once in a way makes it at once in a way makes it at once makes it at once once in a way makes it at once in a way makes it at once in a way. After this it is left that if it is as wide as less than that as it is as wide as less than that it is as wide as less than that. Never happen to have been in even evenly never to have been in even never to have been in even never even to have happen never to have happen to even to have even have been never even to have happen to have been even as for the paint let should not been more as it caught is not the name very easily.

How can there very well be a bell as bell upon as hunting upon as hunting had as there is upon a hunting dog there is.

Pass paper pass please pass pass trees pass trees please pass please pass please pass please as paper as pass as trees. Very likely very nearly likely nearly likely very. Nearly likely very. Nearly very. It is very easy to like to like to pass very likely it is very near nearly to like to pass grass. Farmers or do it. Farmers or do it no one should mix what is heard with what is seen. No one should mix seen and heard. In this way. In this way. Leaves leave it. In this way. Leaves in this way leaves leave it in this way leaves in this way leaves in this way. Not at all to like as alike not at all as this way not trouble some in this way not in this way in this way to have and did it in this way. Different, after having seen one having seen some having seen some. Having seen some. Not having between not having between as long as a field not having between not having seen between as long as a field not having between.

The right was down on the side of the road and the left was on the road. The left was on the road and the right was down on the side of the road. The right was down at the side of the road and the left was on the road. The left was on the road and the right was down by the side of the road.

Let it be for them to know.

Not as much as they could say.

When it is where they have been.

Not to be too much to see that it is so.

There when did it leave to have to come to have given, how did it leave it come to there there there more no. No and acknowledge.

Oh yes of course below.

Because she is because she is Julia because she is Julia because she is and English Julia and Julia Ford.

Never to have been a two one one two one one never to have been a two one one.

To not be surprised if it should rain.

They are to not be surprised if it should rain.

They are to not be surprised if it should rain. There is a difference between rain wind and paper. What is the difference between rain wind and paper. There is a difference between rain wind and paper.

After a little while there is a difference between rain and wind. After a little while there is a difference between wind rain and wind rain and paper and between rain wind and paper and there is after a while there is a difference between rain wind and paper. Thank you very much as much as very much thank you very much as very much as much there is thank you very much there is a difference after a while there is a difference between rain wind and paper thank you very much there is a difference between rain wind and paper thank you very much thank you as much. Let it be that they came there. It was quite as if it was not only not to be not only not to be satisfactory but to be perfectly satisfactory satisfactory satisfactory.

Very well to do it to it to it very well to do it to it to it very well to do it to it very well to do it to it very well to do it to it very well. Why do very small very small marshes very small marshes give pleasure very small marshes give pleasure very small marshes.

Little pieces of that have been where that has made while

that is there need it as it can be said to be more and more
and more and more and more to be sure come to be what is
it for the next and to be sure more and as it is as when they
need to be their with their to their be there like might it be
come to be mine come to be next when if if it is not might
when for spare and let in that come to come with as need it
for the have to be nicely near if they consider an acre an acre
an acre an acre like much seem when if this let in sign and
side two sent which which is a relief if it is sure sure sure surely
now how there is a difference in climbing a hill with or without climbing a hill with or without climbing a hill.

Could be a little marsh.

Promise not to be so yet if this is so and this is more and
when it is as it was for them if it can and is to be left it alone
so that it can if when if it is by that who in that case and can
and it is as if it is as if it is as it was to them to them to them
to if it was as if it was to them to them and let it come to this
for this for this let it as if as if in spite and mean to share let
it be come to be beside with them in that in that and could
and have and did and like and like and why and in and must
and do in do and do leave do leave do leave not without that
with with come come come to to to be sure where if if when
is when is it when is it all not this to be there and sent when
if should have come to be spoken like like like it is alike alike
for it is because it is used to it.

There made a mistake.

Do be like it for that which is why when it is not as if in
their being made for that in their being to being made to be
what is it not as like as if they had had to be when is it that
if they could have it be which is as well. He is very certain to
be sure to be sure to be sure to be sure not to be sure not to
be sure not to be sure to not to be sure to be sure to be sure
not to be sure not to be sure not to be sure not to be sure
to be sure. Not to be sure. Let it be when it is mine to be
sure let it be when it is mine when it is mine let it be to be
sure when it is mine to be sure let it be let it be let it be to
be sure let it be to be sure when it is mine to be sure let it
to be sure when it is mine let it be to be sure let it be to be
sure to be sure let it be to be sure let it be to be sure to be
sure let it be to be sure let it be to be sure let it be to be sure

let it be mine to be sure let it be to be sure to be mine to be
sure to be mine to be sure to be mine let it be to be mine let
it be to be sure to be mine to be sure let it be to be mine let
it be to be sure let it be to be sure to be sure let it to be sure
mine to be sure let it be mine to let it be to be sure to let it
be mine when to be sure when to be sure to let it to be sure
to be mine.

Well there there there very well very well there there there
there well there well there there well there and easily counted
there there counted easily there there there counted there
there there there. Everybody knows everybody knows everybody knows that there there they are easily counted there
there there there they are easily there there they are easily
counted. Not easily counted as easily seen in between as easily
counted not as easily seen counted easily seen there there
there easily counted in between as easily seen there. There is
no use explaining that melons can be used when melons can
be used when melons can be used yellow melons can be used.
That if as it might be left to be that if they are as corn as
many as corn as many as many as corn as seen as many as corn
as seen. There has come a decision that everything and named.

Much as much as if to to be remember that it is to be
remember much as much as if to be as much as much as if to
be remember that as much as much as if to be remember that
as much as much as much as much as if to be remember that
as much as much as much as much as much as if to be remember that as much as much as much as much as much as
much as much as if to be remember that as if to be as much
as much as much as much as much as if to remember that as
if to be to be as if to remember that as if to be as much as if
to be as much as to remember as much as if to be as much as
remember as much as if to be as if to be remember as if as
much with wide with wide as much as if to be remember if
as much as if as to be as if as much as if to be as much as if
as wide as much as if to be to remember as if to be to remember as much to remember as if as much to be as wide as
if to be as much. Very naturally they can be if is when last in
for be by beside made is in can for that in light and need and
made made why can fit this in this and that there leave come
easily need why make it be once again to that which is why

they can have both grapes and apples and pears. That is might it if when is it in and at a time by which by which by which by which it is very much inclined inclined to inclination which is seized that makes it naturally believe be like and to have it faster than at first. We thought not at all. Go might it be all coming which is why which is why which is which is which is which is a very nearly certain certainly letting and let it much as it does when the moon rises. It is very pleasant to see the moon in day-light.

It was easy to be sure that it looked so far away pansy as the let it be as much which is when it is might be so much as much further which which very wide very well and very not and mount. Pansy. Not having counted the pansies it is impossible to say just how many pansies are in it. Very much let it be last which having it be worn and where can it be if it can be that there is no difference between ridges and between ridges. There is a difference between ridges and between ridges and between there is a difference between there there and ridges between there there there and ridges there is a difference between there there there there and ridges there is a difference between no difference between pansies and there between pansies and there between not between not telling between not telling the difference between ridges there there there pansies there there there difference there between difference distance there there between distance difference ridges there there there there distance between and very place as much as place as much as place as much how many trees are there place as much as nectarines nectarines is a mixture of vineyard peaches and counted plums and careful very careful very careful of pears. This makes pansies one time at one time at one time pansies not pansies at one time let it at one time two rosy on two rosy in two in two rosy in at one time in and it is true the little pieces are where they are and those that are are a pair a pair of all around it.

An acquaintance with description asking an acquaintance with description asking for an acquaintance with description. All around it asking for an acquaintance with description.

It is very remarkable. Not that. It is very remarkable that that this is after it has been not only that it is when would it be laughed laughed at and about about to do about to do so and about about what where it is by whom by whose after all by whose having had which it for this as this is in a stream a stream can wash celery celery to be sure there there to be certain to be certain there there cultivate to be most to be most and very to be most most which is moistened by their their arranging wool wool which when very much in the meantime greatly greatly influenced by as much as if in this case in each case and arrangement. Let it be not for this when when is it it is not fortunately that they were understood that the same renting relenting buying rebuying referring referring which is it that is not why then and very much an advantage. The situation in respect to what is seen when there is letting it be carefully to-day. It was not not likely that that it was was to be left to them to decide. Let us unify four things principally and pansies, very reasonably and rightly, come to be as much theirs as it was, and left to be not only thirty but thirty trees.

Do not do not what climb the hills hills which are hills and hills which are hills which are strawberry plants and strawberry plants and in and in that when there is none noon there is should shall and might might be an eraser. Very nearly what they did to-day. Should shall be in case of and never be by this this that leave not with this look again.

Find as much.

Not as to bird this year. Let to this why not if it is not as where that is undoubtedly not from to be that this now touch when leaving leaving lay lane much at behold behold for let this inches inches make make please why they can. What happened was this a bee a wasp which tried when there believe behind make that not before when in this into a bank which is made of shrubs which do not grow in California.

Like this.

Once two three.

Once two three again two three two three.

How do you do happily happily with that happily with that. There is a difference between twice one one and leaving it be chosen that they do not any of them always like that. Not only if this is theirs too to have it be that it can send and consent and finally letting letting that if when after that it should be not only recalled but estimated not in case and care for that to be as much as much as much to be sure leaving leaving it for this at once nearly by all. All of it at one time easily.

Might it be that it can be that it can be might it be that it can be that it can be might it be that that it can be might it be that might it be that it can be might it be that it can be might it be that it can be might it be that it can be might it be that that it can be might it be that it can be might it be might it be that might it that it might be might it be that it can be. Very many who have come very many who have come very many who have come who have come very many who have come very many who have come very many who have come. There is to be sure what is there to be sure what there is to be sure that there is what is what is there to be sure there is what there is to be sure. They might be not might be be seated might be not might not might be not might not might be seated not might be not might be not might be not be seated not be seated not might be not might be seated might be not might not might not might not be seated might be. Leading theirs to this and sown sown makes which when when then an indicative nearly an indirectly as satisfied for that as immediately near and lessen too be what is never with it as in minding fairly should it be the carefully resting and left which is it that that let it have it to be fall of the year how is it if the minding minding to be heard let it alone after much leaving so very much to them to them in this how to be sure surely nearly very very well welcome and for that for that. Any one can know that a house which when when it it was was placed having having having at that distance distance was not not by that which is what is what is it let it be while at one time. In this way a very large house looks small and so that is true two roofs that is true, not two to three that that is true that is true not why not why not why not why that is true not why that is true it is why must it be what must it be after this is heard heard heard, the daughters can cannot go.

Nevertheless if there is distress and they planted two hundred more when it was certainly not what was needed trees not what what was needed vines not what was needed places

and not what was needed and now not what was needed and
nearly not what was needed and not what was needed and so
not what was needed very well in exchange. Did her brother
if he was twenty-five years old was he did he like to leave it
here. If her sister who was seventeen years old did she need
to be left to be here need to be left to be here need to be left
need to be left to be here and if her mother who had been
sixteen years or a widow need to be left to be here and if she
needed to be left to be here and it was not to be undoubtedly
that it was not to be undoubtedly that it was not to be not
to be needed to be left to be here. It is certainly very much
better that if that would that to be that when and might and
make it and this that and that to be with to be with that to
be with that to be with to be with that to be with that to be
with to be with that very much as if when not and nearly to
be nearly which with that there are might to be not for this
not because not not because this this and water with with and
fruit in in as much and left let it be carried. They might be
indifferent. Need it to be left to be their own. With it for
them in as much as while while at last neither with nor by and
when it is in no way as an estimation which can which can
place pleases and colouring collected could it be that they had
been waiting. She was very nearly easily seated. Like and like
it. Not can it with much left to them now. That which is suited
to irresistible irresistibly be very likely need needing needless
and needed needed and needed and needed and needed and
needed now and now and now and needed needed there is
there is there is there is there is there there there will they will
they will they hearing made easily made made made come to
be making to be made very who is under very well very well.
We said the elder he said who is under very well the who
is very well who is very well who is very well very well who
is under the very who is under the very well the elder who is
very well the under the very well. Having five white roses and
one having three white roses and very likely two of them were
mislaid. Not is to be mean to be to be to be very necessarily
that after that after that then and not as well as October after
November. Even a wind can be must be could be that and
were were not not to come let it be what is not as to a place
have this. It never could be nearly when to be when to be

when to be would they care to see this now as candles. This now as candles this now as fruit and this now as this now as this now as this now as this now as this.

There to be like alike in here to be like it thank you very much as when do not when do not do more than it is prepare for this and and come to this to the let it shall for this come to this not as much as if letting in in to not nor can it have to be nearly in this come to be in considerable, if it was not for this at that time come to be sure to win and leave and leave and leave and in as if and in are to be come to be in liking let it not when can this and call seen for his and surely to compare it let it not to be near than nearer than this is now what is it come in to when it is not left and left and fairly not to be in when come to be mine. There is when it can to be sure which is left in liking when nearly near come with it welcome for this use and used and very well should it be letting it come to this this this this half of it half of the time they know and now can it be left to them bread and chance to be which is with pears and not to let it come that is when if not coming to in them shut if not as it must at all come to be did it not not to not only left it there. Having watched a further than it is beside. This makes it not which is it nearly nearly never had to be left to them how do they know the difference between bulls and vines and pears and houses and leaves and hares and houses and theirs and by the time it was to be near nearly nearly there there there there can it there there there was it that it was not only in as much as much as not as not at all. It is very easy easily to know to know to do so do so to so so to wish wish wish leave it to need need in case of this which one two cows one two sheep one two ducks one two trees one two not one two not one two not one two not one two not not at once one two one one two not one two one one one two. One two.

Description from the way to have been at the time if not to be certain that it is left to be fallen down there and if it had been then the terrace and it is not by reason of their not only allowed but nevertheless changing not because their nearly having it be like after all shall and by this time. Very readily see see that from the terrace if there is a flooring flooring fixed fixed it so nearly at a while from distance come to be with it in hand. Looking at it last have hand and share. Three places not three not found there not not much at a time it is easier to rent than to buy than to rent than to buy.

One at a time a meadow at a time a distance at a time and half a house a house at a time and and at a time and then at a time and there there at a time. Who has who had who has who held held it in pieces of theirs beside.

Let leave leant learn line let it make it be it have have have here and might might it try try it try not it as come to be in where they might do it too mix which come there leave and allowance allowance handle handle they make which is it as as likely very likely to be or sure and feeling and faintly faintly there make a mistake useful need a glance shall it be near them the same at once.

There is a great difference between people and places.

Once again have them too all the time might and while to be sure plainly as will not can for this as be shall kind and there. When is it.

When is it that they might see them.

One at a time and a peculiarity of interchanging need it be this to-day to-day clearly which is might it be when if reasonable and liking meaning fortunately exchange by wishes left alone nearly and coming very well to prepare bread.

Bread.

Come to that come to that come to that come to that.

Might it be around. Come to that. Full and feel this place eight days fourteen days really days why will days for the days it need it needed it needed braid it needed braid it needed it is not sound it needed it needed if it needed soldered it needed with it it needed could if it needed with with it with it with it with it it with it which is if the difference if this which soldered which which if be and bear and break and be and bear and be and share it find and not at all either not much not as much feel it white make it last.

It is very easy to cook bread in a communal oven. Why because it is prepared in a basket and easily being fluid it remains in place on a pail and the oven being very nearly stone it is longer heated than it was. An hour two an hour too and hour an hour and a half not as very not by the way in standing. Not an acquaintance not an acquaintance with not an acquaintance with description not an acquaintance with with description not an acquaintance with not an acquaintance with description.

Now be by the way. Ellis now be now be by now be by the way Ellis now need now be now be now be now by the way Ellis now be now be now need now be now by now be now be now by the way.

Now Ellis.

Now be now by the way.

To know.

What is there in difference which is what is when it is there most. Like it like it like it for them to them like it very much by which they went.

Fellow follow for fell feel for likely by a stretch of time time to be mostly and usual usually they make make which in strangely let it very likely be which is when there is in January to be there. Who makes might it mountains.

An acquaintance with then with description and leaving which it matters matters very much to them. An acquaintance with description. With them.

Ellis with them.

An acquaintance with their an acquaintance with description which may be which may be pleased and pressed as planted planted makes it be nearly there as choosing choosing and losing who knows. Can we be see. An acquaintance with description nearly very nearly.

Let it be not nearly five which follow cows which follow cows sheep which follow cows let it be not nearly which follow cows sheep. That is one thing. Let it be which when when not for this is like that to theirs allow come satisfaction remount and more over let this come to be to see might it have should it now come this let it for them must it for near now nearly. This is at one time. There is just as much letting it be when is it not to have been nicely recommenced and a lake. Very frequently there is no sunshine very frequently even then it is not very cold even then. Now and now and now roses. Very white and roses very pretty very pretty very pretty large very pretty large very pretty large very pretty roses very pretty very pretty very pretty very pretty very pretty as very pretty roses very pretty large very pretty very pretty very pretty large very pretty. Some some some he did not like to hear it said to him some some some some he did not like to hear it said to him that in place of then to then to then and as in place twenty as in place now could it after which is letting letting letting. A fish where hare where straw where apples where there there any day a way away and kindly. She preferred to have it named after he had he had he had she must five is five so often as often as often one as often, having half and nearly Jenny too, too too too. Jenny is a drop. This is clear clearly. You do leave it here here here here Chambery.

Look up look her up look her up look her up look her look her look her look her up and down. Mr. Pernollet does not supply it yet Mrs. Press does not express lady fingers which are here she was very likely to be really two at most, Mr. Baird Mr. Baird makes it better to do so if he likes it which is what what is it it is what very much makes theirs start to finish, Mrs. Father has a daughter they do they know they know they do they do they do. Mrs. Middle has a husband really two and two really freshly really freshly freshly really she really very really very very come too, Mr. Bourg is now at peace if he goes if he goes if he goes, can two one of them older and the sister of his mother which is why his wife was is leave it to him, not now that is why liking by it soon. Never to tell well.

What is the difference between a park and a field.

When is a meadow under water when it is a marsh and after which is higher there is always something not might not after this very which is that.

Has it been to be.

If it is when she.

Let it can it be.

If you can and three.

If you see the mountain clearly it means that it will be rainy if you see the mountain it means that it will not be rainy if you see the mountain clearly if you can see the mountain clearly it means that it will not be rainy if you can see the mountain clearly it means it will be rainy if you see the mountain clearly it means that it will be rainy. After this they went to be nearly four nearly five nearly after this they went to be nearly five nearly five nearly four nearly, after this they went away nearly five nearly after this they went away.

Having stopped to gather butter butter can be made to fruiten fruiten can be made to butter having nearly having made to butter having made to fruiten having made to butter fruiten having made to nearly having made to butter fruiten.

Leave which is mine nearly always after it has been the contrary the country nearly which is mine which has been the country which has been the contrary nearly which has been nearly which is mine the country. Leaves which is mine.

Needless to say that it is very needless to say that it is in every way a pleasant month of October as to weather.

There can be flower too flour too flower too there can be corn flour too when there is this and more. There can be this and too when there is corn and too there can be flour too corn flour and this and too. What is the difference between them and grapes grapes are sweeter, what is not what is not ivy what not and ivy which is join and Paulette. Paul and Paulette which is elder older white and next older elder which is left to be now. Does anybody suggest suggest that he can find can find a house with that with that when could eight brothers and their sisters work harder and how. How and how. Could they work harder and how how and how. They kneel knee can it be and see see sat which which is when is this every in the can there make which is why this will this cake if eggs are purchased. Leave it for them to them with them in them and then then like it for its use when this can be nicely left to come to which very little which is not their likely why can it be claimed at once. To like it. Therese can be compared to Therese can be compared to Therese can be compared, very likely very likely which is why it is with that. It is very well very well well enough come to this. Helen has rounder sounder found her found her found her. Think then could it be trout. Trout how. Very likely. Not now not all.

It would be in this little way of placing everything that they believe them it must be as if it is when that it is not as when as when believe it for this which makes nicely not in with and for them this with and for them to be certainly let it be not for this in instance. First they made what is what is let it let it need to be what is meant and unexpectedly have them be theirs. Let us imagine what they do spy what they do spy what they do do what they do with with with spy with spy with

with with in what they do. A place which makes when it is
not only as high as which can be two see, under like it make
and for which is which is why they have to be in pleasing let
it be nicely that four houses are mentioned. Four houses are
mentioned. Four houses are mentioned. Four houses are mentioned. One for one for one for one for one after that three
which may be and not needing it now they cannot them and
not needing it now they cannot them and two at once two at
once two at once more two at once more more more more
two two two more two at once and one to one and to one
one and to one to one to one one, have can have one which
when a duck two cries makes cannot cannot one can cannot
can one can one one, two two which two and one which one.
Georgie would like a letter. Not about it. But rather for pleasure. To be sure to be having could it leave it for this might
a lieutenant be what is after after all after all small small small
after all nicely in decide decide train and nearly which, after
this while needs to needs to to needs to needs needs to this
next fall as if if water flowing flowing with no flow flowing
with no flow flowing need cows cows be fruit and fruit be
mentioned mentioned moon as likely as if to intend let it not
have it have it in this come it come it and committee and after
all never having returned an answer as to the name of that
that let it be not to be when to be then to be Xenobie. It is
very surprising that a young girl about to be certain that one
preparation is better than another is named Marie.

The Life of Juan Gris
The Life and Death of Juan Gris

Juan Gris was one of the younger children of a well to do merchant of Madrid. The earliest picture he has of himself is at about five years of age dressed in a little lace dress standing beside his mother who was very sweet and pleasantly maternal looking. When he was about seven years old his father failed in business honourably and the family fell upon very hard times but in one way and another two sons and a daughter lived to grow up well educated and on the whole prosperous. Juan went to the school of engineering at Madrid and when about seventeen came to Paris to study. He tells delightful stories of his father and Spanish ways which strangely enough he never liked. He had very early a very great attraction and love for french culture. French culture has always seduced me he was fond of saying. It seduces me and then I am seduced over again. He used to tell how Spaniards love not to resist temptation. In order to please them the better class merchants such as his father would always have to leave many little things about everything else being packages carefully tied up and in the back on shelves. He used to dwell upon the lack of trust and comradeship in Spanish life. Each one is a general or does not fight and if he does not fight each one is a general. No one that is no Spaniard can help any one because no one no Spaniard can help any one. And this being so and it is so Juan Gris was a brother and comrade to every one being one as no one ever had been one. That is the proportion. One to any one number of millions. That is any proportion. Juan Gris was that one. French culture was always a seduction. Braque who was such a one was always a seduction seducing french culture seducing again and again. Josette equable intelligent faithful spontaneous delicate courageous delightful fore-thoughtful, the school of Fontainebleau delicate deliberate measured and free all these things seduced. I am seduced and then I am seduced over again he was fond of saying. He had his own Spanish gift of intimacy. We were intimate. Juan knew what he did. In the beginning he did all sorts of things he used to draw for humourous illustrated papers he had a child a boy named George he lived about he was not young and enthusiastic. The first serious exhibition of his pictures was at the Galerie Kahnweiler rue Vignon in 1914. As a Spaniard he knew Cubism and had stepped through into it. He had stepped through it. There was beside this perfection. To have it shown you. Then came the war and desertion. There was little aid. Four years partly illness much perfection and rejoining beauty and perfection and then at the end there came a definite creation of something. This is what is to be measured. He made something that is to be measured. And that is that something.

Therein Juan Gris is not anything but more than anything. He made that thing. He made the thing. He made a thing to be measured.

Later having done it he could be sorry it was not why they liked it. And so he made it very well loving and he made it with plainly playing. And he liked a knife and all but reasonably. This is what is made to be and he then did some stage setting. We liked it but nobody else could see that something is everything. It is everything if it is what is it. Nobody can ask about measuring. Unfortunately. Juan could go on living. No one can say that Henry Kahnweiler can be left out of him. I remember he said "Kahnweiler goes on but no one buys anything and I said it to him and he smiled so gently and said I was everything." This is the history of Juan Gris.

Patriarchal Poetry

As long as it took fasten it back to a place where after all he would be carried away, he would be carried away as long as it took fasten it back to a place where he would be carried away as long as it took.

For before let it before to be before spell to be before to be before to have to be to be for before to be tell to be to having held to be to be for before to call to be for to be before to till until to be till before to be for before to be until to be for before to for to be for before will for before to be shall to be to be for to be for to be before still to be will before to be before for to be to be for before to be before such to be for to be much before to be for before will be for to be for before to be well to be well before to be before for before might while to be might before to be might while to be might before while to be might to be while before for might to be for before to for while to be while for before while before to for which as for before had for before had for before to for to before.

Hire hire let it have to have to hire representative to hire to representative to representative hire to representative to hire wire to representative to hire representative to hire.

There never was a mistake in addition.

Ought ought my prize my ought ought prize with a denies with a denies to be ought ought to denies with a to ought to ought ought with a denies plainly detained practically to be next. With a with a would it last with a with a have it passed come to be with this and theirs there is a million of it shares and stairs and stairs to right about. How can you change from their to be sad to sat. Coming again yesterday.

Once to be when once to be when once to be having an advantage all the time.

Little pieces of their leaving which makes it put it there to be theirs for the beginning of left altogether practically for the sake of relieving it partly.

As your as to your as to your able to be told too much as to your as to as able to receive their measure or rather whether intermediary and left to the might it be letting having when win. When win makes it dark when win makes it dark to held to beheld behold be as particularly in respect to not letting half of it be by. Be by in this away.

To lay when in please and letting it be known to be come to this not in not in not in nightingale in which is not in land in hand there is it leaving light out out in this or this or this beside which may it for it to be in it lest and louder louder to be known which is could might this near special have near nearly reconcile oblige and indestructible and mainly in this use.

Mainly will fill remaining sad had which is to be following dukedom duke in their use say to amount with a part let it go as if with should it might my makes it a leader.

Feels which is there.

To change a boy with a cross from there to there.

Let him have him have him heard let him have him heard him third let him have him have him intend let him have him have him defend let him have him have him third let him have him have him heard let him have him have him occurred let him have him have him third.

Forty-nine Clive as well forty-nine Clive as well forty-nine sixty-nine seventy-nine eighty-nine one hundred and nine Clive as well forty-nine Clive as well which is that it presses it to be or to be stay or to be twenty a day or to be next to be or to be twenty to stay or to be which never separates two more two women.

Fairly letting it see that the change is as to be did Nelly and Lily love to be did Nelly and Lily went to see and to see which is if could it be that so little is known was known if so little was known shown stone come bestow bestown so little as was known could which that for them recognisably.

Wishing for Patriarchal Poetry.

Once threes letting two sees letting two three threes letting it be after these two these threes can be two near threes in threes twos letting two in two twos slower twos choose twos threes never came twos two twos relieve threes twos threes. Threes twos relieves twos to twos to twos to twos relieve to twos to relieve two threes to relieves two relieves threes twos two to relieve threes relieves threes relieve twos relieves threes

two twos slowly twos relieve threes threes to twos relieve relieve two to relieve threes twos twos relieves twos threes threes
relieves twos two relieve twos relieves relieve twos relieves
threes relieve twos slowly twos to relieves relieve threes relieve
threes twos two relieve twos threes relieves relieve relieves
twos two twos threes relieves threes two twos relieve relieves
relieves threes relieve relieves threes relieves as two so threes
twos relieves twos relieve.

Who hears whom once once to snow they might if they
trained fruit-trees they might if they leaned over there they
might look like it which when it could if it as if when it left
to them to their use of pansies and daisies use of them use of
them of use of pansies and daisies use of pansies and daisies
use of them use of them of use use of pansies and use of
pansies and use of pansies and use use of them use of pansies
and daisies use of use of them which is what they which is
what they they do they which is what they do there out and
out and leave it to the meaning of their by their with their
allowance making allowed what is it.

They have it with it reconsider it with it they with it reconsider it with it they have it with it reconsider it have it they
with it reconsider it they have it they with it reconsider it they
with it they reconsider it have it they have it reconsider it with
it have it reconsider it have it with it. She said an older sister
not an older sister she said an older sister not an older sister
she said an older sister have it with it reconsider it with it
reconsider it have it an older sister have it with it. She said
she had followed flowers she had said she had said she had
followed she had said she had said she had followed she had
said with it have it reconsider it have it with it she had said
have followed have said have had have followed have said followed had followed had said followed flowers which she had
had will it reconsider it with it have it had said followed had
followed had followed flowers had said had with it had followed flowers had have had with it had said had have had
with it.

Is no gain.
Is no gain.
To is no gain.
Is to to is no gain.

Is to is to to is no gain.

Is to is no is to is no gain.

Is no gain.

Is to is no gain.

Is to is to is no gain.

Is no gain.

Is to is no gain.

With it which it as it if it is to be to be to come to in which to do in that place.

As much as if it was like as if might be coming to see me.

What comes to be the same as lilies. An ostrich egg and their after lines.

It made that be alike and with it an indefinable reconciliation with roads and better to be not as much as felt to be as well very well as the looking like not only little pieces there. Comparing with it.

Not easily very much very easily, with to be wish to be rest to be like not easily rest to be not like not like rest to be not like it rest to not like rest to be not like it.

How is it to be rest to be receiving rest to be how like it rest to be receiving to be like it. Compare something else to something else. To be rose.

Such a pretty bird.

Not to such a pretty bird. Not to not to not to not to such a pretty bird.

Not to such a pretty bird.

Not to such a pretty bird.

As to as such a pretty bird. As to as to as such a pretty bird.

To and such a pretty bird.

And to and such a pretty bird.

And to as to not to as to and such a pretty bird.

As to and to not to as to and such a pretty bird and to as such a pretty bird and to not to as such a pretty bird and to as to not to and to and such a pretty bird as to and such a pretty bird and to and such a pretty bird not to and to as such a pretty bird as to as such a pretty bird and to as such a pretty bird and to as to and to not to and to as to as such a pretty bird and to as such a pretty bird and to as to not to as to and to and such a pretty bird and to and such a pretty bird as to and such a pretty bird not to and such a pretty bird not to

and such a pretty bird as to and such a pretty bird and to and
such a pretty bird as to and to and such a pretty bird not to
as to and such a pretty bird and to not as to and to not to as
such as pretty bird and such a pretty bird not to and such a
pretty bird as to and such a pretty bird as such a pretty bird
and to as such a pretty bird and to and such a pretty bird not
to and such a pretty bird as to and such a pretty bird not to
as such a pretty bird not to and such a pretty bird as to and
such a pretty bird not to as to and to not to as such a pretty
bird and to not to and to and such a pretty bird as to and
such a pretty bird and to as such a pretty bird as to as such a
pretty bird not to and to as to and such a pretty bird as to
and to and to as to as such a pretty bird as such a pretty bird
and to as such a pretty bird and to and such a pretty bird and
to and such and to and to and such a pretty bird and to and
to and such a pretty bird and to and such a pretty bird and to
and and a pretty bird and to and such a pretty bird and to
and such a pretty bird and to as to and to and such a pretty
bird and to as to as such a pretty bird and to and to and such
a pretty bird and such a pretty bird and to and such a pretty
bird and to and to and such a pretty bird and to and such a
pretty bird.

Was it a fish was heard was it a bird was it a cow was stirred
was it a third was it a cow was stirred was it a third was it a
bird was heard was it a third was it a fish was heard was it a
third. Fishes a bird cows were stirred a bird fishes were heard
a bird cows were stirred a third. A third is all. Come too.

Patriarchal means suppose patriarchal means and close patriarchal means and chose chose Monday Patriarchal means in
close some day patriarchal means and chose chose Sunday patriarchal means and chose chose one day patriarchal means and
close close Tuesday. Tuesday is around Friday and welcomes
as welcomes not only a cow but introductory. This aways patriarchal as sweet.

Patriarchal make it ready.

Patriarchal in investigation and renewing of an intermediate
rectification of the initial boundary between cows and fishes.
Both are admittedly not inferior in which case they may be
obtained as the result of organisation industry concentration
assistance and matter of fact and by this this is their chance

and to appear and to reunite as to their date and their estate. They have been in no need of stretches stretches of their especial and apart and here now.

Favoured by the by favoured by let it by the by favoured by the by. Patriarchal poetry and not meat on Monday patriarchal poetry and meat on Tuesday. Patriarchal poetry and venison on Wednesday Patriarchal poetry and fish on Friday Patriarchal poetry and birds on Sunday Patriarchal poetry and chickens on Tuesday patriarchal poetry and beef on Thursday. Patriarchal poetry and ham on Monday patriarchal poetry and pork on Thursday patriarchal poetry and beef on Tuesday patriarchal poetry and fish on Wednesday Patriarchal poetry and eggs on Thursday patriarchal poetry and carrots on Friday patriarchal poetry and extras on Saturday patriarchal poetry and venison on Sunday patriarchal poetry and lamb on Tuesday patriarchal poetry and jellies on Friday patriarchal poetry and turkeys on Tuesday.

They made hitherto be by and by.

It can easily be returned ten when this, two might it be too just inside, not as if chosen that not as if chosen, withal if it had been known to be going to be here and this needed to be as as green. This is what has been brought here.

Once or two makes that be not at all practically their choice practically their choice.

Might a bit of it be all the would be might be if a bit of it be all they would be if it if it would be all be if it would be a bit of all of it would be, a very great difference between making money peaceably and making money peaceably a great difference between making money making money peaceably making money peaceably making money peaceably.

Reject rejoice rejuvenate rejuvenate rejoice reject rejoice rejuvenate reject rejuvenate reject rejoice. Not as if it was tried. How kindly they receive the the then there this at all.

In change.

Might it be while it is not as it is undid undone to be theirs awhile yet. Not in their mistake which is why it is not after or not further in at all to their cause. Patriarchal poetry partly. In an as much to be in exactly their measure. Patriarchal poetry partly.

Made to be precisely this which is as she is to be connectedly leave it when it is to be admittedly continued to be which is which is to be that it is which it is as she connectedly to be which is as she continued as to this to be continuously not to be connected to be which to be admittedly continued to be which is which is which it is to be. They might change it as it can be made to be which is which is the next left out of it in this and this occasionally settled to the same as the left of it to the undertaking of the regular regulation of it which is which is which is which is what it is when it is needed to be left about to this when to this and they have been undetermined and as likely as it is which it is which it is which is it which is it not as in time and at a time when it is not to be certain certain makes it to be makes it to be makes it to be makes it to be makes it to be that there is not in that in consideration of the preparation of the change which is their chance inestimably.

Let it be as likely why that they have it as they try to manage. Follow. If any one decides that a year is a year beginning and end if any one decides that a year is a year beginning if any one decides that a year is a year if any one decides that a year simultaneously recognised. In recognition.

Once when if the land was there beside once when if the land was there beside.

Once when if the land was there beside.

Once when if the land was there beside.

If any one decided that a year was a year when once if any one decided that a year was a year if when once if once if any one when once if any one decided that a year was a year beside.

Patriarchal poetry includes when it is Wednesday and patriarchal includes when it is Wednesday and patriarchal poetry includes when it is Wednesday.

Never like to bother to be sure never like to bother to be sure never like to bother to be sure never like never like to never like to bother to be sure never like to bother never like to bother to be sure.

Three things which are when they are prepared. Three things which are when they are prepared. Let it alone to be let it alone to be let it alone to be to be sure. Let it alone to be sure.

Three things which are when they had had this to their best arrangement meaning never having had it here as soon.

She might be let it be let it be here as soon. She might be let it be let it be let it be here as soon. She might be let it be here as soon. She might be let it be let it be she might be she might be let it be she might be let it be she might be let it be here as soon. Theirs which way marguerites. Theirs might be let it there as soon.

When is and thank and is and and and is when is when is and when thank when is and when and thank. When is and when is and thank. This when is and when thank and thank. When is and when thank and this when is and thank.

Have hear which have hear which have hear which leave and leave her have hear which have hear which leave her hear which leave her hear she leave her hear which. They might by by they might by by which might by which they might by which they by which they might which they might by which they by which they might by which. In face of it.

Let it be which is it be which is it be which is it let it let it which is it let it which let it which is it let it be which is it be which let it be which let it which is it which is it let it let it which is it let it. Near which with it which with near which with which with near which with near which with near which with it near which near which with near which near which with which with it.

Leave it with it let it go able to be shiny so with it can be is it near let it have it as it may come well be. This is why after all at a time that is which is why after all at the time this is why it is after all at the time this is why this is why this is after all after why this is after all at the time. This is why this is why this is after all this is why this is after all at the time.

Not a piece of which is why a wedding left have wedding left which is why which is why not which is why not a piece of why a a wedding having why a wedding left. Which is what is why is why is why which is what is why is why is why a wedding left.

Leaving left which is why they might be here be here be here. Be here be here. Which is why is why is why is why is which is why is why is why which is here. Not commence to to to be to leave to come to see to let it be to be to be at once mind it mind timely always change timely to kindly kindly to timely timely to kindly timely to kindly always to change kindly to timely kindly to timely always to change timely to kindly.

If he is not used to it he is not used to it, this is the beginning of their singling singling makes Africa shortly if he is not used to it he is not used to it this makes oriole shortly if he is not used to it if he is not used to it if he is not used to it if he is not used if he is not used to it if he is not used to it if he is not used to it he if he is not used to it he is not used to it and this makes an after either after it. She might be likely as to renew prune and see prune. This is what order does.

Next to vast which is which is it.

Next to vast which is why do I be behind the chair because of a chimney fire and higher why do I beside belie what is it when is it which is it well all to be tell all to be well all to be never do do the difference between effort and be in be in within be mine be in be within be within in.

To be we to be to be we to be to be to be we to be we to be to be to be to be to be to be to be to be we we to be to be to be we to be. Once. To be we to be to be to be we to be. Once. To be to be to be to be to be we to be. Once. To be we to be to be to be.

We to be. Once. We to be. Once. We to be be to be we to be. Once. We to be.

Once. We to be we to be. Once. To be. Once. We to be. Once. To be. Once. To be we to be. Once. To be. Once. To be we to be. We to be. Once. To be. We to be. Once.

To be we to be. Once. To be. Once. To be. Once. To be. Once. To be. Once. We to be. To be we to be. We to be. To be we to be. We to be. Once. To be to be to be. We to be. We to be. To be. Once. We to be.

Once. We to be.

Once. We to be. We to be. Once. To be we to be. Once. To be. Once. To be we to be. Once. We to be. To be. We to be. Once. Once. To be. Once. To be. Once. We to be. Once. We to be. We to be. Once. To be. Once. We to be. We to be. We to be. To be. Once. To be. We to be.

Their origin and their history patriarchal poetry their origin and their history patriarchal poetry their origin and their history.

Patriarchal Poetry.

Their origin and their history.

Patriarchal Poetry their origin and their history their history patriarchal poetry their origin patriarchal poetry their history their origin patriarchal poetry their history patriarchal poetry their origin patriarchal poetry their history their origin.

That is one case.

Able sweet and in a seat.

Patriarchal poetry their origin their history their origin. Patriarchal poetry their history their origin.

Two makes it do three make it five four make it more five make it arrive and sundries.

Letters and leaves tables and plainly restive and recover and bide away, away to say regularly.

Never to mention patriarchal poetry altogether.

Two two two occasionally two two as you say two two two not in their explanation two two must you be very well apprised that it had had such an effect that only one out of a great many and there were a great many believe in three relatively and moreover were you aware of the fact that interchangeable and interchangeable was it while they were if not avoided. She knew that is to say she had really informed herself. Patriarchal poetry makes no mistake.

Never to have followed farther there and knitting, is knitting knitting if it is only what is described as called that they should not come to say and how do you do every new year Saturday. Every new year Saturday is likely to bring pleasure is likely to give pleasure is likely to bring pleasure every new year Saturday is likely to bring pleasure.

Day which is what is which is what is day which is what is day which is which is what is which is what is day.

I double you, of course you do. You double me, very likely to be. You double I double I double you double. I double you double me I double you you double me.

When this you see remarkably.

Patriarchal poetry needs rectification and there about it.

Come to a distance and it still bears their name.

Prosperity and theirs prosperity left to it.

To be told to be harsh to be told to be harsh to be to them.
One.

To be told to be harsh to be told to be harsh to them.
None.

To be told to be harsh to be told to be harsh to them.
When.

To be told to be harsh to be told to be harsh to them.
Then.

What is the result.

The result is that they know the difference between instead and instead and made and made and said and said.

The result is that they might be as very well two and as soon three and to be sure, four and which is why they might not be.

Elegant replaced by delicate and tender, delicate and tender replaced by one four there instead of five four there, there is not there this is what has happened evidently.

Why while while why while why why identity identity why while while why. Why while while while while identity.

Patriarchal Poetry is the same as patriarchal poetry is the same as patriarchal poetry is the same as patriarchal poetry is the same as patriarchal poetry is the same.

Patriarchal poetry is the same.

If in in crossing there is a if in crossing if in in crossing nearly there is a distance if in crossing there is a distance between measurement and exact if in in crossing if in in crossing there is a measurement between and in in exact she says I must be careful and I will.

If in in crossing there is an opportunity not only but also and in in looking in looking in regarding if in in looking if in in regarding if in in regarding there is an opportunity if in in looking there is an opportunity if in in regarding there is an opportunity to verify verify sometimes as more sometimes as more sometimes as more.

Fish eggs commonly fish eggs. Architects commonly fortunately indicatively architects indicatively architects. Elaborated at a time with it with it at a time with it at a time attentively to-day.

Does she know how to ask her brother is there any difference between turning it again again and again and again or turning it again and again. In resembling two brothers.

That makes patriarchal poetry apart.

Intermediate or patriarchal poetry.

If at once sixty-five have come one by one if at once sixty five have come one by one if at once sixty-five have come one by one. This took two and two have been added to by Jenny. Never to name Jenny. Have been added to by two. Never have named Helen Jenny never have named Agnes Helen never have named Helen Jenny. There is no difference between having been born in Brittany and having been born in Algeria.

These words containing as they do neither reproaches nor satisfaction may be finally very nearly rearranged and why, because they mean to be partly left alone. Patriarchal poetry and kindly, it would be very kind in him in him of him of him to be as much obliged as that. Patriarchal poetry. It would be as plainly an advantage if not only but altogether repeatedly it should be left not only to them but for them but for them. Explain to them by for them. Explain shall it be explain will it be explain can it be explain as it is to be explain letting it be had as if he had had more than wishes. More than wishes.

Patriarchal poetry more than wishes.

Assigned to Patriarchal Poetry.

Assigned to patriarchal poetry too sue sue sue sue shall sue sell and magnificent can as coming let the same shall shall shall shall let it share is share is share shall shall shall shall shell shell shall share is share shell can shell be shell be shell moving in in in inner moving move inner in in inner in meant meant might might may collect collected recollected to refuse what it is is it.

Having started at once at once.

Put it with it with it and it and it come to ten.

Put it with it with it and it and it for it for it made to be extra.

With it put it put it prepare it prepare it add it add it or it or it would it would it and make it all at once.

Put it with it with it and it and it in it in it add it add it at it at it with it with it put it put it to this to understand.

Put it with it with it add it add it at it at it or it or it to be placed intend.

Put it with it with it in it in it at it at it add it add it or it or it letting it be while it is left as it might could do their danger.

Could it with it with it put it put it place it place it stand it stand it two doors or two doors two tables or two tables two let two let two let two to be sure.

Put it with it with it and it and it in it in it add it add it or it or it to it to be added to it.

There is no doubt about it.

Actually.

To be sure.

Left to the rest if to be sure that to be sent come to be had in to be known or to be liked and to be to be to be to be to be mine.

It always can be one two three it can be always can can always be one two three. It can always be one two three.

It is very trying to have him have it have it have him have it as she said the last was very very much and very much to very much to distance to distance them.

Every time there is a wish wish it. Every time there is a wish wish it. Every time there is a wish wish it.

Every time there is a wish wish it.

Dedicated to all the way through. Dedicated to all the way through.

Dedicated too all the way through. Dedicated too all the way through.

Apples and fishes day-light and wishes apples and fishes day-light and wishes day-light at seven.

All the way through dedicated to you.

Day-light and wishes apples and fishes, dedicated to you all the way through day-light and fishes apples and wishes dedicated to all the way through dedicated to you dedicated to you all the way through day-light and fishes apples and fishes day-light and wishes apples and fishes dedicated to you all the way through day-light and fishes apples and wishes apples and fishes day-light and wishes dedicated to dedicated through all the way through dedicated to.

Not at once Tuesday.

They might be finally their name name same came came

came came or share sharer article entreat coming in letting
this be there letting this be there.

Patriarchal poetry come too.

When with patriarchal poetry when with patriarchal poetry
come too.

There must be more french in France there must be more
French in France patriarchal poetry come too.

Patriarchal poetry come too there must be more french in
France patriarchal come too there must be more french in
France.

Patriarchal Poetry come to.

There must be more french in France.

Helen greatly relieves Alice patriarchal poetry come too
there must be patriarchal poetry come too.

In a way second first in a way first second in a way in a way
first second in a way.

Rearrangement is nearly rearrangement. Finally nearly rearrangement is finally nearly rearrangement nearly not now
finally nearly nearly finally rearrangement nearly rearrangement and not now how nearly finally rearrangement. If two
tables are near together finally nearly not now.

Finally nearly not now.

Able able nearly nearly nearly nearly able able finally nearly
able nearly not now finally finally nearly able.

They make it be very well three or nearly three at a time.

Splendid confidence in the one addressed and equal distrust
of the one who has done everything that is necessary. Finally
nearly able not now able finally nearly not now.

Rearrangement is a rearrangement a rearrangement is
widely known a rearrangement is widely known. A rearrangement is widely known. As a rearrangement is widely known.

As a rearrangement is widely known.

So can a rearrangement which is widely known be a rearrangement which is widely known which is widely known.

Let her be to be to be to be let her be to be to be let her
to be let her to be let her be to be when is it that they are
shy.

Very well to try.

Let her be that is to be let her be that is to be let her be
let her try.

Let her be let her be let her be to be to be shy let her be
to be let her be to be let her try.

Let her try.

Let her be let her be let her be let her be to be to be let
her be let her try.

To be shy.

Let her be.

Let her try.

Let her be let her let her let her be let her be let her be let
her be shy let her be let her be let her try.

Let her try.

Let her be.

Let her be shy.

Let her be.

Let her be let her be let her let her try.

Let her try to be let her try to be let her be shy let her try
to be let her try to be let her be let her be let her try.

Let her be shy.

Let her try.

Let her try.

Let her be

Let her let her be shy.

Let her try.

Let her be.

Let her let her be shy.

Let her be let her let her be shy

Let her let her let her let her try.

Let her try.

Let her try.

Let her try.

Let her be.

Let her be let her

Let her try.

Let her be let her.

Let her be let her let her try.

Let her try.

Let her

Let her try.

Let her be shy.

Let her

Let her
Let her be.
Let her be shy.
Let her be let her try.
Let her try.
Let her try.
Let her try.
Let her let her try
Let her be shy.
Let her try
Let her let her try to be let her try.
Let her try.
Just let her try.
Let her try.
Never to be what he said.
Never to be what he said.
Never to be what he said.
Let her to be what he said.
Let her to be what he said.
Not to let her to be what he said not to let her to be what he said.
Never to be let her to be never let her to be what he said. Never let her to be what he said.
Never to let her to be what he said. Never to let her to be let her to be let her to be let her what he said.
Near near near nearly pink near nearly pink nearly near near nearly pink. Wet inside and pink outside. Pink outside and wet inside wet inside and pink outside latterly nearly near near pink near near nearly three three pink two gentle one strong three pink all medium medium as medium as medium sized as sized. One as one not mistaken but interrupted. One regularly better adapted if readily readily to-day. This is this this readily. Thursday.
This part the part the part of it.
And let to be coming to have it known.
As a difference.
By two by one by and by.
A hyacinth resembles a rose. A rose resembles a blossom a blossom resembles a calla lily a calla lily resembles a jonquil

and a jonquil resembles a marguerite a marguerite resembles a rose in bloom a rose in bloom resembles a lily of the valley a lily of the valley resembles a violet and a violet resembles a bird.

What is the difference between right away and a pearl there is this difference between right away and a pearl a pearl is milk white and right away is at once. This is indeed an explanation.

Patriarchal poetry or indeed an explanation.

Try to be at night try to be to be at night try to be at night try to be at night try to be to try to be to try to be to try to be at night.

Never which when where to be sent to be sent to be sent to be never which when where never to be sent to be sent to be sent never which when where to be sent never to be sent never to be sent never which when where to be sent never to be sent never to be sent which when where never to be sent which when where never which when where never which to be sent never which when where to be sent never which when where to be sent which when where to be sent never to be sent never which when where to be sent never which when which when where to be sent never which when where never which when where which when where never to be sent which when where.

Never to be sent which when where.

As fair as fair to them.

It was not without some difficulty.

Five thousand every year.

Three thousand divided by five three thousand divided as five.

Happily very happily.

They happily very happily.

Happily very happily.

In consequence consequently.

Extra extremely additionally.

Intend or intend or intend or intend or intend additionally.

Returning retaining relatively.

This makes no difference between to be told so admittedly.

Patriarchal Poetry connectedly.

Sentence sent once patriarchal poetry sentence sent once.

Patriarchal poetry sentence sent once.

Patriarchal Poetry.

Patriarchal Poetry sentence sent once.

Patriarchal Poetry is used with a spoon.

Patriarchal poetry is used with a spoon with a spoon.

Patriarchal poetry is used with a spoon.

Patriarchal poetry used with a spoon.

Patriarchal poetry in and for the relating of now and ably.

Patriarchal poetry in preferring needless needless needlessly patriarchal poetry precluding needlessly but it can.

How often do we tell tell tell tale tell tale tell tale tell tale might be tell tale.

Supposing never never never never supposing never never is supposed widening.

Remember all of it too.

Patriarchal poetry reasonably.

Patriarchal poetry administratedly.

Patriarchal poetry with them too.

Patriarchal poetry as to mind.

Patriarchal poetry reserved.

Patriarchal poetry interdiminished.

Patriarchal poetry in regular places largely in regular places placed regularly as if it were as if it were placed regularly.

Patriarchal poetry in regular places placed regularly as if it were placed regularly regularly placed regularly as if it were.

Patriarchal poetry every little while. Not once twenty-five not once twenty-five not once slower not once twenty not once twenty-five. Patriarchal poetry every little while not every little while once every little while once every little while once every twenty once every little while once every twenty-five once every little while once every little while every once twenty-five once.

Make it a mistake.

Patriarchal she said what is it I know what it is it is I know I know so that I know what it is I know so I know so I know so I know what it is. Very slowly. I know what it is it is on the one side a to be her to be his to be their to be in an and to be I know what it is it is he who was an known not known was he was at first it was the grandfather then it was not that in that the father not of that grandfather and then she to be

to be sure to be sure to be I know to be sure to be I know
to be sure to be not as good as that. To be sure not to be
sure to be sure correctly saying to be sure to be that. It was
that. She was right. It was that.

Patriarchal Poetry.

A Sonnet.

> To the wife of my bosom.
> All happiness from everything
> And her husband.
> May he be good and considerate
> Gay and cheerful and restful.
> And make her the best wife
> In the world
> The happiest and the most content
> With reason.
> To the wife of my bosom
> Whose transcendent virtues
> Are those to be most admired
> Loved and adored and indeed
> Her virtues are all inclusive
> Her virtues her beauty and her beauties
> Her charms her qualities her joyous nature
> All of it makes of her husband
> A proud and happy man.

Patriarchal poetry makes no mistake makes no mistake in
estimating the value to be placed upon the best and most
arranged of considerations of this in as apt to be not only to
be partially and as cautiously considered as in allowance which
is one at a time. At a chance at a chance encounter it can be
very well as appointed as appointed not only considerately but
as it as use.

Patriarchal poetry to be sure to be sure to be sure candidly
candidly and aroused patriarchal to be sure and candidly and
aroused once in a while and as a circumstance within that
arranged within that arranged to be not only not only not
only not not secretive but as one at a time not in not to
include cautiously cautiously cautiously at one in not to be
finally prepared. Patriarchal poetry may be mistaken may be
undivided may be usefully to be sure settled and they would
be after a while as establish in relatively understanding a

promise of not in time but at a time wholly reconciled to feel
that as well by an instance of escaped and interrelated choice.
That makes it even.

Patriarchal poetry may seem misplaced at one time.

Patriarchal poetry might be what they wanted.

Patriarchal poetry shall be as much as if it was counted from
one to one hundred.

From one to one hundred.

From one to one hundred.

From one to one hundred.

Counted from one to one hundred.

Nobody says soften as often.

From one to one hundred.

Has to say happen as often.

Laying while it was while it was while it was. While it was.

Patriarchal poetry while it was just as close as when they
were then being used not only in here but also out there
which is what was the thing that was not only requested but
also desired which when there is not as much as if they could
be while it can shall have and this was what was all when it
was not used just for that but simply can be not what is it like
when they use it.

As much as that patriarchal poetry as much as that.

Patriarchal poetry as much as that.

To like patriarchal poetry as much as that.

To like patriarchal poetry as much as that is what she did.

Patriarchal poetry usually.

In finally finding this out out and out out and about to find
it out when it is neither there nor by that time by the time it
is not why they had it.

Why they had it.

What is the difference between a glass pen and a pen what
is the difference between a glass pen and a pen what is the
difference between a glass pen and a pen to smile at the difference between a glass pen and a pen.

To smile at the difference between a glass pen and a pen is
what he did.

Patriarchal poetry makes it as usual.

Patriarchal poetry one two three.

Patriarchal poetry accountably.

Patriarchal poetry as much.

Patriarchal Poetry reasonably.

Patriarchal Poetry which is what they did.

One Patriarchal Poetry.

Two Patriarchal Poetry.

Three Patriarchal Poetry.

One two three.

One two three.

One Patriarchal Poetry.

Two Patriarchal Poetry.

Three Patriarchal Poetry.

When she might be what it was to be left to be what they had as they could.

Patriarchal Poetry as if as if it made it be a choice beside.

The Patriarchal Poetry.

At the time that they were sure surely certain certainly aroused arousing laid lessening let letting be it as if it as if it were to be to be as if it were to be letting let it nearly all it could be not be nearly should be which is there which is it there.

Once more a sign.

Signed by them.

Signed by him.

Signed it.

Signed it as it was.

Patriarchal poetry and rushing Patriarchal Poetry and rush-ing.

Having had having had having had who having had who had having having had and not five not four not three not one not three not two not four not one not one done.

Patriarchal Poetry recollected.

Putting three together all the time two together all the time two together all the time two together two together two to-gether all the time putting five together three together all the time. Never to think of Patriarchal Poetry at one time.

Patriarchal poetry at one time.

Allowed allowed allowed makes it be theirs once once as they had had it have having have have having having is the same.

Patriarchal Poetry is the same.

Patriarchal Poetry.

It is very well and nicely done in Patriarchal Poetry which is begun to be begun and this was why if when if when when did they please themselves indeed. When he did not say leave it to that but rather indeed as if it might be that it was not expressed simultaneously was expressed to be no more as it is very well to trouble him. He will attend to it in time. Be very well accustomed to this in that and plan. There is not only no accounting for tastes but very well identified extra coming out very well identified as repeated verdure and so established as more than for it.

She asked as she came down should she and at that moment there was no answer but if leaving it alone meant all by it out of it all by it very truly and could be used to plainly plainly expressed. She will be determined determined not by but on account of implication implication re-entered which means entered again and upon.

This could be illustrated and is and is and is. There makes more than contain contained mine too. Very well to please please.

Once in a while.

Patriarchal poetry once in a while.

Patriarchal Poetry out of pink once in a while.

Patriarchal Poetry out of pink to be bird once in a while.

Patriarchal Poetry out of pink to be bird left and three once in a while.

Patriarchal Poetry handles once in a while.

Patriarchal Poetry once in a while.

Patriarchal Poetry once in a while.

Patriarchal Poetry to be added.

Patriarchal Poetry reconciled.

Patriarchal Poetry left alone.

Patriarchal Poetry and left of it left of it Patriarchal Poetry left of it Patriarchal poetry left of it as many twice as many patriarchal poetry left to it twice as many once as it was once it was once every once in a while patriarchal poetry every once in a while.

Patriarchal Poetry might have been in two. Patriarchal Poetry added to added to to once to be once in two Patriarchal poetry to be added to once to add to to add to patriarchal poetry to add to to be to be to add to to add to patriarchal poetry to add to.

One little two little one little two little one little at one time one little one little two little two little two little at one at a time.

One little one little two little two little one little two little as to two little as to two little as to one little as to one two little as to two two little two. Two little two little two little one little two one two one two little two. One little one little one little two little two little one little two one little two.

Need which need which as it is need which need which as it is very need which need which it is very warm here is it.

Need which need which need need in need need which need which is it need in need which need which need which is it.

Need in need need which is it.

What is the difference between a fig and an apple. One comes before the other. What is the difference between a fig and an apple one comes before the other what is the difference between a fig and an apple one comes before the other.

When they are here they are here too here too they are here too. When they are here they are here too when they are here they are here too.

As out in it there.

As not out not out in it there as out in it out in it there as put in it there as not out in it there as out in as out in it as out in it there.

Next to next next to Saturday next to next next to Saturday next to next next to Saturday.

This shows it all.

This shows it all next to next next to Saturday this shows it all.

Once or twice or once or twice once or twice or once or twice this shows it all or next to next this shows it all or once or twice or once or twice or once or twice this shows it all or next to next this shows it all or next to next or Saturday or next to next this shows it all or next to next or next to next or Saturday or next to next or once or twice this shows it all or next to next or once or twice this shows it all or Saturday or next to next this shows it all or once or twice this shows it all or Saturday or next to next or once or twice this shows it all or once or twice this shows it all or next to next this shows it all or once or twice this shows it all or next to next or once or twice or once or twice this shows it all or next to next this shows it all or once or twice this shows it all or next to next or once or twice this shows it all or next to next or next to next or next to next or once or twice or once or twice or next to next or next to next or once or twice this shows it all this shows it all or once or twice or next to next this shows it all or next to next this shows it all or next to next this shows it all or next to next this shows it all or next to next this shows it all or next to next this shows it all or once or twice or once or twice this shows it all or once or twice or next to next this shows it all this shows it all or next to next or shows it all or once or twice this shows it all or shows it all or next to next or once or twice or shows it all or once or twice or next to next or next to next or once or twice or next to next or next to next or shows it all or shows it all or next to next or once or twice or shows it all or next to next or shows it all or next to next or shows it all or once or twice or next to next or next to next or next to next or next or next or next or next or shows it all or next or next or next to next or shows it all or next to next to next to next to next.

Not needed near nearest.

Settle it pink with pink.

Pinkily.

Find it a time at most.

Time it at most at most.

Every differs from Avery Avery differs from every within.

As it is as it is as it is as it is in line as it is in line with it.

Next to be with it next to be with it with it with with with it next to it with it with it. Return with it.

Even if it did not touch it would you like to give it would you like to give it give me my even if it did not touch it would you like to give me my. Even if you like to give it if you did not touch it would you like to give me my.

One divided into into what what is it.

As left to left left to it here left to it here which is not queer which is not queer where when when most when most and best what is the difference between breakfast lunch supper and dinner what is the difference between breakfast and lunch and supper and dinner.

She had it here who to who to she had it here who to she had it here who to she had it here who to she had it here who to who to she had it here who to. Who to she had it here who to.

Not and is added added is and not added added is not and added added is and not added added added is not and added added not and is added added is and is added added and is not and added added and is not and added added is and is not added added is and not and added added is and not and added.

Let leave it out be out let leave it out be out be out let leave it out be out let leave it out be out. Let leave it out be out let leave it out be out. Let leave it out be out. Let leave it out. Let leave it out. Let. Let leave it out. Let leave it out. Let leave it out.

Eighty eighty one which is why to be after one one two Seattle blue and feathers they change which is why to blame it once or twice singly to be sure.

A day as to say a day two to say to say a day a day to say to say to say to say a day as to-day to say as to say to-day. To dates dates different from here and there from here and there.

Let it be arranged for them.

What is the difference between Elizabeth and Edith. She knows. There is no difference between Elizabeth and Edith that she knows. What is the difference. She knows. There is no difference as she knows. What is the difference between Elizabeth and Edith that she knows. There is the difference between Elizabeth and Edith which she knows. There is she knows a difference between Elizabeth and Edith which she knows. Elizabeth and Edith as she knows.

Contained in time forty makes forty-nine. Contained in time as forty makes forty-nine contained in time contained in time as forty makes forty-nine contained in time as forty makes forty-nine.

Forty-nine more or at the door.

Forty-nine or more or as before. Forty-nine or fifty-nine or forty-nine.

I wish to sit with Elizabeth who is sitting. I wish to sit with

Elizabeth who is sitting I wish to sit with Elizabeth who is sitting. I wish to sit with Elizabeth who is sitting.

Forty-nine or four attached to them more more than they were as well as they were as often as they are once or twice before.

As peculiarly mine in time.

Reform the past and not the future this is what the past can teach her reform the past and not the future which can be left to be here now here now as it is made to be made to be here now here now.

Reform the future not the past as fast as last as first as third as had as hand it as it happened to be why they did. Did two too two were sent one at once and one afterwards.

Afterwards.

How can patriarchal poetry be often praised often praised.

To get away from me.

She came in.

Wishes.

She went in

Fishes.

She sat in the room

Yes she did.

Patriarchal poetry.

She was where they had it be nearly as nicely in arrangement.

In arrangement.

To be sure.

What is the difference between ardent and ardently.

Leave it alone.

If one does not care to eat if one does not care to eat oysters one has no interest in lambs.

That is as usual.

Everything described as in a way in a way in a way gradually.

Likes to be having it come.

Likes to be.

Having it come.

Have not had that.

Around.

One two three one two three one two three one two three four.

Find it again.
When you said when.
When you said
When you said
When you said when.
Find it again.
Find it again
When you said when.
They said they said.
They said they said they said when they said men.
Men many men many how many many many many men men men said many here.
Many here said many many said many which frequently allowed later in recollection many many said when as naturally to be sure.
Very many as to that which which which one which which which which one.
Patriarchal poetry relined.
It is at least last let letting letting letting letting it be theirs.
Theirs at least letting at least letting it be theirs.
Letting it be at least be letting it be theirs.
Letting it be theirs at least letting it be theirs.
When she was as was she was as was she was not yet neither pronounced so and tempted.
Not this this is the way that they make it theirs not they.
Not they.
Patriarchal Poetry makes mistakes.
One two one two my baby is who one two one two one two my baby or two one two. One two one one or two one one one one one one one one or two. Are to.
It is very nearly a pleasure to be warm.
It is very nearly a pleasure to be warm.
It is very nearly a pleasure to be warm.
A line a day book.
One which is mine.
Two in time
Let it alone
Theirs as well
Having it now
Letting it be their share.

Settled it at once.

Liking it or not

How do you do.

It.

Very well very well seriously.

Patriarchal Poetry defined.

Patriarchal Poetry should be this without which and organisation. It should be defined as once leaving once leaving it here having been placed in that way at once letting this be with them after all. Patriarchal Poetry makes it a master piece like this makes it which which alone makes like it like it previously to know that it that that might that might be all very well patriarchal poetry might be resumed.

How do you do it.

Patriarchal poetry might be withstood.

Patriarchal Poetry at peace.

Patriarchal Poetry a piece.

Patriarchal Poetry in peace.

Patriarchal Poetry in pieces.

Patriarchal Poetry as peace to return to Patriarchal Poetry at peace.

Patriarchal Poetry or peace to return to Patriarchal Poetry or pieces of Patriarchal Poetry.

Very pretty very prettily very prettily very pretty very prettily.

To never blame them for the mischance of eradicating this and that by then.

Not at the time not at that time not in time to do it. Not a time to do it. Patriarchal Poetry or not a time to do it.

Patriarchal Poetry or made a way patriarchal Poetry tenderly.

Patriarchal Poetry or made a way patriarchal poetry or made a way patriarchal poetry as well as even seen even seen clearly even seen clearly and under and over overtake overtaken by it now. Patriarchal Poetry and replace. Patriarchal Poetry and enough. Patriarchal Poetry and at pains to allow them this and that that it would be plentifully as aroused and leaving leaving it exactly as they might with it all be be careful carefully in that and arranging arrangement adapted adapting in regulating regulate and see seat seating send sent by nearly as withstand precluded in this instance veritably in reunion re-union attached to intermediate remarked remarking plentiful and theirs at once. Patriarchal Poetry has that return.

Patriarchal Poetry might be what is left.

Indifferently.

In differently undertaking their being there there to them there to them with them with their pleasure pleasurable recondite and really really relieve relieving remain remade to be sure certainly and in and and on on account account to be nestled and nestling as understood which with regard to it if when and more leave leaving lying where it was as when when in in this this to be in finally to see so so that that should always be refused refusing refusing makes it have have it having having hinted hindered and implicated resist resist was to be exchanged as to be for for it in never having as there can be shared sharing letting it land lie lie to adjacent to see me. When it goes quickly they must choose Patriarchal Poetry originally originate as originating believe believing repudiate repudiating an impulse. It is not left to right to-day to stay. When this you see remember me should never be added to that.

Patriarchal Poetry and remind reminding clearly come came and left instantly with their entire consenting to be enclosed within what is exacting which might and might and partaking of mentioning much of it to be to be this is mine left to them in place of how very nicely it can be planted so as to be productive even if necessarily there is no effort left to them by their having previously made it be nearly able to be found finding where where it is when it is very likely to be this in the demand of remaining. Patriarchal Poetry intimately and intimating that it is to be so as plead. Plead can have to do with room. Room noon and nicely.

Even what was gay.

Easier in left.

Easier in an left.

Easier an left

Easier in an left.

Horticulturally.

Easier in august.

Easier an august.

Easier an in august
Howard.
Easier how housed.
Ivory
Ivoried.
Less
Lest.
Like it can be used in joining gs.
By principally.
Led
Leaden haul
Leaden haul if it hails
Let them you see
Useful makes buttercup buttercup hyacinth too makes it be lilied by water and you.
That is the way they ended.
It.
It was was it.
You jump in the dark, when it is very bright very bright very bright now.
Very bright now.
Might might tell me.
Withstand.
In second second time time to be next next which is not convincing convincing inhabitable that much that much there.
As one to go.
Letting it letting it letting it alone.
Finally as to be sure.
Selecting that that to that selecting that to that to that all that. All and and and and and and it it is very well thought out.
What is it.
Aim less.
What is it.
Aim less
Sword less.
What is it
Sword less
What is it
Aim less

What is it.

What is it aim less what is it.

It did so.

It did so.

Said so

Said it did so.

Said it did so did so said so said it did so just as any one might.

Said it did so just as any one might said it did so said so just as any one might.

If water is softened who softened water.

Patriarchal Poetry means in return for that.

Patriarchal poetry means in return.

Nettles nettles her.

Nettle nettle her.

Nettle nettle nettle her nettles nettles nettles her nettle nettle nettle her nettles nettles nettles her. It nettles her to nettle her to nettle her exchange it nettles her exchange to nettle her exchange it nettles her.

Made a mark remarkable made a remarkable interpretation made a remarkable made a remarkable made a remarkable interpretation made a remarkable interpretation now and made a remarkable made a remarkable interpretation made a mark made a remarkable made a remarkable interpretation made a remarkable interpretation now and here here out here out here. The more to change. Hours and hours. The more to change hours and hours the more to change hours and hours.

It was a pleasant hour however however it was a pleasant hour, it was a pleasant hour however it was a pleasant hour resemble hour however it was a pleasant however it was a pleasant hour resemble hour assemble however hour it was a pleasant hour however.

Patriarchal Poetry in assemble.

Assemble Patriarchal Poetry in assemble it would be assemble assemble Patriarchal Poetry in assemble.

It would be Patriarchal Poetry in assemble.

Assemble Patriarchal Poetry resign resign Patriarchal Poetry to believe in trees.

Early trees.

Assemble moss roses and to try.

Assemble Patriarchal Poetry moss roses resemble patriarchal Poetry assign assign to it assemble Patriarchal Poetry resemble moss roses to try.

Patriarchal Poetry resemble to try.

Moss roses assemble Patriarchal Poetry resign lost a lost to try. Resemble Patriarchal Poetry to love to.

To wish to does.

Patriarchal Poetry to why.

Patriarchal Poetry ally.

Patriarchal Poetry with to try to all ally to ally to wish to why to. Why did it seem originally look as well as very nearly pronounceably satisfy lining.

To by to by that by by a while any any stay stationary.

Stationary has been invalidated.

And not as surprised.

Patriarchal Poetry surprised supposed.

Patriarchal Poetry she did she did.

Did she Patriarchal Poetry.

Is to be periwinkle which she met which is when it is astounded and come yet as she did with this in this and this let in their to be sure it wishes it for them an instance in this as this allows allows it to to be sure now when it is as well as it is and has ever been outlined.

There are three things that are different pillow pleasure prepare and after awhile. There are two things that they prepare maidenly see it and ask it as it if has been where they went. There are enough to go. One thing altogether altogether as he might. Might he.

Never to do never to do never to do to do to do never to do never to do never to do to do to do to do never to do never never to do to do it as if it were an anemone an anemone an anemone to be an anemone to be to be certain to let to let it to let it alone.

What is the difference between two spoonfuls and three. None.

Patriarchal Poetry as signed.

Patriarchal Poetry might which it is very well very well leave it to me very well patriarchal poetry leave it to me leave it to me. Leave it to leave it to me naturally to see the second and third first naturally first naturally to see naturally to first see the second and third first to see to see the second and third to see the second and third naturally to see it first.

Not as well said as she said regret that regret that not as well said as she said Patriarchal Poetry as well said as she said it Patriarchal Poetry untied. Patriarchal Poetry.

Do we.

What is the difference between Mary and May. What is the difference between May and day. What is the difference between day and daughter what is the difference between daughter and there what is the difference between there and day-light what is the difference between day-light and let what is the difference between let and letting what is the difference between letting and to see what is the difference between to see immediately patriarchal poetry and rejoice.

Patriarchal Poetry made and made.

Patriarchal Poetry makes a land a lamb. There is no use at all in reorganising in reorganising. There is no use at all in reorganising chocolate as a dainty.

Patriarchal Poetry reheard.

Patriarchal Poetry to be filled to be filled to be filled to be filled to method method who hears method method who hears who hears who hears method method method who hears who hears who hears and method and method and method and who hears and who who hears and method method is delightful and who and who who hears method is method is method is delightful is who hears is delightful who hears method is who hears method is method is method is delightful is delightful who hears who hears of of delightful who hears of method of delightful who of whom of whom of of who hears of method method is delightful. Unified in their expanse. Unified in letting there there there one two one two three there in a chain a chain how do you laterally in relation to auditors and obliged obliged currently.

Patriarchal Poetry is the same.

Patriarchal Poetry thirteen.

With or with willing with willing mean.

I mean I mean.

Patriarchal Poetry connected with mean.

Queen with willing.

With willing.

Patriarchal Poetry obtained with seize.

Willing.

Patriarchal Poetry in chance to be found.

Patriarchal Poetry obliged as mint to be mint to be mint to be obliged as mint to be.

Mint may be come to be as well as cloud and best.

Patriarchal Poetry deny why.

Patriarchal Poetry come by the way to go.

Patriarchal Poetry interdicted.

Patriarchal Poetry at best.

Best and Most.

Long and Short.

Left and Right.

There and More.

Near and Far.

Gone and come.

Light and Fair.

Here and There.

This and Now.

Felt and How

Next and Near.

In and On.

New and Try

In and This.

Which and Felt.

Come and Leave.

By and Well.

Returned.

Patriarchal Poetry indeed.

Patriarchal Poetry which is let it be come from having a mild and came and same and with it all.

Near.

To be shelled from almond.

Return Patriarchal Poetry at this time.

Begin with a little ruff a little ruffle.

Return with all that.

Returned with all that four and all that returned with four with all that.

How many daisies are there in it.
How many daisies are there in it.
How many daisies are there in it.
How many daisies are there in it.
A line a day book.
How many daisies are there in it.
Patriarchal Poetry a line a day book.
Patriarchal Poetry.
A line a day book.
Patriarchal Poetry.
When there is in it.
When there is in it.
A line a day book.
When there is in it.
Patriarchal Poetry a line a day book when there is in it.
By that time lands lands there.
By that time lands there a line a day book when there is that in it.

Patriarchal Poetry reclaimed renamed replaced and gathered together as they went in and left it more where it is in when it pleased when it was pleased when it can be pleased to be gone over carefully and letting it be a chance for them to lead to lead to lead not only by left but by leaves.

They made it be obstinately in their change and with it with it let it let it leave it in the opportunity. Who comes to be with a glance with a glance at it at it in palms and palms too orderly to orderly in changes of plates and places and beguiled beguiled with a restless impression of having come to be all of it as might as might as might and she encouraged. Patriarchal Poetry might be as useless. With a with a with a won and delay. With a with a with a won and delay.

He might object to it not being there as they were left to them all around. As we went out by the same way we came back again after a detour.

That is one account on one account.

Having found anemones and a very few different shelves we were for a long time just staying by the time that it could have been as desirable. Desirable makes it be left to them.

Patriarchal Poetry includes not being received.

Patriarchal Poetry comes suddenly as around.

And now.

There is no difference between spring and summer none at all.

And wishes.

Patriarchal Poetry there is no difference between spring and summer not at all and wishes.

There is no difference between spring and summer not at all and wishes.

There is no difference not at all between spring and summer not at all and wishes.

Yes as well.

And how many times.

Yes as well and how many times yes as well.

How many times yes as well ordinarily.

Having marked yes as well ordinarily having marked yes as well.

It was to be which is theirs left in this which can have all their thinking it as fine.

It was to be which is theirs left in this which is which is which can which can which may which may which will which will which in which in which are they know they know to care for it having come back without and it would be better if there had not been any at all to find to find to find. It is not desirable to mix what he did with adding adding to choose to choose. Very well part of her part of her very well part of her. Very well part of her. Patriarchal Poetry in pears. There is no choice of cherries.

Will he do.

Patriarchal Poetry in coins.

Not what it is.

Patriarchal Poetry net in it pleases. Patriarchal Poetry surplus if rather admittedly in repercussion instance and glance separating letting dwindling be in knife to be which is not wound wound entirely as white wool white will white change white see white settle white understand white in the way white be lighten lighten let letting bear this nearly nearly made in vain.

Patriarchal Poetry who seats seasons patriarchal poetry in gather meanders patriarchal poetry engaging this in their place their place their allow. Patriarchal Poetry. If he has no farther no farther no farther to no farther to no farther to no to no to farther to not to be right to be known to be even as a chance. Is it best to support Allan Allan will Allan Allan is it best to support Allan Allan patriarchal poetry patriarchal poetry is it best to support Allan Allan will Allan best to support Allan will patriarchal poetry Allan will patriarchal poetry Allan will patriarchal poetry is it best to support Allan patriarchal poetry Allan will is it best Allan will is it best to support Allan patriarchal poetry Allan will best to support patriarchal poetry Allan will is it best Allan will to support patriarchal poetry patriarchal poetry Allan will patriarchal poetry Allan will.

Is it best to support patriarchal poetry Allan will patriarchal poetry.

Patriarchal Poetry makes it incumbent to know on what day races will take place and where otherwise there would be much inconvenience everywhere.

Patriarchal Poetry erases what is eventually their purpose and their inclination and their reception and their without their being beset. Patriarchal poetry an entity.

What is the difference between their charm and to charm.

Patriarchal Poetry in negligence.

Patriarchal Poetry they do not follow that they do not follow that this does not follow that this does not follow that theirs does not follow that theirs does not follow that the not following that the not following that having decided not to abandon a sister for another. This makes patriarchal poetry in their place in their places in their places in the place in the place of is it in the next to it as much as aroused feeling so feeling it feeling at once to be in the wish and what is it of theirs. Suspiciously. Patriarchal poetry for instance. Patriarchal poetry not minded not minded it. In now. Patriarchal poetry left to renown. Renown.

It is very certainly better not to be what is it when it is in the afternoon.

Patriarchal poetry which is it. Which is it after it is after it is after it is after before soon when it is by the time that when they make let it be not only because why should why should why should it all be fine.

Patriarchal poetry they do not do it right.

Patriarchal poetry letting it be alright.

Patriarchal poetry having it placed where it is.

Patriarchal poetry might have it.

Might have it.

Patriarchal poetry a choice.

Patriarchal poetry because of it.

Patriarchal poetry replaced.

Patriarchal Poetry withstood and placated.

Patriarchal Poetry in arrangement.

Patriarchal Poetry that day.

Patriarchal Poetry might it be very likely which is it as it can be very precisely unified as tries.

Patriarchal poetry with them lest they be stated.

Patriarchal poetry. He might be he might be be might be be might be.

Patriarchal poetry a while a way.

Patriarchal poetry if patriarchal poetry is what you say why do you delight in never having positively made it choose.

Patriarchal poetry never linking patriarchal poetry.

Sometime not a thing.

Patriarchal poetry sometimes not anything.

Patriarchal Poetry which which which which is it.

Patriarchal Poetry left to them.

Patriarchal poetry left together.

Patriarchal Poetry does not like to be allowed after a while to be what is more formidably forget me nots anemones china lilies plants articles chances printing pears and likely meant very likely meant to be given to him.

Patriarchal Poetry would concern itself with when it is in their happening to be left about left about now.

There is no interest in resemblances.

Patriarchal poetry one at a time.

This can be so.

To by any way.

Patriarchal poetry in requesting in request in request best patriarchal poetry leave that alone.

Patriarchal poetry noise noiselessly.

Patriarchal poetry not in fact in fact.

After patriarchal poetry.

I defy any one to turn a better heel than that while reading.

Patriarchal poetry reminded.

Patriarchal poetry reminded of it.

Patriarchal poetry reminded of it too.

Patriarchal Poetry reminded of it too to be sure.

Patriarchal Poetry reminded of it too to be sure really. Really left.

Patriarchal Poetry and crackers in that case.

Patriarchal Poetry and left bread in that case.

Patriarchal Poetry and might in that case.

Patriarchal Poetry connected in that case with it.

Patriarchal Poetry make it do a day.

Is he fond of him.

If he is fond of him if he is fond of him is he fond of his birthday the next day. If he is fond of his birthday the next day is he fond of the birthday trimming if he is fond of the birthday the day is he fond of the day before the day before the day of the day before the birthday. Every day is a birthday the day before. Patriarchal Poetry the day before.

Patriarchal Poetry the day that it might.

Patriarchal Poetry does not make it never made it will not have been making it be that way in their behalf.

Patriarchal Poetry insistance.

Insist.

Patriarchal Poetry insist insistance.

Patriarchal Poetry which is which is it.

Patriarchal Poetry and left it left it by left it by left it. Patriarchal Poetry what is the difference patriarchal Poetry.

Patriarchal Poetry.

Not patriarchal poetry all at a time.

To find patriarchal poetry about.

Patriarchal Poetry is named patriarchal poetry.

If patriarchal poetry is nearly by nearly means it to be to be so.

Patriarchal Poetry and for them then.

Patriarchal Poetry did he leave his son.

Patriarchal poetry Gabrielle did her share.

Patriarchal poetry it is curious.

Patriarchal poetry please place better.

Patriarchal poetry in come I mean I mean.

Patriarchal poetry they do their best at once more once more once more once more to do to do would it be left to advise advise realise realise dismay dismay delighted with her pleasure.

Patriarchal poetry left to inundate them.

Patriarchal Poetry in pieces. Pieces which have left it as names which have left it as names to to all said all said as delight.

Patriarchal poetry the difference.

Patriarchal poetry needed with weeded with seeded with payed it with left it with out it with me. When this you see give it to me.

Patriarchal poetry makes it be have you it here.

Patriarchal poetry twice.

Patriarchal Poetry in time.

It should be left.

Patriarchal Poetry with him.

Patriarchal Poetry.

Patriarchal Poetry at a time.

Patriarchal Poetry not patriarchal poetry.

Patriarchal Poetry as wishes.

Patriarchal poetry might be found here.

Patriarchal poetry interested as that.

Patriarchal Poetry left.

Patriarchal Poetry left left.

Patriarchal poetry left left left right left.

Patriarchal poetry in justice.

Patriarchal poetry in sight.

Patriarchal poetry in what is what is what is what.

Patriarchal poetry might to-morrow.

Patriarchal poetry might be finished to-morrow.

Dinky pinky dinky pinky dinky pinky dinky pinky once and try. Dinky pinky dinky pinky dinky pinky lullaby. Once sleepy one once does not once need a lullaby. Not to try.

Patriarchal Poetry not to try. Patriarchal Poetry and lullaby. Patriarchal Poetry not to try Patriarchal poetry at once and why patriarchal poetry at once and by by and by Patriarchal poetry has to be which is best for them at three which is best and will be be and why why patriarchal poetry is not to try try twice.

Patriarchal Poetry having patriarchal poetry. Having patriarchal poetry having patriarchal poetry. Having patriarchal poetry. Having patriarchal poetry and twice, patriarchal poetry.

He might have met.

Patriarchal poetry and twice patriarchal poetry.

Four Saints in Three Acts

An Opera To Be Sung

To know to know to love her so.
Four saints prepare for saints.
It makes it well fish.
Four saints it makes it well fish.
Four saints prepare for saints it makes it well well fish
it makes it well fish prepare for saints.
In narrative prepare for saints.
Prepare for saints.
Two saints.
Four saints.
Two saints prepare for saints it two saints prepare for
saints in prepare for saints.
A narrative of prepare for saints in narrative prepare for
saints.
Remain to narrate to prepare two saints for saints.
At least.
In finally.
Very well if not to have and miner.
A saint is one to be for two when three and you make
five and two and cover.
A at most.
Saint saint a saint.
Forgotten saint.
What happened to-day, a narrative.
We had intended if it were a pleasant day to go to the
country it was a very beautiful day and we carried out our
intention. We went to places that we had seen when we were
equally pleased and we found very nearly what we could find
and returning saw and heard that after all they were rewarded
and likewise. This makes it necessary to go again.
He came and said he was hurrying hurrying and hurrying to remain he said he said finally to be and claim it he
said he said feeling very nearly everything as it had been as if
he could be precious be precious to like like it as it had been

that if he was used it would always do it good and now this time that it was as if it had been just the same as longer when as before it made it be left to be sure and soft softly then can be changed to theirs and speck a speck of it makes blue be often sooner which is shared when theirs is in polite and reply that in their be the same with diminish always in respect to not at all and farther farther might be known as counted with it gain to be in retain which it is not be because of most. This is how they do not like it.

Why while while in that way was it after this that to be seen made left it.

He could be hurt at that.

It is very easy to be land.

Imagine four benches separately.

One in the sun.

Two in the sun.

Three in the sun.

One not in the sun.

Not one not in the sun.

Not one.

Four benches used four benches used separately.

Four benches used separately.

That makes it be not be makes it not be at the time.

The time that it is as well as it could be leave it when when it was to be that it was to be when it was went away.

Four benches with leave it.

Might have as would be as would be as within within nearly as out. It is very close close and closed. Closed closed to let letting closed close close close chose in justice in join in joining. This is where to be at at water at snow snow show show one one sun and sun snow show and no water no water unless unless why unless. Why unless why unless they were loaning it here loaning intentionally. Believe two three. What could be sad beside beside very attentively intentionally and bright.

Begin suddenly not with sisters.

If a great many people were deceived who would be by the way.

To mount it up.

Up hill.

Four saints are never three.
Three saints are never four.
Four saints are never left altogether.
Three saints are never idle.
Four saints are leave it to me.
Three saints when this you see.
Begin three saints.
Begin four saints.
Two and two saints.
One and three saints.
In place.
One should do it.
Easily saints.
Very well saints.
Have saints.
Said saints.
As said saints.
And not annoy.
Annoint.
Choice.
Four saints two at a time have to have to have to have to.
Have to have have to have to.
Two saints four at a time a time.
Have to have to at a time.
Four saints have to have to have at a time.

The difference between saints forget me nots and mountains have to have to have to at a time.

It is very easy in winter to remember winter spring and summer it is very easy in winter to remember spring and winter and summer it is very easy in winter to remember summer spring and winter it is very easy in winter to remember spring and summer and winter.

Does it show as if it could be that very successful that very successful that he was very successful that he was with them with them with them as it was not better than at worst that he could follow him to be taking it away away that way a way a way to go.

Some say some say some say so.

Why should every one be at home why should every one be at home why should every one be at home.

Why should every one be at home.
In idle acts.
Why should everybody be at home.
In idle acts.

He made very much more than he did he did make very much of it he did not only add to his part of it but and with it he was at and in a plight.

There is no parti parti-colour in a house there is no parti parti parti-colour in a house. Reflections by the time that they were given the package that had been sent. Very much what they could would do as a decision.

Supposing she said that he had chosen all the miseries that he had observed in fifty of his years what had that to do with hats. They had made hats for her. Not really.

As she was.

Imagine imagine it imagine it in it. When she returned there was considerable rain.

In some on some evening it would be asked was there anything especial.

By and by plain plainly in making acutely a corner not at right angle but in individual in individual is it.

How can it have been have been held.

A narrative who do who does.

A narrative to plan an opera.

Four saints in three acts.

A croquet scene and when they made their habits. Habits not hourly habits habits not hourly at the time that they made their habits not hourly they made their habits.

When they made their habits.

To know when they made their habits.

Large pigeons in small trees.

Large pigeons in small trees.

Come panic come.

Come close.

Acts three acts.

Come close to croquet.

Four saints.

Rejoice saints rejoin saints recommence some reinvite.

Four saints have been sometime in that way that way all hall.

Four saints were not born at one time although they knew each other. One of them had a birthday before the mother of the other one the father. Four saints later to be if to be one to be to be one to be. Might tingle.

Tangle wood tanglewood.

Four saints born in separate places.

Saint saint saint saint.

Four saints an opera in three acts.

My country tis of thee sweet land of liberty of thee I sing.

Saint Therese something like that.

Saint Therese something like that.

Saint Therese would and would and would.

Saint Therese something like that.

Saint Therese.

Saint Therese half in doors and half out out of doors.

Saint Therese not knowing of other saints.

Saint Therese used to go not to to tell them so but to around so that Saint Therese did find that that that and there. If any came.

This is to say that four saints may may never have seen the day, like. Any day like.

Saint Ignatius. Meant and met.

This is to say that four saints may never have. Any day like.

Gradually wait.

Any one can see that any saint to be.

Saint Therese	Saint Ignatius
Saint Martyr	Saint Paul
Saint Settlement	Saint William
Saint Thomasine	Saint Gilbert
Saint Electra	Saint Settle
Saint Wilhelmina	Saint Arthur
Saint Evelyn	Saint Selmer
Saint Pilar	Saint Paul Seize
Saint Hillaire	Saint Cardinal
Saint Bernadine	Saint Plan
	Saint Guiseppe

Any one to tease a saint seriously.

ACT ONE

Saint Therese in a storm at Avila there can be rain and warm snow and warm that is the water is warm the river is not warm the sun is not warm and if to stay to cry. If to stay to if to stay if having to stay to if having to stay if to cry to stay if to cry stay to cry to stay.

Saint Therese half in and half out of doors.

Saint Ignatius not there. Saint Ignatius staying where. Never heard them speak speak of it.

Saint Ignatius silent motive not hidden.

Saint Therese silent. They were never beset.

Come one come one.

No saint to remember to remember. No saint to remember.

Saint Therese knowing young and told.

If it were possible to kill five thousand chinamen by pressing a button would it be done.

Saint Therese not interested.

Repeat First Act.

A pleasure April fool's day a pleasure.

Saint Therese seated.

Not April fool's day a pleasure.

Saint Therese seated.

Not April fool's day a pleasure.

Saint Therese seated.

April fool's day April fool's day as not as pleasure as April fool's day not a pleasure.

Saint Therese seated and not surrounded. There are a great many persons and places near together. Saint Therese not seated there are a great many persons and places near together.

Saint Therese not seated.

There are a great many persons and places near together.

Saint Therese not seated at once. There are a great many places and persons near together.

Saint Therese once seated. There are a great many places and persons near together. Saint Therese seated and not surrounded. There are a great many places and persons near together.

Saint Therese visited by very many as well as the others really visited before she was seated.

There are a great many persons and places close together.

Saint Therese not young and younger but visited like the others by some, who are frequently going there.

Saint Therese very nearly half inside and half outside outside the house and not surrounded.

How do you do. Very well I thank you. And when do you go. I am staying on quite continuously. When is it planned. Not more than as often.

The garden inside and outside of the wall.

Saint Therese about to be.

The garden inside and outside outside and inside of the wall.

Nobody visits more than they do visits them.

Saint Therese   Nobody visits more than they do visits them Saint Therese.

As loud as that as allowed as that.

Saint Therese   Nobody visits more than they do visit them.

Who settles a private life.

Saint Therese   Who settles a private life.
Saint Therese   Who settles a private life.
Saint Therese   Who settles a private life.
Saint Therese   Who settles a private life.

Enact end of an act.

All of it to be not to be not to be left to be to him and standing.

Saint Therese seated.

Left to be not to be not to be left to be left to be and left to be not to be.

Saint Therese seated and if he could be standing and standing and saying and saying left to be.

Introducing Saint Ignatius.

Left to be.

Saint Therese seated seated and left to be if to be if left to be if left if to be

Saint Ignatius standing.

She has no one to say so.

He said so actually.

She can have no one no one can have any one any one can have not any one can have not any one can have can have to say so.

Saint Therese seated and not standing half and half of it and not half and half of it seated and not standing surrounded and not seated and not seated and not standing and not surrounded and not surrounded and not not not seated not seated not seated not surrounded not seated and Saint Ignatius standing standing not seated Saint Therese not standing not standing and Saint Ignatius not standing standing surrounded as if in once yesterday. In place of situations. Saint Therese could be very much interested not only in settlement Saint Settlement and this not with with this wither wither they must be additional.

Saint Therese having not commenced.

Did she want him dead if now.

Saint Therese could be photographed having been dressed like a lady and then they taking out her head changed it to a nun and a nun a saint and a saint so.

Saint Therese seated and not surrounded might be very well inclined to be settled.

Saint Therese actively.

Made to be coming to be here.

How many saints can sit around. A great many saints can sit around with one standing.

Saint Therese a great many saints seated.

They move through the country in winter in winter entirely.

Saint Therese in moving. Now three can be seated in front.

A saint is easily resisted Saint Therese. Let it as land

Saint Therese. As land beside a house. Saint Therese. As land beside a house and at one time Saint Therese.

Saint Therese   As land beside a house to be to this this
                     which theirs beneath Saint Therese.

Saint Therese saints make sugar with a flavour. In different ways when it is practicable.

Saint Therese in invitation.

Saint Therese   Could she know that that he was not not
                     to be to be very to be dead not dead.

Saint Therese so much to be with it withheld with that.

Saint Therese   Nobody can do so.

Saint Therese   Saint Therese must be must be chain left
                     chain right chain chain is it. No one chain
                     is it not chain is it, chained to not to life
                     chained to not to snow chained to chained
                     to go and and gone.

Saint Therese might be come to be in this not indifferently.

Saint Therese   Not this not in this not with this.

Saint Therese must be theirs first.

Saint Therese as a young girl being widowed.

Saint Therese   Can she sing.

Saint Therese   Leave later gaily the troubadour plays his
                     guitar.

Saint Therese might it be Martha.

Saint Louise and Saint Celestine and Saint Louis Paul and Saint Settlement.

Fernande and Ignatius

Saint Therese   Can women have wishes.

Scene Two

Many saints seen and in between many saints seen.

Saint Therese and Saint Therese and Saint Therese.

Many saints as seen and in between as many saints as seen.

Seen as seen.

Many saints as seen.

Saint Therese and sound.
She is to meet her.
Can two saints be one.
Saint Therese and fastening.
Very many go out as they they do.

Saint Therese   And make him prominent.

Saint Therese   Could a negro be be with a beard to see and to be.

Saint Therese   Never have to have seen a negro there and with it so.

Saint Therese   To differ between go and so.

Saint Therese and three saints all me. Saint Settlement Saint Fernande Saint John Seize Saint Paul Six.
Saint Therese with three saints.

           Who separated saints at one time.

Saint Therese   In follow and saints.

Saint Therese   To be somewhere with or without saints.

Saint Therese can never mention the others.

Saint Therese to   Saints not found. All four saints not more them   than all four saints.

Saint Therese come again to be absent.

Scene Three

Saint Therese   To an occasion louder.

Saint Therese coming to be selfish.
Saint Therese allow.
All four saints remembering not to be with them. Could all four saints not only be in brief.

Saint Therese   Contumely

Saint Therese advancing. Who can be shortly in their way.
Saint Therese having heard. In this way as movement. In having been in.

Does she want to be neglectful of hyacinths and find violets. Saint Therese should never change herbs for pansies and dry them.

They think there that it is their share.
And please.
Saint Therese makes as in this to be as stems.

And while.
Saint Therese settled and some come. Some come to be near not near her but the same.

Surround them with the thirds and that.

Saint Therese might be illustrated. Come to be in between.

Beginning earlier.

And anything.

Around.

Saint Therese seated with the name and choosing.   How many are there halving.

Scene Three

Therese in Saint Ignatius and Saint Settlement to be sure.

Saint Therese having known that no snow in vain as snow is not rain.

Saint Therese needed it as she was.

Saint Therese made it be third. Snow third high third there third.

Saint Therese in allowance.

How many saints can remember a house which was built before they can remember.

Ten saints can.

How many saints can be and land be and sand be and on a high plateau there is no sand there is snow and there is made to be so and very much can be what there is to see when there is a wind to have it dry and be what they can understand to undertake to let it be to send it well as much as more to be to be behind. None to be behind. Enclosure.
Saint Therese   None to be behind. Enclosure.
Saint Ignatius could be in porcelain actually.
Saint Ignatius could be in porcelain actually while he was young and standing.
Saint Therese could not be young and standing she could be sitting.
Saint Ignatius could be in porcelain actually actually in porcelain standing.

Saint Therese could be admittedly could be in moving seating.
Saint Therese could be in moving sitting.
Saint Therese could be.
Saint Ignatius could be
Saint Ignatius could be in porcelain actually in porcelain standing.

They might in at most not leave out an egg. An egg and add some. Some and sum. Add sum. Add some.

Let it in around.
With seas.
With knees.
With keys.
With pleases.
Go and know.
In clouded.
Included.
Saint Therese and attachment.
With any one please.
No one to be behind and enclosure. Suddenly two see.
Two and ten.
Saint Two and Saint Ten.

Scene Four

Did wish did want did at most agree that it was not when they had met that they were separated longitudinally.

While it escapes it add to it just as it did when it has and does with it in that to intend to intensively and sound. Is there a difference between a sound a hiss a kiss a as well.

Could they grow and tell it so if it was left to be to go to go to see to see to saw to saw to build to place to come to rest to hand to beam to couple to name to rectify to do.

Saint Ignatius Saint Settlement Saint Paul Seize Saint Anselmo made it be not only obligatory but very much as they did in little patches.

Saint Therese and Saint Therese and Saint Therese Seize and Saint Therese might be very much as she would if she very much as she would if she were to be wary.

They might be that much that far that with that widen

never having seen and press, it was a land in one when altitude by this to which endowed.

Might it be in claim.

Saint Therese and conversation.   In one.

Saint Therese in conversation   And one.

Saint Therese in and in and one and in and one.

Saint Therese left in complete.

Saint Therese and better bowed.

Saint Therese did she and leave bright.

Snow in snow sun in sun one in one out.

What is the difference between a picture of a volcano and that.

Watered and allowed makes a crown.

Oysters brown and rose tree rose he arose and he arose.

Saint Therese not questioned for this with this and because.

They can remain latin latin there and Virgil Virgil Virgil virgin virgin latin there.

Saint Ignatius to twenty.

A scene and withers.

Scene three and scene two.

How can a sister see Saint Therese suitably.

Pear trees cherry blossoms pink blossoms and late apples and surrounded by Spain and lain.

Why when in lean fairly rejoin place dismiss calls.

Whether weather soil.

Saint Therese refuses to bestow.

Saint Therese with account.

Saint Therese having felt it with it.

There can be no peace on earth with calm with calm. There can be no peace on earth with calm with calm. There can be no peace on earth with calm with calm and with whom whose with calm and with whom whose when they well they well they call it there made message especial and come.

This amounts to Saint Therese.

Saint Therese has been and has been.

What is the difference between a picture and pictured.

All Saints make Sunday Monday Sunday Monday Sunday Monday set.

One two three Saints.

Scene Three

Saint Therese has been prepared for there being summer.
Saint Therese has been prepared for there being summer.

Scene Four

To prepare.
One a window.
Two a shutter.
Three a palace
Four a widow
Five an adopted son
Six a parlour
Seven a shawl
Eight an arbour
Nine a seat
Ten a retirement
Saint Therese has been with him.
Saint Therese has been with him they show they show
that summer summer makes a child happening at all to throw
a ball too often to please.
Saint Therese in pain.
Saint Therese with blame
Saint Therese having been following with them here.
In this way to begin to thin.
Those used to winter like winter and summer.
Those used to summer like winter and summer.
Those used to summer like winter and summer.
Those used to summer like winter and summer like
winter and summer.
Those used to summer like winter and summer.
They make this an act One.

ACT TWO

All to you.

SCENE ONE

Some and some.

Scene one.

This is a scene where this is seen. Saint Therese has been a queen not as you might say royalty not as you might say worn not as you might say.

Saint Therese preparing in as you might say.

ACT ONE

Saint Therese   Preparing in as you might say.
Saint Therese was   In as you might say.
pleasing

Saint Therese Act One

Saint Therese has begun to be in act one.
Saint Therese and begun.
Saint Therese as sung.
Saint Therese act one
Saint Therese and begun.
Saint Therese and sing and sung
Saint Therese in an act one.

Saint Therese   How many have been told twenty have
questions   been here as well.

Saint Therese and with if it is as in a rest and well.

Saint Therese does not live around she is very well understood to have been with them then.

She is very intently with might have been seen rested and with it all. It never snows in Easter.

Saint Therese as if it were as they say they say so.

Saint Ignatius might not have been born.

Saint Therese can know the difference between singing and women. Saint Therese can know the difference between snow and thirds. Saint Therese can know the difference between when there is a day to-day to-day. To-day.

Saint Therese with the land and laid. Not observing.

Saint Therese coming to go.

Saint Therese coming and lots of which it is not as soon as if when it can left to change change theirs in glass and yellowish at most most of this can be when is it that it is very necessary not to plant it green. Planting it green means that it is protected from the wind and they never knew about it. They never know about it green and they never know about it she never knew about it they never knew about it they never knew about it she never knew about it. Planting it green it is necessary to protect it from the sun and from the wind and the sun and they never knew about it and she never knew about it and she never knew about it and they never knew about it.

Scene once seen once seen once seen.

SCENE V

Saint Therese unsurrounded by reason of it being so cold that they stayed away.

SCENE VI

Saint Therese using a cart with oxen to go about and as well as if she were there.

SCENE VII

One two three four five six seven all good children go to heaven some are good and some are bad one two three four five six seven. Saint Therese in a cart drawn by oxen moving around.

Scene VIII

Saint Therese in time.

Scene IX

Saint Therese meant to be complete completely.

Saint Therese and their having been it always was what they liked likened because it was moved.

Saint Therese in advance advances advantage advance advantages. Saint Therese when she had been left to come was left to come was left to right was right to left and there. There and not there by left and right. Saint Therese once and once. No one surrounded trees as there were none.

This meant Saint Ignatius Act II

Act II

Saint Ignatius was very well known.

SCENE II

Would it do if there was a Scene II.

SCENE III&IV

Saint Ignatius and more.

Saint Ignatius with as well.

Saint Ignatius needs not be feared.

Saint Ignatius might be very well adapted to plans and a distance.

Barcelona in the distance. Was Saint Ignatius able to tell the difference between palms and Eucalyptus trees.

Saint Ignatius finally.

Saint Ignatius well bound.

Saint Ignatius with it just.

Saint Ignatius might be read.

Saint Ignatius with it Tuesday.

Saint Therese has very well added it.

SCENE IV

Usefully.

SCENE IV

How many nails are there in it.

Have shoe nails and silver nails and silver does not sound valuable.

To be interested in Saint Therese fortunately.

Saint Therese   To be interested in Saint Therese fortu-
                nately.

Saint Ignatius to be interested fortunately.

Fortunately to be interested in Saint Therese.

To be interested fortunately in Saint Therese.

Interested fortunately in Saint Therese fortunately interested in Saint Therese Saint Ignatius and Saints who have been changed from the evening to the morning.

In the morning to be changed from the morning to the morning in the morning. A scene of changing from the morning to the morning.

SCENE V

There are many saints.

SCENE V

They can be left to many saints.

SCENE V

Many saints.

SCENE V

Many many saints can be left to many many saints scene five left to many many saints.

SCENE V

Scene five left to many saints.

SCENE V

They are left to many saints and those saints these saints these saints. Saints four saints. They are left to many saints.

SCENE V

Saint Therese does disgrace her by leaving it alone and shone.

Saint Ignatius might be five.

When three were together one woman sitting and seeing one man lending and choosing one young man saying and selling. This is just as if it was a tube.

SCENE V

Closely.

SCENE V

Scene five Saint Therese had a father photographically. Not a sister.

Saint Therese had no mother and no other appointed to be left at hand.

Saint Therese famously and mind. To mind. To have to have to have have Helen. Saint Therese have to have Helen have to have Helen. Saint Therese have to have to have to have Saint Therese to have to have Helen. An excuse.

Saint Therese as well as that.

Saint Therese robin.

Saint Therese not attached to robin.

Saint Therese   Robin not attached to Robin.

Saint Therese   Attached not attached to Robin.

Saint Therese   Why they could.

Saint Therese   Why they could why they could.

Saint Therese Saint Therese Saint Therese Saint Therese Ignatius why they could Saint Therese.

Saint Ignatius why they could.

SCENE VI

Away away away away a day it took three days and that day. Saint Therese was very well parted and apart apart from that. Harry marry saints in place saints and sainted distributed grace.

Saint Therese in place.

Saint Therese in place of Saint Therese in place.

Saint Therese   Can any one feel any one moving and in moving can any one feel any one and in moving.

Saint Therese   To be belied.

Saint Therese   Having happily married.

Saint Therese   Having happily beside.

Saint Therese   Having happily had with it a spoon.

Saint Therese   Having happily relied upon noon.

Saint Therese with Saint Therese

Saint Therese   In place

Saint Therese and Saint Therese

Saint Therese to trace

Saint Therese and place
Saint Therese beside.
Saint Therese added ride.
Saint Therese with tied.
Saint Therese and might.
Saint Therese   Might with widow.
Saint Therese   Might.
Saint Therese very made her in.
Saint Therese   Settled settlement some so.
Saint Therese Saint Therese
        Saint Therese in in in in Lynn.

SCENE VII

        One two three four five six seven scene seven.
        Saint Therese scene seven.
        Saint Therese scene scene seven.
        Saint Therese could never be mistaken.
        Saint Therese could never be mistaken.
        Saint Therese scene seven.
Saint Therese   Scene seven.
        Saint Settlement Saint Therese Saint Ignatius Saint
Severine Saint William Saint John Saint Ignatius Saint Alex-
ander Saint Lawrence Saint Pilar Saint Celestine Saint Par-
menter Saint Lys Saint Eustace and Saint Plan.
Saint Therese   How many saints are there in it.
Saint Therese   There are very many many saints in it.
Saint Therese   There are as many saints as there are in it.
Saint Therese   How many saints are there in it.
Saint Therese   There are there are there are saints saints
                in it.
        Saint Therese Saint Settlement Saint Ignatius Saint
Lawrence Saint Pilar Saint Plan and Saint Cecilia.
Saint Therese   How many saints are there in it.
Saint Cecilia   How many saints are there in it.
Saint Therese   There are as many saints as there are in it.
Saint Cecilia   There are as many saints as there are saints
                in it.
Saint Cecilia   How many saints are there in it.
Saint Therese   There are many saints in it.

Saint Lawrence Saint Celestine There are saints in it Saint Celestine Saint Lawrence there are as many saints there are as many saints as there are as many saints as there are in it.

Saint Therese	There are many saints there are many saints many saints in it.
Saint Therese	Thank you very much.
Saint Therese	There are as many saints there are many saints in it.

A very long time but not while waiting.

Saint Ignatius	More needily of which more anon.
Saint Ignatius	Of more which more which more.

Saint Ignatius Loyola. A saint to be met by and by by and by continue reading reading read read readily.

Never to be lost again to-day.

To-day to stay.

Saint Ignatius Saint Ignatius Saint Ignatius temporarily.

Saint Jan	Who makes whose be his. I do.

Saint Therese scene seven one two three four five six seven.

Saint Therese	Let it have a place.

Saint Therese Saint Ignatius and Saint Genevieve and Saint Thomas and Saint Chavez.

All four saints have settled it to be what they must know makes it be what it is when they are defended by attacks.

Saint Genevieve can be welcomed any day.

Saint Chavez can be with them then.

Saint Ignatius can be might it be with them and furl. Saint Therese with them in with them alone.

Saint Plan	Can be seen to be any day any day from here to there.

Saint Settlement aroused by the recall of Amsterdam.

Saint Therese	Judging it as a place to be used negligently.

Saint Ignatius by the time that rain has come.

Saint Genevieve meant with it all.

Saint Plan	Might meant with it all.
Saint Paul	Might meant might with it all.
Saint Chavez	Select.

Saints. All Saints.

SCENE EIGHT

All Saints	All Saints At All Saints.
All Saints	Any and all Saints.
All Saints	All and all Saints.
All Saints	All in all Saints.
All Saints	All Saints.
All Saints	Saints all in all Saints
All Saints	Settled in all Saints.
All Saints	Settled all in all Saints.
Saints	Saints settled saints settled all in all saints.
All Saints	Saints in all Saints.
Saint Settlement	Saints all saints all saints.
Saint Chavez	In all saints Saint Plan in saint in saint in all saints saints in all saints.
Saint Ignatius	Settled passing this in having given in which is not two days when everything being ready it is no doubt not at all the following morning that it is very much later very much earlier with then to find it acceptable as about about which which as a river river helping it to be in doubt. Who do who does and does it about about to be as a river and the order of their advance. It is to-morrow on arriving at a place to pass before the last.

Scene eight. To Wait.
Scene one. And begun
Scene two. To and to.
Scene three. Happily be.
Scene four. Attached or.
Scene five. Sent to derive.
Scene six. Let it mix.
Scene seven. Attached eleven.
Scene Eight. To wait.

Saint Therese	Might be there.
Saint Therese	To be sure.
Saint Therese	With them and
Saint Therese	And hand.
Saint Therese	And alright.

Saint Therese	With them then
Saint Therese	Nestle.
Saint Therese	
Saint Therese	With them and a measure. It is easy to measure a settlement.

SCENE IX

Saint Therese	To be asked how much of it is finished.
Saint Therese	To be asked how much of it is finished.
Saint Therese	To ask Saint Therese

Saint Therese to be asked how much of it is finished.

Saint Therese	Ask Saint Therese how much of it is finished.
Saint Therese	To be asked Saint Therese to be asked Saint Therese to be asked ask Saint Therese ask Saint Therese how much of it is finished.
Saint Chavez	Ask how much of it is finished.
Saint Plan	Ask Saint Therese how much of it is finished.
Saint Therese	Ask asking asking Saint Therese how much of it is finished.

Saint Settlement Saint Chavez Saint Plan

Saint Therese	How much of it is finished.
Saint Therese	Ask how much of it is finished.
Saint Chavez	Ask how much of it is finished.
Saint Therese	Ask how much of it is finished.

Saint Settlement Saint Therese Saint Paul Saint Plan Saint Anne Saint Cecile.

Saint Plan	Ask how much of it is finished.

Once in a while.

Saint Therese	Once in a while.
Saint Plan	Once in a while.
Saint Chavez	Once in a while.
Saint Settlement	Once in a while.
Saint Therese	Once in a while.
Saint Chavez	Once in a while.
Saint Cecile	Once in a while.
Saint Genevieve	Once in a while.
Saint Anne	Once in a while.

Saint Settlement	Once in a while.
Saint Therese	Once in a while.
Saint Therese	Once in a while
Saint Ignatius	Once in a while.
Saint Ignatius	Once in a while.
Saint Ignatius	Once in a while.
Saint Settlement	Once in a while.
Saint Therese Saint Therese	Once in a while.
Saint Therese	Once in a while.
Saint Ignatius	Once in a while.
Saint Ignatius Saint Therese	Once in a while.
Saint Therese	Once in a while.
Saint Therese	Once in a while.
Saint Therese	Once in a while.
Saint Plan	Once in a while
Saint Ignatius Saint Therese	Once in a while.

Scene X

Could Four Acts be Three.

Saint Therese	Could Four Acts be three.
Saint Therese	
Saint Therese	Could Four Acts be three saint Therese.
Saint Therese	

Scene X

When

Saint Therese	Could Four Acts be when four acts could be ten Saint Therese Saint Therese Saint Therese Four acts could be four acts could be when when four acts could be ten.
Saint Therese	When.
Saint Settlement	Then.
Saint Genevieve	When.
Saint Cecile	Then.
Saint Ignatius	Then.
Saint Ignatius	Men.

Saint Ignatius	When.
Saint Ignatius	Ten.
Saint Ignatius	Then.
Saint Therese	When.
Saint Chavez	Ten.
Saint Plan	When then.
Saint Settlement	Then.
Saint Anne	Then.
Saint Genevieve	Ten.
Saint Cecile	Then.
Saint Answers	Ten.
Saint Cecile Saint Anne	When then.
Saint Answers	Saints when.
Saint Chavez	Saints when ten.
Saint Cecile	Ten.
Saint Answers	Ten.
Saint Chavez	Ten.
Saint Settlement	Ten.
Saint Plan	Ten.
Saint Anne	Ten.
Saint Plan	Ten.
Saint Plan	Ten.
Saint Plan	Ten.

Scene XI

Saint Therese	With William.
Saint Therese	With Plan
Saint Therese	With William willing and with Plan willing and with Plan and with William willing and with William and with Plan.
Saint Therese	They might be starving.
Saint Therese	And with William
Saint Therese	And with Plan.
Saint Therese	With William.
Saint Therese	And with Plan.
Saint Therese	
Saint Plan	
Saint Placide	How many windows are there in it.

Saint Chavez
 and
Saint Settlement

Saint Therese	How many windows and doors and floors are there in it.
Saint Therese	How many doors how many floors and how many windows are there in it.
Saint Plan	How many windows are there in it how many doors are there in it.
Saint Chavez	How many doors are there in it how many floors are there in it how many doors are there in it how many windows are there in it how many floors are there in it how many windows are there in it how many doors are there in it.

   Changing in between.

Saint Therese	In this and in this and in this and clarity.
Saint Therese	How many are there in this.
Saint Chavez	How many are there in this.
Saint Chavez	How many are there in this.
Saint Settlement	Singularly to be sure and with a Wednesday at noon.
Saint Chavez	In time and mine.
Saint Therese	Settlement and in in and in and all. All to come and go to stand up to kneel and to be around. Around and around and around and as round and as around and as around and as around.

  One two three.

  There is a distance in between.

  There is a distance in between in between others others meet meet meet met wet yet. It is very tearful to be through. Through and through.

Saint Therese	Might be third.
Saint Therese	Might be heard.
Saint Therese	Might be invaded.

   Saint Therese and three saints and there.

   Commencing again yesterday.

Saint Therese	And principally.
Saint Therese	

Scene X

Saint Ignatius	Withdrew with with withdrew.
Saint Ignatius	Occurred.
Saint Ignatius	Occurred withdrew.
Saint Ignatius	Withdrew occurred
Saint Ignatius	Withdrew occurred.

Saint Ignatius occurred Saint Ignatius withdrew occurred withdrew.

Saint Sarah	Having heard that they had gone she said how many eggs are there in it.
Saint Absolom	Having heard that they are gone he said how many had said how many had been where they had never been with them or with it.
Saint Absolom	Might be annointed.
Saint Therese	With responsibility.
Saint Therese	And in allowance.
Saint Settlement	In might have a change from this.
Saint Chavez	A winning.
Saint Cecile	In plenty.
Saint Eustace	Might it be mountains if it were not Barcelona.
Saint Plan	With wisdom.
Saint Chavez	In a minute.
Saint Therese	And circumstances.
Saint Therese	And as much.
Saint Chavez	With them.

An interval.
Abundance.
An interval.

Saint Chavez	Abundance.
Saint Chavez	And an interval.
Saint Sarah	With them near one.
Saint Michael	With them near one with them.
Saint Chavez	Tire
Saint Cecile	
Saint Chavez	
Saint Therese	One two and alike like liked.
and themselves	

Saint Chavez	Windows and windows and ones.
Saint Cecile	Obligation.
Saint Sarah	Their wonder.
Saint Michael	And their wonder.
Saint Chavez	And whether.
Saint Michael	With windows as much as.
Saint Cecile	More to be considered.
Saint Michael Saint Sarah	Considerable.
Saint Chavez	In consideration of everything and that it is done by them as it must be left to them with this as an arrangement. Night and day cannot be different.
Saint Therese	Completely forgetting.
Saint Therese	I will try.
Saint Therese	Theirs and by and by.
Saint Chavez	With noon.

ACT III

With withdrawn.

There is very much announcement and by the time they leave altogether one at a time they do not leave it left and right and in the middle they withdraw what they need when they might meet with what after all is why they are not only with them but in the midst of them and withdrawn and left meaning to be with this as their belonging to it and as it is what is it when they are in the middle of theirs around they might be very nearly alike as if it is understood. Once and one at a time.

Barcelona can be told.

How do you do.

Very well I thank you.

This is how young men and matter. How many nails are there in it.

Who can try.

They can be a little left behind.

Not at all.

As if they liked it very well to live alone.

With withdrawn.
What can they mean by well very well.

Scene One

And seen one. Very likely.

Saint Therese   It is not what is apprehended what is apprehended what is apprehended what is apprehended intended.

Scene One.

Saint Chavez   It is very likely that there are many of them.
Saint Ignatius   Instantly and subsistently.
Saint Stephen   And leading at night.
Saint Plan   Within with went in.
Saint Stephen   In a little time gradually.
Saint Manuel   Would they refuse to sanction it if they were asked and there was no way to have them carry out anything.
Saint Stephen   With then instantly.
Saint Eustace   In place of lurking.
Saint Chavez   By means of it all.
Saint Plan   Within a season of deliberation.
Saint Stephen   And reasonably insisting.
Saint Chavez   At that time.
Saint Ignatius   And all. Then and not. Might it do. Do and doubling with it at once left and right.
Saint Chavez   Left left left right left with what is known.
Saint Chavez   In time.

Scene II

It is easy to resemble it at most.
Most and best.
It is easy to resemble it most and leave it to them with individuality.

Saint Ignatius   In seems.
Saint Ignatius   In seems.

Saint Ignatius	Within it within it within it as a wedding for them in half of the time.
Saint Ignatius	Particularly.
Saint Ignatius	Call it a day.
Saint Ignatius	With a wide water with within with drawn.
Saint Ignatius	As if a fourth class.

Scene II

Pigeons on the grass alas.

Pigeons on the grass alas.

Short longer grass short longer longer shorter yellow grass. Pigeons large pigeons on the shorter longer yellow grass alas pigeons on the grass.

If they were not pigeons what were they.

If they were not pigeons on the grass alas what were they. He had heard of a third and he asked about it it was a magpie in the sky. If a magpie in the sky on the sky can not cry if the pigeon on the grass alas can alas and to pass the pigeon on the grass alas and the magpie in the sky on the sky and to try and to try alas on the grass alas the pigeon on the grass the pigeon on the grass and alas.

They might be very well very well very well they might be they might be very well they might be very well very well they might be.

Let Lucy Lily Lily Lucy Lucy let Lucy Lucy Lily Lily Lily Lily Lily let Lily Lucy Lucy let Lily. Let Lucy Lily.

Scene One

Saint Ignatius prepared to have examples of windows of curtains of hanging of shawls of windows of curtains of windows of curtains of windows of curtains of hangings of shawls of windows of hangings of curtains of windows of hangings of curtains of shawls.

Saint Ignatius and please please please please.

Scene One

One and one.

Scene One

Might they be with they be with them might they be with them. Never to return to distinctions.

Might they be with them with they be with they be with them. Never to return to distinctions.

Saint Ignatius   In line and in in line please say it first in line and in line and please say it first please say it with first in line and in line in line.

Saint Ignatius   Met to be to be to leave me be with him in partly left to find find with it call call with to them to them that have to be with it as when letting letting it announce announced complacently in change change having fallen two to one in restitution in their inability to leave. Leave left as lost. Might white. From the stand-point of white.

Saint Sulpice   A masterpiece.

Saint Ignatius   When it is ordinarily thoughtful and mak-
and friends   ing it be when they were wishing at one time insatiably and with renounced where where ware and wear wear with them with them and where where will it be as long as long as they might with it with it individually removing left to it when it very well way well and crossed crossed in articulately minding what you do.

The friends at once.

What is it when it is perilously left to it where there are more than there were.

And all and as if there is a mound.

He asked for a distant magpie as if they made a difference.

He asked for a distant magpie as if he asked for a distant magpie as if that made a difference.

He asked as if that made a difference.

He asked for a distant magpie.

He asked for a distant magpie.

As if that made a difference he asked for a distant magpie as if that made a difference. He asked as if that made a difference. A distant magpie. He asked for a distant magpie. He asked for a distant magpie.

Saint Ignatius.   Might be admired for himself alone.

Saint Chavez   Saint Ignatius might be admired for himself alone and because of that it might be as much as any one could desire.

Saint Chavez   Because of that it might be as much as any one could desire.

Saint Chavez   Because of that because it might be as much as any one could desire it might be that it could be done as easily as because it might very much as if precisely why they were carried.

Saint Ignatius   Left when there was precious little to be asked by the ones who were overwhelmingly particular about what they were adding to themselves by means of their arrangements which might be why they went away and came again.

It is every once in a while very much what they pleased.

Saint Ignatius   With them and with them and uniformly.

Saint Chavez   To make it and why they were with them just as soon.

Saint Chavez   And roses very well. Very well and roses very well roses smell roses smell and very well and very well as roses smell roses smell very well. If hedge roses are moss roses larger. If moss roses are larger are there questions of how very well there are strangers who have to be known by their walk.

In a minute.

Saint Ignatius   In a minute by the time that it is graciously gratification and might it be with them to be with them to be with them to be to be windowed.

Saint Ignatius   As seen as seen.

Saint Ignatius surrounded by them. Saint Ignatius and one of two.

Saint Ignatius   And one of two.
Saint Ignatius   And one of two literally.
Saint Ignatius   And one of two and one of two.
Saint Ignatius   And one of two literally.
Saint Ignatius   And one of two and one of two. One of
                  two.
Saint Ignatius   Might when when is exchangeable.
Saint Ignatius   Might when.
Saint Chavez   In change.
        Saint Chavez might be with them at that time.
All of them   Might be with them at that time.
        All of them might be with them all of them at that
time.
        Might be with them at that time all of them might be
with them at that time.

Scene II

It is very easy to love alone. Too much too much. There are very sweetly very sweetly Henry very sweetly René very sweetly many very sweetly. They are very sweetly many very sweetly René very sweetly there are many very sweetly.

Scene III

There is a difference between Barcelona and Avila. What difference.

Scene

There is a difference between Barcelona and Avila.
There is a difference between Barcelona. There is a difference between Barcelona and Avila. There is a difference between Barcelona and Avila.

Scene IV

And no more.

Scene V

Saint Ignatius   Left to left left to left left to left. Left right
                  left left right left left to left.

Saint Pellen   There is every reason why industriously
                      there should be resolution and intermit-
                      tence and furnishing of their delight.

By this time with them in intermingling and objection
with them and with them and intermediately and allowance
and left and more and benignly and acceptably accepting in
their and by mischance with them indeterminately finally as
change.

When they do change to.

Saint Vincent   Authority for it.

Saint Gallo   By this clock o'clock. By this clock by this
                      clock by this clock o'clock.

Saint Pilar   In the middle of their pleasurable resolu-
                      tion resolving in their adequate announc-
                      ing left to it by this by this means.

And out.

Saint Chavez   With a plan.

Saint Pellen   In sound.

Saint Gallo   Around.

Saint Pellen   In particular.

Saint Chavez   Innumerably.

Saint Ignatius might be what is underestimately theirs
in plain and plan and for which is left to because in this with
it as much as is in connecting undividedly theirs at that time.
In this. Coming to be thrown.

They might use having it as high.

Left it to right.

Having used might it be with it as with it as mentioning when.

Having it as having it used usually to actually to additionally to integrally to to the owned to the owning owning
out.

Might it be two at one time time and mine mine and
time.

Saint Ignatius returns to come when.

Saint Plan   Without it with them

Saint Chavez
  and   Without it with them with them without
Saint Pilar   it.

Saint Chavez   Without it with them without it.

With them with out it.

Saint Ignatius	Might be memorised.

Saint Chavez Saint Pilar and with them.

With them with it.

Saint Pilar	With them with with with with out with them.
Saint Chavez	Uniting it one at a time individually.
Saint Pilar	Need it in liking what is a choice between floating and adding. Floating and adding makes smiles.
Saint Hilyar	With them and to to to add to add to it.

Might having it we do.

Saint Ignatius	Foundationally marvellously aboundingly illimitably with it as a circumstance. Fundamentally and saints fundamentally and saints and fundamentally and saints.
Saint Chavez	Found round about.
Saint Pilar and Saint Chavez	Additionally in currents.
Saint Chavez	Found round about without.
Saint Chavez Saint Pilar and Saint Fernande	With what and when it is universally leaving it additionally to them as windowed windowed windowed windowed where.

Answerably.

Scene VI

They might have heard about them altogether.

Scene VII

Saint Chavez	It is very well known that that which has been noticed as needing violence and veils may be what they meant when they said it.
Saint Chavez	By that time.
Saint Chavez	What they meant by it when they said it. By that time.
Saint Chavez	There has been an incredible reason for

	their planning what is not by any manner of means their allowance in having let it be theirs by negligence.
Saint Andrew and Saint John Seize	Letting it be third at all.
Saint Sarah and Saint Leonard	By it a chance
Saint Ferdinande and Saint Plan	With this one at at time
Saint Plan and Saint Arthur	With them and must.
Saint Agnes	Letting it alone.
Saint Henry	With me by and by.
Saint Sylvester	Leaning and letting it be what to wish.
Saint Plan	Leaning and letting it be what to wish.
One Saint	Whose has whose has whose has ordered needing white and green as much as orange and with grey and how much and as much and as much and as a circumstance.
Saint Ignatius	Windowing shortly which makes what have they joined to parks and palaces. Undoubtedly. One and two might be through Through certainly.
Saint Therese	With them and for instance.
Saint Therese	Like and it might be as likely it might be very likely that it would be amounting to once in a while as in a way it could be what was meant by that at once. There is a difference between at most at once.

In at the time.

Saint Therese	Intending to be intending to intending to to to to. To do it for me.
Saint Ignatius	Went to.
Saint Ignatius	Two and two.
Saint Chavez	Might be what was when after all a petal two and water three.

Scene V

Alive

Scene VI

With Seven.

Scene VII

With eight.

Scene VIII

Ordinary pigeons and trees.

If a generation all the same between forty and fifty as as. As they were and met. Was it tenderness and seem. Might it be as well as mean with in.

Ordinary pigeons and trees. This is a setting which is as soon which is as soon which is as soon ordinary setting which is as soon which is as soon and noon.

Ordinary pigeons and trees.

Scene IX

Saint Therese	Face and face face about. Face to face face and face face out.
Saint Therese	Add to additional.
Saint Chavez	Might make milk sung.
Saint Chavez	Might make. In place. Saint Therese.
Saint Therese	In face of in face of might make milk sung sung face to face face in face place in place in place of face to face. Milk sung.
Saint Ignatius	Once in a while and where and where around around is a sound and around is a sound and around is a sound and around. Around is a sound around is a sound around is a sound and around. Around differing from annointed now. Now differing from annointed now. Now differing differing. Now differing from annointed now. Now when there is left and with it inte-

grally with it integrally withstood within
without with out with drawn and in as
much as if it could be withstanding what
in might might be so.

Saint Chavez   In in time.

Many might be comfortabler. This is very well known
now. When this you see remember me. It was very well known
to every one. They were very careful of everything. They were
whatever it was necessary to have to alter. They might be as
thankful as they were that they were not perfectly predispos-
sessed to deny when they were able to be very soon there.
There one at a time. Having arranged magpies so only one
showed and also having arranged magpies so that more than
one showed. If magpies are so arranged that one one shows
it is not more noticeable than if they are so arranged than
more than one is showing against the horizon in such a way
that they are placed directly not only where they were but
where they are. Adding coming forward again.

A great deal of the afternoon is used by this as an advantage. It is meritorious that we do not care to share. It is
meritorious by them with them able and ably.

Saint Ignatius   Forty to fifty with fifty and all and a wall
                       and as all and as called called rather.

Saint Therese   A widow weeded way laid way laying and
                       as spelled.

Saint Chavez   Might and right very well to do. It is all
                       coloured by a straw straw laden.

Saint Ignatius   Very nearly with it with it soon soon as
                       said.

Saint Ignatius   Windowing clearly.

Saint Chavez   Having asked additionally theirs instead.

Saint Therese   Once in a minute.

Saint Therese   In a minute.

Saint Ignatius   One two three as are are and are are are to
                       be are with them are with them are with
                       them with are with are with with it.

Scene IX

Letting pin in letting let in let in in in in in let in let
in wet in wed in dead in dead wed led in led wed dead in

dead in led in wed in said in said led wed dead wed dead said led led said wed dead wed dead led in led in wed in wed in said in wed in led in said in dead in dead wed said led led said wed dead in. That makes they have might kind find fined when this arbitrarily makes it be what is it might they can it fairly well to be added to in this at the time that they can candied leaving as with with it by the left of it with with in in the funniest in union.

Across across across coupled across crept a cross crept crept crept crept a cross. They crept a cross.

If they are between thirty and thirty-five and alive who made them see Saturday.

If they are between thirty-five and forty and they are thought to be who made them see Saturday with having it come in and out in and three thirty.

Between thirty-five and forty-five between forty-five and three five as then when when they were forty-five and thirty-five when then they were forty-five and thirty-five when they were then forty-five and thirty-five and thirty-two and to achieve leave relieve and receive their astonishment. Were they to be left to do to do as well as they do mean I mean I mean. Next best to having heading him.

Might it be left after all where they left left right left. Might it be left where they might have having it left after all left right left after all.

When they have heard it mine.

Left to their in their to their to be their to be there all their to be there all their all their time to be there to be there all their to be all their time there.

With wed led said with led dead said with dead led said with said dead led wed said wed dead led dead led said wed.

With be there all their all their time there be there vine there be vine time there be there time there all their time there.

Needed indented.

Can they and chest, choice, choice of a chest.

It is better and best and just as good as if they needed to have and wanted to have and did want to have and did want to have to have had it had it with them when they might just as easily endeavour in every way to have paraphanelia leave it as their habitual reference to when they are not by the time that they have been very likely to needlessly believe that they want to come to come handily as a desperately arranged charm. Might it be why they were not only but also went as well.

Let it be why if they were adding adding comes cunningly to be additionally cunningly in the sense of attracting attracting in the sense of adding adding in the sense of windowing and windowing and panes and pigeons and ordinary trees and while while away.

ACT III

Did he did we did we and did he did he did he did did he did did did he did did he did he categorically and did he did he did he did he did he did he in interruption interruption interruptedly leave letting let it be be all to me to me out and outer and this and this with in indeed deed and drawn and drawn work.

Saint Ferdinande singing soulfully.

Saint Chavez	Singing singing is singing is singing is singing is singing between between singing is singing is between singing is.
Saint Plan	Theirs and sign.
Saint Cecile	Singing theirs and signing mine.
Saint Philip	Will it be less at first that they are there and be left by the time that it is carried as far as further.
Saint Philip	Let it be gone as it has to be gone in plenty of time.
Saint Sarah	She might be coming to have to have infancy.
Saint Michael	With a stand and would it be the same as yet awhile and glance a glance of be very nearly left to be alone.
Saint Therese	One at at time makes two at a time makes one at a time and be there where where there there where where there. Very well as if to say.

Saint Cecile	With it and as if as if it were a left to them and feel. I feel very well.
Saint Chavez	By the time that they were left perfect.
Saint Ignatius	Might be why they were after all after all who came. One hundred and fifty one and a half and a half and after and after and after and all. With it all.
Saint Chavez	A ball might be less than one.

All together one and one.

ACT IV

How many acts are there in it. Acts are there in it.

Supposing a wheel had been added to three wheels how many acts how many how many acts are there in it.

Any saint at all.

How many acts are there in it.

How many saints in all.

How many acts are there in it.

Ring around a rosey.

How many acts are there in it,

Wedded and weeded.

Please be coming to see me.

When this you see you are all to me.

Me which is you you who are true true to be you.

How many how many saints are there in it.

One two three all out but me.

One two three four all out but four.

One two all about but you.

How many saints are there in it.

How many saints are there in it.

How many saints are there in it.

One two three four and there is no door. Or more. Or more. Or door. Or floor or door. One two three all out but me. How many saints are there in it.

Saints and see all out but me.

How many saints are there in it.

How many saints are there in it. One two three four all out but four one two three four four four or four or more.

More or four.
How many acts are there in it.

Four Acts
Act Four.

Saint Therese deliberately. Encouraged by this then when they might be by thirds words eglantine and by this to mean feeling it as most when they do too to be nearly lost to sight in time in time and mind mind it for them. Let us come to this brink.

The sisters and saints assembling and reenacting why they went away to stay.

One at a time regularly regularly by the time that they are in and and in one at at time regularly very fairly better than they came as they came there and where where will they be wishing to stay here here where they are they are here here where they are they are they are here.

Saint Therese	It is very necessary to have arithmetic inestimably and left by this in the manner in which they are not at all as patient as they were patiently were. One at a time in rhyme.
Saint Chavez	The envelopes are on all the fruit of the fruit trees.

Scene II

Saint Chavez	Remembered as knew.
Saint Ignatius	Meant to send and meant to send and meant meant to differ between send and went and end and mend and very nearly one to two.
Saint Cecile	With this and now.
Saint Plan	Made it with with in with with drawn.

Scene III

Let all act as if they went away.

Scene IV

Saint Therese	Who mentioned that one followed another laterally.

All Saints	One at a time.
Saint Chavez	One at a time.
Saint Settlement and	There can be two Saint Annes if you like
Saint Anne	
Saint Philip	With them and still.
Saint Cecile	They will they will.
Saint Therese	Begin to trace begin to race begin to place begin and in in that that is why this is what is left as may may follows June and June follows moon and moon follows soon and it is very nearly ended with bread.
Saint Chavez	Who can think that they can leave it here to me.

When this you see remember me.
They have to be
They have to be
They have to be to see.
To see to say.
Laterally they may.

Scene V

Who makes who makes it do.
Saint Therese and Saint Therese too.
Who does and who does care.
Saint Chavez to care Saint Chavez to care.
Who may be what is it when it is instead.
Saint Plan Saint Plan to may to say to say two may and inclined.
Who makes it be what they had as porcelain.
Saint Ignatius and left and right laterally be lined.
All Saints.
To Saints.
Four Saints.
And Saints.
Five Saints.
To Saints.

Last Act.

Which is a fact.

Virgil Thomson

Yes ally. As ally. Yes ally yes as ally. A very easy failure takes place. Yes ally. As ally. As ally yes a very easy failure takes place. Very good. Very easy failure takes place. Yes very easy failure takes place.

When with a sentence of intended they were he was neighboured by a bean.

Hour by hour counts.

How makes a may day.

Our comes back back comes our.

It is with a replica of seen. That he was neighbored by a bean.

Which is a weeding, weeding a walk, walk may do done delight does in welcome. Welcome daily is a home alone and our in glass turned around. Lain him. Power four lower lay lain as in case, of my whether ewe lain or to less. What was obligation furnish furs fur lease release in dear. Dear darken. It never was or with a call. My waiting. Remain remark taper or tapestry stopping stopped with a lain at an angle colored like make it as stray. Did he does he was or will well and dove as entail cut a pursuit purpose demean different dip in descent diphthong advantage about their this thin couple a outer our in glass pay white. What is it he admires. Are used to it. Owned when it has. For in a way. Dumbfounded. A cloud in superior which is awake a satisfy found. What does it matter as it happens. Their much is a nuisance when they gain as well as own. How much do they like why were they anxious. None make wishing a pastime. When it is confidence in offer which they came. How ever they came out. Like it. All a part. With known. But which is mine. They may. Let us need partly in case. They are never selfish.

These quotations determine that demonstration is arithmetic with laying very much their happening that account in distance day main lay coupled in coming joined. Barred harder. Very fitly elephant. How is it that it has come to pass. Whenever they can take into account. More of which that whatever they are later. Then without it be as pleases. In reflection their told. Made mainly violet in a man. Comfort in our meshes. Without any habit to have called Howard louder. That they are talkative. Most of all rendered. In a mine of their distension. Resting without referring. Just as it is. Come for this lain will in might it have taught as a dustless redoubt where it is heavier than a chair. How much can sought be ours. Wide or leant be beatific very preparedly in a covering now. It is always just as lost.

Harden as wean does carry a chair intake of rather with a better coupled just as a ream.

How could they know that it had happened.

If they were in the habit of not liking one day. By the time they were started. For the sake of their wishes. As it is every once in a while. Liking it for their sake made as it is.

Their is no need of liking their home.

THE AUTOBIOGRAPHY OF
ALICE B. TOKLAS

Alice B. Toklas at the door, photograph by Man Ray

Contents

Illustrations

I.

Before I Came to Paris

I WAS BORN in San Francisco, California. I have in consequence always preferred living in a temperate climate but
it is difficult, on the continent of Europe or even in America,
to find a temperate climate and live in it. My mother's father
was a pioneer, he came to California in '49, he married my
grandmother who was very fond of music. She was a pupil of
Clara Schumann's father. My mother was a quiet charming
woman named Emilie.

My father came of polish patriotic stock. His grand-uncle
raised a regiment for Napoleon and was its colonel. His father
left his mother just after their marriage, to fight at the barri-
cades in Paris, but his wife having cut off his supplies, he soon
returned and led the life of a conservative well to do land
owner.

I myself have had no liking for violence and have always
enjoyed the pleasures of needlework and gardening. I am fond
of paintings, furniture, tapestry, houses and flowers even vegetables and fruit-trees. I like a view but I like to sit with my
back turned to it.

I led in my childhood and youth the gently bred existence
of my class and kind. I had some intellectual adventures at
this period but very quiet ones. When I was about nineteen
years of age I was a great admirer of Henry James. I felt that
The Awkward Age would make a very remarkable play and I
wrote to Henry James suggesting that I dramatise it. I had
from him a delightful letter on the subject and then, when I
felt my inadequacy, rather blushed for myself and did not keep
the letter. Perhaps at that time I did not feel that I was justified in preserving it, at any rate it no longer exists.

Up to my twentieth year I was seriously interested in music.
I studied and practised assiduously but shortly then it seemed
futile, my mother had died and there was no unconquerable
sadness, but there was no real interest that led me on. In the
story Ada in Geography and Plays Gertrude Stein has given a
very good description of me as I was at that time.

From then on for about six years I was well occupied. I led a pleasant life, I had many friends, much amusement many interests, my life was reasonably full and I enjoyed it but I was not very ardent in it. This brings me to the San Francisco fire which had as a consequence that the elder brother of Gertrude Stein and his wife came back from Paris to San Francisco and this led to a complete change in my life.

I was at this time living with my father and brother. My father was a quiet man who took things quietly, although he felt them deeply. The first terrible morning of the San Francisco fire I woke him and told him, the city has been rocked by an earthquake and is now on fire. That will give us a black eye in the East, he replied turning and going to sleep again. I remember that once when my brother and a comrade had gone horse-back riding, one of the horses returned riderless to the hotel, the mother of the other boy began to make a terrible scene. Be calm madam, said my father, perhaps it is my son who has been killed. One of his axioms I always remember, if you must do a thing do it graciously. He also told me that a hostess should never apologise for any failure in her household arrangements, if there is a hostess there is insofar as there is a hostess no failure.

As I was saying we were all living comfortably together and there had been in my mind no active desire or thought of change. The disturbance of the routine of our lives by the fire followed by the coming of Gertrude Stein's older brother and his wife made the difference.

Mrs. Stein brought with her three little Matisse paintings, the first modern things to cross the Atlantic. I made her acquaintance at this time of general upset and she showed them to me, she also told me many stories of her life in Paris. Gradually I told my father that perhaps I would leave San Francisco. He was not disturbed by this, after all there was at that time a great deal of going and coming and there were many friends of mine going. Within a year I also had gone and I had come to Paris. There I went to see Mrs. Stein who had in the meantime returned to Paris, and there at her house I met Gertrude Stein. I was impressed by the coral brooch she wore and by her voice. I may say that only three times in my life have I met a genius and each time a bell within me rang and I was not mistaken, and I may say in each case it was before there was any general recognition of the quality of genius in them. The three geniuses of whom I wish to speak are Gertrude Stein, Pablo Picasso and Alfred Whitehead. I have met many important people, I have met several great people but I have only known three first class geniuses and in each case on sight within me something rang. In no one of the three cases have I been mistaken. In this way my new full life began.

2.

My Arrival in Paris

THIS WAS the year 1907. Gertrude Stein was just seeing through the press Three Lives which she was having privately printed, and she was deep in The Making of Americans, her thousand page book. Picasso had just finished his portrait of her which nobody at that time liked except the painter and the painted and which is now so famous, and he had just begun his strange complicated picture of three women, Matisse had just finished his Bonheur de Vivre, his first big composition which gave him the name of fauve or a zoo. It was the moment Max Jacob has since called the heroic age of cubism. I remember not long ago hearing Picasso and Gertrude Stein talking about various things that had happened at that time, one of them said but all that could not have happened in that one year, oh said the other, my dear you forget we were young then and we did a great deal in a year.

There are a great many things to tell of what was happening then and what had happened before, which led up to then, but now I must describe what I saw when I came.

The home at 27 rue de Fleurus consisted then as it does now of a tiny pavillon of two stories with four small rooms, a kitchen and bath, and a very large atelier adjoining. Now the atelier is attached to the pavillon by a tiny hall passage added in 1914 but at that time the atelier had its own entrance, one rang the bell of the pavillon or knocked at the door of the atelier, and a great many people did both, but more knocked at the atelier. I was privileged to do both. I had been invited to dine on Saturday evening which was the evening when everybody came, and indeed everybody did come. I went to dinner. The dinner was cooked by Hélène. I must tell a little about Hélène.

Hélène had already been two years with Gertrude Stein and her brother. She was one of those admirable bonnes in other words excellent maids of all work, good cooks thoroughly occupied with the welfare of their employers and of themselves, firmly convinced that everything purchasable was far too dear.

Gertrude Stein in front of the atelier door

Oh but it is dear, was her answer to any question. She wasted nothing and carried on the household at the regular rate of eight francs a day. She even wanted to include guests at that price, it was her pride, but of course that was difficult since she for the honour of her house as well as to satisfy her employers always had to give every one enough to eat. She was a most excellent cook and she made a very good soufflé. In those days most of the guests were living more or less precariously, no one starved, some one always helped but still most of them did not live in abundance. It was Braque who said about four years later when they were all beginning to be known, with a sigh and a smile, how life has changed we all now have cooks who can make a soufflé.

Hélène had her opinions, she did not for instance like Matisse. She said a frenchman should not stay unexpectedly to a meal particularly if he asked the servant beforehand what there was for dinner. She said foreigners had a perfect right to do these things but not a frenchman and Matisse had once done it. So when Miss Stein said to her, Monsieur Matisse is staying for dinner this evening, she would say, in that case I will not make an omelette but fry the eggs. It takes the same number of eggs and the same amount of butter but it shows less respect, and he will understand.

Hélène stayed with the household until the end of 1913. Then her husband, by that time she had married and had a little boy, insisted that she work for others no longer. To her great regret she left and later she always said that life at home was never as amusing as it had been at the rue de Fleurus. Much later, only about three years ago, she came back for a year, she and her husband had fallen on bad times and her boy had died. She was as cheery as ever and enormously interested. She said isn't it extraordinary, all those people whom I knew when they were nobody are now always mentioned in the newspapers, and the other night over the radio they mentioned the name of Monsieur Picasso. Why they even speak in the newspapers of Monsieur Braque, who used to hold up the big pictures to hang because he was the strongest, while the janitor drove the nails, and they are putting into the Louvre, just imagine it, into the Louvre, a picture by that little poor Monsieur Rousseau, who was so timid he did not even have courage enough to knock at the door. She was terribly interested in seeing Monsieur Picasso and his wife and child and cooked her very best dinner for him, but how he has changed, she said, well, said she, I suppose that is natural but then he has a lovely son. We thought that really Hélène had come back to give the young generation the once over. She had in a way but she was not interested in them. She said they made no impression on her which made them all very sad because the legend of her was well known to all Paris. After a year things were going better again, her husband was earning more money, and she once more remains at home. But to come back to 1907.

Before I tell about the guests I must tell what I saw. As I said being invited to dinner I rang the bell of the little pavillon and was taken into the tiny hall and then into the small dining room lined with books. On the only free space, the doors, were tacked up a few drawings by Picasso and Matisse. As the other guests had not yet come Miss Stein took me into the atelier. It often rained in Paris and it was always difficult to go from the little pavillon to the atelier door in the rain in evening clothes, but you were not to mind such things as the hosts and most of the guests did not. We went into the atelier which opened with a yale key the only yale key in the quarter at that time, and this was not so much for safety, because in those days the pictures had no value, but because the key was small and could go into a purse instead of being enormous as french keys were. Against the walls were several pieces of large italian renaissance furniture and in the middle of the room was a big renaissance table, on it a lovely inkstand, and at one end of it note-books neatly arranged, the kind of note-books french children use, with pictures of earthquakes and explorations on the outside of them. And on all the walls right up to the ceiling were pictures. At one end of the room was a big cast iron stove that Hélène came in and filled with a rattle, and in one corner of the room was a large table on which were horseshoe nails and pebbles and little pipe cigarette holders which one looked at curiously but did not touch, but which turned out later to be accumulations from the pockets of Picasso and Gertrude Stein. But to return to the pictures. The pictures were so strange that one quite instinctively looked at anything rather than at them just at first. I have refreshed my memory by looking at some snap shots taken inside the atelier at that time. The chairs in the room were also all italian renaissance, not very comfortable for short-legged people and one got the habit of sitting on one's legs. Miss Stein sat near the stove in a lovely high-backed one and she peacefully let her legs hang, which was a matter of habit, and when any one of the many visitors came to ask her a question she lifted herself up out of this chair and usually replied in french, not just now. This usually referred to something they wished to see, drawings which were put away, some german had once spilled ink on one, or some other not to be fulfilled desire. But to return to the pictures. As I say they completely covered the white-washed walls right up to the top of the very high ceiling. The room was lit at this time by high gas fixtures. This was the second stage. They had just been put in. Before that there had only been lamps, and a stalwart guest held up the lamp while the others looked. But gas had just been put in and an ingenious american painter named Sayen, to divert his mind from the birth of his first child, was arranging some mechanical contrivance that would light the high fixtures by themselves. The old landlady extremely conservative did not allow electricity in her houses and electricity was not put in until 1914, the old landlady by that time too old to know the difference, her house agent gave permission. But this time I am really going to tell about the pictures.

It is very difficult now that everybody is accustomed to everything to give some idea of the kind of uneasiness one felt when one first looked at all these pictures on these walls. In those days there were pictures of all kinds there, the time had not yet come when they were only Cézannes, Renoirs, Matisses and Picassos, nor as it was even later only Cézannes and Picassos. At that time there was a great deal of Matisse, Picasso, Renoir, Cézanne but there were also a great many other things. There were two Gauguins, there were Manguins, there was a big nude by Valloton that felt like only it was not like the Odalisque of Manet, there was a Toulouse-Lautrec. Once about this time Picasso looking at this and greatly daring said, but all the same I do paint better than he did. Toulouse-Lautrec had been the most important of his early influences.

I later bought a little tiny picture by Picasso of that epoch. There was a portrait of Gertrude Stein by Valloton that might have been a David but was not, there was a Maurice Denis, a little Daumier, many Cézanne water colours, there was in short everything, there was even a little Delacroix and a moderate sized Greco. There were enormous Picassos of the Harlequin period, there were two rows of Matisses, there was a big portrait of a woman by Cézanne and some little Cézannes, all these pictures had a history and I will soon tell them. Now I was confused and I looked and I looked and I was confused. Gertrude Stein and her brother were so accustomed to this state of mind in a guest that they payed no attention to it. Then there was a sharp tap at the atelier door. Gertrude Stein opened it and a little dark dapper man came in with hair, eyes, face, hands and feet all very much alive. Hullo Alfy, she said, this is Miss Toklas. How do you do Miss Toklas, he said very solemnly. This was Alfy Maurer, an old habitué of the house. He had been there before there were these pictures, when there were only japanese prints, and he was among those who used to light matches to light up a little piece of the Cézanne portrait. Of course you can tell it is a finished picture, he used to explain to the other american painters who came and looked dubiously, you can tell because it has a frame, now whoever heard of anybody framing a canvas if the picture isn't finished. He had followed, followed, followed always humbly always sincerely, it was he who selected the first lot of pictures for the famous Barnes collection some years later faithfully and enthusiastically. It was he who when later Barnes came to the house and waved his cheque-book said, so help me God, I didn't bring him. Gertrude Stein who has an explosive temper, came in another evening and there were her brother, Alfy and a stranger. She did not like the stranger's looks. Who is that, said she to Alfy. I didn't bring him, said Alfy. He looks like a Jew, said Gertrude Stein, he is worse than that, says Alfy. But to return to that first evening. A few minutes after Alfy came in there was a violent knock at the door and, dinner is ready, from Hélène. It's funny the Picassos have not come, said they all, however we won't wait at least Hélène won't wait. So we went into the court and into the pavillon and dining room and began dinner. It's funny, said Miss Stein, Pablo is always promptness itself, he is never early and he is never late, it is his pride that punctuality is the politeness of kings, he even makes Fernande punctual. Of course he often says yes when he has no intention of doing what he says yes to, he can't say no, no is not in his vocabulary and you have to know whether his yes means yes or means no, but when he says a yes that means yes and he did about to-night he is always punctual. These were the days before automobiles and nobody worried about accidents. We had just finished the first course when there was a quick patter of footsteps in the court and Hélène opened the door before the bell rang. Pablo and Fernande as everybody called them at that time walked in. He, small, quick moving but not restless, his eyes having a strange faculty of opening wide and drinking in what he wished to see. He had the isolation and movement of the head of a bull-fighter at the head of their procession. Fernande was a tall beautiful woman with a wonderful big hat and a very evidently new dress, they were both very fussed. I am very upset, said Pablo, but you know very well Gertrude I am never late but Fernande had ordered a dress for the vernissage to-morrow and it didn't come. Well here you are anyway, said Miss Stein, since it's you Hélène won't mind. And we all sat down. I was next to Picasso who was silent and then gradually became peaceful. Alfy paid compliments to Fernande and she was soon calm and placid. After a little while I murmured to Picasso that I liked his portrait of Gertrude Stein. Yes, he said, everybody says that she does not look like it but that does not make any difference, she will, he said. The conversation soon became lively it was all about the opening day of the salon indépendant which was the great event of the year. Everybody was interested in all the scandals that would or would not break out. Picasso never exhibited but as his followers did and there were a great many stories connected with each follower the hopes and fears were vivacious.

While we were having coffee footsteps were heard in the court quite a number of footsteps and Miss Stein rose and said, don't hurry, I have to let them in. And she left.

When we went into the atelier there were already quite a number of people in the room, scattered groups, single and couples all looking and looking. Gertrude Stein sat by the stove talking and listening and getting up to open the door and go up to various people talking and listening. She usually opened the door to the knock and the usual formula was, de la part de qui venez-vous, who is your introducer. The idea was that anybody could come but for form's sake and in Paris you have to have a formula, everybody was supposed to be able to mention the name of somebody who had told them about it. It was a mere form, really everybody could come in and as at that time these pictures had no value and there was no social privilege attached to knowing any one there, only those came who really were interested. So as I say anybody could come in, however, there was the formula. Miss Stein once in opening the door said as she usually did by whose invitation do you come and we heard an aggrieved voice reply, but by yours, madame. He was a young man Gertrude Stein had met somewhere and with whom she had had a long conversation and to whom she had given a cordial invitation and then had as promptly forgotten.

The room was soon very very full and who were they all. Groups of hungarian painters and writers, it happened that some hungarian had once been brought and the word had spread from him throughout all Hungary, any village where there was a young man who had ambitions heard of 27 rue de Fleurus and then he lived but to get there and a great many did get there. They were always there, all sizes and shapes, all degrees of wealth and poverty, some very charming, some simply rough and every now and then a very beautiful young peasant. Then there were quantities of germans, not too popular because they tended always to want to see anything that was put away and they tended to break things and Gertrude Stein has a weakness for breakable objects, she has a horror of people who collect only the unbreakable. Then there was a fair sprinkling of americans, Mildred Aldrich would bring a group or Sayen, the electrician, or some painter and occasionally an architectural student would accidentally get there and then there were the habitués, among them Miss Mars and Miss Squires whom Gertrude Stein afterwards immortalised in her story of Miss Furr and Miss Skeene. On that first night Miss Mars and I talked of a subject then entirely new, how to make up your face. She was interested in types, she knew that there were femme décorative, femme d'intérieur and femme intrigante; there was no doubt that Fernande Picasso was a femme décorative, but what was Madame Matisse, femme d'intérieur, I said, and she was very pleased. From time to time one heard the high spanish whinnying laugh of Picasso the gay contralto outbreak of Gertrude Stein, people came and went, in and out. Miss Stein told me to sit with Fernande. Fernande was always beautiful but heavy in hand. I sat, it was my first sitting with a wife of a genius.

Before I decided to write this book my twenty-five years with Gertrude Stein, I had often said that I would write, The wives of geniuses I have sat with. I have sat with so many. I have sat with wives who were not wives, of geniuses who were real geniuses. I have sat with real wives of geniuses who were not real geniuses. I have sat with wives of geniuses, of near geniuses, of would be geniuses, in short I have sat very often and very long with many wives and wives of many geniuses.

As I was saying Fernande, who was then living with Picasso and had been with him a long time that is to say they were all twenty-four years old at that time but they had been together a long time, Fernande was the first wife of a genius I sat with and she was not the least amusing. We talked hats. Fernande had two subjects hats and perfumes. This first day we talked hats. She liked hats, she had the true french feeling about a hat, if a hat did not provoke some witticism from a man on the street the hat was not a success. Later on once in Montmartre she and I were walking together. She had on a large yellow hat and I had on a much smaller blue one. As we were walking along a workman stopped and called out, there go the sun and the moon shining together. Ah, said Fernande to me with a radiant smile, you see our hats are a success.

Miss Stein called me and said she wanted to have me meet Matisse. She was talking to a medium sized man with a reddish beard and glasses. He had a very alert although slightly heavy presence and Miss Stein and he seemed to be full of hidden meanings. As I came up I heard her say, Oh yes but it would be more difficult now. We were talking, she said, of a lunch party we had in here last year. We had just hung all the pictures and we asked all the painters. You know how painters are, I wanted to make them happy so I placed each one opposite his own picture, and they were happy so happy that we had to send out twice for more bread, when you know France you will know that that means that they were happy, because they cannot eat and drink without bread and we had to send out twice for bread so they were happy. Nobody noticed my little arrangement except Matisse and he did not until just as he left, and now he says it is a proof that I am very wicked, Matisse laughed and said, yes I know Mademoiselle Gertrude, the world is a theatre for you, but there are theatres and theatres, and when you listen so carefully to me and so attentively and do not hear a word I say then I do say that you are very wicked. Then they both began talking about the vernissage of the independent as every one else was doing and of course I did not know what it was all about. But gradually I knew and later on I will tell the story of the pictures, their painters and their followers and what this conversation meant.

Later I was near Picasso, he was standing meditatively. Do you think, he said, that I really do look like your president Lincoln. I had thought a good many things that evening but I had not thought that. You see, he went on, Gertrude, (I wish I could convey something of the simple affection and confidence with which he always pronounced her name and with which she always said, Pablo. In all their long friendship with all its sometimes troubled moments and its complications this has never changed.) Gertrude showed me a photograph of him and I have been trying to arrange my hair to look like his, I think my forehead does. I did not know whether he meant it or not but I was sympathetic. I did not realise then how completely and entirely american was Gertrude Stein. Later I often teased her, calling her a general, a civil war general of either or both sides. She had a series of photographs of the civil war, rather wonderful photographs and she and Picasso used to pore over them. Then he would suddenly remember the spanish war and he became very spanish and very bitter and Spain and America in their persons could say very bitter things about each other's country. But at this my first evening I knew nothing of all this and so I was polite and that was all.

And now the evening was drawing to a close. Everybody

was leaving and everybody was still talking about the vernissage of the independent. I too left carrying with me a card of invitation for the vernissage. And so this, one of the most important evenings of my life, came to an end.

I went to the vernissage taking with me a friend, the invitation I had been given admitting two. We went very early. I had been told to go early otherwise we would not be able to see anything, and there would be no place to sit, and my friend liked to sit. We went to the building just put up for this salon. In France they always put things up just for the day or for a few days and then take them down again. Gertrude Stein's elder brother always says that the secret of the chronic employment or lack of unemployment in France is due to the number of men actively engaged in putting up and taking down temporary buildings. Human nature is so permanent in France that they can afford to be as temporary as they like with their buildings. We went to the long low certainly very very long temporary building that was put up every year for the independents. When after the war or just before, I forget, the independent was given permanent quarters in the big exposition building, the Grand Palais, it became much less interesting. After all it is the adventure that counts. The long building was beautifully alight with Paris light.

In earlier, still earlier days, in the days of Seurat, the independent had its exhibition in a building where the rain rained in. Indeed it was because of this, that in hanging pictures in the rain, poor Seurat caught his fatal cold. Now there was no rain coming in, it was a lovely day and we felt very festive. When we got in we were indeed early as nearly as possible the first to be there. We went from one room to another and quite frankly we had no idea which of the pictures the Saturday evening crowd would have thought art and which were just the attempts of what in France are known as the Sunday painters, workingmen, hair-dressers and veterinaries and visionaries who only paint once a week when they do not have to work. I say we did not know but yes perhaps we did know. But not about the Rousseau, and there was an enormous Rousseau there which was the scandal of the show, it was a picture of the officials of the republic, Picasso now owns it, no that picture we could not know as going to be one of the great pictures, and that as Hélène was to say, would come to be in the Louvre. There was also there if my memory is correct a strange picture by the same douanier Rousseau, a sort of apotheosis of Guillaume Apollinaire with an aged Marie Laurencin behind him as a muse. That also I would not have recognised as a serious work of art. At that time of course I knew nothing about Marie Laurencin and Guillaume Apollinaire but there is a lot to tell about them later. Then we went on and saw a Matisse. Ah there we were beginning to feel at home. We knew a Matisse when we saw it, knew at once and enjoyed it and knew that it was great art and beautiful. It was a big figure of a woman lying in among some cactuses. A picture which was after the show to be at the rue de Fleurus. There one day the five year old little boy of the janitor who often used to visit Gertrude Stein who was fond of him, jumped into her arms as she was standing at the open door of the atelier and looking over her shoulder and seeing the picture cried out in rapture, oh là là what a beautiful body of a woman. Miss Stein used always to tell this story when the casual stranger in the aggressive way of the casual stranger said, looking at this picture, and what is that supposed to represent.

In the same room as the Matisse, a little covered by a partition, was a hungarian version of the same picture by one Czobel whom I remembered to have seen at the rue de Fleurus, it was the happy independent way to put a violent follower opposite the violent but not quite as violent master.

We went on and on, there were a great many rooms and a great many pictures in the rooms and finally we came to a middle room and there was a garden bench and as there were people coming in quite a few people we sat down on the bench to rest.

We had been resting and looking at every body and it was indeed the vie de Bohème just as one had seen it in the opera and they were very wonderful to look at. Just then somebody behind us put a hand on our shoulders and burst out laughing. It was Gertrude Stein. You have seated yourselves admirably, she said. But why, we asked. Because right here in front of you is the whole story. We looked but we saw nothing except two big pictures that looked quite alike but not altogether alike. One is a Braque and one is a Derain, explained Gertrude Stein. They were strange pictures of strangely formed rather wooden blocked figures, one if I remember rightly a sort of man and women, the other three women. Well, she said still laughing. We were puzzled, we had seen so much strangeness we did not know why these two were any stranger. She was quickly lost in an excited and voluble crowd. We recognised Pablo Picasso and Fernande, we thought we recognised many more, to be sure everybody seemed to be interested in our corner and we stayed, but we did not know why they were so especially interested. After a considerable interval Gertrude Stein came back again, this time evidently even more excited and amused. She leaned over us and said solemnly, do you want to take french lessons. We hesitated, why yes we could take french lessons. Well Fernande will give you french lessons, go and find her and tell her how absolutely you are pining to take french lessons. But why should she give us french lessons, we asked. Because, well because she and Pablo have decided to separate forever. I suppose it has happened before but not since I have known them. You know Pablo says if you love a woman you give her money. Well now it is when you want to leave a woman you have to wait until you have enough money to give her. Vollard has just bought out his atelier and so he can afford to separate from her by giving her half. She wants to install herself in a room by herself and give french lessons, so that is how you come in. Well what has that to do with these two pictures, asked my ever curious friend. Nothing, said Gertrude Stein going off with a great shout of laughter.

I will tell the whole story as I afterward learnt it but now I must find Fernande and propose to her to take french lessons from her.

I wandered about and looked at the crowd, never had I imagined there could be so many kinds of men making and looking at pictures. In America, even in San Francisco, I had been accustomed to see women at picture shows and some men, but here there were men, men, men, sometimes women with them but more often three or four men with one woman, sometimes five or six men with two women. Later on I became accustomed to this proportion. In one of these groups of five or six men and two women I saw the Picassos, that is I saw Fernande with her characteristic gesture, one ringed forefinger straight in the air. As I afterwards found out she had the Napoleonic forefinger quite as long if not a shade longer than the middle finger, and this, whenever she was animated, which after all was not very often because Fernande was indolent, always went straight up into the air. I waited not wishing to break into this group of which she at one end and Picasso at the other end were the absorbed centres but finally I summoned up courage to go forward and draw her attention and tell her of my desire. Oh yes, she said sweetly, Gertrude has told me of your desire, it would give me great pleasure to give you lessons, you and your friend, I will be the next few days very busy installing myself in my new apartment. Gertrude is coming to see me the end of the week, if you and your friend would accompany her we could then make all arrangements. Fernande spoke a very elegant french, some lapses of course into montmartrois that I found difficult to follow, but she had been educated to be a schoolmistress, her voice was lovely and she was very very beautiful with a marvellous complexion. She was a big woman but not too big because she was indolent and she had the small round arms that give the characteristic beauty to all french women. It was rather a pity that short skirts ever came in because until then one never imagined the sturdy french legs of the average french woman, one thought only of the beauty of the small rounded arms. I agreed to Fernande's proposal and left her.

On my way back to where my friend was sitting I became more accustomed not so much to the pictures as to the people. I began to realise there was a certain uniformity of type. Many years after, that is just a few years ago, when Juan Gris whom we all loved very much died, (he was after Pablo Picasso Gertrude Stein's dearest friend) I heard her say to Braque, she and he were standing together at the funeral, who are all these people, there are so many and they are so familiar and I do not know who any of them are. Oh, Braque replied, they are all the people you used to see at the vernissage of the independent and the autumn salon and you saw their faces twice a year, year after year, and that is the reason they are all so familiar.

Pablo and Fernande at Montmartre

Gertrude Stein and I about ten days later went to Montmartre, I for the first time. I have never ceased to love it. We go there every now and then and I always have the same tender expectant feeling that I had then. It is a place where you were always standing and sometimes waiting, not for anything to happen, but just standing. The inhabitants of Montmartre did not sit much, they mostly stood which was just as well as the chairs, the dining room chairs of France, did not tempt one to sit. So I went to Montmartre and I began my apprenticeship of standing. We first went to see Picasso and then we went to see Fernande. Picasso now never likes to go to Montmartre, he does not like to think about it much less talk about it. Even to Gertrude Stein he is hesitant about talking of it, there were things that at that time cut deeply into his spanish pride and the end of his Montmartre life was bitterness and disillusion, and there is nothing more bitter than spanish disillusion.

But at this time he was in and of Montmartre and lived in the rue Ravignan.

We went to the Odéon and there got into an omnibus, that is we mounted on top of an omnibus, the nice old horse-pulled omnibuses that went pretty quickly and steadily across Paris and up the hill to the place Blanche. There we got out and climbed a steep street lined with shops with things to eat, the rue Lepic, and then turning we went around a corner and climbed even more steeply in fact almost straight up and came to the rue Ravignan, now place Emile-Goudeau but otherwise unchanged, with its steps leading up to the little flat square with its few but tender little trees, a man carpentering in the corner of it, the last time I was there not very long ago there was still a man carpentering in a corner of it, and a little café just before you went up the steps where they all used to eat, it is still there, and to the left the low wooden building of studios that is still there.

We went up the couple of steps and through the open door passing on our left the studio in which later Juan Gris was to live out his martyrdom but where then lived a certain Vaillant, a nondescript painter who was to lend his studio as a ladies dressing room at the famous banquet for Rousseau, and then we passed a steep flight of steps leading down where Max

Jacob had a studio a little later, and we passed another steep little stairway which led to the studio where not long before a young fellow had committed suicide, Picasso painted one of the most wonderful of his early pictures of the friends gathered round the coffin, we passed all this to a larger door where Gertrude Stein knocked and Picasso opened the door and we went in.

He was dressed in what the french call the singe or monkey costume, overalls made of blue jean or brown, I think his was blue and it is called a singe or monkey because being all of one piece with a belt, if the belt is not fastened, and it very often is not, it hangs down behind and so makes a monkey. His eyes were more wonderful than even I remembered, so full and so brown, and his hands so dark and delicate and alert. We went further in. There was a couch in one corner, a very small stove that did for cooking and heating in the other corner, some chairs, the large broken one Gertrude Stein sat in when she was painted and a general smell of dog and paint and there was a big dog there and Picasso moved her about from one place to another exactly as if the dog had been a large piece of furniture. He asked us to sit down but as all the chairs were full we all stood up and stood until we left. It was my first experience of standing but afterwards I found that they all stood that way for hours. Against the wall was an enormous picture, a strange picture of light and dark colours, that is all I can say, of a group, an enormous group and next to it another in a sort of a red brown, of three women, square and posturing, all of it rather frightening. Picasso and Gertrude Stein stood together talking. I stood back and looked. I cannot say I realised anything but I felt that there was something painful and beautiful there and oppressive but imprisoned. I heard Gertrude Stein say, and mine. Picasso thereupon brought out a smaller picture, a rather unfinished thing that could not finish, very pale almost white, two figures, they were all there but very unfinished and not finishable. Picasso said, but he will never accept it. Yes, I know, answered Gertrude Stein. But just the same it is the only one in which it is all there. Yes, I know, he replied and they fell silent. After that they continued a low toned conversation and then Miss Stein said, well we have to go, we are going to have tea with

Fernande. Yes, I know, replied Picasso. How often do you see her, she said, he got very red and looked sheepish. I have never been there, he said resentfully. She chuckled, well anyway we are going there, she said, and Miss Toklas is going to have lessons in french. Ah the Miss Toklas, he said, with small feet like a spanish woman and earrings like a gypsy and a father who is king of Poland like the Poniatowskis, of course she will take lessons. We all laughed and went to the door. There stood a very beautiful man, oh Agero, said Picasso, you know the ladies. He looks like a Greco, I said in english. Picasso caught the name, a false Greco, he said. Oh I forgot to give you these, said Gertrude Stein handing Picasso a package of newspapers, they will console you. He opened them up, they were the Sunday supplement of american papers, they were the Katzenjammer kids. Oh oui, Oh oui, he said, his face full of satisfaction, merci thanks Gertrude, and we left.

We left then and continued to climb higher up the hill. What did you think of what you saw, asked Miss Stein. Well I did see something. Sure you did, she said, but did you see what it had to do with those two pictures you sat in front of so long at the vernissage. Only that Picassos were rather awful and the others were not. Sure, she said, as Pablo once remarked, when you make a thing, it is so complicated making it that it is bound to be ugly, but those that do it after you they don't have to worry about making it and they can make it pretty, and so everybody can like it when the others make it.

We went on and turned down a little street and there was another little house and we asked for Mademoiselle Bellevallée and we were sent into a little corridor and we knocked and went into a moderate sized room in which was a very large bed and a piano and a little tea table and Fernande and two others.

One of them was Alice Princet. She was rather a madonna like creature, with large lovely eyes and charming hair. Fernande afterwards explained that she was the daughter of a workingman and had the brutal thumbs that of course were a characteristic of workingmen. She had been, so Fernande explained, for seven years with Princet who was in the government employ and she had been faithful to him in the fashion of Montmartre, that is to say she had stuck to him through sickness and health but she had amused herself by the way. Now they were to be married. Princet had become the head of his small department in the government service and it would be necessary for him to invite other heads of departments to his house and so of course he must regularise the relation. They were actually married a few months afterward and it was apropos of this marriage that Max Jacob made his famous remark, it is wonderful to long for a woman for seven years and to possess her at last. Picasso made the more practical one, why should they marry simply in order to divorce. This was a prophecy.

No sooner were they married than Alice Princet met Derain and Derain met her. It was what the french call un coup de foudre, or love at first sight. They went quite mad about each other. Princet tried to bear it but they were married now and it was different. Beside he was angry for the first time in his life and in his anger he tore up Alice's first fur coat which she had gotten for the wedding. That settled the matter, and within six months after the marriage Alice left Princet never to return. She and Derain went off together and they have never separated since. I always liked Alice Derain. She had a certain wild quality that perhaps had to do with her brutal thumbs and was curiously in accord with her madonna face.

The other woman was Germaine Pichot, entirely a different type. She was quiet and serious and spanish, she had the square shoulders and the unseeing fixed eyes of a spanish woman. She was very gentle. She was married to a spanish painter Pichot, who was rather a wonderful creature, he was long and thin like one of those primitive Christs in spanish churches and when he did a spanish dance which he did later at the famous banquet to Rousseau, he was awe inspiringly religious.

Germaine, so Fernande said, was the heroine of many a strange story, she had once taken a young man to the hospital, he had been injured in a fracas at a music hall and all his crowd had deserted him. Germaine quite naturally stood by and saw him through. She had many sisters, she and all of them had been born and bred in Montmartre and they were all of different fathers and married to different nationalities, even to turks and armenians. Germaine, much later was very ill for years and she always had around her a devoted coterie. They used to carry her in her armchair to the nearest cinema and they, and she in the armchair, saw the performance through. They did this regularly once a week. I imagine they are still doing it.

The conversation around the tea table of Fernande was not lively, nobody had anything to say. It was a pleasure to meet, it was even an honour, but that was about all. Fernande complained a little that her charwoman had not adequately dusted and rinsed the tea things, and also that buying a bed and a piano on the instalment plan had elements of unpleasantness. Otherwise we really none of us had much to say.

Finally she and I arranged about the french lessons, I was to pay fifty cents an hour and she was to come to see me two days hence and we were to begin. Just at the end of the visit they were more natural. Fernande asked Miss Stein if she had any of the comic supplements of the american papers left. Gertrude Stein replied that she had just left them with Pablo.

Fernande roused like a lioness defending her cubs. That is a brutality that I will never forgive him, she said. I met him on the street, he had a comic supplement in his hand, I asked him to give it to me to help me to distract myself and he brutally refused. It was a piece of cruelty that I will never forgive. I ask you, Gertrude, to give to me myself the next copies you have of the comic supplement. Gertrude Stein said, why certainly with pleasure.

As we went out she said to me, it is to be hoped that they will be together again before the next comic supplements of the Katzenjammer kids come out because if I do not give them to Pablo he will be all upset and if I do Fernande will make an awful fuss. Well I suppose I will have to lose them or have my brother give them to Pablo by mistake.

Fernande came quite promptly to the appointment and we proceeded to our lesson. Of course to have a lesson in french one has to converse and Fernande had three subjects, hats, we had not much more to say about hats, perfumes, we had something to say about perfumes. Perfumes were Fernande's really great extravagance, she was the scandal of Montmartre because she had once bought a bottle of perfume named

Smoke and had paid eighty francs for it at that time sixteen dollars and it had no scent but such a wonderful colour, like real bottled liquid smoke. Her third subject was the categories of furs. There were three categories of furs, there were first category, sables, second category ermine and chinchilla, third category martin fox and squirrel. It was the most surprising thing I had heard in Paris. I was surprised. Chinchilla second, squirrel called fur and no seal skin.

Our only other conversation was the description and names of the dogs that were then fashionable. This was my subject and after I had described she always hesitated, ah yes, she would say illuminated, you wish to describe a little belgian dog whose name is griffon.

There we were, she was very beautiful but it was a little heavy and monotonous, so I suggested we should meet out of doors, at a tea place or take walks in Montmartre. That was better. She began to tell me things. I met Max Jacob. Fernande and he were very funny together. They felt themselves to be a courtly couple of the first empire, he being le vieux marquis kissing her hand and paying compliments and she the Empress Josephine receiving them. It was a caricature but a rather wonderful one. Then she told me about a mysterious horrible woman called Marie Laurencin who made noises like an animal and annoyed Picasso. I thought of her as a horrible old woman and was delighted when I met the young chic Marie who looked like a Clouet. Max Jacob read my horoscope. It was a great honour because he wrote it down. I did not realise it then but I have since and most of all very lately, as all the young gentlemen who nowadays so much admire Max are so astonished and impressed that he wrote mine down as he has always been supposed never to write them but just to say them off hand. Well anyway I have mine and it is written.

Then she also told me a great many stories about Van Dongen and his dutch wife and dutch little girl. Van Dongen broke into notoriety by a portrait he did of Fernande. It was in that way that he created the type of almond eyes that were later so much the vogue. But Fernande's almond eyes were natural, for good or for bad everything was natural in Fernande.

Of course Van Dongen did not admit that this picture was

a portrait of Fernande, although she had sat for it and there was in consequence much bitterness. Van Dongen in these days was poor, he had a dutch wife who was a vegetarian and they lived on spinach. Van Dongen frequently escaped from the spinach to a joint in Montmartre where the girls paid for his dinner and his drinks.

The Van Dongen child was only four years old but terrific. Van Dongen used to do acrobatics with her and swing her around his head by a leg. When she hugged Picasso of whom she was very fond she used almost to destroy him, he had a great fear of her.

There were many other tales of Germaine Pichot and the circus where she found her lovers and there were tales of all the past and present life of Montmartre. Fernande herself had one ideal. It was Evelyn Thaw the heroine of the moment. And Fernande adored her in the way a later generation adored Mary Pickford, she was so blonde, so pale, so nothing and Fernande would give a heavy sigh of admiration.

The next time I saw Gertrude Stein she said to me suddenly, is Fernande wearing her earrings. I do not know, I said. Well notice, she said. The next time I saw Gertrude Stein I said, yes Fernande is wearing her earrings. Oh well, she said, there is nothing to be done yet, it's a nuisance because Pablo naturally having nobody in the studio cannot stay at home. In another week I was able to announce that Fernande was not wearing her earrings. Oh well it's alright then she has no more money left and it is all over, said Gertrude Stein. And it was. A week later I was dining with Fernande and Pablo at the rue de Fleurus.

I gave Fernande a chinese gown from San Francisco and Pablo gave me a lovely drawing.

And now I will tell you how two americans happened to be in the heart of an art movement of which the outside world at that time knew nothing.

3.

Gertrude Stein in Paris
1903–1907

D URING Gertrude Stein's last two years at the Medical School, Johns Hopkins, Baltimore, 1900–1903, her brother was living in Florence. There he heard of a painter named Cézanne and saw paintings by him owned by Charles Loeser. When he and his sister made their home in Paris the following year they went to Vollard's the only picture dealer who had Cézannes for sale, to look at them.

Vollard was a huge dark man who lisped a little. His shop was on the rue Laffitte not far from the boulevard. Further along this short street was Durand-Ruel and still further on almost at the church of the Martyrs was Sagot the ex-clown. Higher up in Montmartre on the rue Victor-Massé was Mademoiselle Weill who sold a mixture of pictures, books and bric-à-brac and in entirely another part of Paris on the rue Faubourg-Saint-Honoré was the ex-café keeper and photographer Druet. Also on the rue Laffitte was the confectioner Fouquet where one could console oneself with delicious honey cakes and nut candies and once in a while instead of a picture buy oneself strawberry jam in a glass bowl.

The first visit to Vollard has left an indelible impression on Gertrude Stein. It was an incredible place. It did not look like a picture gallery. Inside there were a couple of canvases turned to the wall, in one corner was a small pile of big and little canvases thrown pell mell on top of one another, in the centre of the room stood a huge dark man glooming. This was Vollard cheerful. When he was really cheerless he put his huge frame against the glass door that led to the street, his arms above his head, his hands on each upper corner of the portal and gloomed darkly into the street. Nobody thought then of trying to come in.

They asked to see Cézannes. He looked less gloomy and became quite polite. As they found out afterward Cézanne was the great romance of Vollard's life. The name Cézanne was to him a magic word. He had first learned about Cézanne from Pissarro the painter. Pissarro indeed was the man from whom all the early Cézanne lovers heard about Cézanne. Cézanne at that time was living gloomy and embittered at Aix-en-Provence. Pissarro told Vollard about him, told Fabry, a Florentine, who told Loeser, told Picabia, in fact told everybody who knew about Cézanne at that time.

There were Cézannes to be seen at Vollard's. Later on Gertrude Stein wrote a poem called Vollard and Cézanne, and Henry McBride printed it in the New York Sun. This was the first fugitive piece of Gertrude Stein's to be so printed and it gave both her and Vollard a great deal of pleasure. Later on when Vollard wrote his book about Cézanne, Vollard at Gertrude Stein's suggestion sent a copy of the book to Henry McBride. She told Vollard that a whole page of one of New York's big daily papers would be devoted to his book. He did not believe it possible, nothing like that had ever happened to anybody in Paris. It did happen and he was deeply moved and unspeakably content. But to return to that first visit.

They told Monsieur Vollard they wanted to see some Cézanne landscapes, they had been sent to him by Mr. Loeser of Florence. Oh yes, said Vollard looking quite cheerful and he began moving about the room, finally he disappeared behind a partition in the back and was heard heavily mounting the steps. After a quite long wait he came down again and had in his hand a tiny picture of an apple with most of the canvas unpainted. They all looked at this thoroughly, then they said, yes but you see what we wanted to see was a landscape. Ah yes, sighed Vollard and he looked even more cheerful, after a moment he again disappeared and this time came back with a painting of a back, it was a beautiful painting there is no doubt about that but the brother and sister were not yet up to a full appreciation of Cézanne nudes and so they returned to the attack. They wanted to see a landscape. This time after even a longer wait he came back with a very large canvas and a very little fragment of a landscape painted on it. Yes that was it, they said, a landscape but what they wanted was a smaller canvas but one all covered. They said, they thought they would like to see one like that. By this time the early winter evening of Paris was closing in and just at this moment a very aged charwoman came down the same back stairs, mumbled, bon soir monsieur et madame, and quietly went out of the door, after a moment another old charwoman came down the same stairs, murmured, bon soir messieurs et mesdames and went quietly out of the door. Gertrude Stein began to laugh and said to her brother, it is all nonsense, there is no Cézanne. Vollard goes upstairs and tells these old women what to paint and he does not understand us and they do not understand him and they paint something and he brings it down and it is a Cézanne. They both began to laugh uncontrollably. Then they recovered and once more explained about the landscape. They said what they wanted was one of those marvellously yellow sunny Aix landscapes of which Loeser had several examples. Once more Vollard went off and this time he came back with a wonderful small green landscape. It was lovely, it covered all the canvas, it did not cost much and they bought it. Later on Vollard explained to every one that he had been visited by two crazy americans and they laughed and he had been much annoyed but gradually he found out that when they laughed most they usually bought something so of course he waited for them to laugh.

From that time on they went to Vollard's all the time. They had soon the privilege of upsetting his piles of canvases and finding what they liked in the heap. They bought a tiny little Daumier, head of an old woman. They began to take an interest in Cézanne nudes and they finally bought two tiny canvases of nude groups. They found a very very small Manet painted in black and white with Forain in the foreground and bought it, they found two tiny little Renoirs. They frequently bought in twos because one of them usually liked one more than the other one did, and so the year wore on. In the spring Vollard announced a show of Gauguin and they for the first time saw some Gauguins. They were rather awful but they finally liked them, and bought two Gauguins. Gertrude Stein liked his sun-flowers but not his figures and her brother preferred the figures. It sounds like a great deal now but in those days these things did not cost much. And so the winter went on.

There were not a great many people in and out of Vollard's but once Gertrude Stein heard a conversation there that pleased her immensely. Duret was a well known figure in Paris. He was now a very old and a very handsome man. He had been a friend of Whistler, Whistler had painted him in evening clothes with a white opera cloak over his arm. He was at Vollard's talking to a group of younger men and one of them Roussel, one of the Vuillard, Bonnard, the post impressionist group, said something complainingly about the lack of recognition of himself and his friends, that they were not even allowed to show in the salon. Duret looked at him kindly, my young friend, he said, there are two kinds of art, never forget this, there is art and there is official art. How can you, my poor young friend, hope to be official art. Just look at yourself. Supposing an important personage came to France, and wanted to meet the representative painters and have his portrait painted. My dear young friend, just look at yourself, the very sight of you would terrify him. You are a nice young man, gentle and intelligent, but to the important personage you would not seem so, you would be terrible. No they need as representative painter a medium sized, slightly stout man, not too well dressed but dressed in the fashion of his class, neither bald or well brushed hair and a respectful bow with it. You can see that you would not do. So never say another word about official recognition, or if you do look in the mirror and think of important personages. No, my dear young friend there is art and there is official art, there always has been and there always will be.

Before the winter was over, having gone so far Gertrude Stein and her brother decided to go further, they decided to buy a big Cézanne and then they would stop. After that they would be reasonable. They convinced their elder brother that this last outlay was necessary, and it was necessary as will soon be evident. They told Vollard that they wanted to buy a Cézanne portrait. In those days practically no big Cézanne portraits had been sold. Vollard owned almost all of them. He was enormously pleased with this decision. They now were introduced into the room above the steps behind the partition where Gertrude Stein had been sure the old charwomen painted the Cézannes and there they spent days deciding which portrait they would have. There were about eight to choose from and the decision was difficult. They had often to go and refresh themselves with honey cakes at Fouquet's. Finally they narrowed the choice down to two, a portrait of a man and a portrait of a woman, but this time they could not afford to buy twos and finally they chose the portrait of the woman.

Vollard said of course ordinarily a portrait of a woman always is more expensive than a portrait of a man but, said he looking at the picture very carefully, I suppose with Cézanne it does not make any difference. They put it in a cab and they went home with it. It was this picture that Alfy Maurer used to explain was finished and that you could tell that it was finished because it had a frame.

It was an important purchase because in looking and looking at this picture Gertrude Stein wrote Three Lives.

She had begun not long before as an exercise in literature to translate Flaubert's Trois Contes and then she had this Cézanne and she looked at it and under its stimulus she wrote Three Lives.

The next thing that happened was in the autumn. It was the first year of the autumn salon, the first autumn salon that had ever existed in Paris and they, very eager and excited, went to see it. There they found Matisse's picture afterwards known as La Femme au Chapeau.

This first autumn salon was a step in official recognition of the outlaws of the independent salon. Their pictures were to be shown in the Petit Palais opposite the Grand Palais where the great spring salon was held. That is, those outlaws were to be shown there who had succeeded enough so that they began to be sold in important picture shops. These in collaboration with some rebels from the old salons had created the autumn salon.

The show had a great deal of freshness and was not alarming. There were a number of attractive pictures but there was one that was not attractive. It infuriated the public, they tried to scratch off the paint.

Gertrude Stein liked that picture, it was a portrait of a woman with a long face and a fan. It was very strange in its colour and in its anatomy. She said she wanted to buy it. Her brother had in the meantime found a white-clothed woman on a green lawn and he wanted to buy it. So as usual they

Room with Oil Lamp

decided to buy two and they went to the office of the secretary of the salon to find out about prices. They had never been in the little room of a secretary of a salon and it was very exciting. The secretary looked up the prices in his catalogue. Gertrude Stein has forgotten how much and even whose it was, the white dress and dog on the green grass, but the Matisse was five hundred francs. The secretary explained that of course one never paid what the artist asked, one suggested a price. They asked what price they should suggest. He asked them what they were willing to pay. They said they did not know. He suggested that they offer four hundred and he would let them know. They agreed and left.

The next day they received word from the secretary that Monsieur Matisse had refused to accept the offer and what did they want to do. They decided to go over to the salon and look at the picture again. They did. People were roaring with laughter at the picture and scratching at it. Gertrude Stein could not understand why, the picture seemed to her perfectly natural. The Cézanne portrait had not seemed natural, it had taken her some time to feel that it was natural but this picture by Matisse seemed perfectly natural and she could not understand why it infuriated everybody. Her brother was less attracted but all the same he agreed and they bought it. She then went back to look at it and it upset her to see them all mocking at it. It bothered her and angered her because she did not understand why because to her it was so alright, just as later she did not understand why since the writing was all so clear and natural they mocked at and were enraged by her work.

And so this was the story of the buying of La Femme au Chapeau by the buyers and now for the story from the seller's point of view as told some months after by Monsieur and Madame Matisse. Shortly after the purchase of the picture they all asked to meet each other. Whether Matisse wrote and asked or whether they wrote and asked Gertrude Stein does not remember. Anyway in no time they were knowing each other and knowing each other very well.

The Matisses lived on the quay just off the boulevard Saint-Michel. They were on the top floor in a small three-roomed apartment with a lovely view over Notre Dame and the river.

Matisse painted it in winter. You went up and up the steps. In those days you were always going up stairs and down stairs. Mildred Aldrich had a distressing way of dropping her key down the middle of the stairs where an elevator might have been, in calling out goodbye to some one below, from her sixth story, and then you or she had to go all the way up or all the way down again. To be sure she would often call out, never mind, I am bursting open my door. Only americans did that. The keys were heavy and you either forgot them or dropped them. Sayen at the end of a Paris summer when he was congratulated on looking so well and sun-burned, said, yes it comes from going up and down stairs.

Madame Matisse was an admirable housekeeper. Her place was small but immaculate. She kept the house in order, she was an excellent cook and provider, she posed for all of Matisse's pictures. It was she who was La Femme au Chapeau, lady with a hat. She had kept a little millinery shop to keep them going in their poorest days. She was a very straight dark woman with a long face and a firm large loosely hung mouth like a horse. She had an abundance of dark hair. Gertrude Stein always liked the way she pinned her hat to her head and Matisse once made a drawing of his wife making this characteristic gesture and gave it to Miss Stein. She always wore black. She always placed a large black hat-pin well in the middle of the hat and the middle of the top of her head and then with a large firm gesture, down it came. They had with them a daughter of Matisse, a daughter he had had before his marriage and who had had diphtheria and had had to have an operation and for many years had to wear a black ribbon around her throat with a silver button. This Matisse put into many of his pictures. The girl was exactly like her father and Madame Matisse, as she once explained in her melodramatic simple way, did more than her duty by this child because having read in her youth a novel in which the heroine had done so and been consequently much loved all her life, had decided to do the same. She herself had had two boys but they were neither of them at that time living with them. The younger Pierre was in the south of France on the borders of Spain with Madame Matisse's father and mother, and the elder Jean with

Monsieur Matisse's father and mother in the north of France on the borders of Belgium.

Matisse had an astonishing virility that always gave one an extraordinary pleasure when one had not seen him for some time. Less the first time of seeing him than later. And one did not lose the pleasure of this virility all the time he was with one. But there was not much feeling of life in this virility. Madame Matisse was very different, there was a very profound feeling of life in her for any one who knew her.

Matisse had at this time a small Cézanne and a small Gauguin and he said he needed them both. The Cézanne had been bought with his wife's marriage portion, the Gauguin with the ring which was the only jewel she had ever owned. And they were happy because he needed these two pictures. The Cézanne was a picture of bathers and a tent, the Gauguin the head of a boy. Later on in life when Matisse became a very rich man, he kept on buying pictures. He said he knew about pictures and had confidence in them and he did not know about other things. And so for his own pleasure and as the best legacy to leave his children he bought Cézannes. Picasso also later when he became rich bought pictures but they were his own. He too believed in pictures and wants to leave the best legacy he can to his son and so keeps and buys his own.

The Matisses had had a hard time. Matisse had come to Paris as a young man to study pharmacy. His people were small grain merchants in the north of France. He had become interested in painting, had begun copying the Poussins at the Louvre and become a painter fairly without the consent of his people who however continued to allow him the very small monthly sum he had had as a student. His daughter was born at this time and this further complicated his life. He had at first a certain amount of success. He married. Under the influence of the paintings of Poussin and Chardin he had painted still life pictures that had considerable success at the Champ-de-Mars salon, one of the two big spring salons. And then he fell under the influence of Cézanne, and then under the influence of negro sculpture. All this developed the Matisse of the period of La Femme au Chapeau. The year after his very considerable success at the salon he spent the winter painting a very large picture of a woman setting a table and on the table was a magnificent dish of fruit. It had strained the resources of the Matisse family to buy this fruit, fruit was horribly dear in Paris in those days, even ordinary fruit, imagine how much dearer was this very extraordinary fruit and it had to keep until the picture was completed and the picture was going to take a long time. In order to keep it as long as possible they kept the room as cold as possible, and that under the roof and in a Paris winter was not difficult, and Matisse painted in an overcoat and gloves and he painted at it all winter. It was finished at last and sent to the salon where the year before Matisse had had considerable success, and there it was refused. And now Matisse's serious troubles began, his daughter was very ill, he was in an agonising mental struggle concerning his work, and he had lost all possibility of showing his pictures. He no longer painted at home but in an atelier. It was cheaper so. Every morning he painted, every afternoon he worked at his sculpture, late every afternoon he drew in the sketch classes from the nude, and every evening he played his violin. These were very dark days and he was very despairful. His wife opened a small millinery shop and they managed to live. The two boys were sent away to the country to his and her people and they continued to live. The only encouragement came in the atelier where he worked and where a crowd of young men began to gather around him and be influenced by him. Among these the best known at that time was Manguin, the best known now Derain. Derain was a very young man at that time, he enormously admired Matisse, he went away to the country with them to Collioure near Perpignan, and he was a great comfort to them all. He began to paint landscapes outlining his trees with red and he had a sense of space that was quite his own and which first showed itself in a landscape of a cart going up a road bordered with trees lined in red. His paintings were coming to be known at the independent.

Matisse worked every day and every day and every day and he worked terribly hard. Once Vollard came to see him. Matisse used to love to tell the story. I have often heard him tell it. Vollard came and said he wanted to see the big picture which had been refused. Matisse showed it to him. He did not look at it. He talked to Madame Matisse and mostly about cooking, he liked cooking and eating as a frenchman should, and so did she. Matisse and Madame Matisse were both getting very nervous although she did not show it. And this door, said Vollard interestedly to Matisse, where does that lead to, does that lead into a court or does that lead on to a stairway. Into a court, said Matisse. Ah yes, said Vollard. And then he left.

The Matisses spent days discussing whether there was anything symbolic in Vollard's question or was it idle curiosity. Vollard never had any idle curiosity, he always wanted to know what everybody thought of everything because in that way he found out what he himself thought. This was very well known and therefore the Matisses asked each other and all their friends, why did he ask that question about that door. Well at any rate within the year he had bought the picture at a very low price but he bought it, and he put it away and nobody saw it, and that was the end of that.

From this time on things went neither better nor worse for Matisse and he was discouraged and aggressive. Then came the first autumn salon and he was asked to exhibit and he sent La Femme au Chapeau and it was hung. It was derided and attacked and it was sold.

Matisse was at this time about thirty-five years old, he was depressed. Having gone to the opening day of the salon and heard what was said of his picture and seen what they were trying to do to it he never went again. His wife went alone. He stayed at home and was unhappy. This is the way Madame Matisse used to tell the story.

Then a note came from the secretary of the salon saying that there had been an offer made for the picture, an offer of four hundred francs. Matisse was painting Madame Matisse as a gypsy holding a guitar. This guitar had already had a history. Madame Matisse was very fond of telling the story. She had a great deal to do and she posed beside and she was very healthy and sleepy. One day she was posing, he was painting, she began to nod and as she nodded the guitar made noises. Stop it, said Matisse, wake up. She woke up, he painted, she nodded and the guitar made noises. Stop it, said Matisse, wake up. She woke up and then in a little while she nodded again the guitar made even more noises. Matisse furious seized the guitar and broke it. And added Madame Matisse ruefully, we were very hard up then and we had to have it mended so he could go on with the picture. She was holding this same mended guitar and posing when the note from the secretary of the autumn salon came. Matisse was joyful, of course I will accept, said Matisse. Oh no, said Madame Matisse, if those people (ces gens) are interested enough to make an offer they are interested enough to pay the price you asked, and she added, the difference would make winter clothes for Margot. Matisse hesitated but was finally convinced and they sent a note saying he wanted his price. Nothing happened and Matisse was in a terrible state and very reproachful and then in a day or two when Madame Matisse was once more posing with the guitar and Matisse was painting, Margot brought them a little blue telegram. Matisse opened it and he made a grimace. Madame Matisse was terrified, she thought the worst had happened. The guitar fell. What is it, she said. They have bought it, he said. Why do you make such a face of agony and frighten me so and perhaps break the guitar, she said. I was winking at you, he said, to tell you, because I was so moved I could not speak.

And so, Madame Matisse used to end up the story triumphantly, you see it was I, and I was right to insist upon the original price, and Mademoiselle Gertrude, who insisted upon buying it, who arranged the whole matter.

The friendship with the Matisses grew apace. Matisse at that time was at work at his first big decoration, Le Bonheur de Vivre. He was making small and larger and very large studies for it. It was in this picture that Matisse first clearly realised his intention of deforming the drawing of the human body in order to harmonise and intensify the colour values of all the simple colours mixed only with white. He used his distorted drawing as a dissonance is used in music or as vinegar or lemons are used in cooking or egg shells in coffee to clarify. I do inevitably take my comparisons from the kitchen because I like food and cooking and know something about it. However this was the idea. Cézanne had come to his unfinishedness and distortion of necessity, Matisse did it by intention.

Little by little people began to come to the rue de Fleurus to see the Matisses and the Cézannes, Matisse brought people, everybody brought somebody, and they came at any time and it began to be a nuisance, and it was in this way that Saturday evenings began. It was also at this time that Gertrude Stein got into the habit of writing at night. It was only after eleven o'clock that she could be sure that no one would knock at the studio door. She was at that time planning her long book, The Making of Americans, she was struggling with her sentences, those long sentences that had to be so exactly carried out. Sentences not only words but sentences and always sentences have been Gertrude Stein's life long passion. And so she had then and indeed it lasted pretty well to the war, which broke down so many habits, she had then the habit of beginning her work at eleven o'clock at night and working until the dawn. She said she always tried to stop before the dawn was too clear and the birds were too lively because it is a disagreeable sensation to go to bed then. There were birds in many trees behind high walls in those days, now there are fewer. But often the birds and the dawn caught her and she stood in the court waiting to get used to it before she went to bed. She had the habit then of sleeping until noon and the beating of the rugs into the court, because everybody did that in those days, even her household did, was one of her most poignant irritations.

So the Saturday evenings began.

Gertrude Stein and her brother were often at the Matisses and the Matisses were constantly with them. Madame Matisse occasionally gave them a lunch, this happened most often when some relation sent the Matisses a hare. Jugged hare prepared by Madame Matisse in the fashion of Perpignan was something quite apart. They also had extremely good wine, a little heavy, but excellent. They also had a sort of Madeira called Roncio which was very good indeed. Maillol the sculptor came from the same part of France as Madame Matisse and once when I met him at Jo Davidson's, many years later, he told me about all these wines. He then told me how he had lived well in his student days in Paris for fifty francs a month. To be sure, he said, the family sent me homemade bread every week and when I came I brought enough wine with me to last a year and I sent my washing home every month.

Derain was present at one of these lunches in those early days. He and Gertrude Stein disagreed violently. They discussed philosophy, he basing his ideas on having read the second part of Faust in a french translation while he was doing his military service. They never became friends. Gertrude Stein was never interested in his work. He had a sense of space but for her his pictures had neither life nor depth nor solidity. They rarely saw each other after. Derain at that time was constantly with the Matisses and was of all Matisse's friends the one Madame Matisse liked the best.

It was about this time that Gertrude Stein's brother happened one day to find the picture gallery of Sagot, an ex-circus clown who had a picture shop further up the rue Laffitte. Here he, Gertrude Stein's brother, found the paintings of two young spaniards, one, whose name everybody has forgotten, the other one, Picasso. The work of both of them interested him and he bought a water colour by the forgotten one, a café scene. Sagot also sent him to a little furniture store where there were some paintings being shown by Picasso. Gertrude Stein's brother was interested and wanted to buy one and asked the price but the price asked was almost as expensive as Cézanne. He went back to Sagot and told him. Sagot laughed. He said, that is alright, come back in a few days and I will have a big one. In a few days he did have a big one and it was very cheap. When Gertrude Stein and Picasso tell about those days they are not always in agreement as to what happened but I think in this case they agree that the price asked was a hundred and fifty francs. The picture was the now well known painting of a nude girl with a basket of red flowers.

Gertrude Stein did not like the picture, she found something rather appalling in the drawing of the legs and feet, something that repelled and shocked her. She and her brother almost quarrelled about this picture. He wanted it and she did not want it in the house. Sagot gathering a little of the discussion said, but that is alright if you do not like the legs and feet it is very easy to guillotine her and only take the head. No that would not do, everybody agreed, and nothing was decided.

Room with Bonheur de Vivre and Cézanne

Gertrude Stein and her brother continued to be very divided in this matter and they were very angry with each other. Finally it was agreed that since he, the brother, wanted it so badly they would buy it, and in this way the first Picasso was brought into the rue de Fleurus.

It was just about this time that Raymond Duncan, the brother of Isadora, rented an atelier in the rue de Fleurus. Raymond had just come back from his first trip to Greece and had brought back with him a greek girl and greek clothes. Raymond had known Gertrude Stein's elder brother and his wife in San Francisco. At that time Raymond was acting as advance agent for Emma Nevada who had also with her Pablo Casals the violincellist, at that time quite unknown.

The Duncan family had been then at the Omar Khayyám stage, they had not yet gone greek. They had after that gone italian renaissance, but now Raymond had gone completely greek and this included a greek girl. Isadora lost interest in him, she found the girl too modern a greek. At any rate Raymond was at this time without any money at all and his wife was enceinte. Gertrude Stein gave him coal and a chair for Penelope to sit in, the rest sat on packing cases. They had another friend who helped them, Kathleen Bruce, a very beautiful, very athletic English girl, a kind of sculptress, she later married and became the widow of the discoverer of the South Pole, Scott. She had at that time no money to speak of either and she used to bring a half portion of her dinner every evening for Penelope. Finally Penelope had her baby, it was named Raymond because when Gertrude Stein's brother and Raymond Duncan went to register it they had not thought of a name. Now he is against his will called Menalkas but he might be gratified if he knew that legally he is Raymond. However that is another matter.

Kathleen Bruce was a sculptress and she was learning to model figures of children and she asked to do a figure of Gertrude Stein's nephew. Gertrude Stein and her nephew went to Kathleen Bruce's studio. There they, one afternoon, met H. P. Roché. Roché was one of those characters that are always to be found in Paris. He was a very earnest, very noble, devoted, very faithful and very enthusiastic man who was a general introducer. He knew everybody, he really knew them and he could introduce anybody to anybody. He was going to be a writer. He was tall and red-headed and he never said anything but good good excellent and he lived with his mother and his grandmother. He had done a great many things, he had gone to the austrian mountains with the austrians, he had gone to Germany with the germans and he had gone to Hungary with hungarians and he had gone to England with the english. He had not gone to Russia although he had been in Paris with russians. As Picasso always said of him, Roché is very nice but he is only a translation.

Later he was often at 27 rue de Fleurus with various nationalities and Gertrude Stein rather liked him. She always said of him he is so faithful, perhaps one need never see him again but one knows that somewhere Roché is faithful. He did give her one delightful sensation in the very early days of their acquaintance. Three Lives, Gertrude Stein's first book was just then being written and Roché who could read english was very impressed by it. One day Gertrude Stein was saying something about herself and Roché said good good excellent that is very important for your biography. She was terribly touched, it was the first time that she really realised that some time she would have a biography. It is quite true that although she has not seen him for years somewhere Roché is probably perfectly faithful.

But to come back to Roché at Kathleen Bruce's studio. They all talked about one thing and another and Gertrude Stein happened to mention that they had just bought a picture from Sagot by a young spaniard named Picasso. Good good excellent, said Roché, he is a very interesting young fellow, I know him. Oh do you, said Gertrude Stein, well enough to take somebody to see him. Why certainly, said Roché. Very well, said Gertrude Stein, my brother I know is very anxious to make his acquaintance. And there and then the appointment was made and shortly after Roché and Gertrude Stein's brother went to see Picasso.

It was only a very short time after this that Picasso began the portrait of Gertrude Stein, now so widely known, but just how that came about is a little vague in everybody's mind. I have heard Picasso and Gertrude Stein talk about it often and they neither of them can remember. They can remember the first time that Picasso dined at the rue de Fleurus and they can remember the first time Gertrude Stein posed for her portrait at rue Ravignan but in between there is a blank. How it came about they do not know. Picasso had never had anybody pose for him since he was sixteen years old, he was then twenty-four and Gertrude Stein had never thought of having her portrait painted, and they do not either of them know how it came about. Anyway it did and she posed to him for this portrait ninety times and a great deal happened during that time. To go back to all the first times.

Picasso and Fernande came to dinner, Picasso in those days was, what a dear friend and schoolmate of mine, Nellie Jacot, called, a good-looking bootblack. He was thin dark, alive with big pools of eyes and a violent but not a rough way. He was sitting next to Gertrude Stein at dinner and she took up a piece of bread. This, said Picasso, snatching it back with violence, this piece of bread is mine. She laughed and he looked sheepish. That was the beginning of their intimacy.

That evening Gertrude Stein's brother took out portfolio after portfolio of japanese prints to show Picasso, Gertrude Stein's brother was fond of japanese prints. Picasso solemnly and obediently looked at print after print and listened to the descriptions. He said under his breath to Gertrude Stein, he is very nice, your brother, but like all americans, like Haviland, he shows you japanese prints. Moi j'aime pas ça, no I don't care for it. As I say Gertrude Stein and Pablo Picasso immediately understood each other.

Then there was the first time of posing. The atelier of Picasso I have already described. In those days there was even more disorder, more coming and going, more red-hot fire in the stove, more cooking and more interruptions. There was a large broken armchair where Gertrude Stein posed. There was a couch where everybody sat and slept. There was a little kitchen chair upon which Picasso sat to paint, there was a large easel and there were many very large canvases. It was at the height of the end of the Harlequin period when the canvases were enormous, the figures also, and the groups.

There was a little fox terrier there that had something the matter with it and had been and was again about to be taken to the veterinary. No frenchman or frenchwoman is so poor or so careless or so avaricious but that they can and do constantly take their pet to the vet.

Fernande was as always, very large, very beautiful and very gracious. She offered to read La Fontaine's stories aloud to amuse Gertrude Stein while Gertrude Stein posed. She took her pose, Picasso sat very tight on his chair and very close to his canvas and on a very small palette which was of a uniform brown grey colour, mixed some more brown grey and the painting began. This was the first of some eighty or ninety sittings.

Toward the end of the afternoon Gertrude Stein's two brothers and her sister-in-law and Andrew Green came to see. They were all excited at the beauty of the sketch and Andrew Green begged and begged that it should be left as it was. But Picasso shook his head and said, non.

It is too bad but in those days no one thought of taking a photograph of the picture as it was then and of course no one of the group that saw it then remembers at all what it looked like any more than do Picasso or Gertrude Stein.

Andrew Green, none of them knew how they had met Andrew Green, he was the great-nephew of Andrew Green known as the father of Greater New York. He had been born and reared in Chicago but he was a typical tall gaunt new englander, blond and gentle. He had a prodigious memory and could recite all of Milton's Paradise Lost by heart and also all the translations of chinese poems of which Gertrude Stein was very fond. He had been in China and he was later to live permanently in the South Sea islands after he finally inherited quite a fortune from his great-uncle who was fond of Milton's Paradise Lost. He had a passion for oriental stuffs. He adored as he said a simple centre and a continuous design. He loved pictures in museums and he hated everything modern. Once when during the family's absence he had stayed at the rue de Fleurus for a month, he had outraged Hélène's feelings by having his bed-sheets changed every day and covering all the pictures with cashmere shawls. He said the pictures were very restful, he could not deny that, but he could not bear it. He said that after the month was over that he had of course never come to like the new pictures but the worst of it was that not liking them he had lost his taste for the old

Room with Gas (Femme au chapeau and Picasso Portrait)

and he never again in his life could go to any museum or look at any picture. He was tremendously impressed by Fernande's beauty. He was indeed quite overcome. I would, he said to Gertrude Stein, if I could talk french, I would make love to her and take her away from that little Picasso. Do you make love with words, laughed Gertrude Stein. He went away before I came to Paris and he came back eighteen years later and he was very dull.

This year was comparatively a quiet one. The Matisses were in the South of France all winter, at Collioure on the Mediterranean coast not far from Perpignan, where Madame Matisse's people lived. The Raymond Duncans had disappeared after having been joined first by a sister of Penelope who was a little actress and was very far from being dressed greek, she was as nearly as she possibly could be a little Parisian. She had accompanying her a very large dark greek cousin. He came in to see Gertrude Stein and he looked around and he announced, I am greek, that is the same as saying that I have perfect taste and I do not care for any of these pictures. Very shortly Raymond, his wife and baby, the sister-in-law and the greek cousin disappeared out of the court at 27 rue de Fleurus and were succeeded by a german lady.

This german lady was the niece and god-daughter of german field-marshals and her brother was a captain in the german navy. Her mother was english and she herself had played the harp at the bavarian court. She was very amusing and had some strange friends, both english and french. She was a sculptress and she made a typical german sculpture of little Roger, the concierge's boy. She made three heads of him, one laughing, one crying and one sticking out his tongue, all three together on one pedestal. She sold this piece to the royal museum at Potsdam. The concierge during the war often wept at the thought of her Roger being there, sculptured, in the museum at Potsdam. She invented clothes that could be worn inside out and taken to pieces and be made long or short and she showed these to everybody with great pride. She had as an instructor in painting a weird looking frenchman one who looked exactly like the pictures of Huckleberry Finn's father. She explained that she employed him out of charity, he had won a gold medal at the salon in his youth and after that had

had no success. She also said that she never employed a servant of the servant class. She said that decayed gentlewomen were more appetising and more efficient and she always had some widow of some army officer or functionary sewing or posing for her. She had an austrian maid for a while who cooked perfectly delicious austrian pastry but she did not keep her long. She was in short very amusing and she and Gertrude Stein used to talk to each other in the court. She always wanted to know what Gertrude Stein thought of everybody who came in and out. She wanted to know if she came to her conclusions by deduction, observation, imagination or analysis. She was amusing and then she disappeared and nobody thought anything about her until the war came and then everybody wondered if after all there had not been something sinister about this german woman's life in Paris.

Practically every afternoon Gertrude Stein went to Montmartre, posed and then later wandered down the hill usually walking across Paris to the rue de Fleurus. She then formed the habit which has never left her of walking around Paris, now accompanied by the dog, in those days alone. And Saturday evenings the Picassos walked home with her and dined and then there was Saturday evening.

During these long poses and these long walks Gertrude Stein meditated and made sentences. She was then in the middle of her negro story Melanctha Herbert, the second story of Three Lives and the poignant incidents that she wove into the life of Melanctha were often these she noticed in walking down the hill from the rue Ravignan.

It was at that time that the hungarians began their pilgrimages to the rue de Fleurus. There were strange groups of americans then, Picasso unaccustomed to the virginal quality of these young men and women used to say of them, ils sont pas des hommes, ils sont pas des femmes, ils sont des américains. They are not men, they are not women they are americans. Once there was a Bryn Mawr woman there, wife of a well known portrait painter, who was very tall and beautiful and having once fallen on her head had a strange vacant expression. Her, he approved of, and used to call the Empress. There was a type of american art student, male, that used very much to afflict him, he used to say no it is not he who will

make the future glory of America. He had a characteristic reaction when he saw the first photograph of a sky-scraper.
Good God, he said, imagine the pangs of jealousy a lover
would have while his beloved came up all those flights of stairs
to his top story studio.

It was at this time that a Maurice Denis, a Toulouse-Lautrec
and many enormous Picassos were added to the collection. It
was at this time also that the acquaintance and friendship with
the Vallotons began.

Vollard once said when he was asked about a certain
painter's picture, oh ça c'est un Cézanne pour les pauvres, that
is a Cézanne for the poor collector. Well Valloton was a Manet
for the impecunious. His big nude had all the hardness, the
stillness and none of the quality of the Olympe of Manet and
his portraits had the aridity but none of the elegance of David.
And further he had the misfortune of having married the sister
of an important picture-dealer. He was very happy with his
wife and she was a very charming woman but then there were
the weekly family reunions, and there was also the wealth of
his wife and the violence of his step-sons. He was a gentle
soul, Valloton, with a keen wit and a great deal of ambition
but a feeling of impotence, the result of being the brother-in-
law of picture dealers. However for a time his pictures were
very interesting. He asked Gertrude Stein to pose for him.
She did the following year. She had come to like posing, the
long still hours followed by a long dark walk intensified the
concentration with which she was creating her sentences. The
sentences of which Marcel Brion, the french critic has written,
by exactitude, austerity, absence of variety in light and shade,
by refusal of the use of the subconscious Gertrude Stein
achieves a symmetry which has a close analogy to the symmetry of the musical fugue of Bach.

She often described the strange sensation she had as a result
of the way in which Valloton painted. He was not at that time
a young man as painters go, he had already had considerable
recognition as a painter in the Paris exposition of 1900. When
he painted a portrait he made a crayon sketch and then began
painting at the top of the canvas straight across. Gertrude
Stein said it was like pulling down a curtain as slowly moving
as one of his swiss glaciers. Slowly he pulled the curtain down

and by the time he was at the bottom of the canvas, there you were. The whole operation took about two weeks and then he gave the canvas to you. First however he exhibited it in the autumn salon and it had considerable notice and everybody was pleased.

Everybody went to the Cirque Médrano once a week, at least, and usually everybody went on the same evening. There the clowns had commenced dressing up in misfit clothes instead of the old classic costume and these clothes later so well known on Charlie Chaplin were the delight of Picasso and all his friends in Montmartre. There also were the english jockeys and their costumes made the mode that all Montmartre followed. Not very long ago somebody was talking about how well the young painters of to-day dressed and what a pity it was that they spent money in that way. Picasso laughed. I am quite certain, he said, they pay less for the fashionable complet, their suits of clothes, than we did for our rough and common ones. You have no idea how hard it was and expensive it was in those days to find english tweed or a french imitation that would look rough and dirty enough. And it was quite true one way and another the painters in those days did spend a lot of money and they spent all they got hold of because in those happy days you could owe money for years for your paints and canvases and rent and restaurant and practically everything except coal and luxuries.

The winter went on. Three Lives was written. Gertrude Stein asked her sister-in-law to come and read it. She did and was deeply moved. This pleased Gertrude Stein immensely, she did not believe that any one could read anything she wrote and be interested. In those days she never asked any one what they thought of her work, but were they interested enough to read it. Now she says if they can bring themselves to read it they will be interested.

Her elder brother's wife has always meant a great deal in her life but never more than on that afternoon. And then it had to be typewritten. Gertrude Stein had at that time a wretched little portable typewriter which she never used. She always then and for many years later wrote on scraps of paper in pencil, copied it into french school note-books in ink and then often copied it over again in ink. It was in connection with these various series of scraps of paper that her elder brother once remarked, I do not know whether Gertrude has more genius than the rest of you all, that I know nothing about, but one thing I have always noticed, the rest of you paint and write and are not satisfied and throw it away or tear it up, she does not say whether she is satisfied or not, she copies it very often but she never throws away any piece of paper upon which she has written.

Gertrude Stein tried to copy Three Lives on the typewriter but it was no use, it made her nervous, so Etta Cone came to the rescue. The Miss Etta Cones as Pablo Picasso used to call her and her sister. Etta Cone was a Baltimore connection of Gertrude Stein's and she was spending a winter in Paris. She was rather lonesome and she was rather interested.

Etta Cone found the Picassos appalling but romantic. She was taken there by Gertrude Stein whenever the Picasso finances got beyond everybody and was made to buy a hundred francs' worth of drawings. After all a hundred francs in those days was twenty dollars. She was quite willing to indulge in this romantic charity. Needless to say these drawings became in very much later years the nucleus of her collection.

Etta Cone offered to typewrite Three Lives and she began. Baltimore is famous for the delicate sensibilities and conscientiousness of its inhabitants. It suddenly occurred to Gertrude Stein that she had not told Etta Cone to read the manuscript before beginning to typewrite it. She went to see her and there indeed was Etta Cone faithfully copying the manuscript letter by letter so that she might not by any indiscretion become conscious of the meaning. Permission to read the text having been given the typewriting went on.

Spring was coming and the sittings were coming to an end. All of a sudden one day Picasso painted out the whole head. I can't see you any longer when I look, he said irritably. And so the picture was left like that.

Nobody remembers being particularly disappointed or particularly annoyed at this ending to the long series of posings. There was the spring independent and then Gertrude Stein and her brother were going to Italy as was at that time their habit. Pablo and Fernande were going to Spain, she for the first time, and she had to buy a dress and a hat and perfumes and a cooking stove. All french women in those days when they went from one country to another took along a french oil stove to cook on. Perhaps they still do. No matter where they were going this had to be taken with them. They always paid a great deal of excess baggage, all french women who went travelling. And the Matisses were back and they had to meet the Picassos and to be enthusiastic about each other, but not to like each other very well. And in their wake, Derain met Picasso and with him came Braque.

It may seem very strange to every one nowadays that before this time Matisse had never heard of Picasso and Picasso had never met Matisse. But at that time every little crowd lived its own life and knew practically nothing of any other crowd. Matisse on the Quai Saint-Michel and in the indépendant did not know anything of Picasso and Montmartre and Sagot. They all, it is true, had been in the very early stages bought one after the other by Mademoiselle Weill, the bric-à-brac shop in Montmartre, but as she bought everybody's pictures, pictures brought by any one, not necessarily by the painter, it was not very likely that any painter would, except by some rare chance, see there the paintings of any other painter. They were however all very grateful to her in later years because after all practically everybody who later became famous had sold their first little picture to her.

As I was saying the sittings were over, the vernissage of the independent was over and everybody went away.

It had been a fruitful winter. In the long struggle with the portrait of Gertrude Stein, Picasso passed from the Harlequin, the charming early italian period to the intensive struggle which was to end in cubism. Gertrude Stein had written the story of Melanctha the negress, the second story of Three Lives which was the first definite step away from the nineteenth century and into the twentieth century in literature. Matisse had painted the Bonheur de Vivre and had created the new school of colour which was soon to leave its mark on everything. And everybody went away. That summer the Matisses came to Italy. Matisse did not care about it very much, he preferred France and Morocco but Madame Matisse was deeply touched. It was a girlish dream fulfilled. She said, I say to myself all the time, I am in Italy. And I say it to Henri all the time and he is very sweet about it, but he says, what of it.

The Picassos were in Spain and Fernande wrote long letters describing Spain and the spaniards and earthquakes.

In Florence except for the short visit of the Matisses and a short visit from Alfy Maurer the summer life was in no way related to the Paris life.

Gertrude Stein and her brother rented for the summer a villa on top of the hill at Fiesole near Florence, and there they spent their summers for several years. The year I came to Paris a friend and myself took this villa, Gertrude Stein and her brother having taken a larger one on the other side of Fiesole, having been joined that year by their elder brother, his wife and child. The small one, the Casa Ricci, was very delightful. It had been made livable by a Scotch woman who born Presbyterian became an ardent Catholic and took her old Presbyterian mother from one convent to another. Finally they came to rest in Casa Ricci and there she made for herself a chapel and there her mother died. She then abandoned this for a larger villa which she turned into a retreat for retired priests and Gertrude Stein and her brother rented the Casa Ricci from her. Gertrude Stein delighted in her landlady who looked exactly like a lady-in-waiting to Mary Stuart and with all her trailing black robes genuflected before every Catholic symbol and would then climb up a precipitous ladder and open a little window in the roof to look at the stars. A strange mingling of Catholic and Protestant exaltation.

Hélène the french servant never came down to Fiesole. She had by that time married. She cooked for her husband during the summer and mended the stockings of Gertrude Stein and her brother by putting new feet into them. She also made jam. In Italy there was Maddalena quite as important in Italy as Hélène in Paris, but I doubt if with as much appreciation for notabilities. Italy is too accustomed to the famous and the children of the famous. It was Edwin Dodge who apropos of these said, the lives of great men oft remind us we should leave no sons behind us.

Gertrude Stein adored heat and sunshine although she always says that Paris winter is an ideal climate. In those days it was always at noon that she preferred to walk. I, who have and had no fondness for a summer sun, often accompanied her. Sometimes later in Spain I sat under a tree and wept but she in the sun was indefatigable. She could even lie in the sun and look straight up into a summer noon sun, she said it rested her eyes and head.

There were amusing people in Florence. There were the Berensons and at that time with them Gladys Deacon, a well known international beauty, but after a winter of Montmartre Gertrude Stein found her too easily shocked to be interesting. Then there were the first russians, von Heiroth and his wife, she who afterwards had four husbands and once pleasantly remarked that she had always been good friends with all her husbands. He was foolish but attractive and told the usual russian stories. Then there were the Thorolds and a great many others. And most important there was a most excellent english lending library with all sorts of strange biographies which were to Gertrude Stein a source of endless pleasure. She once told me that when she was young she had read so much, read from the Elizabethans to the moderns, that she was terribly uneasy lest some day she would be without anything to read. For years this fear haunted her but in one way and another although she always reads and reads she seems always to find more to read. Her eldest brother used to complain that although he brought up from Florence every day as many books as he could carry, there always were just as many to take back.

It was during this summer that Gertrude Stein began her great book, The Making of Americans.

It began with an old daily theme that she had written when at Radcliffe,

"Once an angry man dragged his father along the ground through his own orchard. 'Stop!' cried the groaning old man at last. 'Stop! I did not drag my father beyond this tree.'

"It is hard living down the tempers we are born with. We all begin well. For in our youth there is nothing we are more intolerant of than our own sins writ large in others and we fight them fiercely in ourselves; but we grow old and we see that these our sins are of all sins the really harmless ones to own, nay that they give a charm to any character, and so our struggle with them dies away." And it was to be the history of a family. It was a history of a family but by the time I came to Paris it was getting to be a history of all human beings, all who ever were or are or could be living.

Gertrude Stein in all her life has never been as pleased with anything as she is with the translation that Bernard Faÿ and Madame Seillière are making of this book now. She has just been going over it with Bernard Faÿ and as she says, it is wonderful in english and it is even as wonderful in french. Elliot Paul, when editor of transition once said that he was certain that Gertrude Stein could be a best-seller in France. It seems very likely that his prediction is to be fulfilled.

But to return to those old days in the Casa Ricci and the first beginnings of those long sentences which were to change the literary ideas of a great many people.

Gertrude Stein was working tremendously over the beginning of The Making of Americans and came back to Paris under the spell of the thing she was doing. It was at this time that working every night she often was caught by the dawn coming while she was working. She came back to a Paris fairly full of excitement. In the first place she came back to her finished portrait. The day he returned from Spain Picasso sat down and out of his head painted the head in without having seen Gertrude Stein again. And when she saw it he and she were content. It is very strange but neither can remember at all what the head looked like when he painted it out. There is another charming story of the portrait.

Only a few years ago when Gertrude Stein had had her hair cut short, she had always up to that time worn it as a crown on top of her head as Picasso has painted it, when she had had her hair cut, a day or so later she happened to come into a room and Picasso was several rooms away. She had a hat on but he caught sight of her through two doorways and approaching her quickly called out, Gertrude, what is it, what is it. What is what, Pablo, she said. Let me see, he said. She let him see. And my portrait, said he sternly. Then his face softening he added, mais, quand même, tout y est, all the same it is all there.

Matisse was back and there was excitement in the air. Derain, and Braque with him, had gone Montmartre. Braque was a young painter who had known Marie Laurencin when they were both art students, and they had then painted each other's portraits. After that Braque had done rather geographical pictures, rounded hills and very much under the colour influence of Matisse's independent painting. He had come to know Derain, I am not sure but that they had known each other while doing their military service, and now they knew Picasso. It was an exciting moment.

They began to spend their days up there and they all always ate together at a little restaurant opposite, and Picasso was more than ever as Gertrude Stein said the little bull-fighter followed by his squadron of four, or as later in her portrait of him, she called him, Napoleon followed by his four enormous grenadiers. Derain and Braque were great big men, so was Guillaume a heavy set man and Salmon was not small. Picasso was every inch a chief.

This brings the story to Salmon and Guillaume Apollinaire, although Gertrude Stein had known these two and Marie Laurencin a considerable time before all this was happening.

Salmon and Guillaume Apollinaire both lived in Montmartre in these days. Salmon was very lithe and alive but Gertrude Stein never found him particularly interesting. She liked him. Guillaume Apollinaire on the contrary was very wonderful. There was just about that time, that is about the time when Gertrude Stein first knew Apollinaire, the excitement of a duel that he was to fight with another writer. Fernande and Pablo told about it with so much excitement and so much laughter and so much Montmartre slang, this was in the early days of their acquaintance, that she was always a little vague about just what did happen. But the gist of the matter was that Guillaume challenged the other man and Max Jacob was to be the second and witness for Guillaume. Guillaume and his antagonist each sat in their favourite café all day and waited while their seconds went to and fro. How it all ended Gertrude Stein does not know except that nobody fought, but the great excitement was the bill each second and witness brought to his principal. In these was itemised each time they had a cup of coffee and of course they had to have a cup of coffee every time they sat down at one or other café with one or other principal, and again when the two seconds sat with each other. There was also the question under what circumstances were they under the absolute necessity of having a glass of brandy with the cup of coffee. And how often would they have had coffee if they had not been seconds. All this led to endless meetings and endless discussion and endless additional items. It lasted for days, perhaps weeks and months and whether anybody finally was paid, even the café keeper, nobody knows. It was notorious that Apollinaire was parted with the very greatest difficulty from even the smallest piece of money. It was all very absorbing.

Apollinaire was very attractive and very interesting. He had a head like one of the late roman emperors. He had a brother whom one heard about but never saw. He worked in a bank and therefore he was reasonably well dressed. When anybody in Montmartre had to go anywhere where they had to be conventionally clothed, either to see a relation or attend to a business matter, they always wore a piece of a suit that belonged to the brother of Guillaume.

Guillaume was extraordinarily brilliant and no matter what subject was started, if he knew anything about it or not, he quickly saw the whole meaning of the thing and elaborated it by his wit and fancy carrying it further than anybody knowing anything about it could have done, and oddly enough generally correctly.

Once, several years later, we were dining with the Picassos, and in a conversation I got the best of Guillaume. I was very proud, but, said Eve (Picasso was no longer with Fernande), Guillaume was frightfully drunk or it would not have happened. It was only under such circumstances that anybody could successfully turn a phrase against Guillaume. Poor Guillaume. The last time we saw him was after he had come back to Paris from the war. He had been badly wounded in the head and had had a piece of his skull removed. He looked very wonderful with his bleu horizon and his bandaged head. He lunched with us and we all talked a long time together. He was tired and his heavy head nodded. He was very serious almost solemn. We went away shortly after, we were working with the American Fund for French Wounded, and never saw him again. Later Olga Picasso, the wife of Picasso, told us that the night of the armistice Guillaume Apollinaire died, that they were with him that whole evening and it was warm and the windows were open and the crowd passing were shouting, à bas Guillaume, down with William and as every one always called Guillaume Apollinaire Guillaume, even in his death agony it troubled him.

He had really been heroic. As a foreigner, his mother was a pole, his father possibly an italian, it was not at all necessary that he should volunteer to fight. He was a man of full habit, accustomed to a literary life and the delights of the table, and in spite of everything he volunteered. He went into the artillery first. Every one advised this as it was less dangerous and easier than the infantry, but after a while he could not bear this half protection and he changed into the infantry and was wounded in a charge. He was a long time in hospital, recovered a little, it was at this time that we saw him, and finally died on the day of the armistice.

The death of Guillaume Apollinaire at this time made a very serious difference to all his friends apart from their sorrow at his death. It was the moment just after the war when many things had changed and people naturally fell apart. Guillaume would have been a bond of union, he always had a quality of keeping people together, and now that he was gone everybody ceased to be friends. But all that was very much later and now to go back again to the beginning when Gertrude Stein first met Guillaume and Marie Laurencin.

Everybody called Gertrude Stein Gertrude, or at most Mademoiselle Gertrude, everybody called Picasso Pablo and Fernande Fernande and everybody called Guillaume Apollinaire Guillaume and Max Jacob Max but everybody called Marie Laurencin Marie Laurencin.

The first time Gertrude Stein ever saw Marie Laurencin, Guillaume Apollinaire brought her to the rue de Fleurus, not on a Saturday evening, but another evening. She was very interesting. They were an extraordinary pair. Marie Laurencin was terribly near-sighted and of course she never wore eyeglasses, no french woman and few frenchmen did in those days. She used a lorgnette.

She looked at each picture carefully that is, every picture on the line, bringing her eye close and moving over the whole of it with her lorgnette, an inch at a time. The pictures out of reach she ignored. Finally she remarked, as for myself, I prefer portraits and that is of course quite natural, as I myself am a Clouet. And it was perfectly true, she was a Clouet. She had the square thin build of the mediaeval french women in the french primitives. She spoke in a high pitched beautifully modulated voice. She sat down beside Gertrude Stein on the couch and she recounted the story of her life, told that her mother who had always had it in her nature to dislike men had been for many years the mistress of an important personage, had borne her, Marie Laurencin. I have never, she added, dared let her know Guillaume although of course he is so sweet that she could not refuse to like him but better not. Some day you will see her.

And later on Gertrude Stein saw the mother and by that time I was in Paris and I was taken along.

Marie Laurencin, leading her strange life and making her strange art, lived with her mother, who was a very quiet, very pleasant, very dignified woman, as if the two were living in a convent. The small apartment was filled with needlework which the mother had executed after the designs of Marie Laurencin. Marie and her mother acted toward each other exactly as a young nun with an older one. It was all very strange. Later just before the war the mother fell ill and died. Then the mother did see Guillaume Apollinaire and liked him.

After her mother's death Marie Laurencin lost all sense of stability. She and Guillaume no longer saw each other. A relation that had existed as long as the mother lived without the mother's knowledge now that the mother was dead and had seen and liked Guillaume could no longer endure. Marie against the advice of all her friends married a german. When her friends remonstrated with her she said, but he is the only one who can give me a feeling of my mother.

Six weeks after the marriage the war came and Marie had to leave the country, having been married to a german. As she told me later when once during the war we met in Spain, naturally the officials could make no trouble for her, her passport made it clear that no one knew who her father was and they naturally were afraid because perhaps her father might be the president of the french republic.

During these war years Marie was very unhappy. She was

intensely french and she was technically german. When you met her she would say, let me present to you my husband a boche, I do not remember his name. The official french world in Spain with whom she and her husband occasionally came in contact made things very unpleasant for her, constantly referring to Germany as her country. In the meanwhile Guillaume with whom she was in correspondence wrote her passionately patriotic letters. It was a miserable time for Marie Laurencin.

Finally Madame Groult, the sister of Poiret, coming to Spain, managed to help Marie out of her troubles. She finally divorced her husband and after the armistice returned to Paris, at home once more in the world. It was then that she came to the rue de Fleurus again, this time with Erik Satie. They were both Normans and so proud and happy about it.

In the early days Marie Laurencin painted a strange picture, portraits of Guillaume, Picasso, Fernande and herself. Fernande told Gertrude Stein about it. Gertrude Stein bought it and Marie Laurencin was so pleased. It was the first picture of hers any one had ever bought.

It was before Gertrude Stein knew the rue Ravignan that Guillaume Apollinaire had his first paid job, he edited a little pamphlet about physical culture. And it was for this that Picasso made his wonderful caricatures, including one of Guillaume as an exemplar of what physical culture could do.

And now once more to return to the return from all their travels and to Picasso becoming the head of a movement that was later to be known as the cubists. Who called it cubist first I do not know but very likely it was Apollinaire. At any rate he wrote the first little pamphlet about them all and illustrated it with their paintings.

I can so well remember the first time Gertrude Stein took me to see Guillaume Apollinaire. It was a tiny bachelor's apartment on the rue des Martyrs. The room was crowded with a great many small young gentlemen. Who, I asked Fernande, are all these little men. They are poets, answered Fernande. I was overcome. I had never seen poets before, one poet yes but not poets. It was on that night too that Picasso, just a little drunk and to Fernande's great indignation per- sisted in sitting beside me and finding for me in a spanish album of photographs the exact spot where he was born. I came away with rather a vague idea of its situation.

Derain and Braque became followers of Picasso about six months after Picasso had, through Gertrude Stein and her brother, met Matisse. Matisse had in the meantime introduced Picasso to negro sculpture.

At that time negro sculpture had been well known to curio hunters but not to artists. Who first recognised its potential value for the modern artist I am sure I do not know. Perhaps it was Maillol who came from the Perpignan region and knew Matisse in the south and called his attention to it. There is a tradition that it was Derain. It is also very possible that it was Matisse himself because for many years there was a curio-dealer in the rue de Rennes who always had a great many things of this kind in his window and Matisse often went up the rue de Rennes to go to one of the sketch classes.

In any case it was Matisse who first was influenced, not so much in his painting but in his sculpture, by the african statues and it was Matisse who drew Picasso's attention to it just after Picasso had finished painting Gertrude Stein's portrait.

The effect of this african art upon Matisse and Picasso was entirely different. Matisse through it was affected more in his imagination than in his vision. Picasso more in his vision than in his imagination. Strangely enough it is only very much later in his life that this influence has affected his imagination and that may be through its having been re-enforced by the Orientalism of the russians when he came in contact with that through Diaghilev and the russian ballet.

In these early days when he created cubism the effect of the african art was purely upon his vision and his forms, his imagination remained purely spanish. The spanish quality of ritual and abstraction had been indeed stimulated by his painting the portrait of Gertrude Stein. She had a definite impulse then and always toward elemental abstraction. She was not at any time interested in african sculpture. She always says that she liked it well enough but that it has nothing to do with europeans, that it lacks naïveté, that it is very ancient, very narrow, very sophisticated but lacks the elegance of the egyptian sculpture from which it is derived. She says that as an american she likes primitive things to be more savage.

Matisse and Picasso then being introduced to each other by Gertrude Stein and her brother became friends but they were enemies. Now they are neither friends nor enemies. At that time they were both.

They exchanged pictures as was the habit in those days. Each painter chose the one of the other one that presumably interested him the most. Matisse and Picasso chose each one of the other one the picture that was undoubtedly the least interesting either of them had done. Later each one used it as an example, the picture he had chosen, of the weaknesses of the other one. Very evidently in the two pictures chosen the strong qualities of each painter were not much in evidence.

The feeling between the Picassoites and the Matisseites became bitter. And this, you see, brings me to the independent where my friend and I sat without being aware of it under the two pictures which first publicly showed that Derain and Braque had become Picassoites and were definitely not Matisseites.

In the meantime naturally a great many things had happened.

Matisse showed in every autumn salon and every independent. He was beginning to have a considerable following. Picasso, on the contrary, never in all his life has shown in any salon. His pictures at that time could really only be seen at 27 rue de Fleurus. The first time as one might say that he had ever shown at a public show was when Derain and Braque, completely influenced by his recent work, showed theirs. After that he too had many followers.

Matisse was irritated by the growing friendship between Picasso and Gertrude Stein. Mademoiselle Gertrude, he explained, likes local colour and theatrical values. It would be impossible for any one of her quality to have a serious friendship with any one like Picasso. Matisse still came frequently to the rue de Fleurus but there was no longer any frankness of intercourse between them all. It was about this time that Gertrude Stein and her brother gave a lunch for all the painters whose pictures were on the wall. Of course it did not include the dead or the old. It was at this lunch that as I have already said Gertrude Stein made them all happy and made the lunch a success by seating each painter facing his own picture. No one of them noticed it, they were just naturally pleased, until just as they were all leaving Matisse, standing up with his back to the door and looking into the room suddenly realised what had been done.

Matisse intimated that Gertrude Stein had lost interest in his work. She answered him, there is nothing within you that fights itself and hitherto you have had the instinct to produce antagonism in others which stimulated you to attack. But now they follow.

That was the end of the conversation but a beginning of an important part of The Making of Americans. Upon this idea Gertrude Stein based some of her most permanent distinctions in types of people.

It was about this time that Matisse began his teaching. He now moved from the Quai Saint-Michel, where he had lived ever since his marriage, to the boulevard des Invalides. In consequence of the separation of church and state which had just taken place in France the french government had become possessed of a great many convent schools and other church property. As many of these convents ceased to exist, there were at that time a great many of their buildings empty. Among others a very splendid one on the boulevard des Invalides.

These buildings were being rented at very low prices because no lease was given, as the government when it decided how to use them permanently would put the tenants out without warning. It was therefore an ideal place for artists as there were gardens and big rooms and they could put up with the inconveniences of housekeeping under the circumstances. So the Matisses moved in and Matisse instead of a small room to work in had an immense one and the two boys came home and they were all very happy. Then a number of those who had become his followers asked him if he would teach them if they organised a class for him in the same building in which he was then living. He consented and the Matisse atelier began.

The applicants were of all nationalities and Matisse was at first appalled at the number and variety of them. He told with much amusement as well as surprise that when he asked a very little woman in the front row, what in particular she had in mind in her painting, what she was seeking, she replied, Monsieur je cherche le neuf. He used to wonder how they all managed to learn french when he knew none of their languages. Some one got hold of some of these facts and made fun of the school in one of the french weeklies. This hurt Matisse's feelings frightfully. The article said, and where did these people come from, and it was answered, from Massachusetts. Matisse was very unhappy.

But in spite of all this and also in spite of many dissensions the school flourished. There were difficulties. One of the hungarians wanted to earn his living posing for the class and in the intervals when some one else posed go on with his painting. There were a number of young women who protested, a nude model on a model stand was one thing but to have it turn into a fellow student was another. A hungarian was found eating the bread for rubbing out crayon drawings that the various students left on their painting boards and this evidence of extreme poverty and lack of hygiene had an awful effect upon the sensibilities of the americans. There were quite a number of americans. One of these americans under the plea of poverty was receiving his tuition for nothing and then was found to have purchased for himself a tiny Matisse and a tiny Picasso and a tiny Seurat. This was not only unfair, because many of the others wanted and could not afford to own a picture by the master and they were paying their tuition, but, since he also bought a Picasso, it was treason. And then every once in a while some one said something to Matisse in such bad french that it sounded like something very different from what it was and Matisse grew very angry and the unfortunate had to be taught how to apologise properly. All the students were working under such a state of tension that explosions were frequent. One would accuse another of undue influence with the master and then there were long and complicated scenes in which usually some one had to apologise. It was all very difficult since they themselves organised themselves.

Gertrude Stein enjoyed all these complications immensely. Matisse was a good gossip and so was she and at this time they delighted in telling tales to each other.

She began at that time always calling Matisse the C.M. or cher maître. She told him the favourite Western story, pray gentlemen, let there be no bloodshed. Matisse came not unfrequently to the rue de Fleurus. It was indeed at this time that Hélène prepared him the fried eggs instead of an omelet.

Three Lives had been typewritten and now the next thing was to show it to a publisher. Some one gave Gertrude Stein the name of an agent in New York and she tried that. Nothing came of it. Then she tried publishers directly. The only one at all interested was Bobbs-Merrill and they said they could not undertake it. This attempt to find a publisher lasted some time and then without being really discouraged she decided to have it printed. It was not an unnatural thought as people in Paris often did this. Some one told her about the Grafton Press in New York, a respectable firm that printed special historical things that people wanted to have printed. The arrangements were concluded, Three Lives was to be printed and the proofs to be sent.

One day some one knocked at the door and a very nice very american young man asked if he might speak to Miss Stein. She said, yes come in. He said, I have come at the request of the Grafton Press. Yes, she said. You see, he said slightly hesitant, the director of the Grafton Press is under the impression that perhaps your knowledge of english. But I am an american, said Gertrude Stein indignantly. Yes yes I understand that perfectly now, he said, but perhaps you have not had much experience in writing. I suppose, said she laughing, you were under the impression that I was imperfectly educated. He blushed, why no, he said, but you might not have had much experience in writing. Oh yes, she said, oh yes. Well it's alright. I will write to the director and you might as well tell him also that everything that is written in the manuscript is written with the intention of its being so written and all he has to do is to print it and I will take the responsibility. The young man bowed himself out.

Later when the book was noticed by interested writers and newspaper men the director of the Grafton Press wrote Gertrude Stein a very simple letter in which he admitted he had been surprised at the notice the book had received but wished to add that now that he had seen the result he wished to say that he was very pleased that his firm had printed the book. But this last was after I came to Paris.

4.

Gertrude Stein
Before She Came to Paris

O NCE MORE I have come to Paris and now I am one of the habitués of the rue de Fleurus. Gertrude Stein was writing The Making of Americans and she had just commenced correcting the proofs of Three Lives. I helped her correct them.

Gertrude Stein was born in Allegheny, Pennsylvania. As I am an ardent californian and as she spent her youth there I have often begged her to be born in California but she has always remained firmly born in Allegheny, Pennsylvania. She left it when she was six months old and has never seen it again and now it no longer exists being all of it Pittsburgh. She used however to delight in being born in Allegheny, Pennsylvania when during the war, in connection with war work, we used to have papers made out and they always immediately wanted to know one's birth-place. She used to say if she had been really born in California as I wanted her to have been she would never have had the pleasure of seeing the various french officials try to write, Allegheny, Pennsylvania.

When I first knew Gertrude Stein in Paris I was surprised never to see a french book on her table, although there were always plenty of english ones, there were even no french newspapers. But do you never read french, I as well as many other people asked her. No, she replied, you see I feel with my eyes and it does not make any difference to me what language I hear, I don't hear a language, I hear tones of voice and rhythms, but with my eyes I see words and sentences and there is for me only one language and that is english. One of the things that I have liked all these years is to be surrounded by people who know no english. It has left me more intensely alone with my eyes and my english. I do not know if it would have been possible to have english be so all in all to me otherwise. And they none of them could read a word I wrote, most of them did not even know that I did write. No, I like living with so very many people and being all alone with english and myself.

One of her chapters in The Making of Americans begins: I write for myself and strangers.

She was born in Allegheny, Pennsylvania, of a very respectable middle class family. She always says that she is very grateful not to have been born of an intellectual family, she has a horror of what she calls intellectual people. It has always been rather ridiculous that she who is good friends with all the world and can know them and they can know her, has always been the admired of the precious. But she always says some day they, anybody, will find out that she is of interest to them, she and her writing. And she always consoles herself that the newspapers are always interested. They always say, she says, that my writing is appalling but they always quote it and what is more, they quote it correctly, and those they say they admire they do not quote. This at some of her most bitter moments has been a consolation. My sentences do get under their skin, only they do not know that they do, she has often said.

She was born in Allegheny, Pennsylvania, in a house, a twin house. Her family lived in one and her father's brother's family lived in the other one. These two families are the families described in The Making of Americans. They had lived in these houses for about eight years when Gertrude Stein was born. A year before her birth, the two sisters-in-law who had never gotten along any too well were no longer on speaking terms.

Gertrude Stein's mother as she describes her in The Making of Americans, a gentle pleasant little woman with a quick temper, flatly refused to see her sister-in-law again. I don't know quite what had happened but something. At any rate the two brothers who had been very successful business partners broke up their partnership, the one brother went to New York where he and all his family after him became very rich and the other brother, Gertrude Stein's family, went to Europe. They first went to Vienna and stayed there until Gertrude Stein was about three years old. All she remembers of this is that her brother's tutor once, when she was allowed to sit with her brothers at their lessons, described a tiger's snarl and that that pleased and terrified her. Also that in a picture-book that one of her brothers used to show her there was a story of the wanderings of Ulysses who when sitting sat on bent-wood dining room chairs. Also she remembers that they used to play in the public gardens and that often the old Kaiser Francis Joseph used to stroll through the gardens and sometimes a band played the austrian national hymn which she liked. She believed for many years that Kaiser was the real name of Francis Joseph and she never could come to accept the name as belonging to anybody else.

They lived in Vienna for three years, the father having in the meanwhile gone back to America on business and then they moved to Paris. Here Gertrude Stein has more lively memories. She remembers a little school where she and her elder sister stayed and where there was a little girl in the corner of the school yard and the other little girls told her not to go near her, she scratched. She also remembers the bowl of soup with french bread for breakfast and she also remembers that they had mutton and spinach for lunch and as she was very fond of spinach and not fond of mutton she used to trade mutton for spinach with the little girl opposite. She also remembers all her three older brothers coming to see them at the school and coming on horse-back. She also remembers a black cat jumping from the ceiling of their house at Passy and scaring her mother and some unknown person rescuing her.

The family remained in Paris a year and then they came back to America. Gertrude Stein's elder brother charmingly describes the last days when he and his mother went shopping and bought everything that pleased their fancy, seal skin coats and caps and muffs for the whole family from the mother to the small sister Gertrude Stein, gloves dozens of gloves, wonderful hats, riding costumes, and finally ending up with a microscope and a whole set of the famous french history of zoology. Then they sailed for America.

This visit to Paris made a very great impression upon Gertrude Stein. When in the beginning of the war, she and I having been in England and there having been caught by the outbreak of the war and so not returning until October, were back in Paris, the first day we went out Gertrude Stein said, it is strange, Paris is so different but so familiar. And then reflectively, I see what it is, there is nobody here but the french (there were no soldiers or allies there yet), you can see the little children in their black aprons, you can see the streets because there is nobody on them, it is just like my memory of Paris when I was three years old. The pavements smell like they used (horses had come back into use), the smell of french streets and french public gardens that I remember so well.

They went back to America and in New York, the New York family tried to reconcile Gertrude Stein's mother to her sister-in-law but she was obdurate.

This story reminds me of Miss Etta Cone, a distant connection of Gertrude Stein, who typed Three Lives. When I first met her in Florence she confided to me that she could forgive but never forget. I added that as for myself I could forget but not forgive. Gertrude Stein's mother in this case was evidently unable to do either.

The family went west to California after a short stay in Baltimore at the home of her grandfather, the religious old man she describes in The Making of Americans, who lived in an old house in Baltimore with a large number of those cheerful pleasant little people, her uncles and her aunts.

Gertrude Stein has never ceased to be thankful to her mother for neither forgetting or forgiving. Imagine, she has said to me, if my mother had forgiven her sister-in-law and my father had gone into business with my uncle and we had lived and been brought up in New York, imagine, she says, how horrible. We would have been rich instead of being reasonably poor but imagine how horrible to have been brought up in New York.

I as a californian can very thoroughly sympathise.

And so they took the train to California. The only thing Gertrude Stein remembers of this trip was that she and her sister had beautiful big austrian red felt hats trimmed each with a beautiful ostrich feather and at some stage of the trip her sister leaning out of the window had her hat blown off. Her father rang the emergency bell, stopped the train, got the hat to the awe and astonishment of the passengers and the conductor. The only other thing she remembers is that they had a wonderful hamper of food given them by the aunts in Baltimore and that in it was a marvellous turkey. And that later as the food in it diminished it was renewed all along the

Gertrude Stein in Vienna

road whenever they stopped and that that was always exciting. And also that somewhere in the desert they saw some red indians and that somewhere else in the desert they were given some very funny tasting peaches to eat.

When they arrived in California they went to an orange grove but she does not remember any oranges but remembers filling up her father's cigar boxes with little limes which were very wonderful.

They came by slow stages to San Francisco and settled down in Oakland. She remembers there the eucalyptus trees seeming to her so tall and thin and savage and the animal life very wild. But all this and much more, all the physical life of these days, she has described in the life of the Hersland family in her Making of Americans. The important thing to tell about now is her education.

Her father having taken his children to Europe so that they might have the benefit of a european education now insisted that they should forget their french and german so that their american english would be pure. Gertrude Stein had prattled in german and then in french but she had never read until she read english. As she says eyes to her were more important than ears and it happened then as always that english was her only language.

Her bookish life commenced at this time. She read anything that was printed that came her way and a great deal came her way. In the house were a few stray novels, a few travel books, her mother's well bound gift books Wordsworth Scott and other poets, Bunyan's Pilgrim's Progress a set of Shakespeare with notes, Burns, Congressional Records encyclopedias etcetera. She read them all and many times. She and her brothers began to acquire other books. There was also the local free library and later in San Francisco there were the mercantile and mechanics libraries with their excellent sets of eighteenth century and nineteenth century authors. From her eighth year when she absorbed Shakespeare to her fifteenth year when she read Clarissa Harlowe, Fielding, Smollett etcetera and used to worry lest in a few years more she would have read everything and there would be nothing unread to read, she lived continuously with the english language. She read a tremendous amount of history, she often laughs and says she is one of

the few people of her generation that has read every line of
Carlyle's Frederick the Great and Lecky's Constitutional History of England besides Charles Grandison and Wordsworth's
longer poems. In fact she was as she still is always reading.
She reads anything and everything and even now hates to be
disturbed and above all however often she has read a book
and however foolish the book may be no one must make fun
of it or tell her how it goes on. It is still as it always was real
to her.

The theatre she has always cared for less. She says it goes
too fast, the mixture of eye and ear bothers her and her emotion never keeps pace. Music she only cared for during her
adolescence. She finds it difficult to listen to it, it does not
hold her attention. All of which of course may seem strange
because it has been so often said that the appeal of her work
is to the ear and to the subconscious. Actually it is her eyes
and mind that are active and important and concerned in
choosing.

Life in California came to its end when Gertrude Stein was
about seventeen years old. The last few years had been lonesome ones and had been passed in an agony of adolescence.
After the death of first her mother and then her father she
and her sister and one brother left California for the East.
They came to Baltimore and stayed with her mother's people.
There she began to lose her lonesomeness. She has often described to me how strange it was to her coming from the
rather desperate inner life that she had been living for the last
few years to the cheerful life of all her aunts and uncles. When
later she went to Radcliffe she described this experience in the
first thing she ever wrote. Not quite the first thing she ever
wrote. She remembers having written twice before. Once
when she was about eight and she tried to write a Shakespear-
ean drama in which she got as far as a stage direction, the
courtiers make witty remarks. And then as she could not think
of any witty remarks gave it up.

The only other effort she can remember must have been at
about the same age. They asked the children in the public
schools to write a description. Her recollection is that she described a sunset with the sun going into a cave of clouds.
Anyway it was one of the half dozen in the school chosen to

be copied out on beautiful parchment paper. After she had tried to copy it twice and the writing became worse and worse she was reduced to letting some one else copy it for her. This, her teacher considered a disgrace. She does not remember that she herself did.

As a matter of fact her handwriting has always been illegible and I am very often able to read it when she is not.

She has never been able or had any desire to indulge in any of the arts. She never knows how a thing is going to look until it is done, in arranging a room, a garden, clothes or anything else. She cannot draw anything. She feels no relation between the object and the piece of paper. When at the medical school, she was supposed to draw anatomical things she never found out in sketching how a thing was made concave or convex. She remembers when she was very small she was to learn to draw and was sent to a class. The children were told to take a cup and saucer at home and draw them and the best drawing would have as its reward a stamped leather medal and the next week the same medal would again be given for the best drawing. Gertrude Stein went home, told her brothers and they put a pretty cup and saucer before her and each one explained to her how to draw it. Nothing happened. Finally one of them drew it for her. She took it to the class and won the leather medal. And on the way home in playing some game she lost the leather medal. That was the end of the drawing class.

She says it is a good thing to have no sense of how it is done in the things that amuse you. You should have one absorbing occupation and as for the other things in life for full enjoyment you should only contemplate results. In this way you are bound to feel more about it than those who know a little of how it is done.

She is passionately addicted to what the french call métier and she contends that one can only have one métier as one can only have one language. Her métier is writing and her language is english.

Observation and construction make imagination, that is granting the possession of imagination, is what she has taught many young writers. Once when Hemingway wrote in one of his stories that Gertrude Stein always knew what was good in a Cézanne, she looked at him and said, Hemingway, remarks are not literature.

The young often when they have learnt all they can learn accuse her of an inordinate pride. She says yes of course. She realises that in english literature in her time she is the only one. She has always known it and now she says it.

She understands very well the basis of creation and therefore her advice and criticism is invaluable to all her friends. How often I have heard Picasso say to her when she has said something about a picture of his and then illustrated by something she was trying to do, racontez-moi cela. In other words tell me about it. These two even to-day have long solitary conversations. They sit in two little low chairs up in his apartment studio, knee to knee and Picasso says, expliquez-moi cela. And they explain to each other. They talk about everything, about pictures, about dogs, about death, about unhappiness. Because Picasso is a spaniard and life is tragic and bitter and unhappy. Gertrude Stein often comes down to me and says, Pablo has been persuading me that I am as unhappy as he is. He insists that I am and with as much cause. But are you, I ask. Well I don't think I look it, do I, and she laughs. He says, she says, that I don't look it because I have more courage, but I don't think I am, she says, no I don't think I am.

And so Gertrude Stein having been in Baltimore for a winter and having become more humanised and less adolescent and less lonesome went to Radcliffe. There she had a very good time.

She was one of a group of Harvard men and Radcliffe women and they all lived very closely and very interestingly together. One of them, a young philosopher and mathematician who was doing research work in psychology left a definite mark on her life. She and he together worked out a series of experiments in automatic writing under the direction of Münsterberg. The result of her own experiments, which Gertrude Stein wrote down and which was printed in the Harvard Psychological Review was the first writing of hers ever to be printed. It is very interesting to read because the method of writing to be afterwards developed in Three Lives and Making of Americans already shows itself.

The important person in Gertrude Stein's Radcliffe life was

William James. She enjoyed her life and herself. She was the secretary of the philosophical club and amused herself with all sorts of people. She liked making sport of question asking and she liked equally answering them. She liked it all. But the really lasting impression of her Radcliffe life came through William James.

It is rather strange that she was not then at all interested in the work of Henry James for whom she now has a very great admiration and whom she considers quite definitely as her forerunner, he being the only nineteenth century writer who being an american felt the method of the twentieth century. Gertrude Stein always speaks of America as being now the oldest country in the world because by the methods of the civil war and the commercial conceptions that followed it America created the twentieth century, and since all the other countries are now either living or commencing to be living a twentieth century life, America having begun the creation of the twentieth century in the sixties of the nineteenth century is now the oldest country in the world.

In the same way she contends that Henry James was the first person in literature to find the way to the literary methods of the twentieth century. But oddly enough in all of her formative period she did not read him and was not interested in him. But as she often says one is always naturally antagonistic to one's parents and sympathetic to one's grandparents. The parents are too close, they hamper you, one must be alone. So perhaps that is the reason why only very lately Gertrude Stein reads Henry James.

William James delighted her. His personality and his teaching and his way of amusing himself with himself and his students all pleased her. Keep your mind open, he used to say, and when some one objected, but Professor James, this that I say, is true. Yes, said James, it is abjectly true.

Gertrude Stein never had subconscious reactions, nor was she a successful subject for automatic writing. One of the students in the psychological seminar of which Gertrude Stein, although an undergraduate was at William James' particular request a member, was carrying on a series of experiments on suggestions to the subconscious. When he read his paper upon the result of his experiments, he began by explaining that one of the subjects gave absolutely no results and as this much lowered the average and made the conclusion of his experiments false he wished to be allowed to cut this record out. Whose record is it, said James. Miss Stein's, said the student. Ah, said James, if Miss Stein gave no response I should say that it was as normal not to give a response as to give one and decidedly the result must not be cut out.

It was a very lovely spring day, Gertrude Stein had been going to the opera every night and going also to the opera in the afternoon and had been otherwise engrossed and it was the period of the final examinations, and there was the examination in William James' course. She sat down with the examination paper before her and she just could not. Dear Professor James, she wrote at the top of her paper. I am so sorry but really I do not feel a bit like an examination paper in philosophy to-day, and left.

The next day she had a postal card from William James saying, Dear Miss Stein, I understand perfectly how you feel I often feel like that myself. And underneath it he gave her work the highest mark in his course.

When Gertrude Stein was finishing her last year at Radcliffe, William James one day asked her what she was going to do. She said she had no idea. Well, he said, it should be either philosophy or psychology. Now for philosophy you have to have higher mathematics and I don't gather that that has ever interested you. Now for psychology you must have a medical education, a medical education opens all doors, as Oliver Wendell Holmes told me and as I tell you. Gertrude Stein had been interested in both biology and chemistry and so medical school presented no difficulties.

There were no difficulties except that Gertrude Stein had never passed more than half of her entrance examinations for Radcliffe, having never intended to take a degree. However with considerable struggle and enough tutoring that was accomplished and Gertrude Stein entered Johns Hopkins Medical School.

Some years after when Gertrude Stein and her brother were just beginning knowing Matisse and Picasso, William James came to Paris and they met. She went to see him at his hotel. He was enormously interested in what she was doing, interested in her writing and in the pictures she told him about. He went with her to her house to see them. He looked and gasped, I told you, he said, I always told you that you should keep your mind open.

Only about two years ago a very strange thing happened. Gertrude Stein received a letter from a man in Boston. It was evident from the letter head that he was one of a firm of lawyers. He said in his letter that he had not long ago in reading in the Harvard library found that the library of William James had been given as a gift to the Harvard library. Among these books was the copy of Three Lives that Gertrude Stein had dedicated and sent to James. Also on the margins of the book were notes that William James had evidently made when reading the book. The man then went on to say that very likely Gertrude Stein would be very interested in these notes and he proposed, if she wished, to copy them out for her as he had appropriated the book, in other words taken it and considered it as his. We were very puzzled what to do about it. Finally a note was written saying that Gertrude Stein would like to have a copy of William James' notes. In answer came a manuscript the man himself had written and of which he wished Gertrude Stein to give him an opinion. Not knowing what to do about it all, Gertrude Stein did nothing.

After having passed her entrance examinations she settled down in Baltimore and went to the medical school. She had a servant named Lena and it is her story that Gertrude Stein afterwards wrote as the first story of the Three Lives.

The first two years of the medical school were alright. They were purely laboratory work and Gertrude Stein under Llewelys Barker immediately betook herself to research work. She began a study of all the brain tracts, the beginning of a comparative study. All this was later embodied in Llewelys Barker's book. She delighted in Doctor Mall, professor of anatomy, who directed her work. She always quotes his answer to any student excusing him or herself for anything. He would look reflective and say, yes that is just like our cook. There is always a reason. She never brings the food to the table hot. In summer of course she can't because it is too hot, in winter of course she can't because it is too cold, yes there is always a reason. Doctor Mall believed in everybody developing their own technique. He also remarked, nobody teaches anybody anything, at first every student's scalpel is dull and then later every student's scalpel is sharp, and nobody has taught anybody anything.

These first two years at the medical school Gertrude Stein liked well enough. She always liked knowing a lot of people and being mixed up in a lot of stories and she was not awfully interested but she was not too bored with what she was doing and besides she had quantities of pleasant relatives in Baltimore and she liked it. The last two years at the medical school she was bored, frankly openly bored. There was a good deal of intrigue and struggle among the students, that she liked, but the practice and theory of medicine did not interest her at all. It was fairly well known among all her teachers that she was bored, but as her first two years of scientific work had given her a reputation, everybody gave her the necessary credits and the end of her last year was approaching. It was then that she had to take her turn in the delivering of babies and it was at that time that she noticed the negroes and the places that she afterwards used in the second of the Three Lives stories, Melanctha Herbert, the story that was the beginning of her revolutionary work.

As she always says of herself, she has a great deal of inertia and once started keeps going until she starts somewhere else.

As the graduation examinations drew near some of her professors were getting angry. The big men like Halstead, Osler etcetera knowing her reputation for original scientific work made the medical examinations merely a matter of form and passed her. But there were others who were not so amiable. Gertrude Stein always laughed, and this was difficult. They would ask her questions although as she said to her friends, it was foolish of them to ask her, when there were so many eager and anxious to answer. However they did question her from time to time and as she said, what could she do, she did not know the answers and they did not believe that she did not know them, they thought that she did not answer because she did not consider the professors worth answering. It was a difficult situation, as she said, it was impossible to apologise and explain to them that she was so bored she could not remember the things that of course the dullest medical student could not forget. One of the professors said that although all the big men were ready to pass her he intended that she should be given a lesson and he refused to give her a pass mark and so she was not able to take her degree. There was great excitement in the medical school. Her very close friend Marion Walker pleaded with her, she said, but Gertrude Gertrude remember the cause of women, and Gertrude Stein said, you don't know what it is to be bored.

The professor who had flunked her asked her to come to see him. She did. He said, of course Miss Stein all you have to do is to take a summer course here and in the fall naturally you will take your degree. But not at all, said Gertrude Stein, you have no idea how grateful I am to you. I have so much inertia and so little initiative that very possibly if you had not kept me from taking my degree I would have, well, not taken to the practice of medicine, but at any rate to pathological psychology and you don't know how little I like pathological psychology, and how all medicine bores me. The professor was completely taken aback and that was the end of the medical education of Gertrude Stein.

She always says she dislikes the abnormal, it is so obvious. She says the normal is so much more simply complicated and interesting.

It was only a few years ago that Marion Walker, Gertrude Stein's old friend, came to see her at Bilignin where we spend the summer. She and Gertrude Stein had not met since those old days nor had they corresponded but they were as fond of each other and disagreed as violently about the cause of women as they did then. Not, as Gertrude Stein explained to Marion Walker, that she at all minds the cause of women or any other cause but it does not happen to be her business.

During these years at Radcliffe and Johns Hopkins she often spent the summers in Europe. The last couple of years her brother had been settled in Florence and now that everything medical was over she joined him there and later they settled down in London for the winter.

They settled in lodgings in London and were not uncomfortable. They knew a number of people through the Berensons, Bertrand Russell, the Zangwills, then there was Willard (Josiah Flynt) who wrote Tramping With Tramps, and who knew all about London pubs, but Gertrude Stein was not very much amused. She began spending all her days in the British Museum reading the Elizabethans. She returned to her early love of Shakespeare and the Elizabethans, and became absorbed in Elizabethan prose and particularly in the prose of Greene. She had little note-books full of phrases that pleased her as they had pleased her when she was a child. The rest of the time she wandered about the London streets and found them infinitely depressing and dismal. She never really got over this memory of London and never wanted to go back there, but in nineteen hundred and twelve she went over to see John Lane, the publisher and then living a very pleasant life and visiting very gay and pleasant people she forgot the old memory and became very fond of London.

She always said that that first visit had made London just like Dickens and Dickens had always frightened her. As she says anything can frighten her and London when it was like Dickens certainly did.

There were some compensations, there was the prose of Greene and it was at this time that she discovered the novels of Anthony Trollope, for her the greatest of the Victorians. She then got together the complete collection of his work some of it difficult to get and only obtainable in Tauchnitz and it is of this collection that Robert Coates speaks when he tells about Gertrude Stein lending books to young writers. She also bought a quantity of eighteenth century memoirs among them the Creevy papers and Walpole and it is these that she loaned to Bravig Imbs when he wrote what she believes to be an admirable life of Chatterton. She reads books but she is not fussy about them, she cares about neither editions nor make-up as long as the print is not too bad and she is not even very much bothered about that. It was at this time too that, as she says, she ceased to be worried about there being in the future nothing to read, she said she felt that she would always somehow be able to find something.

But the dismalness of London and the drunken women and children and the gloom and the lonesomeness brought back all the melancholy of her adolescence and one day she said she was leaving for America and she left. She stayed in America the rest of the winter. In the meantime her brother also had

Gertrude Stein at Johns Hopkins Medical School

left London and gone to Paris and there later she joined him. She immediately began to write. She wrote a short novel.

The funny thing about this short novel is that she completely forgot about it for many years. She remembered herself beginning a little later writing the Three Lives but this first piece of writing was completely forgotten, she had never mentioned it to me, even when I first knew her. She must have forgotten about it almost immediately. This spring just two days before our leaving for the country she was looking for some manuscript of The Making of Americans that she wanted to show Bernard Faÿ and she came across these two carefully written volumes of this completely forgotten first novel. She was very bashful and hesitant about it, did not really want to read it. Louis Bromfield was at the house that evening and she handed him the manuscript and said to him, you read it.

5.

1907–1914

A ND SO life in Paris began and as all roads lead to Paris, all of us are now there, and I can begin to tell what happened when I was of it.

When I first came to Paris a friend and myself stayed in a little hotel in the boulevard Saint-Michel, then we took a small apartment in the rue Notre-Dame-des-Champs and then my friend went back to California and I joined Gertrude Stein in the rue de Fleurus.

I had been at the rue de Fleurus every Saturday evening and I was there a great deal beside. I helped Gertrude Stein with the proofs of Three Lives and then I began to typewrite The Making of Americans. The little badly made french portable was not strong enough to type this big book and so we bought a large and imposing Smith Premier which at first looked very much out of place in the atelier but soon we were all used to it and it remained until I had an american portable, in short until after the war.

As I said Fernande was the first wife of a genius I was to sit with. The geniuses came and talked to Gertrude Stein and the wives sat with me. How they unroll, an endless vista through the years. I began with Fernande and then there were Madame Matisse and Marcelle Braque and Josette Gris and Eve Picasso and Bridget Gibb and Marjory Gibb and Hadley and Pauline Hemingway and Mrs. Sherwood Anderson and Mrs. Bravig Imbs and the Mrs. Ford Madox Ford and endless others, geniuses, near geniuses and might be geniuses, all having wives, and I have sat and talked with them all all the wives and later on, well later on too, I have sat and talked with all. But I began with Fernande.

I went too to the Casa Ricci in Fiesole with Gertrude Stein and her brother. How well I remember the first summer I stayed with them. We did charming things. Gertrude Stein and I took a Fiesole cab, I think it was the only one and drove in this old cab all the way to Siena. Gertrude Stein had once walked it with a friend but in those hot italian days I preferred a cab. It was a charming trip. Then another time we went to Rome and we brought back a beautiful black renaissance plate. Maddalena, the old italian cook, came up to Gertrude Stein's bedroom one morning to bring the water for her bath. Gertrude Stein had the hiccoughs. But cannot the signora stop it, said Maddalena anxiously. No, said Gertrude Stein between hiccoughs. Maddalena shaking her head sadly went away. In a minute there was an awful crash. Up flew Maddalena, oh signora, signora, she said, I was so upset because the signora had the hiccoughs that I broke the black plate that the signora so carefully brought from Rome. Gertrude Stein began to swear, she has a reprehensible habit of swearing whenever anything unexpected happens and she always tells me she learned it in her youth in California, and as I am a loyal californian I can then say nothing. She swore and the hiccoughs ceased. Maddalena's face was wreathed in smiles. Ah the signorina, she said, she has stopped hiccoughing. Oh no I did not break the beautiful plate, I just made the noise of it and then said I did it to make the signorina stop hiccoughing.

Gertrude Stein is awfully patient over the breaking of even her most cherished objects, it is I, I am sorry to say who usually break them. Neither she nor the servant nor the dog do, but then the servant never touches them, it is I who dust them and alas sometimes accidentally break them. I always beg her to promise to let me have them mended by an expert before I tell her which it is that is broken, she always replies she gets no pleasure out of them if they are mended but alright have it mended and it is mended and it gets put away. She loves objects that are breakable, cheap objects and valuable objects, a chicken out of a grocery shop or a pigeon out of a fair, one just broke this morning, this time it was not I who did it, she loves them all and she remembers them all but she knows that sooner or later they will break and she says that like books there are always more to find. However to me this is no consolation. She says she likes what she has and she likes the adventure of a new one. That is what she always says about young painters, about anything, once everybody knows they are good the adventure is over. And adds Picasso with a sigh, even after everybody knows they are good not any more people really like them than they did when only the few knew they were good.

I did have to take one hot walk that summer. Gertrude Stein insisted that no one could go to Assisi except on foot. She has three favourite saints, Saint Ignatius Loyola, Saint Theresa of Avila and Saint Francis. I alas have only one favourite saint, Saint Anthony of Padua because it is he who finds lost objects and as Gertrude Stein's elder brother once said of me, if I were a general I would never lose a battle, I would only mislay it. Saint Anthony helps me find it. I always put a considerable sum in his box in every church I visit. At first Gertrude Stein objected to this extravagance but now she realises its necessity and if I am not with her she remembers Saint Anthony for me.

It was a very hot italian day and we started as usual about noon, that being Gertrude Stein's favourite walking hour, because it was hottest and beside presumably Saint Francis had walked it then the oftenest as he had walked it at all hours. We started from Perugia across the hot valley. I gradually undressed, in those days one wore many more clothes than one does now, I even, which was most unconventional in those days, took off my stockings, but even so I dropped a few tears before we arrived and we did arrive. Gertrude Stein was very fond of Assisi for two reasons, because of Saint Francis and the beauty of his city and because the old women used to lead instead of a goat a little pig up and down the hills of Assisi. The little black pig was always decorated with a red ribbon. Gertrude Stein had always liked little pigs and she always said that in her old age she expected to wander up and down the hills of Assisi with a little black pig. She now wanders about the hills of the Ain with a large white dog and a small black one, so I suppose that does as well.

She was always fond of pigs, and because of this Picasso made and gave her some charming drawings of the prodigal son among the pigs. And one delightful study of pigs all by themselves. It was about this time too that he made for her the tiniest of ceiling decorations on a tiny wooden panel and it was an hommage à Gertrude with women and angels bringing fruits and trumpeting. For years she had this tacked to the

Gertrude Stein and Alice B. Toklas in front
of Saint Mark's, Venice

ceiling over her bed. It was only after the war that it was put upon the wall.

But to return to the beginning of my life in Paris. It was based upon the rue de Fleurus and the Saturday evenings and it was like a kaleidoscope slowly turning.

What happened in those early years. A great deal happened.

As I said when I became an habitual visitor at the rue de Fleurus the Picassos were once more together, Pablo and Fernande. That summer they went again to Spain and he came back with some spanish landscapes and one may say that these landscapes, two of them still at the rue de Fleurus and the other one in Moscow in the collection that Stchoukine founded and that is now national property, were the beginning of cubism. In these there was no african sculpture influence. There was very evidently a strong Cézanne influence, particularly the influence of the late Cézanne water colours, the cutting up the sky not in cubes but in spaces.

But the essential thing, the treatment of the houses was essentially spanish and therefore essentially Picasso. In these pictures he first emphasised the way of building in spanish villages, the line of the houses not following the landscape but cutting across and into the landscape, becoming undistinguishable in the landscape by cutting across the landscape. It was the principle of the camouflage of the guns and the ships in the war. The first year of the war, Picasso and Eve, with whom he was living then, Gertrude Stein and myself, were walking down the boulevard Raspail a cold winter evening. There is nothing in the world colder than the Raspail on a cold winter evening, we used to call it the retreat from Moscow. All of a sudden down the street came some big cannon, the first any of us had seen painted, that is camouflaged. Pablo stopped, he was spell-bound. C'est nous qui avons fait ça, he said, it is we that have created that, he said. And he was right, he had. From Cézanne through him they had come to that. His foresight was justified.

But to go back to the three landscapes. When they were first put up on the wall naturally everybody objected. As it happened he and Fernande had taken some photographs of the villages which he had painted and he had given copies of these photographs to Gertrude Stein. When people said that the few cubes in the landscapes looked like nothing but cubes, Gertrude Stein would laugh and say, if you had objected to these landscapes as being too realistic there would be some point in your objection. And she would show them the photographs and really the pictures as she rightly said might be declared to be too photographic a copy of nature. Years after Elliot Paul at Gertrude Stein's suggestion had a photograph of the painting by Picasso and the photographs of the village reproduced on the same page in transition and it was extraordinarily interesting. This then was really the beginning of cubism. The colour too was characteristically spanish, the pale silver yellow with the faintest suggestion of green, the colour afterwards so well known in Picasso's cubist pictures, as well as in those of his followers.

Gertrude Stein always says that cubism is a purely spanish conception and only spaniards can be cubists and that the only real cubism is that of Picasso and Juan Gris. Picasso created it and Juan Gris permeated it with his clarity and his exaltation. To understand this one has only to read the life and death of Juan Gris by Gertrude Stein, written upon the death of one of her two dearest friends, Picasso and Juan Gris, both spaniards.

She always says that americans can understand spaniards. That they are the only two western nations that can realise abstraction. That in americans it expresses itself by disembodiedness, in literature and machinery, in Spain by ritual so abstract that it does not connect itself with anything but ritual.

I always remember Picasso saying disgustedly apropos of some germans who said they liked bull-fights, they would, he said angrily, they like bloodshed. To a spaniard it is not bloodshed, it is ritual.

Americans, so Gertrude Stein says, are like spaniards, they are abstract and cruel. They are not brutal they are cruel. They have no close contact with the earth such as most europeans have. Their materialism is not the materialism of existence, of possession, it is the materialism of action and abstraction. And so cubism is spanish.

We were very much struck, the first time Gertrude Stein and I went to Spain, which was a year or so after the beginning of cubism, to see how naturally cubism was made in

Spain. In the shops in Barcelona instead of post cards they had square little frames and inside it was placed a cigar, a real one, a pipe, a bit of handkerchief etcetera, all absolutely the arrangement of many a cubist picture and helped out by cut paper representing other objects. That is the modern note that in Spain had been done for centuries.

Picasso in his early cubist pictures used printed letters as did Juan Gris to force the painted surface to measure up to something rigid, and the rigid thing was the printed letter. Gradually instead of using the printed thing they painted the letters and all was lost, it was only Juan Gris who could paint with such intensity a printed letter that it still made the rigid contrast. And so cubism came little by little but it came.

It was in these days that the intimacy between Braque and Picasso grew. It was in these days that Juan Gris, a raw rather effusive youth came from Madrid to Paris and began to call Picasso cher maître to Picasso's great annoyance. It was apropos of this that Picasso used to address Braque as cher maître, passing on the joke, and I am sorry to say that some foolish people have taken this joke to mean that Picasso looked up to Braque as a master.

But I am once more running far ahead of those early Paris days when I first knew Fernande and Pablo.

In those days then only the three landscapes had been painted and he was beginning to paint some heads that seemed cut out in planes, also long loaves of bread.

At this time Matisse, the school still going on, was really beginning to be fairly well known, so much so that to everybody's great excitement Bernheim jeune, a very middle class firm indeed, was offering him a contract to take all his work at a very good price. It was an exciting moment.

This was happening because of the influence of a man named Fénéon. Il est très fin, said Matisse, much impressed by Fénéon. Fénéon was a journalist, a french journalist who had invented the thing called a feuilleton en deux lignes, that is to say he was the first one to hit off the news of the day in two lines. He looked like a caricature of Uncle Sam made french and he had been painted standing in front of a curtain in a circus picture by Toulouse-Lautrec.

And now the Bernheims, how or wherefor I do not know,

taking Fénéon into their employ, were going to connect themselves with the new generation of painters.

Something happened, at any rate this contract did not last long, but for all that it changed the fortunes of Matisse. He now had an established position. He bought a house and some land in Clamart and he started to move out there. Let me describe the house as I saw it.

This home in Clamart was very comfortable, to be sure the bath-room, which the family much appreciated from long contact with americans, although it must be said that the Matisses had always been and always were scrupulously neat and clean, was on the ground floor adjoining the dining room. But that was alright, and is and was a french custom, in french houses. It gave more privacy to a bath-room to have it on the ground floor. Not so long ago in going over the new house Braque was building the bath-room was again below, this time underneath the dining room. When we said, but why, they said because being nearer the furnace it would be warmer.

The grounds at Clamart were large and the garden was what Matisse between pride and chagrin called un petit Luxembourg. There was also a glass forcing house for flowers. Later they had begonias in them that grew smaller and smaller. Beyond were lilacs and still beyond a big demountable studio. They liked it enormously. Madame Matisse with simple recklessness went out every day to look at it and pick flowers, keeping a cab waiting for her. In those days only millionaires kept cabs waiting and then only very occasionally.

They moved out and were very comfortable and soon the enormous studio was filled with enormous statues and enormous pictures. It was that period of Matisse. Equally soon he found Clamart so beautiful that he could not go home to it, that is when he came into Paris to his hour of sketching from the nude, a thing he had done every afternoon of his life ever since the beginning of things, and he came in every afternoon. His school no longer existed, the government had taken over the old convent to make a Lycée of it and the school had come to an end.

These were the beginning of very prosperous days for the Matisses. They went to Algeria and they went to Tangiers and their devoted german pupils gave them Rhine wines and a very fine black police dog, the first of the breed that any of us had seen.

And then Matisse had a great show of his pictures in Berlin. I remember so well one spring day, it was a lovely day and we were to lunch at Clamart with the Matisses. When we got there they were all standing around an enormous packing case with its top off. We went up and joined them and there in the packing case was the largest laurel wreath that had ever been made, tied with a beautiful red ribbon. Matisse showed Gertrude Stein a card that had been in it. It said on it, To Henri Matisse, Triumphant on the Battlefield of Berlin, and was signed Thomas Whittemore. Thomas Whittemore was a bostonian archeologist and professor at Tufts College, a great admirer of Matisse and this was his tribute. Said Matisse, still more rueful, but I am not dead yet. Madame Matisse, the shock once over said, but Henri look, and leaning down she plucked a leaf and tasted it, it is real laurel, think how good it will be in soup. And, said she still further brightening, the ribbon will do wonderfully for a long time as hair ribbon for Margot.

The Matisses stayed in Clamart more or less until the war. During this period they and Gertrude Stein were seeing less and less of each other. Then after the war broke out they came to the house a good deal. They were lonesome and troubled, Matisse's family in Saint-Quentin, in the north, were within the german lines and his brother was a hostage. It was Madame Matisse who taught me how to knit woollen gloves. She made them wonderfully neatly and rapidly and I learned to do so too. Then Matisse went to live in Nice and in one way and another, although remaining perfectly good friends, Gertrude Stein and the Matisses never see each other.

The Saturday evenings in those early days were frequented by many hungarians, quite a number of germans, quite a few mixed nationalities, a very thin sprinkling of americans and practically no english. These were to commence later, and with them came aristocracy of all countries and even some royalty.

Among the germans who used to come in those early days was Pascin. He was at that time a thin brilliant-looking creature, he already had a considerable reputation as maker of neat little caricatures in Simplicissimus, the most lively of the german comic papers. The other germans told strange stories of him. That he had been brought up in a house of prostitution of unknown and probably royal birth, etcetera.

He and Gertrude Stein had not met since those early days but a few years ago they saw each other at the vernissage of a young dutch painter Kristians Tonny who had been a pupil of Pascin and in whose work Gertrude Stein was then interested. They liked meeting each other and had a long talk.

Pascin was far away the most amusing of the germans although I cannot quite say that because there was Uhde.

Uhde was undoubtedly well born, he was not a blond german, he was a tallish thin dark man with a high forehead and an excellent quick wit. When he first came to Paris he went to every antiquity shop and bric-à-brac shop in the town in order to see what he could find. He did not find much, he found what purported to be an Ingres, he found a few very early Picassos, but perhaps he found other things. At any rate when the war broke out he was supposed to have been one of the super spies and to have belonged to the german staff.

He was said to have been seen near the french war office after the declaration of war, undoubtedly he and a friend had a summer home very near what was afterward the Hindenburg line. Well at any rate he was very pleasant and very amusing. He it was who was the first to commercialise the douanier Rousseau's pictures. He kept a kind of private art shop. It was here that Braque and Picasso went to see him in their newest and roughest clothes and in their best Cirque Médrano fashion kept up a constant fire of introducing each other to him and asking each other to introduce each other.

Uhde used often to come Saturday evening accompanied by very tall blond good-looking young men who clicked their heels and bowed and then all evening stood solemnly at attention. They made a very effective background to the rest of the crowd. I remember one evening when the son of the great scholar Bréal and his very amusing clever wife brought a spanish guitarist who wanted to come and play. Uhde and his bodyguard were the background and it came on to be a lively evening, the guitarist played and Manolo was there. It was the only time I ever saw Manolo the sculptor, by that time

Homage à Gertrude, Ceiling painting by Picasso

a legendary figure in Paris. Picasso very lively undertook to dance a southern spanish dance not too respectable, Gertrude Stein's brother did the dying dance of Isadora, it was very lively, Fernande and Pablo got into a discussion about Frédéric of the Lapin Agile and apaches. Fernande contended that the apaches were better than the artists and her forefinger went up in the air. Picasso said, yes apaches of course have their universities, artists do not. Fernande got angry and shook him and said, you think you are witty, but you are only stupid. He ruefully showed that she had shaken off a button and she very angry said, and you, your only claim to distinction is that you are a precocious child. Things were not in those days going any too well between them, it was just about the time that they were quitting the rue Ravignan to live in an apartment in the boulevard Clichy, where they were to have a servant and to be prosperous.

But to return to Uhde and first to Manolo. Manolo was perhaps Picasso's oldest friend. He was a strange spaniard. He, so the legend said, was the brother of one of the greatest pickpockets in Madrid. Manolo himself was gentle and admirable. He was the only person in Paris with whom Picasso spoke spanish. All the other spaniards had french wives or french mistresses and having so much the habit of speaking french they always talked french to each other. This always seemed very strange to me. However Picasso and Manolo always talked spanish to each other.

There were many stories about Manolo, he had always loved and he had always lived under the protection of the saints. They told the story of how when he first came to Paris he entered the first church he saw and there he saw a woman bring a chair to some one and receive money. So Manolo did the same, he went into many churches and always gave everybody a chair and always got money, until one day he was caught by the woman whose business it was and whose chairs they were and there was trouble.

He once was hard up and he proposed to his friends to take lottery tickets for one of his statues, everybody agreed, and then when everybody met they found they all had the same number. When they reproached him he explained that he did this because he knew his friends would be unhappy if they did not all have the same number. He was supposed to have left Spain while he was doing his military service, that is to say he was in the cavalry and he went across the border, and sold his horse and his accoutrement, and so had enough money to come to Paris and be a sculptor. He once was left for a few days in the house of a friend of Gauguin. When the owner of the house came back all his Gauguin souvenirs and all his Gauguin sketches were gone. Manolo had sold them to Vollard and Vollard had to give them back. Nobody minded. Manolo was like a sweet crazy religiously uplifted spanish beggar and everybody was fond of him. Moréas, the greek poet, who in those days was a very well known figure in Paris was very fond of him and used to take him with him for company whenever he had anything to do. Manolo always went in hopes of getting a meal but he used to be left to wait while Moréas ate. Manolo was always patient and always hopeful although Moréas was as well known then as Guillaume Apollinaire was later, to pay rarely or rather not at all.

Manolo used to make statues for joints in Montmartre in return for meals etcetera, until Alfred Stieglitz heard of him and showed his things in New York and sold some of them and then Manolo returned to the french frontier, Céret and there he has lived ever since, turning night into day, he and his catalan wife.

But Uhde. Uhde one Saturday evening presented his fiancée to Gertrude Stein. Uhde's morals were not all that they should be and as his fiancée seemed a very well to do and very conventional young woman we were all surprised. But it turned out that it was an arranged marriage. Uhde wished to respectabilise himself and she wanted to come into possession of her inheritance, which she could only do upon marriage. Shortly after she married Uhde and shortly after they were divorced. She then married Delaunay the painter who was just then coming into the foreground. He was the founder of the first of the many vulgarisations of the cubist idea, the painting of houses out of plumb, what was called the catastrophic school.

Delaunay was a big blond frenchman. He had a lively little mother. She used to come to the rue de Fleurus with old vicomtes who looked exactly like one's youthful idea of what an old french marquis should look like. These always left their cards and then wrote a solemn note of thanks and never showed in any way how entirely out of place they must have felt. Delaunay himself was amusing. He was fairly able and inordinately ambitious. He was always asking how old Picasso had been when he had painted a certain picture. When he was told he always said, oh I am not as old as that yet. I will do as much when I am that age.

As a matter of fact he did progress very rapidly. He used to come a great deal to the rue de Fleurus. Gertrude Stein used to delight in him. He was funny and he painted one rather fine picture, the three graces standing in front of Paris, an enormous picture in which he combined everybody's ideas and added a certain french clarity and freshness of his own. It had a rather remarkable atmosphere and it had a great success. After that his pictures lost all quality, they grew big and empty or small and empty. I remember his bringing one of these small ones to the house, saying, look I am bringing you a small picture, a jewel. It is small, said Gertrude Stein, but is it a jewel.

It was Delaunay who married the ex-wife of Uhde and they kept up quite an establishment. They took up Guillaume Apollinaire and it was he who taught them how to cook and how to live. Guillaume was extraordinary. Nobody but Guillaume, it was the italian in Guillaume, Stella the New York painter could do the same thing in his early youth in Paris, could make fun of his hosts, make fun of their guests, make fun of their food and spur them to always greater and greater effort.

It was Guillaume's first opportunity to travel, he went to Germany with Delaunay and thoroughly enjoyed himself.

Uhde used to delight in telling how his former wife came to his house one day and dilating upon Delaunay's future career, explained to him that he should abandon Picasso and Braque, the past, and devote himself to the cause of Delaunay, the future. Picasso and Braque at this time it must be remembered were not yet thirty years old. Uhde told everybody this story with a great many witty additions and always adding, I tell you all this sans discrétion, that is tell it to everybody.

The other german who came to the house in those days was

a dull one. He is, I understand a very important man now in his own country and he was a most faithful friend to Matisse, at all times, even during the war. He was the bulwark of the Matisse school. Matisse was not always or indeed often very kind to him. All women loved him, so it was supposed. He was a stocky Don Juan. I remember one big scandinavian who loved him and who would never come in on Saturday evening but stood in the court and whenever the door opened for some one to come in or go out you could see her smile in the dark of the court like the smile of the Cheshire cat. He was always bothered by Gertrude Stein. She did and bought such strange things. He never dared to criticise anything to her but to me he would say, and you, Mademoiselle, do you, pointing to the despised object, do you find that beautiful.

Once when we were in Spain, in fact the first time we went to Spain, Gertrude Stein had insisted upon buying in Cuenca a brand new enormous turtle made of Rhine stones. She had very lovely old jewellery, but with great satisfaction to herself she was wearing this turtle as a clasp. Purrmann this time was dumbfounded. He got me into a corner. That jewel, he said, that Miss Stein is wearing, are those stones real.

Speaking of Spain also reminds me that once we were in a crowded restaurant. Suddenly in the end of the room a tall form stood up and a man bowed solemnly at Gertrude Stein who as solemnly replied. It was a stray hungarian from Saturday evening, surely.

There was another german whom I must admit we both liked. This was much later, about nineteen twelve. He too was a dark tall german. He talked english, he was a friend of Marsden Hartley whom we liked very much, and we liked his german friend, I cannot say that we did not.

He used to describe himself as the rich son of a not so rich father. In other words he had a large allowance from a moderately poor father who was a university professor. Rönnebeck was charming and he was always invited to dinner. He was at dinner one evening when Berenson the famous critic of italian art was there. Rönnebeck had brought with him some photographs of pictures by Rousseau. He had left them in the atelier and we were all in the dining room. Everybody began to talk about Rousseau. Berenson was puzzled, but Rousseau,

Rousseau, he said, Rousseau was an honourable painter but why all this excitement. Ah, he said with a sigh, fashions change, that I know, but really I never thought that Rousseau would come to be the fashion for the young. Berenson had a tendency to be supercilious and so everybody let him go on and on. Finally Rönnebeck said gently, but perhaps Mr. Berenson, you have never heard of the great Rousseau, the douanier Rousseau. No, admitted Berenson, he hadn't, and later when he saw the photographs he understood less than ever and was fairly fussed. Mabel Dodge who was present, said, but Berenson, you must remember that art is inevitable. That, said Berenson recovering himself, you understand, you being yourself a femme fatale.

We were fond of Rönnebeck and beside the first time he came to the house he quoted some of Gertrude Stein's recent work to her. She had loaned some manuscript to Marsden Hartley. It was the first time that anybody had quoted her work to her and she naturally liked it. He also made a translation into german of some of the portraits she was writing at that time and thus brought her her first international reputation. That however is not quite true, Roché the faithful Roché had introduced some young germans to Three Lives and they were already under its spell. However Rönnebeck was charming and we were very fond of him.

Rönnebeck was a sculptor, he did small full figure portraits and was doing them very well, he was in love with an american girl who was studying music. He liked France and all french things and he was very fond of us. We all separated as usual for the summer. He said he had a very amusing summer before him. He had a commission to do a portrait figure of a countess and her two sons, the little counts and he was to spend the summer doing this in the home of the countess who had a magnificent place on the shores of the Baltic.

When we all came back that winter Rönnebeck was different. In the first place he came back with lots of photographs of ships of the german navy and insisted upon showing them to us. We were not interested. Gertrude Stein said, of course, Rönnebeck, you have a navy, of course, we americans have a navy, everybody has a navy, but to anybody but the navy, one big ironclad looks very much like any other, don't be silly. He was different though. He had had a good time. He had photos of himself with all the counts and there was also one with the crown prince of Germany who was a great friend of the countess. The winter, it was the winter of 1913–1914, wore on. All the usual things happened and we gave as usual some dinner parties. I have forgotten what the occasion of one was but we thought Rönnebeck would do excellently for it. We invited him. He sent word that he had to go to Munich for two days but he would travel at night and get back for the dinner party. This he did and was delightful as he always was.

Pretty soon he went off on a trip to the north, to visit the cathedral towns. When he came back he brought us a series of photographs of all these northern towns seen from above. What are these, Gertrude Stein asked. Oh, he said, I thought you would be interested, they are views I have taken of all the cathedral towns. I took them from the tip top of the steeples and I thought you would be interested because see, he said, they look exactly like the pictures of the followers of Delaunay, what you call the earthquake school, he said turning to me. We thanked him and thought no more about it. Later when during the war I found them, I tore them up in a rage.

Then we all began to talk about our summer plans. Gertrude Stein was to go to London in July to see John Lane to sign the contract for Three Lives. Rönnebeck said, why don't you come to Germany instead or rather before or immediately after, he said. Because, said Gertrude Stein, as you know I don't like germans. Yes I know, said Rönnebeck, I know, but you like me and you would have such a wonderful time. They would be so interested and it would mean so much to them, do come, he said. No, said Gertrude Stein, I like you alright but I don't like germans.

We went to England in July and when we got there Gertrude Stein had a letter from Rönnebeck saying that he still awfully wanted us to come to Germany but since we wouldn't had we not better spend the summer in England or perhaps in Spain but not as we had planned come back to Paris. That was naturally the end. I tell the story for what it is worth.

When I first came to Paris there was a very small sprinkling of americans Saturday evenings, this sprinkling grew gradually more abundant but before I tell about americans I must tell all about the banquet to Rousseau.

In the beginning of my stay in Paris a friend and I were living as I have already said in a little apartment on the rue Notre-Dame-des-Champs. I was no longer taking french lessons from Fernande because she and Picasso were together again but she was not an infrequent visitor. Autumn had come and I can remember it very well because I had bought my first winter Paris hat. It was a very fine hat of black velvet, a big hat with a brilliant yellow fantaisie. Even Fernande gave it her approval.

Fernande was lunching with us one day and she said that there was going to be a banquet given for Rousseau and that she was giving it. She counted up the number of the invited. We were included. Who was Rousseau. I did not know but that really did not matter since it was to be a banquet and everybody was to go, and we were invited.

Next Saturday evening at the rue de Fleurus everybody was talking about the banquet to Rousseau and then I found out that Rousseau was the painter whose picture I had seen in that first independent. It appeared that Picasso had recently found in Montmartre a large portrait of a woman by Rousseau, that he had bought it and that this festivity was in honour of the purchase and the painter. It was going to be very wonderful.

Fernande told me a great real about the menu. There was to be riz à la Valenciennes, Fernande had learnt how to cook this on her last trip to Spain, and then she had ordered, I forget now what it was that she had ordered, but she had ordered a great deal at Félix Potin, the chain store of groceries where they made prepared dishes. Everybody was excited. It was Guillaume Apollinaire, as I remember, who knowing Rousseau very well had induced him to promise to come and was to bring him and everybody was to write poetry and songs and it was to be very rigolo, a favourite Montmartre word meaning a jokeful amusement. We were all to meet at the café at the foot of the rue Ravignan and to have an apéritif and then go up to Picasso's atelier and have dinner. I put on my new hat and we all went to Montmartre and all met at the café.

As Gertrude Stein and I came into the café there seemed to be a great many people present and in the midst was a tall thin girl who with her long thin arms extended was swaying forward and back. I did not know what she was doing, it was evidently not gymnastics, it was bewildering but she looked very enticing. What is that, I whispered to Gertrude Stein. Oh that is Marie Laurencin, I am afraid she has been taking too many preliminary apéritifs. Is she the old lady that Fernande told me about who makes noises like animals and annoys Pablo. She annoys Pablo alright but she is a very young lady and she has had too much, said Gertrude Stein going in. Just then there was a violent noise at the door of the café and Fernande appeared very large, very excited and very angry. Félix Potin, said she, has not sent the dinner. Everybody seemed overcome at these awful tidings but I, in my american way said to Fernande, come quickly, let us telephone. In those days in Paris one did not telephone and never to a provision store. But Fernande consented and off we went. Everywhere we went there was either no telephone or it was not working, finally we got one that worked but Félix Potin was closed or closing and it was deaf to our appeals. Fernande was completely upset but finally I persuaded her to tell me just what we were to have had from Félix Potin and then in one little shop and another little shop in Montmartre we found substitutes, Fernande finally announcing that she had made so much riz à la Valenciennes that it would take the place of everything and it did.

When we were back at the café almost everybody who had been there had gone and some new ones had come, Fernande told them all to come along. As we toiled up the hill we saw in front of us the whole crowd. In the middle was Marie Laurencin supported on the one side by Gertrude Stein and on the other by Gertrude Stein's brother and she was falling first into one pair of arms and then into another, her voice always high and sweet and her arms always thin graceful and long. Guillaume of course was not there, he was to bring Rousseau himself after every one was seated.

Fernande passed this slow moving procession, I following her and we arrived at the atelier. It was rather impressive. They had gotten trestles, carpenter's trestles, and on them had placed boards and all around these boards were benches. At the head of the table was the new acquisition, the Rousseau, draped in flags and wreaths and flanked on either side by big statues, I do not remember what statues. It was very magnificent and very festive. The riz à la Valenciennes was presumably cooking below in Max Jacob's studio. Max not being on good terms with Picasso was not present but they used his studio for the rice and for the men's overcoats. The ladies were to put theirs in the front studio which had been Van Dongen's in his spinach days and now belonged to a frenchman by the name of Vaillant. This was the studio which was later to be Juan Gris'.

I had just time to deposit my hat and admire the arrangements, Fernande violently abusing Marie Laurencin all the time, when the crowd arrived. Fernande large and imposing, barred the way, she was not going to have her party spoiled by Marie Laurencin. This was a serious party, a serious banquet for Rousseau and neither she nor Pablo would tolerate such conduct. Of course Pablo, all this time, was well out of sight in the rear. Gertrude Stein remonstrated, she said half in english half in french, that she would be hanged if after the struggle of getting Marie Laurencin up that terrific hill it was going to be for nothing. No indeed and beside she reminded Fernande that Guillaume and Rousseau would be along any minute and it was necessary that every one should be decorously seated before that event. By this time Pablo had made his way to the front and he joined in and said, yes yes, and Fernande yielded. She was always a little afraid of Guillaume Apollinaire, of his solemnity and of his wit, and they all came in. Everybody sat down.

Everybody sat down and everybody began to eat rice and other things, that is as soon as Guillaume Apollinaire and Rousseau came in which they did very presently and were wildly acclaimed. How well I remember their coming, Rousseau a little small colourless frenchman with a little beard, like any number of frenchmen one saw everywhere. Guillaume Apollinaire with finely cut florid features, dark hair and a beautiful complexion. Everybody was presented and everybody sat down again. Guillaume slipped into a seat beside Marie Laurencin. At the sight of Guillaume, Marie who had become comparatively calm seated next to Gertrude Stein, broke out again in wild movements and outcries. Guillaume got her out of the door and downstairs and after a decent interval they came back Marie a little bruised but sober. By this time everybody had eaten everything and poetry began. Oh yes, before this Frédéric of the Lapin Agile and the University of Apaches had wandered in with his usual companion a donkey, was given a drink and wandered out again. Then a little later some italian street singers hearing of the party came in. Fernande rose at the end of the table and flushed and her forefinger straight into the air said it was not that kind of a party, and they were promptly thrown out.

Who was there. We were there and Salmon, André Salmon, then a rising young poet and journalist, Pichot and Germaine Pichot, Braque and perhaps Marcelle Braque but this I do not remember, I know that there was talk of her at that time, the Raynals, the Ageros the false Greco and his wife, and several other pairs whom I did not know and do not remember and Vaillant, a very amiable ordinary young frenchman who had the front studio.

The ceremonies began. Guillaume Apollinaire got up and made a solemn eulogy, I do not remember at all what he said but it ended up with a poem he had written and which he half chanted and in which everybody joined in the refrain, La peinture de ce Rousseau. Somebody else then, possibly Raynal, I don't remember, got up and there were toasts, and then all of a sudden André Salmon who was sitting next to my friend and solemnly discoursing of literature and travels, leaped upon the by no means solid table and poured out an extemporaneous eulogy and poem. At the end he seized a big glass and drank what was in it, then promptly went off his head, being completely drunk, and began to fight. The men all got hold of him, the statues tottered, Braque, a great big chap, got hold of a statue in either arm and stood there holding them while Gertrude Stein's brother another big chap, protected little Rousseau and his violin from harm. The others with Picasso leading because Picasso though small is very strong, dragged Salmon into the front atelier and locked him in. Everybody came back and sat down.

Thereafter the evening was peaceful. Marie Laurencin sang

in a thin voice some charming old norman songs. The wife of Agero sang some charming old limousin songs, Pichot danced a wonderful religious spanish dance ending in making of himself a crucified Christ upon the floor. Guillaume Apollinaire solemnly approached myself and my friend and asked us to sing some of the native songs of the red indians. We did not either of us feel up to that to the great regret of Guillaume and all the company. Rousseau blissful and gentle played the violin and told us about the plays he had written and his memories of Mexico. It was all very peaceful and about three o'clock in the morning we all went into the atelier where Salmon had been deposited and where we had left our hats and coats to get them to go home. There on the couch lay Salmon peacefully sleeping and surrounding him, half chewed, were a box of matches, a petit bleu and my yellow fantaisie. Imagine my feelings even at three o'clock in the morning. However, Salmon woke up very charming and very polite and we all went out into the street together. All of a sudden with a wild yell Salmon rushed down the hill.

Gertrude Stein and her brother, my friend and I, all in one cab, took Rousseau home.

It was about a month later that one dark Paris winter afternoon I was hurrying home and felt myself being followed. I hurried and hurried and the footsteps drew nearer and I heard, mademoiselle, mademoiselle. I turned. It was Rousseau. Oh mademoiselle, he said, you should not be out alone after dark, may I see you home. Which he did.

It was not long after this that Kahnweiler came to Paris. Kahnweiler was a german married to a frenchwoman and they had lived for many years in England. Kahnweiler had been in England in business, saving money to carry out a dream of some day having a picture shop in Paris. The time had come and he started a neat small gallery in the rue Vignon. He felt his way a little and then completely threw in his lot with the cubist group. There were difficulties at first, Picasso always suspicious did not want to go too far with him. Fernande did the bargaining with Kahnweiler but finally they all realised the genuineness of his interest and his faith, and that he could and would market their work. They all made contracts with him and until the war he did everything for them all. The afternoons with the group coming in and out of his shop were for Kahnweiler really afternoons with Vasari. He believed in them and their future greatness. It was only the year before the war that he added Juan Gris. It was just two months before the outbreak of the war that Gertrude Stein saw the first Juan Gris paintings at Kahnweiler's and bought three of them.

Picasso always says that he used in those days to tell Kahnweiler that he should become a french citizen, that war would come and there would be the devil to pay. Kahnweiler always said he would when he had passed the military age but that he naturally did not want to do military service a second time. The war came, Kahnweiler was in Switzerland with his family on his vacation and he could not come back. All his possessions were sequestrated.

The auction sale by the government of Kahnweiler's pictures, practically all the cubist pictures of the three years before the war, was the first occasion after the war where everybody of the old crowd met. There had been quite a conscious effort on the part of all the older merchants, now that the war was over, to kill cubism. The expert for the sale, who was a well known picture dealer, had avowed this as his intention. He would keep the prices down as low as possible and discourage the public as much as possible. How could the artists defend themselves.

We happened to be with the Braques a day or two before the public show of pictures for the sale and Marcelle Braque, Braque's wife, told us that they had come to a decision. Picasso and Juan Gris could do nothing they were spaniards, and this was a french government sale. Marie Laurencin was technically a german, Lipschitz was a russian at that time not a popular thing to be. Braque a frenchman, who had won the croix de guerre in a charge, who had been made an officer and had won the légion d'honneur and had had a bad head wound could do what he pleased. He had a technical reason too for picking a quarrel with the expert. He had sent in a list of the people likely to buy his pictures, a privilege always accorded to an artist whose pictures are to be publicly sold, and catalogues had not been sent to these people. When we arrived Braque had already done his duty. We came in just at the end of the fray. There was a great excitement.

Braque had approached the expert and told him that he had neglected his obvious duties. The expert had replied that he had done and would do as he pleased and called Braque a norman pig. Braque had hit him. Braque is a big man and the expert is not and Braque tried not to hit hard but nevertheless the expert fell. The police came in and they were taken off to the police station. There they told their story. Braque of course as a hero of the war was treated with all due respect, and when he spoke to the expert using the familiar thou the expert completely lost his temper and his head and was publicly rebuked by the magistrate. Just after it was over Matisse came in and wanted to know what had happened and was happening. Gertrude Stein told him. Matisse said, and it was a Matisse way to say it, Braque a raison, celui-là a volé la France, et on sait bien ce que c'est que voler la France.

As a matter of fact the buyers were frightened off and all the pictures except those of Derain went for little. Poor Juan Gris whose pictures went for very little tried to be brave. They after all did bring an honourable price, he said to Gertrude Stein, but he was sad.

Fortunately Kahnweiler, who had not fought against France, was allowed to come back the next year. The others no longer needed him but Juan needed him desperately and Kahnweiler's loyalty and generosity to Juan Gris all those hard years can only be matched by Juan's loyalty and generosity when at last just before his death and he had become famous tempting offers from other dealers were made to him.

Kahnweiler coming to Paris and taking on commercially the cause of the cubists made a great difference to all of them. Their present and future were secure.

The Picassos moved from the old studio in the rue Ravignan to an apartment in the boulevard Clichy. Fernande began to buy furniture and have a servant and the servant of course made a soufflé. It was a nice apartment with lots of sunshine. On the whole however Fernande was not quite as happy as she had been. There were a great many people there and even afternoon tea. Braque was there a great deal, it was the height of the intimacy between Braque and Picasso, it was at that time they first began to put musical instruments into their pictures. It was also the beginning of Picasso's making constructions. He made still lifes of objects and photographed them. He made paper constructions later, he gave one of these to Gertrude Stein. It is perhaps the only one left in existence.

This was also the time when I first heard of Poiret. He had a houseboat on the Seine and he had given a party on it and he had invited Pablo and Fernande. He gave Fernande a handsome rose-coloured scarf with gold fringe and he also gave her a spun glass fantaisie to put on a hat, an entirely new idea in those days. This she gave to me and I wore it on a little straw pointed cap for years after. I may even have it now.

Then there was the youngest of the cubists. I never knew his name. He was doing his military service and was destined for diplomacy. How he drifted in and whether he painted I do not know. All I know is that he was known as the youngest of the cubists.

Fernande had at this time a new friend of whom she often spoke to me. This was Eve who was living with Marcoussis. And one evening all four of them came to the rue de Fleurus, Pablo, Fernande, Marcoussis and Eve. It was the only time we ever saw Marcoussis until many many years later.

I could perfectly understand Fernande's liking for Eve. As I said Fernande's great heroine was Evelyn Thaw, small and negative. Here was a little french Evelyn Thaw, small and perfect.

Not long after this Picasso came one day and told Gertrude Stein that he had decided to take an atelier in the rue Ravignan. He could work better there. He could not get back his old one but he took one on the lower floor. One day we went to see him there. He was not in and Gertrude Stein as a joke left her visiting card. In a few days we went again and Picasso was at work on a picture on which was written ma jolie and at the lower corner painted in was Gertrude Stein's visiting card. As we went away Gertrude Stein said, Fernande is certainly not ma jolie, I wonder who it is. In a few days we knew. Pablo had gone off with Eve.

This was in the spring. They all had the habit of going to Céret near Perpignan for the summer probably on account of Manolo, and they all in spite of everything went there again. Fernande was there with the Pichots and Eve was there with

Pablo. There were some redoubtable battles and then every-body came back to Paris.

One evening, we too had come back, Picasso came in. He and Gertrude Stein had a long talk alone. It was Pablo, she said when she came in from having bade him goodbye, and he said a marvellous thing about Fernande, he said her beauty always held him but he could not stand any of her little ways. She further added that Pablo and Eve were now settled on the boulevard Raspail and we would go and see them to-morrow.

In the meanwhile Gertrude Stein had received a letter from Fernande, very dignified, written with the reticence of a frenchwoman. She said that she wished to tell Gertrude Stein that she understood perfectly that the friendship had always been with Pablo and that although Gertrude had always shown her every mark of sympathy and affection now that she and Pablo were separated, it was naturally impossible that in the future there should be any intercourse between them be-cause the friendship having been with Pablo there could of course be no question of a choice. That she would always remember their intercourse with pleasure and that she would permit herself, if ever she were in need, to throw herself upon Gertrude's generosity.

And so Picasso left Montmartre never to return.

When I first came to the rue de Fleurus Gertrude Stein was correcting the proofs of Three Lives. I was soon helping her with this and before very long the book was published. I asked her to let me subscribe to Romeike's clipping bureau, the advertisement for Romeike in the San Francisco Argonaut having been one of the romances of my childhood. Soon the clippings began to come in.

It is rather astonishing the number of newspapers that no-ticed this book, printed privately and by a perfectly unknown person. The notice that pleased Gertrude Stein most was in the Kansas City Star. She often asked then and in later years who it was who might have written it but she never found out. It was a very sympathetic and a very understanding re-view. Later on when she was discouraged by what others said she would refer to it as having given her at that time great comfort. She says in Composition and Explanation, when you write a thing it is perfectly clear and then you begin to be doubtful about it, but then you read it again and you lose yourself in it again as when you wrote it.

The other thing in connection with this her first book that gave her pleasure was a very enthusiastic note from H. G. Wells. She kept this for years apart, it had meant so much to her. She wrote to him at that time and they were often to meet but as it happened they never did. And they are not likely to now.

Gertrude Stein was at that time writing The Making of Americans. It had changed from being a history of a family to being the history of everybody the family knew and then it became the history of every kind and of every individual human being. But in spite of all this there was a hero and he was to die. The day he died I met Gertrude Stein at Mildred Aldrich's apartment. Mildred was very fond of Gertrude Stein and took a deep interest in the book's ending. It was over a thousand pages long and I was typewriting it.

I always say that you cannot tell what a picture really is or what an object really is until you dust it every day and you cannot tell what a book is until you type it or proofread it. It then does something to you that only reading never can do. A good many years later Jane Heap said that she had never appreciated the quality of Gertrude Stein's work until she proof-read it.

When The Making of Americans was finished, Gertrude Stein began another which also was to be long and which she called A Long Gay Book but it did not turn out to be long, neither that nor one begun at the same time Many Many Women because they were both interrupted by portrait writing. This is how portrait writing began.

Hélène used to stay at home with her husband Sunday evening, that is to say she was always willing to come but we often told her not to bother. I like cooking, I am an extremely good five-minute cook, and beside, Gertrude Stein liked from time to time to have me make american dishes. One Sunday evening I was very busy preparing one of these and then I called Gertrude Stein to come in from the atelier for supper. She came in much excited and would not sit down. Here I want to show you something, she said. No I said it has to be eaten hot. No, she said, you have to see this first. Gertrude Stein never likes her food hot and I do like mine hot, we never agree about this. She admits that one can wait to cool it but one cannot heat it once it is on a plate so it is agreed that I have it served as hot as I like. In spite of my protests and the food cooling I had to read. I can still see the little tiny pages of the note-book written forward and back. It was the portrait called Ada, the first in Geography and Plays. I began it and I thought she was making fun of me and I protested, she says I protest now about my autobiography. Finally I read it all and was terribly pleased with it. And then we ate our supper.

This was the beginning of the long series of portraits. She has written portraits of practically everybody she has known, and written them in all manners and in all styles.

Ada was followed by portraits of Matisse and Picasso, and Stieglitz who was much interested in them and in Gertrude Stein printed them in a special number of Camera Work.

She then began to do short portraits of everybody who came in and out. She did one of Arthur Frost, the son of A. B. Frost the american illustrator. Frost was a Matisse pupil and his pride when he read his portrait and found that it was three full pages longer than either the portrait of Matisse or the portrait of Picasso was something to hear.

A. B. Frost complained to Pat Bruce who had led Frost to Matisse that it was a pity that Arthur could not see his way to becoming a conventional artist and so earning fame and money. You can lead a horse to water but you cannot make him drink, said Pat Bruce. Most horses drink, Mr. Bruce, said A. B. Frost.

Bruce, Patrick Henry Bruce, was one of the early and most ardent Matisse pupils and soon he made little Matisses, but he was not happy. In explaining his unhappiness he told Gertrude Stein, they talk about the sorrows of great artists, the tragic unhappiness of great artists but after all they are great artists. A little artist has all the tragic unhappiness and the sorrows of a great artist and he is not a great artist.

She did portraits of Nadelman, also of the protégés of the sculptress Mrs. Whitney, Lee and Russell also of Harry Phelan Gibb, her first and best english friend. She did portraits of

Manguin and Roché and Purrmann and David Edstrom, the fat swedish sculptor who married the head of the Christian Science Church in Paris and destroyed her. And Brenner, Brenner the sculptor who never finished anything. He had an admirable technique and a great many obsessions which kept him from work. Gertrude Stein was very fond of him and still is. She once posed to him for weeks and he did a fragmentary portrait of her that is very fine. He and Cody later published some numbers of a little review called Soil and they were among the very early ones to print something of Gertrude Stein. The only little magazine that preceded it was one called Rogue, printed by Allan Norton and which printed her description of the Galérie Lafayette. This was of course all much later and happened through Carl Van Vechten.

She also did portraits of Miss Etta Cone and her sister Doctor Claribel Cone. She also did portraits of Miss Mars and Miss Squires under the title of Miss Furr and Miss Skeene. There were portraits of Mildred Aldrich and her sister. Everybody was given their portrait to read and they were all pleased and it was all very amusing. All this occupied a great deal of that winter and then we went to Spain.

In Spain Gertrude Stein began to write the things that led to Tender Buttons.

I liked Spain immensely. We went several times to Spain and I always liked it more and more. Gertrude Stein says that I am impartial on every subject except that of Spain and spaniards.

We went straight to Avila and I immediately lost my heart to Avila, I must stay in Avila forever I insisted. Gertrude Stein was very upset, Avila was alright but, she insisted, she needed Paris. I felt that I needed nothing but Avila. We were both very violent about it. We did however stay there for ten days and as Saint Theresa was a heroine of Gertrude Stein's youth we thoroughly enjoyed it. In the opera Four Saints written a few years ago she describes the landscape that so profoundly moved me.

We went on to Madrid and there we met Georgiana King of Bryn Mawr, an old friend of Gertrude Stein from Baltimore days. Georgiana King wrote some of the most interesting of the early criticisms of Three Lives. She was then re-editing Street on the cathedrals of Spain and in connection with this she had wandered all over Spain. She gave us a great deal of very good advice.

In these days Gertrude Stein wore a brown corduroy suit, jacket and skirt, a small straw cap, always crocheted for her by a woman in Fiesole, sandals, and she often carried a cane. That summer the head of the cane was of amber. It is more or less this costume without the cap and the cane that Picasso has painted in his portrait of her. This costume was ideal for Spain, they all thought of her as belonging to some religious order and we were always treated with the most absolute respect. I remember that once a nun was showing us the treasures in a convent church in Toledo. We were near the steps of the altar. All of a sudden there was a crash, Gertrude Stein had dropped her cane. The nun paled, the worshippers startled. Gertrude Stein picked up her cane and turning to the frightened nun said reassuringly, no it is not broken.

I used in those days of spanish travelling to wear what I was wont to call my spanish disguise. I always wore a black silk coat, black gloves and a black hat, the only pleasure I allowed myself were lovely artificial flowers on my hat. These always enormously interested the peasant women and they used to very courteously ask my permission to touch them, to realise for themselves that they were artificial.

We went to Cuenca that summer, Harry Gibb the english painter had told us about it. Harry Gibb is a strange case of a man who foresaw everything. He had been a successful animal painter in his youth in England, he came from the north of England, he had married and gone to Germany, there he had become dissatisfied with what he had been doing and heard about the new school of painting in Paris. He came to Paris and was immediately influenced by Matisse. He then became interested in Picasso and he did some very remarkable painting under their combined influences. Then all this together threw him into something else something that fairly completely achieved what the surréalistes after the war tried to do. The only thing he lacked is what the french call saveur, what may be called the graciousness of a picture. Because of this lack it was impossible for him to find a french audience. Naturally in those days there was no english audience. Harry Gibb fell on bad days. He was always falling upon bad days. He and his wife Bridget one of the pleasantest of the wives of a genius I have sat with were full of courage and they faced everything admirably, but there were always very difficult days. And then things were a little better. He found a couple of patrons who believed in him and it was at this time, 1912–1913, that he went to Dublin and had rather an epoch-making show of his pictures there. It was at that time that he took with him several copies of the portrait of Mabel Dodge at the Villa Curonia, Mabel Dodge had had it printed in Florence, and it was then that the Dublin writers in the cafés heard Gertrude Stein read aloud. Doctor Gogarty, Harry Gibb's host and admirer, loved to read it aloud himself and have others read it aloud.

After that there was the war and eclipse for poor Harry, and since then a long sad struggle. He has had his ups and downs, more downs than up, but only recently there was a new turn of the wheel. Gertrude Stein who loved them both dearly always was convinced that the two painters of her generation who would be discovered after they were dead, they being predestined to a life of tragedy, were Juan Gris and Harry Gibb. Juan Gris dead these five years is beginning to come into his own. Harry Gibb still alive is still unknown. Gertrude Stein and Harry Gibb have always been very loyal and very loving friends. One of the very good early portraits she did she did of him, it was printed in the Oxford Review and then in Geography and Plays.

So Harry Gibb told us about Cuenca and we went on a little railroad that turned around curves and ended in the middle of nowhere and there was Cuenca.

We delighted in Cuenca and the population of Cuenca delighted in us. It delighted in us so much that it was getting uncomfortable. Then one day when we were out walking, all of a sudden the population, particularly the children, kept their distance. Soon a uniformed man came up and saluting said that he was a policeman of the town and that the governor of the province had detailed him to always hover in the distance as we went about the country to prevent our being annoyed by the population and that he hoped that this would not inconvenience us. It did not, he was charming and he took us to lovely places in the country where we could not very well have gone by ourselves. Such was Spain in the old days.

We finally came back to Madrid again and there we discovered the Argentina and bull-fights. The young journalists of Madrid had just discovered her. We happened upon her in a music hall, we went to them to see spanish dancing, and after we saw her the first time we went every afternoon and every evening. We went to the bull-fights. At first they upset me and Gertrude Stein used to tell me, now look, now don't look, until finally I was able to look all the time.

We finally came to Granada and stayed there for some time and there Gertrude Stein worked terrifically. She was always very fond of Granada. It was there she had her first experience of Spain when still at college just after the spanish-american war when she and her brother went through Spain. They had a delightful time and she always tells of sitting in the dining room talking to a bostonian and his daughter when suddenly there was a terrific noise, the hee-haw of a donkey. What is it, said the young bostonian trembling. Ah, said the father, it is the last sigh of the Moor.

We enjoyed Granada, we met many amusing people english and spanish and it was there and at that time that Gertrude Stein's style gradually changed. She says hitherto she had been interested only in the insides of people, their character and what went on inside them, it was during that summer that she first felt a desire to express the rhythm of the visible world.

It was a long tormenting process, she looked, listened and described. She always was, she always is, tormented by the problem of the external and the internal. One of the things that always worries her about painting is the difficulty that the artist feels and which sends him to painting still lifes, that after all the human being essentially is not paintable. Once again and very recently she has thought that a painter has added something to the solution of this problem. She is interested in Picabia in whom hitherto she has never been interested because he at least knows that if you do not solve your painting problem in painting human beings you do not solve it at all. There is also a follower of Picabia's, who is facing the problem, but will he solve it. Perhaps not. Well anyway it is that of which she is always talking and now her own long struggle with it was to begin.

These were the days in which she wrote Susie Asado and Preciosilla and Gypsies in Spain. She experimented with everything in trying to describe. She tried a bit inventing words but she soon gave that up. The english language was her medium and with the english language the task was to be achieved, the problem solved. The use of fabricated words offended her, it was an escape into imitative emotionalism.

No, she stayed with her task, although after the return to Paris she described objects, she described rooms and objects, which joined with her first experiments done in Spain, made the volume Tender Buttons.

She always however made her chief study people and therefore the never ending series of portraits.

We came back to the rue de Fleurus as usual.

One of the people who had impressed me very much when I first came to the rue de Fleurus was Mildred Aldrich.

Mildred Aldrich was then in her early fifties, a stout vigorous woman with a George Washington face, white hair and admirably clean fresh clothes and gloves. A very striking figure and a very satisfying one in the crowd of mixed nationalities. She was indeed one of whom Picasso could say and did say, c'est elle qui fera la gloire de l'Amérique. She made one very satisfied with one's country, which had produced her.

Her sister having left for America she lived alone on the top floor of a building on the corner of the boulevard Raspail and the half street, rue Boissonade. There she had at the window an enormous cage filled with canaries. We always thought it was because she loved canaries. Not at all. A friend had once left her a canary in a cage to take care of during her absence. Mildred as she did everything else, took excellent care of the canary in the cage. Some friend seeing this and naturally concluding that Mildred was fond of canaries gave her another canary. Mildred of course took excellent care of both canaries and so the canaries increased and the size of the cage grew until in 1914 she moved to Huiry to the Hilltop on the Marne and gave her canaries away. Her excuse was that in the country cats would eat the canaries. But her real reason she once told me was that she really could not bear canaries.

Mildred was an excellent housekeeper. I was very surprised, having had a very different impression of her, going up to see her one afternoon, finding her mending her linen and doing it beautifully.

Mildred adored cablegrams, she adored being hard up, or rather she adored spending money and as her earning capacity although great was limited, Mildred was chronically hard up. In those days she was making contracts to put Maeterlinck's Blue Bird on the american stage. The arrangements demanded endless cablegrams, and my early memories of Mildred were of her coming to our little apartment in the rue Notre-Dame-des-Champs late in the evening and asking me to lend her the money for a long cable. A few days later the money was returned with a lovely azalea worth five times the money. No wonder she was always hard up. But everybody listened to her. No one in the world could tell stories like Mildred. I can still see her at the rue de Fleurus sitting in one of the big armchairs and gradually the audience increasing around her as she talked.

She was very fond of Gertrude Stein, very interested in her work, enthusiastic about Three Lives, deeply impressed but slightly troubled by The Making of Americans, quite upset by Tender Buttons, but always loyal and convinced that if Gertrude Stein did it it had something in it that was worth while.

Her joy and pride when in nineteen twenty-six Gertrude Stein gave her lecture at Cambridge and Oxford was touching. Gertrude Stein must come out and read it to her before leaving. Gertrude Stein did, much to their mutual pleasure.

Mildred Aldrich liked Picasso and even liked Matisse, that is personally, but she was troubled. One day she said to me, Alice, tell me is it alright, are they really alright, I know Gertrude thinks so and Gertrude knows, but really is it not all fumisterie, is it not all false.

In spite of these occasional doubtful days Mildred Aldrich liked it all. She liked coming herself and she liked bringing other people. She brought a great many. It was she who brought Henry McBride who was then writing on the New York Sun. It was Henry McBride who used to keep Gertrude

Stein's name before the public all those tormented years. Laugh if you like, he used to say to her detractors, but laugh with and not at her, in that way you will enjoy it all much better.

Henry McBride did not believe in worldly success. It ruins you, it ruins you, he used to say. But Henry, Gertrude Stein used to answer dolefully, don't you think I will ever have any success, I would like to have a little, you know. Think of my unpublished manuscripts. But Henry McBride was firm, the best that I can wish you, he always said, is to have no success. It is the only good thing. He was firm about that.

He was however enormously pleased when Mildred was successful and he now says he thinks the time has come when Gertrude Stein could indulge in a little success. He does not think that now it would hurt her.

It was about this time that Roger Fry first came to the house. He brought Clive Bell and Mrs. Clive Bell and later there were many others. In these days Clive Bell went along with the other two. He was rather complainful that his wife and Roger Fry took too much interest in capital works of art. He was quite funny about it. He was very amusing, later when he became a real art critic he was less so.

Roger Fry was always charming, charming as a guest and charming as a host; later when we went to London we spent a day with him in the country.

He was filled with excitement at the sight of the portrait of Gertrude Stein by Picasso. He wrote an article about it in the Burlington Review and illustrated it by two photographs side by side, one the photograph of this portrait and the other a photograph of a portrait by Raphael. He insisted that these two pictures were equal in value. He brought endless people to the house. Very soon there were throngs of englishmen, Augustus John and Lamb, Augustus John amazing looking and not too sober, Lamb rather strange and attractive.

It was about this time that Roger Fry had many young disciples. Among them was Wyndham Lewis. Wyndham Lewis, tall and thin, looked rather like a young frenchman on the rise, perhaps because his feet were very french, or at least his shoes. He used to come and sit and measure pictures. I can not say that he actually measured with a measuring-rod but he gave all the effect of being in the act of taking very careful measurement of the canvas, the lines within the canvas and everything that might be of use. Gertrude Stein rather liked him. She particularly liked him one day when he came and told all about his quarrel with Roger Fry. Roger Fry had come in not many days before and had already told all about it. They told exactly the same story only it was different, very different.

This was about the time too that Prichard of the Museum of Fine Arts, Boston and later of the Kensington Museum began coming. Prichard brought a great many young Oxford men. They were very nice in the room, and they thought Picasso wonderful. They felt and indeed in a way it was true that he had a halo. With these Oxford men came Thomas Whittemore of Tufts College. He was fresh and engaging and later to Gertrude Stein's great delight he one day said, all blue is precious.

Everybody brought somebody. As I said the character of the Saturday evenings was gradually changing, that is to say, the kind of people who came had changed. Somebody brought the Infanta Eulalia and brought her several times. She was delightful and with the flattering memory of royalty she always remembered my name even some years after when we met quite by accident in the place Vendôme. When she first came into the room she was a little frightened. It seemed a strange place but gradually she liked it very much.

Lady Cunard brought her daughter Nancy, then a little girl, and very solemnly bade her never forget the visit.

Who else came. There were so many. The bavarian minister brought quantities of people. Jacques-Emile Blanche brought delightful people, so did Alphonse Kann. There was Lady Otoline Morrell looking like a marvellous feminine version of Disraeli and tall and strange shyly hesitating at the door. There was a dutch near royalty who was left by her escort who had to go and find a cab and she looked during this short interval badly frightened.

There was a roumanian princess, and her cabman grew impatient. Hélène came in to announce violently that the cabman would not wait. And then after a violent knock, the cabman himself announced that he would not wait.

It was an endless variety. And everybody came and no one made any difference. Gertrude Stein sat peacefully in a chair and those who could did the same, the rest stood. There were the friends who sat around the stove and talked and there were the endless strangers who came and went. My memory of it is very vivid.

As I say everybody brought people. William Cook brought a great many from Chicago, very wealthy stout ladies and equally wealthy tall good-looking thin ones. That summer having found the Balearic Islands on the map, we went to the island of Mallorca and on the little boat going over was Cook. He too had found it on the map. We stayed only a little while but he settled down for the summer, and then later he went back and was the solitary first of all the big crowd of americans who have discovered Palma since. We all went back again during the war.

It was during this summer that Picasso gave us a letter to a friend of his youth one Raventos in Barcelona. But does he talk french, asked Gertrude Stein, Pablo giggled, better than you do Gertrude, he answered.

Raventos gave us a good time, he and a descendant of de Soto took us about for two long days, the days were long because so much of them were night. They had an automobile, even in those early days, and they took us up into the hills to see early churches. We would rush up a hill and then happily come down a little slower and every two hours or so we ate a dinner. When we finally came back to Barcelona about ten o'clock in the evening they said, now we will have an apéritif and then we will eat dinner. It was exhausting eating so many dinners but we enjoyed ourselves.

Later on much later on indeed only a few years ago Picasso introduced us to another friend of his youth.

Sabartes and he have known each other ever since they were fifteen years old but as Sabartes had disappeared into South America, Montevideo, Uruguay, before Gertrude Stein met Picasso, she had never heard of him. One day a few years ago Picasso sent word that he was bringing Sabartes to the house. Sabartes, in Uruguay, had read some things of Gertrude Stein in various magazines and he had conceived a great admiration for her work. It never occurred to him that Picasso would know her. Having come back for the first time in all these years to Paris he went to see Picasso and he told him about this Gertrude Stein. But she is my only friend, said Picasso, it is the only home I go to. Take me, said Sabartes, and so they came.

Gertrude Stein and spaniards are natural friends and this time too the friendship grew.

It was about this time that the futurists, the italian futurists, had their big show in Paris and it made a great deal of noise. Everybody was excited and this show being given in a very well known gallery everybody went. Jacques-Emile Blanche was terribly upset by it. We found him wandering tremblingly in the garden of the Tuileries and he said, it looks alright but is it. No it isn't, said Gertrude Stein. You do me good, said Jacques-Emile Blanche.

The futurists all of them led by Severini thronged around Picasso. He brought them all to the house. Marinetti came by himself later as I remember. In any case everybody found the futurists very dull.

Epstein the sculptor came to the rue de Fleurus one evening. When Gertrude Stein first came to Paris in nineteen hundred and four, Epstein was a thin rather beautiful rather melancholy ghost who used to slip in and out among the Rodin statues in the Luxembourg museum. He had illustrated Hutchins Hapgood's studies of the ghetto and with the funds he came to Paris and was very poor. Now when I first saw him, he had come to Paris to place his sphynx statue to Oscar Wilde over Oscar Wilde's grave. He was a large rather stout man, not unimpressive but not beautiful. He had an english wife who had a very remarkable pair of brown eyes, of a shade of brown I had never before seen in eyes.

Doctor Claribel Cone of Baltimore came majestically in and out. She loved to read Gertrude Stein's work out loud and she did read it out loud extraordinarily well. She liked ease and graciousness and comfort. She and her sister Etta Cone were travelling. The only room in the hotel was not comfortable. Etta bade her sister put up with it as it was only for one night. Etta, answered Doctor Claribel, one night is as important as any other night in my life and I must be comfortable. When the war broke out she happened to be in Munich engaged in scientific work. She could never leave because it was never comfortable to travel. Everybody delighted in Doctor Claribel. Much later Picasso made a drawing of her.

Emily Chadbourne came, it was she who brought Lady Otoline Morrell and she also brought many bostonians.

Mildred Aldrich once brought a very extraordinary person Myra Edgerly. I remembered very well that when I was quite young and went to a fancy-dress ball, a Mardi Gras ball in San Francisco, I saw a very tall and very beautiful and very brilliant woman there. This was Myra Edgerly young. Genthe, the well known photographer did endless photographs of her, mostly with a cat. She had come to London as a miniaturist and she had had one of those phenomenal successes that americans do have in Europe. She had miniatured everybody, and the royal family, and she had maintained her earnest gay careless out-spoken San Francisco way through it all. She now came to Paris to study a little. She met Mildred Aldrich and became very devoted to her. Indeed it was Myra who in nineteen thirteen, when Mildred's earning capacity was rapidly dwindling secured an annuity for her and made it possible for Mildred to retire to the Hilltop on the Marne.

Myra Edgerly was very earnestly anxious that Gertrude Stein's work should be more widely known. When Mildred told her about all those unpublished manuscripts Myra said something must be done. And of course something was done.

She knew John Lane slightly and she said Gertrude Stein and I must go to London. But first Myra must write letters and then I must write letters to everybody for Gertrude Stein. She told me the formula I must employ. I remember it began, Miss Gertrude Stein as you may or may not know, is, and then you went on and said everything you had to say.

Under Myra's strenuous impulsion we went to London in the winter of nineteen twelve, thirteen, for a few weeks. We did have an awfully good time.

Myra took us with her to stay with Colonel and Mrs. Rogers at Riverhill in Surrey. This was in the vicinity of Knole and of Ightham Mote, beautiful houses and beautiful parks. This was my first experience of country-house visiting in England since, as a small child, I had only been in the nursery. I enjoyed every minute of it. The comfort, the open fires, the tall maids who were like annunciation angels, the beautiful gardens, the children, the ease of it all. And the quantity of objects and of beautiful things. What is that, I would ask Mrs. Rogers, ah that I know nothing about, it was here when I came. It gave me a feeling that there had been so many lovely brides in that house who had found all these things there when they came.

Gertrude Stein liked country-house visiting less than I did. The continuous pleasant hesitating flow of conversation, the never ceasing sound of the human voice speaking in english, bothered her.

On our next visit to London and when because of being caught by the war we stayed in country houses with our friends a very long time, she managed to isolate herself for considerable parts of the day and to avoid at least one of the three or four meals, and so she liked it better.

We did have a good time in England. Gertrude Stein completely forgot her early dismal memory of London and has liked visiting there immensely ever since.

We went to Roger Fry's house in the country and were charmingly entertained by his quaker sister. We went to Lady Otoline Morrell and met everybody. We went to Clive Bell's. We went about all the time, we went shopping and ordered things. I still have my bag and jewel box. We had an extremely good time. And we went very often to see John Lane. In fact we were supposed to go every Sunday afternoon to his house for tea and Gertrude Stein had several interviews with him in his office. How well I knew all the things in all the shops near the Bodley Head because while Gertrude Stein was inside with John Lane while nothing happened and then when finally something happened I waited outside and looked at everything.

The Sunday afternoons at John Lane's were very amusing. As I remember during that first stay in London we went there twice.

John Lane was very interested. Mrs. John Lane was a Boston woman and very kind.

Tea at the John Lane's Sunday afternoons was an experience. John Lane had copies of Three Lives and The Portrait of Mabel Dodge. One did not know why he selected the people he did to show it to. He did not give either book to any one to read. He put it into their hands and took it away again and inaudibly he announced that Gertrude Stein was here. Nobody was introduced to anybody. From time to time John Lane would take Gertrude Stein into various rooms and show her his pictures, odd pictures of English schools of all periods, some of them very pleasing. Sometimes he told a story about how he had come to get it. He never said anything else about a picture. He also showed her a great many Beardsley drawings and they talked about Paris.

The second Sunday he asked her to come again to the Bodley Head. This was a long interview. He said that Mrs. Lane had read Three Lives and thought very highly of it and that he had the greatest confidence in her judgment. He asked Gertrude Stein when she was coming back to London. She said she probably was not coming back to London. Well, he said, when you come in July I imagine we will be ready to arrange something. Perhaps, he added, I may see you in Paris in the early spring.

And so we left London. We were on the whole very pleased with ourselves. We had had a very good time and it was the first time that Gertrude Stein had ever had a conversation with a publisher.

Mildred Aldrich often brought a whole group of people to the house Saturday evening. One evening a number of people came in with her and among them was Mabel Dodge. I remember my impression of her very well.

She was a stoutish woman with a very sturdy fringe of heavy hair over her forehead, heavy long lashes and very pretty eyes and a very old fashioned coquetry. She had a lovely voice. She reminded me of a heroine of my youth, the actress Georgia Cayvan. She asked us to come to Florence to stay with her. We were going to spend the summer as was then our habit in Spain but we were going to be back in Paris in the fall and perhaps we then would. When we came back there were several urgent telegrams from Mabel Dodge asking us to come to the Villa Curonia and we did.

We had a very amusing time. We liked Edwin Dodge and we liked Mabel Dodge but we particularly liked Constance Fletcher whom we met there.

Constance Fletcher came a day or so after we arrived and I
went to the station to meet her. Mabel Dodge had described
her to me as a very large woman who would wear a purple
robe and who was deaf. As a matter of fact she was dressed
in green and was not deaf but very short sighted, and she was
delightful.

Her father and mother came from and lived in Newbury-
port, Massachusetts. Edwin Dodge's people came from the
same town and this was a strong bond of union. When
Constance was twelve years old her mother fell in love with
the english tutor of Constance's younger brother. Constance
knew that her mother was about to leave her home. For a
week Constance laid on her bed and wept and then accompanied her mother and her future step-father to Italy. Her
step-father being an englishman Constance became passionately an english woman. The step-father was a painter
who had a local reputation among the english residents in
Italy.

When Constance Fletcher was eighteen years old she wrote
a best-seller called Kismet and was engaged to be married to
Lord Lovelace the descendant of Byron.

She did not marry him and thereafter lived always in Italy.
Finally she became permanently fixed in Venice. This was after
the death of her mother and father. I always liked as a californian her description of Joaquin Miller in Rome, in her
younger days.

Now in her comparative old age she was attractive and impressive. I am very fond of needlework and I was fascinated
by her fashion of embroidering wreaths of flowers. There was
nothing drawn upon her linen, she just held it in her hands,
from time to time bringing it closely to one eye, and eventually the wreath took form. She was very fond of ghosts.
There were two of them in the Villa Curonia and Mabel was
very fond of frightening visiting americans with them which
she did in her suggestive way very effectively. Once she drove
a house party consisting of Jo and Yvonne Davidson, Florence
Bradley, Mary Foote and a number of others quite mad with
fear. And at last to complete the effect she had the local priest
in to exorcise the ghosts. You can imagine the state of mind
of her guests. But Constance Fletcher was fond of ghosts and

particularly attached to the later one, who was a wistful ghost of an english governess who had killed herself in the house.

One morning I went in to Constance Fletcher's bedroom to ask her how she was, she had not been very well the night before.

I went in and closed the door. Constance Fletcher very large and very white was lying in one of the vast renaissance beds with which the villa was furnished. Near the door was a very large renaissance cupboard. I had a delightful night, said Constance Fletcher, the gentle ghost visited me all night, indeed she has just left me. I imagine she is still in the cupboard, will you open it please. I did. Is she there, asked Constance Fletcher. I said I saw nothing. Ah yes, said Constance Fletcher.

We had a delightful time and Gertrude Stein at that time wrote The Portrait of Mabel Dodge. She also wrote the portrait of Constance Fletcher that was later printed in Geography and Plays. Many years later indeed after the war in London I met Siegfried Sassoon at a party given by Edith Sitwell for Gertrude Stein. He spoke of Gertrude Stein's portrait of Constance Fletcher which he had read in Geography and Plays and said that he had first become interested in Gertrude Stein's work because of this portrait. And he added, and did you know her and if you did can you tell me about her marvellous voice. I said, very much interested, then you did not know her. No, he said, I never saw her but she ruined my life. How, I asked excitedly. Because, he answered, she separated my father from my mother.

Constance Fletcher had written one very successful play which had had a long run in London called Green Stockings, but her real life had been in Italy. She was more italian than the italians. She admired her step-father and therefore was english but she was really dominated by the fine italian hand of Machiavelli. She could and did intrigue in the italian way better than even the italians and she was a disturbing influence for many years in Venice not only among the english but also among the italians.

André Gide turned up while we were at the Villa Curonia. It was rather a dull evening. It was then also that we first met Muriel Draper and Paul Draper. Gertrude Stein always liked Paul very much. She delighted in his american enthusiasm, and explanation of all things musical and human. He had had a great deal of adventure in the West and that was another bond between them. When Paul Draper left to return to London Mabel Dodge received a telegram saying, pearls missing suspect the second man. She came to Gertrude Stein in great agitation asking what she should do about it. Don't wake me, said Gertrude Stein, do nothing. And then sitting up, but that is a nice thing to say, suspect the second man, that is charming, but who and what is the second man. Mabel explained that the last time they had a robbery in the villa the police said that they could do nothing because nobody suspected any particular person and this time Paul to avoid that complication suspected the second man servant. While this explanation was being given another telegram came, pearls found. The second man had put the pearls in the collar box.

Haweis and his wife, later Mina Loy were also in Florence. Their home had been dismantled as they had had workmen in it but they put it all in order to give us a delightful lunch. Both Haweis and Mina were among the very earliest to be interested in the work of Gertrude Stein. Haweis had been fascinated with what he had read in manuscript of The Making of Americans. He did however plead for commas. Gertrude Stein said commas were unnecessary, the sense should be intrinsic and not have to be explained by commas and otherwise commas were only a sign that one should pause and take breath but one should know of oneself when one wanted to pause and take breath. However, as she liked Haweis very much and he had given her a delightful painting for a fan, she gave him two commas. It must however be added that on re-reading the manuscript she took the commas out.

Mina Loy equally interested was able to understand without the commas. She has always been able to understand.

Gertrude Stein having written The Portrait of Mabel Dodge, Mabel Dodge immediately wanted it printed. She had three hundred copies struck off and bound in Florentine paper. Constance Fletcher corrected the proofs and we were all awfully pleased. Mabel Dodge immediately conceived the idea that Gertrude Stein should be invited from one country house to another and do portraits and then end up doing portraits of american millionaires which would be a very exciting and lucrative career. Gertrude Stein laughed. A little later we went back to Paris.

It was during this winter that Gertrude Stein began to write plays. They began with the one entitled, It Happened a Play. This was written about a dinner party given by Harry and Bridget Gibb. She then wrote Ladies' Voices. Her interest in writing plays continues. She says a landscape is such a natural arrangement for a battle-field or a play that one must write plays.

Florence Bradley, a friend of Mabel Dodge, was spending a winter in Paris. She had had some stage experience and had been interested in planning a little theatre. She was vitally interested in putting these plays on the stage. Demuth was in Paris too at this time. He was then more interested in writing than in painting and particularly interested in these plays. He and Florence Bradley were always talking them over together.

Gertrude Stein has never seen Demuth since. When she first heard that he was painting she was much interested. They never wrote to each other but they often sent messages by mutual friends. Demuth always sent word that some day he would do a little picture that would thoroughly please him and then he would send it to her. And sure enough after all these years, two years ago some one left at the rue de Fleurus during our absence a little picture with a message that this was the picture that Demuth was ready to give to Gertrude Stein. It is a remarkable little landscape in which the roofs and windows are so subtle that they are as mysterious and as alive as the roofs and windows of Hawthorne or Henry James.

It was not long after this that Mabel Dodge went to America and it was the winter of the armoury show which was the first time the general public had a chance to see any of these pictures. It was there that Marcel Duchamp's Nude Descending the Staircase was shown.

It was about this time that Picabia and Gertrude Stein met. I remember going to dinner at the Picabias' and a pleasant dinner it was, Gabrielle Picabia full of life and gaiety, Picabia dark and lively, and Marcel Duchamp looking like a young norman crusader.

I was always perfectly able to understand the enthusiasm that Marcel Duchamp aroused in New York when he went there in the early years of the war. His brother had just died from the effect of his wounds, his other brother was still at the front and he himself was inapt for military service. He was very depressed and he went to America. Everybody loved him. So much so that it was a joke in Paris that when any american arrived in Paris the first thing he said was, and how is Marcel. Once Gertrude Stein went to see Braque, just after the war, and going into the studio in which there happened just then to be three young americans, she said to Braque, and how is Marcelle. The three young americans came up to her breathlessly and said, have you seen Marcel. She laughed, and having become accustomed to the inevitableness of the american belief that there was only one Marcel, she explained that Braque's wife was named Marcelle and it was Marcelle Braque about whom she was enquiring.

In those days Picabia and Gertrude Stein did not get to be very good friends. He annoyed her with his incessantness and what she called the vulgarity of his delayed adolescence. But oddly enough in this last year they have gotten to be very fond of each other. She is very much interested in his drawing and in his painting. It began with his show just a year ago. She is now convinced that although he has in a sense not a painter's gift he has an idea that has been and will be of immense value to all time. She calls him the Leonardo da Vinci of the movement. And it is true, he understands and invents everything.

As soon as the winter of the armoury show was over Mabel Dodge came back to Europe and she brought with her what Jacques-Emile Blanche called her collection des jeunes gens assortis, a mixed assortment of young men. In the lot were Carl Van Vechten, Robert Jones and John Reed. Carl Van Vechten did not come to the rue de Fleurus with her. He came later in the spring by himself. The other two came with her. I remember the evening they all came. Picasso was there too. He looked at John Reed critically and said, le genre de Braque mais beaucoup moins rigolo, Braque's kind but much less diverting. I remember also that Reed told me about his trip through Spain. He told me he had seen many strange sights there, that he had seen witches chased through the street of Salamanca. As I had been spending months in Spain and he only weeks I neither liked his stories nor believed them.

Robert Jones was very impressed by Gertrude Stein's looks. He said he would like to array her in cloth of gold and he wanted to design it then and there. It did not interest her.

Among the people that we had met at John Lane's in London was Gordon Caine and her husband. Gordon Caine had been a Wellesley girl who played the harp with which she always travelled, and who always re-arranged the furniture in the hotel room completely, even if she was only to stay one night. She was tall, rosy-haired and very good-looking. Her husband was a well known humorous english writer and one of John Lane's authors. They had entertained us very pleasantly in London and we asked them to dine with us their first night in Paris. I don't know quite what happened but Hélène cooked a very bad dinner. Only twice in all her long service did Hélène fail us. This time and when about two weeks later Carl Van Vechten turned up. That time too she did strange things, her dinner consisting of a series of hors d'œuvres. However that is later.

During dinner Mrs. Caine said that she had taken the liberty of asking her very dear friend and college mate Mrs. Van Vechten to come in after dinner because she was very anxious that she should meet Gertrude Stein as she was very depressed and unhappy and Gertrude Stein could undoubtedly have an influence for the good in her life. Gertrude Stein said that she had a vague association with the name of Van Vechten but could not remember what it was. She has a bad memory for names. Mrs. Van Vechten came. She too was a very tall woman, it would appear that a great many tall ones go to Wellesley, and she too was good-looking. Mrs. Van Vechten told the story of the tragedy of her married life but Gertrude Stein was not particularly interested.

It was about a week later that Florence Bradley asked us to go with her to see the second performance of the Sacre du Printemps. The russian ballet had just given the first performance of it and it had made a terrible uproar. All Paris was excited about it. Florence Bradley had gotten three tickets in a box, the box held four, and asked us to go with her. In the meantime there had been a letter from Mabel Dodge introducing Carl Van Vechten, a young New York journalist. Gertrude Stein invited him to dine the following Saturday evening.

We went early to the russian ballet, these were the early great days of the russian ballet with Nijinsky as the great dancer. And a great dancer he was. Dancing excites me tremendously and it is a thing I know a great deal about. I have seen three very great dancers. My geniuses seem to run in threes, but that is not my fault, it happens to be a fact. The three really great dancers I have seen are the Argentina, Isadora Duncan and Nijinsky. Like the three geniuses I have known they are each one of a different nationality.

Nijinsky did not dance in the Sacre du Printemps but he created the dance of those who did dance.

We arrived in the box and sat down in the three front chairs leaving one chair behind. Just in front of us in the seats below was Guillaume Apollinaire. He was dressed in evening clothes and he was industriously kissing various important looking ladies' hands. He was the first one of his crowd to come out into the great world wearing evening clothes and kissing hands. We were very amused and very pleased to see him do it. It was the first time we had seen him doing it. After the war they all did these things but he was the only one to commence before the war.

Just before the performance began the fourth chair in our box was occupied. We looked around and there was a tall well-built young man, he might have been a dutchman, a scandinavian or an american and he wore a soft evening shirt with the tiniest pleats all over the front of it. It was impressive, we had never even heard that they were wearing evening shirts like that. That evening when we got home Gertrude Stein did a portrait of the unknown called a Portrait of One.

The performance began. No sooner had it commenced when the excitement began. The scene now so well known with its brilliantly coloured background now not at all extraordinary, outraged the Paris audience. No sooner did the music begin and the dancing than they began to hiss. The defenders began to applaud. We could hear nothing, as a matter of fact I never did hear any of the music of the Sacre du Printemps because it was the only time I ever saw it and one literally could not, throughout the whole performance, hear the sound of music. The dancing was very fine and that we could see although our attention was constantly distracted by a man in the box next to us flourishing his cane, and finally in a violent altercation with an enthusiast in the box next to him, his cane came down and smashed the opera hat the other had just put on in defiance. It was all incredibly fierce.

The next Saturday evening Carl Van Vechten was to come to dinner. He came and he was the young man of the soft much-pleated evening shirt and it was the same shirt. Also of course he was the hero or villain of Mrs. Van Vechten's tragic tale.

As I said Hélène did for the second time in her life make an extraordinarily bad dinner. For some reason best known to herself she gave us course after course of hors d'œuvres finishing up with a sweet omelet. Gertrude Stein began to tease Carl Van Vechten by dropping a word here and there of intimate knowledge of his past life. He was naturally bewildered. It was a curious evening.

Gertrude Stein and he became dear friends.

He interested Allan and Louise Norton in her work and induced them to print in the little magazine they founded, The Rogue, the first thing of Gertrude Stein's ever printed in a little magazine, The Galérie Lafayette. In another number of this now rare little magazine, he printed a little essay on the work of Gertrude Stein. It was he who in one of his early books printed as a motto the device on Gertrude Stein's notepaper, a rose is a rose is a rose is a rose. Just recently she has had made for him by our local potter at the foot of the hill at Belley some plates in the yellow clay of the country and around the border is a rose is a rose is a rose is a rose and in the centre is to Carl.

In season and out he kept her name and her work before the public. When he was beginning to be well known and they asked him what he thought the most important book of the year he replied Three Lives by Gertrude Stein. His loyalty and his effort never weakened. He tried to make Knopf publish The Making of Americans and he almost succeeded but of course they weakened.

Speaking of the device of rose is a rose is a rose is a rose, it was I who found it in one of Gertrude Stein's manuscripts and insisted upon putting it as a device on the letter paper, on the table linen and anywhere that she would permit that I would put it. I am very pleased with myself for having done so.

Carl Van Vechten has had a delightful habit all these years of giving letters of introduction to people who he thought would amuse Gertrude Stein. This he has done with so much discrimination that she has liked them all.

The first and perhaps the one she has liked the best was Avery Hopwood. The friendship lasted until Avery's death a few years ago. When Avery came to Paris he always asked Gertrude Stein and myself to dine with him. This custom began in the early days of the acquaintance. Gertrude Stein is not a very enthusiastic diner-out but she never refused Avery. He always had the table charmingly decorated with flowers and the menu most carefully chosen. He sent us endless petits bleus, little telegrams, arranging this affair and we always had a good time. In these early days, holding his head a little on one side and with his tow-coloured hair, he looked like a lamb. Sometimes in the latter days as Gertrude Stein told him the lamb turned into a wolf. Gertrude Stein would I know at this moment say, dear Avery. They were very fond of each other. Not long before his death he came into the room one day and said I wish I could give you something else beside just dinner, he said, perhaps I could give you a picture. Gertrude Stein laughed, it is alright, she said to him, Avery, if you will always come here and take just tea. And then in the future beside the petit bleu in which he proposed our dining with him he would send another petit bleu saying that he would come one afternoon to take just tea. Once he came and brought with him Gertrude Atherton. He said so sweetly, I want the two Gertrudes whom I love so much to know each other. It was a perfectly delightful afternoon. Every one was pleased and charmed and as for me a californian, Gertrude Atherton had been my youthful idol and so I was very content.

The last time we saw Avery was on his last visit to Paris. He sent his usual message asking us to dinner and when he came to call for us he told Gertrude Stein that he had asked some of his friends to come because he was going to ask her to do something for him. You see, he said, you have never gone to Montmartre with me and I have a great fancy that you should to-night. I know it was your Montmartre long before it was mine but would you. She laughed and said, of course Avery.

We did after dinner go up to Montmartre with him. We went to a great many queer places and he was so proud and pleased. We were always going in a cab from one place to another and Avery Hopwood and Gertrude Stein went together and they had long talks and Avery must have had some premonition that it was the last time because he had never talked so openly and so intimately. Finally we left and he came out and put us into a cab and he told Gertrude Stein it had been one of the best evenings of his life. He left the next day for the south and we for the country. A little while after Gertrude Stein had a postal from him telling her how happy he had been to see her again and the same morning there was the news of his death in the Herald.

It was about nineteen twelve that Alvin Langdon Coburn turned up in Paris. He was a queer american who brought with him a queer english woman, his adopted mother. Alvin Langdon Coburn had just finished a series of photographs that he had done for Henry James. He had published a book of photographs of prominent men and he wished now to do a companion volume of prominent women. I imagine it was Roger Fry who had told him about Gertrude Stein. At any rate he was the first photographer to come and photograph her as a celebrity and she was nicely gratified. He did make some very good photographs of her and gave them to her and then he disappeared and though Gertrude Stein has often asked about him nobody seems ever to have heard of him since.

This brings us pretty well to the spring of nineteen fourteen. During this winter among the people who used to come to the house was the younger step-daughter of Bernard Berenson. She brought with her a young friend, Hope Mirlees and Hope said that when we went to England in the summer we must go down to Cambridge and stay with her people. We promised that we would.

During the winter Gertrude Stein's brother decided that he would go to Florence to live. They divided the pictures that they had bought together, between them. Gertrude Stein kept the Cézannes and the Picassos and her brother the Matisses and Renoirs, with the exception of the original Femme au Chapeau.

We planned that we would have a little passage-way made between the studio and the little house and as that entailed cutting a door and plastering we decided that we would paint the atelier and repaper the house and put in electricity. We proceeded to have all this done. It was the end of June before this was accomplished and the house had not yet been put in order when Gertrude Stein received a letter from John Lane saying he would be in Paris the following day and would come to see her.

We worked very hard, that is I did and the concierge and Hélène and the room was ready to receive him.

He brought with him the first copy of Blast by Wyndham Lewis and he gave it to Gertrude Stein and wanted to know what she thought of it and would she write for it. She said she did not know.

John Lane then asked her if she would come to London in July as he had almost made up his mind to republish the Three Lives and would she bring another manuscript with her. She said she would and she suggested a collection of all the portraits she had done up to that time. The Making of Americans was not considered because it was too long. And so that having been arranged John Lane left.

In those days Picasso having lived rather sadly in the rue Schœlcher was to move a little further out to Montrouge. It was not an unhappy time for him but after the Montmartre days one never heard his high whinnying spanish giggle. His friends, a great many of them, had followed him to Montparnasse but it was not the same. The intimacy with Braque was waning and of his old friends the only ones he saw frequently were Guillaume Apollinaire and Gertrude Stein. It was in that year that he began to use ripolin paints instead of the usual colours used by painters. Just the other day he was talking a long time about the ripolin paints. They are, said he gravely, la santé des couleurs, that is they are the basis of good health for paints. In those days he painted pictures and every-thing with ripolin paints as he still does, and as so many of his followers young and old do.

He was at this time too making constructions in paper, in tin and in all sorts of things, the sort of thing that made it possible for him afterwards to do the famous stage setting for Parade.

It was in these days that Mildred Aldrich was preparing to retire to the Hilltop on the Marne. She too was not unhappy but rather sad. She wanted us often in those spring evenings to take a cab and have what she called our last ride together. She more often than ever dropped her house key all the way down the centre of the stairway while she called good-night to us from the top story of the apartment house on the rue Boissonade.

We often went out to the country with her to see her house. Finally she moved in. We went out and spent the day with her. Mildred was not unhappy but she was very sad. My cur-tains are all up, my books in order, everything is clean and what shall I do now, said Mildred. I told her that when I was a little girl, my mother said that I always used to say, what shall I do now, which was only varied by now what shall I do. Mildred said that the worst of it was that we were going to London and that she would not see us all summer. We assured her that we would only stay away a month, in fact we had return tickets, and so we had to, and as soon as we got home we would go out to see her. Anyway she was happy that at last Gertrude Stein was going to have a publisher who would publish her books. But look out for John Lane, he is a fox, she said, as we kissed her and left.

Hélène was leaving 27 rue de Fleurus because, her husband having recently been promoted to be foreman in his work shop he insisted that she must not work out any longer but must stay at home.

In short in this spring and early summer of nineteen four-teen the old life was over.

6.

The War

AMERICANS living in Europe before the war never really believed that there was going to be war. Gertrude Stein always tells about the little janitor's boy who, playing in the court, would regularly every couple of years assure her that papa was going to the war. Once some cousins of hers were living in Paris, they had a country girl as a servant. It was the time of the russian-japanese war and they were all talking about the latest news. Terrified she dropped the platter and cried, and are the germans at the gates.

William Cook's father was an Iowan who at seventy years of age was making his first trip in Europe in the summer of nineteen fourteen. When the war was upon them he refused to believe it and explained that he could understand a family fighting among themselves, in short a civil war, but not a serious war with one's neighbours.

Gertrude Stein in 1913 and 1914 had been very interested reading the newspapers. She rarely read french newspapers, she never read anything in french, and she always read the Herald. That winter she added the Daily Mail. She liked to read about the suffragettes and she liked to read about Lord Roberts' campaign for compulsory military service in England. Lord Roberts had been a favourite hero of hers early in her life. His Forty-One Years In India was a book she often read and she had seen Lord Roberts when she and her brother, then taking a college vacation, had seen Edward the Seventh's coronation procession. She read the Daily Mail, although, as she said, she was not interested in Ireland.

We went to England July fifth and went according to programme to see John Lane at his house Sunday afternoon.

There were a number of people there and they were talking of many things but some of them were talking about war. One of them, some one told me he was an editorial writer on one of the big London dailies, was bemoaning the fact that he would not be able to eat figs in August in Provence as was his habit. Why not, asked some one. Because of the war, he answered. Some one else, Walpole or his brother I think it was, said that there was no hope of beating Germany as she had such an excellent system, all her railroad trucks were numbered in connection with locomotives and switches. But, said the eater of figs, that is all very well as long as the trucks remain in Germany on their own lines and switches, but in an aggressive war they will leave the frontiers of Germany and then, well I promise you then there will be a great deal of numbered confusion.

This is all I remember definitely of that Sunday afternoon in July.

As we were leaving, John Lane said to Gertrude Stein that he was going out of town for a week and he made a rendez-vous with her in his office for the end of July, to sign the contract for Three Lives. I think, he said, in the present state of affairs I would rather begin with that than with something more entirely new. I have confidence in that book. Mrs. Lane is very enthusiastic and so are the readers.

Having now ten days on our hands we decided to accept the invitation of Mrs. Mirlees, Hope's mother, and spend a few days in Cambridge. We went there and thoroughly enjoyed ourselves.

It was a most comfortable house to visit. Gertrude Stein liked it, she could stay in her room or in the garden as much as she liked without hearing too much conversation. The food was excellent, scotch food, delicious and fresh, and it was very amusing meeting all the University of Cambridge dignitaries. We were taken into all the gardens and invited into many of the homes. It was lovely weather, quantities of roses, morris-dancing by all the students and girls and generally delightful. We were invited to lunch at Newnham, Miss Jane Harrison, who had been Hope Mirlees' pet enthusiasm, was much interested in meeting Gertrude Stein. We sat up on the dais with the faculty and it was very awe inspiring. The conversation was not however particularly amusing. Miss Harrison and Gertrude Stein did not particularly interest each other.

We had been hearing a good deal about Doctor and Mrs. Whitehead. They no longer lived in Cambridge. The year before Doctor Whitehead had left Cambridge to go to London University. They were to be in Cambridge shortly and they were to dine at the Mirlees'. They did and I met my third genius.

It was a pleasant dinner. I sat next to Housman, the Cambridge poet, and we talked about fishes and David Starr Jordan but all the time I was more interested in watching Doctor Whitehead. Later we went into the garden and he came and sat next to me and we talked about the sky in Cambridge.

Gertrude Stein and Doctor Whitehead and Mrs. Whitehead all became interested in each other. Mrs. Whitehead asked us to dine at her house in London and then to spend a week end, the last week end in July with them in their country home in Lockridge, near Salisbury Plain. We accepted with pleasure.

We went back to London and had a lovely time. We were ordering some comfortable chairs and a comfortable couch covered with chintz to replace some of the italian furniture that Gertrude Stein's brother had taken with him. This took a great deal of time. We had to measure ourselves into the chairs and into the couch and to choose chintz that would go with the pictures, all of which we successfully achieved. These chairs and this couch, and they are comfortable, in spite of war came to the door one day in January, nineteen fifteen at the rue de Fleurus and were greeted by us with the greatest delight. One needed such comforting and such comfort in those days. We dined with the Whiteheads and liked them more than ever and they liked us more than ever and were kind enough to say so.

Gertrude Stein kept her appointment with John Lane at the Bodley Head. They had a very long conversation, this time so long that I quite exhausted all the shop windows of that region for quite a distance, but finally Gertrude Stein came out with a contract. It was a gratifying climax.

Then we took the train to Lockridge to spend the week end with the Whiteheads. We had a week-end trunk, we were very proud of our week-end trunk, we had used it on our first visit and now we were actively using it again. As one of my friends said to me later, they asked you to spend the week end and you stayed six weeks. We did.

There was quite a house party when we arrived, some Cambridge people, some young men, the younger son of the

Whiteheads, Eric, then fifteen years old but very tall and flower-like, and the daughter Jessie just back from Newnham. There could not have been much serious thought of war because they were all talking of Jessie Whitehead's coming trip to Finland. Jessie always made friends with foreigners from strange places, she had a passion for geography and a passion for the glory of the British Empire. She had a friend, a finn, who had asked her to spend the summer with her people in Finland and had promised Jessie a possible uprising against Russia. Mrs. Whitehead was hesitating but had practically consented. There was an older son North who was away at the time.

Then suddenly, as I remember, there were the conferences to prevent the war, Lord Grey and the russian minister of foreign affairs. And then before anything further could happen the ultimatum to France. Gertrude Stein and I were completely miserable as was Evelyn Whitehead, who had french blood and who had been raised in France and had strong french sympathies. Then came the days of the invasion of Belgium and I can still hear Doctor Whitehead's gentle voice reading the papers out loud and then all of them talking about the destruction of Louvain and how they must help the brave little belgians. Gertrude Stein desperately unhappy said to me, where is Louvain. Don't you know, I said. No, she said, nor do I care, but where is it.

Our week end was over and we told Mrs. Whitehead that we must leave. But you cannot get back to Paris now, she said. No, we answered, but we can stay in London. Oh no, she said, you must stay with us until you can get back to Paris. She was very sweet and we were very unhappy and we liked them and they liked us and we agreed to stay. And then to our infinite relief England came into the war.

We had to go to London to get our trunks, to cable to people in America and to draw money, and Mrs. Whitehead wished to go in to see if she and her daughter could do anything to help the belgians. I remember that trip so well. There seemed so many people about everywhere, although the train was not overcrowded, but all the stations even little country ones, were filled with people, not people at all troubled but just a great many people. At the junction where we were to change trains we met Lady Astley, a friend of Myra Edgerly's whom we had met in Paris. Oh how do you do, she said in a cheerful loud voice, I am going to London to say goodbye to my son. Is he going away, we said politely. Oh yes, she said, he is in the guards you know, and is leaving to-night for France.

In London everything was difficult. Gertrude Stein's letter of credit was on a french bank but mine luckily small was on a California one. I say luckily small because the banks would not give large sums but my letter of credit was so small and so almost used up that they without hesitation gave me all that there was left of it.

Gertrude Stein cabled to her cousin in Baltimore to send her money, we gathered in our trunks, we met Evelyn Whitehead at the train and we went back with her to Lockridge. It was a relief to get back. We appreciated her kindness because to have been at a hotel in London at that moment would have been too dreadful.

Then one day followed another and it is hard to remember just what happened. North Whitehead was away and Mrs. Whitehead was terribly worried lest he should rashly enlist. She must see him. So they telegraphed to him to come at once. He came. She had been quite right. He had immediately gone to the nearest recruiting station to enlist and luckily there had been so many in front of him that the office closed before he was admitted. She immediately went to London to see Kitchener. Doctor Whitehead's brother was a bishop in India and he had in his younger days known Kitchener very intimately. Mrs. Whitehead had this introduction and North was given a commission. She came home much relieved. North was to join in three days but in the meantime he must learn to drive a motor car. The three days passed very quickly and North was gone. He left immediately for France and without much equipment. And then came the time of waiting.

Evelyn Whitehead was very busy planning war work and helping every one and I as far as possible helped her. Gertrude Stein and Doctor Whitehead walked endlessly around the country. They talked of philosophy and history, it was during these days that Gertrude Stein realised how completely it was Doctor Whitehead and not Russell who had had the ideas for their great book. Doctor Whitehead, the gentlest and most simply generous of human beings never claimed anything for himself and enormously admired anyone who was brilliant, and Russell undoubtedly was brilliant.

Gertrude Stein used to come back and tell me about these walks and the country still the same as in the days of Chaucer, with the green paths of the early britons that could still be seen in long stretches, and the triple rainbows of that strange summer. They used, Doctor Whitehead and Gertrude Stein, to have long conversations with game-keepers and mole-catchers. The mole-catcher had said, but sir, England has never been in a war but that she has been victorious. Doctor Whitehead turned to Gertrude Stein with a gentle smile. I think we may say so, he said. The game-keeper, when Doctor Whitehead seemed discouraged said to him, but Doctor Whitehead, England is the predominant nation, is she not. I hope she is, yes I hope she is, replied Doctor Whitehead gently.

The germans were getting nearer and nearer Paris. One day Doctor Whitehead said to Gertrude Stein, they were just going through a rough little wood and he was helping her, have you any copies of your writings or are they all in Paris. They are all in Paris, she said. I did not like to ask, said Doctor Whitehead, but I have been worrying.

The germans were getting nearer and nearer Paris and the last day Gertrude Stein could not leave her room, she sat and mourned. She loved Paris, she thought neither of manuscripts nor of pictures, she thought only of Paris and she was desolate. I came up to her room, I called out, it is alright Paris is saved, the germans are in retreat. She turned away and said, don't tell me these things. But it's true, I said, it is true. And then we wept together.

The first description that any one we knew received in England of the battle of the Marne came in a letter to Gertrude Stein from Mildred Aldrich. It was practically the first letter of her book the Hilltop on the Marne. We were delighted to receive it, to know that Mildred was safe, and to know all about it. It was passed around and everybody in the neighbourhood read it.

Later when we returned to Paris we had two other descrip-

tions of the battle of the Marne. I had an old school friend
from California, Nellie Jacot who lived in Boulogne-sur-Seine
and I was very worried about her. I telegraphed to her and
she telegraphed back characteristically, Nullement en danger
ne t'inquiète pas, there is no danger don't worry. It was Nellie
who used to call Picasso in the early days a good-looking
bootblack and used to say of Fernande, she is alright but I
don't see why you bother about her. It was also Nellie who
made Matisse blush by cross-questioning him about the different ways he saw Madame Matisse, how she looked to him
as a wife and how she looked to him as a picture, and how
he could change from one to the other. It was also Nellie who
told the story which Gertrude Stein loved to quote, of a
young man who once said to her, I love you Nellie, Nellie is
your name, isn't it. It was also Nellie who when we came back
from England and we said that everybody had been so kind,
said, oh yes, I know that kind.

Nellie described the battle of the Marne to us. You know,
she said, I always come to town once a week to shop and I
always bring my maid. We come in in the street car because
it is difficult to get a taxi in Boulogne and we go back in a
taxi. Well we came in as usual and didn't notice anything and
when we had finished our shopping and had had our tea we
stood on a corner to get a taxi. We stopped several and when
they heard where we wanted to go they drove on. I know that
sometimes taxi drivers don't like to go out to Boulogne so I
said to Marie tell them we will give them a big tip if they will
go. So she stopped another taxi with an old driver and I said
to him, I will give you a very big tip to take us out to Boulogne. Ah, said he laying his finger on his nose, to my great
regret madame it is impossible, no taxi can leave the city limits
to-day. Why, I asked. He winked in answer and drove off. We
had to go back to Boulogne in a street car. Of course we
understood later, when we heard about Gallieni and the taxis,
said Nellie and added, and that was the battle of the Marne.

Another description of the battle of the Marne when we
first came back to Paris was from Alfy Maurer. I was sitting,
said Alfy at a café and Paris was pale, if you know what I mean,
said Alfy, it was like a pale absinthe. Well I was sitting there
and then I noticed lots of horses pulling lots of big trucks

going slowly by and there were some soldiers with them and on the boxes was written Banque de France. That was the gold going away just like that, said Alfy, before the battle of the Marne.

In those dark days of waiting in England of course a great many things happened. There were a great many people coming and going in the Whiteheads' home and there was of course plenty of discussion. First there was Lytton Strachey. He lived in a little house not far from Lockridge.

He came one evening to see Mrs. Whitehead. He was a thin sallow man with a silky beard and a faint high voice. We had met him the year before when we had been invited to meet George Moore at the house of Miss Ethel Sands. Gertrude Stein and George Moore, who looked very like a prosperous Mellins Food baby, had not been interested in each other. Lytton Strachey and I talked together about Picasso and the russian ballet.

He came in this evening and he and Mrs. Whitehead discussed the possibility of rescuing Lytton Strachey's sister who was lost in Germany. She suggested that he apply to a certain person who could help him. But, said Lytton Strachey faintly, I have never met him. Yes, said Mrs. Whitehead, but you might write to him and ask to see him. Not, replied Lytton Strachey faintly, if I have never met him.

Another person who turned up during that week was Bertrand Russell. He came to Lockridge the day North Whitehead left for the front. He was a pacifist and argumentative and although they were very old friends Doctor and Mrs. Whitehead did not think they could bear hearing his views just then. He came and Gertrude Stein, to divert everybody's mind from the burning question of war or peace, introduced the subject of education. This caught Russell and he explained all the weaknesses of the american system of education, particularly their neglect of the study of greek. Gertrude Stein replied that of course England which was an island needed Greece which was or might have been an island. At any rate greek was essentially an island culture, while America needed essentially the culture of a continent which was of necessity latin. This argument fussed Mr. Russell, he became very eloquent. Gertrude Stein then became very earnest and gave a long discourse on the value of greek to the english, aside from its being an island, and the lack of value of greek culture for the americans based upon the psychology of americans as different from the psychology of the english. She grew very eloquent on the disembodied abstract quality of the american character and cited examples, mingling automobiles with Emerson, and all proving that they did not need greek, in a way that fussed Russell more and more and kept everybody occupied until everybody went to bed.

There were many discussions in those days. The bishop, the brother of Doctor Whitehead and his family came to lunch. They all talked constantly about how England had come into the war to save Belgium. At last my nerves could bear it no longer and I blurted out, why do you say that, why do you not say that you are fighting for England, I do not consider it a disgrace to fight for one's country.

Mrs. Bishop, the bishop's wife was very funny on this occasion. She said solemnly to Gertrude Stein, Miss Stein you are I understand an important person in Paris. I think it would come very well from a neutral like yourself to suggest to the french government that they give us Pondichéry. It would be very useful to us. Gertrude Stein replied politely that to her great regret her importance such as it was was among painters and writers and not with politicians. But that, said Mrs. Bishop, would make no difference. You should I think suggest to the french government that they give us Pondichéry. After lunch Gertrude Stein said to me under her breath, where the hell is Pondichéry.

Gertrude Stein used to get furious when the english all talked about german organisation. She used to insist that the germans had no organisation, they had method but no organisation. Don't you understand the difference, she used to say angrily, any two americans, any twenty americans, any millions of americans can organise themselves to do something but germans cannot organise themselves to do anything, they can formulate a method and this method can be put upon them but that isn't organisation. The germans, she used to insist, are not modern, they are a backward people who have made a method of what we conceive as organisation, can't you see. They cannot therefore possibly win this war because they are not modern.

Then another thing that used to annoy us dreadfully was the english statement that the germans in America would turn America against the allies. Don't be silly, Gertrude Stein used to say to any and all of them, if you do not realise that the fundamental sympathy in America is with France and England and could never be with a mediaeval country like Germany, you cannot understand America. We are republican, she used to say with energy, profoundly intensely and completely a republic and a republic can have everything in common with France and a great deal in common with England but whatever its form of government nothing in common with Germany. How often I have heard her then and since explain that americans are republicans living in a republic which is so much a republic that it could never be anything else.

The long summer wore on. It was beautiful weather and beautiful country, and Doctor Whitehead and Gertrude Stein never ceased wandering around in it and talking about all things.

From time to time we went to London. We went regularly to Cook's office to know when we might go back to Paris and they always answered not yet. Gertrude Stein went to see John Lane. He was terribly upset. He was passionately patriotic. He said of course he was doing nothing at present but publishing war-books but soon very soon things would be different or perhaps the war would be over.

Gertrude Stein's cousin and my father sent us money by the United States cruiser Tennessee. We went to get it. We were each one put on the scale and our heights measured and then they gave the money to us. How, said we to one another, can a cousin who has not seen you in ten years and a father who has not seen me for six years possibly know our heights and our weights. It had always been a puzzle. Four years ago Gertrude Stein's cousin came to Paris and the first thing she said to him was, Julian how did you know my weight and height when you sent me money by the Tennessee. Did I know it, he said. Well, she said, at any rate they had written it down that you did. I cannot remember of course, he said, but if any one were to ask me now I would naturally send to Washington for a copy of your passport and I probably did that then. And so was the mystery solved.

We also had to go to the american embassy to get temporary passports to go back to Paris. We had no papers, nobody had any papers in those days. Gertrude Stein as a matter of fact had what they called in Paris a papier de matriculation which stated that she was an american and a french resident.

The embassy was very full of not very american looking citizens waiting their turn. Finally we were ushered in to a very tired looking young american. Gertrude Stein remarked upon the number of not very american looking citizens that were waiting. The young american sighed. They are easier, he said, because they have papers, it is only the native born american who has no papers. Well what do you do about them, asked Gertrude Stein. We guess, he said, and we hope we guess right. And now, said he, will you take the oath. Oh dear, he said, I have said it so often I have forgotten it.

By the fifteenth of October Cook's said we could go back to Paris. Mrs. Whitehead was to go with us. North, her son, had left without an overcoat, and she had secured one and she was afraid he would not get it until much later if she sent it the ordinary way. She arranged to go to Paris and deliver it to him herself or find some one who would take it to him directly. She had papers from the war office and Kitchener and we started.

I remember the leaving London very little, I cannot even remember whether it was day-light or not but it must have been because when we were on the channel boat it was daylight. The boat was crowded. There were quantities of belgian soldiers and officers escaped from Antwerp, all with tired eyes. It was our first experience of the tired but watchful eyes of soldiers. We finally were able to arrange a seat for Mrs. Whitehead who had been ill and soon we were in France. Mrs. Whitehead's papers were so overpowering that there were no delays and soon we were in the train and about ten o'clock at night we were in Paris. We took a taxi and drove through Paris, beautiful and unviolated, to the rue de Fleurus. We were once more at home.

Everybody who had seemed so far away came to see us. Alfy

Maurer described being on the Marne at his favourite village, he always fished the Marne, and the mobilisation locomotive coming and the germans were coming and he was so frightened and he tried to get a conveyance and finally after terrific efforts he succeeded and got back to Paris. As he left Gertrude Stein went with him to the door and came back smiling. Mrs. Whitehead said with some constraint, Gertrude you have always spoken so warmly of Alfy Maurer but how can you like a man who shows himself not only selfish but a coward and at a time like this. He thought only of saving himself and he after all was a neutral. Gertrude Stein burst out laughing. You foolish woman, she said, didn't you understand, of course Alfy had his girl with him and he was scared to death lest she should fall into the hands of the germans.

There were not many people in Paris just then and we liked it and we wandered around Paris and it was so nice to be there, wonderfully nice. Soon Mrs. Whitehead found means of sending her son's coat to him and went back to England and we settled down for the winter.

Gertrude Stein sent copies of her manuscripts to friends in New York to keep for her. We hoped that all danger was over but still it seemed better to do so and there were Zeppelins to come. London had been completely darkened at night before we left. Paris continued to have its usual street lights until January.

How it all happened I do not at all remember but it was through Carl Van Vechten and had something to do with the Nortons, but at any rate there was a letter from Donald Evans proposing to publish three manuscripts to make a small book and would Gertrude Stein suggest a title for them. Of these three manuscripts two had been written during our first trip into Spain and Food, Rooms etcetera, immediately on our return. They were the beginning, as Gertrude Stein would say, of mixing the outside with the inside. Hitherto she had been concerned with seriousness and the inside of things, in these studies she began to describe the inside as seen from the outside. She was awfully pleased at the idea of these three things being published, and immediately consented, and suggested the title of Tender Buttons. Donald Evans called his firm the Claire Marie and he sent over a contract just like any other contract. We took it for granted that there was a Claire Marie but there evidently was not. There were printed of this edition I forget whether it was seven hundred and fifty or a thousand copies but at any rate it was a very charming little book and Gertrude Stein was enormously pleased, and it, as every one knows, had an enormous influence on all young writers and started off columnists in the newspapers of the whole country on their long campaign of ridicule. I must say that when the columnists are really funny, and they quite often are, Gertrude Stein chuckles and reads them aloud to me.

In the meantime the dreary winter of fourteen and fifteen went on. One night, I imagine it must have been about the end of January, I had as was and is my habit gone to bed very early, and Gertrude Stein was down in the studio working, as was her habit. Suddenly I heard her call me gently. What is it, I said. Oh nothing, said she, but perhaps if you don't mind putting on something warm and coming downstairs I think perhaps it would be better. What is it, I said, a revolution. The concierges and the wives of the concierges were all always talking about a revolution. The french are so accustomed to revolutions, they have had so many, that when anything happens they immediately think and say, revolution. Indeed Gertrude Stein once said rather impatiently to some french soldiers when they said something about a revolution, you are silly, you have had one perfectly good revolution and several not quite so good ones; for an intelligent people it seems to me foolish to be always thinking of repeating yourselves. They looked very sheepish and said, bien sûr mademoiselle, in other words, sure you're right.

Well I too said when she woke me, is it a revolution and are there soldiers. No, she said, not exactly. Well what is it, said I impatiently. I don't quite know, she answered, but there has been an alarm. Anyway you had better come. I started to turn on the light. No, she said, you had better not. Give me your hand and I will get you down and you can go to sleep down stairs on the couch. I came. It was very dark. I sat down on the couch and then I said, I'm sure I don't know what is the matter with me but my knees are knocking together. Gertrude Stein burst out laughing, wait a minute, I will get you a blanket, she said. No don't leave me, I said. She managed to find something to cover me and then there was a loud boom, then several more. It was a soft noise and then there was the sound of horns blowing in the streets and then we knew it was all over. We lighted the lights and went to bed.

I must say I would not have believed it was true that knees knocked together as described in poetry and prose if it had not happened to me.

The next time there was a Zeppelin alarm and it was not very long after this first one, Picasso and Eve were dining with us. By this time we knew that the two-story building of the atelier was no more protection than the roof of the little pavillon under which we slept and the concierge had suggested that we should go into her room where at least we would have six stories over us. Eve was not very well these days and fearful so we all went into the concierge's room. Even Jeanne Poule the Breton servant who had succeeded Hélène, came too. Jeanne soon was bored with this precaution and so in spite of all remonstrance, she went back to her kitchen, lit her light, in spite of the regulations, and proceeded to wash the dishes. We soon too got bored with the concierge's loge and went back to the atelier. We put a candle under the table so that it would not make much light, Eve and I tried to sleep and Picasso and Gertrude Stein talked until two in the morning when the all's clear sounded and they went home.

Picasso and Eve were living these days on the rue Schœlcher in a rather sumptuous studio apartment that looked over the cemetery. It was not very gay. The only excitement were the letters from Guillaume Apollinaire who was falling off of horses in the endeavour to become an artilleryman. The only other intimates at that time were a russian whom they called G. Apostrophe and his sister the baronne. They bought all the Rousseaus that were in Rousseau's atelier when he died. They had an apartment in the boulevard Raspail above Victor Hugo's tree and they were not unamusing. Picasso learnt the russian alphabet from them and began putting it into some of his pictures.

It was not a very cheerful winter. People came in and out, new ones and old ones. Ellen La Motte turned up, she was very heroic but gun shy. She wanted to go to Servia and Emily Chadbourne wanted to go with her but they did not go.

Gertrude Stein wrote a little novelette about this event.

Ellen La Motte collected a set of souvenirs of the war for her cousin Dupont de Nemours. The stories of how she got them were diverting. Everybody brought you souvenirs in those days, steel arrows that pierced horses' heads, pieces of shell, ink-wells made out of pieces of shell, helmets, some one even offered us a piece of a Zeppelin or an aeroplane, I forget which, but we declined. It was a strange winter and nothing and everything happened. If I remember rightly it was at this time that some one, I imagine it was Apollinaire on leave, gave a concert and a reading of Blaise Cendrars' poems. It was then that I first heard mentioned and first heard the music of Erik Satie. I remember this took place in some one's atelier and the place was crowded. It was in these days too that the friendship between Gertrude Stein and Juan Gris began. He was living in the rue Ravignan in the studio where Salmon had been shut up when he ate my yellow fantaisie.

We used to go there quite often. Juan was having a hard time, no one was buying pictures and the french artists were not in want because they were at the front and their wives or their mistresses if they had been together a certain number of years were receiving an allowance. There was one bad case, Herbin, a nice little man but so tiny that the army dismissed him. He said ruefully the pack he had to carry weighed as much as he did and it was no use, he could not manage it. He was returned home inapt for service and he came near starving. I don't know who told us about him, he was one of the early simple earnest cubists. Luckily Gertrude Stein succeeded in interesting Roger Fry. Roger Fry took him and his painting over to England where he made and I imagine still has a considerable reputation.

Juan Gris' case was more difficult. Juan was in those days a tormented and not particularly sympathetic character. He was very melancholy and effusive and as always clear sighted and intellectual. He was at that time painting almost entirely in black and white and his pictures were very sombre. Kahnweiler who had befriended him was an exile in Switzerland, Juan's sister in Spain was able to help him only a little. His situation was desperate.

It was just at this time that the picture dealer who afterwards, as the expert in the Kahnweiler sale said he was going to kill cubism, undertook to save cubism and he made contracts with all the cubists who were still free to paint. Among them was Juan Gris and for the moment he was saved.

As soon as we were back in Paris we went to see Mildred Aldrich. She was within the military area so we imagined we would have to have a special permit to go and see her. We went to the police station of our quarter and asked them what we should do. He said what papers have you. We have american passports, french matriculation papers, said Gertrude Stein taking out a pocket full. He looked at them all and said and what is this, of another yellow paper. That, said Gertrude Stein, is a receipt from my bank for the money I have just deposited. I think, said he solemnly, I would take that along too. I think, he added, with all those you will not have any trouble.

We did not as a matter of fact have to show any one any papers. We stayed with Mildred several days.

She was much the most cheerful person we knew that winter. She had been through the battle of the Marne, she had had the Uhlans in the woods below her, she had watched the battle going on below her and she had become part of the country-side. We teased her and told her she was beginning to look like a french peasant and she did, in a funny kind of way, born and bred new englander that she was. It was always astonishing that the inside of her little french peasant house with french furniture, french paint and a french servant and even a french poodle, looked completely american. We saw her several times that winter.

At last the spring came and we were ready to go away for a bit. Our friend William Cook after nursing a while in the american hospital for french wounded had gone again to Palma de Mallorca. Cook who had always earned his living by painting was finding it difficult to get on and he had retired to Palma where in those days when the spanish exchange was very low one lived extremely well for a few francs a day.

We decided we would go to Palma too and forget the war a little. We had only the temporary passports that had been given to us in London so we went to the embassy to get permanent ones with which we might go to Spain. We were first interviewed by a kindly old gentleman most evidently not in the diplomatic service. Impossible, he said, why, said he, look at me, I have lived in Paris for forty years and come of a long line of americans and I have no passport. No, he said, you can have a passport to go to America or you can stay in France without a passport. Gertrude Stein insisted upon seeing one of the secretaries of the embassy. We saw a flushed reddish-headed one. He told us exactly the same thing. Gertrude Stein listened quietly. She then said, but so and so who is exactly in my position, a native born american, has lived the same length of time in Europe, is a writer and has no intention of returning to America at present, has just received a regular passport from your department. I think, said the young man still more flushed, there must be some error. It is very simple, replied Gertrude Stein, to verify it by looking the matter up in your records. He disappeared and presently came back and said, yes you are quite correct but you see it was a very special case. There can be, said Gertrude Stein severely, no privilege extended to one american citizen which is not to be, given similar circumstances, accorded to any other american citizen. He once more disappeared and came back and said, yes yes now may I go through the preliminaries. He then explained that they had orders to give out as few passports as possible but if any one really wanted one why of course it was quite alright. We got ours in record time.

And we went to Palma thinking to spend only a few weeks but we stayed the winter. First we went to Barcelona. It was extraordinary to see so many men on the streets. I did not imagine there could be so many men left in the world. One's eyes had become so habituated to menless streets, the few men one saw being in uniform and therefore not being men but soldiers, that to see quantities of men walking up and down the Ramblas was bewildering. We sat in the hotel window and looked. I went to bed early and got up early and Gertrude Stein went to bed late and got up late and so in a way we overlapped but there was not a moment when there were not quantities of men going up and down the Ramblas.

We arrived in Palma once again and Cook met us and arranged everything for us. William Cook could always be depended upon. In those days he was poor but later when he had inherited money and was well to do and Mildred Aldrich had fallen upon very bad days and Gertrude Stein was not able to help any more, William Cook gave her a blank cheque and said, use that as much as you need for Mildred, you know my mother loved to read her books.

William Cook often disappeared and one knew nothing of him and then when for one reason or another you needed him there he was. He went into the american army later and at that time Gertrude Stein and myself were doing war work for the American Fund for French Wounded and I had often to wake her up very early. She and Cook used to write the most lugubrious letters to each other about the unpleasantness of sunrises met suddenly. Sunrises were, they contended, alright when approached slowly from the night before, but when faced abruptly from the same morning they were awful. It was William Cook too who later on taught Gertrude Stein how to drive a car by teaching her on one of the old battle of the Marne taxis. Cook being hard up had become a taxi driver in Paris, that was in sixteen and Gertrude Stein was to drive a car for the American Fund for French Wounded. So on dark nights they went out beyond the fortifications and the two of them sitting solemnly on the driving seat of one of those old two-cylinder before-the-war Renault taxis, William Cook taught Gertrude Stein how to drive. It was William Cook who inspired the only movie Gertrude Stein ever wrote in english, I have just published it in Operas and Plays in the Plain Edition. The only other one she ever wrote, also in Operas and Plays, many years later and in french, was inspired by her white poodle dog called Basket.

But to come back to Palma de Mallorca. We had been there two summers before and had liked it and we liked it again. A great many americans seem to like it now but in those days Cook and ourselves were the only americans to inhabit the island. There were a few english, about three families there. There was a descendant of one of Nelson's captains, a Mrs. Penfold, a sharp-tongued elderly lady and her husband. It was she who said to young Mark Gilbert, an english boy of sixteen with pacifist tendencies who had at tea at her house refused cake, Mark you are either old enough to fight for your country or young enough to eat cake. Mark ate cake.

There were several french families there, the french consul, Monsieur Marchand with a charming italian wife whom we soon came to know very well. It was he who was very much amused at a story we had to tell him of Morocco. He had been attached to the french residence at Tangiers at the moment the french induced Moulai Hafid the then sultan of Morocco to abdicate. We had been in Tangiers at that time for ten days, it was during that first trip to Spain when so much happened that was important to Gertrude Stein.

We had taken on a guide Mohammed and Mohammed had taken a fancy to us. He became a pleasant companion rather than a guide and we used to take long walks together and he used to take us to see his cousins' wonderfully clean arab middle class homes and drink tea. We enjoyed it all. He also told us all about politics. He had been educated in Moulai Hafid's palace and he knew everything that was happening. He told us just how much money Moulai Hafid would take to abdicate and just when he would be ready to do it. We liked these stories as we liked all Mohammed's stories always ending up with, and when you come back there will be street cars and then we won't have to walk and that will be nice. Later in Spain we read in the papers that it had all happened exactly as Mohammed had said it would and we paid no further attention. Once in talking of our only visit to Morocco we told Monsieur Marchand this story. He said, yes that is diplomacy, probably the only people in the world who were not arabs who knew what the french government wanted so desperately to know were you two and you knew it quite by accident and to you it was of no importance.

Life in Palma was pleasant and so instead of travelling any more that summer we decided to settle down in Palma. We sent for our french servant Jeanne Poule and with the aid of the postman we found a little house on the calle de Dos de Mayo in Terreno, just outside of Palma, and we settled down. We were very content. Instead of spending only the summer we stayed until the following spring.

We had been for some time members of Mudie's Library in London and wherever we went Mudie's Library books came to us. It was at this time that Gertrude Stein read aloud to me all of Queen Victoria's letters and she herself became interested in missionary autobiographies and diaries. There were a great many in Mudie's Library and she read them all.

It was during this stay at Palma de Mallorca that most of the plays afterwards published in Geography and Plays were written. She always says that a certain kind of landscape induces plays and the country around Terreno certainly did.

We had a dog, a mallorcan hound, the hounds slightly crazy, who dance in the moonlight, striped, not all one colour as the spanish hound of the continent. We called this dog Polybe because we were pleased with the articles in the Figaro signed Polybe. Polybe was, as Monsieur Marchand said, like an arab, bon accueil à tout le monde et fidèle à personne. He had an incurable passion for eating filth and nothing would stop him. We muzzled him to see if that would cure him, but this so outraged the russian servant of the english consul that we had to give it up. Then he took to annoying sheep. We even took to quarrelling with Cook about Polybe. Cook had a fox terrier called Marie-Rose and we were convinced that Marie-Rose led Polybe into mischief and then virtuously withdrew and let him take the blame. Cook was convinced that we did not know how to bring up Polybe. Polybe had one nice trait. He would sit in a chair and gently smell large bunches of tube-roses with which I always filled a vase in the centre of the room on the floor. He never tried to eat them, he just gently smelled them. When we left we left Polybe behind us in the care of one of the guardians of the old fortress of Belver. When we saw him a week after he did not know us or his name. Polybe comes into many of the plays Gertrude Stein wrote at that time.

The feelings of the island at that time were very mixed as to the war. The thing that impressed them the most was the amount of money it cost. They could discuss by the hour, how much it cost a year, a month, a week, a day, an hour and even a minute. We used to hear them of a summer evening, five million pesetas, a million pesetas, two million pesetas, good-night, good-night, and know they were busy with their endless calculations of the cost of the war. As most of the men even those of the better middle classes read, wrote and ciphered with difficulty and the women not at all, it can be imagined how fascinating and endless a subject the cost of the war was.

One of our neighbours had a german governess and whenever there was a german victory she hung out a german flag. We responded as well as we could, but alas just then there were not many allied victories. The lower classes were strong for the allies. The waiter at the hotel was always looking forward to Spain's entry into the war on the side of the allies. He was certain that the spanish army would be of great aid as it could march longer on less food than any army in the world. The maid at the hotel took great interest in my knitting for the soldiers. She said, of course madame knits very slowly, all ladies do. But, said I hopefully, if I knit for years may I not come to knit quickly, not as quickly as you but quickly. No, said she firmly, ladies knit slowly. As a matter of fact I did come to knit very quickly and could even read and knit quickly at the same time.

We led a pleasant life, we walked a great deal and ate extremely well, and were well amused by our breton servant.

She was patriotic and always wore the tricolour ribbon around her hat. She once came home very excited. She had just been seeing another french servant and she said, imagine, Marie has just had news that her brother was drowned and has had a civilian funeral. How did that happen, I asked also much excited. Why, said Jeanne, he had not yet been called to the army. It was a great honour to have a brother have a civilian funeral during the war. At any rate it was rare. Jeanne was content with spanish newspapers, she had no trouble reading them, as she said, all the important words were in french.

Jeanne told endless stories of french village life and Gertrude Stein could listen a long time and then all of a sudden she could not listen any more.

Life in Mallorca was pleasant until the attack on Verdun began. Then we all began to be very miserable. We tried to console each other but it was difficult. One of the frenchmen, an engraver who had palsy and in spite of the palsy tried every few months to get the french consul to accept him for the army, used to say we must not worry if Verdun is taken, it is not an entry into France, it is only a moral victory for the germans. But we were all desperately unhappy. I had been so confident and now I had an awful feeling that the war had gotten out of my hands.

In the port of Palma was a german ship called the Fangturm which sold pins and needles to all the Mediterranean ports before the war and further, presumably, because it was a very big steamer. It had been caught in Palma when the war broke out and had never been able to leave. Most of the officers and sailors had gotten away to Barcelona but the big ship remained in the harbour. It looked very rusty and neglected and it was just under our windows. All of a sudden as the attack on Verdun commenced, they began painting the Fangturm. Imagine our feelings. We were all pretty unhappy and this was despair. We told the french consul and he told us and it was awful.

Day by day the news was worse and one whole side of the Fangturm was painted and then they stopped painting. They knew it before we did. Verdun was not going to be taken. Verdun was safe. The germans had given up hoping to take it.

When it was all over we none of us wanted to stay in Mallorca any longer, we all wanted to go home. It was at this time that Cook and Gertrude Stein spent all their time talking about automobiles. They neither of them had ever driven but they were getting very interested. Cook also began to wonder how he was going to earn his living when he got to Paris. His tiny income did for Mallorca but it would not keep him long in Paris. He thought of driving horses for Félix Potin's delivery wagons, he said after all he liked horses better than automobiles. Anyway he went back to Paris and when we got there, we went a longer way, by way of Madrid, he was driving a Paris taxi. Later on he became a trier-out of cars for the Renault works and I can remember how exciting it was when he described how the wind blew out his cheeks when he made eighty kilometres an hour. Then later he joined the american army.

We went home by way of Madrid. There we had a curious experience. We went to the american consul to have our passports visaed. He was a great big flabby man and he had a filipino as an assistant. He looked at our passports, he measured them, weighed them, looked at them upside down and finally said that he supposed they were alright but how could he tell. He then asked the filipino what he thought. The filipino seemed inclined to agree that the consul could not tell. I tell you what you do, he said ingratiatingly, you go to the french consul since you are going to France and you live in Paris and if the french consul says they are alright, why the consul will sign. The consul sagely nodded.

We were furious. It was an awkward position that a french consul, not an american one should decide whether american passports were alright. However there was nothing else to do so we went to the french consul.

When our turn came the man in charge took our passports and looked them over and said to Gertrude Stein, when were you last in Spain. She stopped to think, she never can remember anything when anybody asks her suddenly, and she said she did not remember but she thought it was such and such a date. He said no, and mentioned another year. She said very likely he was right. Then he went on to give all the dates of her various visits to Spain and finally he added a visit when she was still at college when she was in Spain with her brother just after the spanish war. It was all in a way rather frightening to me standing by but Gertrude Stein and the assistant consul seemed to be thoroughly interested in fixing dates. Finally he said, you see I was for many years in the letter of credit department of the Crédit Lyonnais in Madrid and I have a very good memory and I remember, of course I remember you very well. We were all very pleased. He signed the passports and told us to go back and tell our consul to do so also.

At the time we were furious with our consul but now I wonder if it was not an arrangement between the two offices that the american consul should not sign any passport to enter France until the french consul had decided whether its owner was or was not desirable.

We came back to an entirely different Paris. It was no longer gloomy. It was no longer empty. This time we did not settle down, we decided to get into the war. One day we were walking down the rue des Pyramides and there was a ford car being backed up the street by an american girl and on the car it said,

American Fund for French Wounded. There, said I, that is what we are going to do. At least, said I to Gertrude Stein, you will drive the car and I will do the rest. We went over and talked to the american girl and then interviewed Mrs. Lathrop, the head of the organisation. She was enthusiastic, she was always enthusiastic and she said, get a car. But where, we asked. From America, she said. But how, we said. Ask somebody, she said, and Gertrude Stein did, she asked her cousin and in a few months the ford car came. In the meanwhile Cook had taught her to drive his taxi.

As I said it was a changed Paris. Everything was changed, and everybody was cheerful.

During our absence Eve had died and Picasso was now living in a little home in Montrouge. We went out to see him. He had a marvellous rose pink silk counterpane on his bed. Where did that come from Pablo, asked Gertrude Stein. Ah ça, said Picasso with much satisfaction, that is a lady. It was a well known chilean society woman who had given it to him. It was a marvel. He was very cheerful. He was constantly coming to the house, bringing Paquerette a girl who was very nice or Irene a very lovely woman who came from the mountains and wanted to be free. He brought Erik Satie and the Princesse de Polignac and Blaise Cendrars.

It was a great pleasure to know Erik Satie. He was from Normandy and very fond of it. Marie Laurencin comes from Normandy, so also does Braque. Once when after the war Satie and Marie Laurencin were at the house for lunch they were delightfully enthusiastic about each other as being normans. Erik Satie liked food and wine and knew a lot about both. We had at that time some very good eau de vie that the husband of Mildred Aldrich's servant had given us and Erik Satie, drinking his glass slowly and with appreciation, told stories of the country in his youth.

Only once in the half dozen times that Erik Satie was at the house did he talk about music. He said that it had always been his opinion and he was glad that it was being recognised that modern french music owed nothing to modern Germany. That after Debussy had led the way french musicians had either followed him or found their own french way.

He told charming stories, usually of Normandy, he had a

playful wit which was sometimes very biting. He was a charming dinner-guest. It was many years later that Virgil Thomson, when we first knew him in his tiny room near the Gare Saint-Lazare, played for us the whole of Socrate. It was then that Gertrude Stein really became a Satie enthusiast.

Ellen La Motte and Emily Chadbourne, who had not gone to Serbia, were still in Paris. Ellen La Motte, who was an ex Johns Hopkins nurse, wanted to nurse near the front. She was still gun shy but she did want to nurse at the front, and they met Mary Borden-Turner who was running a hospital at the front and Ellen La Motte did for a few months nurse at the front. After that she and Emily Chadbourne went to China and after that became leaders of the anti-opium campaign.

Mary Borden-Turner had been and was going to be a writer. She was very enthusiastic about the work of Gertrude Stein and travelled with what she had of it and volumes of Flaubert to and from the front. She had taken a house near the Bois and it was heated and during that winter when the rest of us had no coal it was very pleasant going to dinner there and being warm. We liked Turner. He was a captain in the British army and was doing contre-espionage work very successfully. Although married to Mary Borden he did not believe in millionaires. He insisted upon giving his own Christmas party to the women and children in the village in which he was billeted and he always said that after the war he would be collector of customs for the British in Düsseldorf or go out to Canada and live simply. After all, he used to say to his wife, you are not a millionaire, not a real one. He had british standards of millionairedom. Mary Borden was very Chicago. Gertrude Stein always says that chicagoans spend so much energy losing Chicago that often it is difficult to know what they are. They have to lose the Chicago voice and to do so they do many things. Some lower their voices, some raise them, some get an english accent, some even get a german accent, some drawl, some speak in a very high tense voice, and some go chinese or spanish and do not move the lips. Mary Borden was very Chicago and Gertrude Stein was immensely interested in her and in Chicago.

All this time we were waiting for our ford truck which was on its way and then we waited for its body to be built. We waited a great deal. It was then that Gertrude Stein wrote a great many little war poems, some of them have since been published in the volume Useful Knowledge which has in it only things about America.

Stirred by the publication of Tender Buttons many newspapers had taken up the amusement of imitating Gertrude Stein's work and making fun of it. Life began a series that were called after Gertrude Stein.

Gertrude Stein suddenly one day wrote a letter to Masson who was then editor of Life and said to him that the real Gertrude Stein was as Henry McBride had pointed out funnier in every way than the imitations, not to say much more interesting, and why did they not print the original. To her astonishment she received a very nice letter from Mr. Masson saying that he would be glad to do so. And they did. They printed two things that she sent them, one about Wilson and one longer thing about war work in France. Mr. Masson had more courage than most.

This winter Paris was bitterly cold and there was no coal. We finally had none at all. We closed up the big room and stayed in a little room but at last we had no more coal. The government was giving coal away to the needy but we did not feel justified in sending our servant to stand in line to get it. One afternoon it was bitterly cold, we went out and on a street corner was a policeman and standing with him was a sergeant of police. Gertrude Stein went up to them. Look here, she said to them, what are we to do. I live in a pavillon on the rue de Fleurus and have lived there many years. Oh yes, said they nodding their heads, certainly madame we know you very well. Well, she said, I have no coal not even enough to heat one small room. I do not want to send my servant to get it for nothing, that does not seem right. Now, she said, it is up to you to tell me what to do. The policeman looked at his sergeant and the sergeant nodded. Alright, they said.

We went home. That evening the policeman in civilian clothes turned up with two sacks of coal. We accepted thankfully and asked no questions. The policeman, a stalwart breton became our all in all. He did everything for us, he cleaned our home, he cleaned our chimneys, he got us in and he got us out and on dark nights when Zeppelins came it was comfortable to know that he was somewhere outside.

There were Zeppelin alarms from time to time, but like everything else we had gotten used to them. When they came at dinner time we went on eating and when they came at night Gertrude Stein did not wake me, she said I might as well stay where I was if I was asleep because when asleep it took more than even the siren that they used then to give the signal, to wake me.

Our little ford was almost ready. She was later to be called Auntie after Gertrude Stein's aunt Pauline who always behaved admirably in emergencies and behaved fairly well most times if she was properly flattered.

One day Picasso came in and with him and leaning on his shoulder was a slim elegant youth. It is Jean, announced Pablo, Jean Cocteau and we are leaving for Italy.

Picasso had been excited at the prospect of doing the scenery for a russian ballet, the music to be by Satie, the drama by Jean Cocteau. Everybody was at the war, life in Montparnasse was not very gay, Montrouge with even a faithful servant was not very lively, he too needed a change. He was very lively at the prospect of going to Rome. We all said goodbye and we all went our various ways.

The little ford car was ready. Gertrude Stein had learned to drive a french car and they all said it was the same. I have never driven any car, but it would appear that it is not the same. We went outside of Paris to get it when it was ready and Gertrude Stein drove it in. Of course the first thing she did was to stop dead on the track between two street cars. Everybody got out and pushed us off the track. The next day when we started off to see what would happen we managed to get as far as the Champs Elysées and once more stopped dead. A crowd shoved us to the side walk and then tried to find out what was the matter. Gertrude Stein cranked, the whole crowd cranked, nothing happened. Finally an old chauffeur said, no gasoline. We said proudly, oh yes at least a gallon, but he insisted on looking and of course there was none. Then the crowd stopped a whole procession of military trucks that were going up the Champs Elysées. They all stopped and a couple of them brought over an immense tank of gasoline and tried to pour it into the little ford. Naturally the process was not successful. Finally getting into a taxi I went to a store in our quarter where they sold brooms and gasoline and where they knew me and I came back with a tin of gasoline and we finally arrived at the Alcazar d'Eté, the then headquarters of the American Fund for French Wounded.

Mrs. Lathrop was waiting for one of the cars to take her to Montmartre. I immediately offered the service of our car and went out and told Gertrude Stein. She quoted Edwin Dodge to me. Once Mabel Dodge's little boy said he would like to fly from the terrace to the lower garden. Do, said Mabel. It is easy, said Edwin Dodge, to be a spartan mother.

However Mrs. Lathrop came and the car went off. I must confess to being terribly nervous until they came back but come back they did.

We had a consultation with Mrs. Lathrop and she sent us off to Perpignan, a region with a good many hospitals that no american organisation had ever visited. We started. We had never been further from Paris than Fontainebleau in the car and it was terribly exciting.

We had a few adventures, we were caught in the snow and I was sure that we were on the wrong road and wanted to turn back. Wrong or right, said Gertrude Stein, we are going on. She could not back the car very successfully and indeed I may say even to this day when she can drive any kind of a car anywhere she still does not back a car very well. She goes forward admirably, she does not go backwards successfully. The only violent discussions that we have had in connection with her driving a car have been on the subject of backing.

On this trip South we picked up our first military god-son. We began the habit then which we kept up all through the war of giving any soldier on the road a lift. We drove by day and we drove by night and in very lonely parts of France and we always stopped and gave a lift to any soldier, and never had we any but the most pleasant experiences with these soldiers. And some of them were as we sometimes found out pretty hard characters. Gertrude Stein once said to a soldier who was doing something for her, they were always doing something for her, whenever there was a soldier or a chauffeur or any kind of a man anywhere, she never did anything for herself, neither changing a tyre, cranking the car or repairing it. Gertrude Stein said to this soldier, but you are tellement gentil, very nice and kind. Madame, said he quite simply, all soldiers are nice and kind.

This faculty of Gertrude Stein of having everybody do anything for her puzzled the other drivers of the organisation. Mrs. Lathrop who used to drive her own car said that nobody did those things for her. It was not only soldiers, a chauffeur would get off the seat of a private car in the place Vendôme and crank Gertrude Stein's old ford for her. Gertrude Stein said that the others looked so efficient, of course nobody would think of doing anything for them. Now as for herself she was not efficient, she was good humoured, she was democratic, one person was as good as another, and she knew what she wanted done. If you are like that she says, anybody will do anything for you. The important thing, she insists, is that you must have deep down as the deepest thing in you a sense of equality. Then anybody will do anything for you.

It was not far from Saulieu that we picked up our first military god-son. He was a butcher in a tiny village not far from Saulieu. Our taking him up was a good example of the democracy of the french army. There were three of them walking along the road. We stopped and said we could take one of them on the step. They were all three going home on leave and walking into the country to their homes from the nearest big town. One was a lieutenant, one was a sergeant and one a soldier. They thanked us and then the lieutenant said to each one of them, how far have you to go. They each one named the distance and then they said, and you my lieutenant, how far have you to go. He told them. Then they all agreed that it was the soldier who had much the longest way to go and so it was his right to have the lift. He touched his cap to his sergeant and officer and got in.

As I say he was our first military god-son. We had a great many afterwards and it was quite an undertaking to keep them all going. The duty of a military god-mother was to write a letter as often as she received one and to send a package of comforts or dainties about once in ten days. They liked the packages but they really liked letters even more. And they answered so promptly. It seemed to me, no sooner was my letter written than there was an answer. And then one had to remember all their family histories and once I did a dreadful thing, I mixed my letters and so I asked a soldier whose wife I knew all about and whose mother was dead to remember me to his mother, and the one who had the mother to remember me to his wife. Their return letters were quite mournful. They each explained that I had made a mistake and I could see that they had been deeply wounded by my error.

The most delightful god-son we ever had was one we took on in Nîmes. One day when we were in the town I dropped my purse. I did not notice the loss until we returned to the hotel and then I was rather bothered as there had been a good deal of money in it. While we were eating our dinner the waiter said some one wanted to see us. We went out and there was a man holding the purse in his hand. He said he had picked it up in the street and as soon as his work was over had come to the hotel to give it to us. There was a card of mine in the purse and he took it for granted that a stranger would be at the hotel, beside by that time we were very well known in Nîmes. I naturally offered him a considerable reward from the contents of the purse but he said no. He said however that he had a favour to ask. They were refugees from the Marne and his son Abel now seventeen years old had just volunteered and was at present in the garrison at Nîmes, would I be his god-mother. I said I would, and I asked him to tell his son to come to see me his first free evening. The next evening the youngest, the sweetest, the smallest soldier imaginable came in. It was Abel.

We became very attached to Abel. I always remember his first letter from the front. He began by saying that he was really not very much surprised by anything at the front, it was exactly as it had been described to him and as he had imagined it, except that there being no tables one was compelled to write upon one's knees.

The next time we saw Abel he was wearing the red fourragère, his regiment as a whole had been decorated with the legion of honour and we were very proud of our filleul. Still later when we went into Alsace with the french army, after the armistice, we had Abel come and stay with us a few days and a proud boy he was when he climbed to the top of the Strasbourg cathedral.

When we finally returned to Paris, Abel came and stayed with us a week. We took him to see everything and he said solemnly at the end of his first day, I think all that was worth fighting for. Paris in the evening however frightened him and we always had to get somebody to go out with him. The front had not been scareful but Paris at night was.

Some time later he wrote and said that the family were moving into a different department and he gave me his new address. By some error the address did not reach him and we lost him.

We did finally arrive at Perpignan and began visiting hospitals and giving away our stores and sending word to headquarters if we thought they needed more than we had. At first it was a little difficult but soon we were doing all we were to do very well. We were also given quantities of comfort-bags and distributing these was a perpetual delight, it was like a continuous Christmas. We always had permission from the head of the hospital to distribute these to the soldiers themselves which was in itself a great pleasure but also it enabled us to get the soldiers to immediately write postal cards of thanks and these we used to send off in batches to Mrs. Lathrop who sent them to America to the people who had sent the comfort-bags. And so everybody was pleased.

Then there was the question of gasoline. The American Fund for French Wounded had an order from the french government giving them the privilege of buying gasoline. But there was no gasoline to buy. The french army had plenty of it and were ready to give it to us but they could not sell it and we were privileged to buy it but not to receive it for nothing. It was necessary to interview the officer in command of the commissary department.

Gertrude Stein was perfectly ready to drive the car anywhere, to crank the car as often as there was nobody else to do it, to repair the car, I must say she was very good at it, even if she was not ready to take it all down and put it back again for practice as I wanted her to do in the beginning, she was even resigned to getting up in the morning, but she flatly refused to go inside of any office and interview any official. I was officially the delegate and she was officially the driver but I had to go and interview the major.

He was a charming major. The affair was very long drawn out, he sent me here and he sent me there but finally the matter was straightened out. All this time of course he called me Mademoiselle Stein because Gertrude Stein's name was on all the papers that I presented to him, she being the driver. And so now, he said, Mademoiselle Stein, my wife is very anxious to make your acquaintance and she has asked me to ask you to dine with us. I was very confused. I hesitated. But I am not Mademoiselle Stein, I said. He almost jumped out of his chair. What, he shouted, not Mademoiselle Stein. Then who are you. It must be remembered this was war time and Perpignan almost at the spanish frontier. Well, said I, you see Mademoiselle Stein. Where is Mademoiselle Stein, he said. She is downstairs, I said feebly, in the automobile. Well what does all this mean, he said. Well, I said, you see Mademoiselle Stein is the driver and I am the delegate and Mademoiselle Stein has no patience, she will not go into offices and wait and interview people and explain, so I do it for her while she sits in the automobile. But what, said he sternly, would you have done if I had asked you to sign something. I would have told you, I said, as I am telling you now. Indeed, he said, let us go downstairs and see this Mademoiselle Stein.

We went downstairs and Gertrude Stein was sitting in the driver's seat of the little ford and he came up to her. They immediately became friends and he renewed his invitation and we went to dinner. We had a good time. Madame Dubois came from Bordeaux, the land of food and wine. And what food above all the soup. It still remains to me the standard of comparison with all the other soups in the world. Sometimes some approach it, a very few have equalled it but none have surpassed it.

Perpignan is not far from Rivesaltes and Rivesaltes is the birthplace of Joffre. It had a little hospital and we got it extra supplies in honour of Papa Joffre. We had also the little ford car showing the red cross and the A.F.F.W. sign and ourselves in it photographed in front of the house in the little street where Joffre was born and had this photograph printed and sent to Mrs. Lathrop. The postal cards were sent to America

Gertrude Stein and Alice B. Toklas
in front of Joffre's birthplace

and sold for the benefit of the fund. In the meantime the U.S. had come into the war and we had some one send us a lot of ribbon with the stars and stripes printed on it and we cut this up and gave it to all the soldiers and they and we were pleased.

Which reminds me of a french peasant. Later in Nîmes we had an american ambulance boy in the car with us and we were out in the country. The boy had gone off to visit a waterfall and I had gone off to see a hospital and Gertrude Stein stayed with the car. She told me when I came back that an old peasant had come up to her and asked her what uniform the young man was wearing. That, she had said proudly, is the uniform of the american army, your new ally. Oh, said the old peasant. And then contemplatively, I ask myself what will we accomplish together, je me demande je me demande qu'est-ce que nous ferons ensemble.

Our work in Perpignan being over we started back to Paris. On the way everything happened to the car. Perhaps it had been too hot even for a ford car in Perpignan. Perpignan is below sea level near the Mediterranean and it is hot. Gertrude Stein who had always wanted it hot and hotter has never been really enthusiastic about heat after this experience. She said she had been just like a pancake, the heat above and the heat below and cranking a car beside. I do not know how often she used to swear and say, I am going to scrap it, that is all there is about it I am going to scrap it. I encouraged and remonstrated until the car started again.

It was in connection with this that Mrs. Lathrop played a joke on Gertrude Stein. After the war was over we were both decorated by the french government, we received the Reconnaissance Française. They always in giving you a decoration give you a citation telling why you have been given it. The account of our valour was exactly the same, except in my case they said that my devotion was sans relache, with no abatement, and in her case they did not put in the words sans relache.

On the way back to Paris we, as I say had everything happen to the car but Gertrude Stein with the aid of an old tramp on the road who pushed and shoved at the critical moments managed to get it to Nevers where we met the first piece of the american army. They were the quartermasters department and the marines, the first contingent to arrive in France. There we first heard what Gertrude Stein calls the sad song of the marines, which tells how everybody else in the american army has at sometime mutinied, but the marines never.

Immediately on entering Nevers, we saw Tarn McGrew, a californian and parisian whom we had known very slightly but he was in uniform and we called for help. He came. We told him our troubles. He said, alright get the car into the garage of the hotel and to-morrow some of the soldiers will put it to rights. We did so.

That evening we spent at Mr. McGrew's request at the Y.M.C.A. and saw for the first time in many years americans just americans, the kind that would not naturally ever have come to Europe. It was quite a thrilling experience. Gertrude Stein of course talked to them all, wanted to know what state and what city they came from, what they did, how old they were and how they liked it. She talked to the french girls who were with the american boys and the french girls told her what they thought of the american boys and the american boys told her all they thought about the french girls.

The next day she spent with California and Iowa in the garage, as she called the two soldiers who were detailed to fix up her car. She was pleased with them when every time there was a terrific noise anywhere, they said solemnly to each other, that french chauffeur is just changing gears. Gertrude Stein, Iowa and California enjoyed themselves so thoroughly that I am sorry to say the car did not last out very well after we left Nevers, but at any rate we did get to Paris.

It was at this time that Gertrude Stein conceived the idea of writing a history of the United States consisting of chapters wherein Iowa differs from Kansas, and wherein Kansas differs from Nebraska etcetera. She did do a little of it which also was printed in the book, Useful Knowledge.

We did not stay in Paris very long. As soon as the car was made over we left for Nîmes, we were to do the three departments the Gard, the Bouches-du-Rhône and the Vaucluse.

We arrived in Nîmes and settled down to a very comfortable life there. We went to see the chief military doctor in the town, Doctor Fabre and through his great kindness and that of his wife we were soon very much at home in Nîmes, but before we began our work there, Doctor Fabre asked a favour of us. There were no automobile ambulances left in Nîmes. At the military hospital was a pharmacist, a captain in the army, who was very ill, certain to die, and wanted to die in his own home. His wife was with him and would sit with him and we were to have no responsibility for him except to drive him home. Of course we said we would and we did.

It had been a long hard ride up into the mountains and it was dark long before we were back. We were still some distance from Nîmes when suddenly on the road we saw a couple of figures. The old ford car's lights did not light up much of anything on the road, and nothing along the side of the road and we did not make out very well who it was. However we stopped as we always did when anybody asked us to give them a lift. One man, he was evidently an officer said, my automobile has broken down and I must get back to Nîmes. Alright we said, both of you climb into the back, you will find a mattress and things, make yourselves comfortable. We went on to Nîmes. As we came into the city I called through the little window, where do you want to get down, where are you going, a voice replied. To the Hôtel Luxembourg, I said. That will do alright, the voice replied. We arrived in front of the Hôtel Luxembourg and stopped. Here there was plenty of light. We heard a scramble in the back and then a little man, very fierce with the cap and oak leaves of a full general and the legion of honour medal at his throat, appeared before us. He said, I wish to thank you but before I do so I must ask you who you are. We, I replied cheerfully are the delegates of the American Fund for French Wounded and we are for the present stationed at Nîmes. And I, he retorted, am the general who commands here and as I see by your car that you have a french military number you should have reported to me immediately. Should we, I said, I did not know, I am most awfully sorry. It is alright, he said aggressively, if you should ever want or need anything let me know.

We did let him know very shortly because of course there was the eternal gasoline question and he was kindness itself and arranged everything for us.

The little general and his wife came from the north of France and had lost their home and spoke of themselves as refugees. When later the big Bertha began to fire on Paris and one shell hit the Luxembourg gardens very near the rue de Fleurus, I must confess I began to cry and said I did not want to be a miserable refugee. We had been helping a good many of them. Gertrude Stein said, General Frotier's family are refugees and they are not miserable. More miserable than I want to be, I said bitterly.

Soon the american army came to Nîmes. One day Madame Fabre met us and said that her cook had seen some american soldiers. She must have mistaken some english soldiers for them, we said. Not at all, she answered, she is very patriotic. At any rate the american soldiers came, a regiment of them of the S.O.S. the service of supply, how well I remember how they used to say it with the emphasis on the of.

We soon got to know them all well and some of them very well. There was Duncan, a southern boy with such a very marked southern accent that when he was well into a story I was lost. Gertrude Stein whose people all come from Baltimore had no difficulty and they used to shout with laughter together, and all I could understand was that they had killed him as if he was a chicken. The people in Nîmes were as much troubled as I was. A great many of the ladies in Nîmes spoke english very well. There had always been english governesses in Nîmes and they, the nîmoises had always prided themselves on their knowledge of english but as they said not only could they not understand these americans but these americans could not understand them when they spoke english. I had to admit that it was more or less the same with me.

The soldiers were all Kentucky, South Carolina etcetera and they were hard to understand.

Duncan was a dear. He was supply-sergeant to the camp and when we began to find american soldiers here and there in french hospitals we always took Duncan along to give the american soldier pieces of his lost uniform and white bread. Poor Duncan was miserable because he was not at the front. He had enlisted as far back as the expedition to Mexico and here he was well in the rear and no hope of getting away because he was one of the few who understood the complicated system of army book-keeping and his officers would not

recommend him for the front. I will go, he used to say bitterly, they can bust me if they like I will go. But as we told
him there were plenty of A.W.O.L. absent without leave the
south was full of them, we were always meeting them and
they would say, say any military police around here. Duncan
was not made for that life. Poor Duncan. Two days before
the armistice, he came in to see us and he was drunk and
bitter. He was usually a sober boy but to go back and face his
family never having been to the front was too awful. He was
with us in a little sitting-room and in the front room were
some of his officers and it would not do for them to see him
in that state and it was time for him to get back to the camp.
He had fallen half asleep with his head on the table. Duncan,
said Gertrude Stein sharply, yes, he said. She said to him, listen
Duncan. Miss Toklas is going to stand up, you stand up too
and you fix your eyes right on the back of her head, do you
understand. Yes, he said. Well then she will start to walk and
you follow her and don't you for a moment move your eyes
from the back of her head until you are in my car. Yes, he
said. And he did and Gertrude Stein drove him to the camp.

Dear Duncan. It was he who was all excited by the news
that the americans had taken forty villages at Saint-Mihiel. He
was to go with us that afternoon to Avignon to deliver some
cases. He was sitting very straight on the step and all of a
sudden his eye was caught by some houses. What are they, he
asked. Oh just a village, Gertrude Stein said. In a minute there
were some more houses. And what are those houses, he asked.
Oh just a village. He fell very silent and he looked at the
landscape as he had never looked at it before. Suddenly with
a deep sigh, forty villages ain't so much, he said.

We did enjoy the life with these doughboys. I would like
to tell nothing but doughboy stories. They all got on amaz-
ingly well with the french. They worked together in the repair
sheds of the railroad. The only thing that bothered the americans were the long hours. They worked too concentratedly
to keep it up so long. Finally an arrangement was made that
they should have their work to do in their hours and the
french in theirs. There was a great deal of friendly rivalry. The
american boys did not see the use of putting so much finish

on work that was to be shot up so soon again, the french said that they could not complete work without finish. But both lots thoroughly liked each other.

Gertrude Stein always said the war was so much better than just going to America. Here you were with America in a kind of way that if you only went to America you could not possibly be. Every now and then one of the american soldiers would get into the hospital at Nîmes and as Doctor Fabre knew that Gertrude Stein had had a medical education he always wanted her present with the doughboy on these occasions. One of them fell off the train. He did not believe that the little french trains could go fast but they did, fast enough to kill him.

This was a tremendous occasion. Gertrude Stein in company with the wife of the préfet, the governmental head of the department and the wife of the general were the chief mourners. Duncan and two others blew on the bugle and everybody made speeches. The Protestant pastor asked Gertrude Stein about the dead man and his virtues and she asked the doughboys. It was difficult to find any virtue. Apparently he had been a fairly hard citizen. But can't you tell me something good about him, she said despairingly. Finally Taylor, one of his friends, looked up solemnly and said, I tell you he had a heart as big as a washtub.

I often wonder, I have often wondered if any of all these doughboys who knew Gertrude Stein so well in those days ever connected her with the Gertrude Stein of the newspapers.

We led a very busy life. There were all the americans, there were a great many in the small hospitals round about as well as in the regiment in Nîmes and we had to find them all and be good to them, then there were all the french in the hospitals, we had them to visit as this was really our business, and then later came the spanish grippe and Gertrude Stein and one of the military doctors from Nîmes used to go to all the villages miles around to bring into Nîmes the sick soldiers and officers who had fallen ill in their homes while on leave.

It was during these long trips that she began writing a great deal again. The landscape, the strange life stimulated her. It was then that she began to love the valley of the Rhône, the landscape that of all landscapes means the most to her. We are still here in Bilignin in the valley of the Rhône.

She wrote at that time the poem of The Deserter, printed almost immediately in Vanity Fair. Henry McBride had interested Crowninshield in her work.

One day when we were in Avignon we met Braque. Braque had been badly wounded in the head and had come to Sorgues near Avignon to recover. It was there that he had been staying when the mobilisation orders came to him. It was awfully pleasant seeing the Braques again. Picasso had just written to Gertrude Stein announcing his marriage to a jeune fille, a real young lady, and he had sent Gertrude Stein a wedding present of a lovely little painting and a photograph of a painting of his wife.

That lovely little painting he copied for me many years later on tapestry canvas and I embroidered it and that was the beginning of my tapestrying. I did not think it possible to ask him to draw me something to work but when I told Gertrude Stein she said, alright, I'll manage. And so one day when he was at the house she said, Pablo, Alice wants to make a tapestry of that little picture and I said I would trace it for her. He looked at her with kindly contempt, if it is done by anybody, he said, it will be done by me. Well, said Gertrude Stein, producing a piece of tapestry canvas, go to it, and he did. And I have been making tapestry of his drawings ever since and they are very successful and go marvellously with old chairs. I have done two small Louis fifteenth chairs in this way. He is kind enough now to make me drawings on my working canvas and to colour them for me.

Braque also told us that Apollinaire too had married a real young lady. We gossiped a great deal together. But after all there was little news to tell.

Time went on, we were very busy and then came the armistice. We were the first to bring the news to many small villages. The french soldiers in the hospitals were relieved rather than glad. They seemed not to feel that it was going to be such a lasting peace. I remember one of them saying to Gertrude Stein when she said to him, well here is peace, at least for twenty years, he said.

The next morning we had a telegram from Mrs. Lathrop. Come at once want you to go with the french armies to Alsace. We did not stop on the way. We made it in a day. Very shortly after we left for Alsace.

We left for Alsace and on the road had our first and only accident. The roads were frightful, mud, ruts, snow, slush, and covered with the french armies going into Alsace. As we passed, two horses dragging an army kitchen kicked out of line and hit our ford, the mud-guard came off and the tool-chest, and worst of all the triangle of the steering gear was badly bent. The army picked up our tools and our mud-guard but there was nothing to do about the bent triangle. We went on, the car wandering all over the muddy road, up hill and down hill, and Gertrude Stein sticking to the wheel. Finally after about forty kilometres, we saw on the road some american ambulance men. Where can we get our car fixed. Just a little farther, they said. We went a little farther and there found an american ambulance outfit. They had no extra mud-guard but they could give us a new triangle. I told our troubles to the sergeant, he grunted and said a word in an undertone to a mechanic. Then turning to us he said gruffly, run-her-in. Then the mechanic took off his tunic and threw it over the radiator. As Gertrude Stein said when any american did that the car was his.

We had never realised before what mud-guards were for but by the time we arrived in Nancy we knew. The french military repair shop fitted us out with a new mud-guard and tool-chest and we went on our way.

Soon we came to the battle-fields and the lines of trenches of both sides. To any one who did not see it as it was then it is impossible to imagine it. It was not terrifying it was strange. We were used to ruined houses and even ruined towns but this was different. It was a landscape. And it belonged to no country.

I remember hearing a french nurse once say and the only thing she did say of the front was, c'est un paysage passionant, an absorbing landscape. And that was what it was as we saw it. It was strange. Camouflage, huts, everything was there. It was wet and dark and there were a few people, one did not know whether they were chinamen or europeans. Our fan-belt had stopped working. A staff car stopped and fixed it with a hairpin, we still wore hairpins.

Another thing that interested us enormously was how different the camouflage of the french looked from the camouflage of the germans, and then once we came across some very very neat camouflage and it was american. The idea was the same but as after all it was different nationalities who did it the difference was inevitable. The colour schemes were different, the designs were different, the way of placing them was different, it made plain the whole theory of art and its inevitability.

Finally we came to Strasbourg and then went on to Mulhouse. Here we stayed until well into May.

Our business in Alsace was not hospitals but refugees. The inhabitants were returning to their ruined homes all over the devastated country and it was the aim of the A.F.F.W. to give a pair of blankets, underclothing and children's and babies' woollen stockings and babies' booties to every family. There was a legend that the quantity of babies' booties sent to us came from the gifts sent to Mrs. Wilson who was supposed at that time to be about to produce a little Wilson. There were a great many babies' booties but not too many for Alsace.

Our headquarters was the assembly-room of one of the big school-buildings in Mulhouse. The german school teachers had disappeared and french school teachers who happened to be in the army had been put in temporarily to teach. The head of our school was in despair, not about the docility of his pupils nor their desire to learn french, but on account of their clothes. French children are all always neatly clothed. There is no such thing as a ragged child, even orphans farmed out in country villages are neatly dressed, just as all french women are neat, even the poor and the aged. They may not always be clean but they are always neat. From this standpoint the parti-coloured rags of even the comparatively prosperous alsatian children was deplorable and the french schoolmasters suffered. We did our best to help him out with black children's aprons but these did not go far, beside we had to keep them for the refugees.

We came to know Alsace and the alsatians very well, all kinds of them. They were astonished at the simplicity with which the french army and french soldiers took care of themselves. They had not been accustomed to that in the german army. On the other hand the french soldiers were rather mistrustful of the alsatians who were too anxious to be french and yet were not french. They are not frank, the french soldiers said. And it is quite true. The french whatever else they may be are frank. They are very polite, they are very adroit but sooner or later they always tell you the truth. The alsatians are not adroit, they are not polite and they do not inevitably tell you the truth. Perhaps with renewed contact with the french they will learn these things.

We distributed. We went into all the devastated villages. We usually asked the priest to help us with the distribution. One priest who gave us a great deal of good advice and with whom we became very friendly had only one large room left in his house. Without any screens or partitions he had made himself three rooms, the first third had his parlour furniture, the second third his dining room furniture and the last third his bedroom furniture. When we lunched with him and we lunched well and his alsatian wines were very good, he received us in his parlour, he then excused himself and withdrew into his bedroom to wash his hands, and then he invited us very formally to come into the dining room, it was like an old fashioned stage setting.

We distributed, we drove around in the snow we talked to everybody and everybody talked to us and by the end of May it was all over and we decided to leave.

We went home by way of Metz, Verdun and Mildred Aldrich.

We once more returned to a changed Paris. We were restless. Gertrude Stein began to work very hard, it was at this time that she wrote her Accents in Alsace and other political plays, the last plays in Geography and Plays. We were still in the shadow of war work and we went on doing some of it, visiting hospitals and seeing the soldiers left in them, now pretty well neglected by everybody. We had spent a great deal of our money during the war and we were economising, servants were difficult to get if not impossible, prices were high. We settled down for the moment with a femme de ménage for only a few hours a day. I used to say Gertrude Stein was the chauffeur and I was the cook. We used to go over early in the morning to the public markets and get in our provisions. It was a confused world.

Jessie Whitehead had come over with the peace commission as secretary to one of the delegations and of course we were very interested in knowing all about the peace. It was then that Gertrude Stein described one of the young men of the peace commission who was holding forth, as one who knew all about the war, he had been here ever since the peace. Gertrude Stein's cousins came over, everybody came over, everybody was dissatisfied and every one was restless. It was a restless and disturbed world.

Gertrude Stein and Picasso quarrelled. They neither of them ever quite knew about what. Anyway they did not see each other for a year and then they met by accident at a party at Adrienne Monnier's. Picasso said, how do you do to her and said something about her coming to see him. No I will not, she answered gloomily. Picasso came to me and said, Gertrude says she won't come to see me, does she mean it. I am afraid if she says it she means it. They did not see each other for another year and in the meantime Picasso's little boy was born and Max Jacob was complaining that he had not been named god-father. A very little while after this we were somewhere at some picture gallery and Picasso came up and put his hand on Gertrude Stein's shoulder and said, oh hell, let's be friends. Sure, said Gertrude Stein and they embraced. When can I come to see you, said Picasso, let's see, said Gertrude Stein, I am afraid we are busy but come to dinner the end of the week. Nonsense, said Picasso, we are coming to dinner to-morrow, and they came.

It was a changed Paris. Guillaume Apollinaire was dead. We saw a tremendous number of people but none of them as far as I can remember that we had ever known before. Paris was crowded. As Clive Bell remarked, they say that an awful lot of people were killed in the war but it seems to me that an extraordinary large number of grown men and women have suddenly been born.

As I say we were restless and we were economical and all

day and all evening we were seeing people and at last there was the defile, the procession under the Arc de Triomphe, of the allies.

The members of the American Fund for French Wounded were to have seats on the benches that were put up the length of the Champs Elysées but quite rightly the people of Paris objected as these seats would make it impossible for them to see the parade and so Clemenceau promptly had them taken down. Luckily for us Jessie Whitehead's room in her hotel looked right over the Arc de Triomphe and she asked us to come to it to see the parade. We accepted gladly. It was a wonderful day.

We got up at sunrise, as later it would have been impossible to cross Paris in a car. This was one of the last trips Auntie made. By this time the red cross was painted off it but it was still a truck. Very shortly after it went its honourable way and was succeeded by Godiva, a two-seated runabout, also a little ford. She was called Godiva because she had come naked into the world and each of our friends gave us something with which to bedeck her.

Auntie then was making practically her last trip. We left her near the river and walked up to the hotel. Everybody was on the streets, men, women, children, soldiers, priests, nuns, we saw two nuns being helped into a tree from which they would be able to see. And we ourselves were admirably placed and we saw perfectly.

We saw it all, we saw first the few wounded from the Invalides in their wheeling chairs wheeling themselves. It is an old french custom that a military procession should always be preceded by the veterans from the Invalides. They all marched past through the Arc de Triomphe. Gertrude Stein remembered that when as a child she used to swing on the chains that were around the Arc de Triomphe her governess had told her that no one must walk underneath since the german armies had marched under it after 1870. And now everybody except the germans were passing through.

All the nations marched differently, some slowly, some quickly, the french carry their flags the best of all, Pershing and his officer carrying the flag behind him were perhaps the most perfectly spaced. It was this scene that Gertrude Stein described in the movie she wrote about this time that I have published in Operas and Plays in the Plain Edition.

However it all finally came to an end. We wandered up and we wandered down the Champs Elysées and the war was over and the piles of captured cannon that had made two pyramids were being taken away and peace was upon us.

7.

After the War
1919–1932

W E WERE, in these days as I look back at them, constantly
seeing people.

It is a confused memory those first years after the war and
very difficult to think back and remember what happened before or after something else. Picasso once said, I have already
told, when Gertrude Stein and he were discussing dates, you
forget that when we were young an awful lot happened in a
year. During the years just after the war as I look in order to
refresh my memory over the bibliography of Gertrude Stein's
work, I am astonished when I realise how many things happened in a year. Perhaps we were not so young then but there
were a great many young in the world and perhaps that comes
to the same thing.

The old crowd had disappeared. Matisse was now permanently in Nice and in any case although Gertrude Stein and
he were perfectly good friends when they met, they practically
never met. This was the time when Gertrude Stein and Picasso
were not seeing each other. They always talked with the ten-
derest friendship about each other to any one who had known
them both but they did not see each other. Guillaume Apollinaire was dead. Braque and his wife we saw from time to
time, he and Picasso by this time were fairly bitterly on the
outs. I remember one evening Man Ray brought a photograph that he had made of Picasso to the house and Braque
happened to be there. The photograph was being passed
around and when it came to Braque he looked at it and said,
I ought to know who that gentleman is, je dois connaître ce
monsieur. It was a period this and a very considerable time
afterward that Gertrude Stein celebrated under the title, Of
Having for a Long Time Not Continued to be Friends.

Juan Gris was ill and discouraged. He had been very ill and
was never really well again. Privation and discouragement had
had their effect. Kahnweiler came back to Paris fairly early after
the war but all his old crowd with the exception of Juan were

too successful to have need of him. Mildred Aldrich had had her tremendous success with the Hilltop on the Marne, in Mildred's way she had spent royally all she had earned royally and was now still spending and enjoying it although getting a little uneasy. We used to go out and see her about once a month, in fact all the rest of her life we always managed to get out to see her regularly. Even in the days of her very greatest glory she loved a visit from Gertrude Stein better than a visit from anybody else. In fact it was largely to please Mildred that Gertrude Stein tried to get the Atlantic Monthly to print something of hers. Mildred always felt and said that it would be a blue ribbon if the Atlantic Monthly consented, which of course it never did. Another thing used to annoy Mildred dreadfully. Gertrude Stein's name was never in Who's Who in America. As a matter of fact it was in english authors' bibliographies before it ever entered an american one. This troubled Mildred very much. I hate to look at Who's Who in America, she said to me, when I see all those insignificant people and Gertrude's name not in. And then she would say, I know it's alright but I wish Gertrude were not so outlawed. Poor Mildred. And now just this year for reasons best known to themselves Who's Who has added Gertrude Stein's name to their list. The Atlantic Monthly needless to say has not.

The Atlantic Monthly story is rather funny.

As I said Gertrude Stein sent the Atlantic Monthly some manuscripts, not with any hope of their accepting them, but if by any miracle they should, she would be pleased and Mildred delighted. An answer came back, a long and rather argumentative answer from the editorial office. Gertrude Stein thinking that some Boston woman in the editorial office had written, answered the arguments lengthily to Miss Ellen Sedgwick. She received an almost immediate answer meeting all her arguments and at the same time admitting that the matter was not without interest but that of course Atlantic Monthly readers could not be affronted by having these manuscripts presented in the review, but it might be possible to have them introduced by somebody in the part of the magazine, if I remember rightly, called the Contributors' Club. The letter ended by saying that the writer was not Ellen but Ellery Sedgwick.

Gertrude Stein of course was delighted with its being Ellery and not Ellen and accepted being printed in the Contributors' Club, but equally of course the manuscripts did not appear even in the part called Contributors' Club.

We began to meet new people all the time.

Some one told us, I have forgotten who, that an american woman had started a lending library of english books in our quarter. We had in those days of economy given up Mudie's, but there was the American Library which supplied us a little, but Gertrude Stein wanted more. We investigated and we found Sylvia Beach. Sylvia Beach was very enthusiastic about Gertrude Stein and they became friends. She was Sylvia Beach's first annual subscriber and Sylvia Beach was proportionately proud and grateful. Her little place was in a little street near the Ecole de Médecine. It was not then much frequented by americans. There was the author of Beebie the Beebeist and there was the niece of Marcel Schwob and there were a few stray irish poets. We saw a good deal of Sylvia those days, she used to come to the house and also go out into the country with us in the old car. We met Adrienne Monnier and she brought Valéry Larbaud to the house and they were all very interested in Three Lives and Valéry Larbaud, so we understood, meditated translating it. It was at this time that Tristan Tzara first appeared in Paris. Adrienne Monnier was much excited by his advent. Picabia had found him in Switzerland during the war and they had together created dadaism, and out of dadaism, with a great deal of struggle and quarrelling came surréalisme.

Tzara came to the house, I imagine Picabia brought him but I am not quite certain. I have always found it very difficult to understand the stories of his violence and his wickedness, at least I found it difficult then because Tzara when he came to the house sat beside me at the tea table and talked to me like a pleasant and not very exciting cousin.

Adrienne Monnier wanted Sylvia to move to the rue de l'Odéon and Sylvia hesitated but finally she did so and as a matter of fact we did not see her very often afterward. They gave a party just after Sylvia moved in and we went and there Gertrude Stein first discovered that she had a young Oxford following. There were several young Oxford men there and they were awfully pleased to meet her and they asked her to

give them some manuscripts and they published them that
year nineteen twenty, in the Oxford Magazine.

Sylvia Beach from time to time brought groups of people
to the house, groups of young writers and some older women
with them. It was at that time that Ezra Pound came, no that
was brought about in another way. She later ceased coming
to the house but she sent word that Sherwood Anderson had
come to Paris and wanted to see Gertrude Stein and might
he come. Gertrude Stein sent back word that she would be
very pleased and he came with his wife and Rosenfeld, the
musical critic.

For some reason or other I was not present on this occasion, some domestic complication in all probability, at any rate
when I did come home Gertrude Stein was moved and pleased
as she has very rarely been. Gertrude Stein was in those days
a little bitter, all her unpublished manuscripts, and no hope
of publication or serious recognition. Sherwood Anderson
came and quite simply and directly as is his way told her what
he thought of her work and what it had meant to him in his
development. He told it to her then and what was even rarer
he told it in print immediately after. Gertrude Stein and Sherwood Anderson have always been the best of friends but I do
not believe even he realises how much his visit meant to her.
It was he who thereupon wrote the introduction to Geography and Plays.

In those days you met anybody anywhere. The Jewetts were
an american couple who owned a tenth century château near
Perpignan. We had met them there during the war and when
they came to Paris we went to see them. There we met first
Man Ray and later Robert Coates, how either of them happened to get there I do not know.

There were a lot of people in the room when we came in
and soon Gertrude Stein was talking to a little man who sat
in the corner. As we went out she made an engagement with
him. She said he was a photographer and seemed interesting,
and reminded me that Jeanne Cook, William Cook's wife,
wanted her picture taken to send to Cook's people in America.
We all three went to Man Ray's hotel. It was one of the little,
tiny hotels in the rue Delambre and Man Ray had one of the
small rooms, but I have never seen any space, not even a ship's

cabin, with so many things in it and the things so admirably disposed. He had a bed, he had three large cameras, he had several kinds of lighting, he had a window screen, and in a little closet he did all his developing. He showed us pictures of Marcel Duchamp and a lot of other people and he asked if he might come and take photographs of the studio and of Gertrude Stein. He did and he also took some of me and we were very pleased with the result. He has at intervals taken pictures of Gertrude Stein and she is always fascinated with his way of using lights. She always comes home very pleased. One day she told him that she liked his photographs of her better than any that had ever been taken except one snap shot I had taken of her recently. This seemed to bother Man Ray. In a little while he asked her to come and pose and she did. He said, move all you like, your eyes, your head, it is to be a pose but it is to have in it all the qualities of a snap shot. The poses were very long, she, as he requested, moved, and the result, the last photographs he made of her, are extraordinarily interesting.

Robert Coates we also met at the Jewetts' in those early days just after the war. I remember the day very well. It was a cold, dark day, on an upper floor of a hotel. There were a number of young men there and suddenly Gertrude Stein said she had forgotten to put the light on her car and she did not want another fine, we had just had one because I had blown the klaxon at a policeman trying to get him out of our way and she had received one by going the wrong way around a post. Alright, said a red-haired young man and immediately he was down and back. The light is on, he announced. How did you know which my car was, asked Gertrude Stein. Oh I knew, said Coates. We always liked Coates. It is extraordinary in wandering about Paris how very few people you know you meet, but we often met Coates hatless and red-headed in the most unexpected places. This was just about the time of Broom, about which I will tell very soon, and Gertrude Stein took a very deep interest in Coates' work as soon as he showed it to her. She said he was the one young man who had an individual rhythm, his words made a sound to the eyes, most people's words do not. We also liked Coates' address, the City Hotel, on the island, and we liked all his ways.

Gertrude Stein was delighted with the scheme of study that he prepared for the Guggenheim prize. Unfortunately, the scheme of study, which was a most charming little novel, with Gertrude Stein as a backer, did not win a prize.

As I have said there was Broom.

Before the war we had known a young fellow, not known him much but a little, Elmer Harden, who was in Paris studying music. During the war we heard that Elmer Harden had joined the french army and had been badly wounded. It was rather an amazing story. Elmer Harden had been nursing french wounded in the american hospital and one of his patients, a captain with an arm fairly disabled, was going back to the front. Elmer Harden could not content himself any longer nursing. He said to Captain Peter, I am going with you. But it is impossible, said Captain Peter. But I am, said Elmer stubbornly. So they took a taxi and they went to the war office and to a dentist and I don't know where else, but by the end of the week Captain Peter had rejoined and Elmer Harden was in his regiment as a soldier. He fought well and was wounded. After the war we met him again and then we met often. He and the lovely flowers he used to send us were a great comfort in those days just after the peace. He and I always say that he and I will be the last people of our generation to remember the war. I am afraid we both of us have already forgotten it a little. Only the other day though Elmer announced that he had had a great triumph, he had made Captain Peter and Captain Peter is a breton admit that it was a nice war. Up to this time when he had said to Captain Peter, it was a nice war, Captain Peter had not answered, but this time when Elmer said, it was a nice war, Captain Peter said, yes Elmer, it was a nice war.

Kate Buss came from the same town as Elmer, from Medford, Mass. She was in Paris and she came to see us. I do not think Elmer introduced her but she did come to see us. She was much interested in the writings of Gertrude Stein and owned everything that up to that time could be bought. She brought Kreymborg to see us. Kreymborg had come to Paris with Harold Loeb to start Broom. Kreymborg and his wife came to the house frequently. He wanted very much to run The Long Gay Book, the thing Gertrude Stein had written just after The Making of Americans, as a serial. Of course Harold Loeb would not consent to that. Kreymborg used to read out the sentences from this book with great gusto. He and Gertrude Stein had a bond of union beside their mutual liking because the Grafton Press that had printed Three Lives had printed his first book and about the same time.

Kate Buss brought lots of people to the house. She brought Djuna Barnes and Mina Loy and they had wanted to bring James Joyce but they didn't. We were glad to see Mina whom we had known in Florence as Mina Haweis. Mina brought Glenway Wescott on his first trip to Europe. Glenway impressed us greatly by his english accent. Hemingway explained. He said, when you matriculate at the University of Chicago you write down just what accent you will have and they give it to you when you graduate. You can have a sixteenth century or modern, whatever you like. Glenway left behind him a silk cigarette case with his initials, we kept it until he came back again and then gave it to him.

Mina also brought Robert McAlmon. McAlmon was very nice in those days, very mature and very good-looking. It was much later that he published The Making of Americans in the Contact press and that everybody quarrelled. But that is Paris, except that as a matter of fact Gertrude Stein and he never became friends again.

Kate Buss brought Ernest Walsh, he was very young then and very feverish and she was very worried about him. We met him later with Hemingway and then in Belley, but we never knew him very well.

We met Ezra Pound at Grace Lounsbery's house, he came home to dinner with us and he stayed and he talked about japanese prints among other things. Gertrude Stein liked him but did not find him amusing. She said he was a village explainer, excellent if you were a village, but if you were not, not. Ezra also talked about T. S. Eliot. It was the first time any one had talked about T.S. at the house. Pretty soon everybody talked about T.S. Kitty Buss talked about him and much later Hemingway talked about him as the Major. Considerably later Lady Rothermere talked about him and invited Gertrude Stein to come and meet him. They were founding the Criterion. We had met Lady Rothermere through Muriel

Draper whom we had seen again for the first time after many years. Gertrude Stein was not particularly anxious to go to Lady Rothermere's and meet T. S. Eliot, but we all insisted she should, and she gave a doubtful yes. I had no evening dress to wear for this occasion and started to make one. The bell rang and in walked Lady Rothermere and T.S.

Eliot and Gertrude Stein had a solemn conversation, mostly about split infinitives and other grammatical solecisms and why Gertrude Stein used them. Finally Lady Rothermere and Eliot rose to go and Eliot said that if he printed anything of Gertrude Stein's in the Criterion it would have to be her very latest thing. They left and Gertrude Stein said, don't bother to finish your dress, now we don't have to go, and she began to write a portrait of T. S. Eliot and called it the fifteenth of November, that being this day and so there could be no doubt but that it was her latest thing. It was all about wool is wool and silk is silk or wool is woollen and silk is silken. She sent it to T. S. Eliot and he accepted it but naturally he did not print it.

Then began a long correspondence, not between Gertrude Stein and T. S. Eliot, but between T. S. Eliot's secretary and myself. We each addressed the other as Sir, I signing myself A. B. Toklas and she signing initials. It was only considerably afterwards that I found out that his secretary was not a young man. I don't know whether she ever found out that I was not.

In spite of all this correspondence nothing happened and Gertrude Stein mischievously told the story to all the english people coming to the house and at that moment there were a great many english coming in and out. At any rate finally there was a note, it was now early spring, from the Criterion asking would Miss Stein mind if her contribution appeared in the October number. She replied that nothing could be more suitable than the fifteenth of November on the fifteenth of October.

Once more a long silence and then this time came proof of the article. We were surprised but returned the proof promptly. Apparently a young man had sent it without authority because very shortly came an apologetic letter saying that there had been a mistake, the article was not to be printed just yet. This was also told to the passing english with the result that after all it was printed. Thereafter it was reprinted in the Georgian Stories. Gertrude Stein was delighted when later she was told that Eliot had said in Cambridge that the work of Gertrude Stein was very fine but not for us.

But to come back to Ezra. Ezra did come back and he came back with the editor of The Dial. This time it was worse than japanese prints, it was much more violent. In his surprise at the violence Ezra fell out of Gertrude Stein's favourite little armchair, the one I have since tapestried with Picasso designs, and Gertrude Stein was furious. Finally Ezra and the editor of The Dial left, nobody too well pleased. Gertrude Stein did not want to see Ezra again. Ezra did not quite see why. He met Gertrude Stein one day near the Luxembourg gardens and said, but I do want to come to see you. I am so sorry, answered Gertrude Stein, but Miss Toklas has a bad tooth and beside we are busy picking wild flowers. All of which was literally true, like all of Gertrude Stein's literature, but it upset Ezra, and we never saw him again.

During these months after the war we were one day going down a little street and saw a man looking in at a window and going backwards and forwards and right and left and otherwise behaving strangely. Lipschitz, said Gertrude Stein. Yes, said Lipschitz, I am buying an iron cock. Where is it, we asked. Why in there, he said, and in there it was. Gertrude Stein had known Lipschitz very slightly at one time but this incident made them friends and soon he asked her to pose. He had just finished a bust of Jean Cocteau and he wanted to do her. She never minds posing, she likes the calm of it and although she does not like sculpture and told Lipschitz so, she began to pose. I remember it was a very hot spring and Lipschitz's studio was appallingly hot and they spent hours there.

Lipschitz is an excellent gossip and Gertrude Stein adores the beginning and middle and end of a story and Lipschitz was able to supply several missing parts of several stories.

And then they talked about art and Gertrude Stein rather liked her portrait and they were very good friends and the sittings were over.

One day we were across town at a picture show and somebody came up to Gertrude Stein and said something. She said, wiping her forehead, it is hot. He said he was a friend of Lipschitz and she answered, yes it was hot there. Lipschitz was to bring her some photographs of the head he had done but he did not and we were awfully busy and Gertrude Stein sometimes wondered why Lipschitz did not come. Somebody wanted the photos so she wrote to him to bring them. He came. She said why did you not come before. He said he did not come before because he had been told by some one to whom she had said it, that she was bored sitting for him. Oh hell, she said, listen I am fairly well known for saying things about any one and anything, I say them about people, I say them to people, I say them when I please and how I please but as I mostly say what I think, the least that you or anybody else can do is to rest content with what I say to you. He seemed very content and they talked happily and pleasantly and they said à bientôt, we will meet soon. Lipschitz left and we did not see him for several years.

Then Jane Heap turned up and wanted to take some of Lipschitz's things to America and she wanted Gertrude Stein to come and choose them. But how can I, said Gertrude Stein, when Lipschitz is very evidently angry, I am sure I have not the slightest idea why or how but he is. Jane Heap said that Lipschitz said that he was fonder of Gertrude Stein than he was of almost anybody and was heart broken at not seeing her. Oh, said Gertrude Stein, I am very fond of him. Sure I will go with you. She went, they embraced tenderly and had a happy time and her only revenge was in parting to say to Lipschitz, à très bientôt. And Lipschitz said, comme vous êtes méchante. They have been excellent friends ever since and Gertrude Stein has done of Lipschitz one of her most lovely portraits but they have never spoken of the quarrel and if he knows what happened the second time she does not.

It was through Lipschitz that Gertrude Stein again met Jean Cocteau. Lipschitz had told Gertrude Stein a thing which she did not know, that Cocteau in his Potomak had spoken of and quoted The Portrait of Mabel Dodge. She was naturally very pleased as Cocteau was the first french writer to speak of her work. They met once or twice and began a friendship that consists in their writing to each other quite often and liking each other immensely and having many young and old friends in common, but not in meeting.

Jo Davidson too sculptured Gertrude Stein at this time. There, all was peaceful, Jo was witty and amusing and he pleased Gertrude Stein. I cannot remember who came in and out, whether they were real or whether they were sculptured but there were a great many. There were among others Lincoln Steffens and in some queer way he is associated with the beginning of our seeing a good deal of Janet Scudder but I do not well remember just what happened.

I do however remember very well the first time I ever heard Janet Scudder's voice. It was way back when I first came to Paris and my friend and I had a little apartment in the rue Notre-Dame-des-Champs. My friend in the enthusiasm of seeing other people enthusiastic had bought a Matisse and it had just been hung on the wall. Mildred Aldrich was calling on us, it was a warm spring afternoon and Mildred was leaning out of the window. I suddenly heard her say, Janet, Janet come up here. What is it, said a very lovely drawling voice. I want you to come up here and meet my friends Harriet and Alice and I want you to come up and see their new apartment. Oh, said the voice. And then Mildred said, and they have a new big Matisse. Come up and see it. I don't think so, said the voice.

Janet did later see a great deal of Matisse when he lived out in Clamart. And Gertrude Stein and she had always been friends, at least ever since the period when they first began to see a good deal of each other.

Like Doctor Claribel Cone, Janet, always insisting that she understands none of it, reads and feels Gertrude Stein's work and reads it aloud understandingly.

We were going to the valley of the Rhône for the first time since the war and Janet and a friend in a duplicate Godiva were to come too. I will tell about this very soon.

During all these restless months we were also trying to get Mildred Aldrich the legion of honour. After the war was over a great many war-workers were given the legion of honour but they were all members of organisations and Mildred Aldrich was not. Gertrude Stein was very anxious that Mildred Aldrich should have it. In the first place she thought she ought, no one else had done as much propaganda for France as she had by her books which everybody in America read, and beside she knew Mildred would like it. So we began the campaign. It was not a very easy thing to accomplish as naturally the organisations had the most influence. We started different people going. We began to get lists of prominent americans and asked them to sign. They did not refuse, but a list in itself helps, but does not accomplish results. Mr. Jaccaci who had a great admiration for Miss Aldrich was very helpful but all the people that he knew wanted things for themselves first. We got the American Legion interested at least two of the colonels, but they also had other names that had to pass first. We had seen and talked to and interested everybody and everybody promised and nothing happened. Finally we met a senator. He would be helpful but then senators were busy and then one afternoon we met the senator's secretary. Gertrude Stein drove the senator's secretary home in Godiva.

As it turned out the senator's secretary had tried to learn to drive a car and had not succeeded. The way in which Gertrude Stein made her way through Paris traffic with the ease and indifference of a chauffeur, and was at the same time a well known author impressed her immensely. She said she would get Mildred Aldrich's papers out of the pigeon hole in which they were probably reposing and she did. Very shortly after the mayor of Mildred's village called upon her one morning on official business. He presented her with the preliminary papers to be signed for the legion of honour. He said to her, you must remember, Mademoiselle, these matters often start but do not get themselves accomplished. So you must be prepared for disappointment. Mildred answered quietly, monsieur le maire, if my friends have started a matter of this kind they will see to it that it is accomplished. And it was. When we arrived at Avignon on our way to Saint-Rémy there was a telegram telling us that Mildred had her decoration. We were delighted and Mildred Aldrich to the day of her death never lost her pride and pleasure in her honour.

During these early restless years after the war Gertrude Stein worked a great deal. Not as in the old days, night after night, but anywhere, in between visits, in the automobile while she was waiting in the street while I did errands, while posing. She was particularly fond in these days of working in the automobile while it stood in the crowded streets.

It was then that she wrote Finer Than Melanctha as a joke. Harold Loeb, at that time editing Broom all by himself, said he would like to have something of hers that would be as fine as Melanctha, her early negro story in Three Lives.

She was much influenced by the sound of the streets and the movement of the automobiles. She also liked then to set a sentence for herself as a sort of tuning fork and metronome and then write to that time and tune. Mildred's Thoughts, published in The American Caravan, was one of these experiments she thought most successful. The Birthplace of Bonnes, published in The Little Review, was another one. Moral Tales of 1920–1921, American Biography, and One Hundred Prominent Men, when as she said she created out of her imagination one hundred men equally men and all equally prominent were written then. These two were later printed in Useful Knowledge.

It was also about this time that Harry Gibb came back to Paris for a short while. He was very anxious that Gertrude Stein should publish a book of her work showing what she had been doing in those years. Not a little book, he kept saying, a big book, something they can get their teeth into. You must do it, he used to say. But no publisher will look at it now that John Lane is no longer active, she said. It makes no difference, said Harry Gibb violently, it is the essence of the thing that they must see and you must have a lot of things printed, and then turning to me he said, Alice you do it. I knew he was right and that it had to be done. But how.

I talked to Kate Buss about it and she suggested the Four Seas Company who had done a little book for her. I began a correspondence with Mr. Brown, Honest to God Brown as Gertrude Stein called him in imitation of William Cook's phrase when everything was going particularly wrong. The arrangements with Honest to God having finally been made we left for the south in July, nineteen twenty-two.

We started off in Godiva, the runabout ford and followed by Janet Scudder in a second Godiva accompanied by Mrs. Lane. They were going to Grasse to buy themselves a home, they finally bought one near Aix-en-Provence. And we were going to Saint-Rémy to visit in peace the country we had loved during the war.

We were only a hundred or so kilometres from Paris when Janet Scudder tooted her horn which was the signal agreed upon for us to stop and wait. Janet came alongside. I think, said she solemnly, Gertrude Stein always called her The Doughboy, she always said there were only two perfectly solemn things on earth, the doughboy and Janet Scudder. Janet had also, Gertrude Stein always said, all the subtlety of the doughboy and all his nice ways and all his lonesomeness. Janet came alongside, I think, she said solemnly, we are not on the right road, it says Paris-Perpignan and I want to go to Grasse.

Anyway at the time we got no further than Lorme and there we suddenly realised how tired we were. We were just tired.

We suggested that the others should move on to Grasse but they said they too would wait and we all waited. It was the first time we had just stayed still since Palma de Mallorca, since 1916. Finally we moved slowly on to Saint-Rémy and they went further to Grasse and then came back. They asked us what we were going to do and we answered, nothing just stay here. So they went off again and bought a property in Aix-en-Provence.

Janet Scudder, as Gertrude Stein always said, had the real pioneer's passion for buying useless real estate. In every little town we stopped on the way Janet would find a piece of property that she considered purchasable and Gertrude Stein, violently protesting, got her away. She wanted to buy property everywhere except in Grasse where she had gone to buy property. She finally did buy a house and grounds in Aix-en-Provence after insisting on Gertrude Stein's seeing it who told her not to and telegraphed no and telephoned no. However Janet did buy it but luckily after a year she was able to get rid of it. During that year we stayed quietly in Saint-Rémy.

We had intended staying only a month or two but we stayed all winter. With the exception of an occasional interchange of visits with Janet Scudder we saw no one except the people of the country. We went to Avignon to shop, we went now and then into the country we had known so well but for the most part we wandered around Saint-Rémy, we went up into the

Alpilles, the little hills that Gertrude Stein described over and over again in the writing of that winter, we watched the enormous flocks of sheep going up into the mountains led by the donkeys and their water bottles, we sat above the roman monuments and we went often to Les Baux. The hotel was not very comfortable but we stayed on. The valley of the Rhône was once more exercising its spell over us.

It was during this winter that Gertrude Stein meditated upon the use of grammar, poetical forms and what might be termed landscape plays.

It was at this time that she wrote Elucidation, printed in transition in nineteen twenty-seven. It was her first effort to state her problems of expression and her attempts to answer them. It was her first effort to realise clearly just what her writing meant and why it was as it was. Later on much later she wrote her treatises on grammar, sentences, paragraphs, vocabulary etcetera, which I have printed in Plain Edition under the title of How To Write.

It was in Saint-Rémy and during this winter that she wrote the poetry that has so greatly influenced the younger generation. Her Capital Capitals, Virgil Thomson has put to music. Lend a Hand or Four Religions has been printed in Useful Knowledge. This play has always interested her immensely, it was the first attempt that later made her Operas and Plays, the first conception of landscape as a play. She also at that time wrote the Valentine to Sherwood Anderson, also printed in the volume Useful Knowledge, Indian Boy, printed later in the Reviewer, (Carl Van Vechten sent Hunter Stagg to us a young Southerner as attractive as his name), and Saints In Seven, which she used to illustrate her work in her lectures at Oxford and Cambridge, and Talks to Saints in Saint-Rémy.

She worked in those days with slow care and concentration, and was very preoccupied.

Finally we received the first copies of Geography and Plays, the winter was over and we went back to Paris.

This long winter in Saint-Rémy broke the restlessness of the war and the after war. A great many things were to happen, there were to be friendships and there were to be enmities and there were to be a great many other things but there was not to be any restlessness.

Gertrude Stein always says that she only has two real distractions, pictures and automobiles. Perhaps she might now add dogs.

Immediately after the war her attention was attracted by the work of a young french painter, Fabre, who had a natural feeling for objects on a table and landscapes but he came to nothing. The next painter who attracted her attention was André Masson. Masson was at that time influenced by Juan Gris in whom Gertrude Stein's interest was permanent and vital. She was interested in André Masson as a painter particularly as a painter of white and she was interested in his composition in the wandering line in his compositions. Soon Masson fell under the influence of the surréalistes.

The surréalistes are the vulgarisation of Picabia as Delaunay and his followers and the futurists were the vulgarisation of Picasso. Picabia had conceived and is struggling with the problem that a line should have the vibration of a musical sound and that this vibration should be the result of conceiving the human form and the human face in so tenuous a fashion that it would induce such vibration in the line forming it. It is his way of achieving the disembodied. It was this idea that conceived mathematically influenced Marcel Duchamp and produced his The Nude Descending the Staircase.

All his life Picabia has struggled to dominate and achieve this conception. Gertrude Stein thinks that perhaps he is now approaching the solution of his problem. The surréalistes taking the manner for the matter as is the way of the vulgarisers, accept the line as having become vibrant and as therefore able in itself to inspire them to higher flights. He who is going to be the creator of the vibrant line knows that it is not yet created and if it were it would not exist by itself, it would be dependent upon the emotion of the object which compels the vibration. So much for the creator and his followers.

Gertrude Stein, in her work, has always been possessed by the intellectual passion for exactitude in the description of inner and outer reality. She has produced a simplification by this concentration, and as a result the destruction of associational emotion in poetry and prose. She knows that beauty, music, decoration, the result of emotion should never be the cause, even events should not be the cause of emotion nor should they be the material of poetry and prose. Nor should emotion itself be the cause of poetry or prose. They should consist of an exact reproduction of either an outer or an inner reality.

It was this conception of exactitude that made the close understanding between Gertrude Stein and Juan Gris.

Juan Gris also conceived exactitude but in him exactitude had a mystical basis. As a mystic it was necessary for him to be exact. In Gertrude Stein the necessity was intellectual, a pure passion for exactitude. It is because of this that her work has often been compared to that of mathematicians and by a certain french critic to the work of Bach.

Picasso by nature the most endowed had less clarity of intellectual purpose. He was in his creative activity dominated by spanish ritual, later by negro ritual expressed in negro sculpture (which has an arab basis the basis also of spanish ritual) and later by russian ritual. His creative activity being tremendously dominant, he made these great rituals over into his own image.

Juan Gris was the only person whom Picasso wished away. The relation between them was just that.

In the days when the friendship between Gertrude Stein and Picasso had become if possible closer than before, (it was for his little boy, born February fourth to her February third, that she wrote her birthday book with a line for each day in the year) in those days her intimacy with Juan Gris displeased him. Once after a show of Juan's pictures at the Gallérie Simon he said to her with violence, tell me why you stand up for his work, you know you do not like it; and she did not answer him.

Later when Juan died and Gertrude Stein was heart broken Picasso came to the house and spent all day there. I do not know what was said but I do know that at one time Gertrude Stein said to him bitterly, you have no right to mourn, and he said, you have no right to say that to me. You never realised his meaning because you did not have it, she said angrily. You know very well I did, he replied.

The most moving thing Gertrude Stein has ever written is The Life and Death of Juan Gris. It was printed in transition and later on translated into german for his retrospective show in Berlin.

A Transatlantic, painting by Juan Gris

Picasso never wished Braque away. Picasso said once when he and Gertrude Stein were talking together, yes, Braque and James Joyce, they are the incomprehensibles whom anybody can understand. Les incompréhensibles que tout le monde peut comprendre.

The first thing that happened when we were back in Paris was Hemingway with a letter of introduction from Sherwood Anderson.

I remember very well the impression I had of Hemingway that first afternoon. He was an extraordinarily good-looking young man, twenty-three years old. It was not long after that that everybody was twenty-six. It became the period of being twenty-six. During the next two or three years all the young men were twenty-six years old. It was the right age apparently for that time and place. There were one or two under twenty, for example George Lynes but they did not count as Gertrude Stein carefully explained to them. If they were young men they were twenty-six. Later on, much later on they were twenty-one and twenty-two.

So Hemingway was twenty-three, rather foreign looking, with passionately interested, rather than interesting eyes. He sat in front of Gertrude Stein and listened and looked.

They talked then, and more and more, a great deal together. He asked her to come and spend an evening in their apartment and look at his work. Hemingway had then and has always a very good instinct for finding apartments in strange but pleasing localities and good femmes de ménage and good food. This his first apartment was just off the place du Tertre. We spent the evening there and he and Gertrude Stein went over all the writing he had done up to that time. He had begun the novel that it was inevitable he would begin and there were the little poems afterwards printed by Mc-Almon in the Contact Edition. Gertrude Stein rather liked the poems, they were direct, Kiplingesque, but the novel she found wanting. There is a great deal of description in this, she said, and not particularly good description. Begin over again and concentrate, she said.

Hemingway was at this time Paris correspondent for a canadian newspaper. He was obliged there to express what he called the canadian viewpoint.

He and Gertrude Stein used to walk together and talk together a great deal. One day she said to him, look here, you say you and your wife have a little money between you. Is it enough to live on if you live quietly. Yes, he said. Well, she said, then do it. If you keep on doing newspaper work you will never see things, you will only see words and that will not do, that is of course if you intend to be a writer. Hemingway said he undoubtedly intended to be a writer. He and his wife went away on a trip and shortly after Hemingway turned up alone. He came to the house about ten o'clock in the morning and he stayed, he stayed for lunch, he stayed all afternoon, he stayed for dinner and he stayed until about ten o'clock at night and then all of a sudden he announced that his wife was enceinte and then with great bitterness, and I, I am too young to be a father. We consoled him as best we could and sent him on his way.

When they came back Hemingway said that he had made up his mind. They would go back to America and he would work hard for a year and with what he would earn and what they had they would settle down and he would give up newspaper work and make himself a writer. They went away and well within the prescribed year they came back with a new born baby. Newspaper work was over.

The first thing to do when they came back was as they thought to get the baby baptised. They wanted Gertrude Stein and myself to be god-mothers and an english war comrade of Hemingway was to be god-father. We were all born of different religions and most of us were not practising any, so it was rather difficult to know in what church the baby could be baptised. We spent a great deal of time that winter, all of us, discussing the matter. Finally it was decided that it should be baptised episcopalian and episcopalian it was. Just how it was managed with the assortment of god-parents I am sure I do not know, but it was baptised in the episcopalian chapel.

Writer or painter god-parents are notoriously unreliable. That is, there is certain before long to be a cooling of friendship. I know several cases of this, poor Paulot Picasso's god-parents have wandered out of sight and just as naturally it is a long time since any of us have seen or heard of our Hemingway god-child.

However in the beginning we were active god-parents, I particularly. I embroidered a little chair and I knitted a gay coloured garment for the god-child. In the meantime the god-child's father was very earnestly at work making himself a writer.

Gertrude Stein never corrects any detail of anybody's writing, she sticks strictly to general principles, the way of seeing what the writer chooses to see, and the relation between that vision and the way it gets down. When the vision is not complete the words are flat, it is very simple, there can be no mistake about it, so she insists. It was at this time that Hemingway began the short things that afterwards were printed in a volume called In Our Time.

One day Hemingway came in very excited about Ford Madox Ford and the Transatlantic. Ford Madox Ford had started the Transatlantic some months before. A good many years before, indeed before the war, we had met Ford Madox Ford who was at that time Ford Madox Hueffer. He was married to Violet Hunt and Violet Hunt and Gertrude Stein were next to each other at the tea table and talked a great deal together. I was next to Ford Madox Hueffer and I liked him very much and I liked his stories of Mistral and Tarascon and I liked his having been followed about in that land of the french royalist, on account of his resemblance to the Bourbon claimant. I had never seen the Bourbon claimant but Ford at that time undoubtedly might have been a Bourbon.

We had heard that Ford was in Paris, but we had not happened to meet. Gertrude Stein had however seen copies of the Transatlantic and found it interesting but had thought nothing further about it.

Hemingway came in then very excited and said that Ford wanted something of Gertrude Stein's for the next number and he, Hemingway, wanted The Making of Americans to be run in it as a serial and he had to have the first fifty pages at once. Gertrude Stein was of course quite overcome with her excitement at this idea, but there was no copy of the manuscript except the one that we had had bound. That makes no difference, said Hemingway, I will copy it. And he and I between us did copy it and it was printed in the next number of the Transatlantic. So for the first time a piece of the monumental work which was the beginning, really the beginning of modern writing, was printed, and we were very happy. Later on when things were difficult between Gertrude Stein and Hemingway, she always remembered with gratitude that after all it was Hemingway who first caused to be printed a piece of The Making of Americans. She always says, yes sure I have a weakness for Hemingway. After all he was the first of the young men to knock at my door and he did make Ford print the first piece of The Making of Americans.

I myself have not so much confidence that Hemingway did do this. I have never known what the story is but I have always been certain that there was some other story behind it all. That is the way I feel about it.

Gertrude Stein and Sherwood Anderson are very funny on the subject of Hemingway. The last time that Sherwood was in Paris they often talked about him. Hemingway had been formed by the two of them and they were both a little proud and a little ashamed of the work of their minds. Hemingway had at one moment, when he had repudiated Sherwood Anderson and all his works, written him a letter in the name of american literature which he, Hemingway, in company with his contemporaries was about to save, telling Sherwood just what he, Hemingway thought about Sherwood's work, and, that thinking, was in no sense complimentary. When Sherwood came to Paris Hemingway naturally was afraid. Sherwood as naturally was not.

As I say he and Gertrude Stein were endlessly amusing on the subject. They admitted that Hemingway was yellow, he is, Gertrude Stein insisted, just like the flat-boat men on the Mississippi river as described by Mark Twain. But what a book, they both agreed, would be the real story of Hemingway, not those he writes but the confessions of the real Ernest Hemingway. It would be for another audience than the audience Hemingway now has but it would be very wonderful. And then they both agreed that they have a weakness for Hemingway because he is such a good pupil. He is a rotten pupil, I protested. You don't understand, they both said, it is so flattering to have a pupil who does it without understanding it, in other words he takes training and anybody who takes training is a favourite pupil. They both admit it to be a weakness. Gertrude Stein added further, you see he is like Derain. You remember Monsieur de Tuille said, when I did not understand why Derain was having the success he was having that it was because he looks like a modern and he smells of the museums. And that is Hemingway, he looks like a modern and he smells of the museums. But what a story that of the real Hem, and one he should tell himself but alas he never will. After all, as he himself once murmured, there is the career, the career.

But to come back to the events that were happening.

Hemingway did it all. He copied the manuscript and corrected the proof. Correcting proofs is, as I said before, like dusting, you learn the values of the thing as no reading suffices to teach it to you. In correcting these proofs Hemingway learned a great deal and he admired all that he learned. It was at this time that he wrote to Gertrude Stein saying that it was she who had done the work in writing The Making of Americans and he and all his had but to devote their lives to seeing that it was published.

He had hopes of being able to accomplish this. Some one, I think by the name of Sterne, said that he could place it with a publisher. Gertrude Stein and Hemingway believed that he could, but soon Hemingway reported that Sterne had entered into his period of unreliability. That was the end of that.

In the meantime and sometime before this Mina Loy had brought McAlmon to the house and he came from time to time and he brought his wife and brought William Carlos Williams. And finally he wanted to print The Making of Americans in the Contact Edition and finally he did. I will come to that.

In the meantime McAlmon had printed the three poems and ten stories of Hemingway and William Bird had printed In Our Time and Hemingway was getting to be known. He was coming to know Dos Passos and Fitzgerald and Bromfield and George Antheil and everybody else and Harold Loeb was once more in Paris. Hemingway had become a writer. He was also a shadow-boxer, thanks to Sherwood, and he heard about bull-fighting from me. I have always loved spanish dancing and spanish bull-fighting and I loved to show the photographs of bull-fighters and bull-fighting. I also loved to show the photograph where Gertrude Stein and I were in the front row and had our picture taken there accidentally. In these days Hemingway was teaching some young chap how to box. The boy did not know how, but by accident he knocked Hemingway out. I believe this sometimes happens. At any rate in these days Hemingway although a sportsman was easily tired. He used to get quite worn out walking from his house to ours. But then he had been worn by the war. Even now he is, as Hélène says all men are, fragile. Recently a robust friend of his said to Gertrude Stein, Ernest is very fragile, whenever he does anything sporting something breaks, his arm, his leg, or his head.

In those early days Hemingway liked all his contemporaries except Cummings. He accused Cummings of having copied everything, not from anybody but from somebody. Gertrude Stein who had been much impressed by The Enormous Room said that Cummings did not copy, he was the natural heir of the New England tradition with its aridity and its sterility, but also with its individuality. They disagreed about this. They also disagreed about Sherwood Anderson. Gertrude Stein contended that Sherwood Anderson had a genius for using the sentence to convey a direct emotion, this was in the great american tradition, and that really except Sherwood there was no one in America who could write a clear and passionate sentence. Hemingway did not believe this, he did not like Sherwood's taste. Taste has nothing to do with sentences, contended Gertrude Stein. She also added that Fitzgerald was the only one of the younger writers who wrote naturally in sentences.

Gertrude Stein and Fitzgerald are very peculiar in their relation to each other. Gertrude Stein had been very much impressed by This Side of Paradise. She read it when it came out and before she knew any of the young american writers. She said of it that it was this book that really created for the public the new generation. She has never changed her opinion about this. She thinks this equally true of The Great Gatsby. She thinks Fitzgerald will be read when many of his well known contemporaries are forgotten. Fitzgerald always says that he thinks Gertrude Stein says these things just to annoy him by making him think that she means them, and he adds in his favourite way, and her doing it is the cruellest thing I ever heard. They always however have a very good time when they meet. And the last time they met they had a good time with themselves and Hemingway.

Then there was McAlmon. McAlmon had one quality that appealed to Gertrude Stein, abundance, he could go on writing, but she complained that it was dull.

There was also Glenway Wescott but Glenway Wescott at no time interested Gertrude Stein. He has a certain syrup but it does not pour.

So then Hemingway's career was begun. For a little while we saw less of him and then he began to come again. He used to recount to Gertrude Stein the conversations that he afterwards used in The Sun Also Rises and they talked endlessly about the character of Harold Loeb. At this time Hemingway was preparing his volume of short stories to submit to publishers in America. One evening after we had not seen him for a while he turned up with Shipman. Shipman was an amusing boy who was to inherit a few thousand dollars when he came of age. He was not of age. He was to buy the Transatlantic Review when he came of age, so Hemingway said. He was to support a surrealist review when he came of age, André Masson said. He was to buy a house in the country when he came of age, Josette Gris said. As a matter of fact when he came of age nobody who had known him then seemed to know what he did do with his inheritance. Hemingway brought him with him to the house to talk about buying the Transatlantic and incidentally he brought the manuscript he intended sending to America. He handed it to Gertrude Stein. He had added to his stories a little story of meditations and in these he said that The Enormous Room was the greatest book he had ever read. It was then that Gertrude Stein said, Hemingway, remarks are not literature.

After this we did not see Hemingway for quite a while and then we went to see some one, just after The Making of Americans was printed, and Hemingway who was there came up to Gertrude Stein and began to explain why he would not be able to write a review of the book. Just then a heavy hand fell on his shoulder and Ford Madox Ford said, young man it is I who wish to speak to Gertrude Stein. Ford then said to her, I wish to ask your permission to dedicate my new book to you. May I. Gertrude Stein and I were both awfully pleased and touched.

For some years after this Gertrude Stein and Hemingway did not meet. And then we heard that he was back in Paris and telling a number of people how much he wanted to see her. Don't you come home with Hemingway on your arm, I used to say when she went out for a walk. Sure enough one day she did come back bringing him with her.

They sat and talked a long time. Finally I heard her say, Hemingway, after all you are ninety percent Rotarian. Can't you, he said, make it eighty percent. No, said she regretfully, I can't. After all, as she always says, he did, and I may say, he does have moments of disinterestedness.

After that they met quite often. Gertrude Stein always says she likes to see him, he is so wonderful. And if he could only tell his own story. In their last conversation she accused him of having killed a great many of his rivals and put them under the sod. I never, said Hemingway, seriously killed anybody but one man and he was a bad man and, he deserved it, but if I killed anybody else I did it unknowingly, and so I am not responsible.

It was Ford who once said of Hemingway, he comes and sits at my feet and praises me. It makes me nervous. Hemingway also said once, I turn my flame which is a small one down and down and then suddenly there is a big explosion. If there were nothing but explosions my work would be so exciting nobody could bear it.

However, whatever I say, Gertrude Stein always says, yes I know but I have a weakness for Hemingway.

Jane Heap turned up one afternoon. The Little Review had printed the Birthplace of Bonnes and The Valentine to Sherwood Anderson. Jane Heap sat down and we began to talk. She stayed to dinner and she stayed the evening and by dawn the little ford car Godiva which had been burning its lights all night waiting to be taken home could hardly start to take Jane home. Gertrude Stein then and always liked Jane Heap immensely, Margaret Anderson interested her much less.

It was now once more summer and this time we went to the Côte d'Azur and joined the Picassos at Antibes. It was there I first saw Picasso's mother. Picasso looks extraordinarily like her. Gertrude Stein and Madame Picasso had difficulty in talking not having a common language but they talked enough to amuse themselves. They were talking about Picasso when Gertrude Stein first knew him. He was remarkably beautiful then, said Gertrude Stein, he was illuminated as if he wore a halo. Oh, said Madame Picasso, if you thought him beautiful then I assure you it was nothing compared to his looks when he was a boy. He was an angel and a devil in beauty, no one could cease looking at him. And now, said Picasso a little resentfully. Ah now, said they together, ah now there is no such beauty left. But, added his mother, you are very sweet and as a son very perfect. So he had to be satisfied with that.

It was at this time that Jean Cocteau who prides himself on being eternally thirty was writing a little biography of Picasso, and he sent him a telegram asking him to tell him the date of his birth. And yours, telegraphed back Picasso.

There are so many stories about Picasso and Jean Cocteau. Picasso like Gertrude Stein is easily upset if asked to do something suddenly and Jean Cocteau does this quite successfully. Picasso resents it and revenges himself at greater length. Not long ago there was a long story.

Picasso was in Spain, in Barcelona, and a friend of his youth who was editor of a paper printed, not in spanish but in catalan, interviewed him. Picasso knowing that the interview to be printed in catalan was probably never going to be printed in spanish, thoroughly enjoyed himself. He said that Jean Cocteau was getting to be very popular in Paris, so popular that you could find his poems on the table of any smart coiffeur.

As I say he thoroughly enjoyed himself in giving this interview and then returned to Paris.

Some catalan in Barcelona sent the paper to some catalan friend in Paris and the catalan friend in Paris translated it to a french friend and the french friend printed the interview in a french paper.

Picasso and his wife told us the story together of what happened then. As soon as Jean saw the article, he tried to see Pablo. Pablo refused to see him, he told the maid to say that he was always out and for days they could not answer the telephone. Cocteau finally stated in an interview given to the french press that the interview which had wounded him so sorely had turned out to be an interview with Picabia and not an interview with Picasso, his friend. Picabia of course denied this. Cocteau implored Picasso to give a public denial. Picasso remained discreetly at home.

The first evening the Picassos went out they went to the theatre and there in front of them seated was Jean Cocteau's mother. At the first intermission they went up to her, and surrounded by all their mutual friends she said, my dear, you cannot imagine the relief to me and to Jean to know that it was not you that gave out that vile interview, do tell me that it was not.

And as Picasso's wife said, I as a mother could not let a mother suffer and I said of course it was not Picasso and Picasso said, yes yes of course it was not, and so the public retraction was given.

It was this summer that Gertrude Stein, delighting in the movement of the tiny waves on the Antibes shore, wrote the Completed Portrait of Picasso, the Second Portrait of Carl Van Vechten, and The Book Concluding With As A Wife Has A Cow A Love Story this afterwards beautifully illustrated by Juan Gris.

Robert McAlmon had definitely decided to publish The Making of Americans, and we were to correct proofs that summer. The summer before we had intended as usual to meet the Picassos at Antibes. I had been reading the Guide des Gourmets and I had found among other places where one ate well, Pernollet's Hôtel in the town of Belley. Belley is its name and Belley is its nature, as Gertrude Stein's elder brother remarked. We arrived there about the middle of August. On the map it looked as if it were high up in the mountains and Gertrude Stein does not like precipices and as we drove through the gorge I was nervous and she protesting, but finally the country opened out delightfully and we arrived in Belley. It was a pleasant hotel although it had no garden and we had intended that it should have a garden. We stayed on for several days.

Then Madame Pernollet, a pleasant round faced woman said to us that since we were evidently staying on why did we not make rates by the day or by the week. We said we would. In the meanwhile the Picassos wanted to know what had become of us. We replied that we were in Belley. We found that Belley was the birthplace of Brillat-Savarin. We now in Bilignin are enjoying using the furniture from the house of Brillat-Savarin which house belongs to the owner of this house.

We also found that Lamartine had been at school in Belley and Gertrude Stein says that wherever Lamartine stayed any length of time one eats well. Madame Récamier also comes from this region and the place is full of descendants of her husband's family. All these things we found out gradually but for the moment we were comfortable and we stayed on and left late. The following summer we were to correct proofs of The Making of Americans and so we left Paris early and came again to Belley. What a summer it was.

The Making of Americans is a book one thousand pages long, closely printed on large pages. Darantière has told me it has five hundred and sixty-five thousand words. It was written in nineteen hundred and six to nineteen hundred and eight, and except for the sections printed in Transatlantic it was all still in manuscript.

The sentences as the book goes on get longer and longer, they are sometimes pages long and the compositors were french, and when they made mistakes and left out a line the effort of getting it back again was terrific.

We used to leave the hotel in the morning with camp chairs, lunch and proof, and all day we struggled with the errors of French compositors. Proof had to be corrected most of it four times and finally I broke my glasses, my eyes gave out, and Gertrude Stein finished alone.

We used to change the scene of our labours and we found lovely spots but there were always to accompany us those endless pages of printers' errors. One of our favourite hillocks where we could see Mont Blanc in the distance we called Madame Mont Blanc.

Another place we went to often was near a little pool made by a small stream near a country cross-road. This was quite like the middle ages, so many things used to happen there, in a very simple middle age way. I remember once a country-man came up to us leading his oxen. Very politely he said, ladies is there anything the matter with me. Why yes, we replied, your face is covered with blood. Oh, he said, you see my oxen were slipping down the hill and I held them back and I too slipped and I wondered if anything had happened to me. We helped him wash the blood off and he went on.

It was during this summer that Gertrude Stein began two long things, A Novel and the Phenomena of Nature which was to lead later to the whole series of meditations on grammar and sentences.

It led first to An Acquaintance With Description, afterwards printed by the Seizin Press. She began at this time to describe landscape as if anything she saw was a natural phenomenon, a thing existent in itself, and she found it, this exercise, very interesting and it finally led her to the later series of Operas and Plays. I am trying to be as commonplace as I can be, she used to say to me. And then sometimes a little worried, it is not too commonplace. The last thing that she has finished, Stanzas of Meditation, and which I am now typewriting, she considers her real achievement of the commonplace.

But to go back. We returned to Paris, the proofs almost done, and Jane Heap was there. She was very excited. She had a wonderful plan, I have now quite forgotten what it was, but Gertrude Stein was enormously pleased with it. It had something to do with a plan for another edition of The Making of Americans in America.

At any rate in the various complications connected with this matter McAlmon became very angry and not without reason, and The Making of Americans appeared but McAlmon and Gertrude Stein were no longer friends.

When Gertrude Stein was quite young her brother once remarked to her, that she, having been born in February, was very like George Washington, she was impulsive and slow-minded. Undoubtedly a great many complications have been the result.

One day in this same spring we were going to visit a new

spring salon. Jane Heap had been telling us of a young russian in whose work she was interested. As we were crossing a bridge in Godiva we saw Jane Heap and the young russian. We saw his pictures and Gertrude Stein too was interested. He of course came to see us.

In How To Write Gertrude Stein makes this sentence, Painting now after its great period has come back to be a minor art.

She was very interested to know who was to be the leader of this art.

This is the story.

The young russian was interesting. He was painting, so he said, colour that was no colour, he was painting blue pictures and he was painting three heads in one. Picasso had been drawing three heads in one. Soon the russian was painting three figures in one. Was he the only one. In a way he was although there was a group of them. This group, very shortly after Gertrude Stein knew the russian, had a show at one of the art galleries, Druet's I think. The group then consisted of the russian, a frenchman, a very young dutchman, and two russian brothers. All of them except the dutchman about twenty-six years old.

At this show Gertrude Stein met George Antheil who asked to come to see her and when he came he brought with him Virgil Thomson. Gertrude Stein had not found George Antheil particularly interesting although she liked him, but Virgil Thomson she found very interesting although I did not like him.

However all this I will tell about later. To go back now to painting.

The russian Tchelitchev's work was the most vigorous of the group and the most mature and the most interesting. He had already then a passionate enmity against the frenchman whom they called Bébé Bérard and whose name was Christian Bérard and whom Tchelitchev said copied everything.

René Crevel had been the friend of all these painters. Some time later one of them was to have a one man show at the Gallérie Pierre. We were going to it and on the way we met René. We all stopped, he was exhilarated with exasperation. He talked with his characteristic brilliant violence. These painters, he said, sell their pictures for several thousand francs apiece and they have the pretentiousness which comes from being valued in terms of money, and we writers who have twice their quality and infinitely greater vitality cannot earn a living and have to beg and intrigue to induce publishers to publish us; but the time will come, and René became prophetic, when these same painters will come to us to re-create them and then we will contemplate them with indifference.

René was then and has remained ever since a devout surréaliste. He needs and needed, being a frenchman, an intellectual as well as a basal justification for the passionate exaltation in him. This he could not find, being of the immediate postwar generation, in either religion or patriotism, the war having destroyed for his generation, both patriotism and religion as a passion. Surréalisme has been his justification. It has clarified for him the confused negation in which he lived and loved. This he alone of his generation has really succeeded in expressing, a little in his earlier books, and in his last book, The Clavecin of Diderot very adequately and with the brilliant violence that is his quality.

Gertrude Stein was at first not interested in this group of painters as a group but only in the russian. This interest gradually increased and then she was bothered. Granted, she used to say, that the influences which make a new movement in art and literature have continued and are making a new movement in art and literature; in order to seize these influences and create as well as re-create them there needs a very dominating creative power. This the russian manifestly did not have. Still there was a distinctly new creative idea. Where had it come from. Gertrude Stein always says to the young painters when they complain that she changes her mind about their work, it is not I that change my mind about the pictures, but the paintings disappear into the wall, I do not see them any more and then they go out of the door naturally.

In the meantime as I have said George Antheil had brought Virgil Thomson to the house and Virgil Thomson and Gertrude Stein became friends and saw each other a great deal. Virgil Thomson had put a number of Gertrude Stein's things to music, Susie Asado, Preciosilla and Capital Capitals. Gertrude Stein was very much interested in Virgil Thomson's music. He had understood Satie undoubtedly and he had a comprehension quite his own of prosody. He understood a great deal of Gertrude Stein's work, he used to dream at night that there was something there that he did not understand, but on the whole he was very well content with that which he did understand. She delighted in listening to her words framed by his music. They saw a great deal of each other.

Virgil had in his room a great many pictures by Christian Bérard and Gertrude Stein used to look at them a great deal. She could not find out at all what she thought about them.

She and Virgil Thomson used to talk about them endlessly. Virgil said he knew nothing about pictures but he thought these wonderful. Gertrude Stein told him about her perplexity about the new movement and that the creative power behind it was not the russian. Virgil said that there he quite agreed with her and he was convinced that it was Bébé Bérard, baptised Christian. She said that perhaps that was the answer but she was very doubtful. She used to say of Bérard's pictures, they are almost something and then they are just not. As she used to explain to Virgil, the Catholic Church makes a very sharp distinction between a hysteric and a saint. The same thing holds true in the art world. There is the sensitiveness of the hysteric which has all the appearance of creation, but actual creation has an individual force which is an entirely different thing. Gertrude Stein was inclined to believe that artistically Bérard was more hysteric than saint. At this time she had come back to portrait writing with renewed vigour and she, to clarify her mind, as she said, did portraits of the russian and of the frenchman. In the meantime, through Virgil Thomson, she had met a young frenchman named Georges Hugnet. He and Gertrude Stein became very devoted to one another. He liked the sound of her writing and then he liked the sense and he liked the sentences.

At his home were a great many portraits of himself painted by his friends. Among others one by one of the two russian brothers and one by a young englishman. Gertrude Stein was not particularly interested in any of these portraits. There was however a painting of a hand by this young englishman which she did not like but which she remembered.

Every one began at this time to be very occupied with their

own affairs. Virgil Thomson had asked Gertrude Stein to write an opera for him. Among the saints there were two saints whom she had always liked better than any others, Saint Theresa of Avila and Ignatius Loyola, and she said she would write him an opera about these two saints. She began this and worked very hard at it all that spring and finally finished Four Saints and gave it to Virgil Thomson to put to music. He did. And it is a completely interesting opera both as to words and music.

All these summers we had continued to go to the hotel in Belley. We now had become so fond of this country, always the valley of the Rhône, and of the people of the country, and the trees of the country, and the oxen of the country, that we began looking for a house. One day we saw the house of our dreams across a valley. Go and ask the farmer there whose house that is, Gertrude Stein said to me. I said, nonsense it is an important house and it is occupied. Go and ask him, she said. Very reluctantly I did. He said, well yes, perhaps it is for rent, it belongs to a little girl, all her people are dead and I think there is a lieutenant of the regiment stationed in Belley living there now, but I understand they were to leave. You might go and see the agent of the property. We did. He was a kindly old farmer who always told us allez doucement, go slowly. We did. We had the promise of the house, which we never saw any nearer than across the valley, as soon as the lieutenant should leave. Finally three years ago the lieutenant went to Morocco and we took the house still only having seen it from across the valley and we have liked it always more.

While we were still staying at the hotel, Natalie Barney came one day and lunched there bringing some friends, among them, the Duchess of Clermont-Tonnerre. Gertrude Stein and she were delighted with one another and the meeting led to many pleasant consequences, but of that later.

To return to the painters. Just after the opera was finished and before leaving Paris we happened to go to a show of pictures at the Gallérie Bonjean. There we met one of the russian brothers, Genia Berman, and Gertrude Stein was not uninterested in his pictures. She went with him to his studio and looked at everything he had ever painted. He seemed to have a purer intelligence than the other two painters who certainly had not created the modern movement, perhaps the idea had been originally his. She asked him, telling her story as she was fond of telling it at that time to any one who would listen, had he originated the idea. He said with an intelligent inner smile that he thought he had. She was not at all sure that he was not right. He came down to Bilignin to see us and she slowly concluded that though he was a very good painter he was too bad a painter to have been the creator of an idea. So once more the search began.

Again just before leaving Paris at this same picture gallery she saw a picture of a poet sitting by a waterfall. Who did that, she said. A young englishman, Francis Rose, was the reply. Oh yes I am not interested in his work. How much is that picture, she said: It cost very little. Gertrude Stein says a picture is either worth three hundred francs or three hundred thousand francs. She bought this for three hundred and we went away for the summer.

Georges Hugnet had decided to become an editor and he began editing the Editions de la Montagne. Actually it was George Maratier, everybody's friend who began this edition, but he decided to go to America and become an american and Georges Hugnet inherited it. The first book to appear was sixty pages in french of The Making of Americans. Gertrude Stein and Georges Hugnet translated them together and she was very happy about it. This was later followed by a volume of Ten Portraits written by Gertrude Stein and illustrated by portraits of the artists of themselves, and of the others drawn by them, Virgil Thomson by Bérard and a drawing of Bérard by himself, a portrait of Tchelitchev by himself, a portrait of Picasso by himself and one of Guillaume Apollinaire and one of Erik Satie by Picasso, one of Kristians Tonny the young dutchman by himself and one of Bernard Faÿ by Tonny. These volumes were very well received and everybody was pleased.

Once more everybody went away.

Gertrude Stein in winter takes her white poodle Basket to be bathed at a vet's and she used to go to the picture gallery where she had bought the englishman's romantic picture and wait for Basket to dry. Every time she came home she brought more pictures by the englishman. She did not talk much about it but they accumulated. Several people began to tell her about this young man and offered to introduce him. Gertrude Stein declined. She said no she had had enough of knowing young painters, she now would content herself with knowing young painting.

In the meantime Georges Hugnet wrote a poem called Enfance. Gertrude Stein offered to translate it for him but instead she wrote a poem about it. This at first pleased Georges Hugnet too much and then did not please him at all. Gertrude Stein then called the poem Before The Flowers Of Friendship Faded Friendship Faded. Everybody mixed themselves up in all this. The group broke up. Gertrude Stein was very upset and then consoled herself by telling all about it in a delightful short story called From Left to Right and which was printed in the London Harper's Bazaar.

It was not long after this that one day Gertrude Stein called in the concierge and asked him to hang up all the Francis Rose pictures, by this time there were some thirty-odd. Gertrude Stein was very much upset while she was having this done. I asked her why she was doing it if it upset her so much. She said she could not help it, that she felt that way about it but to change the whole aspect of the room by adding these thirty pictures was very upsetting. There the matter rested for some time.

To go back again to those days just after the publication of The Making of Americans. There was at that time a review of Gertrude Stein's book Geography and Plays in the Athenaeum signed Edith Sitwell. The review was long and a little condescending but I liked it. Gertrude Stein had not cared for it. A year later in the London Vogue was an article again by Edith Sitwell saying that since writing her article in the Athenaeum she had spent the year reading nothing but Geography and Plays and she wished to say how important and beautiful a book she had found it to be.

One afternoon at Elmer Harden's we met Miss Todd the editor of the London Vogue. She said that Edith Sitwell was to be shortly in Paris and wanted very much to meet Gertrude Stein. She said that Edith Sitwell was very shy and hesitant about coming. Elmer Harden said he would act as escort.

I remember so well my first impression of her, an impression which indeed has never changed. Very tall, bending slightly,

Bilignin from across the valley, painting by Francis Rose

withdrawing and hesitatingly advancing, and beautiful with the most distinguished nose I have ever seen on any human being. At that time and in conversation between Gertrude Stein and herself afterwards, I delighted in the delicacy and completeness of her understanding of poetry. She and Gertrude Stein became friends at once. This friendship like all friendships has had its difficulties but I am convinced that fundamentally Gertrude Stein and Edith Sitwell are friends and enjoy being friends.

We saw a great deal of Edith Sitwell at this time and then she went back to London. In the autumn of that year nineteen twenty-five Gertrude Stein had a letter from the president of the literary society of Cambridge asking her to speak before them in the early spring. Gertrude Stein quite completely upset at the very idea quite promptly answered no. Immediately came a letter from Edith Sitwell saying that the no must be changed to yes. That it was of the first importance that Gertrude Stein should deliver this address and that moreover Oxford was waiting for the yes to be given to Cambridge to ask her to do the same at Oxford.

There was very evidently nothing to do but to say yes and so Gertrude Stein said yes.

She was very upset at the prospect, peace, she said, had much greater terrors than war. Precipices even were nothing to this. She was very low in her mind. Luckily early in January the ford car began to have everything the matter with it. The better garages would not pay much attention to aged fords and Gertrude Stein used to take hers out to a shed in Montrouge where the mechanics worked at it while she sat. If she were to leave it there there would most likely have been nothing left of it to drive away.

One cold dark afternoon she went out to sit with her ford car and while she sat on the steps of another battered ford watching her own being taken to pieces and put together again, she began to write. She stayed there several hours and when she came back chilled, with the ford repaired, she had written the whole of Composition As Explanation.

Once the lecture written the next trouble was the reading of it. Everybody gave her advice. She read it to anybody who came to the house and some of them read it to her. Prichard

happened to be in Paris just then and he and Emily Chad-
bourne between them gave advice and were an audience.
Prichard showed her how to read it in the english manner but
Emily Chadbourne was all for the american manner and
Gertrude Stein was too worried to have any manner. We went
one afternoon to Natalie Barney's. There there was a very
aged and a very charming french professor of history. Natalie
Barney asked him to tell Gertrude Stein how to lecture. Talk
as quickly as you can and never look up, was his advice.
Prichard had said talk as slowly as possible and never look
down. At any rate I ordered a new dress and a new hat for
Gertrude Stein and early in the spring we went to London.

This was the spring of twenty-six and England was still very
strict about passports. We had ours alright but Gertrude Stein
hates to answer questions from officials, it always worries
her and she was already none too happy at the prospect of
lecturing.

So taking both passports I went down stairs to see the officials. Ah, said one of them, and where is Miss Gertrude
Stein. She is on deck, I replied, and she does not care to come
down. She does not care to come down, he repeated, yes that
is quite right, she does not care to come down, and he affixed
the required signatures. So then we arrived in London. Edith
Sitwell gave a party for us and so did her brother Osbert.
Osbert was a great comfort to Gertrude Stein. He so thoroughly understood every possible way in which one could be
nervous that as he sat beside her in the hotel telling her all
the kinds of ways that he and she could suffer from stage
fright she was quite soothed. She was always very fond of
Osbert. She always said he was like an uncle of a king. He had
that pleasant kindly irresponsible agitated calm that an uncle
of an english king always must have.

Finally we arrived in Cambridge in the afternoon, were
given tea and then dined with the president of the society and
some of his friends. It was very pleasant and after dinner we
went to the lecture room. It was a varied audience, men and
women. Gertrude Stein was soon at her ease, the lecture went
off very well, the men afterwards asked a great many questions and were very enthusiastic. The women said nothing.

Gertrude Stein wondered whether they were supposed not to or just did not.

The day after we went to Oxford. There we lunched with young Acton and then went in to the lecture. Gertrude Stein was feeling more comfortable as a lecturer and this time she had a wonderful time. As she remarked afterwards, I felt just like a prima donna.

The lecture room was full, many standing in the back, and the discussion, after the lecture, lasted over an hour and no one left. It was very exciting. They asked all sorts of questions, they wanted to know most often why Gertrude Stein thought she was right in doing the kind of writing she did. She answered that it was not a question of what any one thought but after all she had been doing as she did for about twenty years and now they wanted to hear her lecture. This did not mean of course that they were coming to think that her way was a possible way, it proved nothing, but on the other hand it did possibly indicate something. They laughed. Then up jumped one man, it turned out afterwards that he was a dean, and he said that in the Saints in Seven he had been very interested in the sentence about the ring around the moon, about the ring following the moon. He admitted that the sentence was one of the most beautifully balanced sentences he had ever heard, but still did the ring follow the moon. Gertrude Stein said, when you look at the moon and there is a ring around the moon and the moon moves does not the ring follow the moon. Perhaps it seems to, he replied. Well, in that case how, she said, do you know that it does not; he sat down. Another man, a don, next to him jumped up and asked something else. They did this several times, the two of them, jumping up one after the other. Then the first man jumped up and said, you say that everything being the same everything is always different, how can that be so. Consider, she replied, the two of you, you jump up one after the other, that is the same thing and surely you admit that the two of you are always different. Touché, he said and the meeting was over. One of the men was so moved that he confided to me as we went out that the lecture had been his greatest experience since he had read Kant's Critique of Pure Reason.

Edith Sitwell, Osbert and Sacheverell were all present and were all delighted. They were delighted with the lecture and they were delighted with the good humoured way in which Gertrude Stein had gotten the best of the hecklers. Edith Sitwell said that Sache chuckled about it all the way home.

The next day we returned to Paris. The Sitwells wanted us to stay and be interviewed and generally go on with it but Gertrude Stein felt that she had had enough of glory and excitement. Not, as she always explains, that she could ever have enough of glory. After all, as she always contends, no artist needs criticism, he only needs appreciation. If he needs criticism he is no artist.

Leonard Woolf some months after this published Composition As Explanation in the Hogarth Essay Series. It was also printed in The Dial.

Mildred Aldrich was awfully pleased at Gertrude Stein's english success. She was a good new englander and to her, recognition by Oxford and Cambridge, was even more important than recognition by the Atlantic Monthly. We went out to see her on our return and she had to have the lecture read to her again and to hear every detail of the whole experience.

Mildred Aldrich was falling upon bad days. Her annuity suddenly ceased and for a long time we did not know it. One day Dawson Johnston, the librarian of the American Library, told Gertrude Stein that Miss Aldrich had written to him to come out and get all her books as she would soon be leaving her home. We went out immediately and Mildred told us that her annuity had been stopped. It seems it was an annuity given by a woman who had fallen into her dotage and she one morning told her lawyer to cut off all the annuities that she had given for many years to a number of people. Gertrude Stein told Mildred not to worry. The Carnegie Fund, approached by Kate Buss, sent five hundred dollars, William Cook gave Gertrude Stein a blank cheque to supply all deficiencies, another friend of Mildred's from Providence Rhode Island came forward generously and the Atlantic Monthly started a fund. Very soon Mildred Aldrich was safe. She said ruefully to Gertrude Stein, you would not let me go elegantly to the poorhouse and I would have gone elegantly, but you have turned this into a poor house and I am the sole inmate. Gertrude Stein comforted her and said that she could be just as elegant in her solitary state. After all, Gertrude Stein used to say to her, Mildred nobody can say that you have not had a good run for your money. Mildred Aldrich's last years were safe.

William Cook after the war had been in Russia, in Tiflis, for three years in connection with Red Cross distribution there. One evening he and Gertrude Stein had been out to see Mildred, it was during her last illness and they were coming home one foggy evening. Cook had a small open car but a powerful searchlight, strong enough to pierce the fog. Just behind them was another small car which kept an even pace with them, when Cook drove faster, they drove faster, and when he slowed down, they slowed down. Gertrude Stein said to him, it is lucky for them that you have such a bright light, their lanterns are poor and they are having the benefit of yours. Yes, said Cook, rather curiously, I have been saying that to myself, but you know after three years of Soviet Russia and the Cheka, even I, an american, have gotten to feel a little queer, and I have to talk to myself about it, to be sure that the car behind us is not the car of the secret police.

I said that René Crevel came to the house. Of all the young men who came to the house I think I liked René the best. He had french charm, which when it is at its most charming is more charming even than american charm, charming as that can be. Marcel Duchamp and René Crevel are perhaps the most complete examples of this french charm. We were very fond of René. He was young and violent and ill and revolutionary and sweet and tender. Gertrude Stein and René are very fond of each other, he writes her most delightful english letters, and she scolds him a great deal. It was he who, in early days, first talked to us of Bernard Faÿ. He said he was a young professor in the University of Clermont-Ferrand and he wanted to take us to his house. One afternoon he did take us there. Bernard Faÿ was not at all what Gertrude Stein expected and he and she had nothing in particular to say to each other.

As I remember during that winter and the next we gave a great many parties. We gave a tea party for the Sitwells.

Carl Van Vechten sent us quantities of negroes beside there were the negroes of our neighbour Mrs. Regan who had brought Josephine Baker to Paris. Carl sent us Paul Robeson. Paul Robeson interested Gertrude Stein. He knew american values and american life as only one in it but not of it could know them. And yet as soon as any other person came into the room he became definitely a negro. Gertrude Stein did not like hearing him sing spirituals. They do not belong to you any more than anything else, so why claim them, she said. He did not answer.

Once a southern woman, a very charming southern woman, was there, and she said to him, where were you born, and he answered, in New Jersey, and she said, not in the south, what a pity and he said, not for me.

Gertrude Stein concluded that negroes were not suffering from persecution, they were suffering from nothingness. She always contends that the african is not primitive, he has a very ancient but a very narrow culture and there it remains. Consequently nothing does or can happen.

Carl Van Vechten himself came over for the first time since those far away days of the pleated shirt. All those years he and Gertrude Stein had kept up a friendship and a correspondence. Now that he was actually coming Gertrude Stein was a little worried. When he came they were better friends than ever. Gertrude Stein told him that she had been worried. I wasn't, said Carl.

Among the other young men who came to the house at the time when they came in such numbers was Bravig Imbs. We liked Bravig, even though as Gertrude Stein said, his aim was to please. It was he who brought Elliot Paul to the house and Elliot Paul brought transition.

We had liked Bravig Imbs but we liked Elliot Paul more. He was very interesting. Elliot Paul was a new englander but he was a saracen, a saracen such as you sometimes see in the villages of France where the strain from some Crusading ancestor's dependents still survives. Elliot Paul was such a one. He had an element not of mystery but of evanescence, actually little by little he appeared and then as slowly he disappeared, and Eugene Jolas and Maria Jolas appeared. These once having appeared, stayed in their appearance.

Elliot Paul was at that time working on the Paris Chicago Tribune and he was there writing a series of articles on the work of Gertrude Stein, the first seriously popular estimation of her work. At the same time he was turning the young journalists and proof-readers into writers. He started Bravig Imbs on his first book, The Professor's Wife, by stopping him suddenly in his talk and saying, you begin there. He did the same thing for others. He played the accordion as nobody else not native to the accordion could play it and he learned and played for Gertrude Stein accompanied on the violin by Bravig Imbs, Gertrude Stein's favourite ditty, The Trail of the Lonesome Pine, My name is June and very very soon.

The Trail of the Lonesome Pine as a song made a lasting appeal to Gertrude Stein. Mildred Aldrich had it among her records and when we spent the afternoon with her at Huiry, Gertrude Stein inevitably would start The Trail of the Lonesome Pine on the phonograph and play it and play it. She liked it in itself and she had been fascinated during the war with the magic of The Trail of the Lonesome Pine as a book for the doughboy. How often when a doughboy in hospital had become particularly fond of her, he would say, I once read a great book, do you know it, it is called The Trail of the Lonesome Pine. They finally got a copy of it in the camp at Nîmes and it stayed by the bedside of every sick soldier. They did not read much of it, as far as she could make out sometimes only a paragraph, in the course of several days, but their voices were husky when they spoke of it, and when they were particularly devoted to her they would offer to lend her this very dirty and tattered copy.

She reads anything and naturally she read this and she was puzzled. It had practically no story to it and it was not exciting, or adventurous, and it was very well written and was mostly description of mountain scenery. Later on she came across some reminiscences of a southern woman who told how the mountaineers in the southern army during the civil war used to wait in turn to read Victor Hugo's Les Misérables, an equally astonishing thing for again there is not much of a story and a great deal of description. However Gertrude Stein admits that she loves the song of The Trail of the Lonesome Pine in the same way that the doughboy loved the book and Elliot Paul played it for her on the accordion.

One day Elliot Paul came in very excitedly, he usually seemed to be feeling a great deal of excitement but neither showed nor expressed it. This time however he did show it and express it. He said he wanted to ask Gertrude Stein's advice. A proposition had been made to him to edit a magazine in Paris and he was hesitating whether he should undertake it. Gertrude Stein was naturally all for it. After all, as she said, we do want to be printed. One writes for oneself and strangers but with no adventurous publishers how can one come in contact with those same strangers.

However she was very fond of Elliot Paul and did not want him to take too much risk. No risk, said Elliot Paul, the money for it is guaranteed for a number of years. Well then, said Gertrude Stein, one thing is certain no one could be a better editor than you would be. You are not egotistical and you know what you feel.

Transition began and of course it meant a great deal to everybody. Elliot Paul chose with great care what he wanted to put into transition. He said he was afraid of its becoming too popular. If ever there are more than two thousand subscribers, I quit, he used to say.

He chose Elucidation Gertrude Stein's first effort to explain herself, written in Saint-Rémy to put into the first number of transition. Later As A Wife Has A Cow A Love Story. He was always very enthusiastic about this story. He liked Made A Mile Away, a description of the pictures that Gertrude Stein has liked and later a novelette of desertion If He Thinks, for transition. He had a perfectly definite idea of gradually opening the eyes of the public to the work of the writers that interested him and as I say he chose what he wanted with great care. He was very interested in Picasso and he became very deeply interested in Juan Gris and after his death printed a translation of Juan Gris' defence of painting which had already been printed in french in the Transatlantic Review, and he printed Gertrude Stein's lament, The Life and Death of Juan Gris and her One Spaniard.

Bernard Faÿ and Gertrude Stein at Bilignin

Elliot Paul slowly disappeared and Eugene and Maria Jolas appeared.

Transition grew more bulky. At Gertrude Stein's request transition reprinted Tender Buttons, printed a bibliography of all her work up to date and later printed her opera, Four Saints. For these printings Gertrude Stein was very grateful. In the last numbers of transition nothing of hers appeared. Transition died.

Of all the little magazines which as Gertrude Stein loves to quote, have died to make verse free, perhaps the youngest and freshest was the Blues. Its editor Charles Henri Ford has come to Paris and he is young and fresh as his Blues and also honest which also is a pleasure. Gertrude Stein thinks that he and Robert Coates alone among the young men have an individual sense of words.

During this time Oxford and Cambridge men turned up from time to time at the rue de Fleurus. One of them brought with him Brewer, one of the firm of Payson and Clarke.

Brewer was interested in the work of Gertrude Stein and though he promised nothing he and she talked over the possibilities of his firm printing something of hers. She had just written a shortish novel called A Novel, and was at the time working at another shortish novel which was called Lucy Church Amiably and which she describes as a novel of romantic beauty and nature and which looks like an engraving. She at Brewer's request wrote a summary of this book as an advertisement and he cabled his enthusiasm. However he wished first to commence with a collection of short things and she suggested in that case he should make it all the short things she had written about America and call it Useful Knowledge. This was done.

There are many Paris picture dealers who like adventure in their business, there are no publishers in America who like adventure in theirs. In Paris there are picture dealers like Durand-Ruel who went broke twice supporting the impressionists, Vollard for Cézanne, Sagot for Picasso and Kahnweiler for all the cubists. They make their money as they can and they keep on buying something for which there is no present sale and they do so persistently until they create its public. And these adventurers are adventurous because that is the way they feel about it. There are others who have not chosen as well and have gone entirely broke. It is the tradition among the more adventurous Paris picture dealers to adventure. I suppose there are a great many reasons why publishers do not. John Lane alone among publishers did. He perhaps did not die a very rich man but he lived well, and died a moderately rich one.

We had a hope that Brewer might be this kind of a publisher. He printed Useful Knowledge, his results were not all that he anticipated and instead of continuing and gradually creating a public for Gertrude Stein's work he procrastinated and then said no. I suppose this was inevitable. However that was the matter as it was and as it continued to be.

I now myself began to think about publishing the work of Gertrude Stein. I asked her to invent a name for my edition and she laughed and said, call it Plain Edition. And Plain Edition it is.

All that I knew about what I would have to do was that I would have to get the book printed and then to get it distributed, that is sold.

I talked to everybody about how these two things were to be accomplished.

At first I thought I would associate some one with me but that soon did not please me and I decided to do it all by myself.

Gertrude Stein wanted the first book Lucy Church Amiably to look like a school book and to be bound in blue. Once having ordered my book to be printed my next problem was the problem of distribution. On this subject I received a great deal of advice. Some of the advice turned out to be good and some of it turned out to be bad. William A. Bradley, the friend and comforter of Paris authors, told me to subscribe to The Publishers' Weekly. This was undoubtedly wise advice. This helped me to learn something of my new business, but the real difficulty was to get to the booksellers. Ralph Church, philosopher and friend, said stick to the booksellers, first and last. Excellent advice but how to get to the booksellers. At this moment a kind friend said that she could get me copied an old list of booksellers belonging to a publisher. This list was sent to me and I began sending out my circulars. The

Alice B. Toklas, painting by Francis Rose

circular pleased me at first but I soon concluded that it was not quite right. However I did get orders from America and I was paid without much difficulty and I was encouraged.

The distribution in Paris was at once easier and more difficult. It was easy to get the book put in the window of all the bookstores in Paris that sold english books. This event gave Gertrude Stein a childish delight amounting almost to ecstasy. She had never seen a book of hers in a bookstore window before, except a french translation of The Ten Portraits, and she spent all her time in her wanderings about Paris looking at the copies of Lucy Church Amiably in the windows and coming back and telling me about it.

The books were sold too and then as I was away from Paris six months in the year I turned over the Paris work to a french agent. This worked very well at first but finally did not work well. However one must learn one's trade.

I decided upon my next book How To Write and not being entirely satisfied with the get up of Lucy Church Amiably, although it did look like a school book, I decided to have the next book printed at Dijon and in the form of an Elzevir. Again the question of binding was a difficulty.

I went to work in the same way to sell How To Write, but I began to realise that my list of booksellers was out of date. Also I was told that I should write following up letters. Ellen du Pois helped me with these. I was also told that I should have reviews. Ellen du Pois came to the rescue here too. And that I should advertise. Advertising would of necessity be too expensive; I had to keep my money to print my books, as my plans were getting more and more ambitious. Getting reviews was a difficulty, there are always plenty of humorous references to Gertrude Stein's work, as Gertrude Stein always says to comfort herself, they do quote me, that means that my words and my sentences get under their skins although they do not know it. It was difficult to get serious reviews. There are many writers who write her letters of admiration but even when they are in a position to do so they do not write themselves down in book reviews. Gertrude Stein likes to quote Browning who at a dinner party met a famous literary man and this man came up to Browning and spoke to him at length and in a very laudatory way about his poems. Browning listened and then said, and are you going to print what you have just said. There was naturally no answer. In Gertrude Stein's case there have been some notable exceptions, Sherwood Anderson, Edith Sitwell, Bernard Faÿ and Louis Bromfield.

I also printed an edition of one hundred copies, very beautifully done at Chartres, of the poem of Gertrude Stein Before The Flowers Of Friendship Faded Friendship Faded. These one hundred copies sold very easily.

I was better satisfied with the bookmaking of How To Write but there was always the question of binding the book. It is practically impossible to get a decent commercial binding in France, french publishers only cover their books in paper. I was very troubled about this.

One evening we went to an evening party at Georges Poupet's, a gentle friend of authors. There I met Maurice Darantière. It was he who had printed The Making of Americans and he was always justly proud of it as a book and as bookmaking. He had left Dijon and had started printing books in the neighbourhood of Paris with a hand-press and he was printing very beautiful books. He is a kind man and I naturally began telling him my troubles. Listen, he said I have the solution. But I interrupted him, you must remember that I do not want to make these books expensive. After all Gertrude Stein's readers are writers, university students, librarians and young people who have very little money. Gertrude Stein wants readers not collectors. In spite of herself her books have too often become collector's books. They pay big prices for Tender Buttons and The Portrait of Mabel Dodge and that does not please her, she wants her books read not owned. Yes yes, he said, I understand. No this is what I propose. We will have your book set by monotype which is comparatively cheap, I will see to that, then I will handpull your books on good but not too expensive paper and they will be beautifully printed and instead of any covers I will have them bound in heavy paper like The Making of Americans, paper just like that, and I will have made little boxes in which they will fit perfectly, well made little boxes and there you are. And will I be able to sell them at a reasonable price. Yes you will see, he said.

I was getting more ambitious I wished now to begin a series of three, beginning with Operas and Plays, going on with Matisse, Picasso and Gertrude Stein and Two Shorter Stories, and then going on with Two Long Poems and Many Shorter Ones.

Maurice Darantière has been as good as his word. He has printed Operas and Plays and it is a beautiful book and reasonable in price and he is now printing the second book Matisse Picasso and Gertrude Stein and Two Shorter Stories. Now I have an up to date list of booksellers and I am once more on my way.

As I was saying after the return from England and lecturing we gave a great many parties, there were many occasions for parties, all the Sitwells came over, Carl Van Vechten came over, Sherwood Anderson came over again. And beside there were many other occasions for parties.

It was then that Gertrude Stein and Bernard Faÿ met again and this time they had a great deal to say to each other. Gertrude Stein found the contact with his mind stimulating and comforting. They were slowly coming to be friends.

I remember once coming into the room and hearing Bernard Faÿ say that the three people of first rate importance that he had met in his life were Picasso, Gertrude Stein and André Gide and Gertrude Stein inquired quite simply, that is quite right but why include Gide. A year or so later in referring to this conversation he said to her, and I am not sure you were not right.

Sherwood came to Paris that winter and he was a delight. He was enjoying himself and we enjoyed him. He was being lionised and I must say he was a very appearing and disappearing lion. I remember his being asked to the Pen Club. Natalie Barney and a long-bearded frenchman were to be his sponsors. He wanted Gertrude Stein to come too. She said she loved him very much but not the Pen Club. Natalie Barney came over to ask her. Gertrude Stein who was caught outside, walking her dog, pleaded illness. The next day Sherwood turned up. How was it, asked Gertrude Stein. Why, said he, it wasn't a party for me, it was a party for a big woman, and she was just a derailed freight car.

We had installed electric radiators in the studio, we were as our finnish servant would say getting modern. She finds it difficult to understand why we are not more modern. Gertrude Stein says that if you are way ahead with your head you naturally are old fashioned and regular in your daily life. And Picasso adds, do you suppose Michael Angelo would have been grateful for a gift of a piece of renaissance furniture, no he wanted a greek coin.

We did install electric radiators and Sherwood turned up and we gave him a Christmas party. The radiators smelled and it was terrifically hot but we were all pleased as it was a nice party. Sherwood looked as usual very handsome in one of his very latest scarf ties. Sherwood Anderson does dress well and his son John follows suit. John and his sister came over with their father. While Sherwood was still in Paris John the son was an awkward shy boy. The day after Sherwood left John turned up, sat easily on the arm of the sofa and was beautiful to look upon and he knew it. Nothing to the outward eye had changed but he had changed and he knew it.

It was during this visit that Gertrude Stein and Sherwood Anderson had all those amusing conversations about Hemingway. They enjoyed each other thoroughly. They found out that they both had had and continued to have Grant as their great american hero. They did not care so much about Lincoln either of them. They had always and still liked Grant. They even planned collaborating on a life of Grant. Gertrude Stein still likes to think about this possibility.

We did give a great many parties in those days and the Duchess of Clermont-Tonnerre came very often.

She and Gertrude Stein pleased one another. They were entirely different in life education and interests but they delighted in each other's understanding. They were also the only two women whom they met who still had long hair. Gertrude Stein had always worn hers well on top of her head, an ancient fashion that she had never changed.

Madame de Clermont-Tonnerre came in very late to one of the parties, almost every one had gone, and her hair was cut. Do you like it, said Madame de Clermont-Tonnerre. I do, said Gertrude Stein. Well, said Madame de Clermont-Tonnerre, if you like it and my daughter likes it and she does like it I am satisfied. That night Gertrude Stein said to me, I guess I will have to too. Cut it off she said and I did.

I was still cutting the next evening, I had been cutting a little more all day and by this time it was only a cap of hair when Sherwood Anderson came in. Well, how do you like it, said I rather fearfully. I like it, he said, it makes her look like a monk.

As I have said, Picasso seeing it, was for a moment angry and said, and my portrait, but very soon added, after all it is all there.

We now had our country house, the one we had only seen across the valley and just before leaving we found the white poodle, Basket. He was a little puppy in a little neighbourhood dog-show and he had blue eyes, a pink nose and white hair and he jumped up into Gertrude Stein's arms. A new puppy and a new ford we went off to our new house and we were thoroughly pleased with all three. Basket although now he is a large unwieldy poodle, still will get up on Gertrude Stein's lap and stay there. She says that listening to the rhythm of his water drinking made her recognise the difference between sentences and paragraphs, that paragraphs are emotional and that sentences are not.

Bernard Faÿ came and stayed with us that summer. Gertrude Stein and he talked out in the garden about everything, about life, and America, and themselves and friendship. They then cemented the friendship that is one of the four permanent friendships of Gertrude Stein's life. He even tolerated Basket for Gertrude Stein's sake. Lately Picabia has given us a tiny mexican dog, we call Byron. Bernard Faÿ likes Byron for Byron's own sake. Gertrude Stein teases him and says naturally he likes Byron best because Byron is an american while just as naturally she likes Basket best because Basket is a frenchman.

Bilignin brings me to a new old acquaintance. One day Gertrude Stein came home from a walk to the bank and bringing out a card from her pocket said, we are lunching to-morrow with the Bromfields. Way back in the Hemingway days Gertrude Stein had met Bromfield and his wife and then from time to time there had been a slight acquaintance, there had even been a slight acquaintance with Bromfield's sister, and now suddenly we were lunching with the Bromfields. Why, I asked, because answered Gertrude Stein quite radiant, he knows all about gardens.

We lunched with the Bromfields and he does know all about gardens and all about flowers and all about soils. Gertrude Stein and he first liked each other as gardeners, then they liked each other as americans and then they liked each other as writers. Gertrude Stein says of him that he is as american as Janet Scudder, as american as a doughboy, but not as solemn.

One day the Jolases brought Furman the publisher to the house. He as have been many publishers was enthusiastic and enthusiastic about The Making of Americans. But it is terribly long, it's a thousand pages, said Gertrude Stein. Well, can't it be cut down, he said to about four hundred. Yes, said Gertrude Stein, perhaps. Well cut it down and I will publish it, said Furman.

Gertrude Stein thought about it and then did it. She spent a part of the summer over it and Bradley as well as she and myself thought it alright.

In the meantime Gertrude Stein had told Elliot Paul about the proposition. It's alright when he is over here, said Elliot Paul, but when he gets back the boys won't let him. Who the boys are I do not know but they certainly did not let him. Elliot Paul was right. In spite of the efforts of Robert Coates and Bradley nothing happened.

In the meantime Gertrude Stein's reputation among the french writers and readers was steadily growing. The translation of the fragments of the Making of Americans, and of the Ten Portraits interested them. It was at this time that Bernard Faÿ wrote his article about her work printed in the Revue Européenne. They also printed the only thing she has ever written in french a little film about the dog Basket.

They were very interested in her later work as well as her earlier work. Marcel Brion wrote a serious criticism of her work in Echange, comparing her work to Bach. Since then, in Les Nouvelles Littéraires, he has written of each of her books as they come out. He was particularly impressed by How To Write.

About this time too Bernard Faÿ was translating a fragment of Melanctha from Three Lives for the volume of Ten American Novelists, this to be introduced by his article printed in the Revue Européenne. He came to the house one afternoon and read his translation of Melanctha aloud to us. Madame de Clermont-Tonnerre was there and she was very impressed by his translation.

One day not long after she asked to come to the house as she wished to talk to Gertrude Stein. She came and she said, the time has now come when you must be made known to a larger public. I myself believe in a larger public. Gertrude Stein too believes in a larger public but the way has always been barred. No, said Madame de Clermont-Tonnerre, the way can be opened. Let us think.

She said it must come from the translation of a big book, an important book. Gertrude Stein suggested the Making of Americans and told her how it had been prepared for an American publisher to make about four hundred pages. That will do exactly, she said. And went away.

Finally and not after much delay, Monsieur Bouteleau of Stock saw Gertrude Stein and he decided to publish the book. There was some difficulty about finding a translator, but finally that was arranged. Bernard Faÿ aided by the Baronne Seillière undertook the translation, and it is this translation which is to appear this spring, and that this summer made Gertrude Stein say, I knew it was a wonderful book in english, but it is even, well, I cannot say almost really more wonderful but just as wonderful in french.

Last autumn the day we came back to Paris from Bilignin I was as usual very busy with a number of things and Gertrude Stein went out to buy some nails at the bazaar of the rue de Rennes. There she met Guevara, a chilean painter and his wife. They are our neighbours, and they said, come to tea to-morrow. Gertrude Stein said, but we are just home, wait a bit. Do come, said Méraude Guevara. And then added, there will be some one there you will like to see. Who is it, said Gertrude Stein with a never failing curiosity. Sir Francis Rose, they said. Alright, we'll come, said Gertrude Stein. By this time she no longer objected to meeting Francis Rose. We met then and he of course immediately came back to the house with her. He was, as may be imagined, quite pink with emotion. And what, said he, did Picasso say when he saw my paintings.

When he first saw them, Gertrude Stein answered, he said, at least they are less bêtes than the others. And since, he asked. And since he always goes into the corner and turns the canvas over to look at them but he says nothing.

Since then we have seen a great deal of Francis Rose but Gertrude Stein has not lost interest in the pictures. He has this summer painted the house from across the valley where we first saw it and the waterfall celebrated in Lucy Church Amiably. He has also painted her portrait. He likes it and I like it but she is not sure whether she does, but as she has just said, perhaps she does. We had a pleasant time this summer, Bernard Faÿ and Francis Rose both charming guests.

A young man who first made Gertrude Stein's acquaintance by writing engaging letters from America is Paul Frederick Bowles. Gertrude Stein says of him that he is delightful and sensible in summer but neither delightful nor sensible in the winter. Aaron Copeland came to see us with Bowles in the summer and Gertrude Stein liked him immensely. Bowles told Gertrude Stein and it pleased her that Copeland said threateningly to him when as usual in the winter he was neither delightful nor sensible, if you do not work now when you are twenty when you are thirty, nobody will love you.

For some time now many people, and publishers, have been asking Gertrude Stein to write her autobiography and she had always replied, not possibly.

She began to tease me and say that I should write my autobiography. Just think, she would say, what a lot of money you would make. She then began to invent titles for my autobiography. My Life With The Great, Wives of Geniuses I Have Sat With, My Twenty-five Years With Gertrude Stein.

Then she began to get serious and say, but really seriously you ought to write your autobiography. Finally I promised that if during the summer I could find time I would write my autobiography.

When Ford Madox Ford was editing the Transatlantic Review he once said to Gertrude Stein, I am a pretty good writer and a pretty good editor and a pretty good business man but I find it very difficult to be all three at once.

I am a pretty good housekeeper and a pretty good gardener and a pretty good needlewoman and a pretty good secretary

Chapter **Part I**

I

Before I came to Paris

I was born in San Francisco, Cal.

I have in consequence always preferred

living in a temperate climate but

it is difficult on the continent

of Europe or even in America to

find a temperate climate and

First page of manuscript of this book

and a pretty good editor and a pretty good vet for dogs and I have to do them all at once and I found it difficult to add being a pretty good author.

About six weeks ago Gertrude Stein said, it does not look to me as if you were ever going to write that autobiography. You know what I am going to do. I am going to write it for you. I am going to write it as simply as Defoe did the autobiography of Robinson Crusoe. And she has and this is it.

CHRONOLOGY

NOTE ON THE TEXTS

NOTES

Chronology

1874 Born February 3 in Allegheny, Pennsylvania, the youngest of five surviving children of Daniel Stein and Amelia ("Milly") Keyser. (Parents both belonged to German-Jewish immigrant families who settled in Baltimore before the Civil War. Daniel, born 1832, was a partner with his four brothers in the clothing trade in Baltimore until 1862, when he left to form a clothing business in Pittsburgh with his brother Solomon. He married Amelia, born 1842, in 1864; the newlyweds settled in Allegheny, a northern suburb of Pittsburgh. Their surviving children were Michael, born 1865; Simon, born 1868; Bertha, born 1870; and Leo, born 1872.) Partly because of tensions between the brothers and their families, father moves family to Austria in fall of 1874 to study opportunities in banking business.

1875–79 Father soon returns to the U.S. on business, and is frequently absent during European stay; family remains in Vienna. Stein learns German along with English, and is cared for by a governess. Moves with mother and siblings to Paris in 1878; attends school and learns French. Returns with family to U.S. the following year, living for a while with maternal grandparents in Baltimore.

1880–87 Moves with family to East Oakland, California, in 1880. Father works as stockbroker and invests in San Francisco enterprises, including Omnibus Cable Car Company; family lives at a hotel and a furnished house before settling in April 1881 in large house with a ten-acre yard. Stein attends public schools, Sabbath school, and also has tutors at home; reads widely and goes to the theater; inseparable from brother Leo. Family moves to smaller Oakland house in 1885. Mother becomes ill with cancer.

1888–90 Mother dies in July 1888. Brother Michael returns from Johns Hopkins to manage family business interests. Stein leaves Oakland High School in 1889 (never obtains high school diploma).

1891 Father dies suddenly in January. Michael assumes legal guardianship of Leo and Gertrude and moves family to

San Francisco. He sells off Omnibus holdings and manages estate so efficiently that Leo and Gertrude have small but sufficient incomes.

1892   Stein goes to Baltimore with sister Bertha in July to live with mother's sister, Fannie Bachrach. Leo enrolls in September at Harvard, where Gertrude visits him frequently.

1893–95   Stein enrolls in fall of 1893 in Harvard Annex (re-named Radcliffe the following year); moves into Cambridge boarding house where she will live for the next four years. Attends wedding of brother Michael and Sarah Samuels in March 1894. Studies composition with William Vaughn Moody, philosophy with George Santayana and Josiah Royce, and psychology with Hugo Münsterberg (who supervises her work at Harvard Psychological Laboratory) and William James (later describes herself as deeply influenced by James's ideas on consciousness and perception). Active in philosophy and drama clubs. Has lively social life with group of mostly Jewish students known as "the Crowd." Forms close friendship with philosophy student Leon Solomons, with whom she collaborates on psychology experiments.

1896   Joins Leo (who has been traveling around the world for a year) in Europe for summer; tours Holland and Germany, and visits Paris briefly before settling in London for a month. Research paper "Normal Motor Automatism," co-written with Leon Solomons, published in Harvard publication *The Psychological Review* in September.

1897   Studies with Leo at Woods Hole Marine Biological Laboratory in Massachusetts during summer. Enters Johns Hopkins School of Medicine (where Leo is studying biology) in September; brother and sister share apartment. Forms friendship with physician Claribel Cone and her sister Etta (members of wealthy Jewish family who become important art collectors).

1898–1901 Awarded B.A. from Radcliffe in 1898, after belatedly passing required Latin examination. "Cultivated Motor Automatism: A Study of Character in its Relation to Attention" published in *The Psychological Review* in May

1898. Spends two summers, 1898 and 1899, with Michael and family in San Francisco. Socializes with circle of Bryn Mawr–educated young women at Johns Hopkins, including May Bookstaver (with whom she has affair). Leon Solomons dies February 1900. Stein sails to Europe in June with Leo and mutual friend Mabel Weeks; they travel in Italy and France. Fails four courses; leaves school in spring of 1901 without medical degree. Travels in the summer with Leo, touring in Morocco and Spain before joining the Cone sisters in Paris. Does further research on brain anatomy in Baltimore in the fall, but results are not deemed publishable by advisers at Johns Hopkins.

1902   Sails to Europe in the spring. Joins Leo in Italy and travels with him to England. Makes acquaintance of art historian Bernhard Berenson, his wife, Mary, and philosopher Bertrand Russell. Rents rooms with Leo in Bloomsbury Square, London, in the fall. On her own, studies English literature; shares Leo's interest in Japanese prints.

1903   Sails back to New York in January; stays with Mabel Weeks and other friends at 100th Street and Riverside Drive. Begins early version of long novel *The Making of Americans*, based on the history of her family. Returns to Europe in June; travels to Florence, where she spends time with the Cone sisters. Has emotionally difficult meetings in Rome and Siena with May Bookstaver and her wealthy companion, Mabel Haynes. In the fall joins Leo in Paris, where he is pursuing a career as a painter; settles into his apartment at 27, rue de Fleurus. With Leo, goes regularly to Ambroise Vollard's gallery, where they buy paintings by Cézanne. Writes *Q.E.D.*, novella based on relationship with May Bookstaver.

1904   Michael and his family move to Paris in January. Stein sails to America, visiting friends in New York and Boston; returns to Europe in June with Etta Cone, and spends summer with Leo in Florence, where they see private collection of Cézanne paintings. With unexpected windfall from family estate, Stein and Leo buy paintings by Gauguin, Cézanne, and Renoir from Vollard; subsequently purchase works by Delacroix, Toulouse-Lautrec, Manet, Degas. Stein forms friendship with journalist Mildred Aldrich. Works on novella *Fernhurst*.

1905–6   Begins *Three Lives*, series of three novellas, in spring of 1905 (completed the following year). Spends summer in Italy with Leo. Attends Autumn Salon in Paris, first public showing of Fauvist painters; Stein and Leo, as well as Michael and Sarah Stein, begin collecting work by Henri Matisse and form friendships with Matisse family. Stein and Leo begin buying work by Pablo Picasso; through his dealer, Clovis Sagot, they meet Picasso in November. Stein and Picasso form enduring friendship, and he begins a portrait of her (finished in 1906, by her account after more than 80 sittings). Stein and Leo hold Saturday-night salons which become cultural center of Bohemian Paris and primary showcase of modern art, attended by figures including Guillaume Apollinaire, Georges Braque, Charles Demuth, André Derain, Marcel Duchamp, Marie Laurencin, Mina Loy and husband Stephen Haweis, Henri and Amélie Matisse, and art dealer Daniel-Henry Kahnweiler (who becomes close friend). Resumes work on *The Making of Americans*.

1907   At home of Michael and Sarah in September, is introduced to Alice Babette Toklas (born in San Francisco in 1877), who has just arrived in Paris from California. Toklas rooms with friend Harriet Levy at hotel near rue de Fleurus.

1908   Stein and Toklas spend much of summer together in Italy (Stein stays with Leo, Toklas with Harriet Levy). On return to Paris, the two women are inseparable. Toklas begins to type up manuscript of *The Making of Americans*. William James visits rue de Fleurus.

1909   *Three Lives* published in August by Grafton Press in New York (for $600 fee); receives some favorable reviews.

1910   Tensions and disagreements increase between Stein and Leo. Stein and Toklas spend summer in Italy; send postcards to friends of themselves together in Venice. Toklas moves into 27, rue de Fleurus in December. Stein and Toklas are henceforth permanent companions, always living and traveling together; Toklas serves as homemaker, secretary, typist. Stein composes the first of her portraits, "Ada," in tribute to her relationship with Toklas.

1911   Is introduced to wealthy arts patron Mabel Dodge by
            Mildred Aldrich at rue de Fleurus in the spring; Stein and
            Toklas visit Dodge in Italy. Completes *The Making of
            Americans* in October.

1912   Visited at rue de Fleurus by painter Marsden Hartley,
            of whom Stein becomes friend and patron. Travels with
            Toklas in Spain and Morocco. Portraits "Matisse" and
            "Picasso" published in Alfred Stieglitz's *Camera Work* in
            August. With Toklas, stays at Dodge's villa in September;
            writes "Portrait of Mabel Dodge at the Villa Curonia,"
            which Dodge publishes in private edition.

1913   Stein and Toklas visit England in January; they look un-
            successfully for publishers for her work. Paintings from
            Stein family collections are included in the Armory Show,
            pioneering exhibition of modern art that opens in New
            York in February. Stein writes first play, "What Happened:
            A Five Act Play," in April. Sits for series of portraits
            by photographer Alvin Langdon Coburn; meets painter
            Francis Picabia as well as two major American supporters,
            art critic Henry McBride and, in May, writer and photog-
            rapher Carl Van Vechten, who will become her greatest
            champion and agent. Stein and Leo decide to "disaggre-
            gate" in the fall, dividing up their art collection; Leo,
            openly dismissive of her work and of Cubism, moves to
            Italy (brother and sister never speak again).

1914   Publishes *Tender Buttons* in June with help of Dodge and
            Van Vechten. Relationship with Dodge cools. Buys first
            Juan Gris painting, "Roses." Stein and Toklas go to En-
            gland again in July to negotiate with publishers; in Cam-
            bridge they see classical scholar Jane Harrison and meet
            philosopher Alfred North Whitehead and his wife, Evelyn,
            and are invited to extend their stay at Whitehead home
            when World War I breaks out in mid-July; they return to
            Paris in October.

1915–17   Goes with Toklas to Spain in May 1915, settling in Majorca
            for a year. Returns to Paris in June 1916 after the battle of
            Verdun. Obtains Ford motor van (first of a series of Fords
            she will own) and drives it as supply truck for American
            Fund for French Wounded; goes to Perpignan in March

1917 and afterwards is stationed in Nîmes. They make many acquaintances among American soldiers, and form close friendship with W. G. "Kiddie" Rogers.

1918–21   Stein and Toklas return briefly to Paris after November 1918 armistice, then travel to Alsace to do civilian relief work; they go back to Paris in May 1919, but do not resume Saturday-evening salons. Stein becomes friend of Sylvia Beach and subscriber to Beach's Shakespeare & Company bookstore in Paris. Sits for bust by Jacques Lipschitz in 1920. Stein and Leo glimpse each other for last time, without speaking, on a Paris street in December 1920. Forms friendships with Erik Satie; Jean Cocteau; Sherwood Anderson; Ford Madox Ford; writer Kate Buss, who serves as advocate and agent; and journalist Janet Flanner.

1922   Meets photographer Man Ray, who takes portraits of Stein and Toklas, and the 23-year-old Ernest Hemingway, who visits with a letter of introduction from Sherwood Anderson. Spends summer with Toklas in Saint Rémy. *Geography and Plays*, collection of prose, plays, and poems, published in December.

1923   Stays with Toklas at Hôtel Pernollet in Belley, Ain, in southeastern France, in September (they will continue to spend summers in the region). Sits for bronze portrait by Jo Davidson.

1924   Receives visits from William Carlos Williams in January and T. S. Eliot in November. *The Making of Americans* is partially serialized in Ford Madox Ford's *Transatlantic Review*, April–December.

1925   *The Making of Americans* published by Robert McAlmon's Contact Editions, financed by McAlmon's wife, the novelist Bryher. Introduced by Hemingway to F. Scott and Zelda Fitzgerald in May; meets Edith Sitwell (who introduces her to brothers Osbert and Sacheverell) and, through Van Vechten, Paul Robeson.

1926   Delivers lecture "Composition as Explanation" during summer at Cambridge and Oxford; Leonard and Virginia Woolf's Hogarth Press publishes text. Forms close friendship with Bernard Faÿ, scholar of American history, who becomes translator of her work. Meets composer Virgil Thomson in the fall (he becomes collaborator and pioneer in setting Stein's texts to music). Gradually forms circle of new acquaintances (many of them friends of Thomson) including French poets Georges Hugnet and René Crevel, painters Pavel Tchelitchev, Christian Bérard, and Eugène Berman, and American writer Bravig Imbs. Kahnweiler publishes "A Book Concluding with As a Wife Has a Cow, A Love Story," with illustrations by Juan Gris, in December.

1927   Publishes "Elucidation" (written 1923, early analysis of her own work) in *transition*. Composes "The Life of Juan Gris, the Life and Death of Juan Gris" after Gris' death in May. Agrees to write opera libretto for Virgil Thomson, and completes *Four Saints in Three Acts* in June. Natalie Barney organizes a Gertrude Stein evening at her "Académie des Femmes" salon, at which Thomson performs settings of "Capital Capitals," "Susie Asado," and "Preciosilla."

1928–29   *Useful Knowledge* published in autumn 1928 in New York by Payson & Clarke. Stein and Toklas find summer house in Bilignin near Belley, and begin leasing it in spring 1929 (in future years they will spend summers there).

1930   Sells Picasso's 1905 painting "Woman with a Fan" to finance Plain Edition, small press run by Toklas and dedicated to publishing Stein's work; first book published is *Lucy Church Amiably* (written 1927). Meets Francis Rose, British painter whose work she has begun collecting.

1931   Stein's free adaptation of Hugnet's poem *Enfances* published by Plain Edition as *Before the Flowers of Friendship Faded Friendship Faded*; friendship with Hugnet breaks up over his objections to the looseness of the translation. Visited at Bilignin in the summer by composers Aaron Copland and Paul Bowles.

1932   Publishes *How To Write* (composed 1927–31) and *Operas and Plays* (collection of film treatments, plays, and operas created since 1913) in Plain Edition. While showing unpublished work to novelist Louis Bromfield in April, rediscovers manuscript of *Q.E.D.*; revelations about earlier love affair provoke strains with Toklas. Writes *The Auto-biography of Alice B. Toklas* in six weeks at Bilignin (October–November).

1933   *Matisse Picasso and Gertrude Stein with Two Shorter Sto-ries*, collection of works written before World War I, pub-lished by Plain Edition. Finishes *Four in America* (writings on Ulysses S. Grant, Wilbur Wright, Henry James, and George Washington). Sits for portrait by Picabia. *The Autobiography of Alice B. Toklas* is excerpted in *Atlantic Monthly*; it is published by Harcourt Brace in September and becomes a bestseller. Bennett Cerf of Random House agrees to publish her future work, and reissues *Three Lives* in the Modern Library. *The Making of Americans* is pub-lished in an abridged French translation edited by Stein and Faÿ.

1934   *Four Saints in Three Acts* (directed by John Houseman with all-black cast, choreography by Frederick Ashton, sets and costumes by Florine Stettheimer) opens to acclaim in Hartford in February, then moves to New York for one-month run. Stein agrees to return to America for lecture tour. The abridged version of *The Making of Americans* is published by Harcourt Brace. Sails with Toklas for New York in October; receives wide publicity and gives frequent press and radio interviews (forms friendship with journalist Joseph Alsop, Jr.). Gives first lecture at Colony Club under auspices of Museum of Modern Art on November 2; makes other East Coast appearances at Columbia Univer-sity and Princeton. Random House publishes *Portraits and Prayers* (collection of work from 1909 to 1931) in No-vember. With Toklas, makes first airplane trip to Chicago for performance of *Four Saints*. Lectures at University of Chicago at intervals throughout American visit; faculty member Thornton Wilder becomes friend and advocate. Revisits Harvard and Radcliffe; spends Christmas with Bal-timore relatives. Lectures in Washington, D.C., in Decem-ber; with Toklas, has tea at White House with Eleanor Roosevelt.

1935   Continues lecture tour with engagements in New En-gland; makes recording of her work in New York. Travels with Toklas in South in February. Dismisses "Testimony Against Gertrude Stein," an attack on the accuracy of *The*

Autobiography of Alice B. Toklas by Parisian figures including Matisse, published in February *transition*. *Lectures in America* published by Random House in March. Tours Texas and Oklahoma, March–April. In California, meets Charlie Chaplin, Dashiell Hammett; receives key to city of San Francisco. Stein and Toklas return to childhood homes; Stein finds Oakland home vacant, disagreeable ("there is no there there"); lectures in Berkeley. Returns to New York in late April. Stein and Toklas sail for France in May. Toklas, worried about European political turmoil, begins preparing typescripts of Stein's work for safekeeping by Van Vechten. *Narration*, text of Chicago lectures, published in December with introduction by Wilder.

1936   At Oxford and Cambridge in February, delivers lectures "What Are Masterpieces" and "An American and France." Discusses musical setting of her plays with English composer Lord Gerald Berners, who adapts *They Must. Be Wedded. To Their Wife* as *A Wedding Bouquet*. Forms friendship with photographer Cecil Beaton. *The Geographical History of America* published by Random House in October.

1937   Stein and Toklas fly to London in April for premiere of *A Wedding Bouquet* (choreographed by Frederick Ashton). Accepts Yale University Library proposal to deposit manuscripts there. Anticipating war, Michael Stein family returns to U.S. Memoir *Everybody's Autobiography* published by Random House in December.

1938   Stein and Toklas move to 5, rue Christine in February. Michael Stein dies of cancer in San Francisco. Stein publishes *Picasso* in French (translated into English by Toklas). Finishes play *Doctor Faustus Lights the Lights* in June.

1939   Visited at Bilignin by Clare Booth and Henry Luce; expresses skepticism when they warn her of impending war; rejects similar warnings from other friends. Children's book *The World Is Round* published in August. Following outbreak of war in September, Stein and Toklas spend 36 hours in Paris retrieving papers, clothing, one Cézanne, and Picasso portrait of Stein. Against advice of American officials, they remain in Bilignin.

1940   *Paris France* published in April. As France falls to the Ger-
            mans in June, Stein and Toklas consider leaving the coun-
            try, but at last minute decide to stay in Bilignin, soon to
            be under Vichy rule. "The Winner Loses: A Picture of
            Occupied France" published in November *Atlantic
            Monthly.* Begins *Mrs. Reynolds,* novel dealing allegorically
            with origins of World War II.

1941–43   *Ida: A Novel* published by Random House in February
            1941. Receives protection from Faÿ, who has been ap-
            pointed director of Bibliothèque Nationale in Paris.
            Develops interest in prophecies, including those of 15th-
            century writer Saint Odile; begins translation, later aban-
            doned, of speeches by Vichy leader Marshal Pétain. Stein
            and Toklas subsist on scant rations and food bought on
            black market. Bilignin house reclaimed by landlord in
            1942; Stein institutes a lawsuit against him, drops it when
            she finds another house ("Le Colombier") in nearby Cu-
            loz. Begins diaristic account of the war years (published as
            Wars I Have Seen). Ignores private warning to flee to Swit-
            zerland or be sent to concentration camp. Stein and Toklas
            move to Culoz in February 1943. A German officer and
            his orderly are billeted with them in September.

1944   Two Italian officers and 30 soldiers are billeted in house
            and adjoining park in January. Culoz house comman-
            deered by German officer and men for 24 hours in July.
            French Resistance forces liberate Culoz in August. Amer-
            ican soldiers arrive September 1; correspondents Eric
            Sevareid and Frank Gervasi find Stein and Toklas the next
            day, and Sevareid arranges for Stein to broadcast to U.S.
            from nearby Voiron. Returning to Paris in mid-December,
            learns that art collection in rue Christine apartment is
            mostly intact. Reunites with friends, including Picasso and
            Hemingway.

1945   Treated as celebrity by American soldiers who visit her reg-
            ularly. *Wars I Have Seen* published by Random House in
            March and sells well. Corresponds with Richard Wright.
            Tours U.S. army bases in Germany in June. Lectures to
            American soldiers at Sorbonne. Visits Bernard Faÿ, who
            has been imprisoned for collaboration, and writes testi-
            monial defending him. Begins working with Thomson in
            October on *The Mother of Us All*, opera about Susan B.

Anthony (score is not completed until after her death). Lectures to G.I.'s in Brussels in December; complains of fatigue, and suffers intestinal attacks.

1946   Finishes libretto of *The Mother of Us All* by March. Play *Yes Is For A Very Young Man* (originally *In Savoy*) produced in Pasadena. Meets Richard Wright and family when they arrive in Paris in May. *Brewsie and Willie* published in June. Stein becomes ill while driving to country house of Faÿ, returns to Paris by train; ambulance takes her to American Hospital at Neuilly-sur-Seine, where doctors diagnose stomach cancer. Draws up will on July 23, leaving Picasso portrait to Metropolitan Museum in New York, manuscripts and papers to Yale, and money in care of Van Vechten (who, with Toklas, is named literary executor) for publication of manuscripts. The rest of estate is left for care of Toklas until her death, the residue to pass to nephew Allan Stein and his children. Insists on operation even when told by doctors that she is too weak for it. Awaiting surgery on July 27, asks Toklas, "What is the answer?"; when Toklas remains silent, adds, "In that case, what is the question?" Following operation, dies same day without recovering consciousness. Buried October 22 in Père Lachaise Cemetery, Paris (tombstone designed by Francis Rose; Toklas is buried in same tomb when she dies in March 1967). *Selected Writings of Gertrude Stein* (edited by Van Vechten) published by Random House the same month.

Note on the Texts

This volume contains works written by Gertrude Stein between 1903 and 1932: *Q.E.D.*, *Three Lives*, 36 short works (including portraits, poems, plays, and lectures), and *The Autobiography of Alice B. Toklas*.

Stein's first novel, *Q.E.D.*, was written in 1903. It remained in manuscript form, untyped and unpublished, until after her death. Sometime between 1946 and 1950, Alice B. Toklas produced a typescript that was the basis for the first book version of the novel, published in an edition of 516 copies by the Banyan Press (Pawlet, Vermont) in 1950 under the title *Things As They Are*. The Banyan Press edition regularized Stein's style and altered some names and phrases from the original manuscript, largely in order to protect the privacy of persons still living. In 1971 Liveright published a new edition of the novel in *Fernhurst, Q.E.D., and Other Early Writings* (edited by Leon Katz), which restored most of Stein's original text and changed the title to *Q.E.D.* (following Stein's manuscript title *Quod Erat Demonstrandum*), while regularizing some of Stein's punctuation and grammar. The text printed in the present volume is that of the holograph manuscript, written in two notebooks now housed at the Beinecke Library, Yale University.

Three Lives, a collection of three novellas, was written in 1905–6 and was first published in 1909 by Grafton Press (New York). No typescript is known to be extant. Collation of the holograph manuscript (now in the Beinecke Library) and the first book edition reveals significant differences of a kind suggesting that Stein revised the text before the first publication. The text printed in the present volume is that of the 1909 Grafton Press edition.

The 36 shorter works included in this volume were written between 1910 and 1928. During this period, Stein had difficulty finding publishers for her work, and much of it remained unpublished until long after it was written; some of the works included here were not published until after her death. Between 1907 and 1909, Toklas began systematically typing the holograph manuscripts that Stein composed each night; Stein would then correct and at times revise these typescripts, often sending copies to friends and potential publishers.

In 1935, Toklas grew concerned about political instability in France and began preparing a complete set of typescripts of Stein's work, using carbon copies of some pieces and retyping others; one set of typescripts was sent to Carl Van Vechten in the United States for safekeeping, while Stein and Toklas kept and bound a set for themselves. In addition, by the spring of 1938, Stein had deposited approximately half of her existing papers in the Yale Collection of American Literature, an arrangement facilitated by Thornton Wilder. In 1940, Van Vechten deposited his collection of Stein's typescripts in the Yale Collection of American Literature, and Stein continued to mail papers to Yale until the time of her death. After her death in 1946, Yale received three large boxes filled with Stein's writings, and the Beinecke Library staff completed cataloging these materials in 1996. The Yale Collection of American Literature at the Beinecke Library maintains an almost complete collection of Stein's work, including notebooks, holograph manuscripts, typescripts (both originals and carbon copies), presentation copies, first book editions, foreign publications, and correspondence.

For each of the 36 pieces listed below, the texts of typescripts, first book publications, and most periodical publications have been collated. Except in a few instances described below, the texts printed in the present volume are those of the typescripts prepared under Stein's supervision and often containing her handwritten corrections and revisions. In cases where collation revealed substantive discrepancies between the typescript and the printed versions, the holograph manuscript has been consulted for whatever evidence it contains of Stein's intentions; as a result of these comparisons, published versions have sometimes been preferred. For example, in the first book publication of "Sacred Emily" (written 1913; published 1922 in *Geography and Plays*), two sentences appear that are not in the typescript ("A hand is Willie. Henry Henry Henry."). However, these lines do appear in the manuscript notebook, suggesting that Stein made later corrections, either to the galleys or to a second typescript that is not known to be extant. In the case of "Yet Dish" (written 1913; published 1953 in *Bee Time Vine*), the typographical style of the typescript is changed in the first book edition, which sets the piece as poetry whereas the typescript is arranged as prose, with line breaks only between the numbered sections. The holograph manuscript notebook, however, suggests that the piece was intended to be set as poetry, since each stanza is written on its own page with line breaks that correspond with those in the first book edition. In each of these two cases, the text printed here is that of the first book publication.

The 36 shorter pieces are arranged by the approximate dates of their composition. The large gap that often exists between the dates of composition and publication makes precise dating of composition difficult, particularly for the early pieces, and the scholarship of Richard Bridgman, Edward Burns, Ulla Dydo, Donald Gallup, Robert Bartlett Haas, Leon Katz, Bruce Kellner, and Jayne Walker, in addition to the Stein catalog at the Beinecke Library, has been consulted.

"Ada" was written in 1910 and was first published in *Geography and Plays* (Boston: Four Seas, 1922). A comparison of the first book edition, typescript, and holograph manuscript in the selections from *Geography and Plays* printed in this volume suggests that Stein made later changes (either to a setting typescript not known to be extant or in proofreading) that are not evident in the bound typescripts. The text printed here is from *Geography and Plays*.

"Matisse" was written circa 1910–11 and was first published by Alfred Stieglitz in a special issue of *Camera Work* (August 1912). It was collected in *Portraits and Prayers* (New York: Random House, 1934). The text printed here is that of the typescript, bound volume 9 (pp. 37–44).

"Picasso" was written circa 1910–11 and was first published by Alfred Stieglitz in a special issue of *Camera Work* (August 1912). It was collected in *Portraits and Prayers*. The text printed here is that of the typescript, bound volume 9 (pp. 45–49).

"Orta or One Dancing" was written circa 1911–12 and did not appear in print during Stein's lifetime. It was first collected in *Two: Gertrude Stein and Her Brother, and Other Early Portraits (1908–12)* (New Haven: Yale University Press, 1951), as part of the Yale Edition of the Unpublished Writings of Gertrude Stein. Comparison between the typescript in bound volume 9 (pp. 1–36) and another typescript showing Stein's handwritten corrections suggests that the second typescript is a later version of the piece, since a phrase ("she was then resembling some one, one who was not dancing, one who was writing") that is typed and crossed out in the former typescript is omitted from the latter. The text printed here is that of the typescript showing Stein's handwritten corrections.

"Flirting at the Bon Marche" was written circa 1910–12 and did not appear in print during Stein's lifetime. It was first collected in *Two: Gertrude Stein and Her Brother, and Other Early Portraits (1908–12)*. The text printed here is that of the typescript, bound volume 10 (pp. 70–74).

"Miss Furr and Miss Skeene" was written circa 1910–12 and was collected in *Geography and Plays*. It also appeared in *Vanity Fair* in July 1923. The text printed here is from *Geography and Plays*.

"Tender Buttons" was written in 1912 and was originally published in 1914 in New York by Claire Marie (a private press established by the poet Donald Evans). The text printed here is that of the typescript, bound volume 11 (pp. 1–88).

"Portrait of Mabel Dodge at the Villa Curonia" was written in 1912 and first appeared in *Camera Work* (June 1913). It was collected in *Portraits and Prayers*. The text printed here is that of the typescript, bound volume 11 (pp. 89–94).

"One. Carl Van Vechten" was written in 1913 and was first published in *Geography and Plays*. The text printed here is from *Geography and Plays*.

"Susie Asado" was written in 1913 and was first published in *Geography and Plays*. The text printed here is from *Geography and Plays*.

"Yet Dish" was written in 1913 and did not appear in print during Stein's lifetime. It was first published in *Bee Time Vine* (New Haven: Yale University Press, 1953) as part of the Yale Edition of the Unpublished Writings of Gertrude Stein. Because the typographical style in the book version seems closer than the typescript to Stein's intentions as indicated by the holograph manuscript, the text printed here is from *Bee Time Vine*.

"Americans" was written in 1913 and was first published in *Geography and Plays*. The text printed here is from *Geography and Plays*.

"In the Grass (On Spain)" was written in 1913 and was first published in *Geography and Plays*. The text printed here is from *Geography and Plays*.

"Guillaume Apollinaire" was written in 1913 and was first published in *Portraits and Prayers*. The text printed here is that of the typescript, bound volume 12 (pp. 14–15).

"Preciosilla" was written in 1913. Stein used "Preciosilla" to illustrate her ideas on writing in her lecture "Composition as Explanation," delivered at Oxford and Cambridge in 1926. It first appeared in *Composition as Explanation*, published in London by Leonard and Virginia Woolf at their Hogarth Press in November 1926. The text presented here is that of the typescript, bound volume 12 (pp. 48–50).

"Sacred Emily" was written in 1913 and was first published in *Geography and Plays*. The text printed here is from *Geography and Plays*.

"Turkey and Bones and Eating and We Liked It. A Play" was written in 1916 and was first published in *Geography and Plays*. The text printed here from *Geography and Plays*.

"Lifting Belly" was written between 1915 and 1917 and did not appear in print during Stein's lifetime. It was first published in *Bee Time Vine*. The text printed here is that of the typescript, bound volume 15 (pp. 1–70).

"Marry Nettie" was written in 1917 and did not appear in print during Stein's lifetime. It was first published in *Painted Lace* (New Haven: Yale University Press, 1955) as part of the Yale Gertrude Stein series. The text printed here is that of the typescript, bound volume 15 (pp. 119–29).

"Accents in Alsace. A Reasonable Tragedy" was written in 1919 and was first published in *Geography and Plays*. The text printed here is from *Geography and Plays*.

"A Movie" was written in 1920 and was first published in *Operas and Plays* in 1932 by Plain Edition, a publishing company established by Stein and Toklas in Paris in 1930. The text printed here is that of the typescript, bound volume 15 (pp. 294–97).

"Idem the Same. A Valentine to Sherwood Anderson" was written in 1922 and was first published in *The Little Review* (9:3, Spring 1923). It was later collected in *Useful Knowledge* (New York: Payson & Clarke, Ltd., 1928) and in *Portraits and Prayers*. The text printed here that of the typescript, bound volume 17 (pp. 165–70).

"An Instant Answer or a Hundred Prominent Men" was written in 1922 and was first published in *transition* 13 (Summer 1929); it was later collected in *Useful Knowledge*. The text presented here is that of the typescript, bound volume 17 (pp. 51–68).

"Erik Satie" was written in 1922 and was first published in *Portraits and Prayers*. The text printed here is from *Portraits and Prayers* (the typescript is not known to be extant).

"Cezanne" was written in 1923 and was first published in *Portraits and Prayers*. The text printed is that of the typescript, bound volume 17 (p. 197).

"A Book Concluding With As a Wife Has a Cow A Love Story" was written in 1923 and was first published in Paris by Editions de la Galerie Simon in 1926. It appeared in *transition* 3 (June 1927). The text printed here is that of the typescript, bound volume 18 (pp. 54–66).

"Van or Twenty Years After. A Second Portrait of Carl Van Vechten" was written in 1923 and was first published in *The Reviewer* (4:3, April 1924). It was collected in *Useful Knowledge* and in *Portraits and Prayers*. The text printed here is that of the typescript, bound volume 18 (pp. 67–69).

"If I Told Him. A Completed Portrait of Picasso" was written in 1923 and was first published in *Portraits and Prayers*. The text printed here is that of the typescript, bound volume 18 (pp. 83–87).

"Geography" was written in 1923 and did not appear in print during Stein's lifetime. It was first published in *Painted Lace*. The text printed here is that of the typescript, bound volume 18 (pp. 88–93).

"The Difference Between the Inhabitants of France and the Inhabitants of the United States of America" was written in 1924 and was first published in *Useful Knowledge*. The text printed here is that of the typescript, bound volume 18 (pp. 200-8).

"Composition as Explanation" was written and delivered as a lecture at Oxford and Cambridge in 1926. It appeared in *The Dial* (81: 4, October 1926) and was published in *Composition as Explanation*. The text printed here is that of the typescript, bound volume 19 (pp. 218–32).

"An Acquaintance with Description" was written in 1926 and was published by the Seizin Press, hand-set by Robert Graves and Laura Riding, in London, April 1929. The text printed here is that of the typescript, bound volume 19 (pp. 245–88).

"The Life of Juan Gris. The Life and Death of Juan Gris" was written in 1927 and was first published in *transition* 4 (July 1927); it was later collected in *Portraits and Prayers*. The text printed here is that of *transition* 4 (see note 566.24–26 in this volume).

"Patriarchal Poetry" was written in 1927 and did not appear in print during Stein's lifetime. It was first published in *Bee Time Vine*. The text printed here is that of the typescript.

"Four Saints in Three Acts" was written in 1927 and was excerpted in *transition* 16/17 (June 1929). It was published in its entirety in *Operas and Plays*. The text printed here is that of the typescript.

"Virgil Thomson" was written in 1928 and was first published in *Portraits and Prayers*. No typescript is known to be extant. The text printed here is from *Portraits and Prayers*.

No typescript is known to be extant for *The Autobiography of Alice B. Toklas*, which Stein wrote in 1932. The book first appeared serially in *The Atlantic Monthly* from May to July 1933, and was published by Harcourt Brace and Co. in New York later that year. The text presented here is that of the 1933 Harcourt Brace edition.

Although Stein's use of language and punctuation was unconventional, she employed standard spelling; therefore words inadvertently misspelled in the holograph manuscript of *Q.E.D.* or in Toklas's typescripts, as well as other obvious slips, have been corrected. However, Stein's omission of the apostrophe in some contractions ("its," "whats," for example) is fairly consistent and so has not been changed. Her British forms of several words such as "realise" and "recognise" have also been retained.

This volume presents the texts of the original printings chosen for inclusion here, but it does not attempt to reproduce features of their typographic design, such as display capitalization of chapter openings. The following is a list of typographical errors in the printed source texts corrected in this volume, cited by page and line number: 73.26, Katie; 88.13, Is'nt; 89.32, Sally's; 110.2, Mrs; 121.17, Sally; 121.19, Sally; 121.22, Sally; 187.11, trouble.; 234.19, doing.; 263.26, it,; 267.17, she she; 465.15, sombody; 465.19, neccesary; 470.25, unbrella; 565.29, Bracque; 565.33, Faintainebleau; 711.31, symmetery; 782.6, Preciocilla; 890.2, audience; 891.23, balance; 904.8, easily [no period].

Notes

In the notes below, the reference numbers denote page and line of this volume (the line count includes headings). No note is made for material included in standard desk-reference books such as Webster's *Collegiate*, *Biographical*, and *Geographical* dictionaries. For references to other studies, and further biographical background than is contained in the Chronology, see Richard Bridgman, *Gertrude Stein in Pieces* (New York: Oxford University Press, 1970); *A Stein Reader*, edited by Ulla E. Dydo (Evanston, Illinois: Northwestern University Press, 1993); Janet Hobhouse, *Everybody Who Was Anybody: A Biography of Gertrude Stein* (New York: G.P. Putnam, 1975); *A Gertrude Stein Companion: content with the example*, edited by Bruce Kellner (Westport, Connecticut: Greenwood Press, 1988); James Mellow, *Charmed Circle: Gertrude Stein & Company* (New York: Praeger Publishers, 1974); Diana Souhami, *Gertrude and Alice* (New York: Pandora Press, 1991); *The Letters of Gertrude Stein and Carl Van Vechten, 1913–1946* (New York: Columbia University Press, 1986), edited by Edward Burns; *The Letters of Gertrude Stein and Thornton Wilder* (New Haven: Yale University Press, 1996), edited by Edward M. Burns and Ulla E. Dydo with William Rice; Linda Wagner-Martin, *"Favored Strangers": Gertrude Stein and Her Family* (New Brunswick: Rutgers University Press, 1995); Brenda Wineapple, *Sister Brother: Gertrude and Leo Stein* (New York: G.P. Putnam's Sons, 1996); *Four Americans in Paris: The Collections of Gertrude Stein and Her Family* (New York: The Museum of Modern Art, 1970); and *Gertrude Stein: A Bibliography*, compiled by Robert A. Wilson (New York: The Phoenix Bookshop, 1974).

Q.E.D.

3.13–15   A little knowledge . . . content.]   In the holograph manuscript, Stein indicates possible partial revisions to this sentence, which would make it read as follows: "A little knowledge is a comfortable thing, it gives a cheerful sense of completeness and content."

5.35   there where]   In the holograph manuscript the phrase "here that" is written in pencil above "there where."

11.1   she really . . . count]   In the holograph manuscript the word "count" is unclear and has also been read as "court."

24.28   Kwasind]   Friend of Hiawatha in Henry Wadsworth Longfellow's *The Song of Hiawatha* (1855).

49.19–21 "Well its the . . . celebrate"] In the holograph manuscript, Stein indicates possible partial revisions to this sentence, which would make it read as follows: "Well its the first and probably the last time in your history that you will ever realise your wrong-doing so lets celebrate".

54.1–2 Like Kate Croy . . . nobody'] Cf. Henry James's *The Wings of the Dove*.

63.8 *Oct. 24, 1903.*] Below the final paragraph and date in the holograph manuscript, the following passage is written in Stein's hand in pencil: "(The actual answer) / I don't <u>know</u> understand what you mean by my having denied that I care for you when have I ever done so. I do love you and I am sorrier than I can say that you should have been so bothered."

THREE LIVES

66.1–2 *Donc . . . la vie.*] Thus I am unhappy and the fault is neither mine nor life's.

71.28–32 Molly . . . swear words.] In the holograph manuscript, this passage reads: "Just what the trouble was with Molly we never really knew. She was an American girl born of German parents and with no people left to her. She had a troublesome cough, an ugly temper, and wonderfully opprobrious language always at command."

86.4–6 Miss Jane . . . Bridgeport.] In the holograph manuscript, this paragraph concludes with an additional sentence: "This was a great relief to Anna that they were not all to go on living in the same old place. This change would make the parting for Miss Mary and her Anna so much simpler."

96.29–34 On Sundays . . . their friends.] In the holograph manuscript, this paragraph concludes with an additional sentence: "The mother sat in her rocking chair out on the porch, glad of these hours when she could be at rest and her husband sat near her on the steps when he was not drinking with his friends."

108.11 girls to keep.] In the holograph manuscript, this passage is followed by an additional paragraph: "Miss Mathilda struggled to make Anna understand it better but it was long before Anna could endure to see the gentle mother friend of Miss Mathilda who had made her so angry and so sore on that dark night."

116.38–39 People . . . no sense] In the holograph manuscript, this line reads "They ain't got no sense . . ."

PORTRAITS AND OTHER SHORT WORKS

285.1 *Orta or One Dancing*] A portrait of Isadora Duncan (1878–1927).

307.1 *Miss Furr and Miss Skeene*] A portrait of Ethel Mars and Maude Hunt Squire, friends of Stein.

362.1   *Susie Asado*]   This portrait was suggested by Antonia Marce (1890–1936), a flamenco dancer known as "La Argentina."

386.1   *Preciosilla*]   This portrait was suggested by the stage name of a singer in Madrid.

492.5   Andrew D. White]   Andrew Dickson White (1832–1918), founder and first president of Cornell University, United States minister to Russia (1892–94), and ambassador to Germany (1896–1904).

520.26   Lord Grey]   Sir Edward Grey (1862–1933), Viscount Grey of Fallodon, diplomat involved in peace negotiations after World War I; author of *Twenty-Five Years (1892–1916)*.

566.24–26   I remember . . . everything."]   In different published versions of this piece, the quotation marks in this passage have been variously positioned, leading to ambiguity about the identity of the speaker. The confusion about punctuation has led some readers to believe that Stein is speaking of herself when she writes, "I was everything." Erasures and cross-outs in the holograph manuscript indicate that Stein revised this sentence extensively; "I" in "I said it to him" and "said I was everything" was at one point changed to "Juan," and then back to "I," and there appears to be a set of single quotation marks (within the quoted sentence itself) around the final phrase "I was everything."

590.29   Avery]   Avery Hopwood (1882–1928), American playwright and a close friend of Stein.

THE AUTOBIOGRAPHY OF ALICE B. TOKLAS

662.12   Max Jacob]   French writer and artist (1876–1944) whose works include *The Dice Cup* (1917), a collection of prose poems.

668.17   Alfy Maurer]   Alfred Maurer (1868–1932), pioneering American modernist painter born in New York City.

668.27   Barnes collection]   The Philadelphia pharmacologist Albert Coombs Barnes (1872–1951) began his collection of 19th- and 20th-century French art in 1905, and in 1922 established the Barnes Foundation in Merion, Pennsylvania, as a permanent home for it.

681.15   Katzenjammer kids]   The cartoon characters first appeared in Rudolph Dirks' *The Cruise of the Katzenjammer Kids* (1907), and were later featured in a long-running comic strip.

685.15   Evelyn Thaw]   Evelyn Nesbit, a chorus girl, married the millionaire Harry Thaw; in June 1906 he murdered her former lover, the architect Stanford White, in the Madison Square Roof Garden.

687.10   Henry McBride]   American art critic (1867–1962), who wrote for the *New York Sun* and *The Dial*.

703.37   H. P. Roché] Henri-Pierre Roché (1880–1959), French novelist, author of *Jules and Jim* (1953).

715.35   Edwin Dodge] Wealthy Boston architect, husband of Mabel Dodge (later Mabel Dodge Luhan); they married in 1905 and settled in the Villa Curonia in Florence (they were divorced in 1916).

715.36–37   the lives . . . behind us] Cf. Longfellow, "A Psalm of Life": "Lives of great men all remind us / We can make our lives sublime, / And, departing, leave behind us / Footprints on the sands of time."

717.9   Elliot Paul] American writer (1891–1958), co-editor with Eugene Jolas of the magazine *transition* and author of many books including *The Life and Death of a Spanish Town* (1937).

718.14   Salmon] André Salmon (1881–1969), French poet, novelist, and art critic.

735.36   Clarissa Harlowe] *Clarissa, or, The History of a Young Lady* (1747–48), novel by Samuel Richardson.

736.3   Charles Grandison] *Sir Charles Grandison* (1753–54), novel by Samuel Richardson.

741.33   Doctor Mall] Franklin Payne Mall (1862–1917), anatomist and embryologist, professor of anatomy at Johns Hopkins from 1893.

743.39   Willard] Josiah Flynt Willard (1869–1907), American sociologist whose study *Tramping with Tramps* appeared in 1899.

744.23   Tauchnitz] Series of paperback English-language editions of British and American novels published in Leipzig, for sale on the Continent only; the series was founded by Christian Bernhard von Tauchnitz (1816–95).

744.24   Robert Coates] Coates (1897–1973), American writer, art critic for *The New Yorker* (1937–67), and author of books including *The Eater of Darkness* (1929) and *The Outlaw Years* (1930).

744.28   Bravig Imbs] American poet and novelist (1904–46).

753.12   Stchoukine] Sergei Shchukin, wealthy Russian connoisseur whose collection of modern painting was housed in the Troubetskoy Palace in Moscow until 1918, when it was expropriated by the Soviet government.

755.33   Fénéon] Felix Fénéon (1861–1944), art critic, literary editor, and supporter of anarchism.

758.1   Simplicissimus] German satirical review (1896–1944), celebrated for its innovative graphic art.

758.39   Manolo] Catalan sculptor (real name Manuel Martínez Hugué).

762.11   Moréas] Jean Moréas (real name Iannis Pappadiamontopoulos, 1856–1910), Greek-born French poet who founded a neo-classical literary group, *l'Ecole romane*.

773.14–15   Braque . . . voler la France.]   Braque is right, that one robbed France, and one knows what it is to rob France.

776.24   Jane Heap]   Co-editor (1887–1964), with Margaret Anderson, of *The Little Review*.

777.25   Pat Bruce]   Patrick Bruce (1880–1937), American abstractionist who destroyed most of his canvases.

780.27–28   One of the very . . . of him]   "A Portrait of One: Harry Phelan Gibb."

785.27   Lady Cunard . . . Nancy]   Emerald Cunard's daughter Nancy Cunard (1896–1965) was a writer and political activist.

787.25   Hutchins Hapgood]   American writer (1869–1944) whose works included *The Story of a Lover* (1919); he was also a columnist for the *New York Globe*.

788.10   Genthe]   Arnold Genthe (1869–1942), American photographer noted for his celebrity portraits and documentary street photographs.

790.39–40   Constance Fletcher]   English writer (1858–1938), friend of Oscar Wilde and Henry James, and author of popular novels including *Kismet* (1876).

793.16   Haweis and . . . Mina Loy]   British painter Stephen Haweis (Hugh Oscar William Haweis) married British poet and painter Mina Loy (1882–1966) in 1903; they were divorced in 1917. Loy's *Lunar Baedecker* appeared in 1923.

796.35–36   Sacre du Printemps]   Ballet (1913) by Igor Stravinsky, which provoked a tumultuous public response when first performed in Paris by the Ballet Russe.

797.10   the Argentina]   See note 362.1.

798.21   Allan . . . Norton]   Allan Norton was editor of the New York–based little magazine *Rogue* (March–September 1915).

800.20   Alvin Langdon Coburn]   American photographer (1882–1966) associated with the Photo-Secession Group.

814.28   Donald Evans]   American poet and publisher (1885–1921), whose verse collections included *Sonnets from the Patagonian* (1914), and who founded Claire Marie Publishers.

840.1   big Bertha]   Popular Allied name for German gun used to shell Paris, March–August 1918.

847.17   Adrienne Monnier]   Proprietor of the bookstore La Maison des Amis des Livres on the rue de l'Odeon in Paris, a center of avant-garde literary activity.

852.16   Marcel Schwob]   French writer and scholar (1867–1905) whose stories are collected in *The King in the Golden Mask* (1892) and *Imaginary Lives* (1896).

854.35   Broom]   Little magazine (1921–24) first edited by novelist Harold A. Loeb and poet Alfred Kreymborg (1883–1966).

856.11   Glenway Wescott]   American novelist (1901–87) whose works include *The Apple of the Eye* (1924) and *The Grandmothers* (1927).

856.19   Robert McAlmon]   Expatriate American writer and publisher (1896–1956), author of *Village* (1924) and *The Portrait of a Generation* (1926).

856.25   Ernest Walsh]   Expatriate American writer who (with Ethel Moorhead) edited the first three issues of the little magazine *This Quarter* (1925–27).

859.29–30   à très bientôt . . . méchante.]   See you very soon . . . How naughty you are.

860.9   Janet Scudder]   American sculptor (1874–1940), resident in France from 1894.

869.16   George Lynes]   George Platt Lynes (1907–55), American ballet photographer.

871.21   Violet Hunt]   English novelist (1866–1942); her works include *The Maiden's Progress* (1894) and *Unkist, Unkind* (1897).

879.21   Darantière]   Maurice Darantière, French printer who oversaw the Contact edition of *The Making of Americans* and the volumes of Stein's work published by Plain Edition.

881.34–35   Christian Bérard]   French painter and stage designer (1902–49); he frequently collaborated with Jean Cocteau.

881.36   René Crevel]   French surrealist novelist and poet, born 1900, who committed suicide in 1935.

884.29   Natalie Barney]   American-born Parisian hostess (1876–1972) whose Friday-night salons attracted major figures from literature, the arts, and politics.

884.37   Genia Berman]   Eugene Berman (1899–1972), Russian-born painter who settled in Paris after the Russian revolution.

894.33   transition]   Little magazine (1927–38) edited by Elliot Paul and Eugene Jolas; one of the most influential organs of experimental literature and art, its contributors included Stein, James Joyce, André Breton, William Carlos Williams, and Hart Crane.

899.11   Charles Henri Ford]   American poet (b. 1913), editor of the little magazine *Blues* (1929–30).

900.31   William A. Bradley]   American literary agent (1879–1939) who settled in France after World War I; his clients included Ezra Pound, Thornton
Wilder, and Anais Nin.

900.35   Ralph Church]   Friend of Sherwood Anderson who later taught
philosophy at Cornell University; author of *Analysis of Resemblance* (1952).

Library of Congress Cataloging-in-Publication Data

Stein, Gertrude, 1874–1946.
   [Selections. 1998]
   Writings, 1903–1932 / Gertrude Stein.
      p.   cm. — (The library of America ; 99)
  ISBN 1–883011–40–X (alk. paper)
  I. Title.   II. Title. Q.E.D.   III. Title. Three lives.
  IV. Title. Autobiography of Alice B. Toklas.   V. Series.
  PS3537.T323A6   1998
  818'.5209—dc21   97–28915
                                                      CIP

THE LIBRARY OF AMERICA SERIES

This book is set in 10 point Linotron Galliard,
a face designed for photocomposition by Matthew Carter
and based on the sixteenth-century face Granjon. The paper is
acid-free Ecusta Nyalite and meets the requirements for permanence
of the American National Standards Institute. The binding
material is Brillianta, a woven rayon cloth made by
Van Heek-Scholco Textielfabrieken, Holland.
The composition is by The Clarinda
Company. Printing and binding by
R.R.Donnelley & Sons Company.
Designed by Bruce Campbell.